Works of
Edith Wharton

THE HOUSE OF MIRTH

Works of Edith Wharton

Ethan Frome

The House of Mirth

Tales of Men and Ghosts

ILLUSTRATED

With an Introduction by

Ruth Lake Tepper

AVENEL BOOKS

New York

Publisher's Note: Selections in this work contain racial references and language which the modern reader may find offensive. These references and language are part of the time period and environment written about, and do not reflect the attitudes of the editors or publisher of this current edition.

This 1987 edition is published by Avenel Books, distributed by Crown Publishers, Inc., 225 Park Avenue South, New York, New York 10003.

Printed and bound in the United States of America

Library of Congress Cataloging-in-Publication Data

Wharton, Edith, 1862–1937.
Works of Edith Wharton.

Contents: Ethan Frome—The house of mirth—Tales of men and ghosts.
I. Title.
PS3545.H16A6 1987 813′.52 87-11575
ISBN 0-517-62855-4

h g f e d c b a

Contents

Introduction

IN the two great novels and ten short stories gathered in this collection, Edith Wharton has written superbly about a wide spectrum—truly a rainbow arc—of people and places: from rich to poor, from city to country. Here is the poignant story of exquisitely beautiful Lily Bart, the stylish, but unsophisticated, impulsive heroine of *The House of Mirth,* who seeks a rich husband in the luxurious town houses and country estates of New York's high society. At the other end of the spectrum is the tragic story of the impoverished, troubled farmer in *Ethan Frome,* hopelessly in love, eking out a bare living in the gloomy back country of Starkfield, Massachusetts. And in *Tales of Men and Ghosts,* there are stories of the lofty and the lowly, of art experts, scientists, secretaries, writers, governesses, philosophers, and philanthropists, caught in moments of crisis or conflict, set in the cities and towns of America and Europe.

Ethan Frome is Edith Wharton's most famous, popular, and enduring work; in it, her skills as a novelist and her insight and compassion reached a new high. Though it was not known at the time the book was published, the characters and events of the story had their roots in the hidden reality of Edith Wharton's life. Many years after her death, it was discovered that in the three years before *Ethan Frome* appeared, from 1908 to 1910, when she was in her midforties, the author led a secret and impassioned life (which will be touched upon later) and it became clear that much of the book was based on it.*

Although Mrs. Wharton was born to inherited wealth, in *Ethan Frome* she showed a remarkable understanding of poverty; she knew how it felt to be penniless and realized the depth of despair felt by a poor man trapped by circumstances.

We meet Ethan Frome for the first time when he is fifty-two, "the most striking figure in Starkfield . . . but the ruin of a man." He is tall, gray-haired, badly lamed and scarred, yet with a powerful look about him. But there is "something bleak and unapproachable in his face," and the villagers hint that there is a shocking, mysterious happening in his past.

We meet Ethan again in a flashback, twenty-four years earlier. Young and sensitive, he is desperately but silently in love with Mattie, his wife Zeena's poor, orphaned cousin. A slight, lively, dark-haired young woman, Mattie has been living with Ethan and his wife for a year as an unpaid household helper to Zeena. During the year, she has come to love and cherish Ethan, but her love, like Ethan's, remains unspoken. Zeena, a tall, gaunt, complaining woman seven years older than Ethan, spends most of her time doctoring her symptoms and ailments. Ethan had married her out of fear of loneliness and a feeling of obligation—she had helped nurse his sick mother before she died.

*R.W.B. Lewis recounts in his revelatory work, *Edith Wharton: A Biography,* Harper & Row, Publishers, Inc., New York, 1975, how, more than thirty years after Mrs. Wharton's death, he and Marion Mainwaring unearthed letters and poems relating to Morton Fullerton and her secret love affair with him.

These three live in an isolated, run-down farmhouse two miles from Starkfield. It is winter, and the farmhouse is buried in snow. Winter or summer, the small farm yields little more than a day-to-day living. There is a dearth of cash—years ago, before Zeena's time, Ethan's father had gone "soft in the brain" and, before he died, had given away the money that would have enabled the family to live in comfort.

Seemingly out of the blue, but really because she had become aware of Ethan's interest in Mattie, Zeena declares that her doctor has advised her to hire a girl stronger than Mattie to help in the house: Mattie must go. Unmoved by Ethan's angry pleading, Zeena is adamant, implacable; she is literally and figuratively casting Mattie into the cold.

The seeds of disaster, dormant till now, have been sown. Mattie has no place to go, and Ethan cannot bear to lose her. "All his life was lived in the sight and sound of Mattie Silver and he could no longer conceive of its being otherwise." This is the agonizing dilemma that Ethan, without funds, must somehow resolve. In the memorable second half of *Ethan Frome,* the story of Ethan and Mattie moves with beauty and pain to its fateful climax and its tragic and surprising end.

The love, the joy, the heartbreak, and the anguish—all of the emotions pervading the pages of the book—flowed from the conflict between Edith Wharton's ostensible life and her secret life—her frustrating marriage to Teddy Wharton and her passionate love affair with Morton Fullerton.

Teddy Wharton was thirteen years older than Edith; he was a wealthy, handsome sportsman with no intellectual or artistic interests. (This was not unusual in the leisure class at the time; it was Edith who was "different.") As Edith became a well-known writer, Teddy unhappily found himself more and more out of place in her circle of literary friends. The marriage, which had been amicable, if loveless, deteriorated.

Morton Fullerton, a dapper, prominent American journalist in London and Paris, was divorced but involved with several women when he met Edith in late 1907. Two years younger than she, he shared her interests and was an ardent lover; there is no doubt that he had an irresistible way with women. Edith, at age 46, fell deeply in love for the first time. It was an idyllic, rapturous episode in her life. After three years, the affair began to lose its passion; it was time for Fullerton to move on, and Edith was distracted by her terrible problems with Teddy. He was ill both physically and emotionally and, probably in a spirit of revenge for being cut out of her life, he had embezzled many thousands of dollars of Edith's money, establishing a home for his mistress at the same time.

Although the characters' roles in the love triangle in *Ethan Frome* are reversed from those of the affair in the author's life, the parallels are strong: it appears likely that Edith is Ethan, Morton is Mattie, and Teddy has been transformed into the vengeful Zeena.

While Edith Wharton chose to title *Ethan Frome* with the name of its star character, she did not name *The House of Mirth* for Lily Bart, its unforgettable heroine, whose fate she chronicles. Instead, she took the title from Ecclesiastes in the Old Testament:

> The heart of the wise is in the house of mourning;
> But the heart of fools is in the house of mirth.

It was chosen to reflect Mrs. Wharton's main aim in writing the novel: the depiction, as the leisure class saw it, of the vulgar "new" New York society that was successfully invading refined "old" New York society. In Mrs. Wharton's view, this *nouveau riche* class consisted of millionaires who had *earned* their money in the recent past, most likely by shady and ruthless means; who had built ostentatious city and country homes; who were morally bankrupt and, above all, ill-mannered. This is the society with which the vulnerable Lily Bart is involved.

A portrait of old New York society emerges from the author's memoir, *A Backward Glance*. Of that exclusive upper class, which traced its ancestry back to colonial times and to which her family and her husband's family belonged, she writes "that no retail dealer, no matter . . . how tempting his millions, was received in New York society until long after I was grown up." It was a society closed to all but those who lived on income from "old money" and inherited real estate; who shunned work; who, when not traveling in Europe, spent their time, elegantly dressed, visiting each other and entertaining each other at elaborate dinners (of which there are appetizing descriptions). "My readers," writes Mrs. Wharton, ". . . may be wondering what were the particular merits, private and civic, of these amiable persons." She goes on to say that they had "education and good manners, and . . . a strict standard of uprightness in affairs."

As *The House of Mirth* opens, Lily Bart, low in funds, is on her way to visit friends at their country estate. She knows she may meet a rich, eligible bachelor there, and in exchange for the invitation, she is willing to be used as a bridge partner, secretary, driver, and companion; her stylishness, great beauty, and knowledge of society customs are also of use to her hosts—Lily lends an aura of elegance to any scene.

Missing her train at Grand Central Station, she runs into Lawrence Selden, a friend she sees from time to time. He is a tall, good-looking lawyer, who, struck anew by her "amazing" beauty, invites her to have tea at his apartment until the next train is due. Lily is twenty-nine. It is 1905 and she knows it is not proper for a single young woman to visit a bachelor's apartment, yet she accepts.

Intelligent, a book collector by avocation, Selden, who is somewhat aloof from his upper-class compatriots, lives fairly comfortably but is not rich; Lily does not regard him as a prospective husband. Selden knows that Lily, an orphan left penniless first by the death of her "old New York society" father and then of her extravagant and less well-bred mother, is presently living in New York with her wealthy aunt, also of "old society," who gives Lily a miserly allowance. He also knows, as does Lily's entire circle, that she is looking for a rich husband; she has an extreme horror of poverty.

After tea, Lily refuses Selden's offer to accompany her back to the station. Then, as she is leaving the building, she meets Simon Rosedale, much to her annoyance. Rosedale is a millionaire, an "impossible" Jew. Embarrassed, she tells him that she has been visiting her dressmaker. Rosedale, amused, informs Lily that he owns the building and didn't know there were any dressmakers there. Lily realizes she has compromised herself by lying and fears she may somehow have put herself in Rosedale's power.

To digress for a moment: Mrs. Wharton forgot her good manners when it came to writing about Jews. Though she had allowed herself two Jewish friends (Bernard Berenson, the famous art expert, and the Comtesse Robert de Fitz-James), her prejudice against "the race," as she referred to Jews, turned Simon Rosedale into a caricature rather than a character. While there are no heroes in *The House of Mirth,* Mrs. Wharton created a Jew as villain. (These are some of the words she used to describe Rosedale: fat, shiny, intrusive, insolent, base, gross, rapacious, repugnant, predatory, unscrupulous.) His greatest villainy is wanting to enter New York society. To satisfy his outrageous ambition, he stoops so low as to ask Lily to blackmail one of her friends who had been involved in an adulterous affair. As R. W. B. Lewis remarks about Mrs. Wharton in his biography: "She entertained prejudices that . . . one can only find regrettable."

There is a prevalence of adultery in *The House of Mirth*: among the most unfortunate and damaging things that happen to Lily in the course of the story is her involvement, through indiscretion and accident, in her society friends' extramarital affairs. When *The House of Mirth* was published, Mrs. Wharton had not yet had her affair with Fullerton; she looked with great disfavor on adultery, and considered it a preoccupation of New York society. It is interesting that during her own affair she felt the need somehow to justify it, morally and religiously. She accomplished this by thinking and writing of her relationship with her lover as a return to pre-Christian times when all love was sanctified by nature.

In *The House of Mirth* there is yet a third person who becomes important to Lily—Lawrence Selden's cousin, Gerty Farish. In many ways the antithesis of Lily—plain and steady—Gerty volunteers as a welfare worker among the very poor; she lives in mean, dingy quarters, asking little of life herself, and she is foolishly in love with Selden. But Gerty and Lily are friends, and Lily turns to her in times of trouble and stress.

Selden, Rosedale, and Gerty are not members of the rich social crowd; they move about it rather peripherally. Lily, however, is in the thick of it and, undermined by her own dreamy naiveté, squeamishness, and habit of procrastination, is cruelly treated by it. There is no doubt that she does foolish things; believing that one can get something for nothing, she asks a prominent investor for financial help and, when he gives it, she is shocked to find he expects something in return; when an eligible bachelor is within her grasp, she chooses not to keep an appointment and loses him. But there is also no doubt that terrible things are done to her: though innocent, she becomes a victim of scandalous gossip; and she is used by her society friends as a scapegoat to cover up their own follies.

In Lily, Edith Wharton has created an extremely appealing and provocative heroine. Her beauty is almost ethereal. As Selden walks with her from Grand Central to his apartment, he takes "a luxurious pleasure in her nearness. . . . Everything about her . . . exquisite." He has "a confused sense that she must have cost a great deal to make, that a great many dull and ugly people must, in some mysterious way, have been sacrificed to produce her."

Brought to vivid life by Mrs. Wharton's pen, Lily moves us in many ways. When she is honest and sincere, we love her; when she makes mistakes and bad judgments, she exasperates us. We admire her sensitivity and good taste, but shake our heads over her indecisiveness; we feel terrible when her vile friends do her harm. We root for her, wish her well, and worry with sinking hearts about her future.

The House of Mirth made a sensational debut in 1905; it was both a popular and a critical success, a best seller. It made Mrs. Wharton famous in America and Europe, and opened to her the doors of aristocratic French society, much to her delight and gratification.

Spinners of tales who keep the listener or reader spellbound are often referred to as "born storytellers." Edith Wharton was literally a "born storyteller." When she was three or four years old, before she knew how to read or write, she started "making up," as she called it. This involved holding an open book in her hands, walking up and down a room, alone, and reading aloud a "story" of her own making. So rapidly did she speak, her parents and nurse, listening at the door, could not take down her words.

Mrs. Wharton's awesome storytelling talent is readily apparent in *Tales of Men and Ghosts*. Although it includes only two stories involving ghostly visions (in "The Eyes," a hallucination; in "Afterward," an apparition), many of the stories are dark, and all have surprising twists and ironic endings.

In "The Eyes," a mature man, to please a plain-looking young cousin whom he had offended, proposes marriage; she accepts and he then flees to England without a word to her. A few years later, in Rome, he tells a young writer the novel he has written is great, although it is really awful; he does this to avoid hurting the young man. Around these two actions, Mrs. Wharton has woven a masterful psychological tale that has become known as one of her best. "Afterward," another notable tale, was dramatized and shown on public television. It concerns an American couple who buy an old house in England and are delighted to learn that it has a ghost. But it's an odd ghost, they are told, that will not be known "till long, long afterward."

Many a novel or short story has been made from the stuff of its author's life. In *Tales of Men and Ghosts,* two stories can be traced to their biographical sources: one, "His Father's Son," is based on the rumor of Mrs. Wharton's illegitimate birth; the other, "The Letters," relates to her love affair with Morton Fullerton.

Although it was fairly well circulated in the social circle into which she was born, the rumor that Edith Wharton was an illegitimate child was never proven. It may have started when Mrs. Wharton began showing literary talent: her desire to write was regarded with dismay in her circle. Rich young women were born not to be writers but to ornament their husbands' lives. There were no writers or intellectuals in Edith's family history; where *did* she come from? While Edith was growing up, her two older brothers were being tutored at home by a cultivated young Englishman; the rumor spread that he was her father. Edith was very fond of her real father, George Frederic Jones, who had taught her how to read and in whose library she had spent many happy hours. Though she probably knew about the rumor, she never wrote about it directly, but illegitimacy was a theme in several of her works. In her story "His Father's Son," a successful and snobbish young man comes to believe that he is the illegitimate child of a famous pianist, not the son of the buckle manufacturer who brought him up. How the buckle manufacturer handles this situation makes a wonderful tale.

During Edith's love affair with Fullerton, she was often in America while he was in Europe, and as they both were writers, a great correspondence flowed between them. Even while they were in the same city, letters were often exchanged—Fullerton's letters were precious to Edith. "The Letters" is the story of a young American teacher in Paris who falls in love with the father of her pupil. He is an unsuccessful painter who goes to America to settle his dead wife's estate; the teacher continues to write to him long after his letters stop arriving—she pleads in vain for a word. After three years of silence, he returns. Some years later, the letters she had written to him create a crisis in her life.

Mrs. Wharton was a remarkable woman on several counts: she was a superior writer, in fact, the first American woman to win the Pulitzer Prize for fiction (1921); she became one of the most popular and famous American authors of the twentieth century; and she was a liberated woman, attaining this status against great odds. In this anthology, the reader will find some of the most famous, the best, and the most varied of Edith Wharton's writings.

RUTH LAKE TEPPER

New York City
1987

About the Illustrations
Acknowledgments

As Edith Wharton's prose has not had an abundance of illustrators, despite her long and brilliant publishing history, the period illustrations in this volume were culled from a number of sources. Considerable research was done in that connection, and the editor would like to acknowledge with gratitude the helpful assistance and suggestions of Ruth Lake Tepper; Marion Adler, children's and rare book specialist of Stockbridge, Massachusetts; Kathleen M. Reilly, Research Assistant, Local History and Literature Services at Berkshire Atheneum, Pittsfield, Massachusetts; Denis Leshieur, Head Librarian, Lenox Library, Lenox, Massachusetts; Patricia Middleton, Public Services Reference Librarian, Beinecke Library, Yale University; Barbara Farnsworth, rare book dealer of Cornwall, Connecticut; and Sarah Baldwin, of E. Wharton & Co., Winchester, Massachusetts.

CLAIRE BOOSS

Editorial Note

The editions that were chosen for this collection are, in all cases, the early or first ones. The modern reader may be surprised to discover old-fashioned styles of punctuation and spelling, but these have been kept in order to retain the flavor and authenticity of the originals.

C.B.

Ethan Frome

I HAD the story, bit by bit, from various people, and, as generally happens in such cases, each time it was a different story.

If you know Starkfield, Massachusetts, you know the post-office. If you know the post-office you must have seen Ethan Frome drive up to it, drop the reins on his hollow-backed bay and drag himself across the brick pavement to the white colonnade; and you must have asked who he was.

It was there that, several years ago, I saw him for the first time; and the sight pulled me up sharp. Even then he was the most striking figure in Starkfield, though he was but the ruin of a man. It was not so much his great height that marked him, for the "natives" were easily singled out by their lank longitude from the stockier foreign breed: it was the careless powerful look he had, in spite of a lameness checking each step like the jerk of a chain. There was something bleak and unapproachable in his face, and he was so stiffened and grizzled that I took him for an old man and was surprised to hear that he was not more than fifty-two. I had this from Harmon Gow, who had driven the stage from Bettsbridge to Starkfield in pre-trolley days and knew the chronicle of all the families on his line.

"He's looked that way ever since he had his smash-up; and that's twenty-four years ago come next February," Harmon threw out between reminiscent pauses.

The "smash-up" it was—I gathered from the same informant—which, besides drawing the red gash across Ethan Frome's forehead, had so shortened and warped his right side that it cost him a visible effort to take the few steps from his buggy to the post-office window. He used to drive in from his farm every day at about noon, and as that was my own hour for fetching my mail I often passed him in the porch or stood beside him while we waited on the motions of the distributing hand behind the grating. I noticed that, though he came so punctually, he seldom received anything but a copy of the *Bettsbridge Eagle*, which he put without a glance into his sagging pocket. At intervals, however, the post-master would hand him an envelope addressed to Mrs. Zenobia—or Mrs. Zeena—Frome, and usually bearing conspicuously in the upper left-hand corner the address of some manufacturer of patent medicine and the name of his specific. These documents my neighbor would also pocket without a glance, as if too much used to them to wonder at their number and variety, and would then turn away with a silent nod to the post-master.

Every one in Starkfield knew him and gave him a greeting tempered to his own grave mien; but his taciturnity was respected and it was only on rare occasions that one of the older men of the place detained him for a word. When this happened he would listen quietly, his blue eyes on the speaker's face, and answer in so low a tone that his words never reached me; then he would climb stiffly into his buggy, gather up the reins in his left hand and drive slowly away in the direction of his farm.

"It was a pretty bad smash-up?" I questioned Harmon, looking after Frome's retreating figure, and thinking how gallantly his lean brown head, with its shock of light hair, must have sat on his strong shoulders before they were bent out of shape.

"Wust kind," my informant assented. "More'n enough to kill most men. But the Fromes are tough. Ethan'll likely touch a hundred."

"Good God!" I exclaimed. At the moment Ethan Frome, after climbing to his seat, had leaned over to assure himself of the security of a wooden box—also with a druggist's label on it—which he had placed in the back of the buggy, and I saw his face as it probably looked when he thought himself alone. "*That* man touch a hundred? He looks as if he was dead and in hell now!"

Harmon drew a slab of tobacco from his pocket, cut off a wedge and pressed it into the leather pouch of his cheek. "Guess he's been in Starkfield too many winters. Most of the smart ones get away."

"Why didn't *he?*"

"Somebody had to stay and care for the folks. There warn't ever anybody but Ethan. Fust his father—then his mother—then his wife."

"And then the smash-up?"

Harmon chuckled sardonically. "That's so. He *had* to stay then."

"I see. And since then they've had to care for him?"

Harmon thoughtfully passed his tobacco to the other cheek. "Oh, as to that: I guess it's always Ethan done the caring."

Though Harmon Gow developed the tale as far as his mental and moral reach permitted there were perceptible gaps between his facts, and I had the sense that the deeper meaning of the story was in the gaps. But one phrase stuck in my memory and served as the nucleus about which I grouped my subsequent inferences: "Guess he's been in Starkfield too many winters."

Before my own time there was up I had learned to know what that meant. Yet I had come in the degenerate day of trolley, bicycle and rural delivery, when communication was easy between the scattered mountain villages, and the bigger towns in the valleys, such as Bettsbridge and Shadd's Falls, had libraries, theatres and Y. M. C. A. halls to which the youth of the hills could descend for recreation. But when winter shut down on Starkfield, and the village lay under a sheet of snow perpetually renewed from the pale skies, I began to see what life there—or rather its negation—must have been in Ethan Frome's young manhood.

I had been sent up by my employers on a job connected with the big power-house at Corbury Junction, and a long-drawn carpenters' strike had so delayed the work that I found myself anchored at Starkfield—the nearest habitable spot—for the best part of the winter. I chafed at first, and then, under the hypnotizing effect of routine, gradually began to find a grim satisfaction in the life. During the early part of my stay I had been struck by the contrast between the vitality of the climate and the deadness of the community. Day by day, after the December snows were over, a blazing blue sky poured down torrents of light and air on the white landscape, which gave them back in an intenser glitter. One would have supposed that such an atmosphere must quicken the emotions as well as the blood; but it seemed to produce no change except that of retarding still more the sluggish pulse of Starkfield. When I had been there a little longer, and had seen this phase of crystal clearness followed by long stretches of sunless cold; when the storms of February had pitched their white tents about the devoted village and the wild cavalry of March winds had charged down to their support; I began to understand why Starkfield emerged from its six months' siege like a starved garrison capitulating without quarter. Twenty years earlier the means of resistance must have been far fewer, and the enemy in command of almost all the lines of access between the beleaguered villages; and, considering these things, I felt the sinister force of Harmon's phrase: "Most of the smart ones get away." But if that were the case, how could any combination of obstacles have hindered the flight of a man like Ethan Frome?

During my stay at Starkfield I lodged with a middle-aged widow colloquially known as Mrs. Ned Hale. Mrs. Hale's father had been the village lawyer of the previous generation, and "lawyer Varnum's house," where my landlady still lived with her mother, was the most considerable mansion in the village. It stood at one end of the main street, its classic portico and small-paned windows looking down a flagged path between Norway spruces to the slim white steeple of the Congregational church. It was clear that the Varnum fortunes were at the ebb, but the two women did what they could to preserve a decent dignity; and Mrs. Hale, in particular, had a certain wan refinement not out of keeping with her pale old-fashioned house.

In the "best parlor," with its black horse-hair and mahogany weakly illuminated by a gurgling Carcel lamp, I listened every evening to another and more delicately shaded version of the Starkfield chronicle. It was not that Mrs. Ned Hale felt, or affected, any social superiority to the people about her; it was only that the accident of a finer sensibility and a little more education had put just enough distance between herself and her neighbors to enable her to judge them with detachment. She was not unwilling to exercise this faculty, and I had great hopes of getting from her the missing facts of Ethan Frome's story, or rather such a key to his character as should co-ordinate the facts I knew. Her mind was a store-house of innocuous anecdote and any question about her acquaintances brought forth a volume of detail; but on the subject of Ethan Frome I found her unexpectedly reticent. There was no hint of disapproval in her reserve; I merely felt in her an insurmountable reluctance to speak of him or his affairs, a low "Yes, I knew them both . . . it was awful . . ." seeming to be the utmost concession that her distress could make to my curiosity.

So marked was the change in her manner, such depths of sad initiation did it imply, that, with some doubts as to my delicacy, I put the case anew to my village oracle, Harmon Gow; but got for my pains only an uncomprehending grunt.

"Ruth Varnum was always as nervous as a rat; and, come to think of it, she was the first one to see 'em after they was picked up. It happened right below lawyer Varnum's, down at the bend of the Corbury road, just round about the time that Ruth got engaged to Ned Hale. The young folks was all friends, and I guess she just can't bear to talk about it. She's had troubles enough of her own."

All the dwellers in Starkfield, as in more notable communities, had had troubles enough of their own to make them comparatively indifferent to those of their neighbors; and though all conceded that Ethan Frome's had been beyond the common measure, no one gave me an explanation of the look in his face which, as I persisted in thinking, neither poverty nor physical suffering could have put there. Nevertheless, I might have contented myself with the story pieced together from these hints had it not been for the provocation of Mrs. Hale's silence, and—a little later—for the accident of personal contact with the man.

On my arrival at Starkfield, Denis Eady, the rich Irish grocer, who was the proprietor of Starkfield's nearest approach to a livery stable, had entered into an agreement to send me over daily to Corbury Flats, where I had to pick up my train for the Junction. But about the middle of the winter Eady's horses fell ill of a local epidemic. The illness spread to the other Starkfield stables and for a day or two I was put to it to find a means of transport. Then Harmon Gow suggested that Ethan Frome's bay was still on his legs and that his owner might be glad to drive me over.

I stared at the suggestion. "Ethan Frome? But I've never even spoken to him. Why on earth should he put himself out for me?"

Harmon's answer surprised me still more. "I don't know as he would; but I know he wouldn't be sorry to earn a dollar." I had been told that Frome was poor, and that the saw-mill and the arid acres of his farm yielded scarcely enough to keep his household through the winter; but I had not supposed him to be in such want as Harmon's words implied, and I expressed my wonder.

"Well, matters ain't gone any too well with him," Harmon said. "When a man's been setting round like a hulk for twenty years or more, seeing things that want doing, it eats inter him, and he loses his grit. That Frome farm was always 'bout as bare's a milkpan when the cat's been round; and you know what one of them old water-mills is wuth nowadays. When Ethan could sweat over 'em both from sun-up to dark he kinder choked a living out of 'em; but his folks ate up most everything, even then, and I don't see how he makes out now. Fust his father got a kick, out haying, and went soft in the brain, and gave away money like Bible texts afore he died. Then his mother got queer and dragged along for years as weak as a baby; and his wife Zeena, she's always been the greatest hand at doctoring in the county. Sickness and trouble: that's what Ethan's had his plate full up with, ever since the very first helping."

The next morning, when I looked out, I saw the hollow-backed bay between the Varnum spruces, and Ethan Frome, throwing back his worn bearskin, made room for me in the sleigh at his side. After that, for a week, he drove me over every morning to Corbury Flats, and on my return in the afternoon met me again and carried me back through the icy night to Starkfield. The distance each way was barely three miles, but the old bay's pace was slow, and even with firm snow under the runners we were nearly an hour on the way. Ethan Frome drove in silence, the reins loosely held in his left hand, his brown seamed profile, under the helmet-like peak of the cap, relieved against the banks of snow like the bronze image of a hero. He never turned his face to mine, or answered, except in monosyllables, the questions I put, or such slight pleasantries as I ventured. He seemed a part of the mute melancholy landscape, an incarnation of its frozen woe, with all that was warm and sentient in him fast bound below the surface; but there was nothing unfriendly in his silence. I simply felt that he lived in a depth of moral isolation too remote for casual access, and I had the sense that his loneliness was not merely the result of his personal plight, tragic as I guessed that to be, but had in it, as Harmon Gow had hinted, the profound accumulated cold of many Starkfield winters.

Only once or twice was the distance between us bridged for a moment; and the glimpses thus gained confirmed my desire to know more. Once I happened to speak of an engineering job I had been on the previous year in Florida, and of the contrast between the winter landscape about us and that in which I had found myself the year before; and to my surprise Frome said suddenly: "Yes: I was down there once, and for a good while afterward I could call up the sight of it in winter. But now it's all snowed under."

He drove the sleigh every morning, and came back through the icy night.

He said no more, and I had to guess the rest from the inflection of his voice and his sharp relapse into silence.

Another day, on getting into my train at the Flats, I missed a volume of popular science—I think it was on some recent discoveries in bio-chemistry—which I had carried with me to read on the way. I thought no more about it till I got into the sleigh again that evening, and saw the book in Frome's hand.

"I found it after you were gone," he said.

I put the volume into my pocket and we dropped back into our usual silence; but as we began to crawl up the long hill from Corbury Flats to the Starkfield ridge I became aware in the dusk that he had turned his face to mine.

"There are things in that book that I didn't know the first word about," he said.

I wondered less at his words than at the queer note of resentment in his voice. He was evidently surprised and slightly aggrieved at his own ignorance.

"Does that sort of thing interest you?" I asked.

"It used to."

"There are one or two rather new things in the book: there have been some big strides lately in that particular line of research." I waited a moment for an answer that did not come; then I said: "If you'd like to look the book through I'd be glad to leave it with you."

He hesitated, and I had the impression that he felt himself about to yield to a stealing tide of inertia; then, "Thank you— I'll take it," he answered shortly.

I hoped that this incident might set up some more direct communication between us. Frome was so simple and straightforward that I was sure his curiosity about the book was based on a genuine interest in its subject. Such tastes and acquirements in a man of his condition made the contrast more poignant between his outer situation and his inner needs, and I hoped that the chance of giving expression to the latter might at least unseal his lips. But something in his past history, or in his present way of living, had apparently driven him too deeply into himself for any casual impulse to draw him back to his kind. At our next meeting he made no allusion to the book, and our intercourse seemed fated to remain as negative and one-sided as if there had been no break in his reserve.

Frome had been driving me over to the Flats for about a week when one morning I looked out of my window into a thick snow-fall. The height of the white waves massed against the garden-fence and along the wall of the church showed that the storm must have been going on all night, and that the drifts were likely to be heavy in the open. I thought it probable that my train would be delayed; but I had to be at the power-house for an hour or two that afternoon, and I decided, if Frome turned up, to push through to the Flats and wait there till my train came in. I don't know why I put it in the conditional, however, for I never doubted that Frome would appear. He was not the kind of man to be turned from his business by any commotion of the elements; and at the appointed hour his sleigh glided up through the snow like a stage-apparition behind thickening veils of gauze.

I was getting to know him too well to express either wonder or gratitude at his keeping his appointment; but I exclaimed in surprise as I saw him turn his horse in a direction opposite to that of the Corbury road.

"The railroad's blocked by a freight-train that got stuck in a drift below the Flats," he explained, as we jogged off into the stinging whiteness.

"But look here—where are you taking me, then?"

"Straight to the Junction, by the shortest way," he answered, pointing up School House Hill with his whip.

"To the Junction—in this storm? Why, it's a good ten miles!"

"The bay'll do it if you give him time. You said you had some business there this afternoon. I'll see you get there."

He said it so quietly that I could only answer: "You're doing me the biggest kind of a favor."

"That's all right," he rejoined.

Abreast of the schoolhouse the road forked, and we dipped down a lane to the left, between hemlock boughs bent inward to their trunks by the weight of the snow. I had often walked that way on Sundays, and knew that the solitary roof showing through bare branches near the bottom of the hill was that of Frome's saw-mill. It looked exanimate enough, with its idle wheel looming above the black stream dashed with yellow-white spume, and its cluster of sheds sagging under their white load. Frome did not even turn his head as we drove by, and still in silence we began to mount the next slope. About a mile farther, on a road I had never traveled, we came to an orchard of starved apple-trees writhing over a hillside among outcroppings of slate that nuzzled up through the snow like animals pushing out their noses to breathe. Beyond the orchard lay a field or two, their boundaries lost under drifts; and above the fields, huddled against the white immensities of land and sky, one of those lonely New England farm-houses that make the landscape lonelier.

"That's my place," said Frome, with a sideway jerk of his lame elbow; and in the distress and oppression of the scene I did not know what to answer. The snow had ceased, and a flash of watery sunlight exposed the house on the slope above us in all its plaintive ugliness. The black wraith of a deciduous creeper flapped from the porch, and the thin wooden walls, under their worn coat of paint, seemed to shiver in the wind that had risen with the ceasing of the snow.

"The house was bigger in my father's time: I had to take down the 'L,' a while back," Frome continued, checking with a twitch of the left rein the bay's evident intention of turning in through the broken-down gate.

I saw then that the unusually forlorn and stunted look of the house was partly due to the loss of what is known in New England as the "L": that long deep-roofed adjunct usually built at right angles to the main house, and connecting it, by way of store-rooms and tool-house, with the wood-shed and cow-barn. Whether because of its symbolic sense, the image it presents of a life linked with the soil, and enclosing in itself the chief sources of warmth and nourishment, or whether merely because of the consolatory thought that it enables the dwellers in that harsh climate to get to their morning's work without facing the weather, it is certain that the "L" rather than the house itself seems to be the center, the actual hearth-stone, of the New England farm. Perhaps this connection of ideas, which had often occurred to me in my rambles about Starkfield, caused me to hear a wistful note in Frome's words, and to see in the diminished dwelling the image of his own shrunken body.

"We're kinder side-tracked here now," he added, "but there was considerable passing before the railroad was carried through to the Flats." He roused the lagging bay with another twitch; then, as if the mere sight of the house had let me too deeply into his confidence for any farther pretence of reserve, he went on slowly: "I've always set down the worst of mother's trouble to that. When she got the rheumatism so bad she couldn't move around she used to sit up there and watch the road by the hour; and one year, when they was six months mending the Bettsbridge pike after the floods, and Harmon Gow had to bring his stage round this way, she picked up so that she used to get down to the gate most days to see him. But after the trains begun running nobody ever come by here to speak of, and mother never could get it through her head what had happened, and it preyed on her right along till she died."

As we turned into the Corbury road the snow began to fall again, cutting off our last glimpse of the house; and Frome's silence fell with it, letting down between us the old veil of reticence. This time the wind did not cease with the return of the snow. Instead, it sprang up to a gale which now and then, from a tattered sky, flung pale sweeps of sunlight over a landscape chaotically tossed. But the bay was as good as Frome's word, and we pushed on to the Junction through the wild white scene.

In the afternoon the storm held off, and the clearness in the west seemed to my inexperienced eye the pledge of a fair evening. I finished my business as quickly as possible, and we set out for Starkfield with a good chance of getting there for supper. But at sunset the clouds gathered again, bringing an earlier night, and the snow began to fall straight and steadily from a sky without wind, in a soft universal diffusion more confusing than the gusts and eddies of the morning. It seemed to be a part of the thickening darkness, to be the winter night itself descending on us layer by layer.

The small ray of Frome's lantern was soon lost in this smothering medium, in which even his sense of direction, and the bay's homing instinct, finally ceased to serve us. Two or three times some ghostly landmark sprang up to warn us that we were astray, and then was sucked back into the mist; and when we finally regained our road the old horse began to show signs of exhaustion. I felt myself to blame for having accepted Frome's offer, and after a short discussion I persuaded him to let me get out of the sleigh and walk along through the snow at the bay's side. In this way we struggled on for another mile or two, and at last reached a point where Frome, peering into what seemed to me formless night, said: "That's my gate down yonder."

The last stretch had been the hardest part of the way. The bitter cold and the heavy going had nearly knocked the wind out of me, and I could feel the horse's side ticking like a clock under my hand.

"Look here, Frome," I began, "there's no earthly use in your going any farther—" but he interrupted me: "Nor you neither. There's been about enough of this for anybody."

I understood that he was offering me a night's shelter at the farm, and without answering I turned into the gate at his side, and followed him to the barn, where I helped him to unharness and bed down the tired horse. When this was done he unhooked the lantern from the sleigh, stepped out again into the night, and called to me over his shoulder: "This way."

Far off above us a square of light trembled through the screen of snow. Staggering along in Frome's wake I floundered toward it, and in the darkness almost fell into one of the deep drifts against the front of the house. Frome scrambled up the slippery steps of the porch, digging a way through the snow with his heavily booted foot. Then he lifted his lantern, found the latch, and led the way into the house. I went after him into a low unlit passage, at the back of which a ladder-like staircase rose into obscurity. On our right a line of light marked the door of the room which had sent its ray across the night; and behind the door I heard a woman's voice droning querulously.

Frome stamped on the worn oil-cloth to shake the snow from his boots, and set down his lantern on a kitchen chair which was the only piece of furniture in the hall. Then he opened the door.

"Come in," he said; and as he spoke the droning voice grew still. . .

It was that night that I found the clue to Ethan Frome, and began to put together this vision of his story . . . .

. . . .

. . . .

I

THE village lay under two feet of snow, with drifts at the windy corners. In a sky of iron the points of the Dipper hung like icicles and Orion flashed his cold fires. The moon had set, but the night was so transparent that the white house-fronts between the elms looked gray against the snow, clumps of bushes made black stains on it, and the basement windows of the church sent shafts of yellow light far across the endless undulations.

Young Ethan Frome walked at a quick pace along the deserted street, past the bank and Michael Eady's new brick store and Lawyer Varnum's house with the two black Norway spruces at the gate. Opposite the Varnum gate, where the road fell away toward the Corbury valley, the church reared its slim white steeple and narrow peristyle. As the young man walked toward it the upper windows drew a black arcade along the side wall of the building, but from the lower openings, on the side where the ground sloped steeply down to the Corbury road, the light shot its long bars, illuminating many fresh furrows in the track leading to the basement door, and showing, under an adjoining shed, a line of sleighs with heavily blanketed horses.

The night was perfectly still, and the air so dry and pure that it gave little sensation of cold. The effect produced on Frome was rather of a complete absence of atmosphere, as though nothing less tenuous than ether intervened between the white earth under his feet and the metallic dome overhead. "It's like being in an exhausted receiver," he thought. Four or five years earlier he had taken a year's course at a technological college at Worcester, and dabbled in the laboratory with a friendly professor of physics; and the images supplied by that experience still cropped up, at unexpected moments, through the totally different associations of thought in which he had since been living. His father's death, and the misfortunes following it, had put a premature end to Ethan's studies; but though they had not gone far enough to be of much practical use they had fed his fancy and made him aware of huge cloudy meanings behind the daily face of things.

As he strode along through the snow the sense of such meanings glowed in his brain and mingled with the bodily flush produced by his sharp tramp. At the end of the village he paused before the darkened front of the church. He stood there a moment, breathing quickly, and looking up and down the street, in which not another figure moved. The pitch of the Corbury road, below lawyer Varnum's spruces, was the favorite coasting-ground of Starkfield, and on clear evenings the church corner rang till late with the shouts of the coasters; but tonight not a sled darkened the whiteness of the long declivity. The hush of midnight lay on the village, and all its waking life was gathered behind the church windows, from which strains of dance-music flowed with the broad bands of yellow light.

The young man, skirting the side of the building, went down the slope toward the basement door. To keep out of range of the revealing rays from within he made a circuit through the untrodden snow and gradually approached the farther angle of the basement wall. Thence, still hugging the shadow, he edged his way cautiously forward to the nearest window, holding back his straight spare body and craning his neck till he got a glimpse of the room.

Seen thus, from the pure and frosty darkness in which he stood, it seemed to be seething in a mist of heat. The metal reflectors of the gas-jets sent crude waves of light against the whitewashed walls, and the iron flanks of the stove at the end of the hall looked as though they were heaving with volcanic fires. The floor was thronged with girls and young men. Down the side wall facing the window stood a row of kitchen chairs from which the older women had just risen. By this time the music had stopped, and the musicians—a fiddler, and the young lady who played the harmonium on Sundays—were hastily refreshing themselves at one corner of the supper-table which aligned its devastated pie-dishes and ice-cream saucers on the platform at the end of the hall. The guests were preparing to leave, and the tide had already set toward the passage where coats and wraps were hung, when a young man with a sprightly foot and a shock of black hair shot into the middle of the floor and clapped

The favorite coasting-ground of Starkfield.

his hands. The signal took instant effect. The musicians hurried to their instruments, the dancers—some already half-muffled for departure—fell into line down each side of the room, the older spectators slipped back to their chairs, and the lively young man, after diving about here and there in the throng, drew forth a girl who had already wound a cherry-colored "fascinator" about her head, and, leading her up to the end of the floor, whirled her down its length to the bounding tune of a Virginia reel.

Frome's heart was beating fast. He had been straining for a glimpse of the dark head under the cherry-colored scarf and it vexed him that another eye should have been quicker than his. The leader of the reel, who looked as if he had Irish blood in his veins, danced well, and his partner caught his fire. As she passed down the line, her light figure swinging from hand to hand in circles of increasing swiftness, the scarf flew off her head and stood out behind her shoulders, and Frome, at each turn, caught sight of her laughing panting lips, the cloud of dark hair about her forehead, and the dark eyes which seemed the only fixed points in a maze of flying lines.

The dancers were going faster and faster, and the musicians, to keep up with them, belabored their instruments like jockeys lashing their mounts on the home-stretch; yet it seemed to the young man at the window that the reel would never end. Now and then he turned his eyes from the girl's face to that of her partner, which, in the exhilaration of the dance, had taken on a look of almost impudent ownership. Denis Eady was the son of Michael Eady, the ambitious Irish grocer, whose suppleness and effrontery had given Starkfield its first notion of "smart" business methods, and whose new brick store testified to the success of the attempt. His son seemed likely to follow in his steps, and was meanwhile applying the same arts to the conquest of the Starkfield maidenhood. Hitherto Ethan Frome had been content to think him a mean fellow; but now he positively invited a horse-whipping. It was strange that the girl did not seem aware of it: that she could lift her rapt face to her dancer's, and drop her hands into his, without appearing to feel the offense of his look and touch.

Frome was in the habit of walking into Starkfield to fetch home his wife's cousin, Mattie Silver, on the rare evenings when some chance of amusement drew her to the village. It was his wife who had suggested, when the girl came to live with them, that such opportunities should be put in her way. Mattie Silver came from Stamford, and when she entered the Fromes' household to act as her cousin Zeena's aid it was thought best, as she came without pay, not to let her feel too sharp a contrast between the life she had left and the isolation of a Starkfield farm. But for this—as Frome sardonically reflected—it would hardly have occurred to Zeena to take any thought for the girl's amusement.

When his wife first proposed that they should give Mattie an occasional evening out he had inwardly demurred at having to do the extra two miles to the village and back after his hard day on the farm; but not long afterward he had reached the point of wishing that Starkfield might give all its nights to revelry.

Mattie Silver had lived under his roof for a year, and from early morning till they met at supper he had frequent chances of seeing her; but no moments in her company were comparable to those when, her arm in his, and her light step flying to keep time with his long stride, they walked back through the night to the farm. He had taken to the girl from the first day, when he had driven over to the Flats to meet her, and she had smiled and waved to him from the train, crying out "You must be Ethan!" as she jumped down with her bundles, while he reflected, looking over her slight person: "She don't look much on house-work, but she ain't a fretter, anyhow." But it was not only that the coming to his house of a bit of hopeful young life was like the lighting of a fire on a cold hearth. The girl was more than the bright serviceable creature he had thought her. She had an eye to see and an ear to hear: he could show her things and tell her things, and taste the bliss of feeling that all he imparted left long reverberations and echoes he could wake at will.

It was during their night walks back to the farm that he felt most intensely the sweetness of this communion. He had always been more sensitive than the people about him to the appeal of natural beauty. His unfinished studies had given form to this sensibility and even in his unhappiest moments field and sky spoke to him with a deep and powerful persuasion. But hitherto the emotion had remained in him as a silent ache, veiling with sadness the beauty that evoked it. He did not even know whether any one else in the world felt as he did, or whether he was the sole victim of this mournful privilege. Then he learned that one other spirit had trembled with the same touch of wonder: that at his side, living under his roof and eating his bread, was a creature to whom he could say: "That's Orion down yonder; the big fellow to the right is Aldebaran, and the bunch of little ones—like bees swarming—they're the Pleiades . . ." or whom he could hold entranced before a ledge of granite thrusting up through the fern while he unrolled the huge panorama of the ice age, and the long dim stretches of succeeding time. The fact that admiration for his learning mingled with Mattie's wonder at what he taught was not the least part of his pleasure. And there were other sensations, less definable but more exquisite, which drew them together with a shock of silent joy: the cold red of sunset behind winter hills, the flight of cloud—flocks over slopes of golden stubble, or the intensely blue shadows of hemlocks on sunlit snow. When she said to him once: "It looks just as if it was painted!" it seemed to Ethan that the art of definition could go no farther, and that words had at last been found to utter his secret soul. . . .

As he stood in the darkness outside the church these memories came back with the poignancy of vanished things. Watching Mattie whirl down the floor from hand to hand he wondered how he could ever have thought that his dull talk interested her. To him, who was never gay but in her presence, her gaiety seemed plain proof of indifference. The face she lifted to her dancers was the same which, when she saw him, always looked like a window that has caught the sunset. He even noticed two or three gestures which, in his fatuity, he had thought she kept for him: a way of throwing her head back when she was amused, as if to taste her laugh before she let it out, and a trick of sinking her lids slowly when anything charmed or moved her.

The sight made him unhappy, and his unhappiness roused his latent fears. His wife had never shown any jealousy of Mattie, but of late she had grumbled increasingly over the house-work and found oblique ways of attracting attention to the girl's inefficiency. Zeena had always been what Starkfield called "sickly," and Frome had to admit that, if she were as ailing as she believed, she needed the help of a stronger arm than the one which lay so lightly in his during the night walks to the farm. Mattie had no natural turn for house-keeping, and her training had done nothing to remedy the defect. She was quick to learn, but forgetful and dreamy, and not disposed to take the matter seriously. Ethan had an idea that if she were to marry a man she was fond of the dormant instinct would wake, and her pies and biscuits become the pride of the county; but domesticity in the abstract did not interest her. At first she was so awkward that he could not help laughing at her; but she laughed with him and that made them better friends. He did his best to supplement her unskilled efforts, getting up earlier than usual to light the kitchen fire, carrying in the wood overnight, and neglecting the mill for the farm that he might help her about the house during the day. He even crept down on Saturday nights to scrub the kitchen floor after the women had gone to bed; and Zeena, one day, had surprised him at the churn and had turned away silently, with one of her queer looks.

Of late there had been other signs of her disfavor, as intangible but more disquieting. One cold winter morning, as he dressed in the dark, his candle flickering in the draught of the ill-fitting window, he had heard her speak from the bed behind him.

"The doctor don't want I should be left without anybody to do for me," she said in her flat whine.

He had supposed her to be asleep, and the sound of her voice had startled him, though she was given to abrupt explosions of speech after long intervals of secretive silence.

He turned and looked at her where she lay indistinctly outlined under the dark calico quilt, her high-boned face taking a grayish tinge from the whiteness of the pillow.

"Nobody to do for you?" he repeated.

"If you say you can't afford a hired girl when Mattie goes."

Frome turned away again, and taking up his razor stooped to catch the reflection of his stretched cheek in the blotched looking-glass above the wash-stand.

"Why on earth should Mattie go?"

"Well, when she gets married, I mean," his wife's drawl came from behind him.

"Oh, she'd never leave us as long as you needed her," he returned, scraping hard at his chin.

"I wouldn't ever have it said that I stood in the way of a poor girl like Mattie marrying a smart fellow like Denis Eady," Zeena answered in a tone of plaintive self-effacement.

Ethan, glaring at his face in the glass, threw his head back to draw the razor from ear to chin. His hand was steady, but the attitude was an excuse for not making an immediate reply.

"And the doctor don't want I should be left without anybody,"

Zeena continued. "He wanted I should speak to you about a girl he's heard about, that might come—"

Ethan laid down the razor and straightened himself with a laugh.

"Denis Eady! If that's all I guess there's no such hurry to look round for a girl."

"Well, I'd like to talk to you about it," said Zeena obstinately.

He was getting into his clothes in fumbling haste.

"All right. But I haven't got the time now; I'm late as it is," he returned, holding his old silver turnip-watch to the candle.

Zeena, apparently accepting this as final, lay watching him in silence while he pulled his suspenders over his shoulders and jerked his arms into his coat; but as he went toward the door she said, suddenly and incisively: "I guess you're always late, now you shave every morning."

That thrust had frightened him more than any vague insinuations about Denis Eady. It was a fact that since Mattie Silver's coming he had taken to shaving every day; but his wife always seemed to be asleep when he left her side in the winter darkness, and he had stupidly assumed that she would not notice any change in his appearance. Once or twice in the past he had been faintly disquieted by Zenobia's way of letting things happen without seeming to remark them, and then, weeks afterward, in a casual phrase, revealing that she had all along taken her notes and drawn her inferences. Of late, however, there had been no room in his thoughts for such vague apprehensions. Zeena herself, from an oppressive reality, had faded into an insubstantial shade. All his life was lived in the sight and sound of Mattie Silver, and he could no longer conceive of its being otherwise. But now, as he stood outside the church, and saw Mattie spinning down the floor with Denis Eady, a throng of disregarded hints and menaces wove their cloud about his brain . . .

"I guess you're always late, now you shave every morning."

II

AS the dancers poured out of the hall Frome, drawing back behind the projecting storm-door, watched the segregation of the grotesquely muffled groups, in which a moving lantern ray now and then lit up a face flushed with food and dancing. The villagers, being afoot, were the first to climb the slope to the main street, while the country neighbors packed themselves more slowly into the sleighs under the shed.

"Ain't you riding, Mattie?" a woman's voice called back from the throng about the shed, and Ethan's heart gave a jump. From where he stood he could not see the persons coming out of the hall till they had advanced a few steps beyond the wooden sides of the storm-door; but through its cracks he heard a clear voice answer: "Mercy no! Not on such a night."

She was there, then, close to him, only a thin board between. In another moment she would step forth into the night, and his eyes, accustomed to the obscurity, would discern her as clearly as though she stood in daylight. A wave of shyness pulled him back into the dark angle of the wall, and he stood there in silence instead of making his presence known to her. It had been one of the wonders of their intercourse that from the first, she, the quicker, finer, more expressive, instead of crushing him by the contrast, had given him something of her own ease and freedom; but now he felt as heavy and loutish as in his student days, when he had tried to "jolly" the Worcester girls at a picnic.

He hung back, and she came out alone and paused within a few yards of him. She was almost the last to leave the hall, and she stood looking uncertainly about her as if wondering why he did not show himself. Then a man's figure approached, coming so close to her that under their formless wrappings they seemed merged in one dim outline.

"Gentleman friend gone back on you? Say, Matt, that's tough! No, I wouldn't be mean enough to tell the other girls. I ain't as low-down as that." (How Frome hated his cheap banter!) "But look at here, ain't it lucky I got the old man's cutter down there waiting for us?"

Frome heard the girl's voice, gaily incredulous: "What on earth's your father's cutter doin' down there?"

"Why, waiting for me to take a ride. I got the roan colt too. I kinder knew I'd want to take a ride tonight," Eady, in his triumph, tried to put a sentimental note into his bragging voice.

The girl seemed to waver, and Frome saw her twirl the end of her scarf irresolutely about her fingers. Not for the world would he have made a sign to her, though it seemed to him that his life hung on her next gesture.

"Hold on a minute while I unhitch the colt," Denis called to her, springing toward the shed.

She stood perfectly still, looking after him, in an attitude of tranquil expectancy torturing to the hidden watcher. Frome noticed that she no longer turned her head from side to side, as though peering through the night for another figure. She let Denis Eady lead out the horse, climb into the cutter and fling back the bearskin to make room for her at his side; then, with a swift motion of flight, she turned about and darted up the slope toward the front of the church.

"Good-bye! Hope you'll have a lovely ride!" she called back to him over her shoulder.

Denis laughed, and gave the horse a cut that brought him quickly abreast of her retreating figure.

"Come along! Get in quick! It's as slippery as thunder on this turn," he cried, leaning over to reach out a hand to her.

She laughed back at him: "Good-night! I'm not getting in."

By this time they had passed beyond Frome's earshot and he could only follow the shadowy pantomime of their silhouettes as they continued to move along the crest of the slope above him. He saw Eady, after a moment, jump from the cutter and go toward the girl with the reins over one arm. The other he tried to slip through hers; but she eluded him nimbly, and Frome's heart, which had swung out over a black void, trembled back to safety. A moment later he heard the jingle of departing sleigh bells and discerned a figure advancing alone toward the empty expanse of snow before the church.

In the black shade of the Varnum spruces he caught up with her and she turned with a quick "Oh!"

"Think I'd forgotten you, Matt?" he asked with sheepish glee.

She answered seriously: "I thought maybe you couldn't come back for me."

"Couldn't? What on earth could stop me?"

"I knew Zeena wasn't feeling any too good today."

"Oh, she's in bed long ago." He paused, a question struggling in him. "Then you meant to walk home all alone?"

"Oh, I ain't afraid!" she laughed.

They stood together in the gloom of the spruces, an empty world glimmering about them wide and gray under the stars. He brought his question out.

"If you thought I hadn't come, why didn't you ride back with Denis Eady?"

"Why, where *were* you? How did you know? I never saw you!"

Her wonder and his laughter ran together like spring rills in a thaw. Ethan had the sense of having done something arch and ingenious. To prolong the effect he groped for a dazzling phrase, and brought out, in a growl of rapture: "Come along."

He slipped an arm through hers, as Eady had done, and fancied it was faintly pressed against her side; but neither of them moved. It was so dark under the spruces that he could barely see the shape of her head beside his shoulder. He longed to stoop his cheek and rub it against her scarf. He would have liked to stand there with her all night in the blackness. She moved forward a step or two and then paused again above the dip of the Corbury road. Its icy slope, scored by innumerable runners, looked like a mirror scratched by travelers at an inn.

"There was a whole lot of them coasting before the moon set," she said.

"Would you like to come in and coast with them some night?" he asked.

"Oh, *would* you, Ethan? It would be lovely!"

"We'll come tomorrow if there's a moon."

She lingered, pressing closer to his side. "Ned Hale and Ruth Varnum came just as *near* running into the big elm at the bottom.

We were all sure they were killed." Her shiver ran down his arm. "Wouldn't it have been too awful? They're so happy!"

"Oh, Ned ain't much at steering. I guess I can take you down all right!" he said disdainfully.

He was aware that he was "talking big," like Denis Eady; but his reaction of joy had unsteadied him, and the inflection with which she had said of the engaged couple "They're so happy!" made the words sound as if she had been thinking of herself and him.

"The elm *is* dangerous, though. It ought to be cut down," she insisted.

"Would you be afraid of it, with me?"

"I told you I ain't the kind to be afraid," she tossed back, almost indifferently; and suddenly she began to walk on with a rapid step.

These alterations of mood were the despair and joy of Ethan Frome. The motions of her mind were as incalculable as the flit of a bird in the branches. The fact that he had no right to show his feelings and thus provoke the expression of hers, made him attach a fantastic importance to every change in her look and tone. Now he thought she understood him, and feared; now he was sure she did not, and despaired. Tonight the pressure of accumulated misgivings sent the scale drooping toward despair, and her indifference was the more chilling after the flush of joy into which she had plunged him by dismissing Denis Eady. He mounted School House Hill at her side and walked on in silence till they reached the lane leading to the saw-mill; then the need of some definite assurance grew too strong for him.

"You'd have found me right off if you hadn't gone back to have that last reel with Denis," he brought out awkwardly. He could not pronounce the name without a stiffening of the muscles of his throat.

"Why, Ethan, how could I tell you were there?"

"I suppose what folks say is true," he jerked out at her, instead of answering.

She stopped short, and he felt, in the darkness, that her face was lifted quickly to his. "Why, what do folks say?"

"It's natural enough you should be leaving us," he floundered on, following his thought.

"Is that what they say?" she mocked back at him; then, with a sudden drop of her sweet treble: "You mean that Zeena—ain't suited with me any more?" she faltered.

Their arms had slipped apart and they stood motionless, each seeking to distinguish the other's face.

"I know I ain't anything like as smart as I ought to be," she went on, while he vainly struggled for expression. "There's lots of things a hired girl could do that come awkward to me still—and I haven't got much strength in my arms. But if she'd only tell me I'd try. You know she hardly ever says anything, and sometimes I can see she ain't suited, and yet I don't know why." She turned on him with a sudden flash of indignation. "You'd ought to tell me, Ethan Frome—you'd ought to! Unless *you* want me to go too—"

Unless he wanted her to go too! The cry was balm to his raw wound. The iron heavens seemed to melt and rain down sweetness. Again he struggled for the all-expressive word, and again, his arm in hers, found only a deep "Come along."

They walked on in silence through the blackness of the hemlock-shaded lane, where Ethan's saw-mill gloomed through the night, and out again into the comparative clearness of the fields. On the farther side of the hemlock belt the open country rolled away before them gray and lonely under the stars. Sometimes their way led them under the shade of an overhanging bank or through the thin obscurity of a clump of leafless trees. Here and there a farmhouse stood far back among the fields, mute and cold as a grave-stone. The night was so still that they heard the frozen snow crackle under their feet. The crash of a loaded branch falling far off in the woods reverberated like a musket-shot, and once a fox barked, and Mattie shrank closer to Ethan, and quickened her steps.

At length they sighted the group of larches at Ethan's gate, and as they drew near it the sense that the walk was over brought back his words.

"Then you don't want to leave us, Matt?"

He had to stoop his head to catch her stifled whisper: "Where'd I go, if I did?"

The answer sent a pang through him but the tone suffused him with joy. He forgot what else he had meant to say and pressed her against him so closely that he seemed to feel her warmth in his veins.

"You ain't crying are you, Matt?"

"No, of course I'm not," she quavered.

They turned in at the gate and passed under the shaded knoll where, enclosed in a low fence, the Frome grave-stones slanted at crazy angles through the snow. Ethan looked at them curiously. For years that quiet company had mocked his restlessness, his desire for change and freedom. "We never got away—how should you?" seemed to be written on every headstone; and whenever he went in or out of his gate he thought with a shiver: "I shall just go on living here till I join them." But now all desire for change had vanished, and the sight of the little enclosure gave him a warm sense of continuance and stability.

"I guess we'll never let you go, Matt," he whispered, as though even the dead, lovers once, must conspire with him to keep her; and brushing by the graves, he thought: "We'll always go on living here together, and some day she'll lie there beside me."

He let the vision possess him as they climbed the hill to the house. He was never so happy with her as when he abandoned himself to these dreams. Half-way up the slope Mattie stumbled against some unseen obstruction and clutched his sleeve to steady herself. The wave of warmth that went through him was like the prolongation of his vision. For the first time he stole his arm about her, and she did not resist. They walked on as if they were floating on a summer stream.

Zeena always went to bed as soon as she had had her supper, and the shutterless windows of the house were dark. A dead cucumber-vine dangled from the porch like the crape streamer tied to the door for a death, and the thought flashed through Ethan's brain: "If it was there for Zeena—" Then he had a distinct sight of his wife lying in their bedroom asleep, her mouth slightly open, her false teeth in a tumbler by the bed . . .

They walked around to the back of the house, between the rigid gooseberry bushes. It was Zeena's habit, when they came back late from the village, to leave the key of the kitchen door under the mat.

Ethan stood before the door, his head heavy with dreams, his arm still about Mattie. "Matt—" he began, not knowing what he meant to say.

She slipped out of his hold without speaking, and he stooped down and felt for the key.

"It's not there!" he said, straightening himself with a start.

They strained their eyes at each other through the icy darkness. Such a thing had never happened before.

"Maybe she's forgotten it," Mattie said in a tremulous whisper; but both of them knew that it was not like Zeena to forget.

"It might have fallen off into the snow," Mattie continued, after a pause during which they had stood intently listening.

"It must have been pushed off, then," he rejoined in the same tone. Another wild thought tore through him. What if tramps had been there—what if . . .

Again he listened, fancying he heard a distant sound in the house; then he felt in his pocket for a match, and kneeling down, passed its light slowly over the rough edges of snow about the doorstep.

He was still kneeling when his eyes, on a level with the lower panel of the door, caught a faint ray beneath it. Who could be stirring in that silent house? He heard a step on the stairs, and again for an instant the thought of tramps tore through him. Then the door opened and he saw his wife.

Against the dark background of the kitchen she stood up tall and angular, one hand drawing a quilted counterpane to her flat breast, while the other held a lamp. The light, on a level with her chin, drew out of the darkness her puckered throat and the projecting wrist of the hand that clutched the quilt, and deepened fantastically the hollows and prominences of her high-boned face under its ring of crimping-pins. To Ethan, still in the rosy haze of his hour with Mattie, the sight came with the intense precision of the last dream before waking. He felt as if he had never before known what his wife looked like.

She drew aside without speaking, and Mattie and Ethan passed into the kitchen, which had the deadly chill of a vault after the dry cold of the night.

"Guess you forgot about us, Zeena," Ethan joked, stamping the snow from his boots.

"No. I just felt so mean I couldn't sleep."

Mattie came forward, unwinding her wraps, the color of the cherry scarf in her fresh lips and cheeks. "I'm so sorry, Zeena! Isn't there anything I can do?"

"No; there's nothing." Zeena turned away from her. "You might 'a' shook off that snow outside," she said to her husband.

She walked out of the kitchen ahead of them and pausing in the hall raised the lamp at arm's-length, as if to light them up the stairs.

Ethan paused also, affecting to fumble for the peg on which he hung his coat and cap. The doors of the two bedrooms faced each other across the narrow upper landing, and tonight it was peculiarly repugnant to him that Mattie should see him follow Zeena.

"I guess I won't come up yet awhile," he said, turning as if to go back to the kitchen.

Zeena stopped short and looked at him. "For the land's sake—what you going to do down here?"

"I've got the mill accounts to go over."

She continued to stare at him, the flame of the unshaded lamp bringing out with microscopic cruelty the fretful lines of her face.

"At this time o' night? You'll ketch your death. The fire's out long ago."

Without answering he moved away toward the kitchen. As he did so his glance crossed Mattie's and he fancied that a fugitive warning gleamed through her lashes. The next moment they sank to her flushed cheeks and she began to mount the stairs ahead of Zeena.

"That's so. It *is* powerful cold down here," Ethan assented; and with lowered head he went up in his wife's wake, and followed her across the threshold of their room.

III

THERE was some hauling to be done at the lower end of the wood-lot, and Ethan was out early the next day.

The winter morning was as clear as crystal. The sunrise burned red in a pure sky, the shadows on the rim of the wood-lot were darkly blue, and beyond the white and scintillating fields patches of far-off forest hung like smoke.

It was in the early morning stillness, when his muscles were swinging to their familiar task and his lungs expanding with long draughts of mountain air, that Ethan did his clearest thinking. He and Zeena had not exchanged a word after the door of their room had closed on them. She had measured out some drops from a medicine-bottle on a chair by the bed and, after swallowing them, and wrapping her head in a piece of yellow flannel, had lain down with her face turned away. Ethan undressed hurriedly and blew out the light so that he should not see her when he took his place at her side. As he lay there he could hear Mattie moving about in her room, and her candle, sending its small ray across the landing, drew a scarcely perceptible line of light under his door. He kept his eyes fixed on the light till it vanished. Then the room grew perfectly black, and not a sound was audible but Zeena's asthmatic breathing. Ethan felt confusedly that there were many things he ought to think about, but through his tingling veins and tired brain only one sensation throbbed: the warmth of Mattie's shoulder against his. Why had he not kissed her when he held her there? A few hours earlier he would not have asked himself the question. Even a few minutes earlier, when they had stood alone outside the house, he would not have dared to think of kissing her. But since he had seen her lips in the lamplight he felt that they were his.

Now, in the bright morning air, her face was still before him. It was part of the sun's red and of the pure glitter on the snow. How the girl had changed since she had come to Starkfield! He remembered what a colorless slip of a thing she had looked the day he had met her at the station. And all the first winter, how she had shivered with cold when the northerly gales shook the thin clapboards and the snow beat like hail against the loose-hung windows!

He had been afraid that she would hate the hard life, the cold and loneliness; but not a sign of discontent escaped her. Zeena took the view that Mattie was bound to make the best of Starkfield since she hadn't any other place to go to; but this did not strike Ethan as conclusive. Zeena, at any rate, did not apply the principle in her own case.

He felt all the more sorry for the girl because misfortune had, in a sense, indentured her to them. Mattie Silver was the daughter of a cousin of Zenobia Frome's, who had inflamed his clan with mingled sentiments of envy and admiration by descending from the hills to Connecticut, where he had married a Stamford girl and succeeded to her father's thriving "drug" business. Unhappily Orin Silver, a man of far-reaching aims, had died too soon to prove that the end justifies the means. His accounts revealed merely what the means had been; and these were such that it was fortunate for his wife and daughter that his books were examined only after his impressive funeral. His wife died of the disclosure, and Mattie, at twenty, was left alone to make her way on the fifty dollars obtained from the

How the girl had changed since she had come to Starkfield!

sale of her piano. For this purpose her equipment, though varied, was inadequate. She could trim a hat, make molasses candy, recite "Curfew shall not ring tonight," and play "The Lost Chord" and a pot-pourri from "Carmen." When she tried to extend the field of her activities in the direction of stenography and book-keeping her health broke down, and six months on her feet behind the counter of a department store did not tend to restore it. Her nearest relations had been induced to place their savings in her father's hands, and though, after his death, they ungrudgingly acquitted themselves of the Christian duty of returning good for evil by giving his daughter all the advice at their disposal, they could hardly be expected to supplement it by material aid. But when Zenobia's doctor recommended her looking about for some one to help her with the housework the clan instantly saw the chance of exacting a compensation from Mattie. Zenobia, though doubtful of the girl's efficiency, was tempted by the freedom to find fault without much risk of losing her; and so Mattie came to Starkfield.

Zenobia's fault-finding was of the silent kind, but not the less penetrating for that. During the first months Ethan alternately burned with the desire to see Mattie defy her and trembled with fear of the result. Then the situation grew less strained. The pure air, and the long summer hours in the open, gave back life and elasticity to Mattie, and Zeena, with more leisure to devote to her complex ailments, grew less watchful of the girl's omissions; so that Ethan, struggling on under the burden of his barren farm and failing sawmill, could at least imagine that peace reigned in his house.

There was really, even now, no tangible evidence to the contrary; but since the previous night a vague dread had hung on his sky-line. It was formed of Zeena's obstinate silence, of Mattie's sudden look of warning, of the memory of just such fleeting imperceptible signs as those which told him, on certain stainless mornings, that before night there would be rain.

His dread was so strong that, man-like, he sought to postpone certainty. The hauling was not over till mid-day, and as the lumber was to be delivered to Andrew Hale, the Starkfield builder, it was really easier for Ethan to send Jotham Powell, the hired man, back to the farm on foot, and drive the load down to the village himself. He had scrambled up on the logs, and was sitting astride of them, close over his shaggy grays, when, coming between him and their steaming necks, he had a vision of the warning look that Mattie had given him the night before.

"If there's going to be any trouble I want to be there," was his vague reflection, as he threw to Jotham the unexpected order to unhitch the team and lead them back to the barn.

It was a slow trudge home through the heavy fields, and when the two men entered the kitchen Mattie was lifting the coffee from the stove and Zeena was already at the table. Her husband stopped short at sight of her. Instead of her usual calico wrapper and knitted shawl she wore her best dress of brown merino, and above her thin strands of hair, which still preserved the tight undulations of the crimping-pins, rose a hard perpendicular bonnet, as to which Ethan's clearest notion was that he had to pay five dollars for it at the Bettsbridge Emporium. On the floor beside her stood his old valise and a bandbox wrapped in newspapers.

"Why, where are you going, Zeena?" he exclaimed.

"I've got my shooting pains so bad that I'm going over to Bettsbridge to spend the night with Aunt Martha Pierce and see that new doctor," she answered in a matter-of-fact tone, as if she had said she was going into the store-room to take a look at the preserves, or up to the attic to go over the blankets.

In spite of her sedentary habits such abrupt decisions were not without precedent in Zeena's history. Twice or thrice before she had suddenly packed Ethan's valise and started off to Bettsbridge, or even Springfield, to seek the advice of some new doctor, and her husband had grown to dread these expeditions because of their cost. Zeena always came back laden with expensive remedies, and her last visit to Springfield had been commemorated by her paying twenty dollars for an electric battery of which she had never been able to learn the use. But for the moment his sense of relief was so great as to preclude all other feelings. He had now no doubt that Zeena had spoken the truth in saying, the night before, that she had sat up because she felt "too mean" to sleep: her abrupt resolve to seek medical advice showed that, as usual, she was wholly absorbed in her health.

As if expecting a protest, she continued plaintively; "If you're too busy with the hauling I presume you can let Jotham Powell drive me over with the sorrel in time to ketch the train at the Flats."

Her husband hardly heard what she was saying. During the winter months there was no stage between Starkfield and Bettsbridge, and the trains which stopped at Corbury Flats were slow and infrequent. A rapid calculation showed Ethan that Zeena could not be back at the farm before the following evening. . . .

"If I'd supposed you'd 'a' made any objection to Jotham Powell's driving me over—" she began again, as though his silence had implied refusal. On the brink of departure she was always seized with a flux of words. "All I know is," she continued, "I can't go on the way I am much longer. The pains are clear away down to my ankles now, or I'd 'a' walked in to Starkfield on my own feet, sooner'n put you out, and asked Michael Eady to let me ride over on his wagon to the Flats, when he sends to meet the train that brings his groceries. I'd 'a' had two hours to wait in the station, but I'd sooner 'a' done it, even with this cold, than to have you say—"

"Of course Jotham'll drive you over," Ethan roused himself to answer. He became suddenly conscious that he was looking at Mattie while Zeena talked to him, and with an effort he turned his eyes to his wife. She sat opposite the window, and the pale light reflected from the banks of snow made her face look more than usually drawn and bloodless, sharpened the three parallel creases between ear and cheek, and drew querulous lines from her thin nose to the corners of her mouth. Though she was but seven years her husband's senior, and he was only twenty-eight, she was already an old woman.

Ethan tried to say something befitting the occasion, but there was only one thought in his mind: the fact that, for the first time since Mattie had come to live with them, Zeena was to be away for a night. He wondered if the girl were thinking of it too. . . .

He knew that Zeena must be wondering why he did not offer to drive her to the Flats and let Jotham Powell take the lumber to Starkfield, and at first he could not think of a pretext for not doing so; then he said: "I'd take you over myself, only I've got to collect the cash for the lumber."

As soon as the words were spoken he regretted them, not only because they were untrue—there being no prospect of his receiving cash payment from Hale—but also because he knew from experience the imprudence of letting Zeena think he was in funds on the eve of one of her therapeutic excursions. At the moment, however, his one desire was to avoid the long drive with her behind the ancient sorrel who never went out of a walk.

Zeena made no reply: she did not seem to hear what he had said. She had already pushed her plate aside, and was measuring out a draught from a large bottle at her elbow.

"It ain't done me a speck of good, but I guess I might as well use it up," she remarked; adding, as she pushed the empty bottle toward Mattie:

"If you can get the taste out it'll do for pickles."

IV

AS soon as his wife had driven off Ethan took his coat and cap from the peg. Mattie was washing up the dishes, humming one of the dance tunes of the night before. He said "So long, Matt," and she answered gaily "So long, Ethan," and that was all.

It was warm and bright in the kitchen. The sun slanted through the south window on the girl's moving figure, on the cat dozing in a chair, and on the geraniums brought in from the door-way, where Ethan had planted them in the summer to "make a garden" for Mattie. He would have liked to linger on, watching her tidy up and then settle down to her sewing; but he wanted still more to get the hauling done and be back at the farm before night.

All the way down to the village he continued to think of his return to Mattie. The kitchen was a poor place, not "spruce" and shining as his mother had kept it in his boyhood; but it was surprising what a homelike look the mere fact of Zeena's absence gave it. And he pictured what it would be like that evening, when he and Mattie were there after supper. For the first time they would be alone together indoors, and they would sit there, one on each side of the stove, like a married couple, he in his stocking feet and smoking his pipe, she laughing and talking in that funny way she had, which was always as new to him as if he had never heard her before.

The sweetness of the picture, and the relief of knowing that his fears of "trouble" with Zeena were unfounded, sent up his spirits with a rush, and he, who was usually so silent, whistled and sang aloud as he drove through the snowy fields. There was in him a slumbering spark of sociability which the long Starkfield winters had not yet extinguished. By nature grave and inarticulate, he admired recklessness and gaiety in others and was warmed to the marrow by friendly human intercourse. At Worcester, though he had the name of keeping to himself and not being much of a hand at a good time, he had secretly gloried in being clapped on the back and hailed as "Old Ethe" or "Old Stiff"; and the cessation of such familiarities had increased the chill of his return to Starkfield.

There the silence had deepened about him year by year. Left alone, after his father's accident, to carry the burden of farm and mill, he had had no time for convivial loiterings in the village; and when his mother fell ill the loneliness of the house grew more oppressive than that of the fields. His mother had been a talker in her day, but after her "trouble" the sound of her voice was seldom heard, though she had not lost the power of speech. Sometimes, in the long winter evenings, when in desperation her son asked her why she didn't "say something" she would lift a finger and answer: "Because I'm listening"; and on stormy nights, when the loud wind was about the house, she would complain, if he spoke to her: "They're talking so out there that I can't hear you."

It was only when she drew toward her last illness, and his cousin Zenobia Pierce came over from the next valley to help him nurse her, that human speech was heard again in the house. After the mortal silence of his long imprisonment Zeena's volubility was music in his ears. He felt that he might have "gone like his mother" if the sound of a new voice had not come to steady him. Zeena seemed to understand his case at a glance. She laughed at him for not knowing the simplest sickbed duties and told him to "go right along out" and leave her to see to things. The mere fact of obeying her orders, of feeling free to go about his business again and talk with other men, restored his shaken balance and magnified his sense of what he owed her. Her efficiency shamed and dazzled him. She seemed to possess by instinct all the household wisdom that his long apprenticeship had not instilled in him. When the end came it was she who had to tell him to hitch up and go for the undertaker, and she thought it "funny" that he had not settled beforehand who was to have his mother's clothes and the sewing-machine. After the funeral, when he saw her preparing to go away, he was seized with an unreasoning dread of being left alone on the farm; and before he knew what he was doing he had asked her to stay there with him. He had often thought since that it would not have happened if his mother had died in spring instead of winter . . .

When they married it was agreed that, as soon as he could straighten out the difficulties resulting from Mrs. Frome's long illness, they would sell the farm and saw-mill and try their luck in a large town. Ethan's love of nature did not take the form of a taste for agriculture. He had always wanted to be an engineer, and to live in towns, where there were lectures and big libraries and "fellows doing things." A slight engineering job in Florida, put in his way during his period of study at Worcester, increased his faith in his ability as well as his eagerness to see the world; and he felt sure that, with a "smart" wife like Zeena, it would not be long before he had made himself a place in it.

Zeena's native village was slightly larger and nearer to the railway than Starkfield, and she had let her husband see from the first that life on an isolated farm was not what she had expected when she married. But purchasers were slow in coming, and while he waited for them Ethan learned the impossibility of transplanting her. She chose to look down on Starkfield, but she could not have lived in a place which looked down on her. Even Bettsbridge or Shadd's Falls would not have been sufficiently aware of her, and in the greater cities which attracted Ethan she would have suffered a complete loss of identity. And within a year of their marriage she developed the "sickliness" which had since made her notable even in a community rich in pathological instances. When she came to take care of his mother she had seemed to Ethan like the very genius of health, but he soon saw that her skill as a nurse had been acquired by the absorbed observation of her own symptoms.

Then she too fell silent. Perhaps it was the inevitable effect of life on the farm, or perhaps, as she sometimes said, it was because Ethan "never listened." The charge was not wholly unfounded. When she spoke it was only to complain, and to complain of things not in his power to remedy; and to check a tendency to impatient retort he had first formed the habit of not answering her, and finally of thinking of other things while she talked. Of late, however, since he had had reasons for observing her more closely, her silence had begun to trouble him. He recalled his mother's growing taciturnity, and wondered if Zeena were also turning "queer." Women did, he knew. Zeena, who had at her fingers' ends the pathological chart of the whole region, had cited many cases of the kind while she was nursing his mother; and he himself knew of certain lonely farm-houses in the neighborhood where stricken creatures pined, and of others where sudden tragedy had come of their presence. At times, looking at Zeena's shut face, he felt the chill of such forebodings. At other times her silence seemed deliberately assumed to conceal far-reaching intentions, mysterious conclusions drawn from suspicions and resentments impossible to guess. That supposition was even more disturbing than the other; and it was the one which had come to him the night before, when he had seen her standing in the kitchen door.

Now her departure for Bettsbridge had once more eased his mind, and all his thoughts were on the prospect of his evening with Mattie. Only one thing weighed on him, and that was his having told Zeena that he was to receive cash for the lumber. He foresaw so clearly the consequences of this imprudence that with considerable reluctance he decided to ask Andrew Hale for a small advance on his load.

When Ethan drove into Hale's yard the builder was just getting out of his sleigh.

"Hello, Ethe!" he said. "This comes handy."

Andrew Hale was a ruddy man with a big gray moustache and a stubbly double-chin unconstrained by a collar; but his scrupulously clean shirt was always fastened by a small diamond stud. This display of opulence was misleading, for though he did a fairly good business it was known that his easy-going habits and the demands of his large family frequently kept him what Starkfield called "behind." He was an old friend of Ethan's family, and his house one of the few to which Zeena occasionally went, drawn there by the fact that Mrs. Hale, in her youth, had done more "doctoring" than any other woman in Starkfield, and was still a recognized authority on symptoms and treatment.

Hale went up to the grays and patted their sweating flanks.

"Well, sir," he said, "you keep them two as if they was pets."

Ethan set about unloading the logs and when he had finished his job he pushed open the glazed door of the shed which the builder used as his office. Hale sat with his feet up on the stove, his back propped against a battered desk strewn with papers: the place, like the man, was warm, genial and untidy.

"Sit right down and thaw out," he greeted Ethan.

The latter did not know how to begin, but at length he managed to bring out his request for an advance of fifty dollars. The blood rushed to his thin skin under the sting of Hale's astonishment. It was the builder's custom to pay at the end of three months, and there was no precedent between the two men for a cash settlement.

Ethan felt that if he had pleaded an urgent need Hale might have made shift to pay him; but pride, and an instinctive prudence, kept him from resorting to this argument. After his father's death it had taken time to get his head above water, and he did not want Andrew Hale, or any one else in Starkfield, to think he was going under again. Besides, he hated lying; if he wanted the money he wanted it, and it was nobody's business to ask why. He therefore made his demand with the awkwardness of a proud man who will not admit to himself that he is stooping; and he was not much surprised at Hale's refusal.

The builder refused genially, as he did everything else: he treated the matter as something in the nature of a practical joke, and wanted to know if Ethan meditated buying a grand piano or adding a "cupolo" to his house; offering, in the latter case, to give his services free of cost.

Ethan's arts were soon exhausted, and after an embarrassed pause he wished Hale good day and opened the door of the office. As he passed out the builder suddenly called after him: "See here—you ain't in a tight place, are you?"

"Not a bit," Ethan's pride retorted before his reason had time to intervene.

"Well, that's good! Because I *am* a shade. Fact is, I was going to ask you to give me a little extra time on that payment. Business is pretty slack, to begin with, and then I'm fixing up a little house for Ned and Ruth when they're married. I'm glad to do it for 'em, but it costs." His look appealed to Ethan for sympathy. "The young people like things nice. You know how it is yourself: it's not so long ago since you fixed up your own place for Zeena."

Ethan left the grays in Hale's stable and went about some other business in the village. As he walked away the builder's last phrase lingered in his ears, and he reflected grimly that his seven years with Zeena seemed to Starkfield "not so long."

The afternoon was drawing to an end, and here and there a lighted pane spangled the cold gray dusk and made the snow look whiter. The bitter weather had driven every one indoors and Ethan had the long rural street to himself. Suddenly he heard the brisk play of sleigh-bells and a cutter passed him, drawn by a free-going horse. Ethan recognized Michael Eady's roan colt, and young Denis Eady, in a handsome new fur cap, leaned forward and waved a greeting. "Hello, Ethe!" he shouted and spun on.

The cutter was going in the direction of the Frome farm, and Ethan's heart contracted as he listened to the dwindling bells. What more likely than that Denis Eady had heard of Zeena's departure for Bettsbridge, and was profiting by the opportunity to spend an hour with Mattie? Ethan was ashamed of the storm of jealousy in his breast. It seemed unworthy of the girl that his thoughts of her should be so violent.

He walked on to the church corner and entered the shade of the Varnum spruces, where he had stood with her the night before. As he passed into their gloom he saw an indistinct outline just ahead of him. At his approach it melted for an instant into two separate shapes and then conjoined again, and he heard a kiss, and a half-laughing "Oh!" provoked by the discovery of his presence. Again the outline hastily disunited and the Varnum gate slammed on one half while the other hurried on ahead of him. Ethan smiled at the discomfiture he had caused. What did it matter to Ned Hale and Ruth Varnum if they were caught kissing each other? Everybody in Starkfield knew they were engaged. It pleased Ethan to have surprised a pair of lovers on the spot where he and Mattie had stood with such a thirst for each other in their hearts; but he felt a pang at the thought that these two need not hide their happiness.

He fetched the grays from Hale's stable and started on his long climb back to the farm. The cold was less sharp than earlier in the day and a thick fleecy sky threatened snow for the morrow. Here and there a star pricked through, showing behind it a deep well of blue. In an hour or two the moon would push up over the ridge behind the farm, burn a gold-edged rent in the clouds, and then be swallowed by them. A mournful peace hung on the fields, as though they felt the relaxing grasp of the cold and stretched themselves in their long winter sleep.

Ethan's ears were alert for the jingle of sleigh-bells, but not a

As he drew near the farm, he saw a light twinkling in the house.

sound broke the silence of the lonely road. As he drew near the farm he saw, through the thin screen of larches at the gate, a light twinkling in the house above him. "She's up in her room," he said to himself, "fixing herself up for supper"; and he remembered Zeena's sarcastic stare when Mattie, on the evening of her arrival, had come down to supper with smoothed hair and a ribbon at her neck.

He passed by the graves on the knoll and turned his head to glance at one of the older headstones, which had interested him deeply as a boy because it bore his name.

SACRED TO THE MEMORY OF
ETHAN FROME AND ENDURANCE HIS WIFE,
WHO DWELLED TOGETHER IN PEACE
FOR FIFTY YEARS.

He used to think that fifty years sounded like a long time to live together; but now it seemed to him that they might pass in a flash. Then, with a sudden dart of irony, he wondered if, when their turn came, the same epitaph would be written over him and Zeena.

He opened the barn-door and craned his head into the obscurity, half-fearing to discover Denis Eady's roan colt in the stall beside the sorrel. But the old horse was there alone, mumbling his crib with toothless jaws, and Ethan whistled cheerfully while he bedded down the grays and shook an extra measure of oats into their mangers. His was not a tuneful throat, but harsh melodies burst from it as he locked the barn and sprang up the hill to the house. He reached the kitchen-porch and turned the door-handle; but the door did not yield to his touch.

Startled at finding it locked he rattled the handle violently; then he reflected that Mattie was alone and that it was natural she should barricade herself at nightfall. He stood in the darkness expecting to hear her step. It did not come, and after vainly straining his ears he called out in a voice that shook with joy: "Hello, Matt!"

Silence answered; but in a minute or two he caught a sound on the stairs and saw a line of light about the door-frame, as he had seen it the night before. So strange was the precision with which the incidents of the previous evening were repeating themselves that he half expected, when he heard the key turn, to see his wife before him on the threshold; but the door opened, and Mattie faced him.

She stood just as Zeena had stood, a lifted lamp in her hand, against the black background of the kitchen. She held the light at the same level, and it drew out with the same distinctness her slim young throat and the brown wrist no bigger than a child's. Then, striking upward, it threw a lustrous fleck on her lips, edged her eyes with velvet shade, and laid a milky whiteness above the black curve of her brows.

She wore her usual dress of darkish stuff, and there was no bow at her neck; but through her hair she had run a streak of crimson ribbon. This tribute to the unusual transformed and glorified her. She seemed to Ethan taller, fuller, more womanly in shape and motion. She stood aside, smiling silently, while he entered, and then moved away from him with something soft and flowing in her gait. She set the lamp on the table, and he saw that it was carefully laid for supper, with fresh doughnuts, stewed blueberries and his favorite pickles in a dish of gay red glass. A bright fire glowed in the stove and the cat lay stretched before it, watching the table with a drowsy eye.

Ethan was suffocated with the sense of well-being. He went out into the passage to hang up his coat and pull off his wet boots. When he came back Mattie had set the teapot on the table and the cat was rubbing itself persuasively against her ankles.

"Why, Puss! I nearly tripped over you," she cried, the laughter sparkling through her lashes.

Again Ethan felt a sudden twinge of jealousy. Could it be his coming that gave her such a kindled face?

"Well, Matt, any visitors?" he threw off, stooping down carelessly to examine the fastening of the stove.

She nodded and laughed "Yes, one," and he felt a blackness settling on his brows.

"Who was that?" he questioned, raising himself up to slant a glance at her beneath his scowl.

Her eyes danced with malice. "Why, Jotham Powell. He came in after he got back, and asked for a drop of coffee before he went down home."

The blackness lifted and light flooded Ethan's brain. "That all? Well, I hope you made out to let him have it." And after a pause he felt it right to add: "I suppose he got Zeena over to the Flats all right?"

"Oh, yes; in plenty of time."

The name threw a chill between them, and they stood a moment looking sideways at each other before Mattie said with a shy laugh: "I guess it's about time for supper."

They drew their seats up to the table, and the cat, unbidden, jumped between them into Zeena's empty chair. "Oh, Puss!" said Mattie, and they laughed again.

Ethan, a moment earlier, had felt himself on the brink of eloquence; but the mention of Zeena had paralyzed him. Mattie seemed to feel the contagion of his embarrassment, and sat with downcast lids, sipping her tea, while he feigned an insatiable appetite for doughnuts and sweet pickles. At last, after casting about for an effective opening, he took a long gulp of tea, cleared his throat, and said: "Looks as if there'd be more snow."

She feigned great interest. "Is that so? Do you suppose it'll interfere with Zeena's getting back?"

She flushed red as the question escaped her, and hastily set down the cup she was lifting.

Ethan reached over for another helping of pickles.

"You never can tell, this time of year, it drifts so bad on the Flats." The name had benumbed him again, and once more he felt as if Zeena were in the room between them.

"Oh, Puss, you're too greedy!" Mattie cried. The cat, unnoticed, had crept up on muffled paws from Zeena's seat to the table, and was stealthily elongating its body in the direction of the milk-jug, which stood between Ethan and Mattie. The two leaned forward at the same moment and their hands met on the handle of the jug. Mattie's hand was underneath, and Ethan kept his clasped on it a moment longer than was necessary. The cat, profiting by this unusual demonstration, tried to effect an unnoticed retreat, and in doing so backed into the pickle-dish, which fell to the floor with a crash.

Mattie, in an instant, had sprung from her chair and was down on her knees by the fragments.

"Oh, Ethan, Ethan—it's all to pieces! What will Zeena say?"

But this time his courage was up. "Well, she'll have to say it to the cat, any way!" he rejoined with a laugh, kneeling down at Mattie's side to scrape up the swimming pickles.

She lifted stricken eyes to him. "Yes, but, you see, she never meant it should be used, not even when there was company; and I had to get up on the step-ladder to reach it down from the top shelf of the china-closet, where she keeps it with all her best things, and of course she'll want to know why I did it—?"

The case was so serious that it called forth all of Ethan's latent resolution.

"She needn't know anything about it if you keep quiet. I'll get another just like it tomorrow. Where did it come from? I'll go to Shadd's Falls for it if I have to!"

"Oh, you'll never get another even there! It was a wedding present—don't you remember? It came all the way from Philadelphia, from Zeena's aunt that married the minister. That's why she wouldn't ever use it. Oh, Ethan, Ethan, what in the world shall I do?"

She began to cry, and he felt as if every one of her tears were pouring over him like burning lead. "Don't, Matt, don't—oh, *don't!*" he implored her.

She struggled to her feet, and he rose and followed her helplessly while she spread out the pieces of glass on the kitchen dresser. It seemed to him as if the shattered fragments of their evening lay there.

"Here, give them to me," he said in a voice of sudden authority.

She drew aside, instinctively obeying his tone. "Oh, Ethan, what are you going to do?"

Without replying he gathered the pieces of glass into his broad palm and walked out of the kitchen to the passage. There he lit a candle-end, opened the china-closet, and, reaching his long arm up to the highest shelf, laid the pieces together with such accuracy of touch that a close inspection convinced him of the impossibility of detecting from below that the dish was broken. If he glued it together the next morning months might elapse before his wife noticed what had happened, and meanwhile he might after all be able to match the dish at Shadd's Falls or Bettsbridge. Having satisfied himself that there was no risk of immediate discovery he went back to the kitchen with a lighter step, and found Mattie disconsolately removing the last scraps of pickle from the floor.

"It's all right, Matt. Come back and finish supper," he commanded her.

Completely reassured, she shone on him through tear-hung lashes, and his soul swelled with pride as he saw how his tone subdued her. She did not even ask what he had done. Except when he was steering a big log down the mountain to his mill he had never known such a thrilling sense of mastery.

V

THEY finished supper, and while Mattie cleared the table Ethan went to look at the cows and then took a last turn about the house. The earth lay dark under a muffled sky and the air was so still that now and then he heard a lump of snow come thumping down from a tree far off on the edge of the wood-lot.

When he returned to the kitchen Mattie had pushed up his chair to the stove and seated herself near the lamp with a bit of sewing. The scene was just as he had dreamed of it that morning. He sat down, drew his pipe from his pocket and stretched his feet to the glow. His hard day's work in the keen air made him feel at once lazy and light of mood, and he had a confused sense of being in another world, where all was warmth and harmony and time could bring no change. The only drawback to his complete well-being was the fact that he could not see Mattie from where he sat; but he was too indolent to move and after a moment he said: "Come over here and sit by the stove."

Zeena's empty rocking-chair stood facing him. Mattie rose obediently, and seated herself in it. As her young brown head detached itself against the patch-work cushion that habitually framed his wife's gaunt countenance, Ethan had a momentary shock. It was almost as if the other face, the face of the superseded woman, had obliterated that of the intruder. After a moment Mattie seemed to be affected by the same sense of constraint. She changed her position, leaning forward to bend her head above her work, so that he saw only the foreshortened tip of her nose and the streak of red in her hair; then she slipped to her feet, saying "I can't see to sew," and went back to her chair by the lamp.

Ethan made a pretext of getting up to replenish the stove, and when he returned to his seat he pushed it sideways that he might

The cat had been a puzzled observer of these unusual movements.

get a view of her profile and of the lamplight falling on her hands. The cat, who had been a puzzled observer of these unusual movements, jumped up into Zeena's chair, rolled itself into a ball, and lay watching them with narrowed eyes.

Deep quiet sank on the room. The clock ticked above the dresser, a piece of charred wood fell now and then in the stove, and the faint sharp scent of the geraniums mingled with the odor of Ethan's smoke, which began to throw a blue haze about the lamp and to hang its grayish cobwebs in the shadowy corners of the room.

All constraint had vanished between the two, and they began to talk easily and simply. They spoke of every-day things, of the prospect of snow, of the next church sociable, of the loves and quarrels of Starkfield. The commonplace nature of what they said produced in Ethan an illusion of long-established intimacy which no outburst of emotion could have given, and he set his imagination adrift on the fiction that they had always spent their evenings thus and would always go on doing so . . .

"This is the night we were to have gone coasting, Matt," he said at length, with the rich sense, as he spoke, that they could go on any other night they chose, since they had all time before them.

She smiled back at him. "I guess you forgot!"

"No, I didn't forget; but it's as dark as Egypt outdoors. We might go tomorrow if there's a moon."

She laughed with pleasure, her head tilted back, the lamplight sparkling on her lips and teeth. "That would be lovely, Ethan!"

He kept his eyes fixed on her, marvelling at the way her face changed with each turn of their talk, like a wheat-field under a summer breeze. It was intoxicating to find such magic in his clumsy words, and he longed to try new ways of using it.

"Would you be scared to go down the Corbury road with me on a night like this?" he asked.

Her cheeks burned redder. "I ain't any more scared than you are!"

"Well, *I'd* be scared, then; I wouldn't do it. That's an ugly corner down by the big elm. If a fellow didn't keep his eyes open he'd go plumb into it." He luxuriated in the sense of protection and authority which his words conveyed. To prolong and intensify the feeling he added: "I guess we're well enough here."

She let her lids sink slowly, in the way he loved. "Yes, we're well enough here," she sighed.

Her tone was so sweet that he took the pipe from his mouth and drew his chair up to the table. Leaning forward, he touched the farther end of the strip of brown stuff that she was hemming. "Say, Matt," he began with a smile, "what do you think I saw under the Varnum spruces, coming along home just now? I saw a friend of yours getting kissed."

The words had been on his tongue all the evening, but now that he had spoken them they struck him as inexpressibly vulgar and out of place.

Mattie blushed to the roots of her hair and pulled her needle rapidly twice or thrice through her work, insensibly drawing the end of it away from him. "I suppose it was Ruth and Ned," she said in a low voice, as though he had suddenly touched on something grave.

Ethan had imagined that his allusion might open the way to the accepted pleasantries, and these perhaps in turn to a harmless caress, if only a mere touch on her hand. But now he felt as if her blush had set a flaming guard about her. He supposed it was his natural awkwardness that made him feel so. He knew that most young men made nothing at all of giving a pretty girl a kiss, and he remembered that the night before, when he had put his arm about Mattie, she had not resisted. But that had been out-of-doors, under the open irresponsible night. Now, in the warm lamplit room, with all its ancient implications of conformity and order, she seemed infinitely farther away from him and more unapproachable.

To ease his constraint he said: "I suppose they'll be setting a date before long."

"Yes. I shouldn't wonder if they got married some time along in the summer." She pronounced the word *married* as if her voice caressed it. It seemed a rustling covert leading to enchanted glades. A pang shot through Ethan, and he said, twisting away from her in his chair: "It'll be your turn next, I wouldn't wonder."

She laughed a little uncertainly. "Why do you keep on saying that?"

He echoed her laugh. "I guess I do it to get used to the idea."

He drew up to the table again and she sewed on in silence, with dropped lashes, while he sat in fascinated contemplation of the way in which her hands went up and down above the strip of stuff, just as he had seen a pair of birds make short perpendicular flights over a nest they were building. At length, without turning her head or lifting her lids, she said in a low tone: "It's not because you think Zeena's got anything against me, is it?"

His former dread started up full-armed at the suggestion. "Why, what do you mean?" he stammered.

She raised distressed eyes to his, her work dropping on the table between them. "I don't know. I thought last night she seemed to have."

"I'd like to know what," he growled.

"Nobody can tell with Zeena." It was the first time they had ever spoken so openly of her attitude toward Mattie, and the repetition of the name seemed to carry it to the farther corners of the room and send it back to them in long repercussions of sound. Mattie waited, as if to give the echo time to drop, and then went on: "She hasn't said anything to *you?"*

He shook his head. "No, not a word."

She tossed the hair back from her forehead with a laugh. "I guess I'm just nervous, then. I'm not going to think about it any more."

"Oh, no—don't let's think about it, Matt!"

The sudden heat of his tone made her color mount again, not with a rush, but gradually, delicately, like the reflection of a thought stealing slowly across her heart. She sat silent, her hands clasped on her work, and it seemed to him that a warm current flowed toward him along the strip of stuff that still lay unrolled between them. Cautiously he slid his hand palm-downward along the table till his finger-tips touched the end of the stuff. A faint vibration of her lashes seemed to show that she was aware of his gesture, and that it had sent a counter-current back to her; and she let her hands lie motionless on the other end of the strip.

As they sat thus he heard a sound behind him and turned his head. The cat had jumped from Zeena's chair to dart at a mouse in the wainscot, and as a result of the sudden movement the empty chair had set up a spectral rocking.

"She'll be rocking in it herself this time tomorrow," Ethan thought. "I've been in a dream, and this is the only evening we'll ever have together." The return to reality was as painful as the return to consciousness after taking an anæsthetic. His body and brain ached with indescribable weariness, and he could think of nothing to say or to do that should arrest the mad flight of the moments.

His alteration of mood seemed to have communicated itself to

Mattie. She looked up at him languidly, as though her lids were weighted with sleep and it cost her an effort to raise them. Her glance fell on his hand, which now completely covered the end of her work and grasped it as if it were a part of herself. He saw a scarcely perceptible tremor cross her face, and without knowing what he did he stooped his head and kissed the bit of stuff in his hold. As his lips rested on it he felt it glide slowly from beneath them, and saw that Mattie had risen and was silently rolling up her work. She fastened it with a pin, and then, finding her thimble and scissors, put them with the roll of stuff into the box covered with fancy paper which he had once brought to her from Bettsbridge.

He stood up also, looking vaguely about the room. The clock above the dresser struck eleven.

"Is the fire all right?" she asked in a low voice.

He opened the door of the stove and poked aimlessly at the embers. When he raised himself again he saw that she was dragging toward the stove the old soap-box lined with carpet in which the cat made its bed. Then she recrossed the floor and lifted two of the geranium pots in her arms, moving them away from the cold window. He followed her and brought the other geraniums, the hyacinth bulbs in a cracked custard bowl and the German ivy trained over an old croquet hoop.

When these nightly duties were performed there was nothing left to do but to bring in the tin candlestick from the passage, light the candle and blow out the lamp. Ethan put the candlestick in Mattie's hand and she went out of the kitchen ahead of him, the light that she carried before her making her dark hair look like a drift of mist on the moon.

"Good night, Matt," he said as she put her foot on the first step of the stairs.

She turned and looked at him a moment. "Good night, Ethan," she answered, and went up.

When the door of her room had closed on her he remembered that he had not even touched her hand.

VI

THE next morning at breakfast Jotham Powell was between them, and Ethan tried to hide his joy under an air of exaggerated indifference, lounging back in his chair to throw scraps to the cat, growling at the weather, and not so much as offering to help Mattie when she rose to clear away the dishes.

He did not know why he was so irrationally happy, for nothing was changed in his life or hers. He had not even touched the tip of her fingers or looked her full in the eyes. But their evening together had given him a vision of what life at her side might be, and he was glad now that he had done nothing to trouble the sweetness of the picture. He had a fancy that she knew what had restrained him . . .

There was a last load of lumber to be hauled to the village, and Jotham Powell—who did not work regularly for Ethan in winter—had "come round" to help with the job. But a wet snow, melting to sleet, had fallen in the night and turned the roads to glass. There was more wet in the air and it seemed likely to both men that the weather would "milden" toward afternoon and make the going safer. Ethan therefore proposed to his assistant that they should load the sledge at the wood-lot, as they had done on the previous morning, and put off the "teaming" to Starkfield till later in the day. This plan had the advantage of enabling him to send Jotham to the Flats after dinner to meet Zenobia, while he himself took the lumber down to the village.

He told Jotham to go out and harness up the grays, and for a moment he and Mattie had the kitchen to themselves. She had plunged the breakfast dishes into a tin dish-pan and was bending above it with her slim arms bared to the elbow, the steam from the hot water beading her forehead and tightening her rough hair into little brown rings like the tendrils on the traveller's joy.

Ethan stood looking at her, his heart in his throat. He wanted to say: "We shall never be alone again like this." Instead, he reached down his tobacco-pouch from a shelf of the dresser, put it into his pocket and said: "I guess I can make out to be home for dinner."

She answered "All right, Ethan," and he heard her singing over the dishes as he went.

As soon as the sledge was loaded he meant to send Jotham back to the farm and hurry on foot into the village to buy the glue for the pickle-dish. With ordinary luck he should have had time to carry out this plan; but everything went wrong from the start. On the way over to the wood-lot one of the grays slipped on a glare of ice and cut his knee, and when they got him up again Jotham had to go back to the barn for a strip of rag to bind the cut. Then, when the loading finally began, a sleety rain was coming down once more, and the tree trunks were so slippery that it took twice as long as usual to lift them and get them in place on the sledge. It was what Jotham called a sour morning for work, and the horses, shivering and stamping under their wet blankets, seemed to like it as little as the men. It was long past the dinner-hour when the job was done, and Ethan had to give up going to the village because he wanted to lead the injured horse home and wash the cut himself.

He thought that by starting out again with the lumber as soon as he had finished his dinner he might get back to the farm with the glue before Jotham and the old sorrel had had time to fetch Zenobia from the Flats; but he knew the chance was a slight one. It turned on the state of the roads and on the possible lateness of the Bettsbridge train. He remembered afterward, with a grim flash of self-derision, what importance he had attached to the weighing of these probabilities . . .

As soon as dinner was over he set out again for the wood-lot, not daring to linger till Jotham Powell left. The hired man was still drying his wet feet at the stove, and Ethan could only give Mattie a quick look as he said beneath his breath: "I'll be back early."

He fancied that she nodded her comprehension; and with that scant solace he had to trudge off through the rain.

He had driven his load half-way to the village when Jotham Powell overtook him, urging the reluctant sorrel toward the Flats. "I'll have to hurry up to do it," Ethan mused, as the sleigh dropped down ahead of him over the dip of the school-house hill. He worked like ten at the unloading, and when it was over hastened on to Michael Eady's for the glue. Eady and his assistant were both "down street," and young Denis, who seldom deigned to take their place, was lounging by the stove with a knot of the golden youth of Starkfield. They hailed Ethan with ironic compliment and offers of conviviality; but no one knew where to find the glue. Ethan, consumed with the longing for a last moment alone with Mattie, hung about impatiently while Denis made an ineffectual search in the obscurer corners of the store.

"Looks as if we were all sold out. But if you'll wait around till the old man comes along maybe he can put his hand on it."

"I'm obliged to you, but I'll try if I can get it down at Mrs. Homan's," Ethan answered, burning to be gone.

Denis's commercial instinct compelled him to aver on oath that what Eady's store could not produce would never be found at the widow Homan's; but Ethan, heedless of this boast, had already climbed to the sledge and was driving on to the rival establishment. Here, after considerable search, and sympathetic questions as to what he wanted it for, and whether ordinary flour paste wouldn't do as well if she couldn't find it, the widow Homan finally hunted down her solitary bottle of glue to its hiding-place in a medley of cough-lozenges and corset-laces.

"I hope Zeena ain't broken anything she sets store by," she called after him as he turned the grays toward home.

The fitful bursts of sleet had changed into a steady rain and the horses had heavy work even without a load behind them. Once or twice, hearing sleigh-bells, Ethan turned his head, fancying that Zeena and Jotham might overtake him; but the old sorrel was not in sight, and he set his face against the rain and urged on his ponderous pair.

The barn was empty when the horses turned into it and, after giving them the most perfunctory ministrations they had ever received from him, he strode up to the house and pushed open the kitchen door.

Mattie was there alone, as he had pictured her. She was bending over a pan on the stove; but at the sound of his step she turned with a start and sprang to him.

"See, here, Matt, I've got some stuff to mend the dish with! Let me get at it quick," he cried, waving the bottle in one hand while he put her lightly aside; but she did not seem to hear him.

"Oh, Ethan—Zeena's come," she said in a whisper, clutching his sleeve.

They stood and stared at each other, pale as culprits.

"But the sorrel's not in the barn!" Ethan stammered.

"Jotham Powell brought some goods over from the Flats for his wife, and he drove right on home with them," she explained.

He gazed blankly about the kitchen, which looked cold and squalid in the rainy winter twilight.

"How is she?" he asked, dropping his voice to Mattie's whisper.

She looked away from him uncertainly. "I don't know. She went right up to her room."

"She didn't say anything?"

"No."

Ethan let out his doubts in a low whistle and thrust the bottle back into his pocket. "Don't fret; I'll come down and mend it in the night," he said. He pulled on his wet coat again and went back to the barn to feed the grays.

While he was there Jotham Powell drove up with the sleigh, and when the horses had been attended to Ethan said to him: "You might as well come back up for a bite." He was not sorry to assure himself of Jotham's neutralizing presence at the supper table, for Zeena was always "nervous" after a journey. But the hired man, though seldom loth to accept a meal not included in his wages, opened his stiff jaws to answer slowly: "I'm obliged to you, but I guess I'll go along back."

Ethan looked at him in surprise. "Better come up and dry off. Looks as if there'd be something hot for supper."

Jotham's facial muscles were unmoved by this appeal and, his vocabulary being limited, he merely repeated: "I guess I'll go along back."

To Ethan there was something vaguely ominous in this stolid rejection of free food and warmth, and he wondered what had happened on the drive to nerve Jotham to such stoicism. Perhaps Zeena had failed to see the new doctor or had not liked his counsels: Ethan knew that in such cases the first person she met was likely to be held responsible for her grievance.

When he re-entered the kitchen the lamp lit up the same scene of shining comfort as on the previous evening. The table had been as carefully laid, a clear fire glowed in the stove, the cat dozed in its warmth, and Mattie came forward carrying a plate of doughnuts.

She and Ethan looked at each other in silence; then she said, as she had said the night before: "I guess it's about time for supper."

VII

ETHAN went out into the passage to hang up his wet garments. He listened for Zeena's step and, not hearing it, called her name up the stairs. She did not answer, and after a moment's hesitation he went up and opened her door. The room was almost dark, but in the obscurity he saw her sitting by the window, bolt upright, and knew by the rigidity of the outline projected against the pane that she had not taken off her travelling dress.

"Well, Zeena," he ventured from the threshold.

She did not move, and he continued: "Supper's about ready. Ain't you coming?"

She replied: "I don't feel as if I could touch a morsel."

It was the consecrated formula, and he expected it to be followed, as usual, by her rising and going down to supper. But she remained seated, and he could think of nothing more felicitous than: "I presume you're tired after the long ride."

Turning her head at this, she answered solemnly: "I'm a great deal sicker than you think."

Her words fell on his ear with a strange shock of wonder. He had often heard her pronounce them before—what if at last they were true?

He advanced a step or two into the dim room. "I hope that's not so, Zeena," he said.

She continued to gaze at him through the twilight with a mien of wan authority, as of one consciously singled out for a great fate. "I've got complications," she said.

Ethan knew the word for one of exceptional import. Almost everybody in the neighborhood had "troubles," frankly localized and specified; but only the chosen had "complications." To have them was in itself a distinction, though it was also, in most cases, a death-warrant. People struggled on for years with "troubles," but they almost always succumbed to "complications."

Ethan's heart was jerking to and fro between two extremities of feeling, but for the moment compassion prevailed. His wife looked so hard and lonely, sitting there in the darkness with such thoughts.

"Is that what the new doctor told you?" he asked, instinctively lowering his voice.

"Yes. He says any regular doctor would want me to have an operation."

Ethan was aware that, in regard to the important question of surgical intervention, the female opinion of the neighborhood was divided, some glorying in the prestige conferred by operations while others shunned them as indelicate. Ethan, from motives of economy, had always been glad that Zeena was of the latter faction.

In the agitation caused by the gravity of her announcement he sought a consolatory short cut. "What do you know about this doctor anyway? Nobody ever told you that before."

He saw his blunder before she could take it up: she wanted sympathy, not consolation.

"I didn't need to have anybody tell me I was losing ground every day. Everybody but you could see it. And everybody in Bettsbridge knows about Dr. Buck. He has his office in Worcester, and comes over once a fortnight to Shadd's Falls and Bettsbridge for consultations. Eliza Spears was wasting away with kidney trouble before she went to him, and now she's up and around, and singing in the choir."

"Well, I'm glad of that. You must do just what he tells you," Ethan answered sympathetically.

She was still looking at him. "I mean to," she said. He was struck by a new note in her voice. It was neither whining nor reproachful, but drily resolute.

"What does he want you should do?" he asked, with a mounting vision of fresh expenses.

"He wants I should have a hired girl. He says I oughtn't to have to do a single thing around the house."

"A hired girl?" Ethan stood transfixed.

"Yes. And Aunt Martha found me one right off. Everybody said

I was lucky to get a girl to come away out here, and I agreed to give her a dollar extry to make sure. She'll be over tomorrow afternoon."

Wrath and dismay contended in Ethan. He had foreseen an immediate demand for money, but not a permanent drain on his scant resources. He no longer believed what Zeena had told him of the supposed seriousness of her state: he saw in her expedition to Bettsbridge only a plot hatched between herself and her Pierce relations to foist on him the cost of a servant; and for the moment wrath predominated.

"If you meant to engage a girl you ought to have told me before you started," he said.

"How could I tell you before I started? How did I know what Dr. Buck would say?"

"Oh, Dr. Buck—" Ethan's incredulity escaped in a short laugh. "Did Dr. Buck tell you how I was to pay her wages?"

Her voice rose furiously with his. "No, he didn't. For I'd 'a' been ashamed to tell him that you grudged me the money to get back my health, when I lost it nursing your own mother!"

"*You* lost your health nursing mother?"

"Yes; and my folks all told me at the time you couldn't do no less than marry me after—"

"Zeena!"

Through the obscurity which hid their faces their thoughts seemed to dart at each other like serpents shooting venom. Ethan was seized with horror of the scene and shame at his own share in it. It was as senseless and savage as a physical fight between two enemies in the darkness.

He turned to the shelf above the chimney, groped for matches and lit the one candle in the room. At first its weak flame made no impression on the shadows; then Zeena's face stood grimly out against the uncurtained pane, which had turned from gray to black.

It was the first scene of open anger between the couple in their sad seven years together, and Ethan felt as if he had lost an irretrievable advantage in descending to the level of recrimination. But the practical problem was there and had to be dealt with.

"You know I haven't got the money to pay for a girl, Zeena. You'll have to send her back: I can't do it."

"The doctor says it'll be my death if I go on slaving the way I've had to. He doesn't understand how I've stood it as long as I have."

"Slaving!—" He checked himself again, "You sha'n't lift a hand, if he says so. I'll do everything round the house myself—"

She broke in: "You're neglecting the farm enough already," and this being true, he found no answer, and left her time to add ironically: "Better send me over to the almshouse and done with it . . . I guess there's been Fromes there afore now."

The taunt burned into him, but he let it pass. "I haven't got the money. That settles it."

There was a moment's pause in the struggle, as though the combatants were testing their weapons. Then Zeena said in a level voice: "I thought you were to get fifty dollars from Andrew Hale for that lumber."

"Andrew Hale never pays under three months."

He had hardly spoken when he remembered the excuse he had made for not accompanying his wife to the station the day before; and the blood rose to his frowning brows.

"Why, you told me yesterday you'd fixed it up with him to pay cash down. You said that was why you couldn't drive me over to the Flats."

Ethan had no suppleness in deceiving. He had never before been convicted of a lie, and all the resources of evasion failed him. "I guess that was a misunderstanding," he stammered.

"You ain't got the money?"

"No."

"And you ain't going to get it?"

"No."

"Well, I couldn't know that when I engaged the girl, could I?"

"No." He paused to control his voice. "But you know it now. I'm sorry, but it can't be helped. You're a poor man's wife, Zeena; but I'll do the best I can for you."

For a while she sat motionless, as if reflecting, her arms stretched along the arms of her chair, her eyes fixed on vacancy. "Oh, I guess we'll make out," she said mildly.

The change in her tone reassured him. "Of course we will! There's a whole lot more I can do for you, and Mattie—"

Zeena, while he spoke, seemed to be following out some elaborate mental calculation. She emerged from it to say: "There'll be Mattie's board less, anyhow—"

Ethan, supposing the discussion to be over, had turned to go down to supper. He stopped short, not grasping what he heard. "Mattie's board less—?" he began.

Zeena laughed. It was an odd unfamiliar sound—he did not remember ever having heard her laugh before. "You didn't suppose I was going to keep two girls, did you? No wonder you were scared at the expense!"

He still had but a confused sense of what she was saying. From the beginning of the discussion he had instinctively avoided the mention of Mattie's name, fearing he hardly knew what: criticism, complaints, or vague allusions to the imminent probability of her marrying. But the thought of a definite rupture had never come to him, and even now could not lodge itself in his mind.

"I don't know what you mean," he said. "Mattie Silver's not a hired girl. She's your relation."

"She's a pauper that's hung onto us all after her father'd done his best to ruin us. I've kep' her here a whole year: it's somebody else's turn now."

As the shrill words shot out Ethan heard a tap on the door, which he had drawn shut when he turned back from the threshold.

"Ethan—Zeena!" Mattie's voice sounded gaily from the landing, "do you know what time it is? Supper's been ready half an hour."

Inside the room there was a moment's silence; then Zeena called out from her seat: "I'm not coming down to supper."

"Oh, I'm sorry! Aren't you well? Sha'n't I bring you up a bite of something?"

Ethan roused himself with an effort and opened the door. "Go along down, Matt. Zeena's just a little tired. I'm coming."

He heard her "All right!" and her quick step on the stairs; then he shut the door and turned back into the room. His wife's attitude was unchanged, her face inexorable, and he was seized with the despairing sense of his helplessness.

"You ain't going to do it, Zeena?"

"Do what?" she emitted between flattened lips.

"Send Mattie away—like this?"

"I never bargained to take her for life!"

He continued with rising vehemence: "You can't put her out of the house like a thief—a poor girl without friends or money. She's done her best for you and she's got no place to go to. You may forget she's your kin but everybody else'll remember it. If you do a thing like that what do you suppose folks'll say of you?"

Zeena waited a moment, as if giving him time to feel the full force of the contrast between his own excitement and her composure. Then she replied in the same smooth voice: "I know well enough what they say of my having kep' her here as long as I have."

Ethan's hand dropped from the door-knob, which he had held clenched since he had drawn the door shut on Mattie. His wife's retort was like a knife-cut across the sinews and he felt suddenly weak and powerless. He had meant to humble himself, to argue that Mattie's keep didn't cost much, after all, that he could make out to buy a stove and fix up a place in the attic for the hired girl—but Zeena's words revealed the peril of such pleadings.

"You mean to tell her she's got to go—at once?" he faltered out, in terror of letting his wife complete her sentence.

As if trying to make him see reason she replied impartially; "The girl will be over from Bettsbridge tomorrow, and I presume she's got to have somewheres to sleep."

Ethan looked at her with loathing. She was no longer the listless creature who had lived at his side in a state of sullen self-absorption, but a mysterious alien presence, an evil energy secreted from the long years of silent brooding. It was the sense of his helplessness that sharpened his antipathy. There had never been anything in her that one could appeal to; but as long as he could ignore and command he had remained indifferent. Now she had mastered him and he abhorred her. Mattie was her relation, not his: there were no means by which he could compel her to keep the girl under her roof. All the long misery of his baffled past, of his youth of failure, hardship and vain effort, rose up in his soul in bitterness and seemed to take shape before him in the woman who at every turn had barred his way. She had taken everything else from him; and now she meant to take the one thing that made up for all the others. For a moment such a flame of hate rose in him that it ran down his arm and clenched his fist against her. He took a wild step forward and then stopped.

"You're—you're not coming down?" he said in a bewildered voice.

"No. I guess I'll lay down on the bed a little while," she answered mildly; and he turned and walked out of the room.

In the kitchen Mattie was sitting by the stove, the cat curled up on her knees. She sprang to her feet as Ethan entered and carried the covered dish of meat-pie to the table.

"I hope Zeena isn't sick?" she asked.

"No."

She shone at him across the table. "Well, sit right down then. You must be starving." She uncovered the pie and pushed it over to him. So they were to have one more evening together, her happy eyes seemed to say!

He helped himself mechanically and began to eat; then disgust took him by the throat and he laid down his fork.

Mattie's tender gaze was on him and she marked the gesture.

"Why, Ethan, what's the matter? Don't it taste right?"

"Yes—it's first-rate. Only I—" He pushed his plate away, rose from his chair, and walked around the table to her side. She started up with frightened eyes.

"Ethan, there's something wrong! I *knew* there was!"

She seemed to melt against him in her terror, and he caught her in his arms, held her fast there, felt her lashes beat his cheek like netted butterflies.

"What is it—what is it?" she stammered; but he had found her lips at last and was drinking unconsciousness of everything but the joy they gave him.

She lingered a moment, caught in the same strong current; then she slipped from him and drew back a step or two, pale and troubled. Her look smote him with compunction, and he cried out, as if he saw her drowning in a dream: "You can't go, Matt! I'll never let you!"

"Go—go?" she stammered. "Must I go?"

The words went on sounding between them as though a torch of warning flew from hand to hand through a black landscape.

Ethan was overcome with shame at his lack of self-control in flinging the news at her so brutally. His head reeled and he had to support himself against the table. All the while he felt as if he were still kissing her, and yet dying of thirst for her lips.

"Ethan what has happened? Is Zeena mad with me?"

Her cry steadied him, though it deepened his wrath and pity. "No, no," he assured her, "it's not that. But this new doctor has scared her about herself. You know she believes all they say the first time she sees them. And this one's told her she won't get well unless she lays up and don't do a thing about the house—not for months—"

He paused, his eyes wandering from her miserably. She stood silent a moment, drooping before him like a broken branch. She was so small and weak-looking that it wrung his heart; but suddenly she lifted her head and looked straight at him. "And she wants somebody handier in my place? Is that it?"

"That's what she says tonight."

"If she says it tonight she'll say it tomorrow."

Both bowed to the inexorable truth: they knew that Zeena never changed her mind, and that in her case a resolve once taken was equivalent to an act performed.

There was a long silence between them; then Mattie said in a low voice: "Don't be too sorry, Ethan."

"Oh, God—oh, God," he groaned. The glow of passion he had felt for her had melted to an aching tenderness. He saw her quick lids beating back the tears, and longed to take her in his arms and soothe her.

"You're letting your supper get cold," she admonished him with a pale gleam of gaiety.

"Oh, Matt—Matt—where'll you go to?"

Her lids sank and a tremor crossed her face. He saw that for the first time the thought of the future came to her distinctly. "I might get something to do over at Stamford," she faltered, as if knowing that he knew she had no hope.

He dropped back into his seat and hid his face in his hands. Despair seized him at the thought of her setting out alone to renew the weary quest for work. In the only place where she was known she was surrounded by indifference or animosity; and what chance had she, inexperienced and untrained, among the million bread-seekers of the cities? There came back to him miserable tales he had heard at Worcester, and the faces of girls whose lives had begun as hopefully as Mattie's. . . . It was not possible to think of such things without a revolt of his whole being. He sprang up suddenly.

"You can't go, Matt! I won't let you! She's always had her way, but I mean to have mine now—"

Mattie lifted her hand with a quick gesture, and he heard his wife's step behind him.

Zeena came into the room with her dragging down-at-the-heel step, and quietly took her accustomed seat between them.

"I felt a little mite better, and Dr. Buck says I ought to eat all I can to keep my stren'th up, even if I ain't got any appetite," she said in her flat whine, reaching across Mattie for the teapot. Her "good" dress had been replaced by the black calico and brown knitted shawl which formed her daily wear, and with them she had put on her usual face and manner. She poured out her tea, added a great deal of milk to it, helped herself largely to pie and pickles, and made the familiar gesture of adjusting her false teeth before she began to eat. The cat rubbed itself ingratiatingly against her, and she said "Good Pussy," stooped to stroke it and gave it a scrap of meat from her plate.

Ethan sat speechless, not pretending to eat, but Mattie nibbled valiantly at her food and asked Zeena one or two questions about her visit to Bettsbridge. Zeena answered in her every-day tone and, warming to the theme, regaled them with several vivid descriptions of intestinal disturbances among her friends and relatives. She looked straight at Mattie as she spoke, a faint smile deepening the vertical lines between her nose and chin.

When supper was over she rose from her seat and pressed her hand to the flat surface over the region of her heart. "That pie of yours always sets a mite heavy, Matt," she said, not ill-naturedly. She seldom abbreviated the girl's name, and when she did so it was always a sign of affability.

"I've a good mind to go and hunt up those stomach powders I got last year over in Springfield," she continued. "I ain't tried them for quite a while, and maybe they'll help the heart-burn."

Mattie lifted her eyes. "Can't I get them for you, Zeena?" she ventured.

"No. They're in a place you don't know about," Zeena answered darkly, with one of her secret looks.

She went out of the kitchen and Mattie, rising, began to clear the dishes from the table. As she passed Ethan's chair their eyes met and clung together desolately. The warm still kitchen looked as peaceful as the night before. The cat had sprung to Zeena's rocking-chair, and the heat of the fire was beginning to draw out the faint sharp scent of the geraniums. Ethan dragged himself wearily to his feet.

"I'll go out and take a look round," he said, going toward the passage to get his lantern.

As he reached the door he met Zeena coming back into the room, her lips twitching with anger, a flush of excitement on her sallow face. The shawl had slipped from her shoulders and was dragging at her down-trodden heels, and in her hands she carried the fragments of the red glass pickle-dish.

"I'd like to know who done this," she said, looking sternly from Ethan to Mattie.

There was no answer, and she continued in a trembling voice: "I went to get those powders I'd put away in father's old spectacle-case, top of the china-closet, where I keep the things I set store by, so's folks sha'n't meddle with them—" Her voice broke, and two small tears hung on her lashless lids and ran slowly down her cheeks. "It takes the step-ladder to get at the top shelf, and I put Aunt Philura Maple's pickle-dish up there o' purpose when we was married, and it's never been down since, 'cept for the spring cleaning, and then I always lifted it with my own hands, so's 't it shouldn't get broke." She laid the fragments reverently on the table. "I want to know who done this," she quavered.

At the challenge Ethan turned back into the room and faced her. "I can tell you, then. The cat done it."

"The *cat?*"

"That's what I said."

She looked at him hard, and then turned her eyes to Mattie, who was carrying the dish-pan to the table.

"I'd like to know how the cat got into my china-closet," she said.

"Chasin' mice, I guess," Ethan rejoined. "There was a mouse round the kitchen all last evening."

Zeena continued to look from one to the other; then she emitted her small strange laugh. "I knew the cat was a smart cat,"she said in a high voice, "but I didn't know he was smart enough to pick up the pieces of my pickle-dish and lay 'em edge to edge on the very shelf he knocked 'em off of."

Mattie suddenly drew her arms out of the steaming water. "It wasn't Ethan's fault, Zeena! The cat *did* break the dish; but I got it down from the china-closet, and I'm the one to blame for its getting broken."

Zeena stood beside the ruin of her treasure, stiffening into a stony image of resentment. "*You* got down my pickle-dish—what for?"

A bright flush flew to Mattie's cheeks. "I wanted to make the supper-table pretty," she said.

"You wanted to make the supper-table pretty, and you waited till my back was turned, and took the thing I set most store by of anything I've got, and wouldn't never use it, not even when the minister come to dinner, or Aunt Martha Pierce come over from Bettsbridge—" Zeena paused with a gasp, as if terrified by her own evocation of the sacrilege. "You're a bad girl, Mattie Silver, and I always known it. It's the way your father begun, and I was warned of it when I took you, and I tried to keep my things where you couldn't get at 'em—and now you've took from me the one I cared for most of all—" She broke off in a short spasm of sobs that passed and left her more than ever like a shape of stone.

"If I'd 'a' listened to folks, you'd 'a' gone before now, and this wouldn't 'a' happened," she said; and gathering up the bits of broken glass she went out of the room as if she carried a dead body . . .

VIII

WHEN Ethan was called back to the farm by his father's illness his mother gave him, for his own use, a small room behind the untenanted "best parlor." Here he had nailed up shelves for his books, built himself a box-sofa out of boards and a mattress, laid out his papers on a kitchen-table, hung on the rough plaster wall an engraving of Abraham Lincoln and a calendar with "Thoughts from the Poets," and tried, with these meager properties to produce some likeness to the study of a "minister" who had been kind to him and lent him books when he was at Worcester. He still took refuge there in summer, but when Mattie came to live at the farm he had had to give her his stove, and consequently the room was uninhabitable for several months of the year.

To this retreat he descended as soon as the house was quiet, and Zeena's steady breathing from the bed had assured him that there was to be no sequel to the scene in the kitchen. After Zeena's departure he and Mattie had stood speechless, neither seeking to approach the other. Then the girl had returned to her task of clearing up the kitchen for the night and he had taken his lantern and gone on his usual round outside the house. The kitchen was empty when he came back to it; but his tobacco-pouch and pipe had been laid on the table, and under them was a scrap of paper torn from the back of a seedsman's catalogue, on which three words were written: "Don't trouble, Ethan."

Going into his cold dark "study" he placed the lantern on the table and, stooping to its light, read the message again and again. It was the first time that Mattie had ever written to him, and the possession of the paper gave him a strange new sense of her nearness; yet it deepened his anguish by reminding him that henceforth they would have no other way of communicating with each other. For the life of her smile, the warmth of her voice, only cold paper and dead words!

Confused motions of rebellion stormed in him. He was too young, too strong, too full of the sap of living, to submit so easily to the destruction of his hopes. Must he wear out all his years at the side of a bitter querulous woman? Other possibilities had been in him, possibilities sacrificed, one by one, to Zeena's narrow-mindedness and ignorance. And what good had come of it? She was a hundred times bitterer and more discontented than when he had married her: the one pleasure left her was to inflict pain on him. All the healthy instincts of self-defense rose up in him against such waste . . .

He bundled himself into his old coon-skin coat and lay down on the box-sofa to think. Under his cheek he felt a hard object with strange protuberances. It was a cushion which Zeena had made for him when they were engaged—the only piece of needlework he had ever seen her do. He flung it across the floor and propped his head against the wall . . .

He knew a case of a man over the mountain—a young fellow of about his own age—who had escaped from just such a life of misery by going West with the girl he cared for. His wife had divorced him, and he had married the girl and prospered. Ethan had seen the couple the summer before at Shadd's Falls, where they had come to visit relatives. They had a little girl with fair curls, who wore a gold locket and was dressed like a princess. The deserted wife had not done badly either. Her husband had given her the farm and she had managed to sell it, and with that and the alimony she had started a lunch-room at Bettsbridge and bloomed into activity and importance.

Ethan was fired by the thought. Why should he not leave with Mattie the next day, instead of letting her go alone? He would hide his valise under the seat of the sleigh, and Zeena would suspect nothing till she went upstairs for her afternoon nap and found a letter on the bed . . .

His impulses were still near the surface, and he sprang up, re-lit the lantern, and sat down at the table. He rummaged in the drawer for a sheet of paper, found one, and began to write.

"Zeena, I've done all I could for you, and I don't see as it's been any use. I don't blame you, nor I don't blame myself. Maybe both of us will do better separate. I'm going to try my luck West, and you can sell the farm and mill, and keep the money—"

His pen paused on the word, which brought home to him the relentless conditions of his lot. If he gave the farm and mill to Zeena what would be left him to start his own life with? Once in the West he was sure of picking up work—he would not have feared to try his chance alone. But with Mattie depending on him the case was different. And what of Zeena's fate? Farm and mill were mortgaged to the limit of their value, and even if she found a purchaser—in itself an unlikely chance—it was doubtful if she could clear a thousand dollars on the sale. Meanwhile, how could she keep the farm going? It was only by incessant labor and personal supervision that Ethan drew a meager living from his land, and his wife, even if she were in better health than she imagined, could never carry such a burden alone.

Well, she could go back to her people, then, and see what they would do for her. It was the fate she was forcing on Mattie—why not let her try it herself? By the time she had discovered his whereabouts, and brought suit for divorce, he would probably—wherever he was—be earning enough to pay her a sufficient alimony. And the alternative was to let Mattie go forth alone, with far less hope of ultimate provision . . .

He had scattered the contents of the table-drawer in his search for a sheet of paper, and as he took up his pen his eye fell on an old copy of the *Bettsbridge Eagle*. The advertising sheet was folded uppermost, and he read the seductive words: "Trips to the West: Reduced Rates."

He drew the lantern nearer and eagerly scanned the fares; then the paper fell from his hand and he pushed aside his unfinished

It was only by incessant labor that Ethan drew a meager living from his land.

letter. A moment ago he had wondered what he and Mattie were to live on when they reached the West; now he saw that he had not even the money to take her there. Borrowing was out of the question: six months before he had given his only security to raise funds for necessary repairs to the mill, and he knew that without security no one at Starkfield would lend him ten dollars. The inexorable facts closed in on him like prison-warders hand-cuffing a convict. There was no way out—none. He was a prisoner for life, and now his one ray of light was to be extinguished.

He crept back heavily to the sofa, stretching himself out with limbs so leaden that he felt as if they would never move again. Tears rose in his throat and slowly burned their way to his lids.

As he lay there, the window-pane that faced him, growing gradually lighter, inlaid upon the darkness a square of moon-suffused sky. A crooked tree-branch crossed it, a branch of the apple-tree under which, on summer evenings, he had sometimes found Mattie sitting when he came up from the mill. Slowly the rim of the rainy vapors caught fire and burnt away, and a pure moon swung into the blue. Ethan, rising on his elbow, watched the landscape whiten and shape itself under the sculpture of the moon. This was the night on which he was to have taken Mattie coasting, and there hung the lamp to light them! He looked out at the slopes bathed in lustre, the silver-edged darkness of the woods, the spectral purple of the hills against the sky, and it seemed as though all the beauty of the night had been poured out to mock his wretchedness . . .

He fell asleep, and when he woke the chill of the winter dawn was in the room. He felt cold and stiff and hungry, and ashamed of being hungry. He rubbed his eyes and went to the window. A red sun stood over the gray rim of the fields, behind trees that looked black and brittle. He said to himself: "This is Matt's last day," and tried to think what the place would be without her.

As he stood there he heard a step behind him and she entered.

"Oh, Ethan—were you here all night?"

She looked so small and pinched, in her poor dress, with the red scarf wound about her, and the cold light turning her paleness sallow, that Ethan stood before her without speaking.

"You must be frozen," she went on, fixing lustreless eyes on him.

He drew a step nearer. "How did you know I was here?"

"Because I heard you go down stairs again after I went to bed, and I listened all night, and you didn't come up."

All his tenderness rushed to his lips. He looked at her and said: "I'll come right along and make up the kitchen fire."

They went back to the kitchen, and he fetched the coal and kindlings and cleared out the stove for her, while she brought in the milk and the cold remains of the meat-pie. When warmth began to radiate from the stove, and the first ray of sunlight lay on the kitchen floor, Ethan's dark thoughts melted in the mellower air. The sight of Mattie going about her work as he had seen her on so many mornings made it seem impossible that she should ever cease to be a part of the scene. He said to himself that he had doubtless exaggerated the significance of Zeena's threats, and that she too, with the return of daylight, would come to a saner mood.

He went up to Mattie as she bent above the stove, and laid his hand on her arm. "I don't want you should trouble either," he said, looking down into her eyes with a smile.

She flushed up warmly and whispered back: "No, Ethan, I ain't going to trouble."

"I guess things'll straighten out," he added.

There was no answer but a quick throb of her lids, and he went on: "She ain't said anything this morning?"

"No. I haven't seen her yet."

"Don't you take any notice when you do."

With this injunction he left her and went out to the cow-barn. He saw Jotham Powell walking up the hill through the morning mist, and the familiar sight added to his growing conviction of security.

As the two men were clearing out the stalls Jotham rested on his pitch-fork to say: "Dan'l Byrne's goin' over to the Flats today noon, an' he c'd take Mattie's trunk along, and make it easier ridin' when I take her over in the sleigh."

Ethan looked at him blankly, and he continued: "Mis' Frome said the new girl'd be at the Flats at five, and I was to take Mattie then, so's 't she could ketch the six o'clock train for Stamford."

Ethan felt the blood drumming in his temples. He had to wait a moment before he could find a voice to say: "Oh, it ain't so sure about Mattie's going—"

"That so?" said Jotham indifferently; and they went on with their work.

When they returned to the kitchen the two women were already at breakfast. Zeena had an air of unusual alertness and activity. She drank two cups of coffee and fed the cat with the scraps left in the pie dish; then she rose from her seat and, walking over to the window, snipped two or three yellow leaves from the geraniums. "Aunt Martha's ain't got a faded leaf on 'em; but they pine away when they ain't cared for," she said reflectively. Then she turned to Jotham and asked: "What time'd you say Dan'l Byrne'd be along?"

The hired man threw a hesitating glance at Ethan. "Round about noon," he said.

Zeena turned to Mattie. "That trunk of yours is too heavy for the sleigh, and Dan'l Byrne'll be round to take it over to the Flats," she said.

"I'm much obliged to you, Zeena," said Mattie.

"I'd like to go over things with you first," Zeena continued in an unperturbed voice. "I know there's a huckabuck towel missing; and I can't make out what you done with that match-safe 't used to stand behind the stuffed owl in the parlor."

She went out, followed by Mattie, and when the men were alone Jotham said to his employer: "I guess I better let Dan'l come round, then."

Ethan finished his usual morning tasks about the house and barn; then he said to Jotham: "I'm going down to Starkfield. Tell them not to wait dinner."

The passion of rebellion had broken out in him again. That which had seemed incredible in the sober light of day had really come to pass, and he was to assist as a helpless spectator at Mattie's banishment. His manhood was humbled by the part he was compelled to play and by the thought of what Mattie must think of him. Confused impulses struggled in him as he strode along to the village. He had made up his mind to do something, but he did not know what it would be.

The early mist had vanished and the fields lay like a silver shield under the sun. It was one of the days when the glitter of winter shines through a pale haze of spring. Every yard of the road was alive with Mattie's presence, and there was hardly a branch against the sky or a tangle of brambles on the bank in which some bright shred of memory was not caught. Once, in the stillness, the call of a bird in a mountain ash was so like her laughter that his heart tightened and then grew large; and all these things made him see that something must be done at once.

Suddenly it occurred to him that Andrew Hale, who was a kind-hearted man, might be induced to reconsider his refusal and advance a small sum on the lumber if he were told that Zeena's ill-health made it necessary to hire a servant. Hale, after all, knew enough of Ethan's situation to make it possible for the latter to renew his appeal without too much loss of pride; and, moreover, how much did pride count in the ebullition of passions in his breast?

The more he considered his plan the more hopeful it seemed. If he could get Mrs. Hale's ear he felt certain of success, and with fifty dollars in his pocket nothing could keep him from Mattie . . .

His first object was to reach Starkfield before Hale had started for his work; he knew the carpenter had a job down the Corbury road and was likely to leave his house early. Ethan's long strides grew more rapid with the accelerated beat of his thoughts, and as he reached the foot of School House Hill he caught sight of Hale's sleigh in the distance. He hurried forward to meet it, but as it drew nearer he saw that it was driven by the carpenter's youngest boy and that the figure at his side, looking like a large upright cocoon in spectacles, was that of Mrs. Hale. Ethan signed to them to stop, and Mrs. Hale leaned forward, her pink wrinkles twinkling with benevolence.

"Mr. Hale? Why, yes, you'll find him down home now. He ain't going to his work this forenoon. He woke up with a touch o' lumbago, and I just made him put on one of old Dr. Kidder's plasters and set right up into the fire."

Beaming maternally on Ethan, she bent over to add: "I on'y just heard from Mr. Hale 'bout Zeena's going over to Bettsbridge to see that new doctor. I'm real sorry she's feeling so bad again! I hope he thinks he can do something for her? I don't know anybody round here's had more sickness than Zeena. I always tell Mr. Hale I don't know what she'd 'a' done if she hadn't 'a' had you to look after her; and I used to say the same thing 'bout your mother. You've had an awful mean time, Ethan Frome."

She gave him a last nod of sympathy while her son chirped to the horse; and Ethan, as she drove off, stood in the middle of the road and stared after the retreating sleigh.

It was a long time since anyone had spoken to him as kindly as

Mrs. Hale. Most people were either indifferent to his troubles, or disposed to think it natural that a young fellow of his age should have carried without repining the burden of three crippled lives. But Mrs. Hale had said "You've had an awful mean time, Ethan Frome," and he felt less alone with his misery. If the Hales were sorry for him they would surely respond to his appeal . . .

He started down the road toward their house, but at the end of a few yards he pulled up sharply, the blood in his face. For the first time, in the light of the words he had just heard, he saw what he was about to do. He was planning to take advantage of the Hales' sympathy to obtain money from them on false pretences. That was a plain statement of the cloudy purpose which had driven him in headlong to Starkfield.

With the sudden perception of the point to which his madness had carried him, the madness fell and he saw his life before him as it was. He was a poor man, the husband of a sickly woman, whom his desertion would leave alone and destitute; and even if he had had the heart to desert her he could have done so only by deceiving two kindly people who had pitied him.

He turned and walked slowly back to the farm.

IX

AT the kitchen door Daniel Byrne sat in his sleigh behind a big-boned gray who pawed the snow and swung his long head restlessly from side to side.

Ethan went into the kitchen and found his wife by the stove. Her head was wrapped in her shawl, and she was reading a book called "Kidney Troubles And Their Cure" on which he had had to pay extra postage only a few days before.

Zeena did not move or look up when he entered, and after a moment he asked: "Where's Mattie?"

Without lifting her eyes from the page she replied: "I presume she's getting down her trunk."

The blood rushed to his face. "Getting down her trunk—alone?"

"Jotham Powell's down in the wood-lot, and Dan'l Byrne says he darsn't leave that horse," she returned.

Her husband, without stopping to hear the end of the phrase, had left the kitchen and sprung up the stairs. The door of Mattie's room was shut, and he wavered a moment on the landing. "Matt," he said in a low voice; but there was no answer, and he put his hand on the door-knob.

He had never been in her room except once, in the early summer, when he had gone there to plaster up a leak in the eaves, but he remembered exactly how everything had looked: the red and white quilt on her narrow bed, the pretty pin-cushion on the chest of drawers, and over it the enlarged photograph of her mother, in an oxydized frame, with a bunch of dyed grasses at the back. Now these and all other tokens of her presence had vanished, and the room looked as bare and comfortless as when Zeena had shown her into it on the day of her arrival. In the middle of the floor stood her trunk, and on the trunk she sat in her Sunday dress, her back turned to the door and her face in her hands. She had not heard Ethan's call because she was sobbing; and she did not hear his step till he stood close behind her and laid his hands on her shoulders.

"Matt—oh, don't—oh, *Matt!*"

She started up, lifting her wet face to his. "Ethan—I thought I wasn't ever going to see you again!"

He took her in his arms, pressing her close, and with a trembling hand smoothed away the hair from her forehead.

"Not see me again? What do you mean?"

She sobbed out: "Jotham said you told him we wasn't to wait dinner for you, and I thought—"

"You thought I meant to cut it?" he finished for her grimly.

She clung to him without answering, and he laid his lips on her hair, which was soft yet springy, like certain mosses on warm slopes, and had the faint woody fragrance of fresh sawdust in the sun.

Through the door they heard Zeena's voice calling out from below: "Dan'l Byrne says you better hurry up if you want him to take that trunk."

They drew apart with stricken faces. Words of resistance rushed to Ethan's lips and died there. Mattie found her handkerchief and dried her eyes; then, bending down, she took hold of a handle of the trunk.

Ethan put her aside. "You let go, Matt," he ordered her.

She answered: "It takes two to coax it round the corner"; and submitting to this argument he grasped the other handle, and together they maneuvered the heavy trunk out to the landing.

"Now let go," he repeated; then he shouldered the trunk and carried it down the stairs and across the passage to the kitchen. Zeena, who had gone back to her seat by the stove, did not lift her head from her book as he passed. Mattie followed him out of the door and helped him to lift the trunk into the back of the sleigh. When it was in place they stood side by side on the door-step, watching Daniel Byrne plunge off behind his fidgety horse.

It seemed to Ethan that his heart was bound with cords which an unseen hand was tightening with every tick of the clock. Twice he opened his lips to speak to Mattie and found no breath. At length, as she turned to re-enter the house, he laid a detaining hand on her.

"I'm going to drive you over, Matt," he whispered.

She murmured back: "I think Zeena wants I should go with Jotham."

"I'm going to drive you over," he repeated; and she went into the kitchen without answering.

At dinner Ethan could not eat. If he lifted his eyes they rested on Zeena's pinched face, and the corners of her straight lips seemed to quiver away into a smile. She ate well, declaring that the mild weather made her feel better, and pressed a second helping of beans on Jotham Powell, whose wants she generally ignored.

Mattie, when the meal was over, went about her usual task of clearing the table and washing up the dishes. Zeena, after feeding the cat, had returned to her rocking-chair by the stove, and Jotham Powell, who always lingered last, reluctantly pushed back his chair and moved toward the door.

On the threshold he turned back to say to Ethan: "What time'll I come round for Mattie?"

Ethan was standing near the window, mechanically filling his pipe while he watched Mattie move to and fro. He answered: "You needn't come round; I'm going to drive her over myself."

He saw the rise of the color in Mattie's averted cheek, and the quick lifting of Zeena's head.

"I want you should stay here this afternoon, Ethan," his wife said. "Jotham can drive Mattie over."

Mattie flung an imploring glance at him, but he repeated curtly: "I'm going to drive her over myself."

Zeena continued in the same even tone: "I wanted you should stay and fix up that stove in Mattie's room afore the girl gets here. It ain't been drawing right for nigh on a month now."

Ethan's voice rose indignantly. "If it was good enough for Mattie I guess it's good enough for a hired girl."

"That girl that's coming told me she was used to a house where they had a furnace," Zeena persisted with the same monotonous mildness.

"She'd better ha' stayed there then," he flung back at her; and turning to Mattie he added in a hard voice: "You be ready by three, Matt; I've got business at Corbury."

Jotham Powell had started for the barn, and Ethan strode down after him aflame with anger. The pulses in his temples throbbed and a fog was in his eyes. He went about his task without knowing what force directed him, or whose hands and feet were fulfilling its orders. It was not till he led out the sorrel and backed him between the shafts of the sleigh that he once more became conscious of what he was doing. As he passed the bridle over the horse's head, and wound the traces around the shafts, he remembered the day when he had made the same preparations in order to drive over and meet his wife's cousin at the Flats. It was little more than a year ago, on just such a soft afternoon, with a "feel" of spring in the air. The sorrel, turning the same big ringed eye on him, nuzzled the palm of his hand in the same way; and one by one all the days between rose up and stood before him . . .

He flung the bearskin into the sleigh, climbed to the seat, and drove up to the house. When he entered the kitchen it was empty, but Mattie's bag and shawl lay ready by the door. He went to the foot of the stairs and listened. No sound reached him from above, but presently he thought he heard some one moving about in his deserted study, and pushing open the door he saw Mattie, in her hat and jacket, standing with her back to him near the table.

She started at his approach and turning quickly, said: "Is it time?"

"What are you doing here, Matt?" he asked her.

She looked at him timidly. "I was just taking a look round— that's all," she answered, with a wavering smile.

They went back into the kitchen without speaking, and Ethan picked up her bag and shawl.

"Where's Zeena?" he asked.

"She went upstairs right after dinner. She said she had those shooting pains again, and didn't want to be disturbed."

"Didn't she say good-bye to you?"

"No. That was all she said."

Ethan, looking slowly about the kitchen, said to himself with a shudder that in a few hours he would be returning to it alone. Then the sense of unreality overcame him once more, and he could not bring himself to believe that Mattie stood there for the last time before him.

"Come on," he said almost gaily, opening the door and putting her bag into the sleigh. He sprang to his seat and bent over to tuck the rug about her as she slipped into the place at his side. "Now then, go 'long," he said, with a shake of the reins that sent the sorrel placidly jogging down the hill.

"We got lots of time for a good ride, Matt!" he cried, seeking her hand beneath the fur and pressing it in his. His face tingled and he felt dizzy, as if he had stopped in at the Starkfield saloon on a zero day for a drink.

At the gate, instead of making for Starkfield, he turned the sorrel to the right, up the Bettsbridge road. Mattie sat silent, giving no sign of surprise; but after a moment she said: "Are you going round by Shadow Pond?"

He laughed and answered: "I knew you'd know!"

She drew closer under the bearskin, so that, looking sideways around his coat-sleeve, he could just catch the tip of her nose and a blown brown wave of hair. They drove slowly up the road between fields glistening under the pale sun, and then bent to the right down a lane edged with spruce and larch. Ahead of them, a long way off, a range of hills stained by mottlings of black forest flowed away in round white curves against the sky. The lane passed into a pine-wood with boles reddening in the afternoon sun and delicate blue shadows on the snow. As they entered it the breeze fell and a warm stillness seemed to drop from the branches with the dropping needles. Here the snow was so pure that the tiny tracks of wood-animals had left on it intricate lace-like patterns, and the bluish cones caught in its surface stood out like ornaments of bronze.

Ethan drove on in silence till they reached a part of the wood where the pines were more widely spaced; then he drew up and helped Mattie to get out of the sleigh. They passed between the aromatic trunks, the snow breaking crisply under their feet, till they came to a small sheet of water with steep wooded sides. Across its frozen surface, from the farther bank, a single hill rising against the western sun threw the long conical shadow which gave the lake its name. It was a shy secret spot, full of the same dumb melancholy that Ethan felt in his heart.

He looked up and down the little pebbly beach till his eye lit on a fallen tree-trunk half submerged in snow.

"There's where we sat at the picnic," he reminded her.

The entertainment of which he spoke was one of the few that they had taken part in together: a "church picnic" which, on a long afternoon of the preceding summer, had filled the retired place with merry-making. Mattie had begged him to go with her but he had refused. Then, toward sunset, coming down from the mountain where he had been felling timber, he had been caught by some strayed revellers and drawn into the group by the lake, where Mattie, encircled by facetious youths, and bright as a blackberry under her spreading hat, was brewing coffee over a gipsy fire. He remembered the shyness he had felt at approaching her in his uncouth clothes, and then the lighting up of her face, and the way she had broken through the group to come to him with a cup in her hand. They had sat for a few minutes on the fallen log by the pond, and she had missed her gold locket, and set the young men searching for it; and it was Ethan who had spied it in the moss . . . That was all; but all their intercourse had been made up of just such inarticulate flashes, when they seemed to come suddenly upon happiness as if they had surprised a butterfly in the winter woods . . .

"It was right there I found your locket," he said, pushing his foot into a dense tuft of blueberry bushes.

"I never saw anybody with such sharp eyes!" she answered.

She sat down on the tree-trunk in the sun and he sat down beside her.

"You were as pretty as a picture in that pink hat," he said.

She laughed with pleasure. "Oh, I guess it was the hat!" she rejoined.

They had never before avowed their inclination so openly, and

Ethan, for a moment, had the illusion that he was a free man, wooing the girl he meant to marry. He looked at her hair and longed to touch it again, and to tell her that it smelt of the woods; but he had never learned to say such things.

Suddenly she rose to her feet and said: "We mustn't stay here any longer."

He continued to gaze at her vaguely, only half-roused from his dream. "There's plenty of time," he answered.

They stood looking at each other as if the eyes of each were straining to absorb and hold fast the other's image. There were things he had to say to her before they parted, but he could not say them in that place of summer memories, and he turned and followed her in silence to the sleigh. As they drove away the sun sank behind the hill and the pine-boles turned from red to gray.

By a devious track between the fields they wound back to the Starkfield road. Under the open sky the light was still clear, with a reflection of cold red on the eastern hills. The clumps of trees in the snow seemed to draw together in ruffled lumps, like birds with their heads under their wings; and the sky, as it paled, rose higher, leaving the earth more alone.

As they turned into the Starkfield road Ethan said: "Matt, what do you mean to do?"

She did not answer at once, but at length she said: "I'll try to get a place in a store."

"You know you can't do it. The bad air and the standing all day nearly killed you before."

"I'm a lot stronger than I was before I came to Starkfield."

"And now you're going to throw away all the good it's done you!"

There seemed to be no answer to this, and again they drove on for a while without speaking. With every yard of the way some spot where they had stood, and laughed together or been silent, clutched at Ethan and dragged him back.

"Isn't there any of your father's folks could help you?"

"There isn't any of 'em I'd ask."

He lowered his voice to say: "You know there's nothing I wouldn't do for you if I could."

"I know there isn't."

"But I can't—"

She was silent, but he felt a slight tremor in the shoulder against his.

"Oh, Matt," he broke out, "if I could ha' gone with you now I'd ha' done it—"

She turned to him, pulling a scrap of paper from her breast. "Ethan—I found this," she stammered. Even in the failing light he saw it was the letter to his wife that he had begun the night before and forgotten to destroy. Through his astonishment there ran a fierce thrill of joy. "Matt—" he cried; "if I could ha' done it, would you?"

"Oh, Ethan, Ethan—what's the use?" With a sudden movement she tore the letter in shreds and sent them fluttering off into the snow.

"Tell me, Matt! Tell me!" he adjured her.

She was silent for a moment; then she said, in such a low tone that he had to stoop his head to hear her: "I used to think of it sometimes, summer nights, when the moon was so bright I couldn't sleep."

His heart reeled with the sweetness of it. "As long ago as that?"

She answered, as if the date had long been fixed for her: "The first time was at Shadow Pond."

"Was that why you gave me my coffee before the others?"

"I don't know. Did I? I was dreadfully put out when you wouldn't go to the picnic with me; and then, when I saw you coming down the road, I thought maybe you'd gone home that way o' purpose; and that made me glad."

They were silent again. They had reached the point where the road dipped to the hollow by Ethan's mill and as they descended the darkness descended with them, dropping down like a black veil from the heavy hemlock boughs.

"I'm tied hand and foot, Matt. There isn't a thing I can do," he began again.

"You must write to me sometimes, Ethan."

"Oh, what good'll writing do? I want to put my hand out and touch you. I want to do for you and care for you. I want to be there when you're sick and when you're lonesome."

"You mustn't think but what I'll do all right."

"You won't need me, you mean? I suppose you'll marry!"

"Oh, Ethan!" she cried.

"I don't know how it is you make me feel, Matt. I'd a'most rather have you dead than that!"

"Oh, I wish I was, I wish I was!" she sobbed.

The sound of her weeping shook him out of his dark anger, and he felt ashamed.

"Don't let's talk that way," he whispered.

"Why shouldn't we, when it's true? I've been wishing it every minute of the day."

"Matt! You be quiet! Don't you say it."

"There's never anybody been good to me but you."

"Don't say that either, when I can't lift a hand for you!"

"Yes; but it's true just the same."

They had reached the top of School House Hill and Starkfield lay below them in the twilight. A cutter, mounting the road from the village, passed them by in a joyous flutter of bells, and they straightened themselves and looked ahead with rigid faces. Along the main street lights had begun to shine from the house-fronts and stray figures were turning in here and there at the gates. Ethan, with a touch of his whip, roused the sorrel to a languid trot.

As they drew near the end of the village the cries of children reached them, and they saw a knot of boys, with sleds behind them, scattering across the open space before the church.

"I guess this'll be their last coast for a day or two," Ethan said, looking up at the mild sky.

Mattie was silent, and he added: "We were to have gone down last night."

Still she did not speak and, prompted by an obscure desire to help himself and her through their miserable last hour, he went on discursively: "Ain't it funny we haven't been down together but just that once last winter?"

She answered: "It wasn't often I got down to the village."

"That's so," he said.

They had reached the crest of the Corbury road, and between the indistinct white glimmer of the church and the black curtain of the Varnum spruces the slope stretched away below them without a sled on its length. Some erratic impulse prompted Ethan to say: "How'd you like me to take you down now?"

She forced a laugh. "Why, there isn't time!"

"There's all the time we want. Come along!" His one desire now was to postpone the moment of turning the sorrel toward the Flats.

"But the girl," she faltered. "The girl'll be waiting at the station."

"Well, let her wait. You'd have to if she didn't. Come!"

The note of authority in his voice seemed to subdue her, and when he had jumped from the sleigh she let him help her out, saying only, with a vague feint of reluctance: "But there isn't a sled round any wheres."

"Yes, there is! Right over there under the spruces."

He threw the bearskin over the sorrel, who stood passively by the roadside, hanging a meditative head. Then he caught Mattie's hand and drew her after him toward the sled.

She seated herself obediently and he took his place behind her, so close that her hair brushed his face. "All right, Matt?" he called out, as if the width of the road had been between them.

She turned her head to say: "It's dreadfully dark. Are you sure you can see?"

He laughed contemptuously: "I could go down this coast with my eyes tied!" and she laughed with him, as if she liked his audacity. Nevertheless he sat still a moment, straining his eyes down the long hill, for it was the most confusing hour of the evening, the hour when the last clearness from the upper sky is merged with the rising night in a blur that disguises landmarks and falsifies distances.

"Now!" he cried.

The sled started with a bound, and they flew on through the dusk, gathering smoothness and speed as they went, with the hollow night opening out below them and the air singing by like an organ. Mattie sat perfectly still, but as they reached the bend at the foot of the hill, where the big elm thrust out a deadly elbow, he fancied that she shrank a little closer.

"Don't be scared, Matt!" he cried exultantly, as they spun safely past it and flew down the second slope; and when they reached the level ground beyond, and the speed of the sled began to slacken, he heard her give a little laugh of glee.

They sprang off and started to walk back up the hill. Ethan dragged the sled with one hand and passed the other through Mattie's arm.

"Were you scared I'd run you into the elm?" he asked with a boyish laugh.

"I told you I was never scared with you," she answered.

The strange exaltation of his mood had brought on one of his rare fits of boastfulness. "It *is* a tricky place, though. The least swerve, and we'd never ha' come up again. But I can measure distances to a hair's-breadth—always could."

She murmured: "I always say you've got the surest eye . . ."

Deep silence had fallen with the starless dusk, and they leaned on each other without speaking; but at every step of their climb Ethan said to himself: "It's the last time we'll ever walk together."

They mounted slowly to the top of the hill. When they were abreast of the church he stooped his head to her to ask: "Are you tired?" and she answered, breathing quickly: "It was splendid!"

With a pressure of his arm he guided her toward the Norway spruces. "I guess this sled must be Ned Hale's. Anyhow I'll leave it where I found it." He drew the sled up to the Varnum gate and rested it against the fence. As he raised himself he suddenly felt Mattie close to him among the shadows.

"Is this where Ned and Ruth kissed each other?" she whispered breathlessly, and flung her arms about him. Her lips, groping for his, swept over his face, and he held her fast in a rapture of surprise.

"Good-bye—good-bye," she stammered, and kissed him again.

"Oh, Matt I can't let you go!" broke from him in the same old cry.

She freed herself from his hold and he heard her sobbing. "Oh, I can't go either!" she wailed.

"Matt! What'll we do? What'll we do?"

They clung to each other's hands like children, and her body shook with desperate sobs.

Through the stillness they heard the church clock striking five.

"Oh, Ethan, it's time!" she cried.

He drew her back to him. "Time for what? You don't suppose I'm going to leave you now?"

"If I missed my train where'd I go?"

"Where are you going if you catch it?"

She stood silent, her hands lying cold and relaxed in his.

"What's the good of either of us going anywheres without the other one now?" he said.

She remained motionless, as if she had not heard him. Then she snatched her hands from his, threw her arms about his neck, and pressed a sudden drenched cheek against his face. "Ethan! Ethan! I want you to take me down again!"

"Down where?"

"The coast. Right off," she panted. "So 't we'll never come up any more."

"Matt! What on earth do you mean?"

She put her lips close against his ear to say: "Right into the big elm. You said you could. So 't we'd never have to leave each other any more."

"Why, what are you talking of? You're crazy!"

"I'm not crazy; but I will be if I leave you."

"Oh, Matt, Matt—" he groaned.

She tightened her fierce hold about his neck. Her face lay close to his face.

"Ethan, where'll I go if I leave you? I don't know how to get along alone. You said so yourself just now. Nobody but you was ever good to me. And there'll be that strange girl in the house . . . and she'll sleep in my bed, where I used to lay nights and listen to hear you come up the stairs . . ."

The words were like fragments torn from his heart. With them came the hated vision of the house he was going back to—of the stairs he would have to go up every night, of the woman who would wait for him there. And the sweetness of Mattie's avowal, the wild wonder of knowing at last that all that had happened to him had happened to her too, made the other vision more abhorrent, the other life more intolerable to return to . . .

Her pleadings still came to him between short sobs, but he no longer heard what she was saying. Her hat had slipped back and he was stroking her hair. He wanted to get the feeling of it into his hand, so that it would sleep there like a seed in winter. Once he found her mouth again, and they seemed to be by the pond together in the burning August sun. But his cheek touched hers, and it was cold and full of weeping, and he saw the road to the Flats under the night and heard the whistle of the train up the line.

The spruces swathed them in blackness and silence. They might have been in their coffins underground. He said to himself: "Perhaps it'll feel like this . . ." and then again: "After this I sha'n't feel anything . . ."

Suddenly he heard the old sorrel whinny across the road, and thought: "He's wondering why he doesn't get his supper . . ."

"Come," Mattie whispered, tugging at his hand.

Her somber violence constrained him: she seemed the embodied instrument of fate. He pulled the sled out, blinking like a night-bird as he passed from the shade of the spruces into the transparent dusk of the open. The slope below them was deserted. All Starkfield was at supper, and not a figure crossed the open space before the church.

The sky, swollen with the clouds that announce a thaw, hung as low as before a summer storm. He strained his eyes through the dimness, and they seemed less keen, less capable than usual.

He took his seat on the sled and Mattie instantly placed herself in front of him. Her hat had fallen into the snow and his lips were in her hair. He stretched out his legs, drove his heels into the road to keep the sled from slipping forward, and bent her head back between his hands. Then suddenly he sprang up again.

"Get up," he ordered her.

It was the tone she always heeded, but she cowered down in her seat, repeating vehemently: "No, no, no!"

"Get up!"

"Why?"

"I want to sit in front."

"No, no! How can you steer in front?"

"I don't have to. We'll follow the track."

They spoke in smothered whispers, as though the night were listening.

"Get up! Get up!" he urged her; but she kept on repeating: "Why do you want to sit in front?"

"Because I—because I want to feel you holding me," he stammered, and dragged her to her feet.

The answer seemed to satisfy her, or else she yielded to the power of his voice. He bent down, feeling in the obscurity for the glassy slide worn by preceding coasters, and placed the runners carefully between its edges. She waited while he seated himself with crossed legs in the front of the sled; then she crouched quickly down at his back and clasped her arms about him. Her breath in his neck set him shuddering again, and he almost sprang from his seat. But in a flash he remembered the alternative. She was right: this was better than parting. He leaned back and drew her mouth to his . . .

Just as they started he heard the sorrel's whinny again, and the familiar wistful call, and all the confused images it brought with it, went with him down the first reach of the road. Half-way down there was a sudden drop, then a rise, and after that another long delirious descent. As they took wing for this it seemed to him that they were flying indeed, flying far up into the cloudy night, with Starkfield immeasurably below them, falling away like a speck in space . . . Then the big elm shot up ahead, lying in wait for them at the bend of the road, and he said between his teeth: "We can fetch it; I know we can fetch it—"

As they flew toward the tree Mattie pressed her arms tighter, and her blood seemed to be in his veins. Once or twice the sled swerved a little under them. He slanted his body to keep it headed for the elm, repeating to himself again and again: "I know we can fetch it"; and little phrases she had spoken ran through his head and danced before him on the air. The big tree loomed bigger and closer, and as they bore down on it he thought: "It's waiting for us: it seems to know." But suddenly his wife's face, with twisted monstrous lineaments, thrust itself between him and his goal, and he made an instinctive movement to brush it aside. The sled swerved in response, but he righted it again, kept it straight, and drove down on the black projecting mass. There was a last instant when the air shot past him like millions of fiery wires; and then the elm . . .

The sky was still thick, but looking straight up he saw a single star, and tried vaguely to reckon whether it were Sirius, or—or—The effort tired him too much, and he closed his heavy lids and thought that he would sleep . . . The stillness was so profound that he heard a little animal twittering somewhere near by under the snow. It made a small frightened cheep like a field mouse, and he wondered languidly if it were hurt. Then he understood that it must be in pain: pain so excruciating that he seemed, mysteriously, to feel it shooting through his own body. He tried in vain to roll over in the direction of the sound, and stretched his left arm out across the snow. And now it was as though he felt rather than heard the twittering; it seemed to be under his palm, which rested on something soft and springy. The thought of the animal's suffering was intolerable to him and he struggled to raise himself, and could not because a rock, or some huge mass, seemed to be lying on him. But he continued to finger about cautiously with his left hand, thinking he might get hold of the little creature and help it; and all at once he knew that the soft thing he had touched was Mattie's hair and that his hand was on her face.

He dragged himself to his knees, the monstrous load on him moving with him as he moved, and his hand went over and over her face, and he felt that the twittering came from her lips . . .

He got his face down close to hers, with his ear to her mouth, and in the darkness he saw her eyes open and heard her say his name.

"Oh, Matt, I thought we'd fetched it," he moaned; and far off, up the hill, he heard the sorrel whinny, and thought: "I ought to be getting him his feed . . ."

. . . .
. . . .
. . . .

THE querulous drone ceased as I entered Frome's kitchen, and of the two women sitting there I could not tell which had been the speaker.

One of them, on my appearing, raised her tall bony figure from her seat, not as if to welcome me—for she threw me no more than a brief glance of surprise—but simply to set about preparing the meal which Frome's absence had delayed. A slatternly calico wrapper hung from her shoulders and the wisps of her thin gray hair were drawn away from a high forehead and fastened at the back by a broken comb. She had pale opaque eyes which revealed nothing and reflected nothing, and her narrow lips were of the same sallow color as her face.

The other woman was much smaller and slighter. She sat huddled in an arm-chair near the stove, and when I came in she turned her head quickly toward me, without the least corresponding movement of her body. Her hair was as gray as her companion's, her face as bloodless and shrivelled, but amber-tinted, with swarthy shadows sharpening the nose and hollowing the temples. Under her shapeless dress her body kept its limp immobility, and her dark eyes had the bright witch-like stare that disease of the spine sometimes gives.

Even for that part of the country the kitchen was a poor-looking place. With the exception of the dark-eyed woman's chair, which looked like a soiled relic of luxury bought at a country auction, the furniture was of the roughest kind. Three coarse china plates and a broken-nosed milk-jug had been set on a greasy table scored with knife-cuts, and a couple of straw-bottomed chairs and a kitchen dresser of unpainted pine stood meagerly against the plaster walls.

"My, it's cold here! The fire must be 'most out," Frome said, glancing about him apologetically as he followed me in.

The tall woman, who had moved away from us toward the dresser, took no notice; but the other, from her cushioned niche, answered complainingly, in a high thin voice: "It's on'y just been made up this very minute. Zeena fell asleep and slep' ever so long, and I thought I'd be frozen stiff before I could wake her up and get her to 'tend to it."

I knew then that it was she who had been speaking when we entered.

Her companion, who was just coming back to the table with the remains of a cold mince-pie in a battered pie-dish, set down her unappetizing burden without appearing to hear the accusation brought against her.

Frome stood hesitatingly before her as she advanced; then he looked at me and said: "This is my wife, Mis' Frome." After another interval he added, turning toward the figure in the arm-chair: "And this is Miss Mattie Silver . . ."

. . . .

Mrs. Hale, tender soul, had pictured me as lost in the Flats and buried under a snow-drift; and so lively was her satisfaction on seeing me safely restored to her the next morning that I felt my peril had caused me to advance several degrees in her favor.

Great was her amazement, and that of old Mrs. Varnum, on learning that Ethan Frome's old horse had carried me to and from Corbury Junction through the worst blizzard of the winter; greater still their surprise when they heard that his master had taken me in for the night.

Beneath their wondering exclamations I felt a secret curiosity to know what impressions I had received from my night in the Frome household, and divined that the best way of breaking down their reserve was to let them try to penetrate mine. I therefore confined myself to saying, in a matter-of-fact tone, that I had been received with great kindness, and that Frome had made a bed for me in a room on the ground-floor which seemed in happier days to have been fitted up as a kind of writing-room or study.

"Well," Mrs. Hale mused, "in such a storm I suppose he felt he couldn't do less than take you in—but I guess it went hard with Ethan. I don't believe but what you're the only stranger has set foot in that house for over twenty years. He's that proud he don't even like his oldest friends to go there; and I don't know as any do, any more, except myself and the doctor . . ."

"You still go there, Mrs. Hale?" I ventured.

"I used to go a good deal after the accident, when I was first married; but after awhile I got to think it made 'em feel worse to see us. And then one thing and another came, and my own troubles . . . But I generally make out to drive over there round about New Year's, and once in the summer. Only I always try to pick a day when Ethan's off somewheres. It's bad enough to see the two women sitting there—but *his* face, when he looks round that bare place, just kills me . . . You see, I can look back and call it up in his mother's day, before their troubles."

Old Mrs. Varnum, by this time, had gone up to bed, and her daughter and I were sitting alone, after supper, in the austere seclusion of the horse-hair parlor. Mrs. Hale glanced at me tentatively, as though trying to see how much footing my conjectures gave her; and I guessed that if she had kept silence till now it was because she had been waiting, through all the years, for some one who should see what she alone had seen.

I waited to let her trust in me gather strength before I said: "Yes, it's pretty bad, seeing all three of them there together."

She drew her mild brows into a frown of pain. "It was just awful from the beginning. I was here in the house when they were carried up—they laid Mattie Silver in the room you're in. She and I were great friends, and she was to have been my brides-maid in the spring . . . When she came to I went up to her and stayed all night. They gave her things to quiet her, and she didn't know much till to'rd morning, and then all of a sudden she woke up just like herself, and looked straight at me out of her big eyes, and said . . . Oh, I don't know why I'm telling you all this," Mrs. Hale broke off, crying.

She took off her spectacles, wiped the moisture from them, and put them on again with an unsteady hand. "It got about the next day," she went on, "that Zeena Frome had sent Mattie off in a hurry because she had a hired girl coming, and the folks here could never rightly tell what she and Ethan were doing that night coasting, when

"But his face, *when he looks round that bare place, just kills me."*

they'd ought to have been on their way to the Flats to ketch the train . . . I never knew myself what Zeena thought—I don't to this day. Nobody knows Zeena's thoughts. Anyhow, when she heard o' the accident she came right in and stayed with Ethan over to the minister's, where they'd carried him. And as soon as the doctors said that Mattie could be moved, Zeena sent for her and took her back to the farm."

"And there she's been ever since?"

Mrs. Hale answered simply: "There was nowhere else for her to go"; and my heart tightened at the thought of the hard compulsions of the poor.

"Yes, there she's been," Mrs. Hale continued, "and Zeena's done for her, and done for Ethan, as good as she could. It was a miracle, considering how sick she was—but she seemed to be raised right up just when the call came to her. Not as she's ever given up doctoring, and she's had sick spells right along; but she's had the strength given her to care for those two for over twenty years, and before the accident came she thought she couldn't even care for herself."

Mrs. Hale paused a moment, and I remained silent, plunged in the vision of what her words evoked. "It's horrible for them all," I murmured.

"Yes: it's pretty bad. And they ain't any of 'em easy people either. Mattie *was,* before the accident; I never knew a sweeter nature. But she's suffered too much—that's what I always say when folks tell me how she's soured. And Zeena, she was always cranky. Not but what she bears with Mattie wonderful—I've seen that myself. But sometimes the two of them get going at each other, and then Ethan's face'd break your heart . . . When I see that, I think it's him that suffers most . . . anyhow it ain't Zeena, because she ain't got the time . . . It's a pity, though," Mrs. Hale ended, sighing, "that they're all shut up there'n that one kitchen. In the summertime, on pleasant days, they move Mattie into the parlor, or out in the door-yard, and that makes it easier . . . but winters there's the fires to be thought of; and there ain't a dime to spare up at the Fromes'."

Mrs. Hale drew a deep breath, as though her memory were eased of its long burden, and she had no more to say; but suddenly an impulse of complete avowal seized her.

She took off her spectacles again, leaned toward me across the bead-work table-cover, and went on with lowered voice: "There was one day, about a week after the accident, when they all thought Mattie couldn't live. Well, I say it's a pity she *did*. I said it right out to our minister once, and he was shocked at me. Only he wasn't with me that morning when she first came to . . . And I say, if she'd ha' died, Ethan might ha' lived; and the way they are now, I don't see's there's much difference between the Fromes up at the farm and the Fromes down in the graveyard; 'cept that down there they're all quiet, and the women have got to hold their tongues."

The House of Mirth

Book One

I

SELDEN paused in surprise. In the afternoon rush of the Grand Central Station his eyes had been refreshed by the sight of Miss Lily Bart.

It was a Monday in early September, and he was returning to his work from a hurried dip into the country; but what was Miss Bart doing in town at that season? If she had appeared to be catching a train, he might have inferred that he had come on her in the act of transition between one and another of the country-houses which disputed her presence after the close of the Newport season; but her desultory air perplexed him. She stood apart from the crowd, letting it drift by her to the platform or the street, and wearing an air of irresolution which might, as he surmised, be the mask of a very definite purpose. It struck him at once that she was waiting for someone, but he hardly knew why the idea arrested him. There was nothing new about Lily Bart, yet he could never see her without a faint movement of interest: it was characteristic of her that she always roused speculation, that her simplest acts seemed the result of far-reaching intentions.

An impulse of curiosity made him turn out of his direct line to the door, and stroll past her. He knew that if she did not wish to be seen she would contrive to elude him; and it amused him to think of putting her skill to the test.

"Mr. Selden—what good luck!"

She came forward smiling, eager almost, in her resolve to intercept him. One or two persons, in brushing past them, lingered to look; for Miss Bart was a figure to arrest even the suburban traveller rushing to his last train.

Selden had never seen her more radiant. Her vivid head, relieved against the dull tints of the crowd, made her more conspicuous than in a ballroom, and under her dark hat and veil she regained the girlish smoothness, the purity of tint, that she was beginning to lose after eleven years of late hours and indefatigable dancing. Was it really eleven years, Selden found himself wondering, and had she indeed reached the nine-and-twentieth birthday with which her rivals credited her?

"What luck!" she repeated. "How nice of you to come to my rescue!"

He responded joyfully that to do so was his mission in life, and asked what form the rescue was to take.

"Oh, almost any—even to sitting on a bench and talking to me. One sits out a cotillion—why not sit out a train? It isn't a bit hotter here than in Mrs. Van Osburgh's conservatory—and some of the women are not a bit uglier."

She broke off, laughing, to explain that she had come up to town from Tuxedo, on her way to the Gus Trenors' at Bellomont, and had missed the three-fifteen train to Rhinebeck.

"And there isn't another till half-past five." She consulted the little jewelled watch among her laces. "Just two hours to wait. And I don't know what to do with myself. My maid came up this morning to do some shopping for me, and was to go on to Bellomont at one o'clock, and my aunt's house is closed, and I don't know a soul in town." She glanced plaintively about the station. "It *is* hotter than Mrs. Van Osburgh's, after all. If you can spare the time, do take me somewhere for a breath of air."

He declared himself entirely at her disposal: the adventure struck him as diverting. As a spectator, he had always enjoyed Lily Bart; and his course lay so far out of her orbit that it amused him to be drawn for a moment into the sudden intimacy which her proposal implied.

"Shall we go over to Sherry's for a cup of tea?"

She smiled assentingly, and then made a slight grimace.

"So many people come up to town on a Monday—one is sure to meet a lot of bores. I'm as old as the hills, of course, and it ought not to make any difference; but if *I'm* old enough, you're not," she objected gaily. "I'm dying for tea—but isn't there a quieter place?"

He answered her smile, which rested on him vividly. Her discretions interested him almost as much as her imprudences: he was so sure that both were part of the same carefully-elaborated plan. In judging Miss Bart, he had always made use of the "argument from design."

"The resources of New York are rather meagre," he said; "but I'll find a hansom first, and then we'll invent something."

He led her through the throng of returning holiday-makers, past sallow-faced girls in preposterous hats, and flat-chested women struggling with paper bundles and palm-leaf fans. Was it possible that she belonged to the same race? The dinginess, the crudity of this average section of womanhood made him feel how highly specialized she was.

A rapid shower had cooled the air, and clouds still hung refreshingly over the moist street.

"How delicious! Let us walk a little," she said as they emerged from the station.

They turned into Madison Avenue and began to stroll northward. As she moved beside him, with her long light step, Selden was conscious of taking a luxurious pleasure in her nearness: in the modelling of her little ear, the crisp upward wave of her hair—was it ever so slightly brightened by art?—and the thick planting of her straight black lashes. Everything about her was at once vigorous and exquisite, at once strong and fine. He had a confused sense that she must have cost a great deal to make, that a great many dull and ugly people must, in some mysterious way, have been sacrificed to produce her. He was aware that the qualities distinguishing her from the herd of her sex were chiefly external: as though a fine glaze of beauty and fastidiousness had been applied to vulgar clay. Yet the analogy left him unsatisfied, for a coarse texture will not take a high finish; and was it not possible that the material was fine, but that circumstance had fashioned it into a futile shape?

As he reached this point in his speculations the sun came out, and her lifted parasol cut off his enjoyment. A moment or two later she paused with a sigh.

"Oh, dear, I'm so hot and thirsty—and what a hideous place New York is!" She looked despairingly up and down the dreary thoroughfare. "Other cities put on their best clothes in summer, but

New York seems to sit in its shirt-sleeves." Her eyes wandered down one of the side-streets. "Someone has had the humanity to plant a few trees over there. Let us go into the shade."

"I am glad my street meets with your approval," said Selden as they turned the corner.

"Your street? Do you live here?"

She glanced with interest along the new brick and limestone house-fronts, fantastically varied in obedience to the American craving for novelty, but fresh and inviting with their awnings and flower-boxes.

"Ah, yes—to be sure: *The Benedick*. What a nice-looking building! I don't think I've ever seen it before." She looked across at the flat-house with its marble porch and pseudo-Georgian façade. "Which are your windows? Those with the awnings down?"

"On the top floor—yes."

"And that nice little balcony is yours? How cool it looks up there!"

He paused a moment. "Come up and see," he suggested. "I can give you a cup of tea in no time—and you won't meet any bores."

Her color deepened—she still had the art of blushing at the right time—but she took the suggestion as lightly as it was made.

"Why not? It's too tempting—I'll take the risk," she declared.

"Oh, I'm not dangerous," he said in the same key. In truth, he had never liked her as well as at that moment. He knew she had accepted without afterthought: he could never be a factor in her calculations, and there was a surprise, a refreshment almost, in the spontaneity of her consent.

On the threshold he paused a moment, feeling for his latch-key.

"There's no one here; but I have a servant who is supposed to come in the mornings, and it's just possible he may have put out the tea-things and provided some cake."

He ushered her into a slip of a hall hung with old prints. She noticed the letters and notes heaped on the table among his gloves and sticks; then she found herself in a small library, dark but cheerful, with its walls of books, a pleasantly faded Turkey rug, a littered desk, and, as he had foretold, a tea-tray on a low table near the window. A breeze had sprung up, swaying inward the muslin curtains, and bringing a fresh scent of mignonette and petunias from the flower-box on the balcony.

Lily sank with a sigh into one of the shabby leather chairs.

"How delicious to have a place like this all to one's self! What a miserable thing it is to be a woman." She leaned back in a luxury of discontent.

Selden was rummaging in a cupboard for the cake.

"Even women," he said, "have been known to enjoy the privileges of a flat."

"Oh, governesses—or widows. But not girls—not poor, miserable, marriageable girls!"

"I even know a girl who lives in a flat."

She sat up in surprise. "You do?"

"I do," he assured her, emerging from the cupboard with the sought-for cake.

"Oh, I know—you mean Gerty Farish." She smiled a little unkindly. "But I said *marriageable*—and besides, she has a horrid little place, and no maid, and such queer things to eat. Her cook does the washing and the food tastes of soap. I should hate that, you know."

"You shouldn't dine with her on wash-days," said Selden, cutting the cake.

They both laughed, and he knelt by the table to light the lamp under the kettle, while she measured out the tea into a little teapot of green glaze. As he watched her hand, polished as a bit of old ivory, with its slender pink nails, and the sapphire bracelet slipping over her wrist, he was struck with the irony of suggesting to her such a life as his cousin Gertrude Farish had chosen. She was so evidently the victim of the civilization which had produced her, that the links of her bracelet seemed like manacles chaining her to her fate.

She seemed to read his thought. "It was horrid of me to say that of Gerty," she said with charming compunction. "I forgot she was your cousin. But we're so different, you know: she likes being good, and I like being happy. And besides, she is free and I am not. If I were, I daresay I could manage to be happy even in her flat. It must be pure bliss to arrange the furniture just as one likes, and give all the horrors to the ash-man. If I could only do over my aunt's drawing-room I know I should be a better woman."

"Is it so very bad?" he asked sympathetically.

She smiled at him across the teapot which she was holding up to be filled.

"That shows how seldom you come there. Why don't you come oftener?"

"When I do come, it's not to look at Mrs. Peniston's furniture."

"Nonsense," she said. "You don't come at all—and yet we get on so well when we meet."

"Perhaps that's the reason," he answered promptly. "I'm afraid I haven't any cream, you know—shall you mind a slice of lemon instead?"

"I shall like it better." She waited while he cut the lemon and dropped a thin disk into her cup. "But that is not the reason," she insisted.

"The reason for what?"

"For your never coming." She leaned forward with a shade of perplexity in her charming eyes. "I wish I knew—I wish I could make you out. Of course I know there are men who don't like me—one can tell that at a glance. And there are others who are afraid of me: they think I want to marry them." She smiled up at him frankly. "But I don't think you dislike me—and you can't possibly think I want to marry you."

"No—I absolve you of that," he agreed.

"Well, then——?"

He had carried his cup to the fireplace, and stood leaning against the chimney-piece and looking down on her with an air of indolent amusement. The provocation in her eyes increased his amusement—he had not supposed she would waste her powder on such small game; but perhaps she was only keeping her hand in; or perhaps a girl of her type had no conversation but of the personal kind. At any rate, she was amazingly pretty, and he had asked her to tea and must live up to his obligations.

"Well, then," he said with a plunge, "perhaps *that's* the reason."

"What?"

"The fact that you don't want to marry me. Perhaps I don't regard it as such a strong inducement to go and see you." He felt a slight shiver down his spine as he ventured this, but her laugh reassured him.

"Dear Mr. Selden, that wasn't worthy of you. It's stupid of you to make love to me, and it isn't like you to be stupid." She leaned back, sipping her tea with an air so enchantingly judicial that, if they had been in her aunt's drawing-room, he might almost have tried to disprove her deduction.

She smiled at him across the teapot which she was holding.

"Don't you see," she continued, "that there are men enough to say pleasant things to me, and that what I want is a friend who won't be afraid to say disagreeable ones when I need them? Sometimes I have fancied you might be that friend—I don't know why, except that you are neither a prig nor a bounder, and that I shouldn't have to pretend with you or be on my guard against you." Her voice had dropped to a note of seriousness, and she sat gazing up at him with the troubled gravity of a child.

"You don't know how much I need such a friend," she said. "My aunt is full of copy-book axioms, but they were all meant to apply to conduct in the early fifties. I always feel that to live up to them would include wearing book-muslin with gigot sleeves. And the other women—my best friends—well, they use me or abuse me; but they don't care a straw what happens to me. I've been about too long—people are getting tired of me; they are beginning to say I ought to marry."

There was a moment's pause, during which Selden meditated one or two replies calculated to add a momentary zest to the situation; but he rejected them in favor of the simple question: "Well, why don't you?"

She colored and laughed. "Ah, I see you *are* a friend after all, and that is one of the disagreeable things I was asking for."

"It wasn't meant to be disagreeable," he returned amicably. "Isn't marriage your vocation? Isn't it what you're all brought up for?"

She sighed. "I suppose so. What else is there?"

"Exactly. And so why not take the plunge and have it over?"

She shrugged her shoulders. "You speak as if I ought to marry the first man who came along."

"I didn't mean to imply that you are as hard put to it as that. But there must be someone with the requisite qualifications."

She shook her head wearily. "I threw away one or two good chances when I first came out—I suppose every girl does; and you know I am horribly poor—and very expensive. I must have a great deal of money."

Selden had turned to reach for a cigarette-box on the mantelpiece.

"What's become of Dillworth?" he asked.

"Oh, his mother was frightened—she was afraid I should have all the family jewels reset. And she wanted me to promise that I wouldn't do over the drawing-room."

"The very thing you are marrying for!"

"Exactly. So she packed him off to India."

"Hard luck—but you can do better than Dillworth."

He offered the box, and she took out three or four cigarettes, putting one between her lips and slipping the others into a little gold case attached to her long pearl chain.

"Have I time? Just a whiff, then." She leaned forward, holding the tip of her cigarette to his. As she did so, he noted, with a purely impersonal enjoyment, how evenly the black lashes were set in her smooth white lids, and how the purplish shade beneath them melted into the pure pallor of the cheek.

She began to saunter about the room, examining the book-shelves between the puffs of her cigarette-smoke. Some of the volumes had the ripe tints of good tooling and old morocco, and her eyes lingered on them caressingly, not with the appreciation of the expert, but with the pleasure in agreeable tones and textures that was one of her inmost susceptibilities. Suddenly her expression changed from desultory enjoyment to active conjecture, and she turned to Selden with a question.

"You collect, don't you—you know about first editions and things?"

"As much as a man may who has no money to spend. Now and then I pick up something in the rubbish heap; and I go and look on at the big sales."

She had again addressed herself to the shelves, but her eyes now swept them inattentively, and he saw that she was preoccupied with a new idea.

"And Americana—do you collect Americana?"

Selden stared and laughed.

"No, that's rather out of my line. I'm not really a collector, you see; I simply like to have good editions of the books I am fond of."

She made a slight grimace. "And Americana are horribly dull, I suppose?"

"I should fancy so—except to the historian. But your real collector values a thing for its rarity. I don't suppose the buyers of Americana sit up reading them all night—old Jefferson Gryce certainly didn't."

She was listening with keen attention. "And yet they fetch fabulous prices, don't they? It seems so odd to want to pay a lot for an ugly badly-printed book that one is never going to read! And I suppose most of the owners of Americana are not historians either?"

"No; very few of the historians can afford to buy them. They have to use those in the public libraries or in private collections. It seems to be the mere rarity that attracts the average collector."

He had seated himself on an arm of the chair near which she was standing, and she continued to question him, asking which were the rarest volumes, whether the Jefferson Gryce collection was really considered the finest in the world, and what was the largest price ever fetched by a single volume.

It was so pleasant to sit there looking up at her, as she lifted now one book and then another from the shelves, fluttering the pages between her fingers, while her drooping profile was outlined against the warm background of old bindings, that he talked on without pausing to wonder at her sudden interest in so unsuggestive a subject. But he could never be long with her without trying to find a reason for what she was doing, and as she replaced his first edition of La Bruyère and turned away from the bookcases, he began to ask himself what she had been driving at. Her next question was not of a nature to enlighten him. She paused before him with a smile which seemed at once designed to admit him to her familiarity, and to remind him of the restrictions it imposed.

"Don't you ever mind," she asked suddenly, "not being rich enough to buy all the books you want?"

He followed her glance about the room, with its worn furniture and shabby walls.

"Don't I just? Do you take me for a saint on a pillar?"

"And having to work—do you mind that?"

"Oh, the work itself is not so bad—I'm rather fond of the law."

"No; but the being tied down: the routine—don't you ever want to get away, to see new places and people?"

"Horribly—especially when I see all my friends rushing to the steamer."

She drew a sympathetic breath. "But do you mind enough—to marry to get out of it?"

Selden broke into a laugh. "God forbid!" he declared.

She rose with a sigh, tossing her cigarette into the grate.

"Ah, there's the difference—a girl must, a man may if he chooses." She surveyed him critically. "Your coat's a little shabby—but who cares? It doesn't keep people from asking you to dine. If I were shabby no one would have me: a woman is asked out as much for her clothes as for herself. The clothes are the background, the frame, if you like: they don't make success, but they are a part of it. Who wants a dingy woman? We are expected to be pretty and well-dressed till we drop—and if we can't keep it up alone, we have to go into partnership."

Selden glanced at her with amusement: it was impossible, even with her lovely eyes imploring him, to take a sentimental view of her case.

"Ah, well, there must be plenty of capital on the look-out for such an investment. Perhaps you'll meet your fate tonight at the Trenors'."

She returned his look interrogatively.

"I thought you might be going there—oh, not in that capacity! But there are to be a lot of your set—Gwen Van Osburgh, the Wetheralls, Lady Cressida Raith—and the George Dorsets."

She paused a moment before the last name, and shot a query through her lashes; but he remained imperturbable.

"Mrs. Trenor asked me; but I can't get away till the end of the week; and those big parties bore me."

"Ah, so they do me," she exclaimed.

"Then why go?"

"It's part of the business—you forget! And besides, if I didn't, I should be playing bézique with my aunt at Richfield Springs."

"That's almost as bad as marrying Dillworth," he agreed, and they both laughed for pure pleasure in their sudden intimacy.

She glanced at the clock.

"Dear me! I must be off. It's after five."

She paused before the mantelpiece, studying herself in the mirror while she adjusted her veil. The attitude revealed the long slope of her slender sides, which gave a kind of wild-wood grace to her outline—as though she were a captured dryad subdued to the conventions of the drawing-room; and Selden reflected that it was the same streak of sylvan freedom in her nature that lent such savor to her artificiality.

He followed her across the room to the entrance-hall; but on the threshold she held out her hand with a gesture of leave-taking.

"It's been delightful; and now you will have to return my visit."

"But don't you want me to see you to the station?"

"No; goodbye here, please."

She let her hand lie in his a moment, smiling up at him adorably.

"Goodbye, then—and good luck at Bellomont!" he said, opening the door for her.

On the landing she paused to look about her. There were a thousand chances to one against her meeting anybody, but one could never tell, and she always paid for her rare indiscretions by a violent reaction of prudence. There was no one in sight, however, but a char-woman who was scrubbing the stairs. Her own stout person and its surrounding implements took up so much room that Lily, to pass her, had to gather up her skirts and brush against the wall. As she did so, the woman paused in her work and looked up curiously, resting her clenched red fists on the wet cloth she had just drawn from her pail. She had a broad sallow face, slightly pitted with smallpox, and thin straw-colored hair through which her scalp shone unpleasantly.

"I beg your pardon," said Lily, intending by her politeness to convey a criticism of the other's manner.

The woman, without answering, pushed her pail aside, and continued to stare as Miss Bart swept by with a murmur of silken linings. Lily felt herself flushing under the look. What did the creature suppose? Could one never do the simplest, the most harmless thing, without subjecting one's self to some odious conjecture? Half way down the next flight, she smiled to think that a char-woman's stare should so perturb her. The poor thing was probably dazzled by such an unwonted apparition. But *were* such apparitions unwonted on Selden's stairs? Miss Bart was not familiar with the moral code of bachelors' flat-houses, and her color rose again as it occurred to her that the woman's persistent gaze implied a groping among past associations. But she put aside the thought with a smile at her own fears, and hastened downward, wondering if she should find a cab short of Fifth Avenue.

Under the Georgian porch she paused again, scanning the street for a hansom. None was in sight, but as she reached the sidewalk she ran against a small glossy-looking man with a gardenia in his coat, who raised his hat with a surprised exclamation.

"Miss Bart? Well—of all people! This *is* luck," he declared; and she caught a twinkle of amused curiosity between his screwed-up lids.

"Oh, Mr. Rosedale—how are you?" she said, perceiving that the irrepressible annoyance on her face was reflected in the sudden intimacy of his smile.

Mr. Rosedale stood scanning her with interest and approval. He was a plump rosy man of the blond Jewish type, with smart London clothes fitting him like upholstery, and small sidelong eyes which gave him the air of appraising people as if they were bric-a-brac. He glanced up interrogatively at the porch of the Benedick.

"Been up to town for a little shopping, I suppose?" he said, in a tone which had the familiarity of a touch.

Miss Bart shrank from it slightly, and then flung herself into precipitate explanations.

"Yes—I came up to see my dress-maker. I am just on my way to catch the train to the Trenors'."

"Ah—your dress-maker; just so," he said blandly. "I didn't know there were any dress-makers in the Benedick."

"The Benedick?" She looked gently puzzled. "Is that the name of this building?"

"Yes, that's the name: I believe it's an old word for bachelor, isn't it? I happen to own the building—that's the way I know." His smile deepened as he added with increasing assurance: "But you must let me take you to the station. The Trenors are at Bellomont, of course? You've barely time to catch the five-forty. The dress-maker kept you waiting, I suppose."

Lily stiffened under the pleasantry.

"Oh, thanks," she stammered; and at that moment her eye caught a hansom drifting down Madison Avenue, and she hailed it with a desperate gesture.

"You're very kind; but I couldn't think of troubling you," she said, extending her hand to Mr. Rosedale; and heedless of his protestations, she sprang into the rescuing vehicle, and called out a breathless order to the driver.

II

IN the hansom she leaned back with a sigh.

Why must a girl pay so dearly for her least escape from routine? Why could one never do a natural thing without having to screen it behind a structure of artifice? She had yielded to a passing impulse in going to Lawrence Selden's rooms, and it was so seldom that she could allow herself the luxury of an impulse! This one, at any rate, was going to cost her rather more than she could afford. She was vexed to see that, in spite of so many years of vigilance, she had blundered twice within five minutes. That stupid story about her dress-maker was bad enough—it would have been so simple to tell Rosedale that she had been taking tea with Selden! The mere statement of the fact would have rendered it innocuous. But, after having let herself be surprised in a falsehood, it was doubly stupid to snub the witness of her discomfiture. If she had had the presence of mind to let Rosedale drive her to the station, the concession might have purchased his silence. He had his race's accuracy in the appraisal of values, and to be seen walking down the platform at the crowded afternoon hour in the company of Miss Lily Bart would have been money in his pocket, as he might himself have phrased it. He knew, of course, that there would be a large house-party at Bellomont, and the possibility of being taken for one of Mrs. Trenor's guests was doubtless included in his calculations. Mr. Rosedale was still at a stage in his social ascent when it was of importance to produce such impressions.

The provoking part was that Lily knew all this—knew how easy it would have been to silence him on the spot, and how difficult it might be to do so afterward. Mr. Simon Rosedale was a man who made it his business to know everything about every one, whose idea of showing himself to be at home in society was to display an inconvenient familiarity with the habits of those with whom he wished to be thought intimate. Lily was sure that within twenty-four hours the story of her visiting her dress-maker at the Benedick would be in active circulation among Mr. Rosedale's acquaintances. The worst of it was that she had always snubbed and ignored him. On his first appearance—when her improvident cousin, Jack Stepney, had obtained for him (in return for favors too easily guessed) a card to one of the vast impersonal Van Osburgh "crushes"—Rosedale, with that mixture of artistic sensibility and business astuteness which characterizes his race, had instantly gravitated toward Miss Bart. She understood his motives, for her own course was guided by as nice calculations. Training and experience had taught her to be hospitable to newcomers, since the most unpromising might be useful later on, and there were plenty of available *oubliettes* to swallow them if they were not. But some intuitive repugnance, getting the better of years of social discipline, had made her push Mr. Rosedale into his *oubliette* without a trial. He had left behind only the ripple of amusement which his speedy despatch had caused among her friends; and though later (to shift the metaphor) he reappeared lower down the stream, it was only in fleeting glimpses, with long submergences between.

Hitherto Lily had been undisturbed by scruples. In her little set Mr. Rosedale had been pronounced "impossible," and Jack Stepney roundly snubbed for his attempt to pay his debts in dinner invitations. Even Mrs. Trenor, whose taste for variety had led her into some hazardous experiments, resisted Jack's attempts to disguise Mr. Rosedale as a novelty, and declared that he was the same little Jew who had been served up and rejected at the social board a dozen times within her memory; and while Judy Trenor was obdurate there was small chance of Mr. Rosedale's penetrating beyond the outer limbo of the Van Osburgh crushes. Jack gave up the contest with a laughing "You'll see," and, sticking manfully to his guns, showed himself with Rosedale at the fashionable restaurants, in company with the personally vivid if socially obscure ladies who are available for such purposes. But the attempt had hitherto been vain, and as Rosedale undoubtedly paid for the dinners, the laugh remained with his debtor.

Mr. Rosedale, it will be seen, was thus far not a factor to be feared—unless one put one's self in his power. And this was precisely what Miss Bart had done. Her clumsy fib had let him see that she had something to conceal; and she was sure he had a score to settle with her. Something in his smile told her he had not forgotten. She turned from the thought with a little shiver, but it hung on her all the way to the station, and dogged her down the platform with the persistency of Mr. Rosedale himself.

She had just time to take her seat before the train started; but having arranged herself in her corner with the instinctive feeling for effect which never forsook her, she glanced about in the hope of seeing some other member of the Trenors' party. She wanted to get away from herself, and conversation was the only means of escape that she knew.

Her search was rewarded by the discovery of a very blond young man with a soft reddish beard, who, at the other end of the carriage, appeared to be dissembling himself behind an unfolded newspaper. Lily's eye brightened, and a faint smile relaxed the drawn lines of her mouth. She had known that Mr. Percy Gryce was to be at Bellomont, but she had not counted on the luck of having him to herself in the train; and the fact banished all perturbing thoughts of Mr. Rosedale. Perhaps, after all, the day was to end more favorably than it had begun.

She began to cut the pages of a novel, tranquilly studying her prey through downcast lashes while she organized a method of attack. Something in his attitude of conscious absorption told her that he was aware of her presence: no one had ever been quite so engrossed in an evening paper! She guessed that he was too shy to come up to her, and that she would have to devise some means of approach which should not appear to be an advance on her part. It amused her to think that any one as rich as Mr. Percy Gryce should be shy; but she was gifted with treasures of indulgence for such idiosyncrasies, and besides, his timidity might serve her purpose better than too much assurance. She had the art of giving self-confidence to the embarrassed, but she was not equally sure of being able to embarrass the self-confident.

She waited till the train had emerged from the tunnel and was racing between the ragged edges of the northern suburbs. Then, as it lowered its speed near Yonkers, she rose from her seat and drifted slowly down the carriage. As she passed Mr. Gryce, the train gave a lurch, and he was aware of a slender hand gripping the back of his chair. He rose with a start, his ingenuous face looking as though it had been dipped in crimson: even the reddish tint in his beard seemed to deepen.

The train swayed again, almost flinging Miss Bart into his arms. She steadied herself with a laugh and drew back; but he was enveloped in the scent of her dress, and his shoulder had felt her fugitive touch.

"Oh, Mr. Gryce, is it you? I'm so sorry—I was trying to find the porter and get some tea."

She held out her hand as the train resumed its level rush, and they stood exchanging a few words in the aisle. Yes—he was going to Bellomont. He had heard she was to be of the party—he blushed again as he admitted it. And was he to be there for a whole week? How delightful!

But at this point one or two belated passengers from the last station forced their way into the carriage, and Lily had to retreat to her seat.

"The chair next to mine is empty—do take it," she said over her shoulder; and Mr. Gryce, with considerable embarrassment, succeeded in effecting an exchange which enabled him to transport himself and his bags to her side.

"Ah—and here is the porter, and perhaps we can have some tea."

She signalled to that official, and in a moment, with the ease that seemed to attend the fulfilment of all her wishes, a little table had been set up between the seats, and she had helped Mr. Gryce to bestow his encumbering properties beneath it.

When the tea came he watched her in silent fascination while her hands flitted above the tray, looking miraculously fine and slender in contrast to the coarse china and lumpy bread. It seemed wonderful to him that any one should perform with such careless ease the difficult task of making tea in public in a lurching train. He would never have dared to order it for himself lest he should attract the notice of his fellow-passengers; but, secure in the shelter of her conspicuousness, he sipped the inky draught with a delicious sense of exhilaration.

Lily, with the flavor of Selden's caravan tea on her lips, had no great fancy to drown it in the railway brew which seemed such nectar to her companion; but, rightly judging that one of the charms of tea is the fact of drinking it together, she proceeded to give the last touch to Mr. Gryce's enjoyment by smiling at him across her lifted cup.

"Is it quite right—I haven't made it too strong?" she asked solicitously; and he replied with conviction that he had never tasted better tea.

"I daresay it is true," she reflected; and her imagination was fired by the thought that Mr. Gryce, who might have sounded the depths of the most complex self-indulgence, was perhaps actually taking his first journey alone with a pretty woman.

It struck her as providential that she should be the instrument of his initiation. Some girls would not have known how to manage him. They would have over-emphasized the novelty of the adventure, trying to make him feel in it the zest of an escapade. But Lily's methods were more delicate. She remembered that her cousin Jack Stepney had once defined Mr. Gryce as the young man who had promised his mother never to go out in the rain without his overshoes; and acting on this hint, she resolved to impart a gently domestic air to the scene, in the hope that her companion, instead of feeling that he was doing something reckless or unusual, would merely be led to dwell on the advantage of always having a companion to make one's tea in the train.

But in spite of her efforts, conversation flagged after the tray had been removed, and she was driven to take a fresh measurement of Mr. Gryce's limitations. It was not, after all, opportunity but imagination that he lacked: he had a mental palate which would never learn to distinguish between railway tea and nectar. There was, however, one topic she could rely on: one spring that she had only to touch to set his simple machinery in motion. She had refrained from touching it because it was a last resource, and she had relied on other arts to stimulate other sensations; but as a settled look of dullness began to creep over his candid features, she saw that extreme measures were necessary.

"And how," she said, leaning forward, "are you getting on with your Americana?"

His eye became a degree less opaque: it was as though an incipient film had been removed from it, and she felt the pride of a skillful operator.

"I've got a few new things," he said, suffused with pleasure, but lowering his voice as though he feared his fellow-passengers might be in league to despoil him.

She returned a sympathetic enquiry, and gradually he was drawn on to talk of his latest purchases. It was the one subject which enabled him to forget himself, or allowed him, rather, to remember himself without constraint, because he was at home in it, and could assert a superiority that there were few to dispute. Hardly any of his acquaintances cared for Americana, or knew anything about them; and the consciousness of this ignorance threw Mr. Gryce's knowledge into agreeable relief. The only difficulty was to introduce the topic and to keep it to the front; most people showed no desire to have their ignorance dispelled, and Mr. Gryce was like a merchant whose warehouses are crammed with an unmarketable commodity.

But Miss Bart, it appeared, really did want to know about Americana; and moreover, she was already sufficiently informed to make the task of farther instruction as easy as it was agreeable. She questioned him intelligently, she heard him submissively; and, prepared for the look of lassitude which usually crept over his listeners' faces, he grew eloquent under her receptive gaze. The "points" she had had the presence of mind to glean from Selden, in anticipation of this very contingency, were serving her to such good purpose that she began to think her visit to him had been the luckiest incident of the day. She had once more shown her talent for profiting by the unexpected, and dangerous theories as to the advisability of yielding to impulse were germinating under the surface of smiling attention which she continued to present to her companion.

Mr. Gryce's sensations, if less definite, were equally agreeable. He felt the confused titillation with which the lower organisms welcome the gratification of their needs, and all his senses floundered in a vague well-being, through which Miss Bart's personality was dimly but pleasantly perceptible.

Mr. Gryce's interest in Americana had not originated with himself: it was impossible to think of him as evolving any taste of his own. An uncle had left him a collection already noted among bibliophiles; the existence of the collection was the only fact that had ever shed glory on the name of Gryce, and the nephew took as much pride in his inheritance as though it had been his own work. Indeed, he gradually came to regard it as such, and to feel a sense of personal complacency when he chanced on any reference to the Gryce Americana. Anxious as he was to avoid personal notice, he took, in the printed mention of his name, a pleasure so exquisite and excessive that it seemed a compensation for his shrinking from publicity.

To enjoy the sensation as often as possible, he subscribed to all the reviews dealing with book-collecting in general, and American history in particular, and as allusions to his library abounded in the pages of these journals, which formed his only reading, he came to regard himself as figuring prominently in the public eye, and to enjoy the thought of the interest which would be excited if the persons he met in the street, or sat among in travelling, were suddenly to be told that he was the possessor of the Gryce Americana.

Most timidities have such secret compensations, and Miss Bart was discerning enough to know that the inner vanity is generally in proportion to the outer self-depreciation. With a more confident person she would not have dared to dwell so long on one topic, or to show such exaggerated interest in it; but she had rightly guessed that Mr. Gryce's egoism was a thirsty soil, requiring constant nurture from without. Miss Bart had the gift of following an undercurrent of thought while she appeared to be sailing on the surface of conversation; and in this case her mental excursion took the form of a rapid survey of Mr. Percy Gryce's future as combined with her own. The Gryces were from Albany, and but lately introduced to the metropolis, where the mother and son had come, after old Jefferson Gryce's death, to take possession of his house in Madison Avenue—an appalling house, all brown stone without and black walnut within, with the Gryce library in a fire-proof annex that looked like a mausoleum. Lily, however, knew all about them: young Mr. Gryce's arrival had fluttered the maternal breasts of New York, and when a girl has no mother to palpitate for her she must needs be on the alert for herself. Lily, therefore, had not only contrived to put herself in the young man's way, but had made the acquaintance of Mrs. Gryce, a monumental woman with the voice of a pulpit orator and a mind preoccupied with the iniquities of her servants, who came sometimes to sit with Mrs. Peniston and learn from that lady how she managed to prevent the kitchen-maid's smuggling groceries out of the house. Mrs. Gryce had a kind of impersonal benevolence: cases of individual need she regarded with suspicion, but she subscribed to Institutions when their annual reports showed an impressive surplus. Her domestic duties were manifold, for they extended from furtive inspections of the servants' bedrooms to unannounced descents to the cellar; but she had never allowed herself many pleasures. Once, however, she had had a special edition of the Sarum Rule printed in rubric and presented to every clergyman in the diocese; and the gilt album in which their letters of thanks were pasted formed the chief ornament of her drawing-room table.

Percy had been brought up in the principles which so excellent a woman was sure to inculcate. Every form of prudence and suspicion had been grafted on a nature originally reluctant and cautious, with the result that it would have seemed hardly needful for Mrs. Gryce to extract his promise about the overshoes, so little likely was he to hazard himself abroad in the rain. After attaining his majority, and coming into the fortune which the late Mr. Gryce had made out of a patent device for excluding fresh air from hotels, the young man continued to live with his mother in Albany; but on Jefferson Gryce's death, when another large property passed into her son's hands, Mrs. Gryce thought that what she called his "interests" demanded his presence in New York. She accordingly installed herself in the Madison Avenue house, and Percy, whose sense of duty was not inferior to his mother's, spent all his week days in the handsome Broad Street office where a batch of pale men on small salaries had grown grey in the management of the Gryce estate, and where he was initiated with becoming reverence into every detail of the art of accumulation.

As far as Lily could learn, this had hitherto been Mr. Gryce's only occupation, and she might have been pardoned for thinking it not too hard a task to interest a young man who had been kept on such low diet. At any rate, she felt herself so completely in command of the situation that she yielded to a sense of security in which all fear of Mr. Rosedale, and of the difficulties on which that fear was contingent, vanished beyond the edge of thought.

The stopping of the train at Garrisons would not have distracted her from these thoughts, had she not caught a sudden look of distress in her companion's eye. His seat faced toward the door, and she guessed that he had been perturbed by the approach of an acquaintance; a fact confirmed by the turning of heads and general sense of commotion which her own entrance into a railway-carriage was apt to produce.

She knew the symptoms at once, and was not surprised to be hailed by the high notes of a pretty woman, who entered the train accompanied by a maid, a bull-terrier, and a footman staggering under a load of bags and dressing-cases.

"Oh, Lily—are you going to Bellomont? Then you can't let me have your seat, I suppose? But I *must* have a seat in this carriage—porter, you must find me a place at once. Can't some one be put somewhere else? I want to be with my friends. Oh, how do you do, Mr. Gryce? Do please make him understand that I must have a seat next to you and Lily."

Mrs. George Dorset, regardless of the mild efforts of a traveller with a carpet-bag, who was doing his best to make room for her by getting out of the train, stood in the middle of the aisle, diffusing about her that general sense of exasperation which a pretty woman on her travels not infrequently creates.

She was smaller and thinner than Lily Bart, with a restless pliability of pose, as if she could have been crumpled up and run through a ring, like the sinuous draperies she affected. Her small pale face seemed the mere setting of a pair of dark exaggerated eyes, of which the visionary gaze contrasted curiously with her self-assertive tone and gestures; so that, as one of her friends observed, she was like a disembodied spirit who took up a great deal of room.

Having finally discovered that the seat adjoining Miss Bart's was at her disposal, she possessed herself of it with a farther displacement of her surroundings, explaining meanwhile that she had come across from Mount Kisco in her motor-car that morning, and had been kicking her heels for an hour at Garrisons, without even the alleviation of a cigarette, her brute of a husband having neglected to replenish her case before they parted that morning.

"And at this hour of the day I don't suppose you've a single one left, have you, Lily?" she plaintively concluded.

Miss Bart caught the startled glance of Mr. Percy Gryce, whose own lips were never defiled by tobacco.

"What an absurd question, Bertha!" she exclaimed, blushing at the thought of the store she had laid in at Lawrence Selden's.

"Why, don't you smoke? Since when have you given it up? What—you never——And you don't either, Mr. Gryce? Ah, of course—how stupid of me—I understand."

And Mrs. Dorset leaned back against her travelling cushions with a smile which made Lily wish there had been no vacant seat beside her own.

III

BRIDGE at Bellomont usually lasted till the small hours; and when Lily went to bed that night she had played too long for her own good.

Feeling no desire for the self-communion which awaited her in her room, she lingered on the broad stairway, looking down into the hall below, where the last card-players were grouped about the tray of tall glasses and silver-collared decanters which the butler had just placed on a low table near the fire.

The hall was arcaded, with a gallery supported on columns of pale yellow marble. Tall clumps of flowering plants were grouped against a background of dark foliage in the angles of the walls. On the crimson carpet a deerhound and two or three spaniels dozed luxuriously before the fire, and the light from the great central lantern overhead shed a brightness on the women's hair and struck sparks from their jewels as they moved.

There were moments when such scenes delighted Lily, when they gratified her sense of beauty and her craving for the external finish of life; there were others when they gave a sharper edge to the meagreness of her own opportunities. This was one of the moments when the sense of contrast was uppermost, and she turned away impatiently as Mrs. George Dorset, glittering in serpentine spangles, drew Percy Gryce in her wake to a confidential nook beneath the gallery.

It was not that Miss Bart was afraid of losing her newly-acquired hold over Mr. Gryce. Mrs. Dorset might startle or dazzle him, but she had neither the skill nor the patience to effect his capture. She was too self-engrossed to penetrate the recesses of his shyness, and besides, why should she care to give herself the trouble? At most it might amuse her to make sport of his simplicity for an evening—

after that he would be merely a burden to her, and knowing this, she was far too experienced to encourage him. But the mere thought of that other woman, who could take a man up and toss him aside as she willed, without having to regard him as a possible factor in her plans, filled Lily Bart with envy. She had been bored all the afternoon by Percy Gryce—the mere thought seemed to waken an echo of his droning voice—but she could not ignore him on the morrow, she must follow up her success, must submit to more boredom, must be ready with fresh compliances and adaptabilities, and all on the bare chance that he might ultimately decide to do her the honor of boring her for life.

It was a hateful fate—but how escape from it? What choice had she? To be herself or a Gerty Farish. As she entered her bedroom, with its softly-shaded lights, her lace dressing-gown lying across the silken bedspread, her little embroidered slippers before the fire, a vase of carnations filling the air with perfume, and the last novels and magazines lying uncut on a table beside the reading-lamp, she had a vision of Miss Farish's cramped flat, with its cheap conveniences and hideous wallpapers. No; she was not made for mean and shabby surroundings, for the squalid compromises of poverty. Her whole being dilated in an atmosphere of luxury; it was the background she required, the only climate she could breathe in. But the luxury of others was not what she wanted. A few years ago it had sufficed her: she had taken her daily meed of pleasure without caring who provided it. Now she was beginning to chafe at the obligations it imposed, to feel herself a mere pensioner on the splendor which had once seemed to belong to her. There were even moments when she was conscious of having to pay her way.

For a long time she had refused to play bridge. She knew she could not afford it, and she was afraid of acquiring so expensive a taste. She had seen the danger exemplified in more than one of her associates—in young Ned Silverton, for instance, the charming fair boy now seated in abject rapture at the elbow of Mrs. Fisher, a striking divorcée with eyes and gowns as emphatic as the headlines of her "case." Lily could remember when young Silverton had stumbled into their circle, with the air of a strayed Arcadian who has published charming sonnets in his college journal. Since then he had developed a taste for Mrs. Fisher and bridge, and the latter at least had involved him in expenses from which he had been more

She lingered on the broad stairway, looking down into the hall below.

than once rescued by harassed maiden sisters, who treasured the sonnets, and went without sugar in their tea to keep their darling afloat. Ned's case was familiar to Lily: she had seen his charming eyes—which had a good deal more poetry in them than the sonnets—change from surprise to amusement, and from amusement to anxiety, as he passed under the spell of the terrible god of chance; and she was afraid of discovering the same symptoms in her own case.

For in the last year she had found that her hostesses expected her to take a place at the card-table. It was one of the taxes she had to pay for their prolonged hospitality, and for the dresses and trinkets which occasionally replenished her insufficient wardrobe. And since she had played regularly the passion had grown on her. Once or twice of late she had won a large sum, and instead of keeping it against future losses, had spent it in dress or jewelry; and the desire to atone for this imprudence, combined with the increasing exhilaration of the game, drove her to risk higher stakes at each fresh venture. She tried to excuse herself on the plea that, in the Trenor set, if one played at all one must either play high or be set down as priggish or stingy; but she knew that the gambling passion was upon her, and that in her present surroundings there was small hope of resisting it.

Tonight the luck had been persistently bad, and the little gold purse which hung among her trinkets was almost empty when she returned to her room. She unlocked the wardrobe, and taking out her jewel-case, looked under the tray for the roll of bills from which she had replenished the purse before going down to dinner. Only twenty dollars were left: the discovery was so startling that for a moment she fancied she must have been robbed. Then she took paper and pencil, and seating herself at the writing-table, tried to reckon up what she had spent during the day. Her head was throbbing with fatigue, and she had to go over the figures again and again; but at last it became clear to her that she had lost three hundred dollars at cards. She took out her check-book to see if her balance was larger than she remembered, but found she had erred in the other direction. Then she returned to her calculations; but figure as she would, she could not conjure back the vanished three hundred dollars. It was the sum she had set aside to pacify her dress-maker—unless she should decide to use it as a sop to the jeweller. At any rate, she had so many uses for it that its very insufficiency had caused her to play high in the hope of doubling it. But of course she had lost—she who needed every penny, while Bertha Dorset, whose husband showered money on her, must have pocketed at least five hundred, and Judy Trenor, who could have afforded to lose a thousand a night, had left the table clutching such a heap of bills that she had been unable to shake hands with her guests when they bade her good night.

A world in which such things could be seemed a miserable place to Lily Bart; but then she had never been able to understand the laws of a universe which was so ready to leave her out of its calculations.

She began to undress without ringing for her maid, whom she had sent to bed. She had been long enough in bondage to other people's pleasure to be considerate of those who depended on hers, and in her bitter moods it sometimes struck her that she and her maid were in the same position, except that the latter received her wages more regularly.

As she sat before the mirror brushing her hair, her face looked hollow and pale, and she was frightened by two little lines near her mouth, faint flaws in the smooth curve of the cheek.

"Oh, I must stop worrying!" she exclaimed. "Unless it's the electric light——" she reflected, springing up from her seat and lighting the candles on the dressing-table.

She turned out the wall-lights, and peered at herself between the candle-flames. The white oval of her face swam out waveringly from a background of shadows, the uncertain light blurring it like a haze; but the two lines about the mouth remained.

Lily rose and undressed in haste.

"It is only because I am tired and have such odious things to think about," she kept repeating; and it seemed an added injustice that petty cares should leave a trace on the beauty which was her only defense against them.

But the odious things were there, and remained with her. She returned wearily to the thought of Percy Gryce, as a wayfarer picks up a heavy load and toils on after a brief rest. She was almost sure she had "landed" him: a few days' work and she would win her reward. But the reward itself seemed unpalatable just then: she could get no zest from the thought of victory. It would be a rest from worry, no more—and how little that would have seemed to her a few years earlier! Her ambitions had shrunk gradually in the desiccating air of failure. But why had she failed? Was it her own fault or that of destiny?

She remembered how her mother, after they had lost their money, used to say to her with a kind of fierce vindictiveness, "But you'll get it all back—you'll get it all back, with your face." . . . The remembrance roused a whole train of association, and she lay in the darkness reconstructing the past out of which her present had grown.

A house in which no one ever dined at home unless there was "company"; a door-bell perpetually ringing; a hall-table showered with square envelopes which were opened in haste, and oblong envelopes which were allowed to gather dust in the depths of a bronze jar; a series of French and English maids giving warning amid a chaos of hurriedly-ransacked wardrobes and dress-closets; an equally changing dynasty of nurses and footmen; quarrels in the pantry, the kitchen and the drawing-room; precipitate trips to Europe, and returns with gorged trunks and days of interminable unpacking; semiannual discussions as to where the summer should be spent, grey interludes of economy and brilliant reactions of expense—such was the setting of Lily Bart's first memories.

Ruling the turbulent element called home was the vigorous and determined figure of a mother still young enough to dance her ball-dresses to rags, while the hazy outline of a neutral-tinted father filled an intermediate space between the butler and the man who came to wind the clocks. Even to the eyes of infancy, Mrs. Hudson Bart had appeared young; but Lily could not recall the time when her father had not been bald and slightly stooping, with streaks of grey in his hair, and a tired walk. It was a shock to her to learn afterward that he was but two years older than her mother.

Lily seldom saw her father by daylight. All day he was "down town"; and in winter it was long after nightfall when she heard his fagged step on the stairs and his hand on the school-room door. He would kiss her in silence, and ask one or two questions of the nurse or the governess; then Mrs. Bart's maid would come to remind him that he was dining out, and he would hurry away with a nod to Lily. In summer, when he joined them for a Sunday at Newport or Southampton, he was even more effaced and silent than in winter. It seemed to tire him to rest, and he would sit for hours staring at the sea-line from a quiet corner of the verandah, while the clatter of his wife's existence went on unheeded a few feet off. Generally, however, Mrs. Bart and Lily went to Europe for the summer, and before the steamer was half way over Mr. Bart had dipped below the horizon. Sometimes his daughter heard him denounced for having neglected to forward Mrs. Bart's remittances; but for the most part he was never mentioned or thought of till his patient stooping figure presented itself on the New York dock as a buffer between the magnitude of his wife's luggage and the restrictions of the American custom-house.

In this desultory yet agitated fashion life went on through Lily's teens: a zig-zag broken course down which the family craft glided on a rapid current of amusement, tugged at by the underflow of a perpetual need—the need of more money. Lily could not recall the time when there had been money enough, and in some vague way her father seemed always to blame for the deficiency. It could certainly not be the fault of Mrs. Bart, who was spoken of by her friends as a "wonderful manager." Mrs. Bart was famous for the unlimited effect she produced on limited means; and to the lady and her acquaintances there was something heroic in living as though one were much richer than one's bank-book denoted.

Lily was naturally proud of her mother's aptitude in this line: she had been brought up in the faith that, whatever it cost, one must have a good cook, and be what Mrs. Bart called "decently dressed." Mrs. Bart's worst reproach to her husband was to ask him if he expected her to "live like a pig"; and his replying in the negative was always regarded as a justification for cabling to Paris for an extra dress or two, and telephoning to the jeweller that he might, after all, send home the turquoise bracelet which Mrs. Bart had looked at that morning.

Lily knew people who "lived like pigs," and their appearance and surroundings justified her mother's repugnance to that form of existence. They were mostly cousins, who inhabited dingy houses with engravings from Cole's Voyage of Life on the drawing-room walls, and slatternly parlor-maids who said "I'll go and see" to visitors calling at an hour when all right-minded persons are conventionally if not actually out. The disgusting part of it was that many of these cousins were rich, so that Lily imbibed the idea that if people lived like pigs it was from choice, and through the lack of any proper standard of conduct. This gave her a sense of reflected superiority, and she did not need Mrs. Bart's comments on the family frumps and misers to foster her naturally lively taste for splendor.

Lily was nineteen when circumstances caused her to revise her view of the universe.

The previous year she had made a dazzling début fringed by a heavy thunder-cloud of bills. The light of the début still lingered on the horizon, but the cloud had thickened; and suddenly it broke. The suddenness added to the horror; and there were still times when Lily relived with painful vividness every detail of the day on which the blow fell. She and her mother had been seated at the luncheon-table, over the *chaufroix* and cold salmon of the previous night's dinner: it was one of Mrs. Bart's few economies to consume in private the expensive remnants of her hospitality. Lily was feeling the pleasant languor which is youth's penalty for dancing till dawn; but her mother, in spite of a few lines about the mouth, and under the yellow waves on her temples, was as alert, determined and high in color as if she had risen from an untroubled sleep.

In the center of the table, between the melting *marrons glacés* and candied cherries, a pyramid of American Beauties lifted their vigorous stems; they held their heads as high as Mrs. Bart, but their rose-color had turned to a dissipated purple, and Lily's sense of fitness was disturbed by their reappearance on the luncheon-table.

"I really think, mother," she said reproachfully, "we might afford a few fresh flowers for luncheon. Just some jonquils or lilies-of-the-valley——"

Mrs. Bart stared. Her own fastidiousness had its eye fixed on the world, and she did not care how the luncheon-table looked when there was no one present at it but the family. But she smiled at her daughter's innocence.

"Lilies-of-the-valley," she said calmly, "cost two dollars a dozen at this season."

Lily was not impressed. She knew very little of the value of money.

"It would not take more than six dozen to fill that bowl," she argued.

"Six dozen what?" asked her father's voice in the doorway.

The two women looked up in surprise; though it was a Saturday, the sight of Mr. Bart at luncheon was an unwonted one. But neither his wife nor his daughter was sufficiently interested to ask an explanation.

Mr. Bart dropped into a chair, and sat gazing absently at the fragment of jellied salmon which the butler had placed before him.

"I was only saying," Lily began, "that I hate to see faded flowers at luncheon; and mother says a bunch of lilies-of-the-valley would not cost more than twelve dollars. Mayn't I tell the florist to send a few every day?"

She leaned confidently toward her father: he seldom refused her anything, and Mrs. Bart had taught her to plead with him when her own entreaties failed.

Mr. Bart sat motionless, his gaze still fixed on the salmon, and his lower jaw dropped; he looked even paler than usual, and his thin hair lay in untidy streaks on his forehead. Suddenly he looked at his daughter and laughed. The laugh was so strange that Lily colored under it: she disliked being ridiculed, and her father seemed to see something ridiculous in the request. Perhaps he thought it foolish that she should trouble him about such a trifle.

"Twelve dollars—twelve dollars a day for flowers? Oh, certainly, my dear—give him an order for twelve hundred." He continued to laugh.

Mrs. Bart gave him a quick glance.

"You needn't wait, Poleworth—I will ring for you," she said to the butler.

The butler withdrew with an air of silent disapproval, leaving the remains of the *chaufroix* on the sideboard.

"What is the matter, Hudson? Are you ill?" said Mrs. Bart severely.

She had no tolerance for scenes which were not of her own making, and it was odious to her that her husband should make a show of himself before the servants.

"Are you ill?" she repeated.

"Ill?——No, I'm ruined," he said.

Lily made a frightened sound, and Mrs. Bart rose to her feet.

"Ruined——?" she cried; but controlling herself instantly, she turned a calm face to Lily.

"Shut the pantry door," she said.

Lily obeyed, and when she turned back into the room her father was sitting with both elbows on the table, the plate of salmon between them and his head bowed on his hands.

Mrs. Bart stood over him with a white face which made her hair unnaturally yellow. She looked at Lily as the latter approached: her look was terrible, but her voice was modulated to a ghastly cheerfulness.

"Your father is not well—he doesn't know what he is saying. It is nothing—but you had better go upstairs; and don't talk to the servants," she added.

Lily obeyed; she always obeyed when her mother spoke in that voice. She had not been deceived by Mrs. Bart's words: she knew at once that they were ruined. In the dark hours which followed, that awful fact overshadowed even her father's slow and difficult dying. To his wife he no longer counted: he had become extinct when he ceased to fulfil his purpose, and she sat at his side with the provisional air of a traveller who waits for a belated train to start. Lily's feelings were softer: she pitied him in a frightened ineffectual way. But the fact that he was for the most part unconscious, and that his attention, when she stole into the room, drifted away from her after a moment, made him even more of a stranger than in the nursery days when he had never come home till after dark. She seemed always to have seen him through a blur—first of sleepiness, then of distance and indifference—and now the fog had thickened till he was almost indistinguishable. If she could have performed any little services for him, or have exchanged with him a few of those affecting words which an extensive perusal of fiction had led her to connect with such occasions, the filial instinct might have stirred in her; but her pity, finding no active expression, remained in a state of spectatorship overshadowed by her mother's grim unflagging resentment. Every look and act of Mrs. Bart's seemed to say: "You are sorry for him now—but you will feel differently when you see what he has done to us."

It was a relief to Lily when her father died.

Then a long winter set in. There was a little money left, but to Mrs. Bart it seemed worse than nothing—the mere mockery of what she was entitled to. What was the use of living if one had to live like a pig? She sank into a kind of furious apathy, a state of inert anger against fate. Her faculty for "managing" deserted her, or she no longer took sufficient pride in it to exert it. It was well enough to "manage" when by so doing one could keep one's own carriage; but when one's best contrivance did not conceal the fact that one had to go on foot, the effort was no longer worth making.

Lily and her mother wandered from place to place, now paying long visits to relations whose house-keeping Mrs. Bart criticized, and who deplored the fact that she let Lily breakfast in bed when the girl had no prospects before her, and now vegetating in cheap continental refuges, where Mrs. Bart held herself fiercely aloof from the frugal tea-tables of her companions in misfortune. She was especially careful to avoid her old friends and the scenes of her former successes. To be poor seemed to her such a confession of failure that it amounted to disgrace; and she detected a note of condescension in the friendliest advances.

Only one thought consoled her, and that was the contemplation of Lily's beauty. She studied it with a kind of passion, as though it were some weapon she had slowly fashioned for her vengeance. It was the last asset in their fortunes, the nucleus around which their life was to be rebuilt. She watched it jealously, as though it were her own property and Lily its mere custodian; and she tried to instill into the latter a sense of the responsibility that such a charge involved. She followed in imagination the career of other beauties, pointing out to her daughter what might be achieved through such a gift, and dwelling on the awful warning of those who, in spite of it, had failed to get what they wanted: to Mrs. Bart, only stupidity could explain the lamentable dénouement of some of her examples. She was not above the inconsistency of charging fate, rather than herself, with her own misfortunes; but she inveighed so acrimoniously against love-matches that Lily would have fancied her own marriage had been of that nature, had not Mrs. Bart frequently assured her that she had been "talked into it"—by whom, she never made clear.

Lily was duly impressed by the magnitude of her opportunities. The dinginess of her present life threw into enchanting relief the existence to which she felt herself entitled. To a less illuminated intelligence Mrs. Bart's counsels might have been dangerous; but Lily understood that beauty is only the raw material of conquest, and that to convert it into success other arts are required. She knew that to betray any sense of superiority was a subtler form of the stupidity her mother denounced, and it did not take her long to learn that a beauty needs more tact than the possessor of an average set of features.

Her ambitions were not as crude as Mrs. Bart's. It had been among that lady's grievances that her husband—in the early days, before he was too tired—had wasted his evenings in what she vaguely described as "reading poetry"; and among the effects packed off to auction after his death were a score or two of dingy volumes which had struggled for existence among the boots and medicine bottles of his dressing-room shelves. There was in Lily a vein of sentiment, perhaps transmitted from this source, which gave an idealizing touch to her most prosaic purposes. She liked to think of her beauty as a power for good, as giving her the opportunity to attain a position where she should make her influence felt in the vague diffusion of refinement and good taste. She was fond of pictures and flowers, and of sentimental fiction, and she could not help thinking that the possession of such tastes ennobled her desire for worldly advantages. She would not indeed have cared to marry a man who was merely rich: she was secretly ashamed of her mother's crude passion for money. Lily's preference would have been for an English nobleman with political ambitions and vast estates; or, for second choice, an Italian prince with a castle in the Apennines and an hereditary office in the Vatican. Lost causes had a romantic charm for her, and she liked to picture herself as standing aloof from the vulgar press of the Quirinal, and sacrificing her pleasure to the claims of an immemorial tradition. . . .

How long ago and how far off it all seemed! Those ambitions were hardly more futile and childish than the earlier ones which had centered about the possession of a French jointed doll with real hair. Was it only ten years since she had wavered in imagination between the English earl and the Italian prince? Relentlessly her mind traveled on over the dreary interval. . . .

After two years of hungry roaming Mrs. Bart had died—died of a deep disgust. She had hated dinginess, and it was her fate to be dingy. Her visions of a brilliant marriage for Lily had faded after the first year.

"People can't marry you if they don't see you—and how can they see you in these holes where we're stuck?" That was the burden of her lament; and her last adjuration to her daughter was to escape from dinginess if she could.

"Don't let it creep up on you and drag you down. Fight your way out of it somehow—you're young and can do it," she insisted.

She had died during one of their brief visits to New York, and there Lily at once became the center of a family council composed of the wealthy relatives whom she had been taught to despise for living like pigs. It may be that they had an inkling of the sentiments in which she had been brought up, for none of them manifested a very lively desire for her company; indeed, the question threatened to remain unsolved till Mrs. Peniston with a sigh announced: "I'll try her for a year."

Every one was surprised, but one and all concealed their surprise, lest Mrs. Peniston should be alarmed by it into reconsidering her decision.

Mrs. Peniston was Mr. Bart's widowed sister, and if she was by no means the richest of the family group, its other members nevertheless abounded in reasons why she was clearly destined by Providence to assume the charge of Lily. In the first place she was alone, and it would be charming for her to have a young companion. Then she sometimes traveled, and Lily's familiarity with foreign customs—deplored as a misfortune by her more conservative relatives—would at least enable her to act as a kind of courier. But as a matter of fact Mrs. Peniston had not been affected by these considerations. She had taken the girl simply because no one else would have her, and because she had the kind of moral *mauvaise honte* which makes the public display of selfishness difficult, though it does not interfere with its private indulgence. It would have been impossible for Mrs. Peniston to be heroic on a desert island, but with the eyes of her little world upon her she took a certain pleasure in her act.

She reaped the reward to which disinterestedness is entitled, and found an agreeable companion in her niece. She had expected to find Lily headstrong, critical and "foreign"—for even Mrs. Peniston, though she occasionally went abroad, had the family dread of foreignness—but the girl showed a pliancy which, to a more penetrating mind than her aunt's, might have been less reassuring than the open selfishness of youth. Misfortune had made Lily supple instead of hardening her, and a pliable substance is less easy to break than a stiff one.

Mrs. Peniston, however, did not suffer from her niece's adaptability. Lily had no intention of taking advantage of her aunt's good nature. She was in truth grateful for the refuge offered her: Mrs. Peniston's opulent interior was at least not externally dingy. But dinginess is a quality which assumes all manner of disguises; and Lily soon found that it was as latent in the expensive routine of her aunt's life as in the makeshift existence of a continental pension.

Mrs. Peniston was one of the episodical persons who form the padding of life. It was impossible to believe that she had herself ever been a focus of activities. The most vivid thing about her was the fact that her grandmother had been a Van Alstyne. This connection with the well-fed and industrious stock of early New York revealed itself in the glacial neatness of Mrs. Peniston's drawing-room and in the excellence of her cuisine. She belonged to the class of old New Yorkers who have always lived well, dressed expensively, and done little else; and to these inherited obligations Mrs. Peniston faithfully conformed. She had always been a looker-on at life, and her mind resembled one of those little mirrors which her Dutch ancestors were accustomed to affix to their upper windows, so that from the depths of an impenetrable domesticity they might see what was happening in the street.

Mrs. Peniston was the owner of a country-place in New Jersey, but she had never lived there since her husband's death—a remote event, which appeared to dwell in her memory chiefly as a dividing point in the personal reminiscences that formed the staple of her conversation. She was a woman who remembered dates with intensity, and could tell at a moment's notice whether the drawing-room curtains had been renewed before or after Mr. Peniston's last illness.

Mrs. Peniston thought the country lonely and trees damp, and cherished a vague fear of meeting a bull. To guard against such contingencies she frequented the more populous watering-places, where she installed herself impersonally in a hired house and looked on at life through the matting screen of her verandah. In the care of such a guardian, it soon became clear to Lily that she was to enjoy only the material advantages of good food and expensive clothing; and, though far from underrating these, she would gladly have exchanged them for what Mrs. Bart had taught her to regard as opportunities. She sighed to think what her mother's fierce energies would have accomplished, had they been coupled with Mrs. Peniston's resources. Lily had abundant energy of her own, but it was restricted by the necessity of adapting herself to her aunt's habits. She saw that at all costs she must keep Mrs. Peniston's favor till, as Mrs. Bart would have phrased it, she could stand on her own legs. Lily had no mind for the vagabond life of the poor relation, and to adapt herself to Mrs. Peniston she had, to some degree, to assume that lady's passive attitude. She had fancied at first that it would be easy to draw her aunt into the whirl of her own activities, but there was a static force in Mrs. Peniston against which her niece's efforts spent themselves in vain. To attempt to bring her into active relation with life was like tugging at a piece of furniture which has been screwed to the floor. She did not, indeed, expect Lily to remain equally immovable: she had all the American guardian's indulgence for the volatility of youth. She had indulgence also for certain other habits of her niece's. It seemed to her natural that Lily should spend all her money on dress, and she supplemented the girl's scanty income by occasional "handsome presents" meant to be applied to the same purpose. Lily, who was intensely practical, would have preferred a fixed allowance; but Mrs. Peniston liked the periodical recurrence of gratitude evoked by unexpected checks, and was perhaps shrewd enough to perceive that such a method of giving kept alive in her niece a salutary sense of dependence.

Beyond this, Mrs. Peniston had not felt called upon to do anything for her charge: she had simply stood aside and let her take the field. Lily had taken it, at first with the confidence of assured possessorship, then with gradually narrowing demands, till now she found herself actually struggling for a foothold on the broad space which had once seemed her own for the asking. How it happened she did not yet know. Sometimes she thought it was because Mrs. Peniston had been too passive, and again she feared it was because she herself had not been passive enough. Had she shown an undue eagerness for victory? Had she lacked patience, pliancy and dissimulation? Whether she charged herself with these faults or absolved herself from them, made no difference in the sum-total of her failure. Younger and plainer girls had been married off by dozens, and she was nine-and-twenty, and still Miss Bart.

She was beginning to have fits of angry rebellion against fate, when she longed to drop out of the race and make an independent life for herself. But what manner of life would it be? She had barely enough money to pay her dress-makers' bills and her gambling debts; and none of the desultory interests which she dignified with the name of tastes was pronounced enough to enable her to live contentedly in obscurity. Ah, no—she was too intelligent not to be honest with herself. She knew that she hated dinginess as much as her mother had hated it, and to her last breath she meant to fight against it, dragging herself up again and again above its flood till she gained the bright pinnacles of success which presented such a slippery surface to her clutch.

IV

THE next morning, on her breakfast tray, Miss Bart found a note from her hostess.

"Dearest Lily," it ran, "if it is not too much of a bore to be down by ten, will you come to my sitting-room to help me with some tiresome things?"

Lily tossed aside the note and subsided on her pillows with a sigh. It *was* a bore to be down by ten—an hour regarded at Bellomont as vaguely synchronous with sunrise—and she knew too well the nature of the tiresome things in question. Miss Pragg, the secretary, had been called away, and there would be notes and dinner-cards to write, lost addresses to hunt up, and other social drudgery to perform. It was understood that Miss Bart should fill the gap in such emergencies, and she usually recognized the obligation without a murmur.

Today, however, it renewed the sense of servitude which the previous night's review of her check-book had produced. Everything in her surroundings ministered to feelings of ease and amenity. The windows stood open to the sparkling freshness of the September morning, and between the yellow boughs she caught a perspective of hedges and parterres leading by degrees of lessening formality to the free undulations of the park. Her maid had kindled a little fire on the hearth, and it contended cheerfully with the sunlight which slanted across the moss-green carpet and caressed the curved sides of an old marquetry desk. Near the bed stood a table holding her breakfast tray, with its harmonious porcelain and silver, a handful of violets in a slender glass, and the morning paper folded beneath her letters. There was nothing new to Lily in these tokens of a studied luxury; but, though they formed a part of her atmosphere, she never lost her sensitiveness to their charm. Mere display left her with a sense of superior distinction; but she felt an affinity to all the subtler manifestations of wealth.

Mrs. Trenor's summons, however, suddenly recalled her state of dependence, and she rose and dressed in a mood of irritability that she was usually too prudent to indulge. She knew that such emotions leave lines on the face as well as in the character, and she had meant to take warning by the little creases which her midnight survey had revealed.

The matter-of-course tone of Mrs. Trenor's greeting deepened her irritation. If one did drag one's self out of bed at such an hour, and come down fresh and radiant to the monotony of note-writing, some special recognition of the sacrifice seemed fitting. But Mrs. Trenor's tone showed no consciousness of the fact.

"Oh, Lily, that's nice of you," she merely sighed across the chaos of letters, bills and other domestic documents which gave an incongruously commercial touch to the slender elegance of her writing-table.

"There are such lots of horrors this morning," she added, clearing a space in the center of the confusion and rising to yield her seat to Miss Bart.

Mrs. Trenor was a tall fair woman, whose height just saved her from redundancy. Her rosy blondness had survived some forty years of futile activity without showing much trace of ill-usage except in a diminished play of feature. It was difficult to define her beyond saying that she seemed to exist only as a hostess, not so much from any exaggerated instinct of hospitality as because she could not sustain life except in a crowd. The collective nature of her interests exempted her from the ordinary rivalries of her sex, and she knew no more personal emotion than that of hatred for the woman who presumed to give bigger dinners or have more amusing house-parties than herself. As her social talents, backed by Mr. Trenor's bank-account, almost always assured her ultimate triumph in such competitions, success had developed in her an unscrupulous good nature toward the rest of her sex, and in Miss Bart's utilitarian classification of her friends, Mrs. Trenor ranked as the woman who was least likely to "go back" on her.

"It was simply inhuman of Pragg to go off now," Mrs. Trenor declared, as her friend seated herself at the desk. "She says her sister is going to have a baby—as if that were anything to having a house-party! I'm sure I shall get most horribly mixed up and there will be some awful rows. When I was down at Tuxedo I asked a lot of people for next week, and I've mislaid the list and can't remember who is coming. And this week is going to be a horrid failure too—and Gwen Van Osburgh will go back and tell her mother how bored people were. I didn't mean to ask the Wetheralls—that was a blunder of Gus's. They disapprove of Carry Fisher, you know. As if one could help having Carry Fisher! It *was* foolish of her to get that second divorce—Carry always overdoes things—but she said the only way to get a penny out of Fisher was to divorce him and make him pay alimony. And poor Carry has to consider every dollar. It's really absurd of Alice Wetherall to make such a fuss about meeting her, when one thinks of what society is coming to. Some one said the other day that there was a divorce and a case of appendicitis in every family one knows. Besides, Carry is the only person who can keep Gus in a good humor when we have bores in the house. Have you noticed that *all* the husbands like her? All, I mean, except her own. It's rather clever of her to have made a specialty of devoting herself to dull people—the field is such a large one, and she has it practically to herself. She finds compensations, no doubt—I know she borrows money of Gus—but then I'd *pay* her to keep him in a good humor, so I can't complain, after all."

Mrs. Trenor paused to enjoy the spectacle of Miss Bart's efforts to unravel her tangled correspondence.

"But it isn't only the Wetheralls and Carry," she resumed, with a fresh note of lament. "The truth is, I'm awfully disappointed in Lady Cressida Raith."

"Disappointed? Hadn't you known her before?"

"Mercy, no—never saw her till yesterday. Lady Skiddaw sent her over with letters to the Van Osburghs, and I heard that Maria Van Osburgh was asking a big party to meet her this week, so I thought it would be fun to get her away, and Jack Stepney, who knew her in India, managed it for me. Maria was furious, and actually had the impudence to make Gwen invite herself here, so that they shouldn't be *quite* out of it—if I'd known what Lady Cressida was like, they could have had her and welcome! But I thought any friend of the Skiddaws' was sure to be amusing. You remember what fun Lady Skiddaw was? There were times when I simply had to send the girls out of the room. Besides, Lady Cressida is the Duchess of

Beltshire's sister, and I naturally supposed she was the same sort; but you never can tell in those English families. They are so big that there's room for all kinds, and it turns out that Lady Cressida is the moral one—married a clergyman and does missionary work in the East End. Think of my taking such a lot of trouble about a clergyman's wife, who wears Indian jewelry and botanizes! She made Gus take her all through the glass-houses yesterday, and bothered him to death by asking him the names of the plants. Fancy treating Gus as if he were the gardener!"

Mrs. Trenor brought this out in a *crescendo* of indignation.

"Oh, well, perhaps Lady Cressida will reconcile the Wetheralls to meeting Carry Fisher," said Miss Bart pacifically.

"I'm sure I hope so! But she is boring all the men horribly, and if she takes to distributing tracts, as I hear she does, it will be too depressing. The worst of it is that she would have been so useful at the right time. You know we have to have the Bishop once a year, and she would have given just the right tone to things. I always have horrid luck about the Bishop's visits," added Mrs. Trenor, whose present misery was being fed by a rapidly rising tide of reminiscence; "last year, when he came, Gus forgot all about his being here, and brought home the Ned Wintons and the Farleys—five divorces and six sets of children between them!"

"When is Lady Cressida going?" Lily enquired.

Mrs. Trenor cast up her eyes in despair. "My dear, if one only knew! I was in such a hurry to get her away from Maria that I actually forgot to name a date, and Gus says she told some one she meant to stop here all winter."

"To stop here? In this house?"

"Don't be silly—in America. But if no one else asks her—you know they *never* go to hotels."

"Perhaps Gus only said it to frighten you."

"No—I heard her tell Bertha Dorset that she had six months to put in while her husband was taking the cure in the Engadine. You should have seen Bertha look vacant! But it's no joke, you know—if she stays here all the autumn she'll spoil everything, and Maria Van Osburgh will simply exult."

At this affecting vision Mrs. Trenor's voice trembled with self-pity.

"Oh, Judy—as if any one were ever bored at Bellomont!" Miss Bart tactfully protested. "You know perfectly well that, if Mrs. Van

Osburgh were to get all the right people and leave you with all the wrong ones, you'd manage to make things go off, and she wouldn't."

Such an assurance would usually have restored Mrs. Trenor's complacency; but on this occasion it did not chase the cloud from her brow.

"It isn't only Lady Cressida," she lamented. "Everything has gone wrong this week. I can see that Bertha Dorset is furious with me."

"Furious with you? Why?"

"Because I told her that Lawrence Selden was coming; but he wouldn't, after all, and she's quite unreasonable enough to think it's my fault."

Miss Bart put down her pen and sat absently gazing at the note she had begun.

"I thought that was all over," she said.

"So it is, on his side. And of course Bertha hasn't been idle since. But I fancy she's out of a job just at present—and someone gave me a hint that I had better ask Lawrence. Well, I *did* ask him—but I couldn't make him come; and now I suppose she'll take it out of me by being perfectly nasty to every one else."

"Oh, she may take it out of *him* by being perfectly charming—to some one else."

Mrs. Trenor shook her head dolefully. "She knows he wouldn't mind. And who else is there? Alice Wetherall won't let Lucius out of her sight. Ned Silverton can't take his eyes off Carry Fisher—poor boy! Gus is bored by Bertha, Jack Stepney knows her too well—and—well, to be sure, there's Percy Gryce!"

She sat up smiling at the thought.

Miss Bart's countenance did not reflect the smile.

"Oh, she and Mr. Gryce would not be likely to hit it off."

"You mean that she'd shock him and he'd bore her? Well, that's not such a bad beginning, you know. But I hope she won't take it into her head to be nice to him, for I asked him here on purpose for you."

Lily laughed. "*Merci du compliment!* I should certainly have no show against Bertha."

"Do you think I am uncomplimentary? I'm not really, you know. Every one knows you're a thousand times handsomer and cleverer than Bertha; but then you're not nasty. And for always getting what she wants in the long run, commend me to a nasty woman."

Miss Bart stared in affected reproval. "I thought you were so fond of Bertha."

"Oh, I am—it's much safer to be fond of dangerous people. But she *is* dangerous—and if I ever saw her up to mischief it's now. I can tell by poor George's manner. That man is a perfect barometer—he always knows when Bertha is going to——"

"To fall?" Miss Bart suggested.

"Don't be shocking! You know he believes in her still. And of course I don't say there's any real harm in Bertha. Only she delights in making people miserable, and especially poor George."

"Well, he seems cut out for the part—I don't wonder she likes more cheerful companionship."

"Oh, George is not as dismal as you think. If Bertha didn't worry him he would be quite different. Or if she'd leave him alone, and let him arrange his life as he pleases. But she doesn't dare lose her hold of him on account of the money, and so when *he* isn't jealous she pretends to be."

Miss Bart went on writing in silence, and her hostess sat following her train of thought with frowning intensity.

"Do you know," she exclaimed after a long pause, "I believe I'll call up Lawrence on the telephone and tell him he simply *must* come?"

"Oh, don't," said Lily, with a quick suffusion of color. The blush surprised her almost as much as it did her hostess, who, though not commonly observant of facial changes, sat staring at her with puzzled eyes.

"Good gracious, Lily, how handsome you are!——Why? Do you dislike him so much?"

"Not at all; I like him. But if you are actuated by the benevolent intention of protecting me from Bertha—I don't think I need your protection."

Mrs. Trenor sat up with an exclamation. "Lily!—*Percy?* Do you mean to say you've actually done it?"

Miss Bart smiled. "I only mean to say that Mr. Gryce and I are getting to be very good friends."

"H'm—I see." Mrs. Trenor fixed a rapt eye upon her. "You know they say he has eight hundred thousand a year—and spends nothing, except on some rubbishy old books. And his mother has heart-disease and will leave him a lot more. *Oh, Lily, do go slowly,*" her friend adjured her.

Miss Bart continued to smile without annoyance. "I shouldn't, for instance," she remarked, "be in any haste to tell him that he had a lot of rubbishy old books."

"No, of course not; I know you're wonderful about getting up people's subjects. But he's horribly shy, and easily shocked, and—and——"

"Why don't you say it, Judy? I have the reputation of being on the hunt for a rich husband?"

"Oh, I don't mean that; he wouldn't believe it of you—at first," said Mrs. Trenor, with candid shrewdness. "But you know things are rather lively here at times—I must give Jack and Gus a hint—and if he thought you were what his mother would call fast—oh, well, you know what I mean. Don't wear your scarlet *crêpe-de-chine* for dinner, and don't smoke if you can help it, Lily dear!"

Lily pushed aside her finished work with a dry smile. "You're very kind, Judy: I'll lock up my cigarettes and wear that last year's dress you sent me this morning. And if you are really interested in my career, perhaps you'll be kind enough not to ask me to play bridge again this evening."

"Bridge? Does he mind bridge, too? Oh, Lily, what an awful life you'll lead! But of course I won't—why didn't you give me a hint last night? There's nothing I wouldn't do, you poor duck, to see you happy!"

And Mrs. Trenor, glowing with her sex's eagerness to smooth the course of true love, enveloped Lily in a long embrace.

"You're quite sure," she added solicitously, as the latter extricated herself, "that you wouldn't like me to telephone for Lawrence Selden?"

"Quite sure," said Lily.

The next three days demonstrated to her own complete satisfaction Miss Bart's ability to manage her affairs without extraneous aid.

As she sat, on the Saturday afternoon, on the terrace at Bellomont, she smiled at Mrs. Trenor's fear that she might go too fast. If such a warning had ever been needful, the years had taught her a salutary lesson, and she flattered herself that she now knew how to adapt her pace to the object of pursuit. In the case of Mr. Gryce she had found it well to flutter ahead, losing herself elusively and luring him on from depth to depth of unconscious intimacy. The surrounding atmosphere was propitious to this scheme of courtship. Mrs. Trenor, true to her word, had shown no signs of expecting Lily at the bridge-table, and had even hinted to the other card-players that they were to betray no surprise at her unwonted defection. In consequence of this hint, Lily found herself the center of that feminine solicitude which envelops a young woman in the mating season. A solitude was tacitly created for her in the crowded existence of Bellomont, and her friends could not have shown a greater readiness for self-effacement had her wooing been adorned with all the attributes of romance. In Lily's set this conduct implied a sympathetic comprehension of her motives, and Mr. Gryce rose in her esteem as she saw the consideration he inspired.

The terrace at Bellomont on a September afternoon was a spot propitious to sentimental musings, and as Miss Bart stood leaning against the balustrade above the sunken garden, at a little distance from the animated group about the tea-table, she might have been lost in the mazes of an inarticulate happiness. In reality, her thoughts were finding definite utterance in the tranquil recapitulation of the blessings in store for her. From where she stood she could see them embodied in the form of Mr. Gryce, who, in a light overcoat and muffler, sat somewhat nervously on the edge of his chair, while Carry Fisher, with all the energy of eye and gesture with which nature and art had combined to endow her, pressed on him the duty of taking part in the task of municipal reform.

Mrs. Fisher's latest hobby was municipal reform. It had been preceded by an equal zeal for socialism, which had in turn replaced an energetic advocacy of Christian Science. Mrs. Fisher was small, fiery and dramatic; and her hands and eyes were admirable instruments in the service of whatever cause she happened to espouse. She had, however, the fault common to enthusiasts of ignoring any slackness of response on the part of her hearers, and Lily was amused by her unconsciousness of the resistance displayed in every angle of Mr. Gryce's attitude. Lily herself knew that his mind was divided between the dread of catching cold if he remained out of doors too long at that hour, and the fear that, if he retreated to the house, Mrs. Fisher might follow him up with a paper to be signed. Mr. Gryce had a constitutional dislike to what he called "committing himself," and tenderly as he cherished his health, he evidently concluded that it was safer to stay out of reach of pen and ink till chance released him from Mrs. Fisher's toils. Meanwhile he cast agonized glances in the direction of Miss Bart, whose only response was to sink into an attitude of more graceful abstraction. She had learned the value of contrast in throwing her charms into relief, and was fully aware of the extent to which Mrs. Fisher's volubility was enhancing her own repose.

She was roused from her musings by the approach of her cousin Jack Stepney who, at Gwen Van Osburgh's side, was returning across the garden from the tennis court.

The couple in question were engaged in the same kind of romance in which Lily figured, and the latter felt a certain annoyance in contemplating what seemed to her a caricature of her own situation. Miss Van Osburgh was a large girl with flat surfaces and no high lights: Jack Stepney had once said of her that she was as reliable as roast mutton. His own taste was in the line of less solid and more highly-seasoned diet; but hunger makes any fare palatable, and there had been times when Mr. Stepney had been reduced to a crust.

Lily considered with interest the expression of their faces: the girl's turned toward her companion's like an empty plate held up to be filled, while the man lounging at her side already betrayed the encroaching boredom which would presently crack the thin veneer of his smile.

"How impatient men are!" Lily reflected. "All Jack has to do to get everything he wants is to keep quiet and let that girl marry him; whereas I have to calculate and contrive, and retreat and advance, as if I were going through an intricate dance, where one misstep would throw me hopelessly out of time."

As they drew nearer she was whimsically struck by a kind of family likeness between Miss Van Osburgh and Percy Gryce. There was no resemblance of feature. Gryce was handsome in a didactic way—he looked like a clever pupil's drawing from a plaster-cast—while Gwen's countenance had no more modelling than a face painted on a toy balloon. But the deeper affinity was unmistakable: the two had the same prejudices and ideals, and the same quality of making other standards nonexistent by ignoring them. This attribute was common to most of Lily's set: they had a force of negation which eliminated everything beyond their own range of perception. Gryce and Miss Van Osburgh were, in short, made for each other by every law of moral and physical correspondence——"Yet they wouldn't look at each other," Lily mused, "they never do. Each of them wants a creature of a different race, of Jack's race and mine, with all sorts of intuitions, sensations and perceptions that they don't even guess the existence of. And they always get what they want."

She stood talking with her cousin and Miss Van Osburgh, till a slight cloud on the latter's brow advised her that even cousinly amenities were subject to suspicion, and Miss Bart, mindful of the necessity of not exciting enmities at this crucial point of her career, dropped aside while the happy couple proceeded toward the tea-table.

Seating herself on the upper step of the terrace, Lily leaned her head against the honeysuckles wreathing the balustrade. The fragrance of the late blossoms seemed an emanation of the tranquil scene, a landscape tutored to the last degree of rural elegance. In the foreground glowed the warm tints of the gardens. Beyond the lawn, with its pyramidal pale-gold maples and velvety firs, sloped pastures dotted with cattle; and through a long glade the river widened like a lake under the silver light of September. Lily did not want to join the circle about the tea-table. They represented the future she had chosen, and she was content with it, but in no haste to anticipate its joys. The certainty that she could marry Percy Gryce when she pleased had lifted a heavy load from her mind, and her money troubles were too recent for their removal not to leave a sense of relief which a less discerning intelligence might have taken for happiness. Her vulgar cares were at an end. She would be able to arrange her life as she pleased, to soar into that empyrean of security where creditors cannot penetrate. She would have smarter gowns than Judy Trenor, and far, far more jewels than Bertha Dorset. She would be free forever from the shifts, the expedients, the humiliations of the relatively poor. Instead of having to flatter, she would be flattered; instead of being grateful, she would receive thanks. There were old scores she could pay off as well as old benefits she could return. And she had no doubts as to the extent of her power. She knew that Mr. Gryce was of the small chary type most inaccessible to impulses and emotions. He had the kind of character in which prudence is a vice, and good advice the most dangerous nourishment. But Lily had known the species before: she was aware that such a guarded nature must find one huge outlet of egoism, and she determined to be to him what his Americana had hitherto been: the one possession in which he took sufficient pride to spend money on it. She knew that this generosity to self is one of the forms of meanness, and she resolved so to identify herself with her husband's vanity that to gratify her wishes would be to him the most exquisite form of self-indulgence. The system might at first necessitate a resort to some of the very shifts and expedients from which she intended it should free her; but she felt sure that in a short time she would be able to play the game in her own way. How should she have distrusted her powers? Her beauty itself was not the mere ephemeral possession it might have been in the hands of inexperience: her skill in enhancing it, the care she took of it, the use she made of it, seemed to give it a kind of permanence. She felt she could trust it to carry her through to the end.

And the end, on the whole, was worth while. Life was not the mockery she had thought it three days ago. There was room for her, after all, in this crowded selfish world of pleasure whence, so short a time since, her poverty had seemed to exclude her. These people whom she had ridiculed and yet envied were glad to make a place for her in the charmed circle about which all her desires revolved. They were not as brutal and self-engrossed as she had fancied—or rather, since it would no longer be necessary to flatter and humor them, that side of their nature became less conspicuous. Society is a revolving body which is apt to be judged according to its place in each man's heaven; and at present it was turning its illuminated face to Lily.

In the rosy glow it diffused her companions seemed full of amiable qualities. She liked their elegance, their lightness, their lack of emphasis: even the self-assurance which at times was so like obtuseness now seemed the natural sin of social ascendency. They were lords of the only world she cared for, and they were ready to admit her to their ranks and let her lord it with them. Already she felt within her a stealing allegiance to their standards, an acceptance of their limitations, a disbelief in the things they did not believe in, a contemptuous pity for the people who were not able to live as they lived.

The early sunset was slanting far across the park. Through the boughs of the long avenue beyond the gardens she caught the flash of wheels, and divined that more visitors were approaching. There was a movement behind her, a scattering of steps and voices: it was evident that the party about the tea-table was breaking up. Presently she heard a tread behind her on the terrace. She supposed that Mr.

Gryce had at last found means to escape from his predicament, and she smiled at the significance of his coming to join her instead of beating an instant retreat to the fireside.

She turned to give him the welcome which such gallantry deserved; but her greeting wavered into a blush of wonder, for the man who had approached her was Lawrence Selden.

"You see I came after all," he said; but before she had time to answer, Mrs. Dorset, breaking away from a lifeless colloquy with her host, had stepped between them with a little gesture of appropriation.

V

THE observance of Sunday at Bellomont was chiefly marked by the punctual appearance of the smart omnibus destined to convey the household to the little church at the gates. Whether any one got into the omnibus or not was a matter of secondary importance, since by standing there it not only bore witness to the orthodox intentions of the family, but made Mrs. Trenor feel, when she finally heard it drive away, that she had somehow vicariously made use of it.

It was Mrs. Trenor's theory that her daughters actually did go to church every Sunday; but their French governess's convictions calling her to the rival fane, and the fatigues of the week keeping their mother in her room till luncheon, there was seldom any one present to verify the fact. Now and then, in a spasmodic burst of virtue—when the house had been too uproarious over night—Gus Trenor forced his genial bulk into a tight frock-coat and routed his daughters from their slumbers; but habitually, as Lily explained to Mr. Gryce, this parental duty was forgotten till the church bells were ringing across the park, and the omnibus had driven away empty.

Lily had hinted to Mr. Gryce that this neglect of religious observances was repugnant to her early traditions, and that during her visits to Bellomont she regularly accompanied Muriel and Hilda to church. This tallied with the assurance, also confidentially imparted, that, never having played bridge before, she had been "dragged into it" on the night of her arrival, and had lost an appalling amount of money in consequence of her ignorance of the game and of the rules of betting. Mr. Gryce was undoubtedly enjoying Bellomont. He liked the ease and glitter of the life, and the lustre conferred on him by being a member of this group of rich and conspicuous people. But he thought it a very materialistic society; there were times when he was frightened by the talk of the men and the looks of the ladies, and he was glad to find that Miss Bart, for all her ease and self-possession, was not at home in so ambiguous an atmosphere. For this reason he had been especially pleased to learn that she would, as usual, attend the young Trenors to church on Sunday morning; and as he paced the gravel sweep before the door, his light overcoat on his arm and his prayer-book in one carefully-gloved hand, he reflected agreeably on the strength of character which kept her true to her early training in surroundings so subversive to religious principles.

For a long time Mr. Gryce and the omnibus had the gravel sweep to themselves; but, far from regretting this deplorable indifference on the part of the other guests, he found himself nourishing the hope that Miss Bart might be unaccompanied. The precious minutes were flying, however; the big chestnuts pawed the ground and flecked their impatient sides with foam; the coachman seemed to be slowly petrifying on the box, and the groom on the doorstep; and still the lady did not come. Suddenly, however, there was a sound of voices and a rustle of skirts in the doorway, and Mr. Gryce, restoring his watch to his pocket, turned with a nervous start; but it was only to find himself handing Mrs. Wetherall into the carriage.

The Wetheralls always went to church. They belonged to the vast group of human automata who go through life without neglecting to perform a single one of the gestures executed by the surrounding puppets. It is true that the Bellomont puppets did not go to church; but others equally important did—and Mr. and Mrs. Wetherall's circle was so large that God was included in their visiting-list. They appeared, therefore, punctual and resigned, with the air of people bound for a dull "At Home," and after them Hilda and Muriel straggled, yawning and pinning each other's veils and ribbons as they came. They had promised Lily to go to church with her, they

It was evident that the party about the tea-table was breaking up.

declared, and Lily was such a dear old duck that they didn't mind doing it to please her, though they couldn't fancy what had put the idea in her head, and though for their own part they would much rather have played lawn tennis with Jack and Gwen, if she hadn't told them she was coming. The Misses Trenor were followed by Lady Cressida Raith, a weather-beaten person in Liberty silk and ethnological trinkets, who, on seeing the omnibus, expressed her surprise that they were not to walk across the park; but at Mrs. Wetherall's horrified protest that the church was a mile away, her ladyship, after a glance at the height of the other's heels, acquiesced in the necessity of driving, and poor Mr. Gryce found himself rolling off between four ladies for whose spiritual welfare he felt not the least concern.

It might have afforded him some consolation could he have known that Miss Bart had really meant to go to church. She had even risen earlier than usual in the execution of her purpose. She had an idea that the sight of her in a grey gown of devotional cut, with her famous lashes drooped above a prayer-book, would put the finishing touch to Mr. Gryce's subjugation, and render inevitable a certain incident which she had resolved should form a part of the walk they were to take together after luncheon. Her intentions in short had never been more definite; but poor Lily, for all the hard glaze of her exterior, was inwardly as malleable as wax. Her faculty for adapting herself, for entering into other people's feelings, if it served her now and then in small contingencies, hampered her in the decisive moments of life. She was like a water-plant in the flux of the tides, and today the whole current of her mood was carrying her toward Lawrence Selden. Why had he come? Was it to see herself or Bertha Dorset? It was the last question which, at that moment, should have engaged her. She might better have contented herself with thinking that he had simply responded to the despairing summons of his hostess, anxious to interpose him between herself and the ill-humor of Mrs. Dorset. But Lily had not rested till she learned from Mrs. Trenor that Selden had come of his own accord.

"He didn't even wire me—he just happened to find the trap at the station. Perhaps it's not over with Bertha after all," Mrs. Trenor musingly concluded; and went away to arrange her dinner-cards accordingly.

Perhaps it was not, Lily reflected; but it should be soon, unless she had lost her cunning. If Selden had come at Mrs. Dorset's call, it was at her own that he would stay. So much the previous evening had told her. Mrs. Trenor, true to her simple principle of making her married friends happy, had placed Selden and Mrs. Dorset next to each other at dinner; but, in obedience to the time-honored traditions of the match-maker, she had separated Lily and Mr. Gryce, sending in the former with George Dorset, while Mr. Gryce was coupled with Gwen Van Osburgh.

George Dorset's talk did not interfere with the range of his neighbor's thoughts. He was a mournful dyspeptic, intent on finding out the deleterious ingredients of every dish and diverted from this care only by the sound of his wife's voice. On this occasion, however, Mrs. Dorset took no part in the general conversation. She sat talking in low murmurs with Selden, and turning a contemptuous and denuded shoulder toward her host, who, far from resenting his exclusion, plunged into the excesses of the *menu* with the joyous irresponsibility of a free man. To Mr. Dorset, however, his wife's attitude was a subject of such evident concern that, when he was not scraping the sauce from his fish, or scooping the moist bread-crumbs from the interior of his roll, he sat straining his thin neck for a glimpse of her between the lights.

Mrs. Trenor, as it chanced, had placed the husband and wife on opposite sides of the table, and Lily was therefore able to observe Mrs. Dorset also, and by carrying her glance a few feet farther, to set up a rapid comparison between Lawrence Selden and Mr. Gryce. It was that comparison which was her undoing. Why else had she suddenly grown interested in Selden? She had known him for eight years or more: ever since her return to America he had formed a part of her background. She had always been glad to sit next to him at dinner, had found him more agreeable than most men, and had vaguely wished that he possessed the other qualities needful to fix her attention; but till now she had been too busy with her own affairs to regard him as more than one of the pleasant accessories of life. Miss Bart was a keen reader of her own heart, and she saw that her sudden preoccupation with Selden was due to the fact that his presence shed a new light on her surroundings. Not that he was notably brilliant or exceptional; in his own profession he was surpassed by more than one man who had bored Lily through many a weary dinner. It was rather that he had preserved a certain social detachment, a happy air of viewing the show objectively, of having points of contact outside the great gilt cage in which they were all huddled for the mob to gape at. How alluring the world outside the cage appeared to Lily, as she heard its door clang on her! In reality, as she knew, the door never clanged: it stood always open; but most of the captives were like flies in a bottle, and having once flown in, could never regain their freedom. It was Selden's distinction that he had never forgotten the way out.

That was the secret of his way of readjusting her vision. Lily, turning her eyes from him, found herself scanning her little world through his retina: it was as though the pink lamps had been shut off and the dusty daylight let in. She looked down the long table, studying its occupants one by one, from Gus Trenor, with his heavy carnivorous head sunk between his shoulders, as he preyed on a jellied plover, to his wife, at the opposite end of the long bank of orchids, suggestive, with her glaring good-looks, of a jeweler's window lit by electricity. And between the two, what a long stretch of vacuity! How dreary and trivial these people were! Lily reviewed them with a scornful impatience: Carry Fisher, with her shoulders, her eyes, her divorces, her general air of embodying a "spicy paragraph"; young Silverton, who had meant to live on proof-reading and write an epic, and who now lived on his friends and had become critical of truffles; Alice Wetherall, an animated visiting-list, whose most fervid convictions turned on the wording of invitations and the engraving of dinner-cards; Wetherall, with his perpetual nervous nod of acquiescence, his air of agreeing with people before he knew what they were saying; Jack Stepney, with his confident smile and anxious eyes, half way between the sheriff and an heiress; Gwen Van Osburgh, with all the guileless confidence of a young girl who has always been told that there is no one richer than her father.

Lily smiled at her classification of her friends. How different they had seemed to her a few hours ago! Then they had symbolized what she was gaining, now they stood for what she was giving up. That very afternoon they had seemed full of brilliant qualities; now she saw that they were merely dull in a loud way. Under the glitter of their opportunities she saw the poverty of their achievement. It was not that she wanted them to be more disinterested; but she would have liked them to be more picturesque. And she had a shamed recollection of the way in which, a few hours since, she had felt the centripetal force of their standards. She closed her eyes an instant, and the vacuous routine of the life she had chosen stretched before her like a long white road without dip or turning: it was true she was to roll over it in a carriage instead of trudging it on foot, but sometimes the pedestrian enjoys the diversion of a short cut which is denied to those on wheels.

She was roused by a chuckle which Mr. Dorset seemed to eject from the depths of his lean throat.

"I say, do look at her," he exclaimed, turning to Miss Bart with lugubrious merriment—"I beg your pardon, but do just look at my wife making a fool of that poor devil over there! One would really suppose she was gone on him—and it's all the other way round, I assure you."

Thus adjured, Lily turned her eyes on the spectacle which was affording Mr. Dorset such legitimate mirth. It certainly appeared, as he said, that Mrs. Dorset was the more active participant in the scene: her neighbor seemed to receive her advances with a temperate zest which did not distract him from his dinner. The sight restored Lily's good humor, and knowing the peculiar disguise which Mr. Dorset's marital fears assumed, she asked gaily: "Aren't you horribly jealous of her?"

Dorset greeted the sally with delight. "Oh, abominably—you've just hit it—keeps me awake at night. The doctors tell me that's what has knocked my digestion out—being so infernally jealous of her.—I can't eat a mouthful of this stuff, you know," he added suddenly, pushing back his plate with a clouded countenance; and Lily, unfailingly adaptable, accorded her radiant attention to his prolonged denunciation of other people's cooks, with a supplementary tirade on the toxic qualities of melted butter.

It was not often that he found so ready an ear; and, being a man as well as a dyspeptic, it may be that as he poured his grievances into it he was not insensible to its rosy symmetry. At any rate he engaged Lily so long that the sweets were being handed when she caught a phrase on her other side, where Miss Corby, the comic woman of the company, was bantering Jack Stepney on his approaching engagement. Miss Corby's rôle was jocularity: she always entered the conversation with a handspring.

"And of course you'll have Sim Rosedale as best man!" Lily heard her fling out as the climax of her prognostications; and Stepney responded, as if struck: "Jove, that's an idea. What a thumping present I'd get out of him!"

Sim Rosedale! The name, made more odious by its diminutive, obtruded itself on Lily's thoughts like a leer. It stood for one of the many hated possibilities hovering on the edge of life. If she did not marry Percy Gryce, the day might come when she would have to be civil to such men as Rosedale. *If she did not marry him?* But she meant to marry him—she was sure of him and sure of herself. She drew back with a shiver from the pleasant paths in which her thoughts had been straying, and set her feet once more in the middle of the long white road. . . . When she went upstairs that night she found that the late post had brought her a fresh batch of bills. Mrs. Peniston, who was a conscientious woman, had forwarded them all to Bellomont.

Miss Bart, accordingly, rose the next morning with the most earnest conviction that it was her duty to go to church. She tore herself betimes from the lingering enjoyment of her breakfast-tray, rang to have her grey gown laid out, and despatched her maid to borrow a prayer-book from Mrs. Trenor.

But her course was too purely reasonable not to contain the germs of rebellion. No sooner were her preparations made than they roused a smothered sense of resistance. A small spark was enough to kindle Lily's imagination, and the sight of the grey dress and the borrowed prayer-book flashed a long light down the years. She would have to go to church with Percy Gryce every Sunday. They would have a front pew in the most expensive church in New York, and his name would figure handsomely in the list of parish charities. In a few years, when he grew stouter, he would be made a warden. Once in the winter the rector would come to dine, and her husband would beg her to go over the list and see that no *divorcées* were included, except those who had showed signs of penitence by being remarried to the very wealthy. There was nothing especially arduous in this round of religious obligations; but it stood for a fraction of that great bulk of boredom which loomed across her path. And who could consent to be bored on such a morning? Lily had slept well, and her bath had filled her with a pleasant glow, which was becomingly reflected in the clear curve of her cheek. No lines were visible this morning, or else the glass was at a happier angle.

And the day was the accomplice of her mood: it was a day for impulse and truancy. The light air seemed full of powdered gold; below the dewy bloom of the lawns the woodlands blushed and smouldered, and the hills across the river swam in molten blue. Every drop of blood in Lily's veins invited her to happiness.

The sound of wheels roused her from these musings, and leaning behind her shutters she saw the omnibus take up its freight. She was too late, then—but the fact did not alarm her. A glimpse of Mr. Gryce's crestfallen face even suggested that she had done wisely in absenting herself, since the disappointment he so candidly betrayed would surely whet his appetite for the afternoon walk. That walk she did not mean to miss; one glance at the bills on her writing-table was enough to recall its necessity. But meanwhile she had the morning to herself, and could muse pleasantly on the disposal of its hours. She was familiar enough with the habits of Bellomont to know that she was likely to have a free field till luncheon. She had seen the Wetheralls, the Trenor girls and Lady Cressida packed safely into the omnibus; Judy Trenor was sure to be having her hair shampooed; Carry Fisher had doubtless carried off her host for a drive, Ned Silverton was probably smoking the cigarette of young despair in his bedroom; and Kate Corby was certain to be playing tennis with Jack Stepney and Miss Van Osburgh. Of the ladies, this left only Mrs. Dorset unaccounted for, and Mrs. Dorset never came down till luncheon: her doctors, she averred, had forbidden her to expose herself to the crude air of the morning.

To the remaining members of the party Lily gave no special thought; wherever they were, they were not likely to interfere with her plans. These, for the moment, took the shape of assuming a dress somewhat more rustic and summerlike in style than the garment she had first selected, and rustling downstairs, sunshade in hand, with the disengaged air of a lady in quest of exercise. The great hall was empty but for the knot of dogs by the fire, who, taking in at a glance the outdoor aspect of Miss Bart, were upon her at once with lavish offers of companionship. She put aside the ramping paws which conveyed these offers, and assuring the joyous volunteers that she might presently have a use for their company, sauntered on through the empty drawing-room to the library at the end of the house. The library was almost the only surviving portion of the old manor-house of Bellomont: a long spacious room, revealing the traditions of the mother-country in its classically-cased doors, the Dutch tiles of the chimney, and the elaborate hob-grate with its shining brass urns. A few family portraits of lantern-jawed gentlemen in tie-wigs, and ladies with large head-dresses and small bodies, hung between the shelves lined with pleasantly-shabby books: books mostly contemporaneous with the ancestors in question, and to which the subsequent Trenors had made no perceptible additions. The library at Bellomont was in fact never used for reading, though it had a certain popularity as a smoking-room or a quiet retreat for flirtation. It had occurred to Lily, however, that it might on this occasion have been resorted to by the only member of the party in the least likely to put it to its original use. She advanced noiselessly over the dense old rug scattered with easy-chairs, and before she reached the middle of the room she saw that she had not been mistaken. Lawrence Selden was in fact seated at its farther end; but though a book lay on his knee, his attention was not engaged with it, but directed to a lady whose lace-clad figure, as she leaned back in an adjoining chair, detached itself with exaggerated slimness against the dusky leather of the upholstery.

Lily paused as she caught sight of the group; for a moment she seemed about to withdraw, but thinking better of this, she announced her approach by a slight shake of her skirts which made the couple raise their heads, Mrs. Dorset with a look of frank displeasure, and Selden with his usual quiet smile. The sight of his composure had a disturbing effect on Lily; but to be disturbed was in her case to make a more brilliant effort at self-possession.

"Dear me, am I late?" she asked, putting a hand in his as he advanced to greet her.

"Late for what?" enquired Mrs. Dorset tartly. "Not for luncheon, certainly—but perhaps you had an earlier engagement?"

"Yes, I had," said Lily confidingly.

"Really? Perhaps I am in the way, then? But Mr. Selden is entirely at your disposal." Mrs. Dorset was pale with temper, and her antagonist felt a certain pleasure in prolonging her distress.

"Oh, dear, no—do stay," she said good-humoredly. "I don't in the least want to drive you away."

"You're awfully good, dear, but I never interfere with Mr. Selden's engagements."

The remark was uttered with a little air of proprietorship not lost on its object, who concealed a faint blush of annoyance by stooping to pick up the book he had dropped at Lily's approach. The latter's eyes widened charmingly and she broke into a light laugh.

"But I have no engagement with Mr. Selden! My engagement was to go to church; and I'm afraid the omnibus has started without me. *Has* it started, do you know?"

She turned to Selden, who replied that he had heard it drive away some time since.

"Ah, then I shall have to walk; I promised Hilda and Muriel to go to church with them. It's too late to walk there, you say? Well, I shall have the credit of trying, at any rate—and the advantage of escaping part of the service. I'm not so sorry for myself, after all!"

And with a bright nod to the couple on whom she had intruded, Miss Bart strolled through the glass doors and carried her rustling grace down the long perspective of the garden walk.

She was taking her way churchward, but at no very quick pace; a fact not lost on one of her observers, who stood in the doorway looking after her with an air of puzzled amusement. The truth is that she was conscious of a somewhat keen shock of disappointment. All her plans for the day had been built on the assumption that it was to see her that Selden had come to Bellomont. She had expected, when she came downstairs, to find him on the watch for her, and she had found him, instead, in a situation which might well denote that he had been on the watch for another lady. Was it possible, after all, that he had come for Bertha Dorset? The latter had acted on the assumption to the extent of appearing at an hour when she never showed herself to ordinary mortals, and Lily, for the moment, saw no way of putting her in the wrong. It did not occur to her that Selden might have been actuated merely by the desire to spend a Sunday out of town: women never learn to dispense with the sentimental motive in their judgments of men. But Lily was not easily disconcerted; competition put her on her mettle, and she reflected that Selden's coming, if it did not declare him to be still in Mrs. Dorset's toils, showed him to be so completely free from them that he was not afraid of her proximity.

These thoughts so engaged her that she fell into a gait hardly likely to carry her to church before the sermon, and at length, having passed from the gardens to the wood-path beyond, so far forgot her intention as to sink into a rustic seat at a bend of the walk. The spot was charming, and Lily was not insensible to the charm, or to the fact that her presence enhanced it; but she was not accustomed to taste the joys of solitude except in company, and the combination of a handsome girl and a romantic scene struck her as too good to be wasted. No one, however, appeared to profit by the opportunity; and after a half hour of fruitless waiting she rose and wandered on. She felt a stealing sense of fatigue as she walked; the sparkle had died out of her, and the taste of life was stale on her lips. She hardly knew what she had been seeking, or why the failure to find it had so blotted the light from her sky: she was only aware of a vague sense of failure, of an inner isolation deeper than the loneliness about her.

Her footsteps flagged, and she stood gazing listlessly ahead, digging the ferny edge of the path with the tip of her sun-shade. As she did so a step sounded behind her, and she saw Selden at her side.

"How fast you walk!" he remarked. "I thought I should never catch up with you."

She answered gaily: "You must be quite breathless! I've been sitting under that tree for an hour."

"Waiting for me, I hope?" he rejoined; and she said with a vague laugh:

"Well—waiting to see if you would come."

"I seize the distinction, but I don't mind it, since doing the one involved doing the other. But weren't you sure that I should come?"

"If I waited long enough—but you see I had only a limited time to give to the experiment."

"Why limited? Limited by luncheon?"

"No, by my other engagement."

"Your engagement to go to church with Muriel and Hilda?"

"No; but to come home from church with another person."

"Ah, I see; I might have known you were fully provided with alternatives. And is the other person coming home this way?"

Lily laughed again. "That's just what I don't know; and to find out, it is my business to get to church before the service is over."

"Exactly; and it is my business to prevent your doing so; in which case the other person, piqued by your absence, will form the desperate resolve of driving back in the omnibus."

Lily received this with fresh appreciation; his nonsense was like the bubbling of her inner mood. "Is that what you would do in such an emergency?" she enquired.

Selden looked at her with solemnity. "I am here to prove to you," he cried, "what I am capable of doing in an emergency!"

"Walking a mile in an hour—you must own that the omnibus would be quicker!"

"Ah—but will he find you in the end? That's the only test of success."

They looked at each other with the same luxury of enjoyment that they had felt in exchanging absurdities over his tea-table; but suddenly Lily's face changed, and she said: "Well, if it is, he has succeeded."

Selden, following her glance, perceived a party of people advancing toward them from the farther bend of the path. Lady Cressida had evidently insisted on walking home, and the rest of the church-goers had thought it their duty to accompany her. Lily's companion looked rapidly from one to the other of the two men of the party; Wetherall walking respectfully at Lady Cressida's side with his little sidelong look of nervous attention, and Percy Gryce bringing up the rear with Mrs. Wetherall and the Trenors.

"Ah—now I see why you were getting up your Americana!" Selden exclaimed with a note of the freest admiration; but the blush in which the sally was received checked whatever amplification he had meant to give it.

That Lily Bart should object to being bantered about her suitors, or even about her means of attracting them, was so new to Selden that he had a momentary flash of surprise, which lit up a number of possibilities; but she rose gallantly to the defense of her confusion, by saying, as its object approached: "That was why I was waiting for you—to thank you for having given me so many points!"

"Ah, you can hardly do justice to the subject in such a short time," said Selden, as the Trenor girls caught sight of Miss Bart; and while she signalled a response to their boisterous greeting, he added quickly: "Won't you devote your afternoon to it? You know I must be off tomorrow morning. We'll take a walk, and you can thank me at your leisure."

VI

THE afternoon was perfect. A deeper stillness possessed the air, and the glitter of the American autumn was tempered by a haze which diffused the brightness without dulling it.

In the woody hollows of the park there was already a faint chill; but as the ground rose the air grew lighter, and ascending the long slopes beyond the high-road, Lily and her companion reached a zone of lingering summer. The path wound across a meadow with scattered trees; then it dipped into a lane plumed with asters and purpling sprays of bramble, whence, through the light quiver of ash-leaves, the country unrolled itself in pastoral distances.

Higher up, the lane showed thickening tufts of fern and of the creeping glossy verdure of shaded slopes; trees began to overhang it, and the shade deepened to the checkered dusk of a beech-grove. The boles of the trees stood well apart, with only a light feathering of undergrowth; the path wound along the edge of the wood, now and then looking out on a sunlit pasture or on an orchard spangled with fruit.

Lily had no real intimacy with nature, but she had a passion for the appropriate and could be keenly sensitive to a scene which was the fitting background of her own sensations. The landscape outspread below her seemed an enlargement of her present mood, and she found something of herself in its calmness, its breadth, its long free reaches. On the nearer slopes the sugar-maples wavered like pyres of light; lower down was a massing of grey orchards, and here and there the lingering green of an oak-grove. Two or three red farm-houses dozed under the apple-trees, and the white wooden spire of a village church showed beyond the shoulder of the hill; while far below, in a haze of dust, the high-road ran between the fields.

"Let us sit here," Selden suggested, as they reached an open ledge of rock above which the beeches rose steeply between mossy boulders.

Lily dropped down on the rock, glowing with her long climb. She sat quiet, her lips parted by the stress of the ascent, her eyes wandering peacefully over the broken ranges of the landscape. Selden stretched himself on the grass at her feet, tilting his hat against the level sun-rays, and clasping his hands behind his head, which rested against the side of the rock. He had no wish to make her talk; her quick-breathing silence seemed a part of the general hush and harmony of things. In his own mind there was only a lazy sense of pleasure, veiling the sharp edges of sensation as the September haze veiled the scene at their feet. But Lily, though her attitude was as calm as his, was throbbing inwardly with a rush of thoughts. There were in her at the moment two beings, one drawing deep breaths of freedom and exhilaration, the other gasping for air in a little black prison-house of fears. But gradually the captive's gasps grew fainter, or the other paid less heed to them: the horizon expanded, the air grew stronger, and the free spirit quivered for flight.

She could not herself have explained the sense of buoyancy which seemed to lift and swing her above the sun-suffused world at her feet. Was it love, she wondered, or a mere fortuitous combination of happy thoughts and sensations? How much of it was owing to the spell of the perfect afternoon, the scent of the fading woods, the thought of the dullness she had fled from? Lily had no definite experience by which to test the quality of her feelings. She had several times been in love with fortunes or careers, but only once with a man. That was years ago, when she first came out, and had been smitten with a romantic passion for a young gentleman named Herbert Melson, who had blue eyes and a little wave in his hair. Mr. Melson, who was possessed of no other negotiable securities, had hastened to employ these in capturing the eldest Miss Van Osburgh: since then he had grown stout and wheezy, and was given to telling anecdotes about his children. If Lily recalled this early emotion it was not to compare it with that which now possessed her; the only point of comparison was the sense of lightness, of emancipation, which she remembered feeling, in the whirl of a waltz or the seclusion of a conservatory, during the brief course of her youthful romance. She had not known again till today that lightness, that glow of freedom; but now it was something more than a blind groping of the blood. The peculiar charm of her feeling for Selden was that she understood it; she could put her finger on every link of the chain that was drawing them together. Though his popularity was of the quiet kind, felt rather than actively expressed among his friends, she had never mistaken his inconspicuousness for obscurity. His reputed cultivation was generally regarded as a slight obstacle to easy intercourse, but Lily, who prided herself on her broad-minded recognition of literature, and always carried an Omar Khayam in her travelling-bag, was attracted by this attribute, which she felt would have had its distinction in an older society. It was, moreover, one of his gifts to look his part; to have a height which lifted his head above the crowd, and the keenly-modelled dark features which, in a land of amorphous types, gave him the air of belonging to a more specialized race, of carrying the impress of a concentrated past. Expansive persons found him a little dry, and very young girls thought him sarcastic; but this air of friendly aloofness, as far removed as possible from any assertion of personal advantage, was the quality which piqued Lily's interest. Everything about him accorded with the fastidious element in her taste, even to the light irony with which he surveyed what seemed to be most sacred. She admired him most of all, perhaps, for being able to convey as distinct a sense of superiority as the richest man she had ever met.

It was the unconscious prolongation of this thought which led her to say presently, with a laugh: "I have broken two engagements for you today. How many have you broken for me?"

"None," said Selden calmly. "My only engagement at Bellomont was with you."

She glanced down at him, faintly smiling.

"Did you really come to Bellomont to see me?"

"Of course I did."

Her look deepened meditatively. "Why?" she murmured, with an accent which took all tinge of coquetry from the question.

"Because you're such a wonderful spectacle: I always like to see what you are doing."

"How do you know what I should be doing if you were not here?"

Selden smiled. "I don't flatter myself that my coming has deflected your course of action by a hair's breadth."

"That's absurd—since, if you were not here, I could obviously not be taking a walk with you."

"No; but your taking a walk with me is only another way of making use of your material. You are an artist and I happen to be the bit of color you are using today. It's a part of your cleverness to be able to produce premeditated effects extemporaneously."

Lily smiled also: his words were too acute not to strike her sense of humor. It was true that she meant to use the accident of his presence as part of a very definite effect; or that, at least, was the secret pretext she had found for breaking her promise to walk with Mr. Gryce. She had sometimes been accused of being too eager—even Judy Trenor had warned her to go slowly. Well, she would not be too eager in this case; she would give her suitor a longer taste of suspense. Where duty and inclination jumped together, it was not in Lily's nature to hold them asunder. She had excused herself from the walk on the plea of a headache: the horrid headache which, in the morning, had prevented her venturing to church. Her appearance at luncheon justified the excuse. She looked languid, full of a suffering sweetness; she carried a scent-bottle in her hand. Mr. Gryce was new to such manifestations; he wondered rather nervously if she were delicate, having far-reaching fears about the future of his progeny. But sympathy won the day, and he besought her not to expose herself: he always connected the outer air with ideas of exposure.

Lily had received his sympathy with languid gratitude, urging him, since she should be such poor company, to join the rest of the party who, after luncheon, were starting in automobiles on a visit to the Van Osburghs at Peekskill. Mr. Gryce was touched by her disinterestedness, and, to escape from the threatened vacuity of the afternoon, had taken her advice and departed mournfully, in a dust-hood and goggles: as the motor-car lunged down the avenue she smiled at his resemblance to a baffled beetle.

Selden had watched her maneuvers with lazy amusement. She had made no reply to his suggestion that they should spend the afternoon together, but as her plan unfolded itself he felt fairly confident of being included in it. The house was empty when at length he heard her step on the stair and strolled out of the billiard-room to join her. She had on a hat and walking-dress, and the dogs were bounding at her feet.

"I thought, after all, the air might do me good," she explained; and he agreed that so simple a remedy was worth trying.

The excursionists would be gone at least four hours; Lily and Selden had the whole afternoon before them, and the sense of leisure and safety gave the last touch of lightness to her spirit. With so much time to talk, and no definite object to be led up to, she could taste the rare joys of mental vagrancy.

She felt so free from ulterior motives that she took up his charge with a touch of resentment.

"I don't know," she said, "why you are always accusing me of premeditation."

"I thought you confessed to it: you told me the other day that you had to follow a certain line—and if one does a thing at all it is a merit to do it thoroughly."

"If you mean that a girl who has no one to think for her is obliged to think for herself, I am quite willing to accept the imputation. But you must find me a dismal kind of person if you suppose that I never yield to an impulse."

"Ah, but I don't suppose that: haven't I told you that your genius lies in converting impulses into intentions?"

"My genius?" she echoed with a sudden note of weariness. "Is there any final test of genius but success? And I certainly haven't succeeded."

Selden pushed his hat back and took a side-glance at her. "Success—what is success? I shall be interested to have your definition."

"Success?" She hesitated. "Why, to get as much as one can out of life, I suppose. It's a relative quality, after all. Isn't that your idea of it?"

"My idea of it? God forbid!" He sat up with sudden energy, resting his elbows on his knees and staring out upon the mellow fields. "My idea of success," he said, "is personal freedom."

"Freedom? Freedom from worries?"

"From everything—from money, from poverty, from ease and anxiety, from all the material accidents. To keep a kind of republic of the spirit—that's what I call success."

She leaned forward with a responsive flash. "I know—I know—it's strange; but that's just what I've been feeling today."

He met her eyes with the latent sweetness of his. "Is the feeling so rare with you?" he said.

She blushed a little under his gaze. "You think me horribly sordid, don't you? But perhaps it's rather that I never had any choice. There was no one, I mean, to tell me about the republic of the spirit."

"There never is—it's a country one has to find the way to one's self."

"But I should never have found my way there if you hadn't told me."

"Ah, there are sign-posts—but one has to know how to read them."

"Well, I have known, I have known!" she cried with a glow of eagerness. "Whenever I see you, I find myself spelling out a letter of the sign—and yesterday—last evening at dinner—I suddenly saw a little way into your republic."

Selden was still looking at her, but with a changed eye. Hitherto he had found, in her presence and her talk, the aesthetic amusement which a reflective man is apt to seek in desultory intercourse with pretty women. His attitude had been one of admiring spectatorship and he would have been almost sorry to detect in her any emotional weakness which should interfere with the fulfillment of her aims. But now the hint of this weakness had become the most interesting thing about her. He had come on her that morning in a moment of disarray; her face had been pale and altered, and the diminution of her beauty had lent her a poignant charm. *That is how she looks when she is alone!* had been his first thought; and the second was to note in her the change which his coming produced. It was the danger-point of their intercourse that he could not doubt the spontaneity of her liking. From whatever angle he viewed their dawning intimacy, he could not see it as part of her scheme of life; and to be the unforeseen element in a career so accurately planned was stimulating even to a man who had renounced sentimental experiments.

"Well," he said, "did it make you want to see more? Are you going to become one of us?"

He had drawn out his cigarettes as he spoke, and she reached her hand toward the case.

"Oh, do give me one—I haven't smoked for days!"

"Why such unnatural abstinence? Everybody smokes at Bellomont."

"Yes—but it is not considered becoming in a *jeune fille à marier;* and at the present moment I am a *jeune fille à marier.*"

"Ah, then I'm afraid we can't let you into the republic."

"Why not? Is it a celibate order?"

"Not in the least, though I'm bound to say there are not many married people in it. But you will marry someone very rich, and it's as hard for rich people to get into as the kingdom of heaven."

"That's unjust, I think, because, as I understand it, one of the conditions of citizenship is not to think too much about money, and the only way not to think about money is to have a great deal of it."

"You might as well say that the only way not to think about air is to have enough to breathe. That is true enough in a sense; but your lungs are thinking about the air, if you are not. And so it is with your rich people—they may not be thinking of money, but they're breathing it all the while; take them into another element and see how they squirm and gasp!"

Lily sat gazing absently through the blue rings of her cigarette-smoke.

"It seems to me," she said at length, "that you spend a good deal of your time in the element you disapprove of."

Selden received this thrust without discomposure. "Yes; but I have tried to remain amphibious: it's all right as long as one's lungs can work in another air. The real alchemy consists in being able to turn gold back again into something else; and that's the secret that most of your friends have lost."

Lily mused. "Don't you think," she rejoined after a moment, "that the people who find fault with society are too apt to regard it as an end and not a means, just as the people who despise money speak as if its only use were to be kept in bags and gloated over? Isn't it fairer to look at them both as opportunities, which may be used either stupidly or intelligently, according to the capacity of the user?"

"That is certainly the sane view; but the queer thing about society is that the people who regard it as an end are those who are in it, and not the critics on the fence. It's just the other way with most shows—the audience may be under the illusion, but the actors know that real life is on the other side of the footlights. The people who take society as an escape from work are putting it to its proper use; but when it becomes the thing worked for it distorts all the relations of life." Selden raised himself on his elbow. "Good heavens!" he went on, "I don't underrate the decorative side of life. It seems to me the sense of splendor has justified itself by what it has produced.

The worst of it is that so much human nature is used up in the process. If we're all the raw stuff of the cosmic effects, one would rather be the fire that tempers a sword than the fish that dyes a purple cloak. And a society like ours wastes such good material in producing its little patch of purple! Look at a boy like Ned Silverton—he's really too good to be used to refurbish anybody's social shabbiness. There's a lad just setting out to discover the universe; isn't it a pity he should end by finding it in Mrs. Fisher's drawing-room?"

"Ned is a dear boy, and I hope he will keep his illusions long enough to write some nice poetry about them; but do you think it is only in society that he is likely to lose them?"

Selden answered her with a shrug. "Why do we call all our generous ideas illusions, and the mean ones truths? Isn't it a sufficient condemnation of society to find one's self accepting such phraseology? I very nearly acquired the jargon at Silverton's age, and I know how names can alter the color of beliefs."

She had never heard him speak with such energy of affirmation. His habitual touch was that of the eclectic, who lightly turns over and compares; and she was moved by this sudden glimpse into the laboratory where his faiths were formed.

"Ah, you are as bad as the other sectarians," she exclaimed; "why do you call your republic a republic? It is a close corporation, and you create arbitrary objections in order to keep people out."

"It is not *my* republic; if it were, I should have a *coup d'état* and seat you on the throne."

"Whereas, in reality, you think I can never even get my foot across the threshold? Oh, I understand what you mean. You despise my ambitions—you think them unworthy of me!"

Selden smiled, but not ironically. "Well, isn't that a tribute? I think them quite worthy of most of the people who live by them."

She had turned to gaze on him gravely. "But isn't it possible that, if I had the opportunities of these people, I might make a better use of them? Money stands for all kinds of things—its purchasing quality isn't limited to diamonds and motor-cars."

"Not in the least: you might expiate your enjoyment of them by founding a hospital."

"But if you think they are what I should really enjoy, you must think my ambitions are good enough for me."

Selden met this appeal with a laugh. "Ah, my dear Miss Bart, I am not divine Providence, to guarantee your enjoying the things you are trying to get!"

"Then the best you can say for me is, that after struggling to get them I probably shan't like them?" She drew a deep breath. "What a miserable future you foresee for me!"

"Well—have you never foreseen it for yourself?"

The slow color rose to her cheek, not a blush of excitement but drawn from the deep wells of feeling; it was as if the effort of her spirit had produced it.

"Often and often," she said. "But it looks so much darker when you show it to me!"

He made no answer to this exclamation, and for a while they sat silent, while something throbbed between them in the wide quiet of the air. But suddenly she turned on him with a kind of vehemence.

"Why do you do this to me?" she cried. "Why do you make the things I have chosen seem hateful to me, if you have nothing to give me instead?"

The words roused Selden from the musing fit into which he had fallen. He himself did not know why he had led their talk along such lines; it was the last use he would have imagined himself making of an afternoon's solitude with Miss Bart. But it was one of those moments when neither seemed to speak deliberately, when an indwelling voice in each called to the other across unsounded depths of feeling.

"No, I have nothing to give you instead," he said, sitting up and turning so that he faced her. "If I had, it should be yours, you know."

She received this abrupt declaration in a way even stranger than the manner of its making: she dropped her face on her hands and he saw that for a moment she wept.

It was for a moment only, however; for when he leaned nearer and drew down her hands with a gesture less passionate than grave, she turned on him a face softened but not disfigured by emotion, and he said to himself, somewhat cruelly, that even her weeping was an art.

The reflection steadied his voice as he asked, between pity and irony: "Isn't it natural that I should try to belittle all the things I can't offer you?"

Her face brightened at this, but she drew her hand away, not with a gesture of coquetry, but as though renouncing something to which she had no claim.

"But you belittle *me*, don't you," she returned gently, "in being so sure they are the only things I care for?"

Selden felt an inner start; but it was only the last quiver of his egoism. Almost at once he answered quite simply: "But you do care for them, don't you? And no wishing of mine can alter that."

He had so completely ceased to consider how far this might carry him that he had a distinct sense of disappointment when she turned on him a face sparkling with derision.

"Ah," she cried, "for all your fine phrases you're really as great a coward as I am, for you wouldn't have made one of them if you hadn't been so sure of my answer."

The shock of this retort had the effect of crystallizing Selden's wavering intentions.

"I am not so sure of your answer," he said quietly. "And I do you the justice to believe that you are not either."

It was her turn to look at him with surprise; and after a moment—"Do you want to marry me?" she asked.

He broke into a laugh. "No, I don't want to—but perhaps I should if you did!"

"That's what I told you—you're so sure of me that you can amuse yourself with experiments." She drew back the hand he had regained, and sat looking down on him sadly.

"I am not making experiments," he returned. "Or if I am, it is not on you but on myself. I don't know what effect they are going to have on me—but if marrying you is one of them, I will take the risk."

She smiled faintly. "It would be a great risk, certainly—I have never concealed from you how great."

"Ah, it's you who are the coward!" he exclaimed.

She had risen, and he stood facing her with his eyes on hers. The soft isolation of the falling day enveloped them: they seemed lifted into a finer air. All the exquisite influences of the hour trembled in their veins, and drew them to each other as the loosened leaves were drawn to the earth.

"It's you who are the coward," he repeated, catching her hands in his.

She leaned on him for a moment, as if with a drop of tired wings: he felt as though her heart were beating rather with the stress of a long flight than the thrill of new distances. Then, drawing back with a little smile of warning—"I shall look hideous in dowdy clothes; but I can trim my own hats," she declared.

They stood silent for a while after this, smiling at each other like adventurous children who have climbed to a forbidden height from which they discover a new world. The actual world at their feet was veiling itself in dimness, and across the valley a clear moon rose in the denser blue.

Suddenly they heard a remote sound, like the hum of a giant insect, and following the high-road, which wound whiter through the surrounding twilight, a black object rushed across their vision.

Lily started from her attitude of absorption; her smile faded and she began to move toward the lane.

"I had no idea it was so late! We shall not be back till after dark," she said, almost impatiently.

Selden was looking at her with surprise: it took him a moment to regain his usual view of her; then he said, with an uncontrollable note of dryness: "That was not one of our party; the motor was going the other way."

"I know—I know——" She paused, and he saw her redden through the twilight. "But I told them I was not well—that I should not go out. Let us go down!" she murmured.

Selden continued to look at her; then he drew his cigarette case from his pocket and slowly lit a cigarette. It seemed to him necessary, at this moment, to proclaim, by some habitual gesture of this sort, his recovered hold on the actual: he had an almost puerile wish to let his companion see that, their flight over, he had landed on his feet.

She waited while the spark flickered under his curved palm; then he held out the cigarettes to her.

She took one with an unsteady hand, and putting it to her lips, leaned forward to draw her light from his. In the indistinctness the little red gleam lit up the lower part of her face, and he saw her mouth tremble into a smile.

"Were you serious?" she asked, with an odd thrill of gaiety which she might have caught up, in haste, from a heap of stock inflections, without having time to select the just note.

Selden's voice was under better control. "Why not?" he returned. "You see I took no risks in being so." And as she continued to stand before him, a little pale under the retort, he added quickly: "Let us go down."

VII

IT spoke much for the depth of Mrs. Trenor's friendship that her voice, in admonishing Miss Bart, took the same note of personal despair as if she had been lamenting the collapse of a house-party.

"All I can say is, Lily, that I can't make you out!" She leaned back, sighing, in the morning abandon of lace and muslin, turning an indifferent shoulder to the heaped-up importunities of her desk, while she considered, with the eye of a physician who has given up the case, the erect exterior of the patient confronting her.

"If you hadn't told me you were going in for him seriously—but I'm sure you made that plain enough from the beginning! Why else did you ask me to let you off bridge, and to keep away Carry and Kate Corby? I don't suppose you did it because he amused you; we could none of us imagine your putting up with him for a moment unless you meant to marry him. And I'm sure everybody played fair! They all wanted to help it along. Even Bertha kept her hands off—I will say that—till Lawrence came down and you dragged him away from her. After that she had a right to retaliate—why on earth did you interfere with her? You've known Lawrence Selden for years—why did you behave as if you had just discovered him? If you had a grudge against Bertha it was a stupid time to show it—you could have paid her back just as well after you were married! I told you Bertha was dangerous. She was in an odious mood when she came here, but Lawrence's turning up put her in a good humor, and if you'd only let her think he came for *her* it would have never occurred to her to play you this trick. Oh, Lily, you'll never do anything if you're not serious!"

Miss Bart accepted this exhortation in a spirit of the purest impartiality. Why should she have been angry? It was the voice of her own conscience which spoke to her through Mrs. Trenor's reproachful accents. But even to her own conscience she must trump up a semblance of defense.

"I only took a day off—I thought he meant to stay on all this week, and I knew Mr. Selden was leaving this morning."

Mrs. Trenor brushed aside the plea with a gesture which laid bare its weakness.

"He did mean to stay—that's the worst of it. It shows that he's run away from you; that Bertha's done her work and poisoned him thoroughly."

Lily gave a slight laugh. "Oh, if he's running I'll overtake him!"

Her friend threw out an arresting hand. "Whatever you do, Lily, do nothing!"

Miss Bart received the warning with a smile. "I don't mean, literally, to take the next train. There are ways——" But she did not go on to specify them.

Mrs. Trenor sharply corrected the tense. "There *were* ways—plenty of them! I didn't suppose you needed to have them pointed out. But don't deceive yourself—he's thoroughly frightened. He has run straight home to his mother, and she'll protect him!"

"Oh, to the death," Lily agreed, dimpling at the vision.

"How you can *laugh*——" her friend rebuked her; and she dropped back to a soberer perception of things with the question: "What was it Bertha really told him?"

"Don't ask me—horrors! She seemed to have raked up everything. Oh, you know what I mean—of course there isn't anything, *really;* but I suppose she brought in Prince Varigliano—and Lord Hubert—and there was some story of your having borrowed money of old Ned Van Alstyne: did you ever?"

"He is my father's cousin," Miss Bart interposed.

"Well, of course she left *that* out. It seems Ned told Carry Fisher; and she told Bertha, naturally. They're all alike, you know: they hold their tongues for years, and you think you're safe, but when their opportunity comes they remember everything."

Lily had grown pale: her voice had a harsh note in it. "It was some money I lost at bridge at the Van Osburghs'. I repaid it, of course."

"Ah, well, they wouldn't remember that; besides, it was the idea of the gambling debt that frightened Percy. Oh, Bertha knew her man—she knew just what to tell him!"

In this strain Mrs. Trenor continued for nearly an hour to

admonish her friend. Miss Bart listened with admirable equanimity. Her naturally good temper had been disciplined by years of enforced compliance, since she had almost always had to attain her ends by the circuitous path of other people's; and, being naturally inclined to face unpleasant facts as soon as they presented themselves, she was not sorry to hear an impartial statement of what her folly was likely to cost, the more so as her own thoughts were still insisting on the other side of the case. Presented in the light of Mrs. Trenor's vigorous comments, the reckoning was certainly a formidable one, and Lily, as she listened, found herself gradually reverting to her friend's view of the situation. Mrs. Trenor's words were moreover emphasized for her hearer by anxieties which she herself could scarcely guess. Affluence, unless stimulated by a keen imagination, forms but the vaguest notion of the practical strain of poverty. Judy knew it must be "horrid" for poor Lily to have to stop to consider whether she could afford real lace on her petticoats, and not to have a motor-car and a steam-yacht at her orders; but the daily friction of unpaid bills, the daily nibble of small temptations to expenditure, were trials as far out of her experience as the domestic problems of the char-woman. Mrs. Trenor's unconsciousness of the real stress of the situation had the effect of making it more galling to Lily. While her friend reproached her for missing the opportunity to eclipse her rivals, she was once more battling in imagination with the mounting tide of indebtedness from which she had so nearly escaped. What wind of folly had driven her out again on those dark seas?

If anything was needed to put the last touch to her self-abasement it was the sense of the way her old life was opening its ruts again to receive her. Yesterday her fancy had fluttered free pinions above a choice of occupations; now she had to drop to the level of the familiar routine, in which moments of seeming brilliancy and freedom alternated with long hours of subjection.

She laid a deprecating hand on her friend's. "Dear Judy! I'm sorry to have been such a bore, and you are very good to me. But you must have some letters for me to answer—let me at least be useful."

She settled herself at the desk, and Mrs. Trenor accepted her resumption of the morning's task with a sigh, which implied that, after all, she had proved herself unfit for higher uses.

The luncheon table showed a depleted circle. All the men but

Jack Stepney and Dorset had returned to town (it seemed to Lily a last touch of irony that Selden and Percy Gryce should have gone in the same train), and Lady Cressida and the attendant Wetheralls had been despatched by motor to lunch at a distant country-house. At such moments of diminished interest it was usual for Mrs. Dorset to keep her room till the afternoon; but on this occasion she drifted in when luncheon was half over, hollowed-eyed and drooping, but with an edge of malice under her indifference.

She raised her eyebrows as she looked about the table. "How few of us are left! I do so enjoy the quiet—don't you, Lily? I wish the men would always stop away—it's really much nicer without them. Oh, you don't count, George: one doesn't have to talk to one's husband. But I thought Mr. Gryce was to stay for the rest of the week?" she added enquiringly. "Didn't he intend to, Judy? He's such a nice boy—I wonder what drove him away? He is rather shy, and I'm afraid we may have shocked him: he has been brought up in such an old-fashioned way. Do you know, Lily, he told me he had never seen a girl play cards for money till he saw you doing it the other night? And he lives on the interest of his income, and always has a lot left over to invest!"

Mrs. Fisher leaned forward eagerly. "I do believe it is some one's duty to educate that young man. It is shocking that he has never been made to realize his duties as a citizen. Every wealthy man should be compelled to study the laws of his country."

Mrs. Dorset glanced at her quietly. "I think he *has* studied the divorce laws. He told me he had promised the Bishop to sign some kind of a petition against divorce."

Mrs. Fisher reddened under her powder, and Stepney said with a laughing glance at Miss Bart: "I suppose he is thinking of marriage, and wants to tinker up the old ship before he goes aboard."

His betrothed looked shocked at the metaphor, and George Dorset exclaimed with a sardonic growl: "Poor devil! It isn't the ship that will do for him, it's the crew."

"Or the stowaways," said Miss Corby brightly. "If I contemplated a voyage with him I should try to start with a friend in the hold."

Miss Van Osburgh's vague feeling of pique was struggling for appropriate expression. "I'm sure I don't see why you laugh at him; I think he's very nice," she exclaimed; "and, at any rate, a girl who married him would always have enough to be comfortable."

She looked puzzled at the redoubled laughter which hailed her words, but it might have consoled her to know how deeply they had sunk into the breast of one of her hearers.

Comfortable! At that moment the word was more eloquent to Lily Bart than any other in the language. She could not even pause to smile over the heiress's view of a colossal fortune as a mere shelter against want: her mind was filled with the vision of what that shelter might have been to her. Mrs. Dorset's pin-pricks did not smart, for her own irony cut deeper: no one could hurt her as much as she was hurting herself, for no one else—not even Judy Trenor—knew the full magnitude of her folly.

She was roused from these unprofitable considerations by a whispered request from her hostess, who drew her apart as they left the luncheon-table.

"Lily, dear, if you've nothing special to do, may I tell Carry Fisher that you intend to drive to the station and fetch Gus? He will be back at four, and I know she has it in her mind to meet him. Of course I'm very glad to have him amused, but I happen to know that she has bled him rather severely since she's been here, and she is so keen about going to fetch him that I fancy she must have got a lot more bills this morning. It seems to me," Mrs. Trenor feelingly concluded, "that most of her alimony is paid by other women's husbands!"

Miss Bart, on her way to the station, had leisure to muse over her friend's words, and their peculiar application to herself. Why should she have to suffer for having once, for a few hours, borrowed money of an elderly cousin, when a woman like Carry Fisher could make a living unrebuked from the good-nature of her men friends and the tolerance of their wives? It all turned on the tiresome distinction between what a married woman might, and a girl might not, do. Of course it was shocking for a married woman to borrow money—and Lily was expertly aware of the implication involved—but still, it was the mere *malum prohibitum* which the world decries but condones, and which, though it may be punished by private vengeance, does not provoke the collective disapprobation of society. To Miss Bart, in short, no such opportunities were possible. She could of course borrow from her women friends—a hundred here or there, at the utmost—but they were more ready to give a gown or a trinket, and looked a little askance when she hinted her preference for a check. Women are not generous lenders, and those among whom her lot was cast were either in the same case as herself, or else too far removed from it to understand its necessities. The result of her meditations was the decision to join her aunt at Richfield. She could not remain at Bellomont without playing bridge, and being involved in other expenses; and to continue her usual series of autumn visits would merely prolong the same difficulties. She had reached a point where abrupt retrenchment was necessary, and the only cheap life was a dull life. She would start the next morning for Richfield.

At the station she thought Gus Trenor seemed surprised, and not wholly unrelieved, to see her. She yielded up the reins of the light runabout in which she had driven over, and as he climbed heavily to her side, crushing her into a scant third of the seat, he said: "Halloo! It isn't often you honor me. You must have been uncommonly hard up for something to do."

The afternoon was warm, and propinquity made her more than usually conscious that he was red and massive, and that beads of moisture had caused the dust of the train to adhere unpleasantly to the broad expanse of cheek and neck which he turned to her; but she was aware also, from the look in his small dull eyes, that the contact with her freshness and slenderness was as agreeable to him as the sight of a cooling beverage.

The perception of this fact helped her to answer gaily: "It's not often I have the chance. There are too many ladies to dispute the privilege with me."

"The privilege of driving me home? Well, I'm glad you won the race, anyhow. But I know what really happened—my wife sent you. Now didn't she?"

He had the dull man's unexpected flashes of astuteness, and Lily could not help joining in the laugh with which he had pounced on the truth.

"You see, Judy thinks I'm the safest person for you to be with; and she's quite right," she rejoined.

"Oh, is she, though? If she is, it's because you wouldn't waste your time on an old hulk like me. We married men have to put up with what we can get: all the prizes are for the clever chaps who've kept a free foot. Let me light a cigar, will you? I've had a beastly day of it."

He drew up in the shade of the village street, and passed the reins to her while he held a match to his cigar. The little flame under his hand cast a deeper crimson on his puffing face, and Lily averted her eyes with a momentary feeling of repugnance. And yet some women thought him handsome!

As she handed back the reins, she said sympathetically: "Did you have such a lot of tiresome things to do?"

"I should say so—rather!" Trenor, who was seldom listened to, either by his wife or her friends, settled down into the rare enjoyment of a confidential talk. "You don't know how a fellow has to hustle to keep this kind of thing going." He waved his whip in the direction of the Bellomont acres, which lay outspread before them in opulent undulations. "Judy has no idea of what she spends—not that there isn't plenty to keep the thing going," he interrupted himself, "but a man has got to keep his eyes open and pick up all the tips he can. My father and mother used to live like fighting-cocks on their income, and put by a good bit of it too—luckily for me—but at the pace we go now, I don't know where I should be if it weren't for taking a flyer now and then. The women all think—I mean Judy thinks—I've nothing to do but to go down town once a month and cut off coupons, but the truth is it takes a devilish lot of hard work to keep the machinery running. Not that I ought to complain today, though," he went on after a moment, "for I did a very neat stroke of business, thanks to Stepney's friend Rosedale: by the way, Miss Lily, I wish you'd try to persuade Judy to be decently civil to that chap. He's going to be rich enough to buy us all out one of these days, and if she'd only ask him to dine now and then I could get almost anything out of him. The man is mad to know the people who don't want to know him, and when a fellow's in that state there is nothing he won't do for the first woman who takes him up."

Lily hesitated a moment. The first part of her companion's discourse had started an interesting train of thought, which was rudely interrupted by the mention of Mr. Rosedale's name. She uttered a faint protest.

"But you know Jack did try to take him about, and he was impossible."

"Oh, hang it—because he's fat and shiny, and has a shoppy manner! Well, all I can say is that the people who are clever enough to be civil to him now will make a mighty good thing of it. A few years from now he'll be in it whether we want him or not, and then he won't be giving away a half-a-million tip for a dinner."

Lily's mind had reverted from the intrusive personality of Mr. Rosedale to the train of thought set in motion by Trenor's first words. This vast mysterious Wall Street world of "tips" and "deals"—might she not find in it the means of escape from her dreary predicament? She had often heard of women making money in this way through their friends: she had no more notion than most of her sex of the exact nature of the transaction, and its vagueness seemed to diminish its indelicacy. She could not, indeed, imagine herself, in any extremity, stooping to extract a "tip" from Mr. Rosedale; but at her side was a man in possession of that precious commodity, and who, as the husband of her dearest friend, stood to her in a relation of almost fraternal intimacy.

In her inmost heart Lily knew it was not by appealing to the fraternal instinct that she was likely to move Gus Trenor, but this way of explaining the situation helped to drape its crudity, and she was always scrupulous about keeping up appearances to herself. Her personal fastidiousness had a moral equivalent, and when she made a tour of inspection in her own mind there were certain closed doors she did not open.

As they reached the gates of Bellomont she turned to Trenor with a smile.

"The afternoon is so perfect—don't you want to drive me a little farther? I've been rather out of spirits all day, and it's so restful to be away from people, with someone who won't mind if I'm a little dull."

She looked so plaintively lovely as she proffered the request, so trustfully sure of his sympathy and understanding, that Trenor felt himself wishing that his wife could see how other women treated him—not battered wire-pullers like Mrs. Fisher, but a girl that most men would have given their boots to get such a look from.

"Out of spirits? Why on earth should you ever be out of spirits? Is your last box of Doucet dresses a failure, or did Judy rook you out of everything at bridge last night?"

Lily shook her head with a sigh. "I have had to give up Doucet; and bridge too—I can't afford it. In fact I can't afford any of the things my friends do, and I am afraid Judy often thinks me a bore because I don't play cards any longer, and because I am not as smartly dressed as the other women. But you will think me a bore too if I talk to you about my worries, and I only mention them because I want you to do me a favor—the very greatest of favors."

Her eyes sought his once more, and she smiled inwardly at the tinge of apprehension that she read in them.

"Why, of course—if it's anything I can manage——" He broke off, and she guessed that his enjoyment was disturbed by the remembrance of Mrs. Fisher's methods.

"The greatest of favors," she rejoined gently. "The fact is, Judy is angry with me, and I want you to make my peace."

"Angry with you? Oh, come, nonsense——" his relief broke through in a laugh. "Why, you know she's devoted to you."

"She is the best friend I have, and that is why I mind having to vex her. But I daresay you know what she has wanted me to do. She has set her heart—poor dear—on my marrying—marrying a great deal of money."

She paused with a slight falter of embarrassment, Trenor, turning abruptly, fixed on her a look of growing intelligence.

"A great deal of money? Oh, by Jove—you don't mean Gryce? What—you do? Oh, no, of course I won't mention it—you can trust me to keep my mouth shut—but Gryce—good Lord, *Gryce!* Did Judy really think you could bring yourself to marry that portentous little ass? But you couldn't, eh? And so you gave him the sack, and that's the reason why he lit out by the first train this morning?" He leaned back, spreading himself farther across the seat, as if dilated by the joyful sense of his own discernment. "How on earth could Judy think you would do such a thing? *I* could have told her you'd never put up with such a little milksop!"

Lily sighed more deeply. "I sometimes think," she murmured, "that men understand a woman's motives better than other women do."

"Some men—I'm certain of it! I could have *told* Judy," he repeated, exulting in the implied superiority over his wife.

"I thought you would understand; that's why I wanted to speak to you," Miss Bart rejoined. "I *can't* make that kind of marriage; it's impossible. But neither can I go on living as all the women in my set do. I am almost entirely dependent on my aunt, and though she is very kind to me she makes me no regular allowance, and lately I've lost money at cards, and I don't dare tell her about it. I have paid my card debts, of course, but there is hardly anything left for my other expenses, and if I go on with my present life I shall be in horrible difficulties. I have a tiny income of my own, but I'm afraid it's badly invested, for it seems to bring in less every year, and I am so ignorant of money matters that I don't know if my aunt's agent, who looks after it, is a good adviser." She paused a moment, and added in a lighter tone: "I didn't mean to bore you with all this, but I want your help in making Judy understand that I can't, at present, go on living as one must live among you all. I am going away tomorrow to join my aunt at Richfield, and I shall stay there for the rest of the autumn, and dismiss my maid and learn how to mend my own clothes."

At this picture of loveliness in distress, the pathos of which was heightened by the light touch with which it was drawn, a murmur of indignant sympathy broke from Trenor. Twenty-four hours earlier, if his wife had consulted him on the subject of Miss Bart's future, he would have said that a girl with extravagant tastes and no money had better marry the first rich man she could get; but with the subject of discussion at his side, turning to him for sympathy, making him feel that he understood her better than her dearest friends, and confirming the assurance by the appeal of her exquisite nearness, he was ready to swear that such a marriage was a desecration, and that, as a man of honor, he was bound to do all he could to protect her from the results of her disinterestedness. This impulse was reinforced by the reflection that if she had married Gryce she would have been surrounded by flattery and approval, whereas, having refused to sacrifice herself to expediency, she was left to bear the whole cost of her resistance. Hang it, if he could find a way out of such difficulties for a professional sponge like Carry Fisher, who was simply a mental habit corresponding to the physical titillations of the cigarette or the cocktail, he could surely do as much for a girl who appealed to his highest sympathies, and who brought her troubles to him with the trustfulness of a child.

Trenor and Miss Bart prolonged their drive till long after sunset; and before it was over he had tried, with some show of success, to prove to her that, if she would only trust him, he could make a handsome sum of money for her without endangering the small amount she possessed. She was too genuinely ignorant of the manipulations of the stock-market to understand his technical explanations, or even perhaps to perceive that certain points in them were slurred; the haziness enveloping the transaction served as a veil for her embarrassment, and through the general blur her hopes dilated like lamps in a fog. She understood only that her modest investments were to be mysteriously multiplied without risk to herself; and the assurance that this miracle would take place within a short time, that there would be no tedious interval for suspense and reaction, relieved her of her lingering scruples.

Again she felt the lightening of her load, and with it the release of repressed activities. Her immediate worries conjured, it was easy to resolve that she would never again find herself in such straits, and as the need of economy and self-denial receded from her foreground she felt herself ready to meet any other demand which life might make. Even the immediate one of letting Trenor, as they drove homeward, lean a little nearer and rest his hand reassuringly on hers, cost her only a momentary shiver of reluctance. It was part of the game to make him feel that her appeal had been an uncalculated impulse, provoked by the liking he inspired; and the renewed sense of power in handling men, while it consoled her wounded vanity, helped also to obscure the thought of the claim at which his manner hinted. He was a coarse dull man who, under all his show of authority, was a mere supernumerary in the costly show for which his money paid: surely, to a clever girl, it would be easy to hold him by his vanity, and so keep the obligation on his side.

VIII

THE first thousand dollar check which Lily received with a blotted scrawl from Gus Trenor strengthened her self-confidence in the exact degree to which it effaced her debts.

The transaction had justified itself by its results: she saw now how absurd it would have been to let any primitive scruple deprive her of this easy means of appeasing her creditors. Lily felt really virtuous as she dispensed the sum in sops to her tradesmen, and the fact that a fresh order accompanied each payment did not lessen her sense of disinterestedness. How many women, in her place, would have given the orders without making the payment!

She had found it reassuringly easy to keep Trenor in a good humor. To listen to his stories, to receive his confidence and laugh at his jokes, seemed for the moment all that was required of her, and the complacency with which her hostess regarded these attentions freed them of the least hint of ambiguity. Mrs. Trenor evidently assumed that Lily's growing intimacy with her husband was simply an indirect way of returning her own kindness.

"I'm so glad you and Gus have become such good friends," she said approvingly. "It's too delightful of you to be so nice to him, and put up with all his tiresome stories. I know what they are, because I had to listen to them when we were engaged—I'm sure he is telling the same ones still. And now I shan't always have to be asking Carry Fisher here to keep him in a good humor. She's a perfect vulture, you know; and she hasn't the least moral sense. She is always getting Gus to speculate for her, and I'm sure she never pays when she loses."

Miss Bart could shudder at this state of things without the embarrassment of a personal application. Her own position was surely quite different. There could be no question of her not paying when she lost, since Trenor had assured her that she was certain not to lose. In sending her the check he had explained that he had made five thousand for her out of Rosedale's "tip," and had put four thousand back in the same venture, as there was the promise of another "big rise"; she understood therefore that he was now speculating with her own money, and that she consequently owed him no more than the gratitude which such a trifling service demanded. She vaguely supposed that, to raise the first sum, he had borrowed on her securities; but this was a point over which her curiosity did not linger. It was concentrated, for the moment, on the probable date of the next "big rise."

The news of this event was received by her some weeks later, on the occasion of Jack Stepney's marriage to Miss Van Osburgh. As a cousin of the bridegroom, Miss Bart had been asked to act as bridesmaid; but she had declined on the plea that, since she was much taller than the other attendant virgins, her presence might mar the symmetry of the group. The truth was, she had attended too many brides to the altar: when next seen there she meant to be the chief figure in the ceremony. She knew the pleasantries made at the expense of young girls who have been too long before the public, and she was resolved to avoid such assumptions of youthfulness as might lead people to think her older than she really was.

The Van Osburgh marriage was celebrated in the village church near the paternal estate on the Hudson. It was the "simple country wedding" to which guests are convoyed in special trains, and from which the hordes of the uninvited have to be fended off by the intervention of the police. While these sylvan rites were taking place, in a church packed with fashion and festooned with orchids, the representatives of the press were threading their way, note-book in hand, through the labyrinth of wedding presents, and the agent of a cinematograph syndicate was setting up his apparatus at the church door. It was the kind of scene in which Lily had often pictured herself as taking the principal part, and on this occasion the fact that she was once more merely a casual spectator, instead of the mystically veiled figure occupying the center of attention, strengthened her resolve to assume the latter part before the year was over. The fact that her immediate anxieties were relieved did not blind her to a possibility of their recurrence; it merely gave her enough buoyancy to rise once more above her doubts and feel a renewed faith in her beauty, her power, and her general fitness to attract a brilliant destiny. It could not be that one conscious of such aptitudes for mastery and enjoyment was doomed to a perpetuity of failure; and her mistakes looked easily reparable in the light of her restored self-confidence.

A special appositeness was given to these reflections by the discovery, in a neighboring pew, of the serious profile and neatly-trimmed beard of Mr. Percy Gryce. There was something almost bridal in his own aspect: his large white gardenia had a symbolic air that struck Lily as a good omen. After all, seen in an assemblage of his kind he was not ridiculous-looking: a friendly critic might have called his heaviness weighty, and he was at his best in the attitude of vacant passivity which brings out the oddities of the restless. She fancied he was the kind of man whose sentimental associations would be stirred by the conventional imagery of a wedding, and she pictured herself, in the seclusion of the Van Osburgh conservatories, playing skillfully upon sensibilities thus prepared for her touch. In fact, when she looked at the other women about her, and recalled the image she had brought away from her own glass, it did not seem as though any special skill would be needed to repair her blunder and bring him once more to her feet.

The sight of Selden's dark head, in a pew almost facing her, disturbed for a moment the balance of her complacency. The rise of her blood as their eyes met was succeeded by a contrary motion, a wave of resistance and withdrawal. She did not wish to see him again, not because she feared his influence, but because his presence always had the effect of cheapening her aspirations, of throwing her whole world out of focus. Besides, he was a living reminder of the worst mistake in her career, and the fact that he had been its cause did not soften her feelings toward him. She could still imagine an ideal state of existence in which, all else being superadded, intercourse with Selden might be the last touch of luxury; but in the world as it was, such a privilege was likely to cost more than it was worth.

"Lily, dear, I never saw you look so lovely! You look as if something delightful had just happened to you!"

The young lady who thus formulated her admiration of her brilliant friend did not, in her own person, suggest such happy possibilities. Miss Gertrude Farish, in fact, typified the mediocre and the ineffectual. If there were compensating qualities in her wide frank glance and the freshness of her smile, these were qualities which only the sympathetic observer would perceive before noticing that her eyes were of a workaday grey and her lips without haunting curves. Lily's own view of her wavered between pity for her limitations and impatience at her cheerful acceptance of them. To Miss Bart, as to her mother, acquiescence in dinginess was evidence of stupidity; and there were moments when, in the consciousness of her own power to look and to be so exactly what the occasion required, she almost felt that other girls were plain and inferior from choice. Certainly no one need have confessed such acquiescence in her lot as was revealed in the "useful" color of Gerty Farish's gown and the subdued lines of her hat: it is almost as stupid to let your clothes betray that you know you are ugly as to have them proclaim that you think you are beautiful.

Of course, being fatally poor and dingy, it was wise of Gerty to have taken up philanthropy and symphony concerts; but there was something irritating in her assumption that existence yielded no higher pleasures, and that one might get as much interest and excitement out of life in a cramped flat as in the splendors of the Van Osburgh establishment. Today, however, her chirping enthusiasms did not irritate Lily. They seemed only to throw her own exceptionalness into becoming relief, and give a soaring vastness to her scheme of life.

"Do let us go and take a peep at the presents before every one else leaves the dining-room!" suggested Miss Farish, linking her arm in her friend's. It was characteristic of her to take a sentimental and unenvious interest in all the details of a wedding: she was the kind of person who always kept her handkerchief out during the service, and departed clutching a box of wedding-cake.

"Isn't everything beautifully done?" she pursued, as they entered the distant drawing-room assigned to the display of Miss Van Osburgh's bridal spoils. "I always say no one does things better than cousin Grace! Did you ever taste anything more delicious than that *mousse* of lobster with champagne sauce? I made up my mind weeks ago that I wouldn't miss this wedding, and just fancy how delightfully it all came about. When Lawrence Selden heard I was coming, he insisted on fetching me himself and driving me to the station, and when we go back this evening I am to dine with him at Sherry's. I really feel as excited as if I were getting married myself!"

Lily smiled: she knew that Selden had always been kind to his dull cousin, and she had sometimes wondered why he wasted so much time in such an unremunerative manner; but now the thought gave her a vague pleasure.

"Do you see him often?" she asked.

"Yes; he is very good about dropping in on Sundays. And now and then we do a play together; but lately I haven't seen much of him. He doesn't look well, and he seems nervous and unsettled. The dear fellow! I do wish he would marry some nice girl. I told him so today, but he said he didn't care for the really nice ones, and the other kind didn't care for him—but that was just his joke, of course. He could never marry a girl who *wasn't* nice. Oh, my dear, did you ever see such pearls?"

They had paused before the table on which the bride's jewels were displayed, and Lily's heart gave an envious throb as she caught the refraction of light from their surfaces—the milky gleam of perfectly matched pearls, the flash of rubies relieved against contrasting velvet, the intense blue rays of sapphires kindled into light by surrounding diamonds: all these precious tints enhanced and deepened by the varied art of their setting. The glow of the stones warmed Lily's veins like wine. More completely than any other expression of wealth they symbolized the life she longed to lead, the life of fastidious aloofness and refinement in which every detail should have the finish of a jewel, and the whole form a harmonious setting to her own jewel-like rareness.

"Oh, Lily, do look at this diamond pendant—it's as big as a dinner-plate! Who can have given it?" Miss Farish bent short-sightedly over the accompanying card. "*Mr. Simon Rosedale*. What, that horrid man? Oh, yes—I remember he's a friend of Jack's, and I suppose cousin Grace had to ask him here today; but she must rather hate having to let Gwen accept such a present from him."

Lily smiled. She doubted Mrs. Van Osburgh's reluctance, but was aware of Miss Farish's habit of ascribing her own delicacies of feeling to the persons least likely to be encumbered by them.

"Well, if Gwen doesn't care to be seen wearing it she can always exchange it for something else," she remarked.

"Ah, here is something so much prettier," Miss Farish continued. "Do look at this exquisite white sapphire. I'm sure the person who chose it must have taken particular pains. What is the name? Percy Gryce? Ah, then I'm not surprised!" She smiled significantly as she replaced the card. "Of course you've heard that he's perfectly devoted to Evie Van Osburgh? Cousin Grace is so pleased about it—it's quite a romance! He met her first at the George Dorsets', only about six weeks ago, and it's just the nicest possible marriage for dear Evie. Oh, I don't mean the money—of course she has plenty of her own—but she's such a quiet stay-at-home kind of girl, and it seems he has just the same tastes; so they are exactly suited to each other."

Lily stood staring vacantly at the white sapphire on its velvet bed. Evie Van Osburgh and Percy Gryce? The names rang derisively through her brain. *Evie Van Osburgh?* The youngest, dumpiest, dullest of the four dull and dumpy daughters whom Mrs. Van Osburgh, with unsurpassed astuteness, had "placed" one by one in enviable niches of existence! Ah, lucky girls who grow up in the shelter of a mother's love—a mother who knows how to contrive opportunities without conceding favors, how to take advantage of propinquity without allowing appetite to be dulled by habit! The cleverest girl may miscalculate where her own interests are concerned, may yield too much at one moment and withdraw too far at the next: it takes a mother's unerring vigilance and foresight to land her daughters safely in the arms of wealth and suitability.

Lily's passing light-heartedness sank beneath a renewed sense of failure. Life was too stupid, too blundering! Why should Percy Gryce's millions be joined to another great fortune, why should this clumsy girl be put in possession of powers she would never know how to use?

She was roused from these speculations by a familiar touch on her arm, and turning saw Gus Trenor beside her. She felt a thrill of vexation: what right had he to touch her? Luckily Gerty Farish had wandered off to the next table, and they were alone.

Trenor, looking stouter than ever in his tight frock-coat, and unbecomingly flushed by the bridal libations, gazed at her with undisguised approval.

"By Jove, Lily, you do look a stunner!" He had slipped insensibly into the use of her Christian name, and she had never found the right moment to correct him. Besides, in her set all the men and women called each other by their Christian names; it was only on Trenor's lips that the familiar address had an unpleasant significance.

"Well," he continued, still jovially impervious to her annoyance, "have you made up your mind which of these little trinkets you mean to duplicate at Tiffany's tomorrow? I've got a check for you in my pocket that will go a long way in that line!"

Lily gave him a startled look: his voice was louder than usual, and the room was beginning to fill with people. But as her glance assured her that they were still beyond ear-shot a sense of pleasure replaced her apprehension.

"Another dividend?" she asked, smiling and drawing near him in the desire not to be overheard.

"Well, not exactly: I sold out on the rise and I've pulled off four thou' for you. Not so bad for a beginner, eh? I suppose you'll begin to think you're a pretty knowing speculator. And perhaps you won't think poor old Gus such an awful ass as some people do."

"I think you the kindest of friends; but I can't thank you properly now."

She let her eyes shine into his with a look that made up for the hand-clasp he would have claimed if they had been alone—and how glad she was that they were not! The news filled her with the glow produced by a sudden cessation of physical pain. The world was not so stupid and blundering after all: now and then a stroke of luck came to the unluckiest. At the thought her spirits began to rise: it was characteristic of her that one trifling piece of good fortune should give wings to all her hopes. Instantly came the reflection that Percy Gryce was not irretrievably lost; and she smiled to think of the excitement of recapturing him from Evie Van Osburgh. What chance could such a simpleton have against her if she chose to exert herself? She glanced about, hoping to catch a glimpse of Gryce; but her eyes lit instead on the glossy countenance of Mr. Rosedale, who was slipping through the crowd with an air half obsequious, half obtrusive, as though, the moment his presence was recognized, it would swell to the dimensions of the room.

Not wishing to be the means of effecting this enlargement, Lily quickly transferred her glance to Trenor, to whom the expression of her gratitude seemed not to have brought the complete gratification she had meant it to give.

"Hang thanking me—I don't want to be thanked, but I *should* like the chance to say two words to you now and then," he grumbled. "I thought you were going to spend the whole autumn with us, and I've hardly laid eyes on you for the last month. Why can't you come back to Bellomont this evening? We're all alone, and Judy is as cross as two sticks. Do come and cheer a fellow up. If you say yes I'll run you over in the motor, and you can telephone your maid to bring your traps from town by the next train."

Lily shook her head with a charming semblance of regret. "I wish I could—but it's quite impossible. My aunt has come back to town, and I must be with her for the next few days."

"Well, I've seen a good deal less of you since we've got to be such pals than I used to when you were Judy's friend," he continued with unconscious penetration.

"When I was Judy's friend? Am I not her friend still? Really, you say the most absurd things! If I were always at Bellomont you would tire of me much sooner than Judy—but come and see me at my aunt's the next afternoon you are in town; then we can have a nice quiet talk, and you can tell me how I had better invest my fortune."

It was true that, during the last three or four weeks, she had absented herself from Bellomont on the pretext of having other visits to pay; but she now began to feel that the reckoning she had thus contrived to evade had rolled up interest in the interval.

The prospect of the nice quiet talk did not appear as all-sufficing to Trenor as she had hoped, and his brows continued to lower as he said: "Oh, I don't know that I can promise you a fresh tip every day. But there's one thing you might do for me; and that is, just to be a little civil to Rosedale. Judy has promised to ask him to dine when we get to town, but I can't induce her to have him at Bellomont, and if you would let me bring him up now it would make a lot of difference. I don't believe two women have spoken to him this afternoon, and I can tell you he's a chap it pays to be decent to."

Miss Bart made an impatient movement, but suppressed the words which seemed about to accompany it. After all, this was an unexpectedly easy way of acquitting her debt; and had she not reasons of her own for wishing to be civil to Mr. Rosedale?

"Oh, bring him by all means," she said smiling; "perhaps I can get a tip out of him on my own account."

Trenor paused abruptly, and his eyes fixed themselves on hers with a look which made her change color.

"I say, you know—you'll please remember he's a blooming bounder," he said; and with a slight laugh she turned toward the open window near which they had been standing.

The throng in the room had increased, and she felt a desire for space and fresh air. Both of these she found on the terrace, where only a few men were lingering over cigarettes and liqueur, while scattered couples strolled across the lawn to the autumn-tinted borders of the flower-garden.

As she emerged, a man moved toward her from the knot of smokers, and she found herself face to face with Selden. The stir of the pulses which his nearness always caused was increased by a slight sense of constraint. They had not met since their Sunday afternoon walk at Bellomont, and that episode was still so vivid to her that she could hardly believe him to be less conscious of it. But his greeting expressed no more than the satisfaction which every pretty woman expects to see reflected in masculine eyes; and the discovery, if distasteful to her vanity, was reassuring to her nerves. Between the relief of her escape from Trenor, and the vague apprehension of her meeting with Rosedale, it was pleasant to rest a moment on the sense of complete understanding which Lawrence Selden's manner always conveyed.

"This is luck," he said smiling. "I was wondering if I should be able to have a word with you before the special snatches us away. I came with Gerty Farish, and promised not to let her miss the train, but I am sure she is still extracting sentimental solace from the wedding presents. She appears to regard their number and value as evidence of the disinterested affection of the contracting parties."

There was not the least trace of embarrassment in his voice, and as he spoke, leaning slightly against the jamb of the window, and letting his eyes rest on her in the frank enjoyment of her grace, she felt with a faint chill of regret that he had gone back without an effort to the footing on which they had stood before their last talk together. Her vanity was stung by the sight of his unscathed smile. She longed to be to him something more than a piece of sentient prettiness, a passing diversion to his eye and brain; and the longing betrayed itself in her reply.

"Ah," she said, "I envy Gerty that power she has of dressing up with romance all our ugly and prosaic arrangements! I have never recovered my self-respect since you showed me how poor and unimportant my ambitions were."

The words were hardly spoken when she realized their infelicity. It seemed to be her fate to appear at her worst to Selden.

"I thought, on the contrary," he returned lightly, "that I had been the means of proving they were more important to you than anything else."

It was as if the eager current of her being had been checked by a sudden obstacle which drove it back upon itself. She looked at him helplessly, like a hurt or frightened child: this real self of hers, which he had the faculty of drawing out of the depths, was so little accustomed to go alone!

The appeal of her helplessness touched in him, as it always did, a latent chord of inclination. It would have meant nothing to him to discover that his nearness made her more brilliant, but this glimpse of a twilight mood to which he alone had the clue seemed once more to set him in a world apart with her.

"At least you can't think worse things of me than you say!" she exclaimed with a trembling laugh; but before he could answer, the flow of comprehension between them was abruptly stayed by the reappearance of Gus Trenor, who advanced with Mr. Rosedale in his wake.

"Hang it, Lily, I thought you'd given me the slip: Rosedale and I have been hunting all over for you!"

His voice had a note of conjugal familiarity: Miss Bart fancied she detected in Rosedale's eye a twinkling perception of the fact, and the idea turned her dislike of him to repugnance.

She returned his profound bow with a slight nod, made more disdainful by the sense of Selden's surprise that she should number Rosedale among her acquaintances. Trenor had turned away, and his companion continued to stand before Miss Bart, alert and expectant, his lips parted in a smile at whatever she might be about to say, and his very back conscious of the privilege of being seen with her.

It was the moment for tact; for the quick bridging over of gaps; but Selden still leaned against the window, a detached observer of the scene, and under the spell of his observation Lily felt herself powerless to exert her usual arts. The dread of Selden's suspecting that there was any need for her to propitiate such a man as Rosedale checked the trivial phrases of politeness. Rosedale still stood before her in an expectant attitude, and she continued to face him in silence, her glance just level with his polished baldness. The look put the finishing touch to what her silence implied.

He reddened slowly, shifting from one foot to the other, fingered the plump black pearl in his tie, and gave a nervous twist to his moustache; then, running his eye over her, he drew back, and said, with a side-glance at Selden: "Upon my soul, I never saw a more ripping get-up. Is that the last creation of the dress-maker you go to see at the Benedick? If so, I wonder all the other women don't go to her too!"

The words were projected sharply against Lily's silence, and she saw in a flash that her own act had given them their emphasis. In ordinary talk they might have passed unheeded; but following on her prolonged pause they acquired a special meaning. She felt, without looking, that Selden had immediately seized it, and would inevitably connect the allusion with her visit to himself. The consciousness increased her irritation against Rosedale, but also her feeling that now, if ever, was the moment to propitiate him, hateful as it was to do so in Selden's presence.

"How do you know the other women don't go to my dress-maker?"

she returned. "You see I'm not afraid to give her address to my friends!"

Her glance and accent so plainly included Rosedale in this privileged circle that his small eyes puckered with gratification, and a knowing smile drew up his moustache.

"By Jove, you needn't be!" he declared. "You could give 'em the whole outfit and win at a canter!"

"Ah, that's nice of you; and it would be nicer still if you would carry me off to a quiet corner, and get me a glass of lemonade or some innocent drink before we all have to rush for the train."

She turned away as she spoke, letting him strut at her side through the gathering groups on the terrace, while every nerve in her throbbed with the consciousness of what Selden must have thought of the scene.

But under her angry sense of the perverseness of things, and the light surface of her talk with Rosedale, a third idea persisted: she did not mean to leave without an attempt to discover the truth about Percy Gryce. Chance, or perhaps his own resolve, had kept them apart since his hasty withdrawal from Bellomont; but Miss Bart was an expert in making the most of the unexpected, and the distasteful incidents of the last few minutes—the revelation to Selden of precisely that part of her life which she most wished him to ignore—increased her longing for shelter, for escape from such humiliating contingencies. Any definite situation would be more tolerable than this buffeting of chances, which kept her in an attitude of uneasy alertness toward every possibility of life.

Indoors there was a general sense of dispersal in the air, as of an audience gathering itself up for departure after the principal actors had left the stage; but among the remaining groups, Lily could discover neither Gryce nor the youngest Miss Van Osburgh. That both should be missing struck her with foreboding; and she charmed Mr. Rosedale by proposing that they should make their way to the conservatories at the farther end of the house. There were just enough people left in the long suite of rooms to make their progress conspicuous, and Lily was aware of being followed by looks of amusement and interrogation, which glanced off as harmlessly from her indifference as from her companion's self-satisfaction. She cared very little at that moment about being seen with Rosedale: all her thoughts were centered on the object of her search. The latter, however, was not discoverable in the conservatories, and Lily, oppressed by a sudden conviction of failure, was casting about for a way to rid herself of her now superfluous companion, when they came upon Mrs. Van Osburgh, flushed and exhausted, but beaming with the consciousness of duty performed.

She glanced at them a moment with the benign but vacant eye of the tired hostess, to whom her guests have become mere whirling spots in a kaleidoscope of fatigue; then her attention became suddenly fixed, and she seized on Miss Bart with a confidential gesture.

"My dear Lily, I haven't had time for a word with you, and now I suppose you are just off. Have you seen Evie? She's been looking everywhere for you: she wanted to tell you her little secret; but I daresay you have guessed it already. The engagement is not to be announced till next week—but you are such a friend of Mr. Gryce's that they both wished you to be the first to know of their happiness."

IX

IN Mrs. Peniston's youth, fashion had returned to town in October; therefore on the tenth day of the month the blinds of her Fifth Avenue residence were drawn up, and the eyes of the Dying Gladiator in bronze who occupied the drawing-room window resumed their survey of that deserted thoroughfare.

The first two weeks after her return represented to Mrs. Peniston the domestic equivalent of a religious retreat. She "went through" the linen and blankets in the precise spirit of the penitent exploring the inner folds of conscience; she sought for moths as the stricken soul seeks for lurking infirmities. The topmost shelf of every closet was made to yield up its secret, cellar and coal-bin were probed to their darkest depths and, as a final stage in the lustral rites, the entire house was swathed in penitential white and deluged with expiatory soapsuds.

It was on this phase of the proceedings that Miss Bart entered on the afternoon of her return from the Van Osburgh wedding. The journey back to town had not been calculated to soothe her nerves. Though Evie Van Osburgh's engagement was still officially a secret, it was one of which the innumerable intimate friends of the family were already possessed; and the trainful of returning guests buzzed with allusions and anticipations. Lily was acutely aware of her own part in this drama of innuendo: she knew the exact quality of the amusement the situation evoked. The crude forms in which her friends took their pleasure included a loud enjoyment of such complications: the zest of surprising destiny in the act of playing a practical joke. Lily knew well enough how to bear herself in difficult situations. She had, to a shade, the exact manner between victory and defeat: every insinuation was shed without an effort by the bright indifference of her manner. But she was beginning to feel the strain of the attitude; the reaction was more rapid, and she lapsed to a deeper self-disgust.

As was always the case with her, this moral repulsion found a physical outlet in a quickened distaste for her surroundings. She revolted from the complacent ugliness of Mrs. Peniston's black walnut, from the slippery gloss of the vestibule tiles, and the mingled odor of sapolio and furniture-polish that met her at the door.

The stairs were still carpetless, and on the way up to her room she was arrested on the landing by an encroaching tide of soapsuds. Gathering up her skirts, she drew aside with an impatient gesture; and as she did so she had the odd sensation of having already found herself in the same situation but in different surroundings. It seemed to her that she was again descending the staircase from Selden's rooms; and looking down to remonstrate with the dispenser of the soapy flood, she found herself met by a lifted stare which had once before confronted her under similar circumstances. It was the charwoman of the Benedick who, resting on crimson elbows, examined her with the same unflinching curiosity, the same apparent reluctance to let her pass. On this occasion, however, Miss Bart was on her own ground.

"Don't you see that I wish to go by? Please move your pail," she said sharply.

The woman at first seemed not to hear; then, without a word of excuse, she pushed back her pail and dragged a wet floor-cloth across the landing, keeping her eyes fixed on Lily while the latter swept by. It was insufferable that Mrs. Peniston should have such creatures about the house; and Lily entered her room resolved that the woman should be dismissed that evening.

Mrs. Peniston, however, was at the moment inaccessible to remonstrance: since early morning she had been shut up with her maid, going over her furs, a process which formed the culminating episode in the drama of household renovation. In the evening also Lily found herself alone, for her aunt, who rarely dined out, had responded to the summons of a Van Alstyne cousin who was passing through town. The house, in its state of unnatural immaculateness and order, was as dreary as a tomb, and as Lily, turning from her brief repast between shrouded sideboards, wandered into the newly-uncovered glare of the drawing-room she felt as though she were buried alive in the stifling limits of Mrs. Peniston's existence.

She usually contrived to avoid being at home during the season of domestic renewal. On the present occasion, however, a variety of reasons had combined to bring her to town; and foremost among them was the fact that she had fewer invitations than usual for the autumn. She had so long been accustomed to pass from one country-house to another, till the close of the holidays brought her friends to town, that the unfilled gaps of time confronting her produced a sharp sense of waning popularity. It was as she had said to Selden—people were tired of her. They would welcome her in a new character, but as Miss Bart they knew her by heart. She knew herself by heart too, and was sick of the old story. There were moments when she longed blindly for anything different, anything strange, remote and untried; but the utmost reach of her imagination did not go beyond picturing her usual life in a new setting. She could not figure herself as anywhere but in a drawing-room, diffusing elegance as a flower sheds perfume.

Meanwhile, as October advanced she had to face the alternative of returning to the Trenors or joining her aunt in town. Even the desolating dullness of New York in October, and the soapy discomforts of Mrs. Peniston's interior, seemed preferable to what might await her at Bellomont; and with an air of heroic devotion she announced her intention of remaining with her aunt till the holidays.

Sacrifices of this nature are sometimes received with feelings as mixed as those which actuate them; and Mrs. Peniston remarked to her confidential maid that, if any of the family were to be with her at such a crisis (though for forty years she had been thought competent to see to the hanging of her own curtains), she would certainly have preferred Miss Grace to Miss Lily. Grace Stepney was an obscure cousin, of adaptable manners and vicarious interests, who "ran in" to sit with Mrs. Peniston when Lily dined out too continuously; who played bézique, picked up dropped stitches, read out the deaths from the Times, and sincerely admired the purple satin drawing-room curtains, the Dying Gladiator in the window, and the seven-by-five painting of Niagara which represented the one artistic excess of Mr. Peniston's temperate career.

Mrs. Peniston, under ordinary circumstances, was as much bored by her excellent cousin as the recipient of such services usually is by the person who performs them. She greatly preferred the brilliant and unreliable Lily, who did not know one end of a crochet-needle from the other, and had frequently wounded her susceptibilities by suggesting that the drawing-room should be "done over." But when it came to hunting for missing napkins, or helping to decide whether the backstairs needed recarpeting, Grace's judgment was certainly sounder than Lily's: not to mention the fact that the latter resented the smell of beeswax and brown soap, and behaved as though she thought a house ought to keep clean of itself, without extraneous assistance.

Seated under the cheerless blaze of the drawing-room chandelier—Mrs. Peniston never lit the lamps unless there was "company"—Lily seemed to watch her own figure retreating down vistas of neutral-tinted dullness to a middle age like Grace Stepney's. When she ceased to amuse Judy Trenor and her friends she would have to fall back on amusing Mrs. Peniston; whichever way she looked she saw only a future of servitude to the whims of others, never the possibility of asserting her own eager individuality.

A ring at the door-bell, sounding emphatically through the empty house, roused her suddenly to the extent of her boredom. It was as though all the weariness of the past months had culminated in the vacuity of that interminable evening. If only the ring meant a summons from the outer world—a token that she was still remembered and wanted!

After some delay a parlor-maid presented herself with the announcement that there was a person outside who was asking to see Miss Bart; and on Lily's pressing for a more specific description, she added:

"It's Mrs. Haffen, Miss; she won't say what she wants."

Lily, to whom the name conveyed nothing, opened the door upon a woman in a battered bonnet, who stood firmly planted under the hall light. The glare of the unshaded gas shone familiarly on her pock-marked face and the reddish baldness visible through thin strands of straw-colored hair. Lily looked at the char-woman in surprise.

"Do you wish to see me?" she asked.

"I should like to say a word to you, Miss." The tone was neither aggressive nor conciliatory: it revealed nothing of the speaker's errand. Nevertheless, some precautionary instinct warned Lily to withdraw beyond earshot of the hovering parlor-maid.

She signed to Mrs. Haffen to follow her into the drawing-room, and closed the door when they had entered.

"What is it that you wish?" she enquired.

The char-woman, after the manner of her kind, stood with her arms folded in her shawl. Unwinding the latter, she produced a small parcel wrapped in dirty newspaper.

"I have something here that you might like to see, Miss Bart." She spoke the name with an unpleasant emphasis, as though her knowing it made a part of her reason for being there. To Lily the intonation sounded like a threat.

"You have found something belonging to me?" she asked, extending her hand.

Mrs. Haffen drew back. "Well, if it comes to that, I guess it's mine as much as anybody's," she returned.

Lily looked at her perplexedly. She was sure, now, that her visitor's manner conveyed a threat; but, expert as she was in certain directions, there was nothing in her experience to prepare her for the exact significance of the present scene. She felt, however, that it must be ended as promptly as possible.

"I don't understand; if this parcel is not mine, why have you asked for me?"

The woman was unabashed by the question. She was evidently prepared to answer it, but like all her class she had to go a long way back to make a beginning, and it was only after a pause that she replied: "My husband was janitor to the Benedick till the first of the month; since then he can't get nothing to do."

Lily remained silent and she continued: "It wasn't no fault of our own, neither: the agent had another man he wanted the place for, and we was put out, bag and baggage, just to suit his fancy. I had a long sickness last winter, and an operation that ate up all we'd put by; and it's hard for me and the children, Haffen being so long out of a job."

After all, then, she had come only to ask Miss Bart to find a place for her husband; or, more probably, to seek the young lady's intervention with Mrs. Peniston. Lily had such an air of always getting what she wanted that she was used to being appealed to as an intermediary, and, relieved of her vague apprehension, she took refuge in the conventional formula.

"I am sorry you have been in trouble," she said.

"Oh, that we have, Miss, and it's on'y just beginning. If on'y we'd 'a got another situation—but the agent, he's dead against us. It ain't no fault of ours, neither, but——"

At this point Lily's impatience overcame her. "If you have anything to say to me——" she interposed.

The woman's resentment of the rebuff seemed to spur her lagging ideas.

"Yes, Miss; I'm coming to that," she said. She paused again, with her eyes on Lily, and then continued, in a tone of diffuse narrative: "When we was at the Benedick I had charge of some of the gentlemen's rooms; leastways, I swep' 'em out on Saturdays. Some of the gentlemen got the greatest sight of letters: I never saw the like of it. Their waste-paper baskets 'd be fairly brimming, and papers falling over on the floor. Maybe havin' so many is how they get so careless. Some of 'em is worse than others. Mr. Selden, Mr. Lawrence Selden, he was always one of the carefullest: burnt his letters in winter, and tore 'em in little bits in summer. But sometimes he'd have so many he'd just bunch 'em together, the way the others did, and tear the lot through once—like this."

While she spoke she had loosened the string from the parcel in her hand, and now she drew forth a letter which she laid on the table between Miss Bart and herself. As she had said, the letter was torn in two; but with a rapid gesture she laid the torn edges together and smoothed out the page.

A wave of indignation swept over Lily. She felt herself in the presence of something vile, as yet but dimly conjectured—the kind of vileness of which people whispered, but which she had never thought of as touching her own life. She drew back with a motion of disgust, but her withdrawal was checked by a sudden discovery: under the glare of Mrs. Peniston's chandelier she had recognized the handwriting of the letter. It was a large disjointed hand, with a flourish of masculinity which but slightly disguised its rambling weakness, and the words, scrawled in heavy ink on pale-tinted note-paper, smote on Lily's ear as though she had heard them spoken.

At first she did not grasp the full import of the situation. She understood only that before her lay a letter written by Bertha Dorset, and addressed, presumably, to Lawrence Selden. There was no date, but the blackness of the ink proved the writing to be comparatively recent. The packet in Mrs. Haffen's hand doubtless contained more letters of the same kind—a dozen, Lily conjectured from its thickness. The letter before her was short, but its few words, which had leapt into her brain before she was conscious of reading them, told a long history—a history over which, for the last four years, the friends of the writer had smiled and shrugged, viewing it merely as one among the countless "good situations" of the mundane comedy. Now the other side presented itself to Lily, the volcanic nether side of the surface over which conjecture and innuendo glide so lightly till the first fissure turns their whisper to a shriek. Lily knew that there is nothing society resents so much as having given its protection to those who have not known how to profit by it: it is for having betrayed its connivance that the body social punishes the offender who is found out. And in this case there was no doubt of the issue. The code of Lily's world decreed that a woman's husband should be the only judge of her conduct: she was technically above suspicion while she had the shelter of his approval, or even of his indifference. But with a man of George Dorset's temper there could be no thought of condonation—the possessor of his wife's letters could overthrow with a touch the whole structure of her existence. And into what hands Bertha Dorset's secret had been delivered! For a moment the irony of the coincidence tinged Lily's disgust with a confused sense of triumph. But the disgust prevailed—all her instinctive resistances, of taste, of training, of blind inherited scruples, rose against the other feeling. Her strongest sense was one of personal contamination.

She moved away, as though to put as much distance as possible between herself and her visitor. "I know nothing of these letters," she said; "I have no idea why you have brought them here."

Mrs. Haffen faced her steadily. "I'll tell you why, Miss. I brought 'em to you to sell, because I ain't got no other way of raising money, and if we don't pay our rent by tomorrow night we'll be put out. I never done anythin' of the kind before, and if you'd speak to Mr. Selden or to Mr. Rosedale about getting Haffen taken on again at the Benedick—I seen you talking to Mr. Rosedale at the steps that day you come out of Mr. Selden's rooms——"

The blood rushed to Lily's forehead. She understood now—Mrs. Haffen supposed her to be the writer of the letters. In the first leap of her anger she was about to ring and order the woman out; but an obscure impulse restrained her. The mention of Selden's name had started a new train of thought. Bertha Dorset's letters were nothing to her—they might go where the current of chance carried them! But Selden was inextricably involved in their fate. Men do not, at worst, suffer much from such exposure; and in this instance the flash of divination which had carried the meaning of the letters to Lily's brain had revealed also that they were appeals—repeated and therefore probably unanswered— for the renewal of a tie which time had evidently relaxed. Nevertheless, the fact that the correspondence had been allowed to fall into strange hands would convict Selden of negligence in a matter where the world holds it least pardonable; and there were graver risks to consider where a man of Dorset's ticklish balance was concerned.

If she weighed all these things it was unconsciously: she was aware only of feeling that Selden would wish the letters rescued, and that therefore she must obtain possession of them. Beyond that her mind did not travel. She had, indeed, a quick vision of returning the packet to Bertha Dorset, and of the opportunities the restitution offered; but this thought lit up abysses from which she shrank back ashamed.

Meanwhile Mrs. Haffen, prompt to perceive her hesitation, had already opened the packet and ranged its contents on the table. All the letters had been pieced together with strips of thin paper. Some were in small fragments, the others merely torn in half. Though there were not many, thus spread out they nearly covered the table. Lily's glance fell on a word here and there—then she said in a low voice: "What do you wish me to pay you?"

Mrs. Haffen's face reddened with satisfaction. It was clear that the young lady was badly frightened, and Mrs. Haffen was the woman to make the most of such fears. Anticipating an easier victory than she had foreseen, she named an exorbitant sum.

But Miss Bart showed herself a less ready prey than might have been expected from her imprudent opening. She refused to pay the price named, and after a moment's hesitation, met it by a counter-offer of half the amount.

Mrs. Haffen immediately stiffened. Her hand traveled toward the outspread letters, and folding them slowly, she made as though to restore them to their wrapping.

"I guess they're worth more to you than to me, Miss, but the poor has got to live as well as the rich," she observed sententiously.

Lily was throbbing with fear, but the insinuation fortified her resistance.

"You are mistaken," she said indifferently. "I have offered all I am willing to give for the letters; but there may be other ways of getting them."

Mrs. Haffen raised a suspicious glance: she was too experienced not to know that the traffic she was engaged in had perils as great as its rewards, and she had a vision of the elaborate machinery of revenge which a word of this commanding young lady's might set in motion.

She applied the corner of her shawl to her eyes, and murmured through it that no good came of bearing too hard on the poor, but that for her part she had never been mixed up in such a business before, and that on her honor as a Christian all she and Haffen had thought of was that the letters mustn't go any farther.

Lily stood motionless, keeping between herself and the charwoman the greatest distance compatible with the need of speaking in low tones. The idea of bargaining for the letters was intolerable to her, but she knew that, if she appeared to weaken, Mrs. Haffen would at once increase her original demand.

She could never afterward recall how long the duel lasted, or what was the decisive stroke which finally, after a lapse of time recorded in minutes by the clock, in hours by the precipitate beat of her pulses, put her in possession of the letters; she knew only that the door had finally closed, and that she stood alone with the packet in her hand.

She had no idea of reading the letters; even to unfold Mrs. Haffen's dirty newspaper would have seemed degrading. But what did she intend to do with its contents? The recipient of the letters had meant to destroy them, and it was her duty to carry out his intention. She had no right to keep them—to do so was to lessen whatever merit lay in having secured their possession. But how destroy them so effectually that there should be no second risk of their falling in such hands? Mrs. Peniston's icy drawing-room grate shone with a forbidding lustre: the fire, like the lamps, was never lit except when there was company.

Miss Bart was turning to carry the letters upstairs when she heard the opening of the outer door, and her aunt entered the drawing-room. Mrs. Peniston was a small plump woman, with a colorless skin lined with trivial wrinkles. Her grey hair was arranged with precision, and her clothes looked excessively new and yet slightly old-fashioned. They were always black and tightly fitting, with an expensive glitter: she was the kind of woman who wore jet at breakfast. Lily had never seen her when she was not cuirassed in shining black, with small tight boots, and an air of being packed and ready to start; yet she never started.

She looked about the drawing-room with an expression of minute scrutiny. "I saw a streak of light under one of the blinds as I drove up: it's extraordinary that I can never teach that woman to draw them down evenly."

Having corrected the irregularity, she seated herself on one of the glossy purple arm-chairs; Mrs. Peniston always sat on a chair, never in it. Then she turned her glance to Miss Bart.

"My dear, you look tired; I suppose it's the excitement of the wedding. Cornelia Van Alstyne was full of it: Molly was there, and Gerty Farish ran in for a minute to tell us about it. I think it was odd, their serving melons before the *consommé:* a wedding breakfast should always begin with *consommé*. Molly didn't care for the bridesmaids' dresses. She had it straight from Julia Melson that they cost three hundred dollars apiece at Céleste's, but she says they didn't look it. I'm glad you decided not to be a bridesmaid; that shade of salmon-pink wouldn't have suited you."

Mrs. Peniston delighted in discussing the minutest details of festivities in which she had not taken part. Nothing would have induced her to undergo the exertion and fatigue of attending the Van Osburgh wedding, but so great was her interest in the event that, having heard two versions of it, she now prepared to extract a third from her niece. Lily, however, had been deplorably careless in noting the particulars of the entertainment. She had failed to observe the color of Mrs. Van Osburgh's gown, and could not even say whether the old Van Osburgh Sévres had been used at the bride's table: Mrs. Peniston, in short, found that she was of more service as a listener than as a narrator.

"Really, Lily, I don't see why you took the trouble to go to the wedding, if you don't remember what happened or whom you saw there. When I was a girl I used to keep the *menu* of every dinner I went to, and write the names of the people on the back; and I never threw away my cotillion favors till after your uncle's death, when it seemed unsuitable to have so many colored things about the house. I had a whole closet-full, I remember; and I can tell to this day what balls I got them at. Molly Van Alstyne reminds me of what I was at that age; it's wonderful how she notices. She was able to tell her mother exactly how the wedding-dress was cut, and we knew at once, from the fold in the back, that it must have come from Paquin."

Mrs. Peniston rose abruptly, and, advancing to the ormulu clock surmounted by a helmeted Minerva, which throned on the chimney-piece between two malachite vases, passed her lace handkerchief between the helmet and its visor.

"I knew it—the parlor-maid never dusts there!" she exclaimed, triumphantly displaying a minute spot on the handkerchief; then, reseating herself, she went on: "Molly thought Mrs. Dorset the best-dressed woman at the wedding. I've no doubt her dress *did* cost more than any one else's, but I can't quite like the idea—a combination of sable and *point de Milan*. It seems she goes to a new man in Paris, who won't take an order till his client has spent a day with him at his villa at Neuilly. He says he must study his subject's home life—a most peculiar arrangement, I should say! But Mrs. Dorset told Molly about it herself: she said the villa was full of the most exquisite things and she was really sorry to leave. Molly said she never saw her looking better; she was in tremendous spirits, and said she had made a match between Evie

Van Osburgh and Percy Gryce. She really seems to have a very good influence on young men. I hear she is interesting herself now in that silly Silverton boy, who has had his head turned by Carry Fisher, and has been gambling so dreadfully. Well, as I was saying, Evie is really engaged: Mrs. Dorset had her to stay with Percy Gryce, and managed it all, and Grace Van Osburgh is in the seventh heaven—she had almost despaired of marrying Evie."

Mrs. Peniston again paused, but this time her scrutiny addressed itself not to the furniture, but to her niece.

"Cornelia Van Alstyne was so surprised: she had heard that you were to marry young Gryce. She saw the Wetheralls just after they had stopped with you at Bellomont, and Alice Wetherall was quite sure there was an engagement. She said that when Mr. Gryce left unexpectedly one morning, they all thought he had rushed to town for the ring."

Lily rose and moved toward the door.

"I believe I *am* tired: I think I will go to bed," she said; and Mrs. Peniston, suddenly distracted by the discovery that the easel sustaining the late Mr. Peniston's crayon-portrait was not exactly in line with the sofa in front of it, presented an absent-minded brow to her kiss.

In her own room Lily turned up the gas jet and glanced toward the grate. It was as brilliantly polished as the one below, but here at least she could burn a few papers with less risk of incurring her aunt's disapproval. She made no immediate motion to do so, however, but dropping into a chair looked wearily about her. Her room was large and comfortably-furnished—it was the envy and admiration of poor Grace Stepney, who boarded; but, contrasted with the light tints and luxurious appointments of the guest-rooms where so many weeks of Lily's existence were spent, it seemed as dreary as a prison. The monumental wardrobe and bedstead of black walnut had migrated from Mr. Peniston's bedroom, and the magenta "flock" wallpaper, of a pattern dear to the early 'sixties, was hung with large steel engravings of an anecdotic character. Lily had tried to mitigate this charmless background by a few frivolous touches, in the shape of a lace-decked toilet table and a little painted desk surmounted by photographs; but the futility of the attempt struck her as she looked about the room. What a contrast to the subtle elegance of the setting she had pictured for herself—an apartment which should surpass the complicated luxury of her friends' surroundings by the whole extent of that artistic sensibility which made her feel herself their superior; in which every tint and line should combine to enhance her beauty and give distinction to her leisure! Once more the haunting sense of physical ugliness was intensified by her mental depression, so that each piece of the offending furniture seemed to thrust forth its most aggressive angle.

Her aunt's words had told her nothing new; but they had revived the vision of Bertha Dorset, smiling, flattered, victorious, holding her up to ridicule by insinuations intelligible to every member of their little group. The thought of the ridicule struck deeper than any other sensation: Lily knew every turn of the allusive jargon which could flay its victims without the shedding of blood. Her cheek burned at the recollection, and she rose and caught up the letters. She no longer meant to destroy them: that intention had been effaced by the quick corrosion of Mrs. Peniston's words.

Instead, she approached her desk, and lighting a taper, tied and sealed the packet; then she opened the wardrobe, drew out a despatch-box, and deposited the letters within it. As she did so, it struck her with a flash of irony that she was indebted to Gus Trenor for the means of buying them.

X

THE autumn dragged on monotonously. Miss Bart had received one or two notes from Judy Trenor, reproaching her for not returning to Bellomont; but she replied evasively, alleging the obligation to remain with her aunt. In truth, however, she was fast wearying of her solitary existence with Mrs. Peniston, and only the excitement of spending her newly-acquired money lightened the dullness of the days.

All her life Lily had seen money go out as quickly as it came in, and whatever theories she cultivated as to the prudence of setting aside a part of her gains, she had unhappily no saving vision of the risks of the opposite course. It was a keen satisfaction to feel that, for a few months at least, she would be independent of her friends' bounty, that she could show herself abroad without wondering whether some penetrating eye would detect in her dress the traces of Judy Trenor's refurbished splendor. The fact that the money freed her temporarily from all minor obligations obscured her sense of the greater one it represented, and having never before known what it was to command so large a sum, she lingered delectably over the amusement of spending it.

It was on one of these occasions that, leaving a shop where she had spent an hour of deliberation over a dressing-case of the most complicated elegance, she ran across Miss Farish, who had entered the same establishment with the modest object of having her watch repaired. Lily was feeling unusually virtuous. She had decided to defer the purchase of the dressing-case till she should receive the bill for her new opera-cloak, and the resolve made her feel much richer than when she had entered the shop. In this mood of self-approval she had a sympathetic eye for others, and she was struck by her friend's air of dejection.

Miss Farish, it appeared, had just left the committee meeting of a struggling charity in which she was interested. The object of the association was to provide comfortable lodgings, with a reading-room and other modest distractions, where young women of the class employed in down town offices might find a home when out of work, or in need of rest, and the first year's financial report showed so deplorably small a balance that Miss Farish, who was convinced of the urgency of the work, felt proportionately discouraged by the small amount of interest it aroused. The other-regarding sentiments had not been cultivated in Lily, and she was often bored by the relation of her friend's philanthropic efforts, but today her quick dramatizing fancy seized on the contrast between her own situation and that represented by some of Gerty's "cases." These were young girls, like herself; some perhaps pretty, some not without a trace of her finer sensibilities. She pictured herself leading such a life as theirs—a life in which achievement seemed as squalid as failure—and the vision made her shudder sympathetically. The price of the dressing-case was still in her pocket; and drawing out her little gold purse she slipped a liberal fraction of the amount into Miss Farish's hand.

The satisfaction derived from this act was all that the most ardent moralist could have desired. Lily felt a new interest in herself as a person of charitable instincts; she had never before thought of doing

She ran across Miss Farish.

good with the wealth she had so often dreamed of possessing, but now her horizon was enlarged by the vision of a prodigal philanthropy. Moreover, by some obscure process of logic, she felt that her momentary burst of generosity had justified all previous extravagances, and excused any in which she might subsequently indulge. Miss Farish's surprise and gratitude confirmed this feeling, and Lily parted from her with a sense of self-esteem which she naturally mistook for the fruits of altruism.

About this time she was farther cheered by an invitation to spend the Thanksgiving week at a camp in the Adirondacks. The invitation was one which, a year earlier, would have provoked a less ready response, for the party, though organized by Mrs. Fisher, was ostensibly given by a lady of obscure origin and indomitable social ambitions, whose acquaintance Lily had hitherto avoided. Now, however, she was disposed to coincide with Mrs. Fisher's view, that it didn't matter who gave the party, as long as things were well done; and doing things well (under competent direction) was Mrs. Wellington Bry's strong point. The lady (whose consort was known as "Welly" Bry on the Stock Exchange and in sporting circles) had already sacrificed one husband, and sundry minor considerations, to her determination to get on; and, having obtained a hold on Carry Fisher, she was astute enough to perceive the wisdom of committing herself entirely to that lady's guidance. Everything, accordingly, was well done, for there was no limit to Mrs. Fisher's prodigality when she was not spending her own money, and as she remarked to her pupil, a good cook was the best introduction to society. If the company was not as select as the *cuisine,* the Welly Brys at least had the satisfaction of figuring for the first time in the society columns in company with one or two noticeable names; and foremost among these was of course Miss Bart's. The young lady was treated by her hosts with corresponding deference; and she was in the mood when such attentions are acceptable, whatever their source. Mrs. Bry's admiration was a mirror in which Lily's self-complacency recovered its lost outline. No insect hangs its nest on threads as frail as those which will sustain the weight of human vanity; and the sense of being of importance among the insignificant was enough to restore to Miss Bart the gratifying consciousness of power. If these people paid court to her it proved that she was still conspicuous in the world to which they aspired; and she was not above a certain enjoyment in dazzling them by her fineness, in developing their puzzled perception of her superiorities.

Perhaps, however, her enjoyment proceeded more than she was aware from the physical stimulus of the excursion, the challenge of crisp cold and hard exercise, the responsive thrill of her body to the influences of the winter woods. She returned to town in a glow of rejuvenation, conscious of a clearer color in her cheeks, a fresh elasticity in her muscles. The future seemed full of a vague promise, and all her apprehensions were swept out of sight on the buoyant current of her mood.

A few days after her return to town she had the unpleasant surprise of a visit from Mr. Rosedale. He came late, at the confidential hour when the tea-table still lingers by the fire in friendly expectancy; and his manner showed a readiness to adapt itself to the intimacy of the occasion.

Lily, who had a vague sense of his being somehow connected with her lucky speculations, tried to give him the welcome he expected; but there was something in the quality of his geniality which chilled her own, and she was conscious of marking each step in their acquaintance by a fresh blunder.

Mr. Rosedale—making himself promptly at home in an adjoining easy-chair, and sipping his tea critically, with the comment: "You ought to go to my man for something really good"—appeared totally unconscious of the repugnance which kept her in frozen erectness behind the urn. It was perhaps her very manner of holding herself aloof that appealed to his collector's passion for the rare and unattainable. He gave, at any rate, no sign of resenting it and seemed prepared to supply in his own manner all the ease that was lacking in hers.

His object in calling was to ask her to go to the opera in his box on the opening night, and seeing her hesitate he said persuasively: "Mrs. Fisher is coming, and I've secured a tremendous admirer of yours, who'll never forgive me if you don't accept."

As Lily's silence left him with this allusion on his hands, he added with a confidential smile: "Gus Trenor has promised to come to town on purpose. I fancy he'd go a good deal farther for the pleasure of seeing you."

Miss Bart felt an inward motion of annoyance: it was distasteful enough to hear her name coupled with Trenor's, and on Rosedale's lips the allusion was peculiarly unpleasant.

"The Trenors are my best friends—I think we should all go a long way to see each other," she said, absorbing herself in the preparation of fresh tea.

Her visitor's smile grew increasingly intimate. "Well, I wasn't thinking of Mrs. Trenor at the moment—they say Gus doesn't always, you know." Then, dimly conscious that he had not struck the right note, he added, with a well-meant effort at diversion: "How's your luck been going in Wall Street, by the way? I hear Gus pulled off a nice little pile for you last month."

Lily put down the tea-caddy with an abrupt gesture. She felt that her hands were trembling, and clasped them on her knee to steady them; but her lip trembled too, and for a moment she was afraid the tremor might communicate itself to her voice. When she spoke, however, it was in a tone of perfect lightness.

"Ah, yes—I had a little bit of money to invest, and Mr. Trenor, who helps me about such matters, advised my putting it in stocks instead of a mortgage, as my aunt's agent wanted me to do; and as it happened, I made a lucky 'turn'—is that what you call it? For you make a great many yourself, I believe."

She was smiling back at him now, relaxing the tension of her attitude, and admitting him, by imperceptible gradations of glance and manner, a step farther toward intimacy. The protective instinct always nerved her to successful dissimulation, and it was not the first time she had used her beauty to divert attention from an inconvenient topic.

When Mr. Rosedale took leave, he carried with him, not only her acceptance of his invitation, but a general sense of having comported himself in a way calculated to advance his cause. He had always believed he had a light touch and a knowing way with women, and the prompt manner in which Miss Bart (as he would have phrased it) had "come into line," confirmed his confidence in his powers of handling the skittish sex. Her way of glossing over the transaction with Trenor he regarded at once as a tribute to his own acuteness, and a confirmation of his suspicions. The girl was evidently nervous, and Mr. Rosedale, if he saw no other means of advancing his acquaintance with her, was not above taking advantage of her nervousness.

He left Lily to a passion of disgust and fear. It seemed incredible that Gus Trenor should have spoken of her to Rosedale. With all his faults, Trenor had the safeguard of his traditions, and was the less likely to overstep them because they were so purely instinctive. But

Lily recalled with a pang that there were convivial moments when, as Judy had confided to her, Gus "talked foolishly": in one of these, no doubt, the fatal word had slipped from him. As for Rosedale, she did not, after the first shock, greatly care what conclusions he had drawn. Though usually adroit enough where her own interests were concerned, she made the mistake, not uncommon to persons in whom the social habits are instinctive, of supposing that the inability to acquire them quickly implies a general dullness. Because a blue-bottle bangs irrationally against a window-pane, the drawing-room naturalist may forget that under less artificial conditions it is capable of measuring distances and drawing conclusions with all the accuracy needful to its welfare; and the fact that Mr. Rosedale's drawing-room manner lacked perspective made Lily class him with Trenor and the other dull men she knew, and assume that a little flattery, and the occasional acceptance of his hospitality, would suffice to render him innocuous. However, there could be no doubt of the expediency of showing herself in his box on the opening night of the opera; and after all, since Judy Trenor had promised to take him up that winter, it was as well to reap the advantage of being first in the field.

For a day or two after Rosedale's visit, Lily's thoughts were dogged by the consciousness of Trenor's shadowy claim, and she wished she had a clearer notion of the exact nature of the transaction which seemed to have put her in his power; but her mind shrank from any unusual application, and she was always helplessly puzzled by figures. Moreover she had not seen Trenor since the day of the Van Osburgh wedding, and in his continued absence the trace of Rosedale's words was soon effaced by other impressions.

When the opening night of the opera came, her apprehensions had so completely vanished that the sight of Trenor's ruddy countenance in the back of Mr. Rosedale's box filled her with a sense of pleasant reassurance. Lily had not quite reconciled herself to the necessity of appearing as Rosedale's guest on so conspicuous an occasion, and it was a relief to find herself supported by any one of her own set—for Mrs. Fisher's social habits were too promiscuous for her presence to justify Miss Bart's.

To Lily, always inspirited by the prospect of showing her beauty in public, and conscious tonight of all the added enhancements of dress, the insistency of Trenor's gaze merged itself in the general stream of admiring looks of which she felt herself the center. Ah, it was good to be young, to be radiant, to glow with the sense of slenderness, strength and elasticity, of well-poised lines and happy tints, to feel one's self lifted to a height apart by that incommunicable grace which is the bodily counterpart of genius!

All means seemed justifiable to attain such an end, or rather, by a happy shifting of lights with which practice had familiarized Miss Bart, the cause shrank to a pinpoint in the general brightness of the effect. But brilliant young ladies, a little blinded by their own effulgence, are apt to forget that the modest satellite drowned in their light is still performing its own revolutions and generating heat at its own rate. If Lily's poetic enjoyment of the moment was undisturbed by the base thought that her gown and opera cloak had been indirectly paid for by Gus Trenor, the latter had not sufficient poetry in his composition to lose sight of these prosaic facts. He knew only that he had never seen Lily look smarter in her life, that there wasn't a woman in the house who showed off good clothes as she did, and that hitherto he, to whom she owed the opportunity of making this display, had reaped no return beyond that of gazing at her in company with several hundred other pairs of eyes.

It came to Lily therefore as a disagreeable surprise when, in the back of the box, where they found themselves alone between two acts, Trenor said, without preamble, and in a tone of sulky authority: "Look here, Lily, how is a fellow ever to see anything of you? I'm in town three or four days in the week, and you know a line to the club will always find me, but you don't seem to remember my existence nowadays unless you want to get a tip out of me."

The fact that the remark was in distinctly bad taste did not make it any easier to answer, for Lily was vividly aware that it was not the moment for that drawing up of her slim figure and surprised lifting of the brows by which she usually quelled incipient signs of familiarity.

"I'm very much flattered by your wanting to see me," she returned, essaying lightness instead, "but, unless you have mislaid my address, it would have been easy to find me any afternoon at my aunt's—in fact, I rather expected you to look me up there."

If she hoped to mollify him by this last concession the attempt was a failure, for he only replied, with the familiar lowering of the brows that made him look his dullest when he was angry: "Hang going to your aunt's, and wasting the afternoon listening to a lot of other chaps talking to you! You know I'm not the kind to sit in a crowd and jaw—I'd always rather clear out when that sort of circus is going on. But why can't we go off somewhere on a little lark together—a nice quiet little expedition like that drive at Bellomont, the day you met me at the station?"

He leaned unpleasantly close in order to convey this suggestion, and she fancied she caught a significant aroma which explained the dark flush on his face and the glistening dampness of his forehead.

The idea that any rash answer might provoke an unpleasant outburst tempered her disgust with caution, and she answered with a laugh: "I don't see how one can very well take country drives in town, but I am not always surrounded by an admiring throng, and if you will let me know what afternoon you are coming I will arrange things so that we can have a nice quiet talk."

"Hang talking! That's what you always say," returned Trenor, whose expletives lacked variety. "You put me off with that at the Van Osburgh wedding—but the plain English of it is that, now you've got what you wanted out of me, you'd rather have any other fellow about."

His voice had risen sharply with the last words, and Lily flushed with annoyance, but she kept command of the situation and laid a persuasive hand on his arm.

"Don't be foolish, Gus; I can't let you talk to me in that ridiculous way. If you really want to see me, why shouldn't we take a walk in the Park some afternoon? I agree with you that it's amusing to be rustic in town, and if you like I'll meet you there, and we'll go and feed the squirrels, and you shall take me out on the lake in the steam-gondola."

She smiled as she spoke, letting her eyes rest on his in a way that took the edge from her banter and made him suddenly malleable to her will.

"All right, then: that's a go. Will you come tomorrow? Tomorrow at three o'clock, at the end of the Mall? I'll be there sharp, remember; you won't go back on me, Lily?"

But to Miss Bart's relief the repetition of her promise was cut short by the opening of the box door to admit George Dorset.

Trenor sulkily yielded his place, and Lily turned a brilliant smile on the newcomer. She had not talked with Dorset since their visit at Bellomont, but something in his look and manner told her that he recalled the friendly footing on which they had last met. He was not a man to whom the expression of admiration came easily: his long sallow face and distrustful eyes seemed always barricaded against the expansive emotions. But, where her own influence was concerned, Lily's intuitions sent out thread-like feelers, and as she made room for him on the narrow sofa she was sure he found a dumb pleasure in being near her. Few women took the trouble to make themselves agreeable to Dorset, and Lily had been kind to him at Bellomont, and was now smiling on him with a divine renewal of kindness.

"Well, here we are, in for another six months of caterwauling," he began complainingly. "Not a shade of difference between this year and last, except that the women have got new clothes and the singers haven't got new voices. My wife's musical, you know—puts me through a course of this every winter. It isn't so bad on Italian nights—then she comes late, and there's time to digest. But when they give Wagner we have to rush dinner, and I pay up for it. And the draughts are damnable—asphyxia in front and pleurisy in the back. There's Trenor leaving the box without drawing the curtain! With a hide like that draughts don't make any difference. Did you ever watch Trenor eat? If you did, you'd wonder why he's alive; I suppose he's leather inside too.—But I came to say that my wife wants you to come down to our place next Sunday. Do for heaven's sake say yes. She's got a lot of bores coming—intellectual ones, I mean; that's her new line, you know, and I'm not sure it ain't worse than the music. Some of 'em have long hair, and they start an argument with the soup, and don't notice when things are handed to them. The consequence is the dinner gets cold, and I have dyspepsia. That silly ass Silverton brings them to the house—he writes poetry, you know, and Bertha and he are getting tremendously thick. She could write better than any of 'em if she chose, and I don't blame her for wanting clever fellows about; all I say is: 'Don't let me see 'em eat!'" The gist of this strange communication gave Lily a distinct thrill of pleasure. Under ordinary circumstances, there would have been nothing surprising in an invitation from Bertha Dorset; but since the Bellomont episode an unavowed hostility had kept the two women apart. Now, with a start of inner wonder, Lily felt that her thirst for retaliation had died out. *If you would forgive your enemy,* says the Malay proverb, *first inflict a hurt on him;* and Lily was experiencing the truth of the apothegm. If she had destroyed Mrs. Dorset's letters, she might have continued to hate her; but the fact that they remained in her possession had fed her resentment to satiety.

She uttered a smiling acceptance, hailing in the renewal of the tie an escape from Trenor's importunities.

XI

MEANWHILE the holidays had gone by and the season was beginning. Fifth Avenue had become a nightly torrent of carriages surging upward to the fashionable quarters about the Park, where illuminated windows and outspread awnings betokened the usual routine of hospitality. Other tributary currents crossed the main stream, bearing their freight to the theaters, restaurants or opera; and Mrs. Peniston, from the secluded watch-tower of her upper window, could tell to a nicety just when the chronic volume of sound was increased by the sudden influx setting toward a Van Osburgh ball, or when the multiplication of wheels meant merely that the opera was over, or that there was a big supper at Sherry's.

Mrs. Peniston followed the rise and culmination of the season as keenly as the most active sharer in its gaieties; and, as a looker-on, she enjoyed opportunities of comparison and generalization such as those who take part must proverbially forego. No one could have kept a more accurate record of social fluctuations, or have put a more unerring finger on the distinguishing features of each season: its dullness, its extravagance, its lack of balls or excess of divorces. She had a special memory for the vicissitudes of the "new people" who rose to the surface with each recurring tide, and were either submerged beneath its rush or landed triumphantly beyond the reach of envious breakers; and she was apt to display a remarkable retrospective insight into their ultimate fate, so that, when they had fulfilled their destiny, she was almost always able to say to Grace

Stepney—the recipient of her prophecies—that she had known exactly what would happen. This particular season Mrs. Peniston would have characterized as that in which everybody "felt poor" except the Welly Brys and Mr. Simon Rosedale. It had been a bad autumn in Wall Street, where prices fell in accordance with that peculiar law which proves railway stocks and bales of cotton to be more sensitive to the allotment of executive power than many estimable citizens trained to all the advantages of self-government. Even fortunes supposed to be independent of the market either betrayed a secret dependence on it, or suffered from a sympathetic affection: fashion sulked in its country-houses, or came to town incognito, general entertainments were discountenanced, and informality and short dinners became the fashion.

But society, amused for a while at playing Cinderella, soon wearied of the hearthside rôle, and welcomed the Fairy God-mother in the shape of any magician powerful enough to turn the shrunken pumpkin back again into the golden coach. The mere fact of growing richer at a time when most people's investments are shrinking, is calculated to attract envious attention; and according to Wall Street rumors, Welly Bry and Rosedale had found the secret of performing this miracle.

Rosedale, in particular, was said to have doubled his fortune, and there was talk of his buying the newly-finished house of one of the victims of the crash, who, in the space of twelve short months, had made the same number of millions, built a house in Fifth Avenue, filled a picture-gallery with old masters, entertained all New York in it, and been smuggled out of the country between a trained nurse and a doctor, while his creditors mounted guard over the old masters, and his guests explained to each other that they had dined with him only because they wanted to see the pictures. Mr. Rosedale meant to have a less meteoric career. He knew he should have to go slowly, and the instincts of his race fitted him to suffer rebuffs and put up with delays. But he was prompt to perceive that the general dullness of the season afforded him an unusual opportunity to shine, and he set about with patient industry to form a background for his growing glory. Mrs. Fisher was of immense service to him at this period. She had set off so many newcomers on the social stage that she was like one of those pieces of stock scenery which tell the experienced spectator exactly what is going to take place. But Mr. Rosedale wanted, in the long run, a more individual environment. He was sensitive to shades of difference which Miss Bart would never have credited him with perceiving, because he had no corresponding variations of manner; and it was becoming more and more clear to him that Miss Bart herself possessed precisely the complementary qualities needed to round off his social personality.

Such details did not fall within the range of Mrs. Peniston's vision. Like many minds of panoramic sweep, hers was apt to overlook the *minutiae* of the foreground, and she was much more likely to know where Carry Fisher had found the Welly Brys' *chef* for them, than what was happening to her own niece. She was not, however, without purveyors of information ready to supplement her deficiencies. Grace Stepney's mind was like a kind of moral fly-paper, to which the buzzing items of gossip were drawn by a fatal attraction, and where they hung fast in the toils of an inexorable memory. Lily would have been surprised to know how many trivial facts concerning herself were lodged in Miss Stepney's head. She was quite aware that she was of interest to dingy people, but she assumed that there is only one form of dinginess, and that admiration for brilliancy is the natural expression of its inferior state. She knew that Gerty Farish admired her blindly, and therefore supposed that she inspired the same sentiments in Grace Stepney, whom she classified as a Gerty Farish without the saving traits of youth and enthusiasm.

In reality, the two differed from each other as much as they differed from the object of their mutual contemplation. Miss Farish's heart was a fountain of tender illusions, Miss Stepney's a precise register of facts as manifested in their relation to herself. She had sensibilities which, to Lily, would have seemed comic in a person with a freckled nose and red eye-lids, who lived in a boarding-house and admired Mrs. Peniston's drawing-room; but poor Grace's limitations gave them a more concentrated inner life, as poor soil starves certain plants into intenser efflorescence. She had in truth no abstract propensity to malice: she did not dislike Lily because the latter was brilliant and predominant, but because she thought that Lily disliked her. It is less mortifying to believe one's self unpopular than insignificant, and vanity prefers to assume that indifference is a latent form of unfriendliness. Even such scant civilities as Lily accorded to Mr. Rosedale would have made Miss Stepney her friend for life; but how could she foresee that such a friend was worth cultivating?

How, moreover, can a young woman who has never been ignored measure the pang which this injury inflicts? And, lastly, how could Lily, accustomed to choose between a pressure of engagements, guess that she had mortally offended Miss Stepney by causing her to be excluded from one of Mrs. Peniston's infrequent dinner-parties?

Mrs. Peniston disliked giving dinners, but she had a high sense of family obligation, and on the Jack Stepneys' return from their honeymoon she felt it incumbent upon her to light the drawing-room lamps and extract her best silver from the Safe Deposit vaults. Mrs. Peniston's rare entertainments were preceded by days of heart-rending vacillation as to every detail of the feast, from the seating of the guests to the pattern of the table-cloth, and in the course of one of these preliminary discussions she had imprudently suggested to her cousin Grace that, as the dinner was a family affair, she might be included in it. For a week the prospect had lighted up Miss Stepney's colorless existence; then she had been given to understand that it would be more convenient to have her another day. Miss Stepney knew exactly what had happened. Lily, to whom family reunions were occasions of unalloyed dullness, had persuaded her aunt that a dinner of "smart" people would be much more to the taste of the young couple, and Mrs. Peniston, who leaned helplessly on her niece in social matters, had been prevailed upon to pronounce Grace's exile. After all, Grace could come any other day; why should she mind being put off?

It was precisely because Miss Stepney could come any other day—and because she knew her relations were in the secret of her unoccupied evenings—that this incident loomed gigantically on her horizon. She was aware that she had Lily to thank for it; and dull resentment was turned to active animosity.

Mrs. Peniston, on whom she had looked in a day or two after the dinner, laid down her crochet-work and turned abruptly from her oblique survey of Fifth Avenue.

"Gus Trenor?—Lily and Gus Trenor?" she said, growing so suddenly pale that her visitor was almost alarmed.

"Oh, cousin Julia . . . of course I don't mean . . . "

"I don't know what you *do* mean," said Mrs. Peniston, with a frightened quiver in her small fretful voice. "Such things were never heard of in my day. And my own niece! I'm not sure I understand you. Do people say he's in love with her?"

Mrs. Peniston's horror was genuine. Though she boasted an unequalled familiarity with the secret chronicles of society, she had the innocence of the school-girl who regards wickedness as a part of "history," and to whom it never occurs that the scandals she reads of in lesson-hours may be repeating themselves in the next street. Mrs. Peniston had kept her imagination shrouded, like the drawing-room furniture. She knew, of course, that society was "very much changed," and that many women her mother would have thought "peculiar" were now in a position to be critical about their visiting-lists; she had discussed the perils of divorce with her rector, and had felt thankful at times that Lily was still unmarried; but the idea that any scandal could attach to a young girl's name, above all that it could be lightly coupled with that of a married man, was so new to her that she was as much aghast as if she had been accused of leaving her carpets down all summer, or of violating any of the other cardinal laws of house-keeping.

Miss Stepney, when her first fright had subsided, began to feel the superiority that greater breadth of mind confers. It was really pitiable to be as ignorant of the world as Mrs. Peniston!

She smiled at the latter's question. "People always say unpleasant things—and certainly they're a great deal together. A friend of mine met them the other afternoon in the Park—quite late, after the lamps were lit. It's a pity Lily makes herself so conspicuous."

"Conspicuous!" gasped Mrs. Peniston. She bent forward, lowering her voice to mitigate the horror. "What sort of things do they say? That he means to get a divorce and marry her?"

Grace Stepney laughed outright. "Dear me, no! He would hardly do that. It—it's a flirtation—nothing more."

"A flirtation? Between my niece and a married man? Do you mean to tell me that, with Lily's looks and advantages, she could find no better use for her time than to waste it on a fat stupid man almost old enough to be her father?" This argument had such a convincing ring that it gave Mrs. Peniston sufficient reassurance to pick up her work, while she waited for Grace Stepney to rally her scattered forces.

But Miss Stepney was on the spot in an instant. "That's the worst of it—people say she isn't wasting her time! Everyone knows, as you say, that Lily is too handsome and—and charming—to devote herself to a man like Gus Trenor unless——"

"Unless?" echoed Mrs. Peniston.

Her visitor drew breath nervously. It was agreeable to shock Mrs. Peniston, but not to shock her to the verge of anger. Miss Stepney was not sufficiently familiar with the classic drama to have recalled in advance how bearers of bad tidings are proverbially received, but she now had a rapid vision of forfeited dinners and a reduced wardrobe as the possible consequence of her disinterestedness. To the honor of her sex, however, hatred of Lily prevailed over more personal considerations. Mrs. Peniston had chosen the wrong moment to boast of her niece's charms.

"Unless," said Grace, leaning forward to speak with low-toned emphasis, "unless there are material advantages to be gained by making herself agreeable to him."

She felt that the moment was tremendous, and remembered suddenly that Mrs. Peniston's black brocade, with the cut jet fringe, would have been hers at the end of the season.

Mrs. Peniston put down her work again. Another aspect of the same idea had presented itself to her, and she felt that it was beneath her dignity to have her nerves racked by a dependent relative who wore her old clothes.

"If you take pleasure in annoying me by mysterious insinuations," she said coldly, "you might at least have chosen a more suitable time than just as I am recovering from the strain of giving a large dinner."

The mention of the dinner dispelled Miss Stepney's last scruples. "I don't know why I should be accused of taking pleasure in telling you about Lily. I was sure I shouldn't get any thanks for it," she returned with a flare of temper. "But I have some family feeling left, and as you are the only person who has any authority over Lily, I thought you ought to know what is being said of her."

"Well," said Mrs. Peniston, "what I complain of is that you haven't told me yet what *is* being said."

"I didn't suppose I should have to put it so plainly. People say that Gus Trenor pays her bills."

"Pays her bills—her bills?" Mrs. Peniston broke into a laugh. "I can't imagine where you can have picked up such rubbish. Lily has her own income—and I provide for her very handsomely——"

"Oh, we all know that," interposed Miss Stepney drily. "But Lily wears a great many smart gowns——"

"I like her to be well-dressed—it's only suitable!"

"Certainly; but then there are her gambling debts besides."

Miss Stepney, in the beginning, had not meant to bring up this point; but Mrs. Peniston had only her own incredulity to blame. She was like the stiff-necked unbelievers of Scripture, who must be annihilated to be convinced.

"Gambling debts? Lily?" Mrs. Peniston's voice shook with anger and bewilderment. She wondered whether Grace Stepney had gone out of her mind. "What do you mean by her gambling debts?"

"Simply that if one plays bridge for money in Lily's set one is liable to lose a great deal—and I don't suppose Lily always wins."

"Who told you that my niece played cards for money?"

"Mercy, cousin Julia, don't look at me as if I were trying to turn you against Lily! Everybody knows she is crazy about bridge. Mrs. Gryce told me herself that it was her gambling that frightened Percy Gryce—it seems he was really taken with her at first. But, of course, among Lily's friends it's quite the custom for girls to play for money. In fact, people are inclined to excuse her on that account—"

"To excuse her for what?"

"For being hard up—and accepting attentions from men like Gus Trenor—and George Dorset——"

Mrs. Peniston gave another cry. "George Dorset? Is there anyone else? I should like to know the worst, if you please."

"Don't put it in that way, cousin Julia. Lately Lily has been a good deal with the Dorsets, and he seems to admire her—but of course that's only natural. And I'm sure there is no truth in the horrid things people say; but she *has* been spending a great deal of money this winter. Evie Van Osburgh was at Céleste's ordering her trousseau the other day—yes, the marriage takes place next month—and she told me that Céleste showed her the most exquisite things she was just sending home to Lily. And people say that Judy Trenor has quarrelled with her on account of Gus; but I'm sure I'm sorry I spoke, though I only meant it as a kindness."

Mrs. Peniston's genuine incredulity enabled her to dismiss Miss Stepney with a disdain which boded ill for that lady's prospect of succeeding to the black brocade; but minds impenetrable to reason have generally some crack through which suspicion filters, and her visitor's insinuations did not glide off as easily as she had expected. Mrs. Peniston disliked scenes, and her determination to avoid them had always led her to hold herself aloof from the details of Lily's life. In her youth, girls had not been supposed to require close supervision. They were generally assumed to be taken up with the legitimate business of courtship and marriage, and interference in such affairs on the part of their natural guardians was considered as unwarrantable as a spectator's suddenly joining in a game. There had of course been "fast" girls even in Mrs. Peniston's early experience; but their fastness, at worst, was understood to be a mere excess of animal spirits, against which there could be no graver charge than that of being "unladylike." The modern fastness appeared synonymous with immorality, and the mere idea of immorality was as offensive to Mrs. Peniston as a smell of cooking in the drawing-room: it was one of the conceptions her mind refused to admit.

She had no immediate intention of repeating to Lily what she had heard, or even of trying to ascertain its truth by means of discreet interrogation. To do so might be to provoke a scene; and a scene, in the shaken state of Mrs. Peniston's nerves, with the effects of her dinner not worn off, and her mind still tremulous with new impressions, was a risk she deemed it her duty to avoid. But there remained in her thoughts a settled deposit of resentment against her niece, all the denser because it was not to be cleared by explanation or discussion. It was horrible of a young girl to let herself be talked about; however unfounded the charges against her, she must be to blame for their having been made. Mrs. Peniston felt as if there had been a contagious illness in the house, and she was doomed to sit shivering among her contaminated furniture.

XII

MISS BART had in fact been treading a devious way, and none of her critics could have been more alive to the fact than herself; but she had a fatalistic sense of being drawn from one wrong turning to another, without ever perceiving the right road till it was too late to take it.

Lily, who considered herself above narrow prejudices, had not imagined that the fact of letting Gus Trenor make a little money for her would ever disturb her self-complacency. And the fact in itself still seemed harmless enough; only it was a fertile source of harmful complications. As she exhausted the amusement of spending the money these complications became more pressing, and Lily, whose mind could be severely logical in tracing the causes of her ill-luck to others, justified herself by the thought that she owed all her troubles to the enmity of Bertha Dorset. This enmity, however, had apparently expired in a renewal of friendliness between the two women. Lily's visit to the Dorsets had resulted, for both, in the discovery that they could be of use to each other; and the civilized instinct finds a subtler pleasure in making use of its antagonist than in confounding him. Mrs. Dorset was, in fact, engaged in a new sentimental experiment, of which Mrs. Fisher's late property, Ned Silverton, was the rosy victim; and at such moments, as Judy Trenor had once remarked, she felt a peculiar need of distracting her husband's attention. Dorset was as difficult to amuse as a savage; but even his self-engrossment was not proof against Lily's arts, or rather these were especially adapted to soothe an uneasy egoism. Her experience with Percy Gryce stood her in good stead in ministering to Dorsets humors, and if the incentive to please was less urgent, the difficulties of her situation were teaching her to make much of minor opportunities.

Intimacy with the Dorsets was not likely to lessen such difficulties on the material side. Mrs. Dorset had none of Judy Trenor's lavish impulses, and Dorset's admiration was not likely to express itself in financial "tips" even had Lily cared to renew her experiences in that line. What she required, for the moment, of the Dorsets' friendship, was simply its social sanction. She knew that people were beginning to talk of her; but this fact did not alarm her as it had alarmed Mrs. Peniston. In her set such gossip was not unusual, and a handsome girl who flirted with a married man was merely assumed to be pressing to the limit of her opportunities. It was Trenor himself who frightened her. Their walk in the Park had not been a success. Trenor had married young, and since his marriage his intercourse with women had not taken the form of the sentimental small-talk which doubles upon itself like the paths in a maze. He was first puzzled and then irritated to find himself always led back to the same starting-point, and Lily felt that she was gradually losing control of the situation. Trenor was in truth in an unmanageable mood. In spite of his understanding with Rosedale he had been somewhat heavily "touched" by the fall in stocks; his household expenses weighed on him, and he seemed to be meeting, on all sides, a sullen opposition to his wishes, instead of the easy good luck he had hitherto encountered.

Mrs. Trenor was still at Bellomont, keeping the town-house open, and descending on it now and then for a taste of the world, but preferring the recurrent excitement of week-end parties to the restrictions of a dull season. Since the holidays she had not urged Lily to return to Bellomont, and the first time they met in town Lily fancied there was a shade of coldness in her manner. Was it merely the expression of her displeasure at Miss Bart's neglect, or had disquieting rumors reached her? The latter contingency seemed improbable, yet Lily was not without a sense of uneasiness. If her roaming sympathies had struck root anywhere, it was in her friendship with Judy Trenor. She believed in the sincerity of her friend's affection, though it sometimes showed itself in self-interested ways, and she shrank with peculiar reluctance from any risk of estranging it. But, aside from this, she was keenly conscious of the way in which such an estrangement would react on herself. The fact that Gus Trenor was Judy's husband was at times Lily's strongest reason for disliking him, and for resenting the obligation under which he had placed her.

To set her doubts at rest, Miss Bart, soon after the New Year, "proposed" herself for a week-end at Bellomont. She had learned in advance that the presence of a large party would protect her from too great assiduity on Trenor's part, and his wife's telegraphic "come by all means" seemed to assure her of her usual welcome.

Judy received her amicably. The cares of a large party always prevailed over personal feelings, and Lily saw no change in her hostess's manner. Nevertheless, she was soon aware that the experiment of coming to Bellomont was destined not to be successful. The party was made up of what Mrs. Trenor called "poky people"—her generic name for persons who did not play bridge—and, it being her habit to group all such obstructionists in one class, she usually invited them together, regardless of their other characteristics. The result was apt to be an irreducible combination of persons having no other quality in common than their abstinence from bridge, and

The recurrent excitement of week-end parties.

the antagonisms developed in a group lacking the one taste which might have amalgamated them, were in this case aggravated by bad weather, and by the ill-concealed boredom of their host and hostess. In such emergencies, Judy would usually have turned to Lily to fuse the discordant elements; and Miss Bart, assuming that such a service was expected of her, threw herself into it with her accustomed zeal. But at the outset she perceived a subtle resistance to her efforts. If Mrs. Trenor's manner toward her was unchanged, there was certainly a faint coldness in that of the other ladies. An occasional caustic allusion to "your friends the Wellington Brys," or to "the little Jew who has bought the Greiner house—some one told us you knew him, Miss Bart,"—showed Lily that she was in disfavor with that portion of society which, while contributing least to its amusement, has assumed the right to decide what forms that amusement shall take. The indication was a slight one, and a year ago Lily would have smiled at it, trusting to the charm of her personality to dispel any prejudice against her. But now she had grown more sensitive to criticism and less confident in her power of disarming it. She knew, moreover, that if the ladies at Bellomont permitted themselves to criticize her friends openly, it was a proof that they were not afraid of subjecting her to the same treatment behind her back. The nervous dread lest anything in Trenor's manner should seem to justify their disapproval made her seek every pretext for avoiding him, and she left Bellomont conscious of having failed in every purpose which had taken her there.

In town she returned to preoccupations which, for the moment, had the happy effect of banishing troublesome thoughts. The Welly Brys, after much debate, and anxious counsel with their newly acquired friends, had decided on the bold move of giving a general entertainment. To attack society collectively, when one's means of approach are limited to a few acquaintances, is like advancing into a strange country with an insufficient number of scouts; but such rash tactics have sometimes led to brilliant victories, and the Brys had determined to put their fate to the touch. Mrs. Fisher, to whom they had entrusted the conduct of the affair, had decided that *tableaux vivants* and expensive music were the two baits most likely to attract the desired prey, and after prolonged negotiations, and the kind of wire-pulling in which she was known to excel, she had induced a dozen fashionable women to exhibit themselves in a series of pictures which, by a farther miracle of persuasion, the distinguished portrait painter, Paul Morpeth, had been prevailed upon to organize.

Lily was in her element on such occasions. Under Morpeth's guidance her vivid plastic sense, hitherto nurtured on no higher food than dress-making and upholstery, found eager expression in the disposal of draperies, the study of attitudes, the shifting of lights and shadows. Her dramatic instinct was roused by the choice of subjects, and the gorgeous reproductions of historic dress stirred an imagination which only visual impressions could reach. But keenest of all was the exhilaration of displaying her own beauty under a new aspect: of showing that her loveliness was no mere fixed quality, but an element shaping all emotions to fresh forms of grace.

Mrs. Fisher's measures had been well-taken, and society, surprised in a dull moment, succumbed to the temptation of Mrs. Bry's hospitality. The protesting minority were forgotten in the throng which abjured and came; and the audience was almost as brilliant as the show.

Lawrence Selden was among those who had yielded to the proffered inducements. If he did not often act on the accepted social axiom that a man may go where he pleases, it was because he had long since learned that his pleasures were mainly to be found in a small group of the like-minded. But he enjoyed spectacular effects, and was not insensible to the part money plays in their production: all he asked was that the very rich should live up to their calling as stage-managers, and not spend their money in a dull way. This the Brys could certainly not be charged with doing. Their recently built house, whatever it might lack as a frame for domesticity, was almost as well-designed for the display of a festal assemblage as one of those airy pleasure-halls which the Italian architects improvised to set off the hospitality of princes. The air of improvisation was in fact strikingly present: so recent, so rapidly-evoked was the whole *mise-en-scène* that one had to touch the marble columns to learn they were not of cardboard, to seat one's self in one of the damask-and-gold armchairs to be sure it was not painted against the wall.

Selden, who had put one of these seats to the test, found himself, from an angle of the ballroom, surveying the scene with frank enjoyment. The company, in obedience to the decorative instinct which calls for fine clothes in fine surroundings, had dressed rather with an eye to Mrs. Bry's background than to herself. The seated throng, filling the immense room without undue crowding, presented a surface of rich tissues and jewelled shoulders in harmony with the festooned and gilded walls, and the flushed splendors of the Venetian ceiling. At the farther end of the room a stage had been constructed behind a proscenium arch curtained with folds of old damask; but in the pause before the parting of the folds there was little thought of what they might reveal, for every woman who had accepted Miss Bry's invitation was engaged in trying to find out how many of her friends had done the same.

Gerty Farish, seated next to Selden, was lost in that indiscriminate and uncritical enjoyment so irritating to Miss Bart's finer perceptions. It may be that Selden's nearness had something to do with the quality of his cousin's pleasure; but Miss Farish was so little accustomed to refer her enjoyment of such scenes to her own share in them, that she was merely conscious of a deeper sense of contentment.

"Wasn't it dear of Lily to get me an invitation? Of course it would never have occurred to Carry Fisher to put me on the list, and I should have been so sorry to miss seeing it all—and especially Lily herself. Someone told me the ceiling was by Veronese—you would know, of course, Lawrence. I suppose it's very beautiful, but his women are so dreadfully fat. Goddesses? Well, I can only say that if they'd been mortals and had to wear corsets, it would have been better for them. I think our women are much handsomer. And this room is wonderfully becoming—every one looks so well! Did you ever see such jewels? Do look at Mrs. George Dorset's pearls—I suppose the smallest of them would pay the rent of our Girls' Club for a year. Not that I ought to complain about the club; every one has been so wonderfully kind. Did I tell you that Lily had given us three hundred dollars? Wasn't it splendid of her? And then she collected a lot of money from her friends—Mrs. Bry gave us five hundred, and Mr. Rosedale a thousand. I wish Lily were not so nice to Mr. Rosedale, but she says it's no use being rude to him, because he doesn't see the difference. She really can't bear to hurt people's feelings—it makes me so angry when I hear her called cold and conceited! The girls at the club don't call her that. Do you know she has been there with me twice?—yes, Lily! And you should have seen their eyes! One of them said it was as good as a day in the country just to look at her. And she sat there, and laughed and talked with them—not a bit as if she were being *charitable,* you know, but as if she liked it as much as they did. They've been asking ever since when she's coming back; and she's promised me——oh!"

Miss Farish's confidences were cut short by the parting of the curtain on the first *tableau*—a group of nymphs dancing across flower-strewn sward in the rhythmic postures of Botticelli's Spring. *Tableaux vivants* depend for their effect not only on the happy disposal of lights and the delusive interposition of layers of gauze, but on a corresponding adjustment of the mental vision. To unfurnished minds they remain, in spite of every enhancement of art, only a superior kind of wax-works; but to the responsive fancy they may give magic glimpses of the boundary world between fact and imagination. Selden's mind was of this order: he could yield to vision-making influences as completely as a child to the spell of a fairy-tale. Mrs. Bry's *tableaux* wanted none of the qualities which go to the producing of such illusions, and under Morpeth's organizing hand the pictures succeeded each other with the rhythmic march of some splendid frieze, in which the fugitive curves of living flesh and the wandering light of young eyes have been subdued to plastic harmony without losing the charm of life.

The scenes were taken from old pictures, and the participators had been cleverly fitted with characters suited to their types. No one, for instance, could have made a more typical Goya than Carry Fisher, with her short dark-skinned face, the exaggerated glow of her eyes, the provocation of her frankly-painted smile. A brilliant Miss Smedden from Brooklyn showed to perfection the sumptuous curves of Titian's Daughter, lifting her gold salver laden with grapes above the harmonizing gold of rippled hair and rich brocade, and a young Mrs. Van Alstyne, who showed the frailer Dutch type, with high blue-veined forehead and pale eyes and lashes, made a characteristic Vandyck, in black satin, against a curtained archway. Then there were Kauffmann nymphs garlanding the altar of Love; a Veronese supper, all sheeny textures, pearl-woven heads and marble architecture; and a Watteau group of lute-playing comedians, lounging by a fountain in a sunlit glade.

Each evanescent picture touched the vision-building faculty in Selden, leading him so far down the vistas of fancy that even Gerty Farish's running commentary—"Oh, how lovely Lulu Melson looks!" or: "That must be Kate Corby, to the right there, in purple"—

did not break the spell of the illusion. Indeed, so skillfully had the personality of the actors been subdued to the scenes they figured in that even the least imaginative of the audience must have felt a thrill of contrast when the curtain suddenly parted on a picture which was simply and undisguisedly the portrait of Miss Bart.

Here there could be no mistaking the predominance of personality—the unanimous "Oh!" of the spectators was a tribute, not to the brush-work of Reynolds's "Mrs. Lloyd" but to the flesh and blood loveliness of Lily Bart. She had shown her artistic intelligence in selecting a type so like her own that she could embody the person represented without ceasing to be herself. It was as though she had stepped, not out of, but into, Reynolds's canvas, banishing the phantom of his dead beauty by the beams of her living grace. The impulse to show herself in a splendid setting—she had thought for a moment of representing Tiepolo's Cleopatra—had yielded to the truer instinct of trusting to her unassisted beauty, and she had purposely chosen a picture without distracting accessories of dress or surroundings. Her pale draperies, and the background of foliage against which she stood, served only to relieve the long dryad-like curves that swept upward from her poised foot to her lifted arm. The noble buoyancy of her attitude, its suggestion of soaring grace, revealed the touch of poetry in her beauty that Selden always felt in her presence, yet lost the sense of when he was not with her. Its expression was now so vivid that for the first time he seemed to see before him the real Lily Bart, divested of the trivialities of her little world, and catching for a moment a note of that eternal harmony of which her beauty was a part.

"Deuced bold thing to show herself in that get-up but, gad, there isn't a break in the lines anywhere, and I suppose she wanted us to know it!"

These words, uttered by that experienced connoisseur, Mr. Ned Van Alstyne, whose scented white moustache had brushed Selden's shoulder whenever the parting of the curtains presented any exceptional opportunity for the study of the female outline, affected their hearer in an unexpected way. It was not the first time that Selden had heard Lily's beauty lightly remarked on, and hitherto the tone of the comments had imperceptibly colored his view of her. But now it woke only a motion of indignant contempt. This was the world she lived in, these were the standards by which she was fated to be measured! Does one go to Caliban for a judgment on Miranda?

In the long moment before the curtain fell, he had time to feel the whole tragedy of her life. It was as though her beauty, thus detached from all that cheapened and vulgarized it, had held out suppliant hands to him from the world in which he and she had once met for a moment, and where he felt an overmastering longing to be with her again.

He was roused by the pressure of ecstatic fingers. "Wasn't she too beautiful, Lawrence? Don't you like her best in that simple dress? It makes her look like the real Lily—the Lily I know."

He met Gerty Farish's brimming gaze. "The Lily *we* know," he corrected; and his cousin, beaming at the implied understanding, exclaimed joyfully: "I'll tell her that! She always says you dislike her."

The performance over, Selden's first impulse was to seek Miss Bart. During the interlude of music which succeeded the *tableaux,* the actors had seated themselves here and there in the audience, diversifying its conventional appearance by the varied picturesqueness of their dress. Lily, however, was not among them, and her absence served to protract the effect she had produced on Selden: it would have broken the spell to see her too soon in the surroundings from which accident had so happily detached her. They had not met since the day of the Van Osburgh wedding, and on his side the avoidance had been intentional. Tonight, however, he knew that, sooner or later, he should find himself at her side; and though he let the dispersing crowd drift him whither it would, without making an immediate effort to reach her, his procrastination was not due to any lingering resistance, but to the desire to luxuriate a moment in the sense of complete surrender.

Lily had not an instant's doubt as to the meaning of the murmur greeting her appearance. No other *tableau* had been received with that precise note of approval: it had obviously been called forth by herself, and not by the picture she impersonated. She had feared at the last moment that she was risking too much in dispensing with the advantages of a more sumptuous setting, and the completeness of her triumph gave her an intoxicating sense of recovered power. Not caring to diminish the impression she had produced, she held herself aloof from the audience till the movement of dispersal before supper, and thus had a second opportunity of showing herself to advantage, as the throng poured slowly into the empty drawing-room where she was standing.

She was soon the center of a group which increased and renewed itself as the circulation became general, and the individual comments on her success were a delightful prolongation of the collective applause. At such moments she lost something of her natural fastidiousness, and cared less for the quality of the admiration received than for its quantity. Differences of personality were merged in a warm atmosphere of praise, in which her beauty expanded like a flower in sunlight; and if Selden had approached a moment or two sooner he would have seen her turning on Ned Van Alstyne and George Dorset the look he had dreamed of capturing for himself.

Fortune willed, however, that the hurried approach of Mrs. Fisher, as whose aide-de-camp Van Alstyne was acting, should break up the group before Selden reached the threshold of the room. One or two of the men wandered off in search of their partners for supper, and the others, noticing Selden's approach, gave way to him in accordance with the tacit free-masonry of the ballroom. Lily was therefore standing alone when he reached her; and finding the expected look in her eye, he had the satisfaction of supposing he had kindled it. The look did indeed deepen as it rested on him, for even in that moment of self-intoxication Lily felt the quicker beat of life that his nearness always produced. She read, too, in his answering gaze the delicious confirmation of her triumph, and for the moment it seemed to her that it was for him only she cared to be beautiful.

Selden had given her his arm without speaking. She took it in silence, and they moved away, not toward the supper-room, but against the tide which was setting thither. The faces about her flowed by like the streaming images of sleep: she hardly noticed where Selden was leading her, till they passed through a glass doorway at the end of the long suite of rooms and stood suddenly in the fragrant hush of a garden. Gravel grated beneath their feet, and about them was the transparent dimness of a midsummer night. Hanging lights made emerald caverns in the depths of foliage, and whitened the spray of a fountain falling among lilies. The magic place was deserted: there was no sound but the plash of the water on the lily-pads, and a distant drift of music that might have been blown across a sleeping lake.

Selden and Lily stood still, accepting the unreality of the scene as a part of their own dream-like sensations. It would not have surprised them to feel a summer breeze on their faces, or to see the lights among the boughs reduplicated in the arch of a starry sky. The strange solitude about them was no stranger than the sweetness of being alone in it together.

At length Lily withdrew her hand, and moved away a step, so that her white-robed slimness was outlined against the dusk of the branches. Selden followed her, and still without speaking they seated themselves on a bench beside the fountain.

Suddenly she raised her eyes with the beseeching earnestness of a child. "You never speak to me—you think hard things of me," she murmured.

"I think of you at any rate, God knows!" he said.

"Then why do we never see each other? Why can't we be friends? You promised once to help me," she continued in the same tone, as though the words were drawn from her unwillingly.

"The only way I can help you is by loving you," Selden said in a low voice.

She made no reply, but her face turned to him with the soft motion of a flower. His own met it slowly, and their lips touched.

She drew back and rose from her seat. Selden rose too, and they stood facing each other. Suddenly she caught his hand and pressed it a moment against her cheek.

"Ah, love me, love me—but don't tell me so!" she sighed with her eyes in his; and before he could speak she had turned and slipped through the arch of boughs, disappearing in the brightness of the room beyond.

Selden stood where she had left him. He knew too well the transiency of exquisite moments to attempt to follow her; but presently he reentered the house and made his way through the deserted rooms to the door. A few sumptuously-cloaked ladies were already gathered in the marble vestibule, and in the coat-room he found Van Alstyne and Gus Trenor.

The former, at Selden's approach, paused in the careful selection of a cigar from one of the silver boxes invitingly set out near the door.

"Hallo, Selden, going too? You're an Epicurean like myself, I see: you don't want to see all those goddesses gobbling terrapin. Gad, what a show of good-looking women; but not one of them could touch that little cousin of mine. Talk of jewels—what's a woman want with jewels when she's got herself to show? The trouble is that all these fal-bals they wear cover up their figures when they've got 'em. I never knew till tonight what an outline Lily has."

"It's not her fault if everybody don't know it now," growled Trenor, flushed with the struggle of getting into his fur-lined coat. "Damned bad taste, I call it—no, no cigar for me. You can't tell what you're smoking in one of these new houses—likely as not the *chef* buys the cigars. Stay for supper? Not if I know it! When people crowd their rooms so that you can't get near any one you want to speak to, I'd as soon sup in the elevated at the rush hour. My wife was dead right to stay away: she says life's too short to spend it in breaking in new people."

XIII

LILY woke from happy dreams to find two notes at her bed-side.

One was from Mrs. Trenor, who announced that she was coming to town that afternoon for a flying visit, and hoped Miss Bart would be able to dine with her.

The other was from Selden. He wrote briefly that an important case called him to Albany, whence he would be unable to return till the evening, and asked Lily to let him know at what hour on the following day she would see him.

Lily, leaning back among her pillows, gazed musingly at his letter. The scene in the Brys' conservatory had been like a part of her dreams; she had not expected to wake to such evidence of its reality. Her first movement was one of annoyance: this unforeseen act of Selden's added another complication to life. It was so unlike him to yield to such an irrational impulse! Did he really mean to ask her to marry him? She had once shown him the impossibility of such a hope, and his subsequent behavior seemed to prove that he had accepted the situation with a reasonableness somewhat mortifying to her vanity. It was all the more agreeable to find that this reasonableness was maintained only at the cost of not seeing her; but, though nothing in life was as sweet as the sense of her power over him, she saw the danger of allowing the episode of the previous night to have a sequel. Since she could not marry him, it would be kinder to him, as well as easier for herself, to write a line amicably evading his request to see her: he was not the man to mistake such a hint, and when next they met it would be on their usual friendly footing.

Lily sprang out of bed, and went straight to her desk. She wanted to write at once, while she could trust to the strength of her resolve. She was still languid from her brief sleep and the exhilaration of the evening, and the sight of Selden's writing brought back the culminating moment of her triumph: the moment when she had read in his eyes that no philosophy was proof against her power. It would be pleasant to have that sensation again . . . no one else could give it to her in its fullness; and she could not bear to mar her mood of luxurious retrospection by an act of definite refusal. She took up her pen and wrote hastily: *"Tomorrow at four;"* murmuring to herself, as she slipped the sheet into its envelope: "I can easily put him off when tomorrow comes."

Judy Trenor's summons was very welcome to Lily. It was the first time she had received a direct communication from Bellomont since the close of her last visit there, and she was still visited by the dread of having incurred Judy's displeasure. But this characteristic command seemed to reestablish their former relations; and Lily smiled at the thought that her friend had probably summoned her in order to hear about the Brys' entertainment. Mrs. Trenor had absented herself from the feast, perhaps for the reason so frankly enunciated by her husband, perhaps because, as Mrs. Fisher somewhat differently put it, she "couldn't bear new people when she hadn't discovered them herself." At any rate, though she remained haughtily at Bellomont, Lily suspected in her a devouring eagerness to hear of what she had missed, and to learn exactly in what measure Mrs. Wellington Bry had surpassed all previous competitors for social recognition. Lily was quite ready to gratify this curiosity, but it happened that she was dining out. She determined, however, to see Mrs. Trenor for a few moments, and ringing for her maid she dispatched a telegram to say that she would be with her friend that evening at ten.

She was dining with Mrs. Fisher, who had gathered at an informal feast a few of the performers of the previous evening. There was to be plantation music in the studio after dinner—for Mrs. Fisher, despairing of the republic, had taken up modelling, and annexed to her small crowded house a spacious apartment, which, whatever its uses in her hours of plastic inspiration, served at other times for the exercise of an indefatigable hospitality. Lily was reluctant to leave, for the dinner was amusing, and she would have liked to lounge over a cigarette and hear a few songs; but she could not break her engagement with Judy, and shortly after ten she asked her hostess to ring for a hansom, and drove up Fifth Avenue to the Trenors'.

She waited long enough on the doorstep to wonder that Judy's presence in town was not signalized by a greater promptness in admitting her; and her surprise was increased when, instead of the expected footman, pushing his shoulders into a tardy coat, a shabby caretaking person in calico let her into the shrouded hall. Trenor, however, appeared at once on the threshold of the drawing-room, welcoming her with unusual volubility while he relieved her of her cloak and drew her into the room.

"Come along to the den; it's the only comfortable place in the house. Doesn't this room look as if it was waiting for the body to be brought down? Can't see why Judy keeps the house wrapped up in this awful slippery white stuff—it's enough to give a fellow pneumonia to walk through these rooms on a cold day. You look a little pinched yourself, by the way: it's rather a sharp night out. I noticed it walking up from the club. Come along, and I'll give you a nip of brandy, and you can toast yourself over the fire and try some of my new Egyptians—that little Turkish chap at the Embassy put me on to a brand that I want you to try, and if you like 'em I'll get out a lot for you: they don't have 'em here yet, but I'll cable."

He led her through the house to the large room at the back, where Mrs. Trenor usually sat, and where, even in her absence, there was an air of occupancy. Here, as usual, were flowers, newspapers, a littered writing-table, and a general aspect of lamp-lit familiarity, so that it was a surprise not to see Judy's energetic figure start up from the armchair near the fire.

It was apparently Trenor himself who had been occupying the seat in question, for it was overhung by a cloud of cigar smoke, and near it stood one of those intricate folding tables which British ingenuity has devised to facilitate the circulation of tobacco and spirits. The sight of such appliances in a drawing-room was not unusual in Lily's set, where smoking and drinking were unrestricted by considerations of time and place, and her first movement was to help herself to one of the cigarettes recommended by Trenor, while she checked his loquacity by asking, with a surprised glance: "Where's Judy?"

Trenor, a little heated by his unusual flow of words, and perhaps by prolonged propinquity with the decanters, was bending over the latter to decipher their silver labels.

"Here, now, Lily, just a drop of cognac in a little fizzy water—you do look pinched, you know: I swear the end of your nose is red. I'll take another glass to keep you company—Judy?—Why, you see, Judy's got a devil of a headache—quite knocked out with it, poor thing—she asked me to explain—make it all right, you know—Do come up to the fire, though; you look dead-beat, really. Now do let me make you comfortable, there's a good girl."

He had taken her hand, half-banteringly, and was drawing her toward a low seat by the hearth; but she stopped and freed herself quietly.

"Do you mean to say that Judy's not well enough to see me? Doesn't she want me to go upstairs?"

Trenor drained the glass he had filled for himself, and paused to set it down before he answered.

"Why, no—the fact is, she's not up to seeing anybody. It came on suddenly, you know, and she asked me to tell you how awfully sorry she was—if she'd known where you were dining she'd have sent you word."

"She did know where I was dining; I mentioned it in my telegram. But it doesn't matter, of course. I suppose if she's so poorly she won't go back to Bellomont in the morning, and I can come and see her then."

"Yes: exactly—that's capital. I'll tell her you'll pop in tomorrow morning. And now do sit down a minute, there's a dear, and let's have a nice quiet jaw together. You won't take a drop, just for sociability? Tell me what you think of that cigarette. Why, don't you like it? What are you chucking it away for?"

"I am chucking it away because I must go, if you'll have the goodness to call a cab for me," Lily returned with a smile.

She did not like Trenor's unusual excitability, with its too evident explanation, and the thought of being alone with him, with her friend out of reach upstairs, at the other end of the great empty house, did not conduce to a desire to prolong their *tête-à-tête*.

But Trenor, with a promptness which did not escape her, had moved between herself and the door.

"Why must you go, I should like to know? If Judy'd been here you'd have sat gossiping till all hours—and you can't even give me five minutes! It's always the same story. Last night I couldn't get near you—I went to that damned vulgar party just to see you, and there was everybody talking about you, and asking me if I'd ever seen anything so stunning, and when I tried to come up and say a word, you never took any notice, but just went on laughing and joking with a lot of asses who only wanted to be able to swagger about afterward, and look knowing when you were mentioned."

He paused, flushed by his diatribe, and fixing on her a look in which resentment was the ingredient she least disliked. But she had regained her presence of mind, and stood composedly in the middle of the room, while her slight smile seemed to put an ever increasing distance between herself and Trenor.

Across it she said: "Don't be absurd, Gus. It's past eleven, and I must really ask you to ring for a cab."

He remained immovable, with the lowering forehead she had grown to detest.

"And supposing I won't ring for one—what'll you do then?"

"I shall go upstairs to Judy if you force me to disturb her."

Trenor drew a step nearer and laid his hand on her arm. "Look here, Lily: won't you give me five minutes of your own accord?"

"Not tonight, Gus: you——"

"Very good, then: I'll take 'em. And as many more as I want." He had squared himself on the threshold, his hands thrust deep in his pockets. He nodded toward the chair on the hearth.

"Go and sit down there, please: I've got a word to say to you."

Lily's quick temper was getting the better of her fears. She drew herself up and moved toward the door.

"If you have anything to say to me, you must say it another time. I shall go up to Judy unless you call a cab for me at once."

He burst into a laugh. "Go upstairs and welcome, my dear; but you won't find Judy. She ain't there."

Lily cast a startled look upon him. "Do you mean that Judy is not in the house—not in town?" she exclaimed.

"That's just what I do mean," returned Trenor, his bluster sinking to sullenness under her look.

"Nonsense—I don't believe you. I am going upstairs," she said impatiently.

He drew unexpectedly aside, letting her reach the threshold unimpeded.

"Go up and welcome; but my wife is at Bellomont."

But Lily had a flash of reassurance. "If she hadn't come she would have sent me word——"

"She did; she telephoned me this afternoon to let you know."

"I received no message."

"I didn't send any."

The two measured each other for a moment, but Lily still saw her opponent through a blur of scorn that made all other considerations indistinct.

"I can't imagine your object in playing such a stupid trick on me; but if you have fully gratified your peculiar sense of humor I must again ask you to send for a cab."

It was the wrong note, and she knew it as she spoke. To be stung by irony it is not necessary to understand it, and the angry streaks on Trenor's face might have been raised by an actual lash.

"Look here, Lily, don't take that high and mighty tone with me." He had again moved toward the door, and in her instinctive shrinking from him she let him regain command of the threshold. "I did play a trick on you; I own up to it; but if you think I'm ashamed you're mistaken. Lord knows I've been patient enough—I've hung round and looked like an ass. And all the while you were letting a lot of other fellows make up to you . . . letting 'em make fun of me, I daresay . . . I'm not sharp, and can't dress my friends up to look funny, as you do . . . but I can tell when it's being done to me . . . I can tell fast enough when I'm made a fool of . . . "

"Ah, I shouldn't have thought that!" flashed from Lily; but her laugh dropped to silence under his look.

"No; you wouldn't have thought it; but you'll know better now. That's what you're here for tonight. I've been waiting for a quiet time to talk things over, and now I've got it I mean to make you hear me out."

His first rush of inarticulate resentment had been followed by a steadiness and concentration of tone more disconcerting to Lily than the excitement preceding it. For a moment her presence of mind forsook her. She had more than once been in situations where a quick sword-play of wit had been needful to cover her retreat; but her frightened heart-throbs told her that here such skill would not avail.

To gain time she repeated: "I don't understand what you want."

Trenor had pushed a chair between herself and the door. He threw himself in it, and leaned back, looking up at her.

"I'll tell you what I want: I want to know just where you and I stand. Hang it, the man who pays for the dinner is generally allowed to have a seat at table."

She flamed with anger and abasement, and the sickening need of having to conciliate where she longed to humble.

"I don't know what you mean—but you must see, Gus, that I can't stay here talking to you at this hour——"

"Gad, you go to men's houses fast enough in broad daylight—strikes me you're not always so deuced careful of appearances."

The brutality of the thrust gave her the sense of dizziness that follows on a physical blow. Rosedale had spoken then—this was the way men talked of her—She felt suddenly weak and defenseless: there was a throb of self-pity in her throat. But all the while another self was sharpening her to vigilance, whispering the terrified warning that every word and gesture must be measured.

"If you have brought me here to say insulting things——" she began.

Trenor laughed. "Don't talk stage-rot. I don't want to insult you. But a man's got his feelings—and you've played with mine too long. I didn't begin this business—kept out of the way, and left the track clear for the other chaps, till you rummaged me out and set to work to make an ass of me—and an easy job you had of it, too. That's the trouble—it was too easy for you—you got reckless—thought you could turn me inside out, and chuck me in the gutter like an empty purse. But, by gad, that ain't playing fair: that's dodging the rules of the game. Of course I know now what you wanted—it wasn't my beautiful eyes you were after—but I tell you what, Miss Lily, you've got to pay up for making me think so——"

He rose, squaring his shoulders aggressively, and stepped toward her with a reddening brow; but she held her footing, though every nerve tore at her to retreat as he advanced.

"Pay up?" she faltered. "Do you mean that I owe you money?"

He laughed again. "Oh, I'm not asking for payment in kind. But there's such a thing as fair play—and interest on one's money—and hang me if I've had as much as a look from you——"

"Your money? What have I to do with your money? You advised me how to invest mine . . . you must have seen I knew nothing of business . . . you told me it was all right——"

"It *was* all right—it is, Lily: you're welcome to all of it, and ten times more. I'm only asking for a word of thanks from you." He was closer still, with a hand that grew formidable; and the frightened self in her was dragging the other down.

"I *have* thanked you; I've shown I was grateful. What more have you done than any friend might do, or anyone accept from a friend?"

Trenor caught her up with a sneer. "I don't doubt you've accepted as much before—and chucked the other chaps as you'd like to chuck me. I don't care how you settled your score with them—if you fooled 'em I'm that much to the good. Don't stare at me like that—I know I'm not talking the way a man is supposed to talk to a girl—but, hang it, if you don't like it you can stop me quick enough—you know I'm mad about you—damn the money, there's plenty more of it—if *that* bothers you . . . I was a brute, Lily—Lily!—just look at me——"

Over and over her the sea of humiliation broke—wave crashing on wave so close that the moral shame was one with the physical dread. It seemed to her that self-esteem would have made her invulnerable—that it was her own dishonor which put a fearful solitude about her.

His touch was a shock to her drowning consciousness. She drew back from him with a desperate assumption of scorn.

"I've told you I don't understand—but if I owe you money you shall be paid——"

Trenor's face darkened to rage: her recoil of abhorrence had called out the primitive man.

"Ah—you'll borrow from Selden or Rosedale—and take your chances of fooling them as you've fooled me. Unless—unless you've settled your other scores already—and I'm the only one left out in the cold!"

She stood silent, frozen to her place. The words—the words were worse than the touch! Her heart was beating all over her body—in her throat, her limbs, her helpless useless hands. Her eyes traveled despairingly about the room—they lit on the bell, and she remembered that help was in call. Yes, but scandal with it—a hideous mustering of tongues. No, she must fight her way out alone. It was enough that the servants knew her to be in the house with Trenor—there must be nothing to excite conjecture in her way of leaving it.

She raised her head, and achieved a last clear look at him.

"I am here alone with you," she said. "What more have you to say?"

To her surprise, Trenor answered the look with a speechless stare. With his last gust of words the flame had died out, leaving him chill and humbled. It was as though a cold air had dispersed the fumes of his libations, and the situation loomed before him black and naked as the ruins of a fire. Old habits, old restraints, the hand of inherited order, plucked back the bewildered mind which passion had jolted from its ruts. Trenor's eye had the haggard look of the sleep-walker waked on a deathly ledge.

"Go home! Go away from here"——he stammered, and turning his back on her walked toward the hearth.

The sharp release from her fears restored Lily to immediate lucidity. The collapse of Trenor's will left her in control, and she heard herself, in a voice that was her own yet outside herself bidding him ring for the servant, bidding him give the order for a hansom, directing him to put her in it when it came. Whence the strength came to her she knew not; but an insistent voice warned her that she must leave the house openly, and nerved her, in the hall before the hovering caretaker, to exchange light words with Trenor, and charge him with the usual messages for Judy, while all the while she shook with inward loathing. On the doorstep, with the street before her, she felt a mad throb of liberation, intoxicating as the prisoner's first draught of free air; but the clearness of brain continued, and she noted the mute aspect of Fifth Avenue, guessed at the lateness of the hour, and even observed a man's figure—was there something half-familiar in its outline?—which, as she entered the hansom, turned from the opposite corner and vanished in the obscurity of the side street.

But with the turn of the wheels reaction came, and shuddering darkness closed on her. "I can't think—I can't think," she moaned, and leaned her head against the rattling side of the cab. She seemed a stranger to herself, or rather there were two selves in her, the one she had always known, and a new abhorrent being to which it found itself chained. She had once picked up, in a house where she was staying, a translation of the *Eumenides,* and her imagination had been seized by the high terror of the scene where Orestes, in the cave of the oracle, finds his implacable huntresses asleep, and snatches an hour's repose. Yes, the Furies might sometimes sleep, but they were there, always there in the dark corners, and now they were awake and the iron clang of their wings was in her brain . . . She opened her eyes and saw the streets passing—the familiar alien streets. All she looked on was the same and yet changed. There was a great gulf fixed between today and yesterday. Everything in the past seemed simple, natural, full of daylight—and she was alone in a place of darkness and pollution.—Alone! It was the loneliness that frightened her. Her eyes fell on an illuminated clock at a street corner, and she saw that the hands marked the half hour after eleven. Only half-past eleven—there were hours and hours left of the night! And she must spend them alone, shuddering sleepless on her bed. Her soft nature recoiled from this ordeal, which had none of the stimulus of conflict to goad her through it. Oh, the slow cold drip of the minutes on her head! She had a vision of herself lying on the black walnut bed—and the darkness would frighten her, and if she left the light burning the dreary details of the room would brand themselves forever on her brain. She had always hated her room at Mrs. Peniston's—its ugliness, its impersonality, the fact that nothing in it was really hers. To a torn heart uncomforted by human nearness a room may open almost human arms, and the being to whom no four walls mean more than any others, is, at such hours, expatriate everywhere.

Lily had no heart to lean on. Her relation with her aunt was as superficial as that of chance lodgers who pass on the stairs. But even had the two been in closer contact, it was impossible to think of Mrs. Peniston's mind as offering shelter or comprehension to such misery as Lily's. As the pain that can be told is but half a pain, so the pity that questions has little healing in its touch. What Lily craved was the darkness made by enfolding arms, the silence which is not solitude, but compassion holding its breath.

She started up and looked forth on the passing streets. Gerty!—they were nearing Gerty's corner. If only she could reach there before this laboring anguish burst from her breast to her lips—if only she could feel the hold of Gerty's arms while she shook in the ague-fit of fear that was coming upon her! She pushed up the door in the roof and called the address to the driver. It was not so late—Gerty might still be waking. And even if she were not, the sound of the bell would penetrate every recess of her tiny apartment, and rouse her to answer her friend's call.

XIV

GERTY FARISH, the morning after the Wellington Brys' entertainment, woke from dreams as happy as Lily's. If they were less vivid in hue, more subdued to the half-tints of her personality and her experience, they were for that very reason better suited to her mental vision. Such flashes of joy as Lily moved in would have blinded Miss Farish, who was accustomed, in the way of happiness, to such scant light as shone through the cracks of other people's lives.

Now she was the center of a little illumination of her own: a mild but unmistakable beam, compounded of Lawrence Selden's growing kindness to herself and the discovery that he extended his liking to Lily Bart. If these two factors seem incompatible to the student of feminine psychology, it must be remembered that Gerty had always been a parasite in the moral order, living on the crumbs of other tables, and content to look through the window at the banquet spread for her friends. Now that she was enjoying a little private feast of her own, it would have seemed incredibly selfish not to lay a plate for a friend; and there was no one with whom she would rather have shared her enjoyment than Miss Bart.

As to the nature of Selden's growing kindness, Gerty would no more have dared to define it than she would have tried to learn a butterfly's color by knocking the dust from its wings. To seize on the wonder would be to brush off its bloom, and perhaps see it fade and stiffen in her hand: better the sense of beauty palpitating out of reach, while she held her breath and watched where it would alight. Yet Selden's manner at the Brys' had brought the flutter of wings so close that they seemed to be beating in her own heart. She had never seen him so alert, so responsive, so attentive to what she had to say. His habitual manner had an absent-minded kindliness which she accepted, and was grateful for, as the liveliest sentiment her presence was likely to inspire; but she was quick to feel in him a change implying that for once she could give pleasure as well as receive it.

And it was so delightful that this higher degree of sympathy should be reached through their interest in Lily Bart! Gerty's affection for her friend—a sentiment that had learned to keep itself alive on the scantiest diet—had grown to active adoration since Lily's restless curiosity had drawn her into the circle of Miss Farish's work. Lily's taste of beneficence had wakened in her a momentary appetite for well-doing. Her visit to the Girls' Club had first brought her in contact with the dramatic contrasts of life. She had always accepted with philosophic calm the fact that such existences as hers were pedestalled on foundations of obscure humanity. The dreary limbo of dinginess lay all around and beneath that little illuminated circle in which life reached its finest efflorescence, as the mud and sleet of a winter night enclose a hot-house filled with tropical flowers. All this was in the natural order of things, and the orchid basking in its artificially created atmosphere could round the delicate curves of its petals undisturbed by the ice on the panes.

But it is one thing to live comfortably with the abstract conception of poverty, another to be brought in contact with its human embodiments. Lily had never conceived of these victims of fate otherwise than in the mass. That the mass was composed of individual lives, innumerable separate centers of sensation, with her own eager reachings for pleasure, her own fierce revulsions from pain—that some of these bundles of feeling were clothed in shapes not so unlike her own, with eyes meant to look on gladness, and young lips shaped for love—this discovery gave Lily one of those sudden shocks of pity that sometimes decentralize a life. Lily's nature was incapable of such renewal: she could feel other demands only through her own, and no pain was long vivid which did not press on an answering nerve. But for the moment she was drawn out of herself by the interest of her direct relation with a world so unlike her own. She had supplemented her first gift by personal assistance to one or two of Miss Farish's most appealing subjects, and the admiration and interest her presence excited among the tired workers at the club ministered in a new form to her insatiable desire to please.

Gerty Farish was not a close enough reader of character to disentangle the mixed threads of which Lily's philanthropy was woven. She supposed her beautiful friend to be actuated by the same motive as herself—that sharpening of the moral vision which makes all human suffering so near and insistent that the other aspects of life fade into remoteness. Gerty lived by such simple formulas that she did not hesitate to class her friend's state with the emotional "change of heart" to which her dealings with the poor had accustomed her; and she rejoiced in the thought that she had been the humble instrument of this renewal. Now she had an answer to all criticisms of Lily's conduct: as she had said, she knew "the real Lily," and the discovery that Selden shared her knowledge raised her placid acceptance of life to a dazzled sense of its possibilities—a sense farther enlarged, in the course of the afternoon, by the receipt of a telegram from Selden asking if he might dine with her that evening.

While Gerty was lost in the happy bustle which this announcement produced in her small household, Selden was at one with her in thinking with intensity of Lily Bart. The case which had called him to Albany was not complicated enough to absorb all his attention, and he had the professional faculty of keeping a part of his mind free when its services were not needed. This part—which at the moment seemed dangerously like the whole—was filled to the brim with the sensations of the previous evening. Selden understood the symptoms: he recognized the fact that he was paying up, as there had always been a chance of his having to pay up, for the voluntary exclusions of his past. He had meant to keep free from permanent ties, not from any poverty of feeling, but because, in a different way, he was, as much as Lily, the victim of his environment. There had been a germ of truth in his declaration to Gerty Farish that he had never wanted to marry a "nice" girl: the adjective connoting, in his cousin's vocabulary, certain utilitarian qualities which are apt to preclude the luxury of charm. Now it had been Selden's fate to have a charming mother: her graceful portrait, all smiles and Cashmere, still emitted a faded scent of the undefinable quality. His father was the kind of man who delights in a charming woman: who quotes her, stimulates her, and keeps her perennially charming. Neither one of the couple cared for money, but their disdain of it took the form of always spending a little more than was prudent. If their house was shabby, it was exquisitely kept; if there were good books on the shelves there were also good dishes on the table. Selden senior had an eye for a picture, his wife an understanding of old lace; and both were so conscious of restraint and discrimination in buying that they never quite knew how it was that the bills mounted up.

Though many of Selden's friends would have called his parents poor, he had grown up in an atmosphere where restricted means were felt only as a check on aimless profusion: where the few possessions were so good that their rarity gave them a merited relief and abstinence was combined with elegance in a way exemplified by Mrs. Selden's knack of wearing her old velvet as if it were new. A man has the advantage of being delivered early from the home point of view, and before Selden left college he had learned that there are as many different ways of going without money as of spending it. Unfortunately, he found no way as agreeable as that practiced at home; and his views of womankind in especial were tinged by the remembrance of the one woman who had given him his sense of "values." It was from her that he inherited his detachment from the sumptuary side of life: the stoic's carelessness of material things, combined with the Epicurean's pleasure in them. Life shorn of either feeling appeared to him a diminished thing; and nowhere was the blending of the two ingredients so essential as in the character of a pretty woman.

It had always seemed to Selden that experience offered a great deal besides the sentimental adventure, yet he could vividly conceive of a love which should broaden and deepen till it became the central fact of life. What he could not accept, in his own case, was the makeshift alternative of a relation that should be less than this: that should leave some portions of his nature unsatisfied, while it put an undue strain on others. He would not, in other words, yield to the growth of an affection which might appeal to pity yet leave the understanding untouched: sympathy should no more delude him than a trick of the eyes, the grace of helplessness than a curve of the cheek.

But now—that little *but* passed like a sponge over all his vows.

His reasoned-out resistances seemed for the moment so much less important than the question as to when Lily would receive his note! He yielded himself to the charm of trivial preoccupations, wondering at what hour her reply would be sent, with what words it would begin. As to its import he had no doubt—he was as sure of her surrender as of his own. And so he had leisure to muse on all its exquisite details, as a hard worker, on a holiday morning, might lie still and watch the beam of light travel gradually across his room. But if the new light dazzled, it did not blind him. He could still discern the outline of facts, though his own relation to them had changed. He was no less conscious than before of what was said of Lily Bart, but he could separate the woman he knew from the vulgar estimate of her. His mind turned to Gerty Farish's words, and the wisdom of the world seemed a groping thing beside the insight of innocence. *Blessed are the pure in heart, for they shall see God*—even the hidden god in their neighbor's breast! Selden was in the state of impassioned self-absorption that the first surrender to love produces. His craving was for the companionship of one whose point of view should justify his own, who should confirm, by deliberate observation, the truth to which his intuitions had leaped. He could not wait for the midday recess, but seized a moment's leisure in court to scribble his telegram to Gerty Farish.

Reaching town, he was driven direct to his club, where he hoped a note from Miss Bart might await him. But his box contained only a line of rapturous assent from Gerty, and he was turning away disappointed when he was hailed by a voice from the smoking room.

"Hallo, Lawrence! Dining here? Take a bite with me—I've ordered a canvas-back."

He discovered Trenor, in his day clothes, sitting, with a tall glass at his elbow, behind the folds of a sporting journal.

Selden thanked him, but pleaded an engagement.

"Hang it, I believe every man in town has an engagement tonight. I shall have the club to myself. You know how I'm living this winter, rattling round in that empty house. My wife meant to come to town today, but she's put it off again, and how is a fellow to dine alone in a room with the looking-glasses covered, and nothing but a bottle of Harvey sauce on the side-board? I say, Lawrence, chuck your engagement and take pity on me—it gives me the blue devils to dine alone, and there's nobody but that canting ass Wetherall in the club."

"Sorry, Gus—I can't do it."

As Selden turned away, he noticed the dark flush on Trenor's face, the unpleasant moisture of his intensely white forehead, the way his jewelled rings were wedged in the creases of his fat red fingers. Certainly the beast was predominating—the beast at the bottom of the glass. And he had heard this man's name coupled with Lily's! Bah—the thought sickened him; all the way back to his rooms he was haunted by the sight of Trenor's fat creased hands——

On his table lay the note: Lily had sent it to his rooms. He knew what was in it before he broke the seal—a grey seal with *Beyond!* beneath a flying ship. Ah, he would take her beyond—beyond the ugliness, the pettiness, the attrition and corrosion of the soul——

Gerty's little sitting-room sparkled with welcome when Selden entered it. Its modest "effects," compact of enamel paint and ingenuity, spoke to him in the language just then sweetest to his ear. It is surprising how little narrow walls and a low ceiling matter, when the roof of the soul has suddenly been raised. Gerty sparkled too; or at least shone with a tempered radiance. He had never before noticed that she had "points"—really, some good fellow might do worse . . . Over the little dinner (and here, again, the effects were wonderful) he told her she ought to marry—he was in a mood to pair off the whole world. She had made the caramel custard with her own hands? It was sinful to keep such gifts to herself. He reflected with a throb of pride that Lily could trim her own hats—she had told him so the day of their walk at Bellomont.

He did not speak of Lily till after dinner. During the little repast he kept the talk on his hostess, who, flattered at being the center of observation, shone as rosy as the candle-shades she had manufactured for the occasion. Selden evinced an extraordinary interest in her household arrangements: complimented her on the ingenuity with which she had utilized every inch of her small quarters, asked how her servant managed about afternoons out, learned that one may improvise delicious dinners in a chafing-dish, and uttered thoughtful generalizations on the burden of a large establishment.

When they were in the sitting-room again, where they fitted as snugly as bits in a puzzle, and she had brewed the coffee, and poured it into her grandmother's egg-shell cups, his eye, as he leaned back, basking in the warm fragrance, lighted on a recent photograph of

Miss Bart, and the desired transition was effected without an effort. The photograph was well enough—but to catch her as she had looked last night! Gerty agreed with him—never had she been so radiant. But could photography capture that light? There had been a new look in her face—something different; yes, Selden agreed there had been something different. The coffee was so exquisite that he asked for a second cup: such a contrast to the watery stuff at the club! Ah, your poor bachelor with his impersonal club fare, alternating with the equally impersonal *cuisine* of the dinner-party! A man who lived in lodgings missed the best part of life—he pictured the flavorless solitude of Trenor's repast, and felt a moment's compassion for the man . . . But to return to Lily—and again and again he returned, questioning, conjecturing, leading Gerty on, draining her inmost thoughts of their stored tenderness for her friend.

At first she poured herself out unstintingly, happy in this perfect communion of their sympathies. His understanding of Lily helped to confirm her own belief in her friend. They dwelt together on the fact that Lily had had no chance. Gerty instanced her generous impulses—her restlessness and discontent. The fact that her life had never satisfied her proved that she was made for better things. She might have married more than once—the conventional rich marriage which she had been taught to consider the sole end of existence—but when the opportunity came she had always shrunk from it. Percy Gryce, for instance, had been in love with her—every one at Bellomont had supposed them to be engaged, and her dismissal of him was thought inexplicable. This view of the Gryce incident chimed too well with Selden's mood not to be instantly adopted by him, with a flash of retrospective contempt for what had once seemed the obvious solution. If rejection there had been—and he wondered now that he had ever doubted it!—then he held the key to the secret, and the hillsides of Bellomont were lit up, not with sunset, but with dawn. It was he who had wavered and disowned the face of opportunity—and the joy now warming his breast might have been a familiar inmate if he had captured it in its first flight.

It was at this point, perhaps, that a joy just trying its wings in Gerty's heart dropped to earth and lay still. She sat facing Selden, repeating mechanically: "No, she has never been understood——" and all the while she herself seemed to be sitting in the center of a great glare of comprehension. The little confidential room, where a moment ago their thoughts had touched elbows like their chairs, grew to unfriendly vastness, separating her from Selden by all the length of her new vision of the future—and that future stretched out interminably, with her lonely figure toiling down it, a mere speck on the solitude.

"She is herself with a few people only; and you are one of them," she heard Selden saying. And again: "Be good to her, Gerty, won't you?" and: "She has it in her to become whatever she is believed to be—you'll help her by believing the best of her?"

The words beat on Gerty's brain like the sound of a language which has seemed familiar at a distance, but on approaching is found to be unintelligible. He had come to talk to her of Lily—that was all! There had been a third at the feast she had spread for him, and that third had taken her own place. She tried to follow what he was saying, to cling to her own part in the talk—but it was all as meaningless as the boom of waves in a drowning head, and she felt, as the drowning may feel, that to sink would be nothing beside the pain of struggling to keep up.

Selden rose, and she drew a deep breath, feeling that soon she could yield to the blessed waves.

"Mrs. Fisher's? You say she was dining there? There's music afterward; I believe I had a card from her." He glanced at the foolish pink-faced clock that was drumming out this hideous hour. "A quarter past ten? I might look in there now; the Fisher evenings are amusing. I haven't kept you up too late, Gerty? You look tired—I've rambled on and bored you." And in the unwonted overflow of his feelings, he left a cousinly kiss upon her cheek.

At Mrs. Fisher's, through the cigar-smoke of the studio, a dozen voices greeted Selden. A song was pending as he entered, and he dropped into a seat near his hostess, his eyes roaming in search of Miss Bart. But she was not there, and the discovery gave him a pang out of all proportion to its seriousness; since the note in his breast-pocket assured him that at four the next day they would meet. To his impatience it seemed immeasurably long to wait, and half-ashamed of the impulse, he leaned to Mrs. Fisher to ask, as the music ceased, if Miss Bart had not dined with her.

"Lily? She's just gone. She had to run off, I forget where. Wasn't she wonderful last night?"

"Who's that? Lily?" asked Jack Stepney, from the depths of a neighboring arm-chair. "Really, you know, I'm no child, but when it comes to a girl standing there as if she was up at auction—I thought seriously of speaking to cousin Julia."

"You didn't know Jack had become our social censor?" Mrs. Fisher said to Selden with a laugh; and Stepney spluttered, amid the general derision: "But she's a cousin, hang it, and when a man's married—*Town Talk* was full of her this morning."

"Yes: lively reading that was," said Mr. Ned Van Alstyne, stroking his moustache to hide the smile behind it. "Buy the dirty sheet? No, of course not; some fellow showed it to me—but I'd heard the stories before. When a girl's as good-looking as that she'd better marry; then no questions are asked. In our imperfectly organized society there is no provision as yet for the young woman who claims the privileges of marriage without assuming its obligations."

"Well, I understand Lily is about to assume them in the shape of Mr. Rosedale," Mrs. Fisher said with a laugh.

"Rosedale—good heavens!" exclaimed Van Alstyne, dropping his eye-glass. "Stepney, that's your fault for foisting the brute on us."

"Oh, confound it, you know, we don't *marry* Rosedale in our family," Stepney languidly protested; but his wife, who sat in oppressive bridal finery at the other side of the room, quelled him with the judicial reflection: "In Lily's circumstances it's a mistake to have too high a standard."

"I hear even Rosedale has been scared by the talk lately," Mrs. Fisher rejoined; "but the sight of her last night sent him off his head. What do you think he said to me after her *tableau?* 'My God, Mrs. Fisher, if I could get Paul Morpeth to paint her like that, the picture'd appreciate a hundred per cent in ten years.'"

"By Jove,—but isn't she about somewhere?" exclaimed Van Alstyne, restoring his glass with an uneasy glance.

"No; she ran off while you were all mixing the punch down stairs. Where was she going, by the way? What's on tonight? I hadn't heard of anything."

"Oh, not a party, I think," said an inexperienced young Farish who had arrived late. "I put her in her cab as I was coming in, and she gave the driver the Trenors' address."

"The Trenors'?" exclaimed Mrs. Jack Stepney. "Why, the house is closed—Judy telephoned me from Bellomont this evening."

"Did she? That's queer. I'm sure I'm not mistaken. Well, come now, Trenor's there, anyhow—I—oh, well, the fact is, I've no head for numbers," he broke off, admonished by the nudge of an adjoining foot, and the smile that circled the room.

In its unpleasant light Selden had risen and was shaking hands with his hostess. The air of the place stifled him, and he wondered why he had stayed in it so long.

On the doorstep he stood still, remembering a phrase of Lily's: "It seems to me you spend a good deal of time in the element you disapprove of."

Well—what had brought him there but the quest of her? It was her element, not his. But he would lift her out of it, take her beyond! That *Beyond!* on her letter was like a cry for rescue. He knew that Perseus's task is not done when he has loosed Andromeda's chains, for her limbs are numb with bondage, and she cannot rise and walk, but clings to him with dragging arms as he beats back to land with his burden. Well, he had strength for both—it was her weakness which had put the strength in him. It was not, alas, a clean rush of waves they had to win through, but a clogging morass of old associations and habits, and for the moment its vapors were in his throat. But he would see clearer, breathe freer in her presence: she was at once the dead weight at his breast and the spar which should float them to safety. He smiled at the whirl of metaphor with which he was trying to build up a defense against the influences of the last hour. It was pitiable that he, who knew the mixed motives on which social judgments depend, should still feel himself so swayed by them. How could he lift Lily to a freer vision of life, if his own view of her was to be colored by any mind in which he saw her reflected?

The moral oppression had produced a physical craving for air, and he strode on, opening his lungs to the reverberating coldness of the night. At the corner of Fifth Avenue Van Alstyne hailed him with an offer of company.

"Walking? A good thing to blow the smoke out of one's head. Now that women have taken to tobacco we live in a bath of nicotine. It would be a curious thing to study the effect of cigarettes on the relation of the sexes. Smoke is almost as great a solvent as divorce: both tend to obscure the moral issue."

Nothing could have been less consonant with Selden's mood than

Van Alstyne's after-dinner aphorisms, but as long as the latter confined himself to generalities his listener's nerves were in control. Happily Van Alstyne prided himself on his summing up of social aspects, and with Selden for audience was eager to show the sureness of his touch. Mrs. Fisher lived in an East side street near the Park, and as the two men walked down Fifth Avenue the new architectural developments of that versatile thoroughfare invited Van Alstyne's comment.

"That Greiner house, now—a typical rung in the social ladder! The man who built it came from a *milieu* where all the dishes are put on the table at once. His façade is a complete architectural meal; if he had omitted a style his friends might have thought the money had given out. Not a bad purchase for Rosedale, though: attracts attention, and awes the Western sight-seer. By and bye he'll get out of that phase, and want something that the crowd will pass and the few pause before. Especially if he marries my clever cousin——"

Selden dashed in with the query: "And the Wellington Brys'? Rather clever of its kind, don't you think?"

They were just beneath the wide white facade, with its rich restraint of line, which suggested the clever corseting of a redundant figure.

"That's the next stage: the desire to imply that one has been to Europe, and has a standard. I'm sure Mrs. Bry thinks her house a copy of the *Trianon;* in America every marble house with gilt furniture is thought to be a copy of the *Trianon*. What a clever chap that architect is, though—how he takes his client's measure! He has put the whole of Mrs. Bry in his use of the composite order. Now for the Trenors, you remember, he chose the Corinthian: exuberant, but based on the best precedent. The Trenor house is one of his best things—doesn't look like a banqueting-hall turned inside out. I hear Mrs. Trenor wants to build out a new ballroom, and that divergence from Gus on that point keeps her at Bellomont. The dimensions of the Brys' ballroom must rankle: you may be sure she knows 'em as well as if she'd been there last night with a yard-measure. Who said she was in town, by the way? That Farish boy? She isn't, I know; Mrs. Stepney was right; the house is dark, you see: I suppose Gus lives in the back."

He had halted opposite the Trenors' corner, and Selden perforce stayed his steps also. The house loomed obscure and uninhabited; only an oblong gleam above the door spoke of provisional occupancy.

"They've bought the house at the back: it gives them a hundred and fifty feet in the side street. There's where the ballroom's to be, with a gallery connecting it: billiard-room and so on above. I suggested changing the entrance, and carrying the drawing-room across the whole Fifth Avenue front: you see the front door corresponds with the windows——"

The walking-stick which Van Alstyne swung in demonstration dropped to a startled "Hallo!" as the door opened and two figures were seen silhouetted against the hall-light. At the same moment a hansom halted at the curb-stone, and one of the figures floated down to it in a haze of evening draperies; while the other, black and bulky, remained persistently projected against the light.

For an immeasurable second the two spectators of the incident were silent; then the house-door closed, the hansom rolled off, and the whole scene slipped by as if with the turn of a stereopticon.

Van Alstyne dropped his eye-glass with a low whistle.

"A—hem—nothing of this, eh, Selden? As one of the family, I know I may count on you—appearances are deceptive—and Fifth Avenue is so imperfectly lighted——"

"Goodnight," said Selden, turning sharply down the side street without seeing the other's extended hand.

Alone with her cousin's kiss, Gerty stared upon her thoughts. He had kissed her before—but not with another woman on his lips. If he had spared her that she could have drowned quietly, welcoming the dark flood as it submerged her. But now the flood was shot through with glory, and it was harder to drown at sunrise than in darkness. Gerty hid her face from the light, but it pierced to the crannies of her soul. She had been so contented, life had seemed so simple and sufficient—why had he come to trouble her with new hopes? And Lily—Lily, her best friend! Woman-like, she accused the woman. Perhaps, had it not been for Lily, her fond imagining might have become truth. Selden had always liked her—had understood and sympathized with the modest independence of her life. He, who had the reputation of weighing all things in the nice balance of fastidious perceptions, had been uncritical and simple in his view of her: his cleverness had never overawed her because she had felt at home in his heart. And now she was thrust out, and the door barred against her by Lily's hand! Lily, for whose admission there she herself had pleaded! The situation was lighted up by a dreary flash of irony. She knew Selden—she saw how the force of her faith in Lily must have helped to dispel his hesitations. She remembered, too, how Lily had talked of him—she saw herself bringing the two together, making them known to each other. On Selden's part, no doubt, the wound inflicted was inconscient; he had never guessed her foolish secret; but Lily—Lily must have known! When, in such matters, are a woman's perceptions at fault? And if she knew, then she had deliberately despoiled her friend, and in mere wantonness of power, since, even to Gerty's suddenly flaming jealousy, it seemed incredible that Lily should wish to be Selden's wife. Lily might be incapable of marrying for money, but she was equally incapable of living without it, and Selden's eager investigations into the small economies of house-keeping made him appear to Gerty as tragically duped as herself.

She remained long in her sitting-room, where the embers were crumbling to cold grey, and the lamp paled under its gay shade. Just beneath it stood the photograph of Lily Bart, looking out imperially on the cheap gim-cracks, the cramped furniture of the little room. Could Selden picture her in such an interior? Gerty felt the poverty, the insignificance of her surroundings: she beheld her life as it must appear to Lily. And the cruelty of Lily's judgments smote upon her memory. She saw that she had dressed her idol with the attributes of her own making. When had Lily ever really felt, or pitied, or understood? All she wanted was the taste of new experiences: she seemed like some cruel creature experimenting in a laboratory.

The pink-faced clock drummed out another hour, and Gerty rose with a start. She had an appointment early the next morning with a district visitor on the East side. She put out her lamp, covered the fire, and went into her bedroom to undress. In the little glass above her dressing-table she saw her face reflected against the shadows of the room, and tears blotted the reflection. What right had she to dream the dreams of loveliness? A dull face invited a dull fate. She cried quietly as she undressed, laying aside her clothes with her habitual precision, setting everything in order for the next day, when the old life must be taken up as though there had been no break in its routine. Her servant did not come till eight o'clock, and she prepared her own tea-tray and placed it beside the bed. Then she locked the door of the flat, extinguished her light and lay down.

But on her bed sleep would not come, and she lay face to face with the fact that she hated Lily Bart. It closed with her in the darkness like some formless evil to be blindly grappled with. Reason, judgment, renunciation, all the sane daylight forces, were beaten back in the sharp struggle for self-preservation. She wanted happiness—wanted it as fiercely and unscrupulously as Lily did, but without Lily's power of obtaining it. And in her conscious impotence she lay shivering, and hated her friend——

A ring at the door-bell caught her to her feet. She struck a light and stood startled, listening. For a moment her heart beat incoherently, then she felt the sobering touch of fact, and remembered that such calls were not unknown in her charitable work. She flung on her dressing-gown to answer the summons, and unlocking her door, confronted the shining vision of Lily Bart.

Gerty's first movement was one of revulsion. She shrank back as though Lily's presence flashed too sudden a light upon her misery. Then she heard her name in a cry, had a glimpse of her friend's face, and felt herself caught and clung to.

"Lily—what is it?" she exclaimed.

Miss Bart released her, and stood breathing brokenly, like one who has gained shelter after a long flight.

"I was so cold—I couldn't go home. Have you a fire?"

Gerty's compassionate instincts, responding to the swift call of habit, swept aside all her reluctances. Lily was simply someone who needed help, for what reason, there was no time to pause and conjecture: disciplined sympathy checked the wonder on Gerty's lips, and made her draw her friend silently into the sitting-room and seat her by the darkened hearth.

"There is kindling wood here: the fire will burn in a minute."

She knelt down, and the flame leapt under her rapid hands. It flashed strangely through the tears which still blurred her eyes, and smote on the white ruin of Lily's face. The girls looked at each other in silence; then Lily repeated: "I couldn't go home."

"No—no—you came here, dear! You're cold and tired—sit quiet, and I'll make you some tea."

Gerty had unconsciously adopted the soothing note of her trade: all personal feeling was merged in the sense of ministry, and experience had taught her that the bleeding must be stayed before the wound is probed.

Lily sat quiet, leaning to the fire: the clatter of cups behind her soothed her as familiar noises hush a child whom silence has kept wakeful. But when Gerty stood at her side with the tea she pushed it away, and turned an estranged eye on the familiar room.

"I came here because I couldn't bear to be alone," she said.

Gerty set down the cup and knelt beside her.

"Lily! Something has happened—can't you tell me?"

"I couldn't bear to lie awake in my room till morning. I hate my room at Aunt Julia's—so I came here——"

She stirred suddenly, broke from her apathy, and clung to Gerty in a fresh burst of fear.

"Oh, Gerty, the furies . . . you know the noise of their wings—alone, at night, in the dark? But you don't know—there is nothing to make the dark dreadful to you——"

The words, flashing back on Gerty's last hours, struck from her a faint derisive murmur; but Lily, in the blaze of her own misery, was blinded to everything outside it.

"You'll let me stay? I shan't mind when daylight comes—Is it late? Is the night nearly over? It must be awful to be sleepless—everything stands by the bed and stares——"

Miss Farish caught her straying hands. "Lily, look at me! Something has happened—an accident? You have been frightened—what has frightened you? Tell me if you can—a word or two—so that I can help you."

Lily shook her head.

"I am not frightened: that's not the word. Can you imagine looking into your glass some morning and seeing a disfigurement—some hideous change that has come to you while you slept? Well, I seem to myself like that—I can't bear to see myself in my own thoughts—I hate ugliness, you know—I've always turned from it—but I can't explain to you—you wouldn't understand."

She lifted her head and her eyes fell on the clock.

"How long the night is! And I know I shan't sleep tomorrow. Some one told me my father used to lie sleepless and think of horrors. And he was not wicked, only unfortunate—and I see now how he must have suffered, lying alone with his thoughts! But I am bad—a bad girl—all my thoughts are bad—I have always had bad people about me. Is that any excuse? I thought I could manage my own life—I was proud—proud! but now I'm on their level——"

Sobs shook her, and she bowed to them like a tree in a dry storm.

Gerty knelt beside her, waiting, with the patience born of experience, till this gust of misery should loosen fresh speech. She had first imagined some physical shock, some peril of the crowded streets, since Lily was presumably on her way home from Carry Fisher's; but she now saw that other nerve-centers were smitten, and her mind trembled back from conjecture.

Lily's sobs ceased, and she lifted her head.

"There are bad girls in your slums. Tell me—do they ever pick themselves up? Ever forget, and feel as they did before?"

"Lily! you mustn't speak so—you're dreaming."

"Don't they always go from bad to worse? There's no turning back—your old self rejects you, and shuts you out."

She rose, stretching her arms as if in utter physical weariness. "Go to bed, dear! You work hard and get up early. I'll watch here by the fire, and you'll leave the light, and your door open. All I want is to feel that you are near me." She laid both hands on Gerty's shoulders, with a smile that was like sunrise on a sea strewn with wreckage.

"I can't leave you, Lily. Come and lie on my bed. Your hands are frozen—you must undress and be made warm." Gerty paused with sudden compunction. "But Mrs. Peniston—it's past midnight! What will she think?"

"She goes to bed. I have a latch-key. It doesn't matter—I can't go back there."

"There's no need to: you shall stay here. But you must tell me where you have been. Listen, Lily—it will help you to speak!" She regained Miss Bart's hands, and pressed them against her. "Try to tell me—it will clear your poor head. Listen—you were dining at Carry Fisher's." Gerty paused and added with a flash of heroism: "Lawrence Selden went from here to find you."

At the word, Lily's face melted from locked anguish to the open misery of a child. Her lips trembled and her gaze widened with tears.

"He went to find me? And I missed him! Oh, Gerty, he tried to help me. He told me—he warned me long ago—he foresaw that I should grow hateful to myself!"

The name, as Gerty saw with a clutch at the heart, had loosened the springs of self-pity in her friend's dry breast, and tear by tear Lily poured out the measure of her anguish. She had dropped sideways in Gerty's big arm-chair, her head buried where lately Selden's had leaned, in a beauty of abandonment that drove home to Gerty's aching senses the inevitableness of her own defeat. Ah, it needed no deliberate purpose on Lily's part to rob her of her dream! To look on that prone loveliness was to see in it a natural force, to recognize that love and power belong to such as Lily, as renunciation and service are the lot of those they despoil. But if Selden's infatuation seemed a fatal necessity, the effect that his name produced shook Gerty's steadfastness with a last pang. Men pass through such superhuman loves and outlive them, they are the probation subduing the heart to human joys. How gladly Gerty would have welcomed the ministry of healing: how willingly have soothed the sufferer back to tolerance of life! But Lily's self-betrayal took this last hope from her. The mortal maid on the shore is helpless against the siren who loves her prey: such victims are floated back dead from their adventure.

Lily sprang up and caught her with strong hands. "Gerty, you know him—you understand him—tell me; if I went to him, if I told him everything—if I said: 'I am bad through and through—I want admiration, I want excitement, I want money—' yes, *money!* That's my shame, Gerty—and it's known, it's said of me—it's what men think of me— If I said it all to him—told him the whole story—said plainly: 'I've sunk lower than the lowest, for I've taken what they take, and not paid as they pay'—oh, Gerty, you know him, you can speak for him: if I told him everything would he loathe me? Or would he pity me, and understand me, and save me from loathing myself?"

Gerty stood cold and passive. She knew the hour of her probation had come, and her poor heart beat wildly against its destiny. As a dark river sweeps by under a lightning flash, she saw her chance of happiness surge past under a flash of temptation. What prevented her from saying: "He is like other men"? She was not so sure of him, after all. But to do so would have been like blaspheming her love. She could not put him before herself in any light but the noblest: she must trust him to the height of her own passion. "Yes: I know him; he will help you," she said; and in a moment Lily's passion was weeping itself out against her breast.

There was but one bed in the little flat, and the two girls lay down on it side by side when Gerty had unlaced Lily's dress and persuaded her to put her lips to the warm tea. The light extinguished, they lay still in the darkness, Gerty shrinking to the outer edge of the narrow couch to avoid contact with her bed-fellow. Knowing that Lily disliked to be caressed, she had long ago learned to check her demonstrative impulses toward her friend. But tonight every fibre in her body shrank from Lily's nearness: it was torture to listen to her breathing, and feel the sheet stir with it. As Lily turned, and settled to completer rest, a strand of her hair swept Gerty's cheek with its fragrance. Everything about her was warm and soft and scented: even the stains of her grief became her as rain-drops do the beaten rose. But as Gerty lay with arms drawn down her side, in the motionless narrowness of an effigy, she felt a stir of sobs from the breathing warmth beside her, and Lily flung out her hand, groped for her friend's, and held it fast.

"Hold me, Gerty, hold me, or I shall think of things," she moaned; and Gerty silently slipped an arm under her, pillowing her head in its hollow as a mother makes a nest for a tossing child. In the warm hollow Lily lay still and her breathing grew low and regular. Her hand still clung to Gerty's as if to ward off evil dreams, but the hold of her fingers relaxed, her head sank deeper into its shelter, and Gerty felt that she slept.

XV

WHEN Lily woke she had the bed to herself, and the winter light was in the room.

She sat up, bewildered by the strangeness of her surroundings; then memory returned, and she looked about her with a shiver. In the cold slant of light reflected from the back wall of a neighboring building, she saw her evening dress and opera cloak lying in a tawdry heap on a chair. Finery laid off is as unappetizing as the remains of a feast, and it occurred to Lily that, at home, her maid's vigilance had always spared her the sight of such incongruities. Her body ached with fatigue, and with the constriction of her attitude in Gerty's bed. All through her troubled sleep she had been conscious of having no space to toss in, and the long effort to remain motionless made her feel as if she had spent her night in a train.

This sense of physical discomfort was the first to assert itself; then she perceived, beneath it, a corresponding mental prostration, a languor of horror more insufferable than the first rush of her disgust. The thought of having to wake every morning with this weight on her breast roused her tired mind to fresh effort. She must find some way out of the slough into which she had stumbled: it was not so much compunction as the dread of her morning thoughts that pressed on her the need of action. But she was unutterably tired; it was weariness to think connectedly. She lay back, looking about the poor slit of a room with a renewal of physical distaste. The outer air, penned between high buildings, brought no freshness through the window; steam-heat was beginning to sing in a coil of dingy pipes, and a smell of cooking penetrated the crack of the door.

The door opened, and Gerty, dressed and hatted, entered with a cup of tea. Her face looked sallow and swollen in the dreary light, and her dull hair shaded imperceptibly into the tones of her skin.

She glanced shyly at Lily, asking in an embarrassed tone how she felt; Lily answered with the same constraint, and raised herself up to drink the tea.

"I must have been over-tired last night; I think I had a nervous attack in the carriage," she said, as the drink brought clearness to her sluggish thoughts.

"You were not well; I am so glad you came here," Gerty returned.

"But how am I to get home? And Aunt Julia——?"

"She knows; I telephoned early, and your maid has brought your things. But won't you eat something? I scrambled the eggs myself."

Lily could not eat; but the tea strengthened her to rise and dress under her maid's searching gaze. It was a relief to her that Gerty was obliged to hasten away: the two kissed silently, but without a trace of the previous night's emotion.

Lily found Mrs. Peniston in a state of agitation. She had sent for Grace Stepney and was taking digitalis. Lily breasted the storm of enquiries as best she could, explaining that she had had an attack of faintness on her way back from Carry Fisher's; that, fearing she would not have strength to reach home, she had gone to Miss Farish's instead; but that a quiet night had restored her, and that she had no need of a doctor.

This was a relief to Mrs. Peniston, who could give herself up to her own symptoms, and Lily was advised to go and lie down, her aunt's panacea for all physical and moral disorders. In the solitude of her own room she was brought back to a sharp contemplation of facts. Her daylight view of them necessarily differed from the cloudy vision of the night. The winged furies were now prowling gossips who dropped in on each other for tea. But her fears seemed the uglier, thus shorn of their vagueness; and besides, she had to act, not rave. For the first time she forced herself to reckon up the exact amount of her debt to Trenor; and the result of this hateful computation was the discovery that she had, in all, received nine thousand dollars from him. The flimsy pretext on which it had been given and received shrivelled up in the blaze of her shame: she knew that not a penny of it was her own, and that to restore her self-respect she must at once repay the whole amount. The inability thus to solace her outraged feelings gave her a paralyzing sense of insignificance. She was realizing for the first time that a woman's dignity may cost more to keep up than her carriage; and that the maintenance of a moral attribute should be dependent on dollars and cents, made the world appear a more sordid place than she had conceived it.

After luncheon, when Grace Stepney's prying eyes had been removed, Lily asked for a word with her aunt. The two ladies went upstairs to the sitting-room, where Mrs. Peniston seated herself in her black satin arm-chair tufted with yellow buttons, beside a bead-work table bearing a bronze box with a miniature of Beatrice Cenci in the lid. Lily felt for these objects the same distaste which the prisoner may entertain for the fittings of the court-room. It was here that her aunt received her rare confidences, and the pink-eyed smirk of the turbaned Beatrice was associated in her mind with the gradual fading of the smile from Mrs. Peniston lips. That lady's dread of a scene gave her an inexorableness which the greatest strength of character could not have produced, since it was independent of all considerations of right or wrong; and knowing this, Lily seldom ventured to assail it. She had never felt less like making the attempt than on the present occasion; but she had sought in vain for any other means of escape from an intolerable situation.

Mrs. Peniston examined her critically. "You're a bad color, Lily:

this incessant rushing about is beginning to tell on you," she said.

Miss Bart saw an opening. "I don't think it's that, Aunt Julia; I've had worries," she replied.

"Ah," said Mrs. Peniston, shutting her lips with the snap of a purse closing against a beggar.

"I'm sorry to bother you with them," Lily continued, "but I really believe my faintness last night was brought on partly by anxious thoughts——"

"I should have said Carry Fisher's cook was enough to account for it. She has a woman who was with Maria Melson in 1891—the spring of the year we went to Aix—and I remember dining there two days before we sailed, and feeling *sure* the coppers hadn't been scoured."

"I don't think I ate much; I can't eat or sleep." Lily paused, and then said abruptly: "The fact is, Aunt Julia, I owe some money."

Mrs. Peniston's face clouded perceptibly, but did not express the astonishment her niece had expected. She was silent, and Lily was forced to continue: "I have been foolish——"

"No doubt you have: extremely foolish," Mrs. Peniston interposed. "I fail to see how any one with your income, and no expenses—not to mention the handsome presents I've always given you——"

"Oh, you've been most generous, Aunt Julia; I shall never forget your kindness. But perhaps you don't quite realize the expense a girl is put to nowadays——"

"I don't realize that *you* are put to any expense except for your clothes and your railway fares. I expect you to be handsomely dressed; but I paid Céleste's bill for you last October."

Lily hesitated: her aunt's implacable memory had never been more inconvenient. "You were as kind as possible; but I have had to get a few things since——"

"What kind of things? Clothes? How much have you spent? Let me see the bill—I daresay the woman is swindling you."

"Oh, no, I think not: clothes have grown so frightfully expensive; and one needs so many different kinds, with country visits, and golf and skating, and Aiken and Tuxedo——"

"Let me see the bill," Mrs. Peniston repeated.

Lily hesitated again. In the first place, Mme. Céleste had not yet sent in her account, and secondly, the amount it represented was only a fraction of the sum that Lily needed.

"She hasn't sent in the bill for my winter things, but I *know* it's large; and there are one or two other things. I've been careless and imprudent—I'm frightened to think of what I owe——"

She raised the troubled loveliness of her face to Mrs. Peniston, vainly hoping that a sight so moving to the other sex might not be without effect upon her own. But the effect produced was that of making Mrs. Peniston shrink back apprehensively.

"Really, Lily, you are old enough to manage your own affairs, and after frightening me to death by your performance of last night you might at least choose a better time to worry me with such matters." Mrs. Peniston glanced at the clock, and swallowed a tablet of digitalis. "If you owe Céleste another thousand, she may send me her account," she added, as though to end the discussion at any cost.

"I am very sorry, Aunt Julia; I hate to trouble you at such a time; but I have really no choice—I ought to have spoken sooner—I owe a great deal more than a thousand dollars."

"A great deal more? Do you owe two? She must have robbed you!"

"I told you it was not only Céleste. I—there are other bills—more pressing—that must be settled."

"What on earth have you been buying? Jewelry? You must have gone off your head," said Mrs. Peniston with asperity. "But if you have run into debt, you must suffer the consequences, and put aside your monthly income till your bills are paid. If you stay quietly here until next spring, instead of racing about all over the country, you will have no expenses at all, and surely in four or five months you can settle the rest of your bills if I pay the dress-maker now."

Lily was again silent. She knew she could not hope to extract even a thousand dollars from Mrs. Peniston on the mere plea of paying Céleste's bill: Mrs. Peniston would expect to go over the dress-maker's account, and would make out the check to her and not to Lily. And yet the money must be obtained before the day was over!

"The debts I speak of are—different—not like tradesmen's bills," she began confusedly; but Mrs. Peniston's look made her almost afraid to continue. Could it be that her aunt suspected anything? The idea precipitated Lily's avowal.

"The fact is, I've played cards a good deal—bridge; the women all do it; girls too—it's expected. Sometimes I've won—won a good deal—but lately I've been unlucky—and of course such debts can't be paid off gradually——"

She paused: Mrs. Peniston's face seemed to be petrifying as she listened.

"Cards—you've played cards for money? It's true, then: when I was told so I wouldn't believe it. I won't ask if the other horrors I was told were true too; I've heard enough for the state of my nerves. When I think of the example you've had in this house! But I suppose it's your foreign bringing-up—no one knew where your mother picked up her friends. And her Sundays were a scandal—that I know." Mrs. Peniston wheeled round suddenly. "You play cards on Sunday?"

Lily flushed with the recollection of certain rainy Sundays at Bellomont and with the Dorsets.

"You're hard on me, Aunt Julia: I have never really cared for cards, but a girl hates to be thought priggish and superior, and one drifts into doing what the others do. I've had a dreadful lesson, and if you'll help me out this time I promise you——"

Mrs. Peniston raised her hand warningly. "You needn't make any promises: it's unnecessary. When I offered you a home I didn't undertake to pay your gambling debts."

"Aunt Julia! You don't mean that you won't help me?"

"I shall certainly not do anything to give the impression that I countenance your behavior. If you really owe your dress-maker, I will settle with her—beyond that I recognize no obligation to assume your debts."

Lily had risen, and stood pale and quivering before her aunt. Pride stormed in her, but humiliation forced the cry from her lips: "Aunt Julia, I shall be disgraced—I——" But she could go no farther. If her aunt turned such a stony ear to the fiction of the gambling debts, in what spirit would she receive the terrible avowal of the truth?

"I consider that you *are* disgraced, Lily; disgraced by your conduct far more than by its results. You say your friends have persuaded you to play cards with them; well, they may as well learn a lesson too. They can probably afford to lose a little money—and at any rate, I am not going to waste any of mine in paying them. And now I must ask you to leave me—this scene has been extremely painful, and I have my own health to consider. Draw down the blinds, please; and tell Jennings I will see no one this afternoon but Grace Stepney."

Lily went up to her own room and bolted the door. She was trembling with fear and anger—the rush of the furies' wings was in her ears. She walked up and down the room with blind irregular steps. The last door of escape was closed—she felt herself shut in with her dishonor——

Suddenly her wild pacing brought her before the clock on the chimney-piece. Its hands stood at half-past three, and she remembered that Selden was to come to her at four. She had meant to put him off with a word—but now her heart leaped at the thought of seeing him. Was there not a promise of rescue in his love? As she had lain at Gerty's side the night before, she had thought of his coming, and of the sweetness of weeping out her pain upon his breast. Of course she had meant to clear herself of its consequences before she met him—she had never really doubted that Mrs. Peniston would come to her aid. And she had felt, even in the full storm of her misery, that Selden's love could not be her ultimate refuge; only it would be so sweet to take a moment's shelter there, while she gathered fresh strength to go on.

But now his love was her only hope, and as she sat alone with her wretchedness the thought of confiding in him became as seductive as the river's flow to the suicide. The first plunge would be terrible—but afterward, what blessedness might come! She remembered Gerty's words: "I know him—he will help you"; and her mind clung to them as a sick person might cling to a healing relic. Oh, if he really understood—if he would help her to gather up her broken life, and put it together in some new semblance in which no trace of the past should remain! He had always made her feel that she was worthy of better things, and she had never been in greater need of such solace. Once and again she shrank at the thought of imperilling his love by her confession: for love was what she needed—it would take the glow of passion to weld together the shattered fragments of her self-esteem. But she recurred to Gerty's words and held fast to them. She was sure that Gerty knew Selden's feeling for her, and it had never dawned upon her blindness that Gerty's own judgment of him was colored by emotions far more ardent than her own.

Four o'clock found her in the drawing-room: she was sure that Selden would be punctual. But the hour came and passed—it moved on feverishly, measured by her impatient heart-beats. She had time to take a fresh survey of her wretchedness, and to fluctuate anew between the impulse to confide in Selden and the dread of destroying his illusions. But as the minutes passed the need of throwing herself on his comprehension became more urgent: she could not bear the weight of her misery alone. There would be a perilous moment, perhaps: but could she not trust to her beauty to bridge it over, to land her safe in the shelter of his devotion?

But the hour sped on and Selden did not come. Doubtless he had been detained, or had misread her hurriedly scrawled note, taking the four for a five. The ringing of the door-bell a few minutes after five confirmed this supposition, and made Lily hastily resolve to write more legibly in future. The sound of steps in the hall, and of the butler's voice preceding them, poured fresh energy into her veins. She felt herself once more the alert and competent molder of emergencies, and the remembrance of her power over Selden flushed her with sudden confidence. But when the drawing-room door opened it was Rosedale who came in.

The reaction caused her a sharp pang, but after a passing movement of irritation at the clumsiness of fate, and at her own carelessness in not denying the door to all but Selden, she controlled herself and greeted Rosedale amicably. It was annoying that Selden, when he came, should find that particular visitor in possession, but Lily was mistress of the art of ridding herself of superfluous company, and to her present mood Rosedale seemed distinctly negligible.

His own view of the situation forced itself upon her after a few moments' conversation. She had caught at the Brys' entertainment as an easy impersonal subject, likely to tide them over the interval till Selden appeared, but Mr. Rosedale, tenaciously planted beside the tea-table, his hands in his pockets, his legs a little too freely extended, at once gave the topic a personal turn.

"Pretty well done—well, yes, I suppose it was: Welly Bry's got his back up and don't mean to let go till he's got the hang of the thing. Of course, there were things here and there—things Mrs. Fisher couldn't be expected to see to—the champagne wasn't cold, and the coats got mixed in the coat-room. I would have spent more money on the music. But that's my character: if I want a thing I'm willing to pay: I don't go up to the counter, and then wonder if the article's worth the price. I wouldn't be satisfied to entertain like the Welly Brys; I'd want something that would look more easy and natural, more as if I took it in my stride. And it takes just two things to do that, Miss Bart: money, and the right woman to spend it."

He paused, and examined her attentively while she affected to rearrange the tea-cups.

"I've got the money," he continued, clearing his throat, "and what I want is the woman—and I mean to have her too."

He leaned forward a little, resting his hands on the head of his walking-stick. He had seen men of Ned Van Alstyne's type bring their hats and sticks into a drawing-room, and he thought it added a touch of elegant familiarity to their appearance.

Lily was silent, smiling faintly, with her eyes absently resting on his face. She was in reality reflecting that a declaration would take some time to make, and that Selden must surely appear before the moment of refusal had been reached. Her brooding look, as of a mind withdrawn yet not averted, seemed to Mr. Rosedale full of a subtle encouragement. He would not have liked any evidence of eagerness.

"I mean to have her too," he repeated, with a laugh intended to strengthen his self-assurance. "I generally *have* got what I wanted in life, Miss Bart. I wanted money, and I've got more than I know how to invest; and now the money doesn't seem to be of any account unless I can spend it on the right woman. That's what I want to do with it: I want my wife to make all the other women feel small. I'd never grudge a dollar that was spent on that. But it isn't every woman can do it, no matter how much you spend on her. There was a girl in some history book who wanted gold shields, or something, and the fellows threw 'em at her, and she was crushed under 'em: they killed her. Well, that's true enough: some women looked buried under their jewelry. What I want is a woman who'll hold her head higher the more diamonds I put on it. And when I looked at you the other night at the Brys, in that plain white dress, looking as if you had a crown on, I said to myself: 'By gad, if she had one she'd wear it as if it grew on her.'"

Still Lily did not speak, and he continued, warming with his theme: "Tell you what it is, though, that kind of woman costs more than all the rest of 'em put together. If a woman's going to ignore her pearls, they want to be better than anybody else's—and so it is with everything else. You know what I mean—you know it's only the showy things that are cheap. Well, I should want my wife to be able to take the earth for granted if she wanted to. I know there's one thing vulgar about money, and that's the thinking about it; and my wife would never have to demean herself in that way." He paused, and then added, with an unfortunate lapse to an earlier manner: "I guess you know the lady I've got in view, Miss Bart."

Lily raised her head, brightening a little under the challenge. Even through the dark tumult of her thoughts, the clink of Mr. Rosedale's millions had a faintly seductive note. Oh, for enough of them to cancel her one miserable debt! But the man behind them grew increasingly repugnant in the light of Selden's expected coming. The contrast was too grotesque: she could scarcely suppress the smile it provoked. She decided that directness would be best.

"If you mean me, Mr. Rosedale, I am very grateful—very much flattered; but I don't know what I have ever done to make you think——"

"Oh, if you mean you're not dead in love with me, I've got sense enough left to see that. And I ain't talking to you as if you were—I presume I know the kind of talk that's expected under those circumstances. I'm confoundedly gone on you—that's about the size of it—and I'm just giving you a plain business statement of the consequences. You're not very fond of me—*yet*—but you're fond of luxury, and style, and amusement, and of not having to worry about cash. You like to have a good time, and not to have to settle for it; and what I propose to do is to provide for the good time and do the settling."

He paused, and she returned with a chilling smile: "You are mistaken in one point, Mr. Rosedale: whatever I enjoy I am prepared to settle for."

She spoke with the intention of making him see that, if his words implied a tentative allusion to her private affairs, she was prepared to meet and repudiate it. But if he recognized her meaning it failed to abash him and he went on in the same tone: "I didn't mean to give offense; excuse me if I've spoken too plainly. But why ain't you straight with me—why do you put up that kind of bluff? You know there've been times when you were bothered—damned bothered—and as a girl gets older, and things keep moving along, why, before she knows it, the things she wants are liable to move past her and not come back. I don't say it's anywhere near that with you yet; but you've had a taste of bothers that a girl like yourself ought never to have known about, and what I'm offering you is the chance to turn your back on them once for all."

The color burned in Lily's face as he ended; there was no mistaking the point he meant to make, and to permit it to pass unheeded was a fatal confession of weakness, while to resent it too openly was to risk offending him at a perilous moment. Indignation quivered on her lip; but it was quelled by the secret voice which warned her that she must not quarrel with him. He knew too much about her, and even at the moment when it was essential that he should show himself at his best, he did not scruple to let her see how much he knew. How then would he use his power when her expression of contempt had dispelled his one motive for restraint? Her whole future might hinge on her way of answering him: she had to stop and consider that, in the stress of her other anxieties, as a breathless fugitive may have to pause at the cross-roads and try to decide coolly which turn to take.

"You are quite right, Mr. Rosedale. I *have* had bothers; and I am grateful to you for wanting to relieve me of them. It is not always easy to be quite independent and self-respecting when one is poor and lives among rich people; I have been careless about money, and have worried about my bills. But I should be selfish and ungrateful if I made that a reason for accepting all you offer, with no better return to make than the desire to be free from my anxieties. You must give me time—time to think of your kindness—and of what I could give you in return for it——"

She held out her hand with a charming gesture in which dismissal was shorn of its rigor. Its hint of future leniency made Rosedale rise in obedience to it, a little flushed with his unhoped-for success, and disciplined by the tradition of his blood to accept what was conceded, without undue haste to press for more. Something in his prompt acquiescence frightened her; she felt behind it the stored force of a patience that might subdue the strongest will. But at least they had parted amicably, and he was out of the house without meeting Selden—Selden, whose continued absence now smote her with a new alarm. Rosedale had remained over an hour, and she understood that it was now too late to hope for Selden. He would write explaining his absence, of course; there would be a note from him by the late post. But her confession would have to be postponed; and the chill of the delay settled heavily on her fagged spirit.

It lay heavier when the postman's last ring brought no note for her, and she had to go upstairs to a lonely night—a night as grim and sleepless as her tortured fancy had pictured it to Gerty. She had never learned to live with her own thoughts, and to be confronted with them through such hours of lucid misery made the confused wretchedness of her previous vigil seem easily bearable.

Daylight disbanded the phantom crew, and made it clear to her that she would hear from Selden before noon; but the day passed without his writing or coming. Lily remained at home, lunching and dining alone with her aunt, who complained of flutterings of the heart, and talked icily on general topics. Mrs. Peniston went to bed early, and when she had gone Lily sat down and wrote a note to Selden. She was about to ring for a messenger to despatch it when her eye fell on a paragraph in the evening paper which lay at her elbow: "Mr. Lawrence Selden was among the passengers sailing this afternoon for Havana and the West Indies on the Windward Liner Antilles."

She laid down the paper and sat motionless, staring at her note. She understood now that he was never coming—that he had gone away because he was afraid that he might come. She rose, and walking across the floor stood gazing at herself for a long time in the brightly-lit mirror above the mantelpiece. The lines in her face came out terribly—she looked old; and when a girl looks old to herself, how does she look to other people? She moved away, and began to wander aimlessly about the room, fitting her steps with mechanical precision between the monstrous roses of Mrs. Peniston's Axminster. Suddenly she noticed that the pen with which she had written to Selden still rested against the uncovered ink-stand. She seated herself again, and taking out an envelope, addressed it rapidly to Rosedale. Then she laid out a sheet of paper, and sat over it with suspended pen. It had been easy enough to write the date, and "Dear Mr. Rosedale"—but after that her inspiration flagged. She meant to tell him to come to her, but the words refused to shape themselves. At length she began: "I have been thinking——" then she laid the pen down, and sat with her elbows on the table and her face hidden in her hands.

Suddenly she started up at the sound of the door-bell. It was not late—barely ten o'clock—and there might still be a note from Selden, or a message—or he might be there himself, on the other side of the door! The announcement of his sailing might have been a mistake—it might be another Lawrence Selden who had gone to Havana—all these possibilities had time to flash through her mind, and build up the conviction that she was after all to see or hear from him, before the drawing-room door opened to admit a servant carrying a telegram.

Lily tore it open with shaking hands, and read Bertha Dorset's name below the message: "Sailing unexpectedly tomorrow. Will you join us on a cruise in Mediterranean?"

Book Two

I

IT came vividly to Selden on the Casino steps that Monte Carlo had, more than any other place he knew, the gift of accommodating itself to each man's humor.

His own, at the moment, lent it a festive readiness of welcome that might well, in a disenchanted eye, have turned to paint and facility. So frank an appeal for participation—so outspoken a recognition of the holiday vein in human nature—struck refreshingly on a mind jaded by prolonged hard work in surroundings made for the discipline of the senses. As he surveyed the white square set in an exotic coquetry of architecture, the studied tropicality of the gardens, the groups loitering in the foreground against mauve mountains which suggested a sublime stage-setting forgotten in a hurried shifting of scenes—as he took in the whole outspread effect of light and leisure, he felt a movement of revulsion from the last few months of his life.

The New York winter had presented an interminable perspective of snow-burdened days, reaching toward a spring of raw sunshine and furious air, when the ugliness of things rasped the eye as the gritty wind ground into the skin. Selden, immersed in his work, had told himself that external conditions did not matter to a man in his state, and that cold and ugliness were a good tonic for relaxed sensibilities. When an urgent case summoned him abroad to confer with a client in Paris, he broke reluctantly with the routine of the office; and it was only now that, having despatched his business, and slipped away for a week in the south, he began to feel the renewed zest of spectatorship that is the solace of those who take an objective interest in life.

The multiplicity of its appeals—the perpetual surprise of its contrasts and resemblances! All these tricks and turns of the show were upon him with a spring as he descended the Casino steps and paused on the pavement at its doors. He had not been abroad for seven years—and what changes the renewed contact produced! If the central depths were untouched, hardly a pin-point of surface remained the same. And this was the very place to bring out the completeness of the renewal. The sublimities, the perpetuities, might have left him as he was: but this tent pitched for a day's revelry spread a roof of oblivion between himself and his fixed sky.

It was mid-April, and one felt that the revelry had reached its climax and that the desultory groups in the square and gardens would soon dissolve and reform in other scenes. Meanwhile the last moments of the performance seemed to gain an added brightness from the hovering threat of the curtain. The quality of the air, the exuberance of the flowers, the blue intensity of sea and sky, produced the effect of a closing *tableau,* when all the lights are turned on at once. This impression was presently heightened by the way in which a consciously conspicuous group of people advanced to the middle front and stood before Selden with the air of the chief performers gathered together by the exigencies of the final effect. Their appearance confirmed the impression that the show had been staged regardless of expense, and emphasized its resemblance to one of those "costume-plays" in which the protagonists walk through the passions without displacing a drapery. The ladies stood in unrelated attitudes calculated to isolate their effects, and the men hung about them as irrelevantly as stage heroes whose tailors are named in the program. It was Selden himself who unwittingly fused the group by arresting the attention of one of its members.

"Why, Mr. Selden!" Mrs. Fisher exclaimed in surprise; and with a gesture toward Mrs. Jack Stepney and Mrs. Wellington Bry, she added plaintively: "We're starving to death because we can't decide where to lunch."

Welcomed into their group, and made the confidant of their difficulty, Selden learned with amusement that there were several places where one might miss something by not lunching, or forfeit something by lunching; so that eating actually became a minor consideration on the very spot consecrated to its rites.

"Of course one gets the best things at the *Terrasse*—but that looks as if one hadn't any other reason for being there: the Americans who don't know any one always rush for the best food. And the Duchess of Beltshire has taken up Bécassin's lately," Mrs. Bry earnestly summed up.

Mrs. Bry, to Mrs. Fisher's despair, had not progressed beyond the point of weighing her social alternatives in public. She could not acquire the air of doing things because she wanted to, and making her choice the final seal of their fitness.

Mr. Bry, a short pale man, with a business face and leisure clothes, met the dilemma hilariously.

"I guess the Duchess goes where it's cheapest, unless she can get her meal paid for. If you offered to blow her off at the *Terrasse* she'd turn up fast enough."

But Mrs. Jack Stepney interposed. "The Grand Dukes go to that little place at the Condamine. Lord Hubert says it's the only restaurant in Europe where they can cook peas."

Lord Hubert Dacey, a slender shabby-looking man, with a charming worn smile, and the air of having spent his best years in piloting the wealthy to the right restaurant, assented with gentle emphasis: "It's quite that."

"Peas?" said Mr. Bry contemptuously. "Can they cook terrapin? It just shows," he continued, "what these European markets are, when a fellow can make a reputation cooking peas!"

Jack Stepney intervened with authority. "I don't know that I quite agree with Dacey: there's a little hole in Paris, off the Quai Voltaire—but in any case, I can't advise the Condamine *gargote;* at least not with ladies."

Stepney, since his marriage, had thickened and grown prudish, as the Van Osburgh husbands were apt to do, but his wife, to his surprise and discomfiture, had developed an earth-shaking fastness of gait which left him trailing breathlessly in her wake.

"That's where we'll go then!" she declared, with a heavy toss of her plumage. "I'm so tired of the *Terrasse:* it's as dull as one of mother's dinners. And Lord Hubert has promised to tell us who all the awful people are at the other place—hasn't he, Carry? Now, Jack, don't look so solemn!"

"Well," said Mrs. Bry, "all I want to know is who their dress-makers are."

"No doubt Dacey can tell you that too," remarked Stepney, with an ironic intention which the other received with the light murmur, "I can at least *find out,* my dear fellow"; and Mrs. Bry having declared that she couldn't walk another step, the party hailed two or three of the light phaetons which hover attentively on the confines of the gardens, and rattled off in procession toward the Condamine.

Their destination was one of the little restaurants overhanging the boulevard which dips steeply down from Monte Carlo to the low intermediate quarter along the quay. From the window in which they presently found themselves installed, they overlooked the intense blue curve of the harbor, set between the verdure of twin promontories: to the right, the cliff of Monaco, topped by the mediaeval silhouette of its church and castle, to the left the terraces and pinnacles of the gambling-house. Between the two, the waters of the bay were furrowed by a light coming and going of pleasure-craft, through which, just at the culminating moment of luncheon, the majestic advance of a great steam-yacht drew the company's attention from the peas.

"By Jove, I believe that's the Dorsets back!" Stepney exclaimed; and Lord Hubert, dropping his single eye-glass, corroborated : "It's the Sabrina—yes."

"So soon? They were to spend a month in Sicily," Mrs. Fisher observed.

"I guess they feel as if they had: there's only one up-to-date hotel in the whole place," said Mr. Bry disparagingly.

"It was Ned Silverton's idea—but poor Dorset and Lily Bart must have been horribly bored." Mrs. Fisher added in an undertone to Selden: "I do hope there hasn't been a row."

"It's most awfully jolly having Miss Bart back," said Lord Hubert, in his mild deliberate voice; and Mrs. Bry added ingenuously: "I daresay the Duchess will dine with us, now that Lily's here."

"The Duchess admires her immensely: I'm sure she'd be charmed to have it arranged," Lord Hubert agreed, with the professional promptness of the man accustomed to draw his profit from facilitating social contacts: Selden was struck by the businesslike change in his manner.

"Lily has been a tremendous success here," Mrs. Fisher continued, still addressing herself confidentially to Selden. "She looks ten years younger—I never saw her so handsome. Lady Skiddaw took her everywhere in Cannes, and the Crown Princess of Macedonia had her to stop for a week at Cimiez. People say that was one reason why Bertha whisked the yacht off to Sicily: the Crown Princess didn't take much notice of her, and she couldn't bear to look on at Lily's triumph."

Selden made no reply. He was vaguely aware that Miss Bart was cruising in the Mediterranean with the Dorsets, but it had not occurred to him that there was any chance of running across her on the Riviera, where the season was virtually at an end. As he leaned back, silently contemplating his filigree cup of Turkish coffee, he was trying to put some order in his thoughts, to tell himself how the news of her nearness was really affecting him. He had a personal detachment enabling him, even in moments of emotional high-pressure, to get a fairly clear view of his feelings, and he was sincerely surprised by the disturbance which the sight of the Sabrina had produced in him. He had reason to think that his three months of engrossing professional work, following on the sharp shock of his disillusionment, had cleared his mind of its sentimental vapors. The feeling he had nourished and given prominence to was one of thankfulness for his escape: he was like a traveller so grateful for rescue from a dangerous accident that at first he is hardly conscious of his bruises. Now he suddenly felt the latent ache, and realized that after all he had not come off unhurt.

An hour later, at Mrs. Fisher's side in the Casino gardens, he was trying to find fresh reasons for forgetting the injury received in the contemplation of the peril avoided. The party had dispersed with the loitering indecision characteristic of social movements at Monte Carlo, where the whole place, and the long gilded hours of the day, seem to offer an infinity of ways of being idle. Lord Hubert Dacey had finally gone off in quest of the Duchess of Beltshire, charged by Mrs. Bry with the delicate negotiation of securing that lady's presence at dinner, the Stepneys had left for Nice in their motor-car, and Mr. Bry had departed to take his place in the pigeon-shooting match which was at the moment engaging his highest faculties.

Mrs. Bry, who had a tendency to grow red and stertorous after luncheon, had been judiciously prevailed upon by Carry Fisher to withdraw to her hotel for an hour's repose; and Selden and his companion were thus left to a stroll propitious to confidences. The stroll soon resolved itself into a tranquil session on a bench overhung with laurel and Banksian roses, from which they caught a dazzle of blue sea between marble balusters, and the fiery shafts of cactus-blossoms shooting meteor-like from the rock. The soft shade of their niche, and the adjacent glitter of the air, were conducive to an easy lounging mood, and to the smoking of many cigarettes; and Selden, yielding to these influences, suffered Mrs. Fisher to unfold to him the history of her recent experiences. She had come abroad with the Welly Brys at the moment when fashion flees the inclemency of the New York spring. The Brys, intoxicated by their first success, already thirsted for new kingdoms, and Mrs. Fisher, viewing the Riviera as an easy introduction to London society, had guided their course thither. She had affiliations of her own in every capital, and a facility for picking them up again after long absences; and the carefully disseminated rumor of the Brys' wealth had at once gathered about them a group of cosmopolitan pleasure-seekers.

"But things are not going as well as I expected," Mrs. Fisher frankly admitted. "It's all very well to say that everybody with money can get into society; but it would be truer to say that *nearly* everybody can. And the London market is so glutted with new Americans that, to succeed there now, they must be either very clever or awfully queer. The Brys are neither. *He* would get on well enough if she'd let him alone; they like his slang and his brag and his blunders. But Louisa spoils it all by trying to repress him and put herself forward. If she'd be natural herself—fat and vulgar and bouncing—it would be all right; but as soon as she meets anybody smart she tries to be slender and queenly. She tried it with the Duchess of Beltshire and Lady Skiddaw, and they fled. I've done my best to make her see her mistake—I've said to her again and again: 'Just let yourself go, Louisa'; but she keeps up the humbug even with me—I believe she keeps on being queenly in her own room, with the door shut.

"The worst of it is," Mrs. Fisher went on, "that she thinks it's all *my* fault. When the Dorsets turned up here six weeks ago, and everybody began to make a fuss about Lily Bart, I could see Louisa thought that if she'd had Lily in tow instead of me she would have been hobnobbing with all the royalties by this time. She doesn't realize that it's Lily's beauty that does it: Lord Hubert tells me Lily is thought even handsomer than when he knew her at Aix ten years ago. It seems she was tremendously admired there. An Italian Prince, rich and the real thing, wanted to marry her; but just at the critical moment a good-looking step-son turned up, and Lily was silly enough to flirt with him while her marriage-settlements with the step-father were being drawn up. Some people said the young man did it on purpose. You can fancy the scandal: there was an awful row between the men, and people began to look at Lily so queerly that Mrs. Peniston had to pack up and finish her cure elsewhere. Not that *she* ever understood: to this day she thinks that Aix didn't suit her, and mentions her having been sent there as proof of the incompetence of French doctors. That's Lily all over, you know: she works like a slave preparing the ground and sowing her seed; but the day she ought to be reaping the harvest she over-sleeps herself or goes off on a picnic."

Mrs. Fisher paused and looked reflectively at the deep shimmer of sea between the cactus-flowers. "Sometimes," she added, "I think it's just flightiness—and sometimes I think it's because, at heart, she despises the things she's trying for. And it's the difficulty of deciding that makes her such an interesting study." She glanced tentatively at Selden's motionless profile, and resumed with a slight sigh: "Well, all I can say is, I wish she'd give me some of her discarded opportunities. I wish we could change places now, for instance. She could make a very good thing out of the Brys if she managed them properly, and I should know just how to look after George Dorset while Bertha is reading Verlaine with Neddy Silverton."

She met Selden's sound of protest with a sharp derisive glance. "Well, what's the use of mincing matters? We all know that's what Bertha brought her abroad for. When Bertha wants to have a good time she has to provide occupation for George. At first I thought Lily was going to play her cards well *this* time, but there are rumors that Bertha is jealous of her success here and at Cannes, and I shouldn't be surprised if there were a break any day. Lily's only safeguard is that Bertha needs her badly—oh, very badly. The Silverton affair is in the acute stage: it's necessary that George's attention should be pretty continuously distracted. And I'm bound to say Lily *does* distract it: I believe he'd marry her tomorrow if he found out there was anything wrong with Bertha. But you know him—he's as blind as he's jealous; and of course Lily's present business is to keep him blind. A clever woman might know just the right moment to tear off the bandage: but Lily isn't clever in that way, and when George does open his eyes she'll probably contrive not to be in his line of vision."

Selden tossed away his cigarette. "By Jove—it's time for my train," he exclaimed, with a glance at his watch; adding, in reply to Mrs. Fisher's surprised comment—"Why, I thought of course you were at

Monte!"—a murmured word to the effect that he was making Nice his headquarters.

"The worst of it is, she snubs the Brys now," he heard irrelevantly flung after him.

Ten minutes later, in the high-perched bedroom of an hotel overlooking the Casino, he was tossing his effects into a couple of gaping portmanteaux, while the porter waited outside to transport them to the cab at the door. It took but a brief plunge down the steep white road to the station to land him safely in the afternoon express for Nice; and not till he was installed in the corner of an empty carriage, did he exclaim to himself, with a reaction of self-contempt: "What the deuce am I running away from?"

The pertinence of the question checked Selden's fugitive impulse before the train had started. It was ridiculous to be flying like an emotional coward from an infatuation his reason had conquered. He had instructed his bankers to forward some important business letters to Nice, and at Nice he would quietly await them. He was already annoyed with himself for having left Monte Carlo, where he had intended to pass the week which remained to him before sailing; but it would now be difficult to return on his steps without an appearance of inconsistency from which his pride recoiled. In his inmost heart he was not sorry to put himself beyond the probability of meeting Miss Bart. Completely as he had detached himself from her, he could not yet regard her merely as a social instance; and viewed in a more personal way she was not likely to be a reassuring object of study. Chance encounters, or even the repeated mention of her name, would send his thoughts back into grooves from which he had resolutely detached them; whereas, if she could be entirely excluded from his life, the pressure of new and varied impressions, with which no thought of her was connected, would soon complete the work of separation. Mrs. Fisher's conversation had, indeed, operated to that end; but the treatment was too painful to be voluntarily chosen while milder remedies were untried; and Selden thought he could trust himself to return gradually to a reasonable view of Miss Bart, if only he did not see her.

Having reached the station early, he had arrived at this point in his reflections before the increasing throng on the platform warned him that he could not hope to preserve his privacy; the next moment there was a hand on the door, and he turned to confront the very face he was fleeing.

Miss Bart, glowing with the haste of a precipitate descent upon the train, headed a group composed of the Dorsets, young Silverton and Lord Hubert Dacey, who had barely time to spring into the carriage, and envelop Selden in ejaculations of surprise and welcome, before the whistle of departure sounded. The party, it appeared, were hastening to Nice in response to a sudden summons to dine with the Duchess of Beltshire and to see the water-fête in the bay; a plan evidently improvised—in spite of Lord Hubert's protesting "Oh, I say, you know,"—for the express purpose of defeating Mrs. Bry's endeavor to capture the Duchess.

During the laughing relation of this maneuver, Selden had time for a rapid impression of Miss Bart, who had seated herself opposite to him in the golden afternoon light. Scarcely three months had elapsed since he had parted from her on the threshold of the Brys' conservatory; but a subtle change had passed over the quality of her beauty. Then it had had a transparency through which the fluctuations of the spirit were sometimes tragically visible; now its impenetrable surface suggested a process of crystallization which had fused her whole being into one hard brilliant substance. The change had struck Mrs. Fisher as a rejuvenation: to Selden it seemed like that moment of pause and arrest when the warm fluidity of youth is chilled into its final shape.

He felt it in the way she smiled on him, and in the readiness and competence with which, flung unexpectedly into his presence, she took up the thread of their intercourse as though that thread had not been snapped with a violence from which he still reeled. Such facility sickened him—but he told himself that it was with the pang which precedes recovery. Now he would really get well—would eject the last drop of poison from his blood. Already he felt himself calmer in her presence than he had learned to be in the thought of her. Her assumptions and elisions, her short-cuts and long *détours,* the skill with which she contrived to meet him at a point from which no inconvenient glimpses of the past were visible, suggested what opportunities she had had for practicing such arts since their last meeting. He felt that she had at last arrived at an understanding with herself: had made a pact with her rebellious impulses, and achieved a uniform system of self-government, under which all vagrant tendencies were either held captive or forced into the service of the state.

And he saw other things too in her manner: saw how it had

adjusted itself to the hidden intricacies of a situation in which, even after Mrs. Fisher's elucidating flashes, he still felt himself agrope. Surely Mrs. Fisher could no longer charge Miss Bart with neglecting her opportunities! To Selden's exasperated observation she was only too completely alive to them. She was "perfect" to every one: subservient to Bertha's anxious predominance, good-naturedly watchful of Dorset's moods, brightly companionable to Silverton and Dacey, the latter of whom met her on an evident footing of old admiration, while young Silverton, portentously self-absorbed, seemed conscious of her only as of something vaguely obstructive. And suddenly, as Selden noted the fine shades of manner by which she harmonized herself with her surroundings, it flashed on him that, to need such adroit handling, the situation must indeed be desperate. She was on the edge of something—that was the impression left with him. He seemed to see her poised on the brink of a chasm, with one graceful foot advanced to assert her unconsciousness that the ground was failing her.

On the Promenade des Anglais, where Ned Silverton hung on him for the half hour before dinner, he received a deeper impression of the general insecurity. Silverton was in a mood of Titanic pessimism. How any one could come to such a damned hole as the Riviera—any one with a grain of imagination—with the whole Mediterranean to choose from: but then, if one's estimate of a place depended on the way they broiled a spring chicken! Gad! what a study might be made of the tyranny of the stomach—the way a sluggish liver or insufficient gastric juices might affect the whole course of the universe, over-shadow everything in reach—chronic dyspepsia ought to be among the "statutory causes"; a woman's life might be ruined by a man's inability to digest fresh bread. Grotesque? Yes—and tragic—like most absurdities. There's nothing grimmer than the tragedy that wears a comic mask. . . . Where was he? Oh—the reason they chucked Sicily and rushed back? Well—partly, no doubt, Miss Bart's desire to get back to bridge and smartness. Dead as a stone to art and poetry—the light never *was* on sea or land for her! And of course she persuaded Dorset that the Italian food was bad for him. Oh, she could make him believe anything—*anything!* Mrs. Dorset was aware of it—oh, perfectly: nothing *she* didn't see! But she could hold her tongue—she'd had to, often enough. Miss Bart was an intimate friend—she wouldn't hear a word

A plan was improvised—in spite of Lord Hubert's protesting, "Oh, I say, you know."

against her. Only it hurts a woman's pride—there are some things one doesn't get used to . . . All this in confidence, of course? Ah—and there were the ladies signalling from the balcony of the hotel. . . He plunged across the Promenade, leaving Selden to a meditative cigar.

The conclusions it led him to were fortified, later in the evening, by some of those faint corroborative hints that generate a light of their own in the dusk of a doubting mind. Selden, stumbling on a chance acquaintance, had dined with him, and adjourned, still in his company, to the brightly lit Promenade, where a line of crowded stands commanded the glittering darkness of the waters. The night was soft and persuasive. Overhead hung a summer sky furrowed with the rush of rockets; and from the east a late moon, pushing up beyond the lofty bend of the coast, sent across the bay a shaft of brightness which paled to ashes in the red glitter of the illuminated boats. Down the lantern-hung Promenade, snatches of band-music floated above the hum of the crowd and the soft tossing of boughs in dusky gardens; and between these gardens and the backs of the stands there flowed a stream of people in whom the vociferous carnival mood seemed tempered by the growing languor of the season.

Selden and his companion, unable to get seats on one of the stands facing the bay, had wandered for a while with the throng, and then found a point of vantage on a high garden-parapet above the Promenade. Thence they caught but a triangular glimpse of the water, and of the flashing play of boats across its surface; but the crowd in the street was under their immediate view, and seemed to Selden, on the whole, of more interest than the show itself. After a while, however, he wearied of his perch and, dropping alone to the pavement, pushed his way to the first corner and turned into the moonlit silence of a side street. Long garden-walls overhung by trees made a dark boundary to the pavement; an empty cab trailed along the deserted thoroughfare, and presently Selden saw two persons emerge from the opposite shadows, signal to the cab, and drive off in it toward the center of the town. The moonlight touched them as they paused to enter the carriage, and he recognized Mrs. Dorset and young Silverton.

Beneath the nearest lamp-post he glanced at his watch and saw that the time was close on eleven. He took another cross street, and without breasting the throng on the Promenade, made his way to the fashionable club which overlooks that thoroughfare. Here, amid the blaze of crowded baccarat tables, he caught sight of Lord Hubert Dacey, seated with his habitual worn smile behind a rapidly dwindling heap of gold. The heap being in due course wiped out, Lord Hubert rose with a shrug, and joining Selden, adjourned with him to the deserted terrace of the club. It was now past midnight, and the throng on the stands was dispersing, while the long trails of red-lit boats scattered and faded beneath a sky repossessed by the tranquil splendor of the moon.

Lord Hubert looked at his watch. "By Jove, I promised to join the Duchess for supper at the *London House;* but it's past twelve, and I suppose they've all scattered. The fact is, I lost them in the crowd soon after dinner, and took refuge here, for my sins. They had seats on one of the stands, but of course they couldn't stop quiet: the Duchess never can. She and Miss Bart went off in quest of what they call adventures—gad, it ain't their fault if they don't have some queer ones!" He added tentatively, after pausing to grope for a cigarette: "Miss Bart's an old friend of yours, I believe? So she told me. —Ah, thanks—I don't seem to have one left." He lit Selden's proffered cigarette, and continued, in his high-pitched drawling tone: "None of my business, of course, but I didn't introduce her to the Duchess. Charming woman, the Duchess, you understand; and a very good friend of mine; but *rather* a liberal education."

Selden received this in silence, and after a few puffs Lord Hubert broke out again: "Sort of thing one can't communicate to the young lady—though young ladies nowadays are so competent to judge for themselves; but in this case—I'm an old friend too, you know . . . and there seemed no one else to speak to. The whole situation's a little mixed, as I see it—but there used to be an aunt somewhere, a diffuse and innocent person, who was great at bridging over chasms she didn't see . . . Ah, in New York, is she? Pity New York's such a long way off!"

II

MISS BART, emerging late the next morning from her cabin, found herself alone on the deck of the Sabrina.

The cushioned chairs, disposed expectantly under the wide awning, showed no signs of recent occupancy, and she presently learned from a steward that Mrs. Dorset had not yet appeared, and that the gentlemen—separately—had gone ashore as soon as they had breakfasted. Supplied with these facts, Lily leaned awhile over the side, giving herself up to a leisurely enjoyment of the spectacle before her. Unclouded sunlight enveloped sea and shore in a bath of purest radiancy. The purpling waters drew a sharp white line of foam at the base of the shore; against its irregular eminences, hotels and villas flashed from the greyish verdure of olive and eucalyptus; and the background of bare and finely-pencilled mountains quivered in a pale intensity of light.

How beautiful it was—and how she loved beauty! She had always felt that her sensibility in this direction made up for certain obtusenesses of feeling of which she was less proud; and during the last three months she had indulged it passionately. The Dorsets' invitation to go abroad with them had come as an almost miraculous release from crushing difficulties; and her faculty for renewing herself in new scenes, and casting off problems of conduct as easily as the surroundings in which they had arisen, made the mere change from one place to another seem, not merely a postponement, but a solution of her troubles. Moral complications existed for her only in the environment that had produced them; she did not mean to slight or ignore them, but they lost their reality when they changed their background. She could not have remained in New York without repaying the money she owed to Trenor; to acquit herself of that odious debt she might even have faced a marriage with Rosedale; but the accident of placing the Atlantic between herself and her obligations made them dwindle out of sight as if they had been milestones and she had traveled past them.

Her two months on the Sabrina had been especially calculated to aid this illusion of distance. She had been plunged into new scenes, and had found in them a renewal of old hopes and ambitions. The cruise itself charmed her as a romantic adventure. She was vaguely touched by the names and scenes amid which she moved, and had listened to Ned Silverton reading Theocritus by moonlight, as the yacht rounded the Sicilian promontories, with a thrill of the nerves that confirmed her belief in her intellectual superiority. But the weeks at Cannes and Nice had really given her more pleasure. The gratification of being welcomed in high company, and of making her own ascendency felt there, so that she found herself figuring once more as the "beautiful Miss Bart" in the interesting journal devoted to recording the least movements of her cosmopolitan companions—all these experiences tended to throw into the extreme background of memory the prosaic and sordid difficulties from which she had escaped.

If she was faintly aware of fresh difficulties ahead, she was sure of her ability to meet them: it was characteristic of her to feel that the only problems she could not solve were those with which she was familiar. Meanwhile she could honestly be proud of the skill with which she had adapted herself to somewhat delicate conditions. She had reason to think that she had made herself equally necessary to her host and hostess; and if only she had seen any perfectly irreproachable means of drawing a financial profit from the situation, there would have been no cloud on her horizon. The truth was that her funds, as usual, were inconveniently low; and to neither Dorset nor his wife could this vulgar embarrassment be safely hinted. Still, the need was not a pressing one; she could worry along, as she had so often done before, with the hope of some happy change of fortune to sustain her; and meanwhile life was gay and beautiful and easy, and she was conscious of figuring not unworthily in such a setting.

She was engaged to breakfast that morning with the Duchess of Beltshire, and at twelve o'clock she asked to be set ashore in the gig. Before this she had sent her maid to enquire if she might see Mrs. Dorset; but the reply came back that the latter was tired, and trying to sleep. Lily thought she understood the reason of the rebuff. Her hostess had not been included in the Duchess's invitation, though she herself had made the most loyal efforts in that direction. But her grace was impervious to hints, and invited or omitted as she chose. It was not Lily's fault if Mrs. Dorset's complicated attitudes did not fall in with the Duchess's easy gait. The Duchess, who seldom explained herself, had not formulated her objection beyond saying: "She's rather a bore, you know. The only one of your friends I like is that little Mr. Bry—*he's* funny——" but Lily knew enough not to press the point, and was not altogether sorry to be thus distinguished at her friend's expense. Bertha certainly *had* grown tiresome since she had taken to poetry and Ned Silverton.

On the whole, it was a relief to break away now and then from the Sabrina; and the Duchess's little breakfast, organized by Lord Hubert with all his usual virtuosity, was the pleasanter to Lily for not including her travelling-companions. Dorset, of late, had grown more than usually morose and incalculable, and Ned Silverton went about with an air that seemed to challenge the universe. The freedom and lightness of the ducal intercourse made an agreeable change from these complications, and Lily was tempted, after luncheon, to adjourn in the wake of her companions to the hectic atmosphere of the Casino. She did not mean to play; her diminished pocket-money offered small scope for the adventure; but it amused her to sit on a divan, under the doubtful protection of the Duchess's back, while the latter hung above her stakes at a neighboring table.

The rooms were packed with the gazing throng which, in the afternoon hours, trickles heavily between the tables, like the Sunday crowd in a lion-house. In the stagnant flow of the mass, identities were hardly distinguishable; but Lily presently saw Mrs. Bry cleaving her determined way through the doors, and, in the broad wake she left, the light figure of Mrs. Fisher bobbing after her like a row-boat at the stern of a tug. Mrs. Bry pressed on, evidently animated by the resolve to reach a certain point in the rooms; but Mrs. Fisher, as she passed Lily, broke from her towing-line, and let herself float to the girl's side.

"Lose her?" she echoed the latter's query, with an indifferent glance at Mrs. Bry's retreating back. "I daresay—it doesn't matter: I *have* lost her already." And, as Lily exclaimed, she added: "We had an awful row this morning. You know, of course, that the Duchess chucked her at dinner last night, and she thinks it was my fault—my want of management. The worst of it is, the message—just a mere word by telephone—came so late that the dinner had to be paid for;

Cruising the Mediterranean on the Sabrina.

and Bécassin *had* run it up—it had been so drummed into him that the Duchess was coming!" Mrs. Fisher indulged in a faint laugh at the remembrance. "Paying for what she doesn't get rankles so dreadfully with Louisa: I can't make her see that it's one of the preliminary steps to getting what you haven't paid for—and as I was the nearest thing to smash, she smashed me to atoms, poor dear!"

Lily murmured her commiseration. Impulses of sympathy came naturally to her, and it was instinctive to proffer her help to Mrs. Fisher.

"If there's anything I can do—if it's only a question of meeting the Duchess! I heard her say she thought Mr. Bry amusing——"

But Mrs. Fisher interposed with a decisive gesture. "My dear, I have my pride: the pride of my trade. *I* couldn't manage the Duchess, and I can't palm off your arts on Louisa Bry as mine. I've taken the final step: I go to Paris tonight with the Sam Gormers. *They're* still in the elementary stage; an Italian Prince is a great deal more than a Prince to them, and they're always on the brink of taking a courier for one. To save them from that is my present mission." She laughed again at the picture. "But before I go I want to make my last will and testament—I want to leave you the Brys."

"Me?" Miss Bart joined in her amusement. "It's charming of you to remember me, dear; but really——"

"You're already so well provided for?" Mrs. Fisher flashed a sharp glance at her. "*Are* you, though, Lily—to the point of rejecting my offer?"

Miss Bart colored slowly. "What I really meant was, that the Brys wouldn't in the least care to be so disposed of."

Mrs. Fisher continued to probe her embarrassment with an unflinching eye. "What you really meant was that you've snubbed the Brys horribly; and you know that they know it——"

"Carry!"

"Oh, on certain sides Louisa bristles with perceptions. If you'd even managed to have them asked once on the Sabrina—especially when royalties were coming! But it's not too late," she ended earnestly, "it's not too late for either of you."

Lily smiled. "Stay over, and I'll get the Duchess to dine with them."

"I shan't stay over—the Gormers have paid for my *salon-lit,"* said Mrs. Fisher with simplicity. "But get the Duchess to dine with them all the same."

Lily's smile again flowed into a slight laugh: her friend's importunity was beginning to strike her as irrelevant. "I'm sorry I have been negligent about the Brys——" she began.

"Oh, as to the Brys—it's you I'm thinking of," said Mrs. Fisher abruptly. She paused, and then, bending forward, with a lowered voice: "You know we all went on to Nice last night when the Duchess chucked us. It was Louisa's idea—I told her what I thought of it."

Miss Bart assented. "Yes—I caught sight of you on the way back, at the station."

"Well, the man who was in the carriage with you and George Dorset—that horrid little Dabham who does 'Society Notes from the Riviera'—had been dining with us at Nice. And he's telling everybody that you and Dorset came back alone after midnight."

"Alone—? When he was with us?" Lily laughed, but her laugh faded into gravity under the prolonged implication of Mrs. Fisher's look. "We *did* come back alone—if that's so very dreadful! But whose fault was it? The Duchess was spending the night at Cimiez with the Crown Princess; Bertha got bored with the show, and went off early, promising to meet us at the station. We turned up on time, but she didn't—she didn't turn up at all!"

Miss Bart made this announcement in the tone of one who presents, with careless assurance, a complete vindication; but Mrs. Fisher received it in a manner almost inconsequent. She seemed to have lost sight of her friend's part in the incident; her inward vision had taken another slant.

"Bertha never turned up at all? Then how on earth did she get back?"

"Oh, by the next train, I suppose; there were two extra ones for the *fête*. At any rate, I know she's safe on the yacht, though I haven't yet seen her; but you see it was not my fault," Lily summed up.

"Not your fault that Bertha didn't turn up? My poor child, if only you don't have to pay for it!" Mrs. Fisher rose—she had seen Mrs. Bry surging back in her direction. "There's Louisa, and I must be off—oh, we're on the best of terms externally; we're lunching together; but at heart it's *me* she's lunching on," she explained; and with a last hand-clasp and a last look, she added: "Remember, I leave her to you; she's hovering now, ready to take you in."

Lily carried the impression of Mrs. Fisher's leave-taking away with her from the Casino doors. She had accomplished, before leaving, the first step toward her reinstatement in Mrs. Bry's good graces. An affable advance—a vague murmur that they must see more of each other—an allusive glance to a near future that was felt to include the Duchess as well as the Sabrina—how easily it was all done, if one possessed the knack of doing it! She wondered at herself, as she had so often wondered, that, possessing the knack, she did not more consistently exercise it. But sometimes she was forgetful—and sometimes, could it be that she was proud? Today, at any rate, she had been vaguely conscious of a reason for sinking her pride, had in fact even sunk it to the point of suggesting to Lord Hubert Dacey, whom she ran across on the Casino steps, that he might really get the Duchess to dine with the Brys, if *she* undertook to have them asked on the Sabrina. Lord Hubert had promised his help, with the readiness on which she could always count: it was his only way of ever reminding her that he had once been ready to do so much more for her. Her path, in short, seemed to smooth itself before her as she advanced; yet the faint stir of uneasiness persisted. Had it been produced, she wondered, by her chance meeting with Selden? She thought not—time and change seemed so completely to have relegated him to his proper distance. The sudden and exquisite reaction from her anxieties had had the effect of throwing the recent past so far back that even Selden, as part of it, retained a certain air of unreality. And he had made it so clear that they were not to meet again; that he had merely dropped down to Nice for a day or two, and had almost his foot on the next steamer. No—that part of the past had merely surged up for a moment on the fleeing surface of events; and now that it was submerged again, the uncertainty, the apprehension persisted.

They grew to sudden acuteness as she caught sight of George Dorset descending the steps of the Hôtel de Paris and making for her across the square. She had meant to drive down to the quay and regain the yacht; but she now had the immediate impression that something more was to happen first.

"Which way are you going? Shall we walk a bit?" he began, putting the second question before the first was answered, and not waiting for a reply to either before he directed her silently toward the comparative seclusion of the lower gardens.

She detected in him at once all the signs of extreme nervous tension. The skin was puffed out under his sunken eyes, and its sallowness had paled to a leaden white against which his irregular eyebrows and long reddish moustache were relieved with a saturnine effect. His appearance, in short, presented an odd mixture of the bedraggled and the ferocious.

He walked beside her in silence, with quick precipitate steps, till they reached the embowered slopes to the east of the Casino; then, pulling up abruptly, he said: "Have you seen Bertha?"

"No—when I left the yacht she was not yet up."

He received this with a laugh like the whirring sound in a disabled clock. "Not yet up? Had she gone to bed? Do you know at what time she came on board? This morning at seven!" he exclaimed.

"At seven?" Lily started. "What happened—an accident to the train?"

He laughed again. "They missed the train—all the trains—they had to drive back."

"Well——?" She hesitated, feeling at once how little even this necessity accounted for the fatal lapse of hours.

"Well, they couldn't get a carriage at once—at that time of night, you know——" the explanatory note made it almost seem as though he were putting the case for his wife—"and when they finally did, it was only a one-horse cab, and the horse was lame!"

"How tiresome! I see," she affirmed, with the more earnestness because she was so nervously conscious that she did not; and after a pause she added: "I'm so sorry—but ought we to have waited?"

"Waited for the one-horse cab? It would scarcely have carried the four of us, do you think?"

She took this in what seemed the only possible way, with a laugh intended to sink the question itself in his humorous treatment of it. "Well, it would have been difficult; we should have had to walk by turns. But it would have been jolly to see the sunrise."

"Yes: the sunrise *was* jolly," he agreed.

"Was it? You saw it, then?"

"I saw it, yes; from the deck. I waited up for them."

"Naturally—I suppose you were worried. Why didn't you call on me to share your vigil?"

He stood still, dragging at his moustache with a lean weak hand.

"I don't think you would have cared for its *dénouement,*" he said with sudden grimness.

Again she was disconcerted by the abrupt change in his tone, and as in one flash she saw the peril of the moment, and the need of keeping her sense of it out of her eyes.

"*Dénouement*—isn't that too big a word for such a small incident? The worst of it, after all, is the fatigue which Bertha has probably slept off by this time."

She clung to the note bravely, though its futility was now plain to her in the glare of his miserable eyes.

"Don't—don't!——" he broke out, with the hurt cry of a child; and while she tried to merge her sympathy, and her resolve to ignore any cause for it, in one ambiguous murmur of deprecation, he dropped down on the bench near which they had paused, and poured out the wretchedness of his soul.

It was a dreadful hour—an hour from which she emerged shrinking and seared, as though her lids had been scorched by its actual glare. It was not that she had never had premonitory glimpses of such an outbreak; but rather because, here and there throughout the three months, the surface of life had shown such ominous cracks and vapors that her fears had always been on the alert for an upheaval. There had been moments when the situation had presented itself under a homelier yet more vivid image—that of a shaky vehicle, dashed by unbroken steeds over a bumping road, while she cowered within, aware that the harness wanted mending, and wondering what would give way first. Well—everything had given way now; and the wonder was that the crazy outfit had held together so long. Her sense of being involved in the crash, instead of merely witnessing it from the road, was intensified by the way in which Dorset, through his furies of denunciation and wild reactions of self-contempt, made her feel the need he had of her, the place she had taken in his life. But for her, what ear would have been open to his cries? And what hand but hers could drag him up again to a footing of sanity and self-respect? All through the stress of the struggle with him, she had been conscious of something faintly maternal in her efforts to guide and uplift him. But for the present, if he clung to her, it was not in order to be dragged up, but to feel someone floundering in the depths with him: he wanted her to suffer with him, not to help him to suffer less.

Happily for both, there was little physical strength to sustain his frenzy. It left him, collapsed and breathing heavily, to an apathy so deep and prolonged that Lily almost feared the passers-by would think it the result of a seizure, and stop to offer their aid. But Monte Carlo is, of all places, the one where the human bond is least close, and odd sights are the least arresting. If a glance or two lingered on the couple, no intrusive sympathy disturbed them; and it was Lily herself who broke the silence by rising from her seat. With the clearing of her vision the sweep of peril had extended, and she saw that the post of danger was no longer at Dorset's side.

"If you won't go back, I must—don't make me leave you!" she urged.

But he remained mutely resistant, and she added: "What are you going to do? You really can't sit here all night."

"I can go to a hotel. I can telegraph my lawyers." He sat up, roused by a new thought. "By Jove, Selden's at Nice—I'll send for Selden!"

Lily, at this, reseated herself with a cry of alarm. "No, no, *no!*" she protested.

He swung round on her distrustfully. "Why not Selden? He's a lawyer, isn't he? One will do as well as another in a case like this."

"As badly as another, you mean. I thought you relied on *me* to help you."

"You do—by being so sweet and patient with me. If it hadn't been for you I'd have ended the thing long ago. But now it's got to end." He rose suddenly, straightening himself with an effort. "You can't want to see me ridiculous."

She looked at him kindly. "That's just it." Then, after a moment's pondering, almost to her own surprise she broke out with a flash of inspiration: "Well, go over and see Mr. Selden. You'll have time to do it before dinner."

"Oh, *dinner*——" he mocked her; but she left him with the smiling rejoinder: "Dinner on board, remember; we'll put it off till nine if you like."

It was past four already; and when a cab had dropped her at the quay, and she stood waiting for the gig to put off for her, she began to wonder what had been happening on the yacht. Of Silverton's whereabouts there had been no mention. Had he returned to the Sabrina? Or could Bertha—the dread alternative sprang on her suddenly—could Bertha, left to herself, have gone ashore to rejoin him? Lily's heart stood still at the thought. All her concern had hitherto been for young Silverton, not only because, in such affairs, the woman's instinct is to side with the man, but because his case made a peculiar appeal to her sympathies. He was so desperately in earnest, poor youth, and his earnestness was of so different a quality from Bertha's, though hers too was desperate enough. The difference was that Bertha was in earnest only about herself while he was in earnest about her. But now, at the actual crisis, this difference seemed to throw the weight of destitution on Bertha's side, since at least he had her to suffer for, and she had only herself.

At any rate, viewed less ideally, all the disadvantages of such a situation were for the woman; and it was to Bertha that Lily's sympathies now went out. She was not fond of Bertha Dorset, but neither was she without a sense of obligation, the heavier for having so little personal liking to sustain it. Bertha had been kind to her, they had lived together, during the last months, on terms of easy friendship, and the sense of friction of which Lily had recently become aware seemed to make it the more urgent that she should work undividedly in her friend's interest.

It was in Bertha's interest, certainly, that she had despatched Dorset to consult with Lawrence Selden. Once the grotesqueness of the situation accepted, she had seen at a glance that it was the safest in which Dorset could find himself. Who but Selden could thus miraculously combine the skill to save Bertha with the obligation of doing so? The consciousness that much skill would be required made Lily rest thankfully in the greatness of the obligation. Since he would *have* to pull Bertha through she could trust him to find a way; and she put the fullness of her trust in the telegram she managed to send him on her way to the quay.

Thus far, then, Lily felt that she had done well; and the conviction strengthened her for the task that remained. She and Bertha had never been on confidential terms, but at such a crisis the barriers of reserve must surely fall: Dorset's wild allusions to the scene of the morning made Lily feel that they were down already, and that any attempt to rebuild them would be beyond Bertha's strength. She pictured the poor creature shivering behind her fallen defenses and awaiting with suspense the moment when she could take refuge in the first shelter that offered. If only that shelter had not already offered itself elsewhere! As the gig traversed the short distance between the quay and the yacht, Lily grew more than ever alarmed at the possible consequences of her long absence. What if the wretched Bertha, finding in all the long hours no soul to turn to—but by this time Lily's eager foot was on the side-ladder, and her first step on the Sabrina showed the worst of her apprehensions to be unfounded; for there, in the luxurious shade of the afterdeck, the wretched Bertha, in full command of her usual attenuated elegance, sat dispensing tea to the Duchess of Beltshire and Lord Hubert.

The sight filled Lily with such surprise that she felt that Bertha, at least, must read its meaning in her look, and she was proportionately disconcerted by the blankness of the look returned. But in an instant she saw that Mrs. Dorset had, of necessity, to look blank before the others, and that, to mitigate the effect of her own surprise, she must at once produce some simple reason for it. The long habit of rapid transitions made it easy for her to exclaim to the Duchess: "Why, I thought you'd gone back to the Princess!" and this sufficed for the lady she addressed, if it was hardly enough for Lord Hubert.

At least it opened the way to a lively explanation of how the Duchess was, in fact, going back the next moment, but had first rushed out to the yacht for a word with Mrs. Dorset on the subject of tomorrow's dinner—the dinner with the Brys, to which Lord Hubert had finally insisted on dragging them.

"To save my neck, you know!" he explained, with a glance that appealed to Lily for some recognition of his promptness; and the Duchess added, with her noble candor: "Mr. Bry has promised him a tip, and he says if we go he'll pass it on to us."

This led to some final pleasantries, in which, as it seemed to Lily, Mrs. Dorset bore her part with astounding bravery, and at the close of which Lord Hubert, from half way down the side-ladder, called back, with an air of numbering heads: "And of course we may count on Dorset too?"

"Oh, count on him," his wife assented gaily. She was keeping up well to the last—but as she turned back from waving her adieux over the side, Lily said to herself that the mask must drop and the soul of fear look out.

Mrs. Dorset turned back slowly; perhaps she wanted time to steady her muscles; at any rate, they were still under perfect control when, dropping once more into her seat behind the tea-table, she remarked to Miss Bart with a faint touch of irony: "I suppose I ought to say good morning."

If it was a cue, Lily was ready to take it, though with only the vaguest sense of what was expected of her in return. There was something unnerving in the contemplation of Mrs. Dorset's composure, and she had to force the light tone in which she answered: "I tried to see you this morning, but you were not yet up."

"No—I got to bed late. After we missed you at the station I thought we ought to wait for you till the last train." She spoke very gently, but with just the least tinge of reproach.

"You missed us? You waited for us at the station?"

Now indeed Lily was too far adrift in bewilderment to measure the other's words or keep watch on her own. "But I thought you didn't get to the station till after the last train had left!"

Mrs. Dorset, examining her between lowered lids, met this with the immediate query: "Who told you that?"

"George—I saw him just now in the gardens."

"Ah, is that George's version? Poor George—he was in no state to remember what I told him. He had one of his worst attacks this morning, and I packed him off to see the doctor. Do you know if he found him?"

Lily, still lost in conjecture, made no reply, and Mrs. Dorset settled herself indolently in her seat. "He'll wait to see him; he was horribly frightened about himself. It's very bad for him to be worried, and whenever anything upsetting happens, it always brings on an attack."

This time Lily felt sure that a cue was being pressed on her; but it was put forth with such startling suddenness, and with so incredible an air of ignoring what it led up to, that she could only falter out doubtfully: "Anything upsetting?"

"Yes—such as having you so conspicuously on his hands in the small hours. You know, my dear, you're rather a big responsibility in such a scandalous place after midnight."

At that—at the complete unexpectedness and the inconceivable audacity of it—Lily could not restrain the tribute of an astonished laugh.

"Well, really—considering it was you who burdened him with the responsibility!"

Mrs. Dorset took this with an exquisite mildness. "By not having the superhuman cleverness to discover you in that frightful rush for the train? Or the imagination to believe that you'd take it without us—you and he all alone—instead of waiting quietly in the station till we *did* manage to meet you?"

Lily's color rose: it was growing clear to her that Bertha was pursuing an object, following a line she had marked out for herself. Only, with such a doom impending, why waste time in these childish efforts to avert it? The puerility of the attempt disarmed Lily's indignation: did it not prove how horribly the poor creature was frightened?

"No; by our simply all keeping together at Nice," she returned.

"Keeping together? When it was you who seized the first opportunity to rush off with the Duchess and her friends? My dear Lily, you are not a child to be led by the hand!"

"No—nor to be lectured, Bertha, really; if that's what you are doing to me now."

Mrs. Dorset smiled on her reproachfully. "Lecture you—I? Heaven forbid! I was merely trying to give you a friendly hint. But it's usually the other way round, isn't it? I'm expected to take hints, not to give them: I've positively lived on them all these last months."

"Hints—from me to you?" Lily repeated.

"Oh, negative ones merely—what not to be and to do and to see. And I think I've taken them to admiration. Only, my dear, if you'll let me say so, I didn't understand that one of my negative duties was *not* to warn you when you carried your imprudence too far."

A chill of fear passed over Miss Bart: a sense of remembered treachery that was like the gleam of a knife in the dusk. But compassion, in a moment, got the better of her instinctive recoil. What was this outpouring of senseless bitterness but the tracked creature's attempt to cloud the medium through which it was fleeing? It was on Lily's lips to exclaim: "You poor soul, don't double and turn—come straight back to me, and we'll find a way out!" But the words died under the impenetrable insolence of Bertha's smile. Lily sat silent, taking the brunt of it quietly, letting it spend itself on her to the last drop of its accumulated falseness; then, without a word, she rose and went down to her cabin.

III

MISS BART'S telegram caught Lawrence Selden at the door of his hotel, and having read it, he turned back to wait for Dorset. The message necessarily left large gaps for conjecture; but all that he had recently heard and seen made these but too easy to fill in. On the whole he was surprised; for though he had perceived that the situation contained all the elements of an explosion, he had often enough, in the range of his personal experience, seen just such combinations subside into harmlessness. Still, Dorset's spasmodic temper, and his wife's reckless disregard of appearances, gave the situation a particular insecurity; and it was less from the sense of any special relation to the case than from a purely professional zeal, that Selden resolved to guide the pair to safety. Whether, in the present instance, safety for either lay in repairing so damaged a tie, it was no business of his to consider; he had only, on general principles, to think of averting a scandal, and his desire to avert it was increased by his fear of its involving Miss Bart. There was nothing specific in this apprehension; he merely wished to spare her the embarrassment of being ever so remotely connected with the public washing of the Dorset linen.

How exhaustive and unpleasant such a process would be, he saw even more vividly after his two hours' talk with poor Dorset. If anything came out at all, it would be such a vast unpacking of accumulated moral rags as left him, after his visitor had gone, with the feeling that he must fling open the windows and have his room swept out. But nothing should come out; and happily for his side of the case, the dirty rags, however pieced together, could not, without considerable difficulty, be turned into a homogeneous grievance. The torn edges did not always fit—there were missing bits, there were disparities of size and color, all of which it was naturally Selden's business to make the most of in putting them under his client's eye. But to a man in Dorset's mood the completest demonstration could not carry conviction, and Selden saw that for the moment all he could do was to soothe and temporize, to offer sympathy and to counsel prudence. He let Dorset depart charged to the brim with the sense that, till their next meeting, he must maintain a strictly noncommittal attitude; that, in short, his share in the game consisted for the present in looking on. Selden knew, however, that he could not long keep such violences in equilibrium; and he promised to meet Dorset, the next morning, at an hotel in Monte Carlo. Meanwhile he counted not a little on the reaction of weakness and self-distrust that, in such natures, follows on every unwonted expenditure of moral force; and his telegraphic reply to Miss Bart consisted simply in the injunction: "Assume that everything is as usual."

On this assumption, in fact, the early part of the following day was lived through. Dorset, as if in obedience to Lily's imperative bidding, had actually returned in time for a late dinner on the yacht. The repast had been the most difficult moment of the day. Dorset was sunk in one of the abysmal silences which so commonly followed on what his wife called his "attacks" that it was easy, before the servants, to refer it to this cause; but Bertha herself seemed, perversely enough, little disposed to make use of this obvious means of protection. She simply left the brunt of the situation on her husband's hands, as if too absorbed in a grievance of her own to suspect that she might be the object of one herself. To Lily this attitude was the most ominous, because the most perplexing, element in the situation. As she tried to fan the weak flicker of talk, to build up, again and again, the crumbling structure of "appearances," her own attention was perpetually distracted by the question: "What on earth can she be driving at?" There was something positively exasperating in Bertha's attitude of isolated defiance. If only she would have given her friend a hint they might still have worked together successfully; but how could Lily be of use, while she was thus obstinately shut out from participation? To be of use was what she honestly wanted; and not for her own sake but for the Dorsets'. She had not thought of her own situation at all: she was simply engrossed in trying to put a little order in theirs. But the close of the short dreary evening left her with a sense of effort hopelessly wasted. She had not tried to see Dorset alone: she had positively shrunk from a renewal of his confidences. It was Bertha whose confidence she sought, and who should as eagerly have invited her own; and Bertha, as if in the infatuation of self-destruction, was actually pushing away her rescuing hand.

Lily, going to bed early, had left the couple to themselves; and it seemed part of the general mystery in which she moved that more than an hour should elapse before she heard Bertha walk down the silent passage and regain her room. The morrow, rising on an apparent continuance of the same conditions, revealed nothing of what had occurred between the confronted pair. One fact alone outwardly proclaimed the change they were all conspiring to ignore; and that was the non-appearance of Ned Silverton. No one referred to it, and this tacit avoidance of the subject kept it in the immediate foreground of consciousness. But there was another change, perceptible only to Lily; and that was that Dorset now avoided her almost as pointedly as his wife. Perhaps he was repenting his rash outpourings of the previous day; perhaps only trying, in his clumsy way, to conform to Selden's counsel to behave "as usual." Such instructions no more make for easiness of attitude than the photographer's behest to "look natural"; and in a creature as unconscious as poor Dorset of the appearance he habitually presented, the struggle to maintain a pose was sure to result in queer contortions.

It resulted, at any rate, in throwing Lily strangely on her own resources. She had learned, on leaving her room, that Mrs. Dorset was still invisible, and that Dorset had left the yacht early; and feeling too restless to remain alone, she too had herself ferried ashore. Straying toward the Casino, she attached herself to a group of acquaintances from Nice, with whom she lunched, and in whose company she was returning to the rooms when she encountered Selden crossing the square. She could not, at the moment, separate herself definitely from her party, who had hospitably assumed that she would remain with them till they took their departure; but she found time for a momentary pause of enquiry, to which he promptly returned: "I've seen him again—he's just left me."

She waited before him anxiously. "Well? what has happened? What *will* happen?"

"Nothing as yet—and nothing in the future, I think."

"It's over, then? It's settled? You're sure?"

He smiled. "Give me time. I'm not sure—but I'm a good deal surer." And with that she had to content herself, and hasten on to the expectant group on the steps.

Selden had in fact given her the utmost measure of his sureness, had even stretched it a shade to meet the anxiety in her eyes. And now, as he turned away, strolling down the hill toward the station, that anxiety remained with him as the visible justification of his own. It was not, indeed, anything specific that he feared: there had been a literal truth in his declaration that he did not think anything would happen. What troubled him was that, though Dorset's attitude had perceptibly changed, the change was not clearly to be accounted for. It had certainly not been produced by Selden's arguments, or by the action of his own soberer reason. Five minutes' talk sufficed to show that some alien influence had been at work, and that it had not so much subdued his resentment as weakened his will, so that he moved under it in a state of apathy, like a dangerous lunatic who has been drugged. Temporarily, no doubt, however exerted, it worked for the general safety: the question was how long it would last, and by what kind of reaction it was likely to be followed. On these points Selden could gain no light; for he saw that one effect of the transformation had been to shut him off from free communion with Dorset. The latter, indeed, was still moved by the irresistible desire to discuss his wrong; but, though he revolved about it with the same forlorn tenacity, Selden was aware that something always restrained him from full expression. His state was one to produce first weariness and then impatience in his hearer; and when their talk was over, Selden began to feel that he had done his utmost, and might justifiably wash his hands of the sequel.

It was in this mind that he had been making his way back to the station when Miss Bart crossed his path; but though, after his brief word with her, he kept mechanically on his course, he was conscious of a gradual change in his purpose. The change had been produced by the look in her eyes; and in his eagerness to define the nature of that look, he dropped into a seat in the gardens, and sat brooding upon the question. It was natural enough, in all conscience, that she should appear anxious: a young woman placed, in the close intimacy of a yachting-cruise, between a couple on the verge of disaster, could hardly, aside from her concern for her friends, be insensible to the awkwardness of her own position. The worst of it was that, in interpreting Miss Bart's state of mind, so many alternative readings were possible; and one of these, in Selden's troubled mind, took the ugly form suggested by Mrs. Fisher. If the girl was afraid, was she afraid for herself or for her friends? And to what degree was her dread of a catastrophe intensified by the sense of being fatally involved in it? The burden of offense lying manifestly with Mrs. Dorset, this conjecture seemed on the face of it gratuitously unkind; but Selden knew that in the most one-sided matrimonial quarrel there are generally counter-charges to be brought, and that they are brought with the greater audacity where the original grievance is so emphatic. Mrs. Fisher had not hesitated to suggest the likelihood of Dorset's marrying Miss Bart "if anything happened"; and though Mrs. Fisher's conclusions were notoriously rash, she was shrewd enough in reading the signs from which they were drawn. Dorset had apparently shown marked interest in the girl, and this interest might be used to cruel advantage in his wife's struggle for rehabilitation. Selden knew that Bertha would fight to the last round of powder: the rashness of her conduct was illogically combined with a cold determination to escape its consequences. She could be as unscrupulous in fighting for herself as she was reckless in courting danger, and whatever came to her hand at such moments was likely to be used as a defensive missile. He did not, as yet, see clearly just what course she was likely to take, but his perplexity increased his apprehension, and with it the sense that, before leaving, he must speak again with Miss Bart. Whatever her share in the situation—and he had always honestly tried to resist judging her by her surroundings—however free she might be from any personal connection with it, she would be better out of the way of a possible crash; and since she had appealed to him for help, it was clearly his business to tell her so.

This decision at last brought him to his feet, and carried him back to the gambling rooms, within whose doors he had seen her disappearing; but a prolonged exploration of the crowd failed to put him on her traces. He saw instead, to his surprise, Ned Silverton loitering somewhat ostentatiously about the tables; and the discovery that this actor in the drama was not only hovering in the wings, but actually inviting the exposure of the footlights, though it might have seemed to imply that all peril was over, served rather to deepen Selden's sense of foreboding. Charged with this impression he returned to the square, hoping to see Miss Bart move across it, as every one in Monte Carlo seemed inevitably to do at least a dozen times a day; but here again he waited vainly for a glimpse of her, and the conclusion was slowly forced on him that she had gone back to the Sabrina. It would be difficult to follow her there, and still more difficult, should he do so, to contrive the opportunity for a private word; and he had almost decided on the unsatisfactory alternative of writing, when the ceaseless diorama of the square suddenly unrolled before him the figures of Lord Hubert and Mrs. Bry.

Hailing them at once with his question, he learned from Lord Hubert that Miss Bart had just returned to the Sabrina in Dorset's company; an announcement so evidently disconcerting to him that Mrs. Bry, after a glance from her companion, which seemed to act like the pressure on a spring, brought forth the prompt proposal that he should come and meet his friends at dinner that evening—"At Bécassin's—a little dinner to the Duchess," she flashed out before Lord Hubert had time to remove the pressure.

Selden's sense of the privilege of being included in such company brought him early in the evening to the door of the restaurant, where he paused to scan the ranks of diners approaching down the brightly lit terrace. There, while the Brys hovered within over the last agitating alternatives of the *menu,* he kept watch for the guests from the Sabrina, who at length rose on the horizon in company with the Duchess, Lord and Lady Skiddaw and the Stepneys. From this group it was easy for him to detach Miss Bart on the pretext of a moment's glance into one of the brilliant shops along the terrace, and to say to her, while they lingered together in the white dazzle of a jeweller's window: "I stopped over to see you—to beg of you to leave the yacht."

The eyes she turned on him showed a quick gleam of her former fear. "To leave—? What do you mean? What has happened?"

"Nothing. But if anything should, why be in the way of it?"

The glare from the jeweller's window, deepening the pallor of her face, gave to its delicate lines the sharpness of a tragic mask. "Nothing will, I am sure; but while there's even a doubt left, how can you think I would leave Bertha?"

The words rang out on a note of contempt—was it possibly of contempt for himself? Well, he was willing to risk its renewal to the extent of insisting, with an undeniable throb of added interest: "You have yourself to think of, you know—" to which, with a strange fall of sadness in her voice, she answered, meeting his eyes: "If you knew how little difference that makes!"

"Oh, well, nothing *will* happen," he said, more for his own reassurance than for hers; and "Nothing, nothing, of course!" she valiantly assented, as they turned to overtake their companions.

In the thronged restaurant, taking their places about Mrs. Bry's illuminated board, their confidence seemed to gain support from the familiarity of their surroundings. Here were Dorset and his wife once more presenting their customary faces to the world, she engrossed in establishing her relation with an intensely new gown, he shrinking with dyspeptic dread from the multiplied solicitations of the *menu*. The mere fact that they thus showed themselves together, with the utmost openness the place afforded, seemed to declare beyond a doubt that their differences were composed. How this end had been attained was still matter for wonder, but it was clear that for the moment Miss Bart rested confidently in the result; and Selden tried to achieve the same view by telling himself that her opportunities for observation had been ampler than his own.

Meanwhile, as the dinner advanced through a labyrinth of courses, in which it became clear that Mrs. Bry had occasionally broken away from Lord Hubert's restraining hand, Selden's general watchfulness began to lose itself in a particular study of Miss Bart. It was one of the days when she was so handsome that to be handsome was enough, and all the rest—her grace, her quickness, her social felicities—seemed the overflow of a bounteous nature. But what especially struck him was the way in which she detached herself by a hundred undefinable shades, from the persons who most abounded in her own style. It was in just such company, the fine flower and complete expression of the state she aspired to, that the differences came out with special poignancy, her grace cheapening the other women's smartness as her finely-discriminated silences made their chatter dull. The strain of the last hours had restored to her face the deeper eloquence which Selden had lately missed in it, and the bravery of her words to him still fluttered in her voice and eyes. Yes, she was matchless—it was the one word for her; and he could give his admiration the freer play because so little personal feeling remained in it. His real detachment from her had taken place, not at the lurid moment of disenchantment, but now, in the sober after-light of discrimination, where he saw her definitely divided from him by the crudeness of a choice which seemed to deny the very differences he felt in her. It was before him again in its completeness—the choice in which she was content to rest: in the stupid costliness of the food and the showy dullness of the talk, in the freedom of speech which never arrived at wit and the freedom of act which never made for romance. The strident setting of the restaurant, in which their table seemed set apart in a special glare of publicity, and the presence at it of little Dabham of the "Riviera Notes," emphasized the ideals of a world where conspicuousness passed for distinction, and the society column had become the roll of fame.

It was as the immortalizer of such occasions that little Dabham, wedged in modest watchfulness between two brilliant neighbors, suddenly became the center of Selden's scrutiny. How much did he know of what was going on, and how much, for his purpose, was still worth finding out? His little eyes were like tentacles thrown out to catch the floating intimations with which, to Selden, the air at moments seemed thick; then again it cleared to its normal emptiness, and he could see nothing in it for the journalist but leisure to note the elegance of the ladies' gowns. Mrs. Dorset's, in particular, challenged all the wealth of Mr. Dabham's vocabulary: it had surprises and subtleties worthy of what he would have called "the literary style." At first, as Selden had noticed, it had been almost too preoccupying to its wearer; but now she was in full command of it, and was even producing her effects with unwonted freedom. Was she not, indeed, too free, too fluent, for perfect naturalness? And was not Dorset, to whom his glance had passed by a natural transition, too jerkily wavering between the same extremes? Dorset indeed was always jerky; but it seemed to Selden that tonight each vibration swung him farther from his center.

The dinner, meanwhile, was moving to its triumphant close, to the evident satisfaction of Mrs. Bry, who, throned in apoplectic majesty between Lord Skiddaw and Lord Hubert, seemed in spirit to be calling on Mrs. Fisher to witness her achievement. Short of Mrs. Fisher her audience might have been called complete; for the restaurant was crowded with persons mainly gathered there for the purpose of spectatorship, and accurately posted as to the names and faces of the celebrities they had come to see. Mrs. Bry, conscious that all her feminine guests came under that heading, and that each one looked her part to admiration, shone on Lily with all the pent-up gratitude that Mrs. Fisher had failed to deserve. Selden, catching the glance, wondered what part Miss Bart had played in organizing the entertainment. She did, at least, a great deal to adorn it; and as he watched the bright security with which she bore herself, he smiled to think that he should have fancied her in need of help. Never had she appeared more serenely mistress of the situation than when, at the moment of dispersal, detaching herself a little from the group about the table, she turned with a smile and a graceful slant of the shoulders to receive her cloak from Dorset.

The dinner had been protracted over Mr. Bry's exceptional cigars and a bewildering array of liqueurs, and many of the other tables were empty; but a sufficient number of diners still lingered to give relief to the leave-taking of Mrs. Bry's distinguished guests. This ceremony was drawn out and complicated by the fact that it involved, on the part of the Duchess and Lady Skiddaw, definite farewells, and pledges of speedy reunion in Paris, where they were to pause and replenish their wardrobes on the way to England. The quality of Mrs. Bry's hospitality, and of the tips her husband had presumably imparted, lent to the manner of the English ladies a general effusiveness which shed the rosiest light over their hostess's future. In its glow Mrs. Dorset and the Stepneys were also visibly included, and the whole scene had touches of intimacy worth their weight in gold to the watchful pen of Mr. Dabham.

A glance at her watch caused the Duchess to exclaim to her sister that they had just time to dash for their train, and the flurry of this departure over, the Stepneys, who had their motor at the door, offered to convey the Dorsets and Miss Bart to the quay. The offer was accepted, and Mrs. Dorset moved away with her husband in attendance. Miss Bart had lingered for a last word with Lord Hubert, and Stepney, on whom Mr. Bry was pressing a final, and still more expensive, cigar, called out: "Come on, Lily, if you're going back to the yacht."

Lily turned to obey; but as she did so, Mrs. Dorset, who had paused on her way out, moved a few steps back toward the table.

"Miss Bart is not going back to the yacht," she said in a voice of singular distinctness.

A startled look ran from eye to eye; Mrs. Bry crimsoned to the verge of congestion, Mrs. Stepney slipped nervously behind her husband, and Selden, in the general turmoil of his sensations, was mainly conscious of a longing to grip Dabham by the collar and fling him out into the street.

Dorset, meanwhile, had stepped back to his wife's side. His face was white, and he looked about him with cowed angry eyes. "Bertha!—Miss Bart . . . this is some misunderstanding . . . some mistake . . . "

"Miss Bart remains here," his wife rejoined incisively.

"And, I think, George, we had better not detain Mrs. Stepney any longer."

Miss Bart, during this brief exchange of words, remained in admirable erectness, slightly isolated from the embarrassed group about her. She had paled a little under the shock of the insult, but the discomposure of the surrounding faces was not reflected in her own. The faint disdain of her smile seemed to lift her high above her antagonist's reach, and it was not till she had given Mrs. Dorset the full measure of the distance

"Miss Bart remains here," his wife rejoined incisively.

between them that she turned and extended her hand to her hostess.

"I am joining the Duchess tomorrow," she explained, "and it seemed easier for me to remain on shore for the night."

She held firmly to Mrs. Bry's wavering eye while she gave this explanation, but when it was over Selden saw her send a tentative glance from one to another of the women's faces. She read their incredulity in their averted looks, and in the mute wretchedness of the men behind them, and for a miserable half-second he thought she quivered on the brink of failure. Then, turning to him with an easy gesture, and the pale bravery of her recovered smile— "Dear Mr. Selden," she said, "you promised to see me to my cab."

Outside, the sky was gusty and overcast, and as Lily and Selden moved toward the deserted gardens below the restaurant, spurts of warm rain blew fitfully against their faces. The fiction of the cab had been tacitly abandoned; they walked on in silence, her hand on his arm, till the deeper shade of the gardens received them, and pausing beside a bench, he said: "Sit down a moment."

She dropped to the seat without answering, but the electric lamp at the bend of the path shed a gleam on the struggling misery of her face. Selden sat down beside her, waiting for her to speak, fearful lest any word he chose should touch too roughly on her wound, and kept also from free utterance by the wretched doubt which had slowly renewed itself within him. What had brought her to this pass? What weakness had placed her so abominably at her enemy's mercy? And why should Bertha Dorset have turned into an enemy at the very moment when she so obviously needed the support of her sex? Even while his nerves raged at the subjection of husbands to their wives, and at the cruelty of women to their kind, reason obstinately harped on the proverbial relation between smoke and fire. The memory of Mrs. Fisher's hints, and the corroboration of his own impressions,while they deepened his pity also increased his constraint, since, whichever way he sought a free outlet for sympathy, it was blocked by the fear of committing a blunder.

Suddenly it struck him that his silence must seem almost as accusatory as that of the men he had despised for turning from her; but before he could find the fitting word she had cut him short with a question.

"Do you know of a quiet hotel? I can send for my maid in the morning."

"An hotel—*here*—that you can go to alone? It's not possible."

She met this with a pale gleam of her old playfulness. "What *is*, then? It's too wet to sleep in the gardens."

"But there must be some one——"

"Some one to whom I can go? Of course—any number—but at *this* hour? You see my change of plan was rather sudden——"

"Good God—if you'd listened to me!" he cried, venting his helplessness in a burst of anger.

She still held him off with the gentle mockery of her smile. "But haven't I?" she rejoined. "You advised me to leave the yacht, and I'm leaving it."

He saw then, with a pang of self-reproach, that she meant neither to explain nor to defend herself; that by his miserable silence he had forfeited all chance of helping her, and that the decisive hour was past.

She had risen, and stood before him in a kind of clouded majesty, like some deposed princess moving tranquilly to exile.

"Lily!" he exclaimed, with a note of despairing appeal; but—"Oh, not now," she gently admonished him; and then, in all the sweetness of her recovered composure: "Since I must find shelter somewhere, and since you're so kindly here to help me——"

He gathered himself up at the challenge. "You will do as I tell you? There's but one thing, then; you must go straight to your cousins, the Stepneys."

"Oh—" broke from her with a movement of instinctive resistance; but he insisted: "Come—it's late, and you must appear to have gone there directly."

He had drawn her hand into his arm, but she held him back with a last gesture of protest. "I can't—I can't—not that—you don't know Gwen: you mustn't ask me."

"I *must* ask you—you must obey me," he persisted, though infected at heart by her own fear.

Her voice sank to a whisper: "And if she refuses?"—but, "Oh, trust me—trust me!" he could only insist in return; and yielding to his touch, she let him lead her back in silence to the edge of the square.

In the cab they continued to remain silent through the brief drive which carried them to the illuminated portals of the Stepneys' hotel. Here he left her outside, in the darkness of the raised hood, while his name was sent up to Stepney, and he paced the showy hall, awaiting the latter's descent. Ten minutes later the two men passed out together between the gold-laced custodians of the threshold; but in the vestibule Stepney drew up with a last flare of reluctance.

"It's understood, then?" he stipulated nervously, with his hand on Selden's arm. "She leaves tomorrow by the early train—and my wife's asleep, and can't be disturbed."

IV

THE blinds of Mrs. Peniston's drawing-room were drawn down against the oppressive June sun, and in the sultry twilight the faces of her assembled relatives took on a fitting shadow of bereavement.

They were all there: Van Alstynes, Stepneys and Melsons—even a stray Peniston or two, indicating, by a greater latitude in dress and manner, the fact of remoter relationship and more settled hopes. The Peniston side was, in fact, secure in the knowledge that the bulk of Mr. Peniston's property "went back"; while the direct connection hung suspended on the disposal of his widow's private fortune and on the uncertainty of its extent. Jack Stepney, in his new character as the richest nephew, tacitly took the lead, emphasizing his importance by the deeper gloss of his mourning and the subdued authority of his manner; while his wife's bored attitude and frivolous gown proclaimed the heiress's disregard of the insignificant interests at stake. Old Ned Van Alstyne, seated next to her in a coat that made affliction dapper, twirled his white moustache to conceal the eager twitch of his lips; and Grace Stepney, red-nosed and smelling of crape, whispered emotionally to Mrs. Herbert Melson: "I couldn't *bear* to see the Niagara anywhere else!"

A rustle of weeds and quick turning of heads hailed the opening of the door, and Lily Bart appeared, tall and noble in her black dress, with Gerty Farish at her side. The women's faces, as she paused interrogatively on the threshold, were a study in hesitation.

She had risen, and stood before him, like some deposed princess moving tranquilly to exile.

One or two made faint motions of recognition, which might have been subdued either by the solemnity of the scene, or by the doubt as to how far the others meant to go; Mrs. Jack Stepney gave a careless nod, and Grace Stepney, with a sepulchral gesture, indicated a seat at her side. But Lily, ignoring the invitation, as well as Jack Stepney's official attempt to direct her, moved across the room with her smooth free gait, and seated herself in a chair which seemed to have been purposely placed apart from the others.

It was the first time that she had faced her family since her return from Europe, two weeks earlier; but if she perceived any uncertainty in their welcome, it served only to add a tinge of irony to the usual composure of her bearing. The shock of dismay with which, on the dock, she had heard from Gerty Farish of Mrs. Peniston's sudden death, had been mitigated, almost at once, by the irrepressible thought that now, at last, she would be able to pay her debts. She had looked forward with considerable uneasiness to her first encounter with her aunt. Mrs. Peniston had vehemently opposed her niece's departure with the Dorsets, and had marked her continued disapproval by not writing during Lily's absence. The certainty that she had heard of the rupture with the Dorsets made the prospect of the meeting more formidable; and how should Lily have repressed a quick sense of relief at the thought that, instead of undergoing the anticipated ordeal, she had only to enter gracefully on a long-assured inheritance? It had been, in the consecrated phrase, "always understood" that Mrs. Peniston was to provide handsomely for her niece; and in the latter's mind the understanding had long since crystallized into fact.

"She gets everything, of course—I don't see what we're here for," Mrs. Jack Stepney remarked with careless loudness to Ned Van Alstyne; and the latter's deprecating murmur—"Julia was always a just woman"—might have been interpreted as signifying either acquiescence or doubt.

"Well, it's only about four hundred thousand," Mrs. Stepney rejoined with a yawn; and Grace Stepney, in the silence produced by the lawyer's preliminary cough, was heard to sob out: "They won't find a towel missing—I went over them with her the very day——"

Lily, oppressed by the close atmosphere, and the stifling odor of fresh mourning, felt her attention straying as Mrs. Peniston's lawyer, solemnly erect behind the Buhl table at the end of the room, began to rattle through the preamble of the will.

"It's like being in church," she reflected, wondering vaguely where Gwen Stepney had got such an awful hat. Then she noticed how stout Jack had grown—he would soon be almost as plethoric as Herbert Melson, who sat a few feet off, breathing puffily as he leaned his black-gloved hands on his stick.

"I wonder why rich people always grow fat—I suppose it's because there's nothing to worry them. If I inherit, I shall have to be careful of my figure," she mused, while the lawyer droned on through a labyrinth of legacies. The servants came first, then a few charitable institutions, then several remoter Melsons and Stepneys, who stirred consciously as their names rang out, and then subsided into a state of impassiveness befitting the solemnity of the occasion. Ned Van Alstyne, Jack Stepney, and a cousin or two followed, each coupled with the mention of a few thousands: Lily wondered that Grace Stepney was not among them. Then she heard her own name—"to my niece Lily Bart ten thousand dollars—" and after that the lawyer again lost himself in a coil of unintelligible periods, from which the concluding phrase flashed out with startling distinctness: "and the residue of my estate to my dear cousin and name-sake, Grace Julia Stepney."

There was a subdued gasp of surprise, a rapid turning of heads, and a surging of sable figures toward the corner in which Miss Stepney wailed out her sense of unworthiness through the crumpled ball of a black-edged handkerchief.

Lily stood apart from the general movement, feeling herself for the first time utterly alone. No one looked at her, no one seemed aware of her presence; she was probing the very depths of insignificance. And under her sense of the collective indifference came the acuter pang of hopes deceived. Disinherited—she had been disinherited—and for Grace Stepney! She met Gerty's lamentable eyes, fixed on her in a despairing effort at consolation, and the look brought her to herself. There was something to be done before she left the house: to be done with all the nobility she knew how to put into such gestures. She advanced to the group about Miss Stepney, and holding out her hand said simply: "Dear Grace, I am so glad."

The other ladies had fallen back at her approach, and a space created itself about her. It widened as she turned to go, and no one advanced to fill it up. She paused a moment, glancing about her, calmly taking the measure of her situation. She heard some one ask a question about the date of the will; she caught a fragment of the lawyer's answer—something about a sudden summons, and an "earlier instrument." Then the tide of dispersal began to drift past her; Mrs. Jack Stepney and Mrs. Herbert Melson stood on the doorstep awaiting their motor; a sympathizing group escorted Grace Stepney to the cab it was felt to be fitting she should take, though she lived but a street or two away; and Miss Bart and Gerty found themselves almost alone in the purple drawing-room, which more than ever, in its stuffy dimness, resembled a well-kept family vault, in which the last corpse had just been decently deposited.

In Gerty Farish's sitting-room, whither a hansom had carried the two friends, Lily dropped into a chair with a faint sound of laughter: it struck her as a humorous coincidence that her aunt's legacy should so nearly represent the amount of her debt to Trenor. The need of discharging that debt had reasserted itself with increased urgency since her return to America, and she spoke her first thought in saying to the anxiously hovering Gerty: "I wonder when the legacies will be paid."

But Miss Farish could not pause over the legacies; she broke into a larger indignation. "Oh, Lily, it's unjust; it's cruel—Grace Stepney must *feel* she has no right to all that money!"

"Any one who knew how to please Aunt Julia has a right to her money," Miss Bart rejoined philosophically.

"But she was devoted to you—she led every one to think——" Gerty checked herself in evident embarrassment, and Miss Bart turned to her with a direct look. "Gerty, be honest: this will was made only six weeks ago. She had heard of my break with the Dorsets?"

"Every one heard, of course, that there had been some disagreement—some misunderstanding——"

"Did she hear that Bertha turned me off the yacht?"

"Lily!"

"That was what happened, you know. She said I was trying to marry George Dorset. She did it to make him think she was jealous. Isn't that what she told Gwen Stepney?"

"I don't know—I don't listen to such horrors."

"I *must* listen to them—I must know where I stand." She paused, and again sounded a faint note of derision. "Did you notice the women? They were afraid to snub me while they thought I was going to get the money—afterward they scuttled off as if I had the plague." Gerty remained silent, and she continued: "I stayed on to see what would happen. They took their cue from Gwen Stepney and Lulu Melson—I saw them watching to see what Gwen would do.—Gerty, I must know just what is being said of me."

"I tell you I don't listen——"

"One hears such things without listening." She rose and laid her resolute hands on Miss Farish's shoulders. "Gerty, are people going to cut me?"

"Your *friends,* Lily—how can you think it?"

"Who are one's friends at such a time? Who, but you, you poor trustful darling? And heaven knows what *you* suspect me of!" She kissed Gerty with a whimsical murmur. "You'd never let it make any difference—but then you're fond of criminals, Gerty! How about the irreclaimable ones, though? For I'm absolutely impenitent, you know."

She drew herself up to the full height of her slender majesty, towering like some dark angel of defiance above the troubled Gerty, who could only falter out: "Lily, Lily—how can you laugh about such things?"

"So as not to weep, perhaps. But no—I'm not of the tearful order. I discovered early that crying makes my nose red, and the knowledge has helped me through several painful episodes." She took a restless turn about the room, and then, reseating herself, lifted the bright mockery of her eyes to Gerty's anxious countenance.

"I shouldn't have minded, you know, if I'd got the money—" and at Miss Farish's protesting "Oh!" she repeated calmly: "Not a straw, my dear; for, in the first place, they wouldn't have quite dared to ignore me; and if they had, it wouldn't have mattered, because I should have been independent of them. But now—!" The irony faded from her eyes, and she bent a clouded face upon her friend.

"How can you talk so, Lily? Of course the money ought to have been yours, but after all that makes no difference. The important thing——" Gerty paused, and then continued firmly: "The important thing is that you should clear yourself—should tell your friends the whole truth."

"The whole truth?" Miss Bart laughed. "What is truth? Where a woman is concerned, it's the story that's easiest to believe. In this case it's a great deal easier to believe Bertha Dorset's story than mine, because she has a big house and an opera box, and it's convenient to be on good terms with her."

Miss Farish still fixed her with an anxious gaze. "But what *is* your story, Lily? I don't believe any one knows it yet."

"My story?—I don't believe I know it myself. You see I never thought of preparing a version in advance as Bertha did—and if I had, I don't think I should take the trouble to use it now."

But Gerty continued with her quiet reasonableness: "I don't want a version prepared in advance—but I want you to tell me exactly what happened from the beginning."

"From the beginning?" Miss Bart gently mimicked her. "Dear Gerty, how little imagination you good people have! Why, the beginning was in my cradle, I suppose—in the way I was brought up, and the things I was taught to care for. Or no—I won't blame anybody for my faults: I'll say it was in my blood, that I got it from some wicked pleasure-loving ancestress, who reacted against the homely virtues of New Amsterdam, and wanted to be back at the court of the Charleses!" And as Miss Farish continued to press her with troubled eyes, she went on impatiently: "You asked me just now for the truth—well, the truth about any girl is that once she's talked about she's done for; and the more she explains her case the worse it looks.—My good Gerty, you don't happen to have a cigarette about you?"

In her stuffy room at the hotel to which she had gone on landing, Lily Bart that evening reviewed her situation. It was the last week in June, and none of her friends were in town. The few relatives who had stayed on, or returned, for the reading of Mrs. Peniston's will, had taken flight again that afternoon to Newport or Long Island; and not one of them had made any offer of hospitality to Lily. For the first time in her life she found herself utterly alone except for Gerty Farish. Even at the actual moment of her break with the Dorsets she had not had so keen a sense of its consequences, for the Duchess of Beltshire, hearing of the catastrophe from Lord Hubert, had instantly offered her protection, and under her sheltering wing Lily had made an almost triumphant progress to London. There she had been sorely tempted to linger on in a society which asked of her only to amuse and charm it, without inquiring too curiously how she had acquired her gift for doing so; but Selden, before they parted, had pressed on her the urgent need of returning at once to her aunt, and Lord Hubert, when he presently reappeared in London, abounded in the same counsel. Lily did not need to be told that the Duchess's championship was not the best road to social rehabilitation and as she was besides aware that her noble defender might at any moment drop her in favor of a new *protégeé,* she reluctantly decided to return to America. But she had not been ten minutes on her native shore before she realized that she had delayed too long to regain it. The Dorsets, the Stepneys, the Brys—all the actors and witnesses in the miserable drama—had preceded her with their version of the case; and, even had she seen the least chance of gaining a hearing for her own, some obscure disdain and reluctance would have restrained her. She knew it was not by explanations and counter-charges that she could ever hope to recover her lost standing; but even had she felt the least trust in their efficacy, she would still have been held back by the feeling which had kept her from defending herself to Gerty Farish—a feeling that was half pride and half humiliation. For though she knew she had been ruthlessly sacrificed to Bertha Dorset's determination to win back her husband, and though her own relation to Dorset had been that of the merest good-fellowship, yet she had been perfectly aware from the outset that her part in the affair was, as Carry Fisher brutally put it, to distract Dorset's attention from his wife. That was what she was "there for": it was the price she had chosen to pay for three months of luxury and freedom from care. Her habit of resolutely facing the facts, in her rare moments of introspection, did not now allow her to put any false gloss on the situation. She had suffered for the very faithfulness with which she had carried out her part of the tacit compact, but the part was not a handsome one at best, and she saw it now in all the ugliness of failure.

She saw, too, in the same uncompromising light, the train of consequences resulting from that failure; and these became clearer to her with every day of her weary lingering in town. She stayed on partly for the comfort of Gerty Farish's nearness, and partly for lack of knowing where to go. She understood well enough the nature of the task before her. She must set out to regain, little by little, the position she had lost; and the first step in the tedious task was to find out, as soon as possible, on how many of her friends she could count. Her hopes were mainly centered on Mrs. Trenor, who had treasures of easy-going tolerance for those who were amusing or useful to her, and in the noisy rush of whose existence the still small voice of detraction was slow to make itself heard. But Judy, though she must have been apprised of Miss Bart's return, had not even recognized it by the formal note of condolence which her friend's bereavement demanded. Any advance on Lily's side might have been perilous: there was nothing to do but to trust to the happy chance of an accidental meeting, and Lily knew that, even so late in the season, there was always a hope of running across her friends in their frequent passages through town.

To this end she assiduously showed herself at the restaurants they frequented, where, attended by the troubled Gerty, she lunched luxuriously, as she said, on her expectations.

"My dear Gerty, you wouldn't have me let the head-waiter see that I've nothing to live on but Aunt Julia's legacy? Think of Grace Stepney's satisfaction if she came in and found us lunching on cold mutton and tea! What sweet shall we have today, dear—*Coupe Jacques* or *Pêches à la Melba?*"

She dropped the *menu* abruptly, with a quick heightening of color, and Gerty, following her glance, was aware of the advance, from an inner room, of a party headed by Mrs. Trenor and Carry Fisher. It was impossible for these ladies and their companions—among whom Lily had at once distinguished both Trenor and Rosedale—not to pass, in going out, the table at which the two girls were seated; and Gerty's sense of the fact betrayed itself in the helpless trepidation of her manner.

Miss Bart, on the contrary, borne forward on the wave of her buoyant grace, and neither shrinking from her friends nor appearing to lie in wait for them, gave to the encounter the touch of naturalness which she could impart to the most strained situations. Such embarrassment as was shown was on Mrs. Trenor's side, and manifested itself in the mingling of exaggerated warmth with imperceptible reservations. Her loudly affirmed pleasure at seeing Miss Bart took the form of a nebulous generalization, which included neither inquiries as to her future nor the expression of a definite wish to see her again.

Lily, well-versed in the language of these omissions, knew that they were equally intelligible to the other members of the party: even Rosedale, flushed as he was with the importance of keeping such company, at once took the temperature of Mrs. Trenor's cordiality, and reflected it in his off-hand greeting of Miss Bart. Trenor, red and uncomfortable, had cut short his salutations on the pretext of a word to say to the head-waiter; and the rest of the group soon melted away in Mrs. Trenor's wake.

It was over in a moment—the waiter, *menu* in hand, still hung on the result of the choice between *Coupe Jacques* and *Pêches à la Melba*—but Miss Bart, in the interval, had taken the measure of her fate. Where Judy Trenor led, all the world would follow; and Lily had the doomed sense of the castaway who has signalled in vain to fleeing sails.

In a flash she remembered Mrs. Trenor's complaints of Carry Fisher's rapacity, and saw that they denoted an unexpected acquaintance with her husband's private affairs. In the large tumultuous disorder of the life at Bellomont, where no one seemed to have time to observe any one else, and private aims and personal interests were swept along unheeded in the rush of collective activities, Lily had fancied herself sheltered from inconvenient scrutiny; but if Judy knew when Mrs. Fisher borrowed money of her husband, was she likely to ignore the same transaction on Lily's part? If she was careless of his affections she was plainly jealous of his pocket; and in that fact Lily read the explanation of her rebuff. The immediate result of these conclusions was the passionate resolve to pay back her debt to Trenor. That obligation discharged, she would have but a thousand dollars of Mrs. Peniston's legacy left, and nothing to live on but her own small income, which was considerably less than Gerty Farish's wretched pittance; but this consideration gave way to the imperative claim of her wounded pride. She must be quits with the Trenors first; after that she would take thought for the future.

In her ignorance of legal procrastinations she had supposed that her legacy would be paid over within a few days of the reading of her aunt's will; and after an interval of anxious suspense, she wrote to inquire the cause of the delay. There was another interval before Mrs. Peniston's lawyer, who was also one of the executors, replied to the effect that, some questions having arisen relative to the interpretation of the will, he and his associates might not be in a position to pay the legacies till the close of the twelvemonth legally allotted for their settlement. Bewildered and indignant, Lily resolved to try the effect of a personal appeal; but she returned from her expedition with a sense of the powerlessness of beauty and charm against the unfeeling process of the law. It seemed intolerable to live on for another year under the weight of her debt; and in her extremity she decided to turn to Miss Stepney, who still lingered in town, immersed in the delectable duty of "going over" her benefactress's effects. It was bitter enough for Lily to ask a favor of Grace Stepney, but the alternative was bitterer still; and one morning she presented herself at Mrs. Peniston's, where Grace, for the facilitation of her pious task, had taken up a provisional abode.

The strangeness of entering as a suppliant the house where she had so long commanded, increased Lily's desire to shorten the ordeal; and when Miss Stepney entered the darkened drawing-room, rustling with the best quality of crape, her visitor went straight to the point: would she be willing to advance the amount of the expected legacy?

Grace, in reply, wept and wondered at the request, bemoaned the inexorableness of the law, and was astonished that Lily had not realized the exact similarity of their positions. Did she think that only the payment of the legacies had been delayed? Why, Miss Stepney herself had not received a penny of her inheritance, and was paying rent—yes, actually—for the privilege of living in a house that belonged to her. She was sure it was not what poor dear cousin Julia would have wished—she had told the executors so to their faces; but they were inaccessible to reason, and there was nothing to do but to wait. Let Lily take example by her and be patient—let them both remember how beautifully patient cousin Julia had always been.

Lily made a movement which showed her imperfect assimilation of this example. "But you will have everything, Grace—it would be easy for you to borrow ten times the amount I am asking for."

"Borrow—easy for me to borrow?" Grace Stepney rose up before her in sable wrath. "Do you imagine for a moment that I would raise money on my expectations from cousin Julia, when I know so well her unspeakable horror of every transaction of the sort? Why, Lily, if you must know the truth, it was the idea of your being in debt that brought on her illness—you remember she had a slight attack before you sailed. Oh, I don't know the particulars, of course—

I don't want to know them—but there were rumors about your affairs that made her most unhappy—no one could be with her without seeing that. I can't help it if you are offended by my telling you this now—if I can do anything to make you realize the folly of your course, and how deeply she disapproved of it, I shall feel it is the truest way of making up to you for her loss."

V

IT seemed to Lily, as Mrs. Peniston's door closed on her, that she was taking a final leave of her old life. The future stretched before her dull and bare as the deserted length of Fifth Avenue, and opportunities showed as meagrely as the few cabs trailing in quest of fares that did not come. The completeness of the analogy was, however, disturbed as she reached the sidewalk by the rapid approach of a hansom which pulled up at sight of her.

From beneath its luggage-laden top, she caught the wave of a signalling hand; and the next moment Mrs. Fisher, springing to the street, had folded her in a demonstrative embrace.

"My dear, you don't mean to say you're still in town? When I saw you the other day at Sherry's I didn't have time to ask——" She broke off, and added with a burst of frankness: "The truth is I was *horrid,* Lily, and I've wanted to tell you so ever since."

"Oh——" Miss Bart protested, drawing back from her penitent clasp; but Mrs. Fisher went on with her usual directness: "Look here, Lily, don't let's beat about the bush: half the trouble in life is caused by pretending there isn't any. That's not my way, and I can only say I'm thoroughly ashamed of myself for following the other women's lead. But we'll talk of that by and bye—tell me now where you're staying and what your plans are. I don't suppose you're keeping house in there with Grace Stepney, eh?—and it struck me you might be rather at loose ends."

In Lily's present mood there was no resisting the honest friendliness of this appeal, and she said with a smile: "I *am* at loose ends for the moment, but Gerty Farish is still in town, and she's good enough to let me be with her whenever she can spare the time."

Mrs. Fisher made a slight grimace. "H'm—that's a temperate joy. Oh, I know—Gerty's a trump, and worth all the rest of us put together; but *à la longue* you're used to a little higher seasoning, aren't you, dear? And besides, I suppose she'll be off herself before long—the first of August, you say? Well, look here, you can't spend your summer in town; we'll talk of that later too. But meanwhile, what do you say to putting a few things in a trunk and coming down with me to the Sam Gormers' tonight?"

And as Lily stared at the breathless suddenness of the suggestion, she continued with her easy laugh: "You don't know them and they don't know you; but that don't make a rap of difference. They've taken the Van Alstyne place at Roslyn, and I've got *carte blanche* to bring my friends down there—the more the merrier. They do things awfully well, and there's to be rather a jolly party there this week——" she broke off, checked by an undefinable change in Miss Bart's expression. "Oh, I don't mean *your* particular set, you know: rather a different crowd, but very good fun. The fact is, the Gormers have struck out on a line of their own: what they want is to have a good time, and to have it in their own way. They gave the other thing a few months' trial, under my distinguished auspices, and they were really doing extremely well—getting on a good deal faster than the Brys, just because they didn't care as much—but suddenly they decided that the whole business bored them, and that what they wanted was a crowd they could really feel at home with. Rather original of them, don't you think so? Mattie Gormer *has* got aspirations still; women always have; but she's awfully easy-going, and Sam won't be bothered, and they both like to be the most important people in sight, so they've started a sort of continuous performance of their own, a kind of social Coney Island, where everybody is welcome who can make noise enough and doesn't put on airs. *I* think it's awfully good fun myself—some of the artistic set, you know, any pretty actress that's going, and so on. This week, for instance, they have Audrey Anstell, who made such a hit last spring in 'The Winning of Winny'; and Paul Morpeth—he's painting Mattie Gormer—and the Dick Bellingers, and Kate Corby—well, every one you can think of who's jolly and makes a row. Now don't stand there with your nose in the air, my dear—it will be a good deal better than a broiling Sunday in town, and you'll find clever people as well as noisy ones—Morpeth, who admires Mattie enormously, always brings one or two of his set."

Mrs. Fisher drew Lily toward the hansom with friendly authority. "Jump in now, there's a dear, and we'll drive round to your hotel and have your things packed, and then we'll have tea, and the two maids can meet us at the train."

It was a good deal better than a broiling Sunday in town—of that no doubt remained to Lily as, reclining in the shade of a leafy verandah, she looked seaward across a stretch of greensward picturesquely dotted with groups of ladies in lace raiment and men in tennis flannels. The huge Van Alstyne house and its rambling dependencies were packed to their fullest capacity with the Gormers' weekend guests, who now, in the radiance of the Sunday forenoon, were dispersing themselves over the grounds in quest of the various distractions the place afforded: distractions ranging from tennis-courts to shooting-galleries, from bridge and whiskey within doors to motors and steam-launches without. Lily had the odd sense of having been caught up into the crowd as carelessly as a passenger is gathered in by an express train. The blonde and genial Mrs. Gormer might, indeed, have figured the conductor, calmly assigning seats to the rush of travellers, while Carry Fisher represented the porter pushing their bags into place, giving them their numbers for the dining-car, and warning them when their station was at hand. The train, meanwhile, had scarcely slackened speed—life whizzed on with a deafening rattle and roar, in which one traveller at least found a welcome refuge from the sound of her own thoughts.

The Gormer *milieu* represented a social outskirt which Lily had always fastidiously avoided; but it struck her, now that she was in it, as only a flamboyant copy of her own world, a caricature approximating the real thing as the "society play" approaches the manners of the drawing-room. The people about her were doing the same things as the Trenors, the Van Osburghs and the Dorsets: the difference lay in a hundred shades of aspect and manner, from the pattern of the men's waistcoats to the inflection of the women's voices. Everything was pitched in a higher key, and there was more of each thing: more noise, more color, more champagne, more familiarity—but also greater good-nature, less rivalry, and a fresher capacity for enjoyment.

Miss Bart's arrival had been welcomed with an uncritical friendliness that first irritated her pride and then brought her to a sharp sense of her own situation—of the place in life which, for the moment, she must accept and make the best of. These people knew her story—of that her first long talk with Carry Fisher had left no doubt: she was publicly branded as the heroine of a "queer" episode—but instead of shrinking from her as her own friends had done, they received her without question into the easy promiscuity of their lives. They swallowed her past as easily as they did Miss Anstell's, and with no apparent sense of any difference in the size of the mouthful: all they asked was that she should—in her own way, for they recognized a diversity of gifts—contribute as much to the general amusement as that graceful actress, whose talents, when off the stage, were of the most varied order. Lily felt at once that any tendency to be "stuck-up," to mark a sense of differences and distinctions, would be fatal to her continuance in the Gormer set. To be taken in on such terms—and into such a world!—was hard enough to the lingering pride in her; but she realized, with a pang of self-contempt, that to be excluded from it would, after all, be harder still. For, almost at once, she had felt the insidious charm of slipping back into a life where every material difficulty was smoothed away. The sudden escape from a stifling hotel in a dusty deserted city to the space and luxury of a great country-house fanned by sea breezes, had produced a state of moral lassitude agreeable enough after the nervous tension and physical discomfort of the past weeks. For the moment she must yield to the refreshment her senses craved—after that she would reconsider her situation, and take counsel with her dignity. Her enjoyment of her surroundings was, indeed, tinged by the unpleasant consideration that she was accepting the hospitality and courting the approval of people she had disdained under other conditions. But she was growing less sensitive on such points: a hard glaze of indifference was fast forming over her delicacies and susceptibilities, and each concession to expediency hardened the surface a little more.

On the Monday, when the party disbanded with uproarious adieux, the return to town threw into stronger relief the charms of the life she was leaving. The other guests were dispersing to take up the same existence in a different setting: some at Newport, some at Bar Harbour, some in the elaborate rusticity of an Adirondack camp.

The huge Van Alstyne house was packed to fullest capacity with the Gormers' weekend guests.

Even Gerty Farish, who welcomed Lily's return with tender solicitude, would soon be preparing to join the aunt with whom she spent her summers on Lake George: only Lily herself remained without plan or purpose, stranded in a backwater of the great current of pleasure. But Carry Fisher, who had insisted on transporting her to her own house, where she herself was to perch for a day or two on the way to the Brys' camp, came to the rescue with a new suggestion.

"Look here, Lily—I'll tell you what it is: I want you to take my place with Mattie Gormer this summer. They're taking a party out to Alaska next month in their private car, and Mattie, who is the laziest woman alive, wants me to go with them, and relieve her of the bother of arranging things; but the Brys want me too—oh, yes, we've made it up: didn't I tell you?—and, to put it frankly, though I like the Gormers best, there's more profit for me in the Brys. The fact is, they want to try Newport this summer, and if I can make it a success for them they—well, they'll make it a success for *me*." Mrs. Fisher clasped her hands enthusiastically. "Do you know, Lily, the more I think of my idea the better I like it—quite as much for you as for myself. The Gormers have both taken a tremendous fancy to you, and the trip to Alaska is—well—the very thing I should want for you just at present."

Miss Bart lifted her eyes with a keen glance. "To take me out of my friends' way, you mean?" she said quietly; and Mrs. Fisher responded with a deprecating kiss: "To keep you out of their sight till they realize how much they miss you."

Miss Bart went with the Gormers to Alaska; and the expedition, if it did not produce the effect anticipated by her friend, had at least the negative advantage of removing her from the fiery center of criticism and discussion. Gerty Farish had opposed the plan with all the energy of her somewhat inarticulate nature. She had even offered to give up her visit to Lake George, and remain in town with Miss Bart, if the latter would renounce her journey; but Lily could disguise her real distaste for this plan under a sufficiently valid reason.

"You dear innocent, don't you see," she protested, "that Carry is quite right, and that I must take up my usual life, and go about among people as much as possible? If my old friends choose to believe lies about me I shall have to make new ones, that's all; and you know beggars mustn't be choosers. Not that I don't like Mattie Gormer—I *do* like her: she's kind and honest and unaffected; and don't you suppose I feel grateful to her for making me welcome at a time when, as you've yourself seen, my own family have unanimously washed their hands of me?"

Gerty shook her head, mutely unconvinced. She felt not only that Lily was cheapening herself by making use of an intimacy she would never have cultivated from choice, but that, in drifting back now to her former manner of life, she was forfeiting her last chance of ever escaping from it. Gerty had but an obscure conception of what Lily's actual experience had been: but its consequences had established a lasting hold on her pity since the memorable night when she had offered up her own secret hope to her friend's extremity. To characters like Gerty's such a sacrifice constitutes a moral claim on the part of the person in whose behalf it has been made. Having once helped Lily, she must continue to help her; and helping her, must believe in her, because faith is the main-spring of such natures. But even if Miss Bart, after her renewed taste of the amenities of life, could have returned to the barrenness of a New York August, mitigated only by poor Gerty's presence, her worldly wisdom would have counselled her against such an act of abnegation. She knew that Carry Fisher was right: that an opportune absence might be the first step toward rehabilitation, and that, at any rate, to linger on in town out of season was a fatal admission of defeat.

From the Gormers' tumultuous progress across their native continent, she returned with an altered view of her situation. The renewed habit of luxury—the daily waking to an assured absence of care and presence of material ease—gradually blunted her appreciation of these values, and left her more conscious of the void they could not fill. Mattie Gormer's undiscriminating good-nature, and the slap-dash sociability of her friends, who treated Lily precisely as they treated each other—all these characteristic notes of difference began to wear upon her endurance; and the more she saw to criticize in her companions, the less justification she found for making use of them. The longing to get back to her former surroundings hardened to a fixed idea; but with the strengthening of her purpose came the inevitable perception that, to attain it, she must exact fresh concessions from her pride. These, for the moment, took the unpleasant form of continuing to cling to her hosts after their return from Alaska. Little as she was in the key of their *milieu,* her immense social facility, her long habit of adapting herself to others without suffering her own outline to be blurred, the skilled manipulation of all the polished implements of her craft, had won for her an important place in the Gormer group. If their resonant hilarity could never be hers, she contributed a note of easy elegance more valuable to Mattie Gormer than the louder passages of the band. Sam Gormer and his special cronies stood indeed a little in awe of her; but Mattie's following, headed by Paul Morpeth, made her feel that they prized her for the very qualities they most conspicuously lacked. If Morpeth, whose social indolence was as great as his artistic activity, had abandoned himself to the easy current of the Gormer existence, where the minor exactions of politeness were unknown or ignored, and a man could either break his engagements, or keep them in a painting-jacket and slippers, he still preserved his sense of differences, and his appreciation of graces he had no time to cultivate. During the preparations for the Brys' *tableaux* he had been immensely struck by Lily's plastic possibilities—"not the face: too self-controlled for expression; but the rest of her—gad, what a model she'd make!"—and though his abhorrence of the world in which he had seen her was too great for him to think of seeking her there, he was fully alive to the privilege of having her to look at and listen to while he lounged in Mattie Gormer's dishevelled drawing-room.

Lily had thus formed, in the tumult of her surroundings, a little nucleus of friendly relations which mitigated the crudeness of her course in lingering with the Gormers after their return. Nor was she without pale glimpses of her own world, especially since the breaking-up of the Newport season had set the social current once more toward Long Island. Kate Corby, whose tastes made her as promiscuous as Carry Fisher was rendered by her necessities, occasionally descended on the Gormers, where, after a first stare of surprise, she took Lily's presence almost too much as a matter of course. Mrs. Fisher, too, appearing frequently in the neighborhood, drove over to impart her experiences and give Lily what she called the latest report from the weather-bureau; and the latter, who had never directly invited her confidence, could yet talk with her more freely than with Gerty Farish, in whose presence it was impossible even to admit the existence of much that Mrs. Fisher conveniently took for granted.

Mrs. Fisher, moreover, had no embarrassing curiosity. She did not wish to probe the inwardness of Lily's situation, but simply to view it from the outside, and draw her conclusions accordingly; and these conclusions, at the end of a confidential talk, she summed up to her friend in the succinct remark: "You must marry as soon as you can."

Lily uttered a faint laugh—for once Mrs. Fisher lacked originality. "Do you mean, like Gerty Farish, to recommend the unfailing panacea of 'a good man's love'?"

"No—I don't think either of my candidates would answer to that description," said Mrs. Fisher after a pause of reflection.

"Either? Are there actually two?"

"Well, perhaps I ought to say one and a half—for the moment."

Miss Bart received this with increasing amusement. "Other things being equal, I think I should prefer a half-husband: who is he?"

"Don't fly out at me till you hear my reasons—George Dorset."

"Oh——" Lily murmured reproachfully; but Mrs. Fisher pressed on unrebuffed. "Well, why not? They had a few weeks' honeymoon when they first got back from Europe, but now things are going badly with them again. Bertha has been behaving more than ever like a madwoman, and George's powers of credulity are very nearly exhausted. They're at their place here, you know, and I spent last Sunday with them. It was a ghastly party—no one else but poor Neddy Silverton, who looks like a galley-slave (they used to talk of my making that poor boy unhappy!)—and after luncheon George carried me off on a long walk, and told me the end would have to come soon."

Miss Bart made an incredulous gesture. "As far as that goes, the end will never come—Bertha will always know how to get him back when she wants him."

Mrs. Fisher continued to observe her tentatively. "Not if he has any one else to turn to! Yes—that's just what it comes to: the poor creature can't stand alone. And I remember him such a good fellow, full of life and enthusiasm." She paused, and went on, dropping her glance from Lily's: "He wouldn't stay with her ten minutes if he *knew*——"

"Knew——?" Miss Bart repeated.

"What *you* must, for instance—with the opportunities you've had! If he had positive proof, I mean——"

Lily interrupted her with a deep blush of displeasure. "Please let us drop the subject, Carry: it's too odious to me." And to divert her companion's attention she added, with an attempt at lightness: "And your second candidate? We must not forget him."

Mrs. Fisher echoed her laugh. "I wonder if you'll cry out just as loud if I say—Sim Rosedale?"

Miss Bart did not cry out: she sat silent, gazing thoughtfully at her friend. The suggestion, in truth, gave expression to a possibility which, in the last weeks, had more than once recurred to her; but after a moment she said carelessly: "Mr. Rosedale wants a wife who can establish him in the bosom of the Van Osburghs and Trenors."

Mrs. Fisher caught her up eagerly. "And so *you* could—with his money! Don't you see how beautifully it would work out for you both?"

"I don't see any way of making him see it," Lily returned, with a laugh intended to dismiss the subject.

But in reality it lingered with her long after Mrs. Fisher had taken leave. She had seen very little of Rosedale since her annexation by the Gormers, for he was still steadily bent on penetrating to the inner Paradise from which she was now excluded; but once or twice, when nothing better offered, he had turned up for a Sunday, and on these occasions he had left her in no doubt as to his view of her situation. That he still admired her was, more than ever, offensively evident; for in the Gormer circle, where he expanded as in his native element, there were no puzzling conventions to check the full expression of his approval. But it was in the quality of his admiration that she read his shrewd estimate of her case. He enjoyed letting the Gormers see that he had known "Miss Lily"—she was "Miss Lily" to him now—before they had had the faintest social existence: enjoyed more especially impressing Paul Morpeth with the distance to which their intimacy dated back. But he let it be felt that intimacy was a mere ripple on the surface of a rushing social current, the kind of relaxation which a man of large interests and manifold preoccupations permits himself in his hours of ease.

The necessity of accepting this view of their past relation, and of meeting it in the key of pleasantry prevalent among her new friends, was deeply humiliating to Lily. But she dared less than ever to quarrel with Rosedale. She suspected that her rejection rankled among the most unforgettable of his rebuffs, and the fact that he knew something of her wretched transaction with Trenor, and was sure to put the basest construction on it, seemed to place her hopelessly in his power. Yet at Carry Fisher's suggestion a new hope had stirred in her. Much as she disliked Rosedale, she no longer absolutely despised him. For he was gradually attaining his object in life, and that, to Lily, was always less despicable than to miss it. With the slow unalterable persistency which she had always felt in him, he was making his way through the dense mass of social antagonisms. Already his wealth, and the masterly use he had made of it, were giving him an enviable prominence in the world of affairs, and placing Wall Street under obligations which only Fifth Avenue could repay. In response to these claims, his name began to figure on municipal committees and charitable boards; he appeared at banquets to distinguished strangers, and his candidacy at one of the fashionable clubs was discussed with diminishing opposition. He had figured once or twice at the Trenor dinners, and had learned to speak with just the right note of disdain of the big Van Osburgh crushes; and all he now needed was a wife whose affiliations would shorten the last tedious steps of his ascent. It was with that object that, a year earlier, he had fixed his affections on Miss Bart; but in the interval he had mounted nearer to the goal, while she had lost the power to abbreviate the remaining steps of the way. All this she saw with the clearness of vision that came to her in moments of despondency. It was success that dazzled her—she could distinguish facts plainly enough in the twilight of failure. And the twilight, as she now sought to pierce it, was gradually lighted by a faint spark of reassurance. Under the utilitarian motive of Rosedale's wooing she had felt, clearly enough, the heat of personal inclination. She would not have detested him so heartily had she not known that he dared to admire her. What, then, if the passion persisted, though the other motive had ceased to sustain it? She had never even tried to please him—he had been drawn to her in spite of her manifest disdain. What if she now chose to exert the power which, even in its passive state, he had felt so strongly? What if she made him marry her for love, now that he had no other reason for marrying her?

VI

AS became persons of their rising consequence, the Gormers were engaged in building a country-house on Long Island; and it was a part of Miss Bart's duty to attend her hostess on frequent visits of inspection to the new estate. There, while Mrs. Gormer plunged into problems of lighting and sanitation, Lily had leisure to wander, in the bright autumn air, along the tree-fringed bay to which the land declined. Little as she was addicted to solitude, there had come to be moments when it seemed a welcome escape from the empty noises of her life. She was weary of being swept passively along a current of pleasure and business in which she had no share; weary of seeing other people pursue amusement and squander money, while she felt herself of no more account among them than an expensive toy in the hands of a spoiled child.

It was in this frame of mind that, striking back from the shore one morning into the windings of an unfamiliar lane, she came suddenly upon the figure of George Dorset. The Dorset place was in the immediate neighborhood of the Gormers' newly-acquired estate, and in her motor-flights thither with Mrs. Gormer, Lily had caught one or two passing glimpses of the couple; but they moved in so different an orbit that she had not considered the possibility of a direct encounter.

Dorset, swinging along with bent head, in moody abstraction, did not see Miss Bart till he was close upon her; but the sight, instead of bringing him to a halt as she had half-expected, sent him toward her with an eagerness which found expression in his opening words.

"Miss Bart!—You'll shake hands, won't you? I've been hoping to meet you—I should have written to you if I'd dared." His face, with its tossed red hair and straggling moustache, had a driven uneasy look, as though life had become an unceasing race between himself and the thoughts at his heels.

The look drew a word of compassionate greeting from Lily, and he pressed on, as if encouraged by her tone: "I wanted to apologize—to ask you to forgive me for the miserable part I played——"

She checked him with a quick gesture. "Don't let us speak of it: I was very sorry for you," she said, with a tinge of disdain which, as she instantly perceived, was not lost on him.

He flushed to his haggard eyes, flushed so cruelly that she repented the thrust. "You might well be; you don't know—you must let me explain. I was deceived: abominably deceived——"

"I am still more sorry for you, then," she interposed, without irony; "but you must see that I am not exactly the person with whom the subject can be discussed."

He met this with a look of genuine wonder. "Why not? Isn't it to you, of all people, that I owe an explanation——"

"No explanation is necessary: the situation was perfectly clear to me."

"Ah——" he murmured, his head drooping again, and his irresolute hand switching at the underbrush along the lane. But as Lily made a movement to pass on, he broke out with fresh vehemence: "Miss Bart, for God's sake don't turn from me! We used to be good friends—you were always kind to me—and you don't know how I need a friend now."

The lamentable weakness of the words roused a motion of pity in Lily's breast. She too needed friends—she had tasted the pang of loneliness; and her resentment of Bertha Dorset's cruelty softened her heart to the poor wretch who was after all the chief of Bertha's victims.

"I still wish to be kind; I feel no ill-will toward you," she said. "But you must understand that after what has happened we can't be friends again—we can't see each other."

"Ah, you *are* kind—you're merciful—you always were!" He fixed his miserable gaze on her. "But why can't we be friends—why not, when I've repented in dust and ashes? Isn't it hard that you should condemn me to suffer for the falseness, the treachery of others? I was punished enough at the time—is there to be no respite for me?"

"I should have thought you had found complete respite in the reconciliation which was effected at my expense," Lily began, with renewed impatience; but he broke in imploringly: "Don't put it in that way—that's been the worst of my punishment. My God! what could I do—wasn't I powerless? You were singled out as a sacrifice: any word I might have said would have been turned against you——"

"I have told you I don't blame you; all I ask you to understand is that, after the use Bertha chose to make of me— after all that her behavior has since implied—it's impossible that you and I should meet."

He continued to stand before her, in his dogged weakness. "Is it—need it be? Mightn't there be circumstances——?" he checked himself, slashing at the wayside weeds in a wider radius. Then he began again: "Miss Bart, listen—give me a minute. If we're not to meet again, at least let me have a hearing now. You say we can't be friends after—after what has happened. But can't I at least appeal to your pity? Can't I move you if I ask you to think of me as a prisoner—a prisoner you alone can set free?"

Lily's inward start betrayed itself in a quick blush: was it possible that this was really the sense of Carry Fisher's adumbrations?

"I can't see how I can possibly be of any help to you," she murmured, drawing back a little from the mounting excitement of his look.

Her tone seemed to sober him, as it had so often done in his stormiest moments. The stubborn lines of his face relaxed, and he said, with an abrupt drop to docility: "You *would* see, if you'd be as merciful as you used to be: and heaven knows I've never needed it more!"

She paused a moment, moved in spite of herself by this reminder of her influence over him. Her fibers had been softened by suffering, and the sudden glimpse into his mocked and broken life disarmed her contempt for his weakness.

"I am very sorry for you—I would help you willingly; but you must have other friends, other advisers."

"I never had a friend like you," he answered simply. "And besides—can't you see?—you're the only person"—his voice dropped to a whisper—"the only person who knows."

Again she felt her color change; again her heart rose in precipitate throbs to meet what she felt was coming.

He lifted his eyes to her entreatingly. "You do see, don't you? You understand? I'm desperate—I'm at the end of my tether. I want to be free, and you can free me. I know you can. You don't want to keep me bound fast in hell, do you? You can't want to take such a vengeance as that. You were always kind—your eyes are kind now. You say you're sorry for me. Well, it rests with you to show it; and heaven knows there's nothing to keep you back. You understand, of course—there wouldn't be a hint of publicity—not a sound or a syllable to connect you with the thing. It would never come to that, you know: all I need is to be able to say definitely: 'I know this—and this—and this'—and the fight would drop, and the way be cleared, and the whole abominable business swept out of sight in a second."

He spoke pantingly, like a tired runner, with breaks of exhaustion between his words; and through the breaks she caught, as through the shifting rents of a fog, great golden vistas of peace and safety. For there was no mistaking the definite intention behind his vague appeal; she could have filled up the blanks without the help of Mrs. Fisher's insinuations. Here was a man who turned to her in the extremity of his loneliness and his humiliation: if she came to him at such a moment he would be hers with all the force of his deluded faith. And the power to make him so lay in her hand—lay there in a completeness he could not even remotely conjecture. Revenge and rehabilitation might be hers at a stroke—there was something dazzling in the completeness of the opportunity.

She stood silent, gazing away from him down the autumnal stretch of the deserted lane. And suddenly fear possessed her—fear of herself and of the terrible force of the temptation. All her past weaknesses were like so many eager accomplices drawing her toward the path their feet had already smoothed. She turned quickly, and held out her hand to Dorset.

"Goodbye—I'm sorry; there's nothing in the world that I can do."

"Nothing? Ah, don't say that," he cried; "say what's true: that you abandon me like the others. You, the only creature who could have saved me!"

"Goodbye—goodbye," she repeated hurriedly; and as she moved away she heard him cry out on a last note of entreaty: "At least you'll let me see you once more?"

Lily, on regaining the Gormer grounds, struck rapidly across the lawn toward the unfinished house, where she fancied that her hostess might be speculating, not too resignedly, on the cause of her delay; for, like many unpunctual persons, Mrs. Gormer disliked to be kept waiting.

As Miss Bart reached the avenue, however, she saw a smart phaeton with a high-stepping pair disappear behind the shrubbery in the direction of the gate; and on the doorstep stood Mrs. Gormer, with a glow of retrospective pleasure on her open countenance. At sight of Lily the glow deepened to an embarrassed red, and she said with a slight laugh: "Did you see my visitor? Oh, I thought you came back by the avenue. It was Mrs. George Dorset—she said she'd dropped in to make a neighborly call."

Lily met the announcement with her usual composure, though her experience of Bertha's idiosyncrasies would not have led her to include the neighborly instinct among them; and Mrs. Gormer, relieved to see that she gave no sign of surprise, went on with a deprecating laugh: "Of course what really brought her was curiosity—she made me take her all over the house. But no one could have been nicer—no airs, you know, and so good-natured: I can quite see why people think her so fascinating."

This surprising event, coinciding too completely with her meeting with Dorset to be regarded as contingent upon it, had yet immediately struck Lily with a vague sense of foreboding. It was not in Bertha's habits to be neighborly, much less to make advances to any one outside the immediate circle of her affinities. She had always consistently ignored the world of outer aspirants, or had recognized its individual members only when prompted by motives of self-interest; and the very capriciousness of her condescensions had, as Lily was aware, given them special value in the eyes of the persons she distinguished. Lily saw this now in Mrs. Gormer's unconcealable complacency, and in the happy irrelevance with which, for the next day or two, she quoted Bertha's opinions and speculated on the origin of her gown. All the secret ambitions which Mrs. Gormer's native indolence, and the attitude of her companions, kept in habitual abeyance, were now germinating afresh in the glow of Bertha's advances; and whatever the cause of the latter, Lily saw that, if they were followed up, they were likely to have a disturbing effect upon her own future.

She had arranged to break the length of her stay with her new friends by one or two visits to other acquaintances as recent; and on her return from this somewhat depressing excursion she was immediately conscious that Mrs. Dorset's influence was still in the air. There had been another exchange of visits, a tea at a country-club, an encounter at a hunt ball; there was even a rumor of an approaching dinner, which Mattie Gormer, with an unnatural effort at discretion, tried to smuggle out of the conversation whenever Miss Bart took part in it.

The latter had already planned to return to town after a farewell Sunday with her friends; and, with Gerty Farish's aid, had discovered a small private hotel where she might establish herself for the winter. The hotel being on the edge of a fashionable neighborhood, the price of the few square feet she was to occupy was considerably in excess of her means; but she found a justification for her dislike of poorer quarters in the argument that, at this particular juncture, it was of the utmost importance to keep up a show of prosperity. In reality, it was impossible for her, while she had the means to pay her way for a week ahead, to lapse into a form of existence like Gerty Farish's. She had never been so near the brink of insolvency; but she could at least manage to meet her weekly hotel bill, and having settled the heaviest of her previous debts out of the money she had received from Trenor, she had a still fair margin of credit to go upon. The situation, however, was not agreeable enough to lull her to complete unconsciousness of its insecurity. Her rooms, with their cramped outlook down a sallow vista of brick walls and fire escapes, her lonely meals in the dark restaurant with its surcharged ceiling and haunting smell of coffee—all these material discomforts, which were yet to be accounted as so many privileges soon to be withdrawn, kept constantly before her the disadvantages of her state, and her mind reverted the more insistently to Mrs. Fisher's counsels. Beat about the question as she would, she knew the outcome of it was that she must try to marry Rosedale; and in this conviction she was fortified by an unexpected visit from George Dorset.

She found him, on the first Sunday after her return to town, pacing her narrow sitting-room to the imminent peril of the few knick-knacks with which she had tried to disguise its plush exuberances; but the sight of her seemed to quiet him, and he said meekly that he hadn't come to bother her—that he asked only to be allowed to sit for half an hour and talk of anything she liked. In reality, as she knew, he had but one subject: himself and his wretchedness; and it was the need of her sympathy that had drawn him back. But he began with a pretence of questioning her about herself and as she replied, she saw that, for the first time, a faint realization of her plight penetrated the dense surface of his self-absorption. Was it possible that her old beast of an aunt had actually cut her off? That she was living alone like this because there was no one else for her to go to, and that she really hadn't more than enough to keep alive on till the wretched little legacy was paid? The fibers of sympathy were nearly atrophied in him, but he was suffering so intensely that he had a faint glimpse of what other sufferings might mean—and, as she perceived, an almost simultaneous perception of the way in which her particular misfortunes might serve him.

When at length she dismissed him, on the pretext that she must dress for dinner, he lingered entreatingly on the threshold to blurt out: "It's been such a comfort—do say you'll let me see you again—" But to this direct appeal it was impossible to give an assent; and she said with friendly decisiveness: "I'm sorry but you know why I can't."

He colored to the eyes, pushed the door shut, and stood before her embarrassed but insistent. "I know how you might, if you would—if things were different—and it lies with you to make them so. It's just a word to say, and you put me out of my misery!"

Their eyes met, and for a second she trembled again with the nearness of the temptation. "You're mistaken; I know nothing; I saw nothing," she exclaimed, striving, by sheer force of reiteration, to build a barrier between herself and her peril; and as he turned away, groaning out "You sacrifice us both," she continued to repeat, as if it were a charm: "I know nothing—absolutely nothing."

Lily had seen little of Rosedale since her illuminating talk with Mrs. Fisher, but on the two or three occasions when they had met she was conscious of having distinctly advanced in his favor. There could be no doubt that he admired her as much as ever, and she believed it rested with herself to raise his admiration to the point where it should bear down the lingering counsels of expediency. The task was not an easy one; but neither was it easy, in her long sleepless nights, to face the thought of what George Dorset was so clearly ready to offer. Baseness for baseness, she hated the other least: there were even moments when a marriage with Rosedale seemed the only honorable solution of her difficulties. She did not indeed let her imagination range beyond the day of plighting: after that everything faded into a haze of material well-being, in which the personality of her benefactor remained mercifully vague. She had learned, in her long vigils, that there were certain things not good to think of, certain midnight images that must at any cost be exorcised—and one of these was the image of herself as Rosedale's wife.

Carry Fisher, on the strength, as she frankly owned, of the Brys' Newport success, had taken for the autumn months a small house at Tuxedo; and thither Lily was bound on the Sunday after Dorset's visit. Though it was nearly dinner-time when she arrived, her hostess was still out, and the firelit quiet of the small silent house descended on her spirit with a sense of peace and familiarity. It may be doubted if such an emotion had ever before been evoked by Carry Fisher's surroundings; but, contrasted to the world in which Lily had lately lived, there was an air of repose and stability in the very placing of the furniture, and in the quiet competence of the parlor-maid who led her up to her room. Mrs. Fisher's unconventionality was, after all, a merely superficial divergence from an inherited social creed, while the manners of the Gormer circle represented their first attempt to formulate such a creed for themselves.

It was the first time since her return from Europe that Lily had found herself in a congenial atmosphere, and the stirring of familiar associations had almost prepared her, as she descended the stairs before dinner, to enter upon a group of her old acquaintances. But this expectation was instantly checked by the reflection that the friends who remained loyal were precisely those who would be least willing to expose her to such encounters; and it was hardly with surprise that she found, instead, Mr. Rosedale kneeling domestically on the drawing-room hearth before his hostess's little girl.

Rosedale in the paternal rôle was hardly a figure to soften Lily; yet she could not but notice a quality of homely goodness in his advances to the child. They were not, at any rate, the premeditated and perfunctory endearments of the guest under his hostess's eye, for he and the little girl had the room to themselves; and something in his attitude made him seem a simple and kindly being compared to the small critical creature who endured his homage. Yes, he would be kind—Lily, from the threshold, had time to feel—kind in his gross, unscrupulous, rapacious way, the way of the predatory creature with his mate. She had but a moment in which to consider whether this glimpse of the fireside man mitigated her repugnance, or gave it, rather, a more concrete and intimate form; for at sight of her he was immediately on his feet again, the florid and dominant Rosedale of Mattie Gormer's drawing-room.

It was no surprise to Lily to find that he had been selected as her only fellow-guest. Though she and her hostess had not met since the latter's tentative discussion of her future, Lily knew that the acuteness which enabled Mrs. Fisher to lay a safe and pleasant course through a world of antagonistic forces was not infrequently exercised for the benefit of her friends. It was, in fact, characteristic of Carry that, while she actively gleaned her own stores from the fields of affluence, her real sympathies were on the other side—with the unlucky, the unpopular, the unsuccessful, with all her hungry fellow-toilers in the shorn stubble of success.

Mrs. Fisher's experience guarded her against the mistake of exposing Lily, for the first evening, to the unmitigated impression of Rosedale's personality. Kate Corby and two or three men dropped in to dinner, and Lily, alive to every detail of her friend's method, saw that such opportunities as had been contrived for her were to be deferred till she had, as it were, gained courage to make effectual use of them. She had a sense of acquiescing in this plan with the passiveness of a sufferer resigned to the surgeon's touch; and this feeling of almost lethargic helplessness continued when, after the departure of the guests, Mrs. Fisher followed her upstairs.

"May I come in and smoke a cigarette over your fire? If we talk in my room we shall disturb the child." Mrs. Fisher looked about her with the eye of the solicitous hostess. "I hope you've managed to make yourself comfortable, dear? Isn't it a jolly little house? It's such a blessing to have a few quiet weeks with the baby."

Carry, in her rare moments of prosperity, became so expansively maternal that Miss Bart sometimes wondered whether, if she could ever get time and money enough, she would not end by devoting them both to her daughter.

"It's a well-earned rest: I'll say that for myself," she continued, sinking down with a sigh of content on the pillowed lounge near the fire. "Louisa Bry is a stern task-master: I often used to wish myself back with the Gormers. Talk of love making people jealous and suspicious—it's nothing to social ambition! Louisa used to lie awake at night wondering whether the women who called on us called on *me* because I was with her, or on *her* because she was with me; and she was always laying traps to find out what I thought. Of course I had to disown my oldest friends, rather than let her suspect she owed me the chance of making a single acquaintance—when, all the while, that was what she had me there for, and what she wrote me a handsome check for when the season was over!"

Mrs. Fisher was not a woman who talked of herself without cause, and the practice of direct speech, far from precluding in her an occasional resort to circuitous methods, served rather, at crucial moments, the purpose of the juggler's chatter while he shifts the contents of his sleeves. Through the haze of her cigarette smoke she continued to gaze meditatively at Miss Bart, who, having dismissed her maid, sat before the toilet-table shaking out over her shoulders the loosened undulations of her hair.

"Your hair's wonderful, Lily. Thinner—? What does that matter, when it's so light and alive? So many women's worries seem to go straight to their hair—but yours looks as if there had never been an anxious thought under it. I never saw you look better than you did this evening. Mattie Gormer told me that Morpeth wanted to paint you—why don't you let him?"

Miss Bart's immediate answer was to address a critical glance to the reflection of the countenance under discussion. Then she said, with a slight touch of irritation: "I don't care to accept a portrait from Paul Morpeth."

Mrs. Fisher mused. "N—no. And just now, especially—well, he can do you after you're married." She waited a moment, and then went on: "By the way, I had a visit from Mattie the other day. She turned up here last Sunday—and with Bertha Dorset, of all people in the world!" She paused again to measure the effect of this announcement on her hearer, but the brush in Miss Bart's lifted hand maintained its unwavering stroke from brow to nape.

"I never was more astonished," Mrs. Fisher pursued. "I don't know two women less predestined to intimacy—from Bertha's standpoint, that is; for of course poor Mattie thinks it natural enough that she should be singled out—I've no doubt the rabbit always thinks it is fascinating the anaconda. Well, you know I've always told you that Mattie secretly longed to bore herself with the really fashionable; and now that the chance has come, I see that she's capable of sacrificing all her old friends to it."

Lily laid aside her brush and turned a penetrating glance upon her friend. "Including *me?*" she suggested.

"Ah, my dear," murmured Mrs. Fisher, rising to push back a log from the hearth.

"That's what Bertha means, isn't it?" Miss Bart went on steadily. "For of course she always means something; and before I left Long Island I saw that she was beginning to lay her toils for Mattie."

Mrs. Fisher sighed evasively. "She has her fast now, at any rate. To think of that loud independence of Mattie's being only a subtler form of snobbishness! Bertha can already make her believe anything she pleases—and I'm afraid she's begun, my poor child, by insinuating horrors about you."

Lily flushed under the shadow of her drooping hair. "The world is too vile," she murmured, averting herself from Mrs. Fisher's anxious scrutiny.

"It's not a pretty place; and the only way to keep a footing in it is to fight it on its own terms—and above all, my dear, not alone!" Mrs. Fisher gathered up her floating implications in a resolute grasp. "You've told me so little that I can only guess what has been happening; but in the rush we all live in there's no time to keep on hating anyone without a cause, and if Bertha is still nasty enough to want to injure you with other people it must be because she's still afraid of you. From her standpoint there's only one reason for being afraid of you; and my own idea is that, if you want to punish her, you hold the means in your hand. I believe you can marry George Dorset tomorrow; but if you don't care for that particular form of retaliation, the only thing to save you from Bertha is to marry somebody else."

VII

THE light projected on the situation by Mrs. Fisher had the cheerless distinctness of a winter dawn. It outlined the facts with a cold precision unmodified by shade or color, and refracted, as it were, from the blank walls of the surrounding limitations: she had opened windows from which no sky was ever visible. But the idealist subdued to vulgar necessities must employ vulgar minds to draw the inferences to which he cannot stoop; and it was easier for Lily to let Mrs. Fisher formulate her case than to put it plainly to herself. Once confronted with it, however, she went the full length of its consequences; and these had never been more clearly present to her than when, the next afternoon, she set out for a walk with Rosedale.

It was one of those still November days when the air is haunted with the light of summer, and something in the lines of the landscape, and in the golden haze which bathed them, recalled to Miss Bart the September afternoon when she had climbed the slopes of Bellomont with Selden. The importunate memory was kept before her by its ironic contrast to her present situation, since her walk with Selden had represented an irresistible flight from just such a climax as the present excursion was designed to bring about. But other memories importuned her also; the recollection of similar situations, as skillfully led up to, but through some malice of fortune, or her own unsteadiness of purpose, always failing of the intended result. Well, her purpose was steady enough now. She saw that the whole weary work of rehabilitation must begin again, and against far greater odds, if Bertha Dorset should succeed in breaking up her friendship with the Gormers; and her longing for shelter and security was intensified by the passionate desire to triumph over Bertha, as only wealth and predominance could triumph over her. As the wife of Rosedale—the Rosedale she felt it in her power to create—she would at least present an invulnerable front to her enemy.

She had to draw upon this thought, as upon some fiery stimulant, to keep up her part in the scene toward which Rosedale was too frankly tending. As she walked beside him, shrinking in every nerve from the way in which his look and tone made free of her, yet telling herself that this momentary endurance of his mood was the price she must pay for her ultimate power over him, she tried to calculate the exact point at which concession must turn to resistance, and the price *he* would have to pay be made equally clear to him. But his dapper self-confidence seemed impenetrable to such hints, and she had a sense of something hard and self-contained behind the superficial warmth of his manner.

They had been seated for some time in the seclusion of a rocky glen above the lake, when she suddenly cut short the culmination of an impassioned period by turning upon him the grave loveliness of her gaze.

"I *do* believe what you say, Mr. Rosedale," she said quietly; "and I am ready to marry you whenever you wish."

Rosedale, reddening to the roots of his glossy hair, received this announcement with a recoil which carried him to his feet, where he halted before her in an attitude of almost comic discomfiture.

"For I suppose that is what you do wish," she continued, in the same quiet tone. "And, though I was unable to consent when you spoke to me in this way before, I am ready, now that I know you so much better, to trust my happiness to your hands."

She spoke with the noble directness which she could command on such occasions, and which was like a large steady light thrown across the tortuous darkness of the situation. In its inconvenient brightness Rosedale seemed to waver a moment, as though conscious that every avenue of escape was unpleasantly illuminated.

Then he gave a short laugh, and drew out a gold cigarette-case, in which, with plump jewelled fingers, he groped for a gold-tipped cigarette. Selecting one, he paused to contemplate it a moment before saying: "My dear Miss Lily, I'm sorry if there's been any little misapprehension between us—but you made me feel my suit was so hopeless that I had really no intention of renewing it."

Lily's blood tingled with the grossness of the rebuff, but she checked the first leap of her anger, and said in a tone of gentle dignity: "I have no one but myself to blame if I gave you the impression that my decision was final."

Her word-play was always too quick for him, and this reply held him in puzzled silence while she extended her hand and added, with the faintest inflection of sadness in her voice: "Before we bid each other goodbye, I want at least to thank you for having once thought of me as you did."

The touch of her hand, the moving softness of her look, thrilled a vulnerable fiber in Rosedale. It was her exquisite inaccessibleness, the sense of distance she could convey without a hint of disdain, that made it most difficult for him to give her up.

"Why do you talk of saying goodbye? Ain't we going to be good friends all the same?" he urged, without releasing her hand.

She drew it away quietly. "What is your idea of being good friends?" she returned with a slight smile. "Making love to me without asking me to marry you?"

Rosedale laughed with a recovered sense of ease. "Well, that's about the size of it, I suppose. I can't help making love to you—I don't see how any man could; but I don't mean to ask you to marry me as long as I can keep out of it."

She continued to smile. "I like your frankness; but I am afraid our friendship can hardly continue on those terms."

She turned away, as though to mark that its final term had in fact been reached, and he followed her for a few steps with a baffled sense of her having after all kept the game in her own hands.

"Miss Lily——" he began impulsively; but she walked on without seeming to hear him.

He overtook her in a few quick strides, and laid an entreating hand on her arm. "Miss Lily—don't hurry away like that. You're beastly hard on a fellow; but if you don't mind speaking the truth I don't see why you shouldn't allow me to do the same."

She had paused a moment with raised brows, drawing away instinctively from his touch, though she made no effort to evade his words.

"I was under the impression," she rejoined, "that you had done so without waiting for my permission."

"Well—why shouldn't you hear my reasons for doing it, then? We're neither of us such new hands that a little plain speaking is going to hurt us. I'm all broken up on you: there's nothing new in that. I'm more in love with you than I was this time last year; but I've got to face the fact that the situation is changed."

She continued to confront him with the same air of ironic composure. "You mean to say that I'm not as desirable a match as you thought me?"

"Yes; that's what I do mean," he answered resolutely. "I won't go into what's happened. I don't believe the stories about you—I don't want to believe them. But they're there, and my not believing them ain't going to alter the situation."

She flushed to her temples, but the extremity of her need checked the retort on her lip and she continued to face him composedly. "If they are not true," she said, "doesn't *that* alter the situation?"

He met this with a steady gaze of his small stock-taking eyes, which made her feel herself no more than some superfine human merchandise. "I believe it does in novels; but I'm certain it don't in real life. You know that as well as I do: if we're speaking the truth, let's speak the whole truth. Last year I was wild to marry you, and you wouldn't look at me: this year—well, you appear to be willing. Now, what has changed in the interval? Your situation, that's all. Then you thought you could do better; now——"

"You think you can?" broke from her ironically.

"Why, yes, I do: in one way, that is." He stood before her, his hands in his pockets, his chest sturdily expanded under its vivid waistcoat. "It's this way, you see: I've had a pretty steady grind of it these last years, working up my social position. Think it's funny I should say that? Why should I mind saying I want to get into society? A man ain't ashamed to say he wants to own a racing stable or a picture gallery. Well, a taste for society's just another kind of hobby. Perhaps I want to get even with some of the people who cold-shouldered me last year—put it that way if it sounds better. Anyhow, I want to have the run of the best houses; and I'm getting it too, little by little. But I know the quickest way to queer yourself with the right people is to be seen with the wrong ones; and that's the reason I want to avoid mistakes."

Miss Bart continued to stand before him in a silence that might have expressed either mockery or a half-reluctant respect for his candor, and after a moment's pause he went on: "There it is, you see. I'm more in love with you than ever, but if I married you now I'd queer myself for good and all, and everything I've worked for all these years would be wasted."

She received this with a look from which all tinge of resentment had faded. After the tissue of social falsehoods in which she had so long moved it was refreshing to step into the open daylight of an avowed expediency.

"I understand you," she said. "A year ago I should have been of use to you, and now I should be all encumbrance; and I like you for telling me so quite honestly." She extended her hand with a smile.

Again the gesture had a disturbing effect upon Mr. Rosedale's self-command. "By George, you're a dead game sport, you are!" he exclaimed; and as she began once more to move away, he broke out suddenly—"Miss Lily—stop. You know I don't believe those stories—I believe they were all got up by a woman who didn't hesitate to sacrifice you to her own convenience——"

Lily drew away with a movement of quick disdain: it was easier to endure his insolence than his commiseration.

"You are very kind; but I don't think we need discuss the matter farther."

But Rosedale's natural imperviousness to hints made it easy for him to brush such resistance aside. "I don't want to discuss anything; I just want to put a plain case before you," he persisted.

She paused in spite of herself, held by the note of a new purpose in his look and tone; and he went on, keeping his eyes firmly upon her: "The wonder to me is that you've waited so long to get square with that woman, when you've had the power in your hands." She continued silent under the rush of astonishment that his words produced, and he moved a step closer to ask with low-toned directness: "Why don't you use those letters of hers you bought last year?"

Lily stood speechless under the shock of the interrogation. In the words preceding it she had conjectured, at most, an allusion to her supposed influence over George Dorset; nor did the astonishing indelicacy of the reference diminish the likelihood of Rosedale's resorting to it. But now she saw how far short of the mark she had fallen; and the surprise of learning that he had discovered the secret of the letters left her, for the moment, unconscious of the special use to which he was in the act of putting his knowledge.

Her temporary loss of self-possession gave him time to press his point; and he went on quickly, as though to secure completer control of the situation: "You see I know where you stand—I know how completely she's in your power. That sounds like stage-talk, don't it?—but there's a lot of truth in some of those old gags; and I don't suppose you bought those letters simply because you're collecting autographs."

She continued to look at him with a deepening bewilderment: her only clear impression resolved itself into a scared sense of his power.

"You're wondering how I found out about 'em?" he went on, answering her look with a note of conscious pride. "Perhaps you've forgotten that I'm the owner of the Benedick—but never mind about that now. Getting on to things is a mighty useful accomplishment in business, and I've simply extended it to my private affairs. For this is partly my affair, you see—at least, it depends on you to make it so. Let's look the situation straight in the eye. Mrs. Dorset, for reasons we needn't go into, did you a beastly bad turn last spring. Everybody knows what Mrs. Dorset is, and her best friends wouldn't believe her on oath where their own interests were concerned; but as long as they're out of the row it's much easier to follow her lead than to set themselves against it, and you've simply been sacrificed to their laziness and selfishness. Isn't that a pretty fair statement of the case?—Well, some people say you've got the neatest kind of an answer in your hands: that George Dorset would marry you tomorrow, if you'd tell him all you know, and give him the chance to show the lady the door. I daresay he would; but you don't seem to care for that particular form of getting even, and, taking a purely business view of the question, I think you're right. In a deal like that, nobody comes out with perfectly clean hands, and the only way for you to start fresh is to get Bertha Dorset to back you up, instead of trying to fight her."

He paused long enough to draw breath, but not to give her time for the expression of her gathering resistance; and as he pressed on, expounding and elucidating his idea with the directness of the man who has no doubts of his cause, she found the indignation gradually freezing on her lip, found herself held fast in the grasp of his argument by the mere cold strength of its presentation. There was no time now to wonder how he had heard of her obtaining the letters: all her world was dark outside the monstrous glare of his scheme for using them. And it was not, after the first moment, the horror of the idea that held her spellbound, subdued to his will; it was rather its subtle affinity to her own inmost cravings. He would marry her tomorrow if she could regain Bertha Dorset's friendship; and to induce the open resumption of that friendship, and the tacit retractation of all that had caused its withdrawal, she had only to put to the lady the latent menace contained in the packet so miraculously delivered into her hands. Lily saw in a flash the advantage of this course over that which poor Dorset had pressed upon her. The other plan depended for its success on the infliction of an open injury, while this reduced the transaction to a private understanding, of which no third person need have the remotest hint. Put by Rosedale in terms of business-like give-and-take, this understanding took on the harmless air of a mutual accommodation, like a transfer of property or a revision of boundary lines. It certainly simplified life to view it as a perpetual adjustment, a play of party politics, in which every concession had its recognized equivalent: Lily's tired mind was fascinated by this escape from fluctuating ethical estimates into a region of concrete weights and measures.

Rosedale, as she listened, seemed to read in her silence not only a gradual acquiescence in his plan, but a dangerously far-reaching perception of the chances it offered; for as she continued to stand before him without speaking, he broke out, with a quick return upon himself: "You see how simple it is, don't you? Well, don't be carried away by the idea that it's *too* simple. It isn't exactly as if you'd started in with a clean bill of health. Now we're talking let's call things by their right names, and clear the whole business up. You know well enough that Bertha Dorset couldn't have touched you if there hadn't been—well—questions asked before—little points of interrogation, eh? Bound to happen to a good-looking girl with stingy relatives, I suppose; anyhow, they *did* happen, and she found the ground prepared for her. Do you see where I'm coming out? You don't want these little questions cropping up again. It's one thing to get Bertha Dorset into line—but what you want is to keep her there. You can frighten her fast enough—but how are you going to keep her frightened? By showing her that you're as powerful as she is. All the letters in the world won't do that for you as you are now; but with a big backing behind you, you'll keep her just where you want her to be. That's *my* share in the business—that's what I'm offering you. You can't put the thing through without me—don't run away with any idea that you can. In six months you'd be back again among your old worries, or worse ones; and here I am, ready to lift you out of 'em tomorrow if you say so. *Do* you say so, Miss Lily?" he added, moving suddenly nearer.

The words, and the movement which accompanied them, combined to startle Lily out of the state of tranced subservience into which she had insensibly slipped. Light comes in devious ways to the groping consciousness, and it came to her now through the disgusted perception that her would-be accomplice assumed, as a matter of course, the likelihood of her distrusting him and perhaps trying to cheat him of his share of the spoils. This glimpse of his inner mind seemed to present the whole transaction in a new aspect, and she saw that the essential baseness of the act lay in its freedom from risk.

She drew back with a quick gesture of rejection, saying, in a voice that was a surprise to her own ears: "You are mistaken—quite mistaken—both in the facts and in what you infer from them."

Rosedale stared a moment, puzzled by her sudden dash in a direction so different from that toward which she had appeared to be letting him guide her.

"Now what on earth does that mean? I thought we understood each other!" he exclaimed; and to her murmur of "Ah, we do *now,*" he retorted with a sudden burst of violence: "I suppose it's because the letters are to *him,* then? Well, I'll be damned if I see what thanks you've got from him!"

VIII

THE autumn days declined to winter. Once more the leisure world was in transition between country and town, and Fifth Avenue, still deserted at the weekend, showed from Monday to Friday a broadening stream of carriages between house-fronts gradually restored to consciousness.

The Horse Show, some two weeks earlier, had produced a passing semblance of reanimation, filling the theaters and restaurants with a human display of the same costly and high-stepping kind as circled daily about its ring. In Miss Bart's world the Horse Show, and the public it attracted, had ostensibly come to be classed among the spectacles disdained of the elect; but, as the feudal lord might sally forth to join in the dance on his village green, so society, unofficially and incidentally, still condescended to look in upon the scene. Mrs. Gormer, among the rest, was not above seizing such an occasion for the display of herself and her horses; and Lily was given one or two opportunities of appearing at her friend's side in the most conspicuous box the house afforded. But this lingering semblance of intimacy made her only the more conscious of a change in the relation between Mattie and herself, of a dawning discrimination, a gradually formed social standard, emerging from Mrs. Gormer's chaotic view of life. It was inevitable that Lily herself should constitute the first sacrifice to this new ideal, and she knew that, once the Gormers were established in town, the whole drift of fashionable life would facilitate Mattie's detachment from her. She had, in short, failed to make herself indispensable; or rather, her attempt to do so had been thwarted by an influence stronger than any she could exert. That influence, in its last analysis, was simply the power of money: Bertha Dorset's social credit was based on an impregnable bank account.

Lily knew that Rosedale had overstated neither the difficulty of her own position nor the completeness of the vindication he offered: once Bertha's match in material resources, her superior gifts would make it easy for her to dominate her adversary. An understanding of what such domination would mean, and of the disadvantages accruing from her rejection of it, was brought home to Lily with increasing clearness during the early weeks of the winter. Hitherto, she had kept up a semblance of movement outside the main flow of the social current; but with the return to town, and the concentrating of scattered activities, the mere fact of not slipping back naturally into her old habits of life marked her as being unmistakably excluded from them. If one were not a part of the season's fixed routine, one swung unsphered in a void of social nonexistence. Lily, for all her dissatisfied dreaming, had never really conceived the possibility of revolving about a different center: it was easy enough to despise the world, but decidedly difficult to find any other habitable region. Her sense of irony never quite deserted her, and she could still note, with self-directed derision, the abnormal value suddenly acquired by the most tiresome and insignificant details of her former life. Its very drudgeries had a charm now that she was involuntarily released from them: card-leaving, note-writing, enforced civilities to the dull and elderly, and the smiling endurance of tedious dinners—how pleasantly such obligations would have filled the emptiness of her days! She did indeed leave cards in plenty; she kept herself, with a smiling and valiant persistence, well in the eye of her world; nor did she suffer any of those gross rebuffs which sometimes produce a wholesome reaction of contempt in their victim. Society did not turn away from her, it simply drifted by, preoccupied and inattentive, letting her feel, to the full measure of her humbled pride, how completely she had been the creature of its favor.

She had rejected Rosedale's suggestion with a promptness of scorn almost surprising to herself: she had not lost her capacity for high flashes of indignation. But she could not breathe long on the heights; there had been nothing in her training to develop any continuity of moral strength: what she craved, and really felt herself entitled to, was a situation in which the noblest attitude should also be the easiest. Hitherto her intermittent impulses of resistance had sufficed to maintain her self-respect. If she slipped she recovered her footing, and it was only afterward that she was aware of having recovered it each time on a slightly lower level. She had rejected Rosedale's offer without conscious effort; her whole being had risen against it; and she did not yet perceive that, by the mere act of listening to him, she had learned to live with ideas which would once have been intolerable to her.

To Gerty Farish, keeping watch over her with a tenderer if less discerning eye than Mrs. Fisher's, the results of the struggle were already distinctly visible. She did not, indeed, know what hostages Lily had already given to expediency; but she saw her passionately and irretrievably pledged to the ruinous policy of "keeping up." Gerty could smile now at her own early dream of her friend's renovation through adversity: she understood clearly enough that Lily was not of those to whom privation teaches the unimportance of what they have lost. But this very fact, to Gerty, made her friend the more piteously in want of aid, the more exposed to the claims of a tenderness she was so little conscious of needing.

Lily, since her return to town, had not often climbed Miss Farish's stairs. There was something irritating to her in the mute interrogation of Gerty's sympathy: she felt the real difficulties of her situation to be incommunicable to any one whose theory of values was so different from her own, and the restrictions of Gerty's life, which had once had the charm of contrast, now reminded her too painfully of the limits to which her own existence was shrinking. When at length, one afternoon, she put into execution the belated resolve to visit her friend, this sense of shrunken opportunities possessed her with unusual intensity. The walk up Fifth Avenue, unfolding before her, in the brilliance of the hard winter sunlight, an interminable procession of fastidiously-equipped carriages—giving her, through the little squares of brougham-windows, peeps of familiar profiles bent above visiting-lists, of hurried hands dispensing notes and cards to attendant footmen—this glimpse of the ever-revolving wheels of the great social machine made Lily more than ever conscious of the steepness and narrowness of Gerty's stairs, and of the cramped blind-alley of life to which they led. Dull stairs destined to be mounted by dull people: how many thousands of insignificant figures were going up and down such stairs all over the world at that very moment—figures as shabby and uninteresting as that of the middle-aged lady in limp black who descended Gerty's flight as Lily climbed to it!

"That was poor Miss Jane Silverton—she came to talk things over with me: she and her sister want to do something to support themselves," Gerty explained, as Lily followed her into the sitting-room.

"To support themselves? Are they so hard up?" Miss Bart asked with a touch of irritation: she had not come to listen to the woes of other people.

"I'm afraid they have nothing left: Ned's debts have swallowed up everything. They had such hopes, you know, when he broke away from Carry Fisher; they thought Bertha Dorset would be such a good influence, because she doesn't care for cards, and—well, she talked quite beautifully to poor Miss Jane about feeling as if Ned were her younger brother, and wanting to carry him off on the yacht, so that he might have a chance to drop cards and racing, and take up his literary work again."

Miss Farish paused with a sigh which reflected the perplexity of her departing visitor. "But that isn't all; it isn't even the worst. It seems that Ned has quarrelled with the Dorsets; or at least Bertha won't allow him to see her, and he is so unhappy about it that he has taken to gambling again, and going about with all sorts of queer people. And cousin Grace Van Osburgh accuses him of having had a very bad influence on Bertie, who left Harvard last spring, and has been a great deal with Ned ever since. She sent for Miss Jane and made a dreadful scene; and Jack Stepney and Herbert Melson, who were there too, told Miss Jane that Bertie was threatening to marry some dreadful woman to whom Ned had introduced him, and that they could do nothing with him because now he's of age he has his own money. You can fancy how poor Miss Jane felt—she came to me at once, and seemed to think that if I could get her something to do she could earn enough to pay Ned's debts and send him away—I'm afraid she has no idea how long it would take her to pay for one of his evenings at bridge. And he was horribly in debt when he came back from the cruise—I can't see why he should have spent so much more money under Bertha's influence than Carry's: can you?"

Lily met this query with an impatient gesture. "My dear Gerty, I always understand how people can spend much more money—never how they can spend any less!"

She loosened her furs and settled herself in Gerty's easy-chair, while her friend busied herself with the tea-cups.

"But what can they do—the Miss Silvertons? How do they mean to support themselves?" she asked, conscious that the note of irritation still persisted in her voice. It was the very last topic she had meant to discuss—it really did not interest her in the least—but she was seized by a sudden perverse curiosity to know how the two colorless shrinking victims of young Silverton's sentimental experiments meant to cope with the grim necessity which lurked so close to her own threshold.

"I don't know—I am trying to find something for them. Miss Jane reads aloud very nicely—but it's so hard to find any one who is willing to be read to. And Miss Annie paints a little——"

"Oh, I know—apple-blossoms on blotting-paper; just the kind of thing I shall be doing myself before long!" exclaimed Lily, starting up with a vehemence of movement that threatened destruction to Miss Farish's fragile tea-table.

Lily bent over to steady the cups; then she sank back into her seat. "I'd forgotten there was no room to dash about in—how beautifully one does have to behave in a small flat! Oh, Gerty, I wasn't meant to be good," she sighed out incoherently.

Gerty lifted an apprehensive look to her pale face, in which the eyes shone with a peculiar sleepless luster.

"You look horribly tired, Lily; take your tea, and let me give you this cushion to lean against."

Miss Bart accepted the cup of tea, but put back the cushion with an impatient hand.

"Don't give me that! I don't want to lean back—I shall go to sleep if I do."

"Well, why not, dear? I'll be as quiet as a mouse," Gerty urged affectionately.

"No—no; don't be quiet; talk to me—keep me awake! I don't sleep at night, and in the afternoon a dreadful drowsiness creeps over me."

"You don't sleep at night? Since when?"

"I don't know—I can't remember." She rose and put the empty cup on the tea-tray. "Another, and stronger, please; if I don't keep awake now I shall see horrors tonight—perfect horrors!"

"But they'll be worse if you drink too much tea."

"No, no—give it to me; and don't preach, please," Lily returned imperiously. Her voice had a dangerous edge, and Gerty noticed that her hand shook as she held it out to receive the second cup.

"But you look so tired: I'm sure you must be ill——"

Miss Bart set down her cup with a start. "Do I look ill? Does my face show it?" She rose and walked quickly toward the little mirror above the writing-table. "What a horrid looking-glass—it's all blotched and discolored. Any one would look ghastly in it!" She turned back, fixing her plaintive eyes on Gerty. "You stupid dear, why do you say such odious things to me? It's enough to make one ill to be told one looks so! And looking ill means looking ugly." She caught Gerty's wrists, and drew her close to the window. "After all, I'd rather know the truth. Look me straight in the face, Gerty, and tell me: am I perfectly frightful?"

"You're perfectly beautiful now, Lily: your eyes are shining, and your cheeks have grown so pink all of a sudden——"

"Ah, they *were* pale, then—ghastly pale, when I came in? Why don't you tell me frankly that I'm a wreck? My eyes are bright now because I'm so nervous—but in the mornings they look like lead. And I can see the lines coming in my face—the lines of worry and disappointment and failure! Every sleepless night leaves a new one—and how can I sleep, when I have such dreadful things to think about?"

"Dreadful things—what things?" asked Gerty, gently detaching her wrists from her friend's feverish fingers.

"What things? Well, poverty, for one—and I don't know any that's more dreadful." Lily turned away and sank with sudden weariness into the easy-chair near the tea-table. "You asked me just now if I could understand why Ned Silverton spent so much money. Of course I understand—he spends it on living with the rich. You think we live *on* the rich, rather than with them: and so we do, in a sense—but it's a privilege we have to pay for! We eat their dinners, and drink their wine, and smoke their cigarettes, and use their carriages and their opera-boxes and their private cars—yes, but there's a tax to pay on every one of those luxuries. The man pays it by big tips to the servants, by playing cards beyond his means, by flowers and presents—and—and—lots of other things that cost; the girl pays it by tips and cards too—oh, yes, I've had to take up bridge again—and by going to the best dress-makers, and having just the right dress for every occasion, and always keeping herself fresh and exquisite and amusing!"

She leaned back for a moment, closing her eyes, and as she sat there, her pale lips slightly parted, and the lids dropped above her fagged brilliant gaze, Gerty had a startled perception of the change in her face—of the way in which an ashen daylight seemed suddenly to extinguish its artificial brightness. She looked up, and the vision vanished.

"It doesn't sound very amusing, does it? And it isn't—I'm sick to death of it! And yet the thought of giving it all up nearly kills me—it's what keeps me awake at night, and makes me so crazy for your strong tea. For I can't go on in this way much longer, you know—I'm nearly at the end of my tether. And then what can I do—how on earth am I to keep myself alive? I see myself reduced to the fate of that poor Silverton woman—slinking about to employment agencies, and trying to sell painted blotting-pads to Women's Exchanges! And there are thousands and thousands of women trying to do the same thing already, and not one of the number who has less idea how to earn a dollar than I have!"

She rose again with a hurried glance at the clock. "It's late, and I must be off—I have an appointment with Carry Fisher. Don't look so worried, you dear thing—don't think too much about the nonsense I've been talking." She was before the mirror again, adjusting her hair with a light hand, drawing down her veil, and giving a dexterous touch to her furs. "Of course, you know, it hasn't come to the employment agencies and the painted blotting-pads yet; but I'm rather hard-up just for the moment, and if I could find something to do—notes to write and visiting-lists to make up, or that kind of thing—it would tide me over till the legacy is paid. And Carry has promised to find somebody who

"What a horrible looking-glass—it's all blotched and discolored."

wants a kind of social secretary—you know she makes a specialty of the helpless rich."

Miss Bart had not revealed to Gerty the full extent of her anxiety. She was in fact in urgent and immediate need of money: money to meet the vulgar weekly claims which could neither be deferred nor evaded. To give up her apartment, and shrink to the obscurity of a boarding-house, or the provisional hospitality of a bed in Gerty Farish's sitting-room, was an expedient which could only postpone the problem confronting her; and it seemed wiser as well as more agreeable to remain where she was and find some means of earning her living. The possibility of having to do this was one which she had never before seriously considered, and the discovery that, as a bread-winner, she was likely to prove as helpless and ineffectual as poor Miss Silverton, was a severe shock to her self-confidence.

Having been accustomed to take herself at the popular valuation, as a person of energy and resource, naturally fitted to dominate any situation in which she found herself, she vaguely imagined that such gifts would be of value to seekers after social guidance; but there was unfortunately no specific head under which the art of saying and doing the right thing could be offered in the market, and even Mrs. Fisher's resourcefulness failed before the difficulty of discovering a workable vein in the vague wealth of Lily's graces. Mrs. Fisher was full of indirect expedients for enabling her friends to earn a living, and could conscientiously assert that she had put several opportunities of this kind before Lily; but more legitimate methods of bread-winning were as much out of her line as they were beyond the capacity of the sufferers she was generally called upon to assist. Lily's failure to profit by the chances already afforded her might, moreover, have justified the abandonment of farther effort on her behalf; but Mrs. Fisher's inexhaustible good-nature made her an adept at creating artificial demands in response to an actual supply. In the pursuance of this end she at once started on a voyage of discovery in Miss Bart's behalf; and as the result of her explorations she now summoned the latter with the announcement that she had "found something."

Left to herself, Gerty mused distressfully upon her friend's plight, and her own inability to relieve it. It was clear to her that Lily, for the present, had no wish for the kind of help she could give. Miss Farish could see no hope for her friend but in a life completely reorganized and detached from its old associations; whereas all Lily's energies were centered in the determined effort to hold fast to those associations, to keep herself visibly identified with them, as long as the illusion could be maintained. Pitiable as such an attitude seemed to Gerty, she could not judge it as harshly as Selden, for instance, might have done. She had not forgotten the night of emotion when she and Lily had lain in each other's arms, and she had seemed to feel her very heart's blood passing into her friend. The sacrifice she had made had seemed unavailing enough; no trace remained in Lily of the subduing influences of that hour; but Gerty's tenderness, disciplined by long years of contact with obscure and inarticulate suffering, could wait on its object with a silent forbearance which took no account of time. She could not, however, deny herself the solace of taking anxious counsel with Lawrence Selden, with whom, since his return from Europe, she had renewed her old relation of cousinly confidence.

Selden himself had never been aware of any change in their relation. He found Gerty as he had left her, simple, undemanding and devoted, but with a quickened intelligence of the heart which he recognized without seeking to explain it. To Gerty herself it would once have seemed impossible that she should ever again talk freely with him of Lily Bart; but what had passed in the secrecy of her own breast seemed to resolve itself, when the mist of the struggle cleared, into a breaking down of the bounds of self, a deflecting of the wasted personal emotion into the general current of human understanding.

It was not till some two weeks after her visit from Lily that Gerty had the opportunity of communicating her fears to Selden. The latter, having presented himself on a Sunday afternoon, had lingered on through the dowdy animation of his cousin's tea-hour, conscious of something in her voice and eye which solicited a word apart; and as soon as the last visitor was gone Gerty opened her case by asking how lately he had seen Miss Bart.

Selden's perceptible pause gave her time for a slight stir of surprise.

"I haven't seen her at all—I've perpetually missed seeing her since she came back."

This unexpected admission made Gerty pause too; and she was still hesitating on the brink of her subject when he relieved her by adding: "I've wanted to see her—but she seems to have been absorbed by the Gormer set since her return from Europe."

"That's all the more reason: she's been very unhappy."

"Unhappy at being with the Gormers?"

"Oh, I don't defend her intimacy with the Gormers; but that too is at an end now, I think. You know people have been very unkind since Bertha Dorset quarrelled with her."

"Ah——" Selden exclaimed, rising abruptly to walk to the window, where he remained with his eyes on the darkening street while his cousin continued to explain: "Judy Trenor and her own family have deserted her too—and all because Bertha Dorset has said such horrible things. And she is very poor—you know Mrs. Peniston cut her off with a small legacy, after giving her to understand that she was to have everything."

"Yes—I know," Selden assented curtly, turning back into the room, but only to stir about with restless steps in the circumscribed space between door and window. "Yes—she's been abominably treated; but it's unfortunately the precise thing that a man who wants to show his sympathy can't say to her."

His words caused Gerty a slight chill of disappointment. "There would be other ways of showing your sympathy," she suggested.

Selden, with a slight laugh, sat down beside her on the little sofa which projected from the hearth. "What are you thinking of, you incorrigible missionary?" he asked.

Gerty's color rose, and her blush was for a moment her only answer. Then she made it more explicit by saying: "I am thinking of the fact that you and she used to be great friends—that she used to care immensely for what you thought of her—and that, if she takes your staying away as a sign of what you think now, I can imagine its adding a great deal to her unhappiness."

"My dear child, don't add to it still more—at least to your conception of it—by attributing to her all sorts of susceptibilities of your own." Selden, for his life, could not keep a note of dryness out of his voice; but he met Gerty's look of perplexity by saying more mildly: "But, though you immensely exaggerate the importance of anything I could do for Miss Bart, you can't exaggerate my readiness to do it—if you ask me to." He laid his hand for a moment on hers, and there passed between them, on the current of the rare contact, one of those exchanges of meaning which fill the hidden reservoirs of affection. Gerty had the feeling that he measured the cost of her request as plainly as she read the significance of his reply; and the sense of all that was suddenly clear between them made her next words easier to find.

"I do ask you, then; I ask you because she once told me that you had been a help to her, and because she needs help now as she has never needed it before. You know how dependent she has always been on ease and luxury—how she has hated what was shabby and ugly and uncomfortable. She can't help it—she was brought up with those ideas, and has never been able to find her way out of them. But now all the things she cared for have been taken from her, and the people who taught her to care for them have abandoned her too; and it seems to me that if some one could reach out a hand and show her the other side—show her how much is left in life and in herself——" Gerty broke off abashed at the sound of her own eloquence, and impeded by the difficulty of giving precise expression to her vague yearning for her friend's retrieval. "I can't help her myself: she's passed out of my reach," she continued. "I think she's afraid of being a burden to me. When she was last here, two weeks ago, she seemed dreadfully worried about her future: she said Carry Fisher was trying to find something for her to do. A few days later she wrote me that she had taken a position as private secretary, and that I was not to be anxious, for everything was all right, and she would come in and tell me about it when she had time; but she has never come, and I don't like to go to her, because I am afraid of forcing myself on her when I'm not wanted. Once, when we were children, and I had rushed up after a long separation, and thrown my arms about her, she said: 'Please don't kiss me unless I ask you to, Gerty'—and she *did* ask me, a minute later; but since then I've always waited to be asked."

Selden had listened in silence, with the concentrated look which his thin dark face could assume when he wished to guard it against any involuntary change of expression. When his cousin ended, he said with a slight smile: "Since you've learned the wisdom of waiting, I don't see why you urge me to rush in——" but the troubled appeal of her eyes made him add, as he rose to take leave: "Still, I'll do what you wish, and not hold you responsible for my failure."

Selden's avoidance of Miss Bart had not been as unintentional as he had allowed his cousin to think. At first, indeed, while the memory of their last hour at Monte Carlo still held the full heat of his indignation, he had anxiously watched for her return; but she had disappointed him by lingering in England, and when she finally reappeared it happened that business had called him to the West, whence he came back only to learn that she was starting for Alaska with the Gormers. The revelation of this suddenly-established intimacy effectually chilled his desire to see her. If, at a moment when her whole life seemed to be breaking up, she could cheerfully commit its reconstruction to the Gormers, there was no reason why such accidents should ever strike her as irreparable. Every step she took seemed in fact to carry her farther from the region where, once or twice, he and she had met for an illumined moment; and the recognition of this fact, when its first pang had been surmounted, produced in him a sense of negative relief. It was much simpler for him to judge Miss Bart by her habitual conduct than by the rare deviations from it which had thrown her so disturbingly in his way; and every act of hers which made the recurrence of such deviations more unlikely, confirmed the sense of relief with which he returned to the conventional view of her.

But Gerty Farish's words had sufficed to make him see how little this view was really his, and how impossible it was for him to live quietly with the thought of Lily Bart. To hear that she was in need of help—even such vague help as he could offer—was to be at once repossessed by that thought; and by the time he reached the street he had sufficiently convinced himself of the urgency of his cousin's appeal to turn his steps directly toward Lily's hotel.

There his zeal met a check in the unforeseen news that Miss Bart had moved away; but, on his pressing his enquiries, the clerk remembered that she had left an address, for which he presently began to search through his books.

It was certainly strange that she should have taken this step without letting Gerty Farish know of her decision; and Selden waited with a vague sense of uneasiness while the address was sought for. The process lasted long enough for uneasiness to turn to apprehension; but when at length a slip of paper was handed him, and he read on it: "Care of Mrs. Norma Hatch, Emporium Hotel," his apprehension passed into an incredulous stare, and this into the gesture of disgust with which he tore the paper in two, and turned to walk quickly homeward.

IX

WHEN Lily woke on the morning after her translation to the Emporium Hotel, her first feeling was one of purely physical satisfaction. The force of contrast gave an added keenness to the luxury of lying once more in a soft-pillowed bed, and looking across a spacious sun-lit room at a breakfast-table set invitingly near the fire. Analysis and introspection might come later; but for the moment she was not even troubled by the excesses of the upholstery or the restless convolutions of the furniture. The sense of being once more lapped and folded in ease, as in some dense mild medium impenetrable to discomfort, effectually stilled the faintest note of criticism.

When, the afternoon before, she had presented herself to the lady to whom Carry Fisher had directed her, she had been conscious of entering a new world. Carry's vague presentment of Mrs. Norma Hatch (whose reversion to her Christian name was explained as the result of her latest divorce) left her under the implication of coming "from the West," with the not unusual extenuation of having brought a great deal of money with her. She was, in short, rich, helpless, unplaced: the very subject for Lily's hand. Mrs. Fisher had not specified the line her friend was to take; she owned herself unacquainted with Mrs. Hatch, whom she "knew about" through Melville Stancy, a lawyer in his leisure moments, and the Falstaff of a certain section of festive club life. Socially, Mr. Stancy might have been said to form a connecting link between the Gormer world and the more dimly-lit region on which Miss Bart now found herself entering. It was, however, only figuratively that the illumination of Mrs. Hatch's world could be described as dim: in actual fact, Lily found her seated in a blaze of electric light, impartially projected from various ornamental excrescences on a vast concavity of pink damask and gilding, from which she rose like Venus from her shell. The analogy was justified by the appearance of the lady, whose large-eyed prettiness had the fixity of something impaled and shown under glass. This did not preclude the immediate discovery that she was some years younger than her visitor, and that under her showiness, her ease, the aggression of her dress and voice, there persisted that ineradicable innocence which, in ladies of her nationality, so curiously coexists with startling extremes of experience.

The environment in which Lily found herself was as strange to her as its inhabitants. She was unacquainted with the world of the fashionable New York hotel—a world over-heated, over-upholstered, and over-fitted with mechanical appliances for the gratification of fantastic requirements, while the comforts of a civilized life were as unattainable as in a desert. Through this atmosphere of torrid splendor moved wan beings as richly upholstered as the furniture, beings without definite pursuits or permanent relations, who drifted on a languid tide of curiosity from restaurant to concert-hall, from palm-garden to music-room, from "art exhibit" to dress-maker's opening. High-stepping horses or elaborately equipped motors waited to carry these ladies into vague metropolitan distances, whence they returned, still more wan from the weight of their sables, to be sucked back into the stifling inertia of the hotel routine. Somewhere behind them, in the background of their lives, there was doubtless a real past, peopled by real human activities: they themselves were probably the product of strong ambitions, persistent energies, diversified contacts with the wholesome roughness of life; yet they had no more real existence than the poet's shades in limbo.

Lily had not been long in this pallid world without discovering that Mrs. Hatch was its most substantial figure. That lady, though still floating in the void, showed faint symptoms of developing an outline; and in this endeavor she was actively seconded by Mr. Melville Stancy. It was Mr. Stancy, a man of large resounding presence, suggestive of convivial occasions and of a chivalry finding expression in "first-night" boxes and thousand dollar bonbonnières, who had transplanted Mrs. Hatch from the scene of her first development to the higher stage of hotel life in the metropolis. It was he who had selected the horses with which she had taken the blue ribbon at the Show, had introduced her to the photographer whose portraits of her formed the recurring ornament of "Sunday Supplements," and had got together the group which constituted her social world. It was a small group still, with heterogeneous figures suspended in large unpeopled spaces; but Lily did not take long to learn that its regulation was no longer in Mr. Stancy's hands. As often happens, the pupil had outstripped the teacher, and Mrs. Hatch was already aware of heights of elegance as well as depths of luxury beyond the world of the Emporium. This discovery at once produced in her a craving for higher guidance, for the adroit feminine hand which should give the right turn to her correspondence, the right "look" to her hats, the right succession to the items of her *menus*. It was, in short, as the regulator of a germinating social life that Miss Bart's guidance was required; her ostensible duties as secretary being restricted by the fact that Mrs. Hatch, as yet, knew hardly any one to write to.

The daily details of Mrs. Hatch's existence were as strange to Lily as its general tenor. The lady's habits were marked by an Oriental indolence and disorder peculiarly trying to her companion. Mrs. Hatch and her friends seemed to float together outside the bounds of time and space. No definite hours were kept; no fixed obligations existed: night and day flowed into one another in a blur of confused and retarded engagements, so that one had the impression of lunching at the tea-hour, while dinner was often merged in the noisy after-theater supper which prolonged Mrs. Hatch's vigil till daylight.

Through this jumble of futile activities came and went a strange throng of hangers-on—manicures, beauty-doctors, hair-dressers, teachers of bridge, of French, of "physical development": figures sometimes indistinguishable, by their appearance, or by Mrs. Hatch's relation to them, from the visitors constituting her recognized society. But strangest of all to Lily was the encounter, in this latter group, of several of her acquaintances. She had supposed, and not without relief, that she was passing, for the moment, completely out of her own circle; but she found that Mr. Stancy, one side of whose sprawling existence overlapped the edge of Mrs. Fisher's world, had drawn several of its brightest ornaments into the circle of the Emporium. To find Ned Silverton among the habitual frequenters of Mrs. Hatch's drawing-room was one of Lily's first astonishments; but she soon discovered that he was not Mr. Stancy's most important recruit. It was on little Freddy Van Osburgh, the small slim heir of the Van Osburgh millions, that the attention of Mrs. Hatch's group was centered. Freddy, barely out of college, had risen above the horizon since Lily's eclipse, and she now saw with surprise what an effulgence he shed on the outer twilight of Mrs. Hatch's existence. This, then, was one of the things that young men "went in" for when released from the official social routine; this was the kind of "previous engagement" that so frequently caused them to disappoint the hopes of anxious hostesses. Lily had an odd sense of being behind the social tapestry, on the side where the threads were knotted and the loose ends hung. For a moment she found a certain amusement in the show, and in her own share of it: the situation had an ease and unconventionality distinctly refreshing after her experience of the irony of conventions. But these flashes of amusement were but brief reactions from the long disgust of her days. Compared with the vast gilded void of Mrs. Hatch's existence, the life of Lily's former friends seemed packed with ordered activities. Even the most irresponsible pretty woman of her acquaintance had her inherited obligations, her conventional benevolences, her share in the working of the great civic machine; and all hung together in the solidarity of these traditional functions. The performance of specific duties would have simplified Miss Bart's position; but the vague attendance on Mrs Hatch was not without its perplexities.

It was not her employer who created these perplexities. Mrs. Hatch showed from the first an almost touching desire for Lily's approval. Far from asserting the superiority of wealth, her beautiful eyes seemed to urge the plea of inexperience: she wanted to do what was "nice," to be taught how to be "lovely." The difficulty was to find any point of contact between her ideals and Lily's.

Mrs. Hatch swam in a haze of indeterminate enthusiasms, of aspirations culled from the stage, the newspapers, the fashion-journals, and a gaudy world of sport still more completely beyond her companion's ken. To separate from these confused conceptions those most likely to advance the lady on her way, was Lily's obvious duty; but its performance was hampered by rapidly-growing doubts. Lily was in fact becoming more and more aware of a certain ambiguity in her situation. It was not that she had, in the conventional sense, any doubt of Mrs. Hatch's irreproachableness. The lady's offenses were always against taste rather than conduct; her divorce record seemed due to geographical rather than ethical conditions; and her worst laxities were likely to proceed from a wandering and extravagant good-nature. But if Lily did not mind her detaining her manicure for luncheon, or offering the "Beauty-Doctor" a seat in Freddy Van Osburgh's box at the play, she was not equally at ease in regard to some less apparent lapses from convention. Ned Silverton's relation to Stancy seemed, for instance, closer and less clear than any natural affinities would warrant; and both appeared united in the effort to cultivate Freddy Van Osburgh's growing taste for Mrs. Hatch. There was as yet nothing definable in the situation, which might well resolve itself into a huge joke on the part of the other two; but Lily had a vague sense that the subject of their experiment was too young, too rich and too credulous. Her embarrassment was increased by the fact that Freddy seemed to regard her as cooperating with himself in the social development of Mrs. Hatch: a view that suggested, on his part, a permanent interest in the lady's future. There were moments when Lily found an ironic amusement in this aspect of the case. The thought of launching such a missile as Mrs. Hatch at the perfidious bosom of society was not without its charm: Miss Bart had even beguiled her leisure with visions of the fair Norma introduced for the first time to a family banquet at the Van Osburghs'. But the thought of being personally connected with the transaction was less agreeable; and her momentary flashes of amusement were followed by increasing periods of doubt.

The sense of these doubts was uppermost when, late one afternoon, she was surprised by a visit from Lawrence Selden. He found her alone in the wilderness of pink damask, for in Mrs. Hatch's world the tea-hour was not dedicated to social rites, and the lady was in the hands of her masseuse.

Selden's entrance had caused Lily an inward start of embarrassment; but his air of constraint had the effect of restoring her self-possession, and she took at once the tone of surprise and pleasure, wondering frankly that he should have traced her to so unlikely a place, and asking what had inspired him to make the search.

Selden met this with an unusual seriousness: she had never seen him so little master of the situation, so plainly at the mercy of any obstructions she might put in his way. "I wanted to see you," he said; and she could not resist observing in reply that he had kept his wishes under remarkable control. She had in truth felt his long absence as one of the chief bitternesses of the last months: his desertion had wounded sensibilities far below the surface of her pride.

Selden met the challenge with directness. "Why should I have come, unless I thought I could be of use to you? It is my only excuse for imagining you could want me."

This struck her as a clumsy evasion, and the thought gave a flash of keenness to her answer. "Then you have come now because you think you can be of use to me?"

He hesitated again. "Yes: in the modest capacity of a person to talk things over with."

For a clever man it was certainly a stupid beginning; and the idea that his awkwardness was due to the fear of her attaching a personal significance to his visit, chilled her pleasure in seeing him. Even under the most adverse conditions, that pleasure always made itself felt: she might hate him, but she had never been able to wish him out of the room. She was very near hating him now; yet the sound of his voice, the way the light fell on his thin dark hair, the way he sat and moved and wore his clothes—she was conscious that even these trivial things were inwoven with her deepest life. In his presence a sudden stillness came upon her, and the turmoil of her spirit ceased; but an impulse of resistance to this stealing influence now prompted her to say: "It's very good of you to present yourself in that capacity; but what makes you think I have anything particular to talk about?"

Though she kept the even tone of light intercourse, the question was framed in a way to remind him that his good offices were unsought; and for a moment Selden was checked by it. The situation between them was one which could have been cleared up only by a sudden explosion of feeling; and their whole training and habit of mind were against the chances of such an explosion. Selden's calmness seemed rather to harden into resistance, and Miss Bart's into a surface of glittering irony, as they faced each other from the opposite corners of one of Mrs. Hatch's elephantine sofas. The sofa in question, and the apartment peopled by its monstrous mates, served at length to suggest the turn of Selden's reply.

"Gerty told me that you were acting as Mrs. Hatch's secretary; and I knew she was anxious to hear how you were getting on."

Miss Bart received this explanation without perceptible softening. "Why didn't she look me up herself, then?" she asked.

"Because, as you didn't send her your address, she was afraid of being importunate." Selden continued with a smile: "You see no such scruples restrained me; but then I haven't as much to risk if I incur your displeasure."

Lily answered his smile. "You haven't incurred it as yet; but I have an idea that you are going to."

"That rests with you, doesn't it? You see my initiative doesn't go beyond putting myself at your disposal."

"But in what capacity? What am I to do with you?" she asked in the same light tone.

Selden again glanced about Mrs. Hatch's drawing-room; then he said, with a decision which he seemed to have gathered from this final inspection: "You are to let me take you away from here."

Lily flushed at the suddenness of the attack; then she stiffened under it and said coldly: "And may I ask where you mean me to go?"

"Back to Gerty in the first place, if you will; the essential thing is that it should be away from here."

The unusual harshness of his tone might have shown her how much the words cost him; but she was in no state to measure his feelings while her own were in a flame of revolt. To neglect her, perhaps even to avoid her, at a time when she had most need of her friends, and then suddenly and unwarrantably to break into her life with this strange assumption of authority, was to rouse in her every instinct of pride and self-defense.

"I am very much obliged to you," she said, "for taking such an interest in my plans; but I am quite contented where I am, and have no intention of leaving."

Selden had risen, and was standing before her in an attitude of uncontrollable expectancy.

"That simply means that you don't know where you are!" he exclaimed.

Lily rose also, with a quick flash of anger. "If you have come here to say disagreeable things about Mrs. Hatch——

"It is only with your relation to Mrs. Hatch that I am concerned."

"My relation to Mrs. Hatch is one I have no reason to be ashamed of. She has helped me to earn a living when my old friends were quite resigned to seeing me starve."

"Nonsense! Starvation is not the only alternative. You know you can always find a home with Gerty till you are independent again."

"You show such an intimate acquaintance with my affairs that I suppose you mean—till my aunt's legacy is paid?"

"I do mean that; Gerty told me of it," Selden acknowledged without embarrassment. He was too much in earnest now to feel any false constraint in speaking his mind.

"But Gerty does not happen to know," Miss Bart rejoined, "that I owe every penny of that legacy."

"Good God!" Selden exclaimed, startled out of his composure by the abruptness of the statement.

"Every penny of it, and more too," Lily repeated; "and you now perhaps see why I prefer to remain with Mrs. Hatch rather than take advantage of Gerty's kindness. I have no money left, except my small income, and I must earn something more to keep myself alive."

Selden hesitated a moment; then he rejoined in a quieter tone: "But with your income and Gerty's—since you allow me to go so far into the details of the situation—you and she could surely contrive a life together which would put you beyond the need of having to support yourself. Gerty, I know, is eager to make such an arrangement, and would be quite happy in it——"

"But I should not," Miss Bart interposed. "There are many reasons why it would be neither kind to Gerty nor wise for myself." She paused a moment, and as he seemed to await a farther explanation, added with a quick lift of her head: "You will perhaps excuse me from giving you these reasons."

"I have no claim to know them," Selden answered, ignoring her tone; "no claim to offer any comment or suggestion beyond the one I have already made. And my right to make that is simply the universal right of a man to enlighten a woman when he sees her unconsciously placed in a false position."

Lily smiled. "I suppose," she rejoined, "that by a false position you mean one outside of what we call society; but you must remember that I had been excluded from those sacred precincts long before I met Mrs. Hatch. As far as I can see, there is very little real difference in being inside or out, and I remember your once telling me that it was only those inside who took the difference seriously."

She had not been without intention in making this allusion to their memorable talk at Bellomont, and she waited with an odd tremor of the nerves to see what response it would bring; but the result of the experiment was disappointing. Selden did not allow the allusion to deflect him from his point; he merely said with completer fullness of emphasis: "The question of being inside or out is, as you say, a small one, and it happens to have nothing to do with the case, except in so far as Mrs. Hatch's desire to be inside may put you in the position I call false."

In spite of the moderation of his tone, each word he spoke had the effect of confirming Lily's resistance. The very apprehensions he aroused hardened her against him: she had been on the alert for the note of personal sympathy, for any sign of recovered power over him; and his attitude of sober impartiality, the absence of all response to her appeal, turned her hurt pride to blind resentment of his interference. The conviction that he had been sent by Gerty, and that, whatever straits he conceived her to be in, he would never voluntarily have come to her aid, strengthened her resolve not to admit him a hair's breadth farther into her confidence. However doubtful she might feel her situation to be, she would rather persist in darkness than owe her enlightenment to Selden.

"I don't know," she said, when he had ceased to speak, "why you imagine me to be situated as you describe; but as you have always told me that the sole object of a bringing-up like mine was to teach a girl to get what she wants, why not assume that that is precisely what I am doing?"

The smile with which she summed up her case was like a clear barrier raised against farther confidences: its brightness held him at such a distance that he had a sense of being almost out of hearing as he rejoined: "I am not sure that I have ever called you a successful example of that kind of bringing-up."

Her color rose a little at the implication, but she steeled herself with a light laugh.

"Ah, wait a little longer—give me a little more time before you decide!" And as he wavered before her, still watching for a break in the impenetrable front she presented: "Don't give me up; I may still do credit to my training!" she affirmed.

X

LOOK at those spangles, Miss Bart—every one of 'em sewed on crooked."

The tall forewoman, a pinched perpendicular figure, dropped the condemned structure of wire and net on the table at Lily's side, and passed on to the next figure in the line.

There were twenty of them in the work-room, their fagged profiles, under exaggerated hair, bowed in the harsh north light above the utensils of their art; for it was something more than an industry, surely, this creation of ever-varied settings for the face of fortunate womanhood. Their own faces were sallow with the unwholesomeness of hot air and sedentary toil, rather than with any actual signs of want: they were employed in a fashionable millinery establishment, and were fairly well clothed and well paid; but the youngest among them was as dull and colorless as the middle-aged. In the whole work-room there was only one skin beneath which the blood still visibly played; and that now burned with vexation as Miss Bart, under the lash of the forewoman's comment, began to strip the hat-frame of its over-lapping spangles.

To Gerty Farish's hopeful spirit a solution appeared to have been reached when she remembered how beautifully Lily could trim hats. Instances of young lady-milliners establishing themselves under fashionable patronage, and imparting to their "creations" that indefinable touch which the professional hand can never give, had flattered Gerty's visions of the future, and convinced even Lily that her separation from Mrs. Norma Hatch need not reduce her to dependence on her friends.

The parting had occurred a few weeks after Selden's visit, and would have taken place sooner had it not been for the resistance set up in Lily by his ill-starred offer of advice. The sense of being involved in a transaction she would not have cared to examine too closely had soon afterward defined itself in the light of a hint from

Mr. Stancy that, if she "saw them through," she would have no reason to be sorry. The implication that such loyalty would meet with a direct reward had hastened her flight, and flung her back, ashamed and penitent, on the broad bosom of Gerty's sympathy. She did not, however, propose to lie there prone, and Gerty's inspiration about the hats at once revived her hopes of profitable activity. Here was, after all, something that her charming listless hands could really do; she had no doubt of their capacity for knotting a ribbon or placing a flower to advantage. And of course only these finishing touches would be expected of her: subordinate fingers, blunt, grey, needle-pricked fingers, would prepare the shapes and stitch the linings, while she presided over the charming little front shop—a shop all white panels, mirrors, and moss-green hangings—where her finished creations, hats, wreaths, aigrettes and the rest, perched on their stands like birds just poising for flight.

But at the very outset of Gerty's campaign this vision of the green-and-white shop had been dispelled. Other young ladies of fashion had been thus "set-up," selling their hats by the mere attraction of a name and the reputed knack of tying a bow; but these privileged beings could command a faith in their powers materially expressed by the readiness to pay their shop-rent and advance a handsome sum for current expenses. Where was Lily to find such support? And even could it have been found, how were the ladies on whose approval she depended to be induced to give her their patronage? Gerty learned that whatever sympathy her friend's case might have excited a few months since had been imperilled, if not lost, by her association with Mrs. Hatch. Once again, Lily had withdrawn from an ambiguous situation in time to save her self-respect, but too late for public vindication. Freddy Van Osburgh was not to marry Mrs. Hatch; he had been rescued at the eleventh hour—some said by the efforts of Gus Trenor and Rosedale—and despatched to Europe with old Ned Van Alstyne; but the risk he had run would always be ascribed to Miss Bart's connivance, and would somehow serve as a summing-up and corroboration of the vague general distrust of her. It was a relief to those who had hung back from her to find themselves thus justified, and they were inclined to insist a little on her connection with the Hatch case in order to show that they had been right.

Gerty's quest, at any rate, brought up against a solid wall of resistance; and even when Carry Fisher, momentarily penitent for her share in the Hatch affair, joined her efforts to Miss Farish's, they met with no better success. Gerty had tried to veil her failure in tender ambiguities; but Carry, always the soul of candor, put the case squarely to her friend.

"I went straight to Judy Trenor; she has fewer prejudices than the others, and besides she's always hated Bertha Dorset. But what *have* you done to her, Lily? At the very first word about giving you a start she flamed out about some money you'd got from Gus; I never knew her so hot before. You know she'll let him do anything but spend money on his friends: the only reason she's decent to me now is that she knows I'm not hard up.—He speculated for you, you say? Well, what's the harm? He had no business to lose. He *didn't* lose? Then what on earth—but I never *could* understand you, Lily!"

The end of it was that, after anxious enquiry and much deliberation, Mrs. Fisher and Gerty, for once oddly united in their effort to help their friend, decided on placing her in the work-room of Mme. Regina's renowned millinery establishment. Even this arrangement was not effected without considerable negotiation, for Mme. Regina had a strong prejudice against untrained assistance, and was induced to yield only by the fact that she owed the patronage of Mrs. Bry and Mrs. Gormer to Carry Fisher's influence. She had been willing from the first to employ Lily in the show-room: as a displayer of hats, a fashionable beauty might be a valuable asset. But to this suggestion Miss Bart opposed a negative which Gerty emphatically supported, while Mrs. Fisher, inwardly unconvinced, but resigned to this latest proof of Lily's unreason, agreed that perhaps in the end it would be more useful that she should learn the trade. To Regina's work-room Lily was therefore committed by her friends, and there Mrs. Fisher left her with a sigh of relief, while Gerty's watchfulness continued to hover over her at a distance.

Lily had taken up her work early in January: it was now two months later, and she was still being rebuked for her inability to sew spangles on a hat-frame. As she returned to her work she heard a titter pass down the tables. She knew she was an object of criticism and amusement to the other work-women. They were, of course, aware of her history—the exact situation of every girl in the room was known and freely discussed by all the others—but the knowledge did not produce in them any awkward sense of class distinction: it merely explained why her untutored fingers were still blundering over the rudiments of the trade. Lily had no desire that they should recognize any social difference in her; but she had hoped to be received as their equal, and perhaps before long to show herself their superior by a special deftness of touch, and it was humiliating to find that, after two months of drudgery, she still betrayed her lack of early training. Remote was the day when she might aspire to exercise the talents she felt confident of possessing; only experienced workers were entrusted with the delicate art of shaping and trimming the hat, and the forewoman still held her inexorably to the routine of preparatory work.

She began to rip the spangles from the frame, listening absently to the buzz of talk which rose and fell with the coming and going of Miss Haines's active figure. The air was closer than usual, because Miss Haines, who had a cold, had not allowed a window to be opened even during the noon recess; and Lily's head was so heavy with the weight of a sleepless night that the chatter of her companions had the incoherence of a dream.

"I *told* her he'd never look at her again; and he didn't. I wouldn't have, either—I think she acted real mean to him. He took her to the Arion Ball, and had a hack for her both ways. . . . She's taken ten bottles, and her headaches don't seem no better—but she's written a testimonial to say the first bottle cured her, and she got five dollars and her picture in the paper. . . . Mrs. Trenor's hat? The one with the green Paradise? Here, Miss Haines—it'll be ready right off. . . . That was one of the Trenor girls here yesterday with Mrs. George Dorset. How'd I know? Why, Madam sent for me to alter the flower in that Virot hat—the blue tulle: she's tall and slight, with her hair fuzzed out—a good deal like Mamie Leach, on'y thinner. . . ."

On and on it flowed, a current of meaningless sound, on which, startlingly enough, a familiar name now and then floated to the surface. It was the strangest part of Lily's strange experience, the hearing of these names, the seeing the fragmentary and distorted image of the world she had lived in reflected in the mirror of the working-girls' minds. She had never before suspected the mixture of insatiable curiosity and contemptuous freedom with which she and her kind were discussed in this underworld of toilers who lived on their vanity and self-indulgence. Every girl in Mme. Regina's work-room knew to whom the headgear in her hands was destined, and had her opinion of its future wearer, and a definite knowledge of the latter's place in the social system. That Lily was a star fallen from that sky did not, after the first stir of curiosity had subsided, materially add to their interest in her. She had fallen, she had "gone under," and true to the ideal of their race, they were awed only by success—by the gross tangible image of material achievement. The consciousness of her different point of view merely kept them at a little distance from her, as though she were a foreigner with whom it was an effort to talk.

"Miss Bart, if you can't sew those spangles on more regular I guess you'd better give the hat to Miss Kilroy."

Lily looked down ruefully at her handiwork. The forewoman was right: the sewing on of the spangles was inexcusably bad. What made her so much more clumsy than usual? Was it a growing distaste for her task, or actual physical disability? She felt tired and confused: it was an effort to put her thoughts together. She rose and handed the hat to Miss Kilroy, who took it with a suppressed smile.

"I'm sorry; I'm afraid I am not well," she said to the forewoman.

Miss Haines offered no comment. From the first she had augured ill of Mme. Regina's consenting to include a fashionable apprentice among her workers. In that temple of art no raw beginners were wanted, and Miss Haines would have been more than human had she not taken a certain pleasure in seeing her forebodings confirmed.

"You'd better go back to binding edges," she said drily.

Lily slipped out last among the band of liberated work-women. She did not care to be mingled in their noisy dispersal: once in the street, she always felt an irresistible return to her old standpoint, an instinctive shrinking from all that was unpolished and promiscuous. In the days—how distant they now seemed!—when she had visited the Girls' Club with Gerty Farish, she had felt an enlightened interest in the working-classes; but that was because she looked down on them from above, from the happy altitude of her grace and her beneficence. Now that she was on a level with them, the point of view was less interesting.

She felt a touch on her arm, and met the penitent eye of Miss Kilroy.

"Miss Bart, I guess you can sew those spangles on as well as I can when you're feeling right. Miss Haines didn't act fair to you."

Lily's color rose at the unexpected advance: it was a long time since real kindness had looked at her from any eyes but Gerty's.

"Oh, thank you: I'm not particularly well, but Miss Haines was right. I *am* clumsy."

"Well, it's mean work for anybody with a headache." Miss Kilroy paused irresolutely. "You ought to go right home and lay down. Ever try orangeine?"

"Thank you." Lily held out her hand. "It's very kind of you—I mean to go home."

She looked gratefully at Miss Kilroy, but neither knew what more to say. Lily was aware that the other was on the point of offering to go home with her, but she wanted to be alone and silent—even kindness, the sort of kindness that Miss Kilroy could give, would have jarred on her just then.

"Thank you," she repeated as she turned away.

She struck westward through the dreary March twilight, toward the street where her boarding-house stood. She had resolutely refused Gerty's offer of hospitality. Something of her mother's fierce shrinking from observation and sympathy was beginning to develop in her, and the promiscuity of small quarters and close intimacy seemed, on the whole, less endurable than the solitude of a hall bedroom in a house where she could come and go unremarked among other workers. For a while she had been sustained by this desire for privacy and independence; but now, perhaps from increasing physical weariness, the lassitude brought about by hours of unwonted confinement, she was beginning to feel acutely the ugliness and discomfort of her surroundings. The day's task done, she dreaded to return to her narrow room, with its blotched wallpaper and shabby paint; and she hated every step of the walk thither, through the degradation of a New York street in the last stages of decline from fashion to commerce.

But what she dreaded most of all was having to pass the chemist's at the corner of Sixth Avenue. She had meant to take another street: she had usually done so of late. But today her steps were irresistibly drawn toward the flaring plate-glass corner; she tried to take the lower crossing, but a laden dray crowded her back, and she struck across the street obliquely, reaching the sidewalk just opposite the chemist's door.

Over the counter she caught the eye of the clerk who had waited on her before, and slipped the prescription into his hand. There could be no question about the prescription: it was a copy of one of Mrs. Hatch's, obligingly furnished by that lady's chemist. Lily was confident that the clerk would fill it without hesitation; yet the nervous dread of a refusal, or even of an expression of doubt, communicated itself to her restless hands as she affected to examine the bottles of perfume stacked on the glass case before her.

The clerk had read the prescription without comment; but in the act of handing out the bottle he paused.

"You don't want to increase the dose, you know," he remarked.

Lily's heart contracted. What did he mean by looking at her in that way?

"Of course not," she murmured, holding out her hand.

"That's all right: it's a queer-acting drug. A drop or two more, and off you go—the doctors don't know why."

The dread lest he should question her, or keep the bottle back, choked the murmur of acquiescence in her throat; and when at length she emerged safely from the shop she was almost dizzy with the intensity of her relief. The mere touch of the packet thrilled her tired nerves with the delicious promise of a night of sleep, and in the reaction from her momentary fear she felt as if the first fumes of drowsiness were already stealing over her.

In her confusion she stumbled against a man who was hurrying down the last steps of the elevated station. He drew back, and she heard her name uttered with surprise. It was Rosedale, fur-coated, glossy and prosperous—but why did she seem to see him so far off, and as if through a mist of splintered crystals? Before she could account for the phenomenon she found herself shaking hands with him. They had parted with scorn on her side and anger upon his; but all trace of these emotions seemed to vanish as their hands met, and she was only aware of a confused wish that she might continue to hold fast to him.

"Why, what's the matter, Miss Lily? You're not well!" he exclaimed; and she forced her lips into a pallid smile of reassurance.

"I'm a little tired—it's nothing. Stay with me a moment, please," she faltered. That she should be asking this service of Rosedale!

He glanced at the dirty and unpropitious corner on which they stood, with the shriek of the "elevated" and the tumult of trams and wagons contending hideously in their ears.

"We can't stay here; but let me take you somewhere for a cup of tea. The *Longworth* is only a few yards off, and there'll be no one there at this hour."

A cup of tea in quiet, somewhere out of the noise and ugliness, seemed for the moment the one solace she could bear. A few steps brought them to the ladies' door of the hotel he had named, and a moment later he was seated opposite to her, and the waiter had placed the tea-tray between them.

"Not a drop of brandy or whiskey first? You look regularly done up, Miss Lily. Well, take your tea strong, then; and, waiter, get a cushion for the lady's back."

Lily smiled faintly at the injunction to take her tea strong. It was the temptation she was always struggling to resist. Her craving for the keen stimulant was forever conflicting with that other craving for sleep—the midnight craving which only the little phial in her hand could still. But today, at any rate, the tea could hardly be too strong: she counted on it to pour warmth and resolution into her empty veins.

As she leaned back before him, her lids drooping in utter lassitude, though the first warm draught already tinged her face with returning life, Rosedale was seized afresh by the poignant surprise of her beauty. The dark pencilling of fatigue under her eyes, the morbid blue-veined pallor of the temples, brought out the brightness of her hair and lips, as though all her ebbing vitality were centered there. Against the dull chocolate-colored background of the restaurant, the purity of her head stood out as it had never done in the most brightly-lit ballroom. He looked at her with a startled uncomfortable feeling, as though her beauty were a forgotten enemy that had lain in ambush and now sprang out on him unawares.

To clear the air he tried to take an easy tone with her. "Why, Miss Lily, I haven't seen you for an age. I didn't know what had become of you."

As he spoke, he was checked by an embarrassing sense of the complications to which this might lead. Though he had not seen her he had heard of her; he knew of her connection with Mrs. Hatch, and of the talk resulting from it. Mrs. Hatch's *milieu* was one which he had once assiduously frequented, and now as devoutly shunned.

Lily, to whom the tea had restored her usual clearness of mind, saw what was in his thoughts and said with a slight smile: "You would not be likely to know about me. I have joined the working classes."

He stared in genuine wonder. "You don't mean——? Why, what on earth are you doing?"

"Learning to be a milliner—at least *trying* to learn," she hastily qualified the statement.

Rosedale suppressed a low whistle of surprise. "Come off—you ain't serious, are you?"

"Perfectly serious. I'm obliged to work for my living."

"But I understood—I thought you were with Norma Hatch."

"You heard I had gone to her as her secretary?"

"Something of the kind, I believe." He leaned forward to refill her cup.

Lily guessed the possibilities of embarrassment which the topic held for him, and raising her eyes to his, she said suddenly: "I left her two months ago."

Rosedale continued to fumble awkwardly with the teapot, and she felt sure that he had heard what had been said of her. But what was there that Rosedale did not hear?

"Wasn't it a soft berth?" he enquired, with an attempt at lightness.

"Too soft—one might have sunk in too deep." Lily rested one arm on the edge of the table, and sat looking at him more intently than she had ever looked before. An uncontrollable impulse was urging her to put her case to this man, from whose curiosity she had always so fiercely defended herself.

"You know Mrs. Hatch, I think? Well, perhaps you can understand that she might make things too easy for one."

Rosedale looked faintly puzzled, and she remembered that allusiveness was lost on him.

"It was no place for you, anyhow," he agreed, so suffused and immersed in the light of her full gaze that he found himself being drawn into strange depths of intimacy. He who had had to subsist on mere fugitive glances, looks winged in flight and swiftly lost under covert, now found her eyes settling on him with a brooding intensity that fairly dazzled him.

"I left," Lily continued, "lest people should say I was helping Mrs. Hatch to marry Freddy Van Osburgh—who is not in the least too good for her—and as they still continue to say it, I see that I might as well have stayed where I was."

"Oh, Freddy——" Rosedale brushed aside the topic with an air of its unimportance which gave a sense of the immense perspective he had acquired. "Freddy don't count—but I knew *you* weren't mixed up in that. It ain't your style."

Lily colored slightly: she could not conceal from herself that the words gave her pleasure. She would have liked to sit there, drinking more tea, and continuing to talk of herself to Rosedale. But the old habit of observing the conventions reminded her that it was time to bring their colloquy to an end, and she made a faint motion to push back her chair.

Rosedale stopped her with a protesting gesture. "Wait a minute—don't go yet; sit quiet and rest a little longer. You look thoroughly played out. And you haven't told me——" He broke off, conscious of going farther than he had meant. She saw the struggle and understood it; understood also the nature of the spell to which he yielded as, with his eyes on her face, he began again abruptly: "What on earth did you mean by saying just now that you were learning to be a milliner?"

"Just what I said. I am an apprentice at Regina's."

"Good Lord—*you?* But what for? I knew your aunt had turned you down: Mrs. Fisher told me about it. But I understood you got a legacy from her——"

"I got ten thousand dollars; but the legacy is not to be paid till next summer."

"Well, but—look here: you could *borrow* on it any time you wanted."

She shook her head gravely. "No; for I owe it already."

"Owe it? The whole ten thousand?"

"Every penny." She paused, and then continued abruptly, with her eyes on his face: "I think Gus Trenor spoke to you once about having made some money for me in stocks."

She waited, and Rosedale, congested with embarrassment, muttered that he remembered something of the kind.

"He made about nine thousand dollars," Lily pursued, in the same tone of eager communicativeness. "At the time, I understood that he was speculating with my own money: it was incredibly stupid of me, but I knew nothing of business. Afterward I found out that he had *not* used my money—that what he said he had made for me he had really given me. It was meant in kindness, of course; but it was not the sort of obligation one could remain under. Unfortunately I had spent the money before I discovered my mistake; and so my legacy will have to go to pay it back. That is the reason why I am trying to learn a trade."

She made the statement clearly, deliberately, with pauses between the sentences, so that each should have time to sink deeply into her hearer's mind. She had a passionate desire that someone should know the truth about this transaction, and also that the rumor of her intention to repay the money should reach Judy Trenor's ears. And it had suddenly occurred to her that Rosedale, who had surprised Trenor's confidence, was the fitting person to receive and transmit her version of the facts. She had even felt a momentary exhilaration at the thought of thus relieving herself of her detested secret; but the sensation gradually faded in the telling, and as she ended her pallor was suffused with a deep blush of misery.

Rosedale continued to stare at her in wonder; but the wonder took the turn she had least expected.

"But see here—if that's the case, it cleans you out altogether?"

He put it to her as if she had not grasped the consequences of her act; as if her incorrigible ignorance of business were about to precipitate her into a fresh act of folly.

"Altogether—yes," she calmly agreed.

He sat silent, his thick hands clasped on the table, his little puzzled eyes exploring the recesses of the deserted restaurant.

"See here—that's fine," he exclaimed abruptly.

Lily rose from her seat with a deprecating laugh. "Oh, no—it's merely a bore," she asserted, gathering together the ends of her feather scarf.

Rosedale remained seated, too intent on his thoughts to notice her movement. "Miss Lily, if you want any backing—I like pluck——" broke from him disconnectedly.

"Thank you." She held out her hand. "Your tea has given me a tremendous backing. I feel equal to anything now."

Her gesture seemed to show a definite intention of dismissal, but her companion had tossed a bill to the waiter, and was slipping his short arms into his expensive overcoat.

"Wait a minute—you've got to let me walk home with you," he said.

Lily uttered no protest, and when he had paused to make sure of his change they emerged from the hotel and crossed Sixth Avenue again. As she led the way westward past a long line of areas which, through the distortion of their paintless rails, revealed with increasing candor the *disjecta membra* of bygone dinners, Lily felt that Rosedale was taking contemptuous note of the neighborhood; and before the doorstep at which she finally paused he looked up with an air of incredulous disgust.

"This isn't the place? Some one told me you were living with Miss Farish."

"No: I am boarding here. I have lived too long on my friends."

He continued to scan the blistered brown stone front, the windows draped with discolored lace, and the Pompeian decoration of the muddy vestibule; then he looked back at her face and said with a visible effort: "You'll let me come and see you some day?"

She smiled, recognizing the heroism of the offer to the point of being frankly touched by it. "Thank you—I shall be very glad," she made answer, in the first sincere words she had ever spoken to him.

That evening in her own room Miss Bart—who had fled early from the heavy fumes of the basement dinner table—sat musing upon the impulse which had led her to unbosom herself to Rosedale. Beneath it she discovered an increasing sense of loneliness—a dread of returning to the solitude of her room, while she could be anywhere else, or in any company but her own. Circumstances, of late, had combined to cut her off more and more from her few remaining friends. On Carry Fisher's part the withdrawal was perhaps not quite involuntary. Having made her final effort on Lily's behalf, and landed her safely in Mme. Regina's work-room, Mrs. Fisher seemed disposed to rest from her labors; and Lily, understanding the reason, could not condemn her. Carry had in fact come dangerously near to being involved in the episode of Mrs. Norma Hatch, and it had taken some verbal ingenuity to extricate herself. She frankly owned to having brought Lily and Mrs. Hatch together, but then she did not know Mrs. Hatch—she had expressly warned Lily that she did not know Mrs. Hatch—and besides, she was not Lily's keeper, and really the girl was old enough to take care of herself. Carry did not put her own case so brutally, but she allowed it to be thus put for her by her latest bosom friend, Mrs. Jack Stepney: Mrs. Stepney, trembling over the narrowness of her only brother's escape, but eager to vindicate Mrs. Fisher, at whose house she could count on the "jolly parties" which had become a necessity to her since marriage had emancipated her from the Van Osburgh point of view.

Lily understood the situation and could make allowances for it. Carry had been a good friend to her in difficult days, and perhaps only a friendship like Gerty's could be proof against such an increasing strain. Gerty's friendship did indeed hold fast; yet Lily was beginning to avoid her also. For she could not go to Gerty's without risk of meeting Selden; and to meet him now would be pure pain. It was pain enough even to think of him, whether she considered him in the distinctness of her waking thoughts, or felt the obsession of his presence through the blur of her tormented nights. That was one of the reasons why she had turned again to Mrs. Hatch's prescription. In the uneasy snatches of her natural dreams he came to her sometimes in the old guise of fellowship and tenderness; and she would rise from the sweet delusion mocked and emptied of her courage. But in the sleep which the phial procured she sank far below such half-waking visitations, sank into depths of dreamless annihilation from which she woke each morning with an obliterated past.

Gradually, to be sure, the stress of the old thoughts would return; but at least they did not importune her waking hour. The drug gave her a momentary illusion of complete renewal, from which she drew strength to take up her daily work. The strength was more and more needed as the perplexities of her future increased. She knew that to Gerty and Mrs. Fisher she was only passing through a temporary period of probation, since they believed that the apprenticeship she was serving at Mme. Regina's would enable her, when Mrs. Peniston's legacy was paid, to realize the vision of the green-and-white shop with the fuller competence acquired by her preliminary training. But to Lily herself, aware that the legacy could not be put to such a use, the preliminary training seemed a wasted effort. She understood clearly enough that, even if she could ever learn to compete with hands formed from childhood for their special work, the small pay she received would not be a sufficient addition to her income to compensate her for such drudgery. And the realization of this fact brought her recurringly face to face with the temptation to use the legacy in establishing her business. Once installed, and in command of her own work-women, she believed she had sufficient tact and ability to attract a fashionable *clientèle;* and if the business succeeded she could gradually lay aside money enough to discharge her debt to Trenor. But the task might take years to accomplish, even if she continued to stint herself to the utmost; and meanwhile her pride would be crushed under the weight of an intolerable obligation.

These were her superficial considerations; but under them lurked the secret dread that the obligation might not always remain intolerable. She knew she could not count on her continuity of purpose, and what really frightened her was the thought that she might gradually accommodate herself to remaining indefinitely in Trenor's debt, as she had accommodated herself to the part allotted her on the Sabrina, and as she had so nearly drifted into acquiescing with Stancy's scheme for the advancement of Mrs. Hatch. Her danger lay, as she knew, in her old incurable dread of discomfort and poverty; in the fear of that mounting tide of dinginess against which her mother had so passionately warned her. And now a new vista of peril opened before her. She understood that Rosedale was ready to lend her money; and the longing to take advantage of his offer began to haunt her insidiously. It was of course impossible to accept a loan from Rosedale; but proximate possibilities hovered temptingly before her. She was quite sure that he would come and see her again, and almost sure that, if he did, she could bring him to the point of offering to marry her on the terms she had previously rejected. Would she still reject them if they were offered? More and more, with every fresh mischance befalling her, did the pursuing furies seem to take the shape of Bertha Dorset; and close at hand, safely locked among her papers, lay the means of ending their pursuit. The temptation, which her scorn of Rosedale had once enabled her to reject, now insistently returned upon her; and how much strength was left her to oppose it?

What little there was must at any rate be husbanded to the utmost; she could not trust herself again to the perils of a sleepless night. Through the long hours of silence the dark spirit of fatigue and loneliness crouched upon her breast, leaving her so drained of bodily strength that her morning thoughts swam in a haze of weakness. The only hope of renewal lay in the little bottle at her bed-side; and how much longer that hope would last she dared not conjecture.

XI

LILY, lingering for a moment on the corner, looked out on the afternoon spectacle of Fifth Avenue.

It was a day in late April, and the sweetness of spring was in the air. It mitigated the ugliness of the long crowded thoroughfare, blurred the gaunt roof-lines, threw a mauve veil over the discouraging perspective of the side streets, and gave a touch of poetry to the delicate haze of green that marked the entrance to the Park.

As Lily stood there, she recognized several familiar faces in the passing carriages. The season was over, and its ruling forces had disbanded; but a few still lingered, delaying their departure for Europe, or passing through town on their return from the South. Among them was Mrs. Van Osburgh, swaying majestically in her C-spring barouche, with Mrs. Percy Gryce at her side, and the new heir to the Gryce millions enthroned before them on his nurse's knees. They were succeeded by Mrs. Hatch's electric victoria, in which that lady reclined in the lonely splendor of a spring toilet obviously designed for company; and a moment or two later came Judy Trenor, accompanied by Lady Skiddaw, who had come over for her annual tarpon fishing and a dip into "the street."

This fleeting glimpse of her past served to emphasize the sense of aimlessness with which Lily at length turned toward home. She had nothing to do for the rest of the day, nor for the days to come; for the season was over in millinery as well as in society, and a week earlier Mme. Regina had notified her that her services were no longer required. Mme. Regina always reduced her staff on the first of May, and Miss Bart's attendance had of late been so irregular—she had so often been unwell, and had done so little work when she came—that it was only as a favor that her dismissal had hitherto been deferred.

Lily did not question the justice of the decision. She was conscious of having been forgetful, awkward and slow to learn. It was bitter to acknowledge her inferiority even to herself, but the fact had been brought home to her that as a bread-winner she could never compete with professional ability. Since she had been brought up to be ornamental, she could hardly blame herself for failing to serve any practical purpose; but the discovery put an end to her consoling sense of universal efficiency.

As she turned homeward her thoughts shrank in anticipation from the fact that there would be nothing to get up for the next morning. The luxury of lying late in bed was a pleasure belonging to the life of ease; it had no part in the utilitarian existence of the boarding-house. She liked to leave her room early, and to return to it as late as possible; and she was walking slowly now in order to postpone the detested approach to her doorstep.

But the doorstep, as she drew near it, acquired a sudden interest from the fact that it was occupied—and indeed filled—by the conspicuous figure of Mr. Rosedale, whose presence seemed to take on an added amplitude from the meanness of his surroundings.

The sight stirred Lily with an irresistible sense of triumph. Rosedale, a day or two after their chance meeting, had called to enquire if she had recovered from her indisposition; but since then she had not seen or heard from him, and his absence seemed to betoken a struggle to keep away, to let her pass once more out of his life. If this were the case, his return showed that the struggle had been unsuccessful, for Lily knew he was not the man to waste his time in an ineffectual sentimental dalliance. He was too busy, too practical, and above all too much preoccupied with his own advancement, to indulge in such unprofitable asides.

In the peacock-blue parlor, with its bunches of dried pampas grass, and discolored steel engravings of sentimental episodes, he looked about him with unconcealed disgust, laying his hat distrustfully on the dusty console adorned with a Rogers statuette.

Lily sat down on one of the plush and rosewood sofas, and he deposited himself in a rocking-chair draped with a starched anti-macassar which scraped unpleasantly against the pink fold of skin above his collar.

"My goodness—you can't go on living here!" he exclaimed.

Lily smiled at his tone. "I am not sure that I can; but I have gone over my expenses very carefully, and I rather think I shall be able to manage it."

"Be able to manage it? That's not what I mean—it's no place for you!"

"It's what *I* mean; for I have been out of work for the last week."

"Out of work—out of work! What a way for you to talk! The idea of your having to work—it's preposterous." He brought out his sentences in short violent jerks, as though they were forced up from a deep inner crater of indignation. "It's a farce—a crazy farce," he repeated, his eyes fixed on the long vista of the room reflected in the blotched glass between the windows.

Lily continued to meet his expostulations with a smile. "I don't know why I should regard myself as an exception——" she began.

"Because you *are;* that's why; and your being in a place like this is a damnable outrage. I can't talk of it calmly."

She had in truth never seen him so shaken out of his usual glibness; and there was something almost moving to her in his inarticulate struggle with his emotions.

He rose with a start which left the rocking-chair quivering on its beam ends, and placed himself squarely before her.

"Look here, Miss Lily, I'm going to Europe next week: going over to Paris and London for a couple of months—and I can't leave you like this. I can't do it. I know it's none of my business—you've let me understand that often enough; but things are worse with you now than they have been before, and you must see that you've got to accept help from somebody. You spoke to me the other day about some debt to Trenor. I know what you mean—and I respect you for feeling as you do about it."

A blush of surprise rose to Lily's pale face, but before she could interrupt him he had continued eagerly: "Well, I'll lend you the money to pay Trenor; and I won't—I—see here, don't take me up till I've finished. What I mean is, it'll be a plain business arrangement, such as one man would make with another. Now, what have you got to say against that?"

Lily's blush deepened to a glow in which humiliation and gratitude were mingled; and both sentiments revealed themselves in the unexpected gentleness of her reply.

"Only this: that it is exactly what Gus Trenor proposed; and that I can never again be sure of understanding the plainest business arrangement." Then, realizing that this answer contained a germ of injustice, she added, even more kindly: "Not that I don't appreciate your kindness—that I'm not grateful for it. But a business arrangement between us would in any case be impossible, because I shall have no security to give when my debt to Gus Trenor has been paid."

Rosedale received this statement in silence: he seemed to feel the note of finality in her voice, yet to be unable to accept it as closing the question between them.

In the silence Lily had a clear perception of what was passing through his mind. Whatever perplexity he felt as to the inexorableness of her course—however little he penetrated its motive—she saw that it unmistakably tended to strengthen her hold over him. It was as though the sense in her of unexplained scruples and resistances had the same attraction as the delicacy of feature, the fastidiousness of manner, which gave her an external rarity, an air of being impossible to match. As he advanced in social experience this uniqueness had acquired a greater value for him, as though he were a collector who had learned to distinguish minor differences of design and quality in some long-coveted object.

Lily, perceiving all this, understood that he would marry her at once, on the sole condition of a reconciliation with Mrs. Dorset; and the temptation was the less easy to put aside because, little by little, circumstances were breaking down her dislike for Rosedale. The dislike, indeed, still subsisted; but it was penetrated here and there by the perception of mitigating qualities in him: of a certain gross kindliness, a rather helpless fidelity of sentiment, which seemed to be struggling through the hard surface of his material ambitions.

Reading his dismissal in her eyes, he held out his hand with a gesture which conveyed something of this inarticulate conflict.

"If you'd only let me, I'd set you up over them all—I'd put you where you could wipe your feet on 'em!" he declared; and it touched her oddly to see that his new passion had not altered his old standard of values.

Lily took no sleeping-drops that night. She lay awake viewing her situation in the crude light which Rosedale's visit had shed on it. In fending off the offer he was so plainly ready to renew, had she not sacrificed to one of those abstract notions of honor that might be called the conventionalities of the moral life? What debt did she owe to a social order which had condemned and banished her without trial? She had never been heard in her own defense; she was innocent of the charge on which she had been found guilty; and the irregularity of her conviction might seem to justify the use of methods as irregular in recovering her lost rights. Bertha Dorset, to save herself, had not scrupled to ruin her by an open falsehood; why should she hesitate to make private use of the facts that chance had put in her way? After all, half the opprobrium of such an act lies in the name attached to it. Call it blackmail and it becomes unthinkable; but explain that it injures no one, and that the rights regained by it were unjustly forfeited, and he must be a formalist indeed who can find no plea in its defense.

The arguments pleading for it with Lily were the old unanswerable ones of the personal situation: the sense of injury, the sense of failure, the passionate craving for a fair chance against the selfish despotism of society. She had learned by experience that she had neither the aptitude nor the moral constancy to remake her life on new lines; to become a worker among workers, and let the world of luxury and pleasure sweep by her unregarded. She could not hold herself much to blame for this ineffectiveness, and she was perhaps less to blame than she believed. Inherited tendencies had combined with early training to make her the highly specialized product she was: an organism as helpless out of its narrow range as the sea-anemone torn from the rock. She had been fashioned to adorn and delight; to what other end does nature round the rose-leaf and paint the humming-bird's breast? And was it her fault that the purely decorative mission is less easily and harmoniously fulfilled among social beings than in the world of nature? That it is apt to be hampered by material necessities or complicated by moral scruples?

These last were the two antagonistic forces which fought out their battle in her breast during the long watches of the night; and when she rose the next morning she hardly knew where the victory lay. She was exhausted by the reaction of a night without sleep, coming after many nights of rest artificially obtained; and in the distorting light of fatigue the future stretched out before her grey, interminable and desolate.

She lay late in bed, refusing the coffee and fried eggs which the friendly Irish servant thrust through her door, and hating the intimate domestic noises of the house and the cries and rumblings of the street. Her week of idleness had brought home to her with exaggerated force these small aggravations of the boarding-house world, and she yearned for that other luxurious world, whose machinery is so carefully concealed that one scene flows into another without perceptible agency.

At length she rose and dressed. Since she had left Mme. Regina's she had spent her days in the streets, partly to escape from the uncongenial promiscuities of the boarding-house, and partly in the hope that physical fatigue would help her to sleep. But once out of the house, she could not decide where to go; for she had avoided Gerty since her dismissal from the milliner's, and she was not sure of a welcome anywhere else.

The morning was in harsh contrast to the previous day. A cold grey sky threatened rain, and a high wind drove the dust in wild spirals up and down the streets. Lily walked up Fifth Avenue toward the Park, hoping to find a sheltered nook where she might sit; but the wind chilled her, and after an hour's wandering under the tossing boughs she yielded to her increasing weariness, and took refuge in a little restaurant in Fifty-ninth Street. She was not hungry, and had meant to go without luncheon; but she was too tired to return home, and the long perspective of white tables showed alluringly through the windows.

The room was full of women and girls, all too much engaged in the rapid absorption of tea and pie to remark her entrance. A hum of shrill voices reverberated against the low ceiling, leaving Lily shut out in a little circle of silence. She felt a sudden pang of profound loneliness. She had lost the sense of time, and it seemed to her as though she had not spoken to any one for days. Her eyes sought the faces about her, craving a responsive glance, some sign of an intuition of her trouble. But the sallow preoccupied women, with their bags and note-books and rolls of music, were all engrossed in their own affairs, and even those who sat by themselves were busy running over proof-sheets or devouring magazines between their hurried gulps of tea. Lily alone was stranded in a great waste of disoccupation.

She drank several cups of the tea which was served with her portion of stewed oysters, and her brain felt clearer and livelier when she emerged once more into the street. She realized now that, as she sat in the restaurant, she had unconsciously arrived at a final decision. The discovery gave her an immediate illusion of activity:

it was exhilarating to think that she had actually a reason for hurrying home. To prolong her enjoyment of the sensation she decided to walk; but the distance was so great that she found herself glancing nervously at the clocks on the way. One of the surprises of her unoccupied state was the discovery that time, when it is left to itself and no definite demands are made on it, cannot be trusted to move at any recognized pace. Usually it loiters; but just when one has come to count upon its slowness, it may suddenly break into a wild irrational gallop.

She found, however, on reaching home, that the hour was still early enough for her to sit down and rest a few minutes before putting her plan into execution. The delay did not perceptibly weaken her resolve. She was frightened and yet stimulated by the reserved force of resolution which she felt within herself: she saw it was going to be easier, a great deal easier, than she had imagined.

At five o'clock she rose, unlocked her trunk, and took out a sealed packet which she slipped into the bosom of her dress. Even the contact with the packet did not shake her nerves as she had half-expected it would. She seemed encased in a strong armor of indifference, as though the vigorous exertion of her will had finally benumbed her finer sensibilities.

She dressed herself once more for the street, locked her door and went out. When she emerged on the pavement, the day was still high, but a threat of rain darkened the sky and cold gusts shook the signs projecting from the basement shops along the street. She reached Fifth Avenue and began to walk slowly northward. She was sufficiently familiar with Mrs. Dorset's habits to know that she could always be found at home after five. She might not, indeed, be accessible to visitors, especially to a visitor so unwelcome, and against whom it was quite possible that she had guarded herself by special orders; but Lily had written a note which she meant to send up with her name, and which she thought would secure her admission.

She had allowed herself time to walk to Mrs. Dorset's, thinking that the quick movement through the cold evening air would help to steady her nerves; but she really felt no need of being tranquillized. Her survey of the situation remained calm and unwavering.

As she reached Fiftieth Street the clouds broke abruptly, and a rush of cold rain slanted into her face. She had no umbrella and the moisture quickly penetrated her thin spring dress. She was still half a mile from her destination, and she decided to walk across to Madison Avenue and take the electric car. As she turned into the side street, a vague memory stirred in her. The row of budding trees, the new brick and limestone house-fronts, the Georgian flat-house with flower-boxes on its balconies, were merged together into the setting of a familiar scene. It was down this street that she had walked with Selden, that September day two years ago; a few yards ahead was the doorway they had entered together. The recollection loosened a throng of benumbed sensations—longings, regrets, imaginings, the throbbing brood of the only spring her heart had ever known. It was strange to find herself passing his house on such an errand. She seemed suddenly to see her action as he would see it—and the fact of his own connection with it, the fact that, to attain her end, she must trade on his name, and profit by a secret of his past, chilled her blood with shame. What a long way she had traveled since the day of their first talk together! Even then her feet had been set in the path she was now following—even then she had resisted the hand he had held out.

All her resentment of his fancied coldness was swept away in this overwhelming rush of recollection. Twice he had been ready to help her—to help her by loving her, as he had said—and if, the third time, he had seemed to fail her, whom but herself could she accuse? . . . Well, that part of her life was over; she did not know why her thoughts still clung to it. But the sudden longing to see him remained; it grew to hunger as she paused on the pavement opposite his door. The street was dark and empty, swept by the rain. She had a vision of his quiet room, of the bookshelves, and the fire on the hearth. She looked up and saw a light in his window; then she crossed the street and entered the house.

XII

THE library looked as she had pictured it. The green-shaded lamps made tranquil circles of light in the gathering dusk, a little fire flickered on the hearth, and Selden's easy-chair, which stood near it, had been pushed aside when he rose to admit her.

He had checked his first movement of surprise, and stood silent, waiting for her to speak, while she paused a moment on the threshold, assailed by a rush of memories.

The scene was unchanged. She recognized the row of shelves from which he had taken down his La Bruyère, and the worn arm of the chair he had leaned against while she examined the precious volume. But then the wide September light had filled the room, making it seem a part of the outer world: now the shaded lamps and the warm hearth, detaching it from the gathering darkness of the street, gave it a sweeter touch of intimacy.

Becoming gradually aware of the surprise under Selden's silence, Lily turned to him and said simply: "I came to tell you that I was sorry for the way we parted—for what I said to you that day at Mrs. Hatch's."

The words rose to her lips spontaneously. Even on her way up the stairs, she had not thought of preparing a pretext for her visit, but she now felt an intense longing to dispel the cloud of misunderstanding that hung between them.

Selden returned her look with a smile. "I was sorry too that we should have parted in that way; but I am not sure I didn't bring it on myself. Luckily I had foreseen the risk I was taking——"

"So that you really didn't care——?" broke from her with a flash of her old irony.

"So that I was prepared for the consequences," he corrected good-humoredly. "But we'll talk of all this later. Do come and sit by the fire. I can recommend that armchair, if you'll let me put a cushion behind you."

While he spoke she had moved slowly to the middle of the room, and paused near his writing-table, where the lamp, striking upward, cast exaggerated shadows on the pallor of her delicately-hollowed face.

"You look tired—do sit down," he repeated gently.

She did not seem to hear the request. "I wanted you to know that I left Mrs. Hatch immediately after I saw you," she said, as though continuing her confession.

"Yes—yes; I know," he assented, with a rising tinge of embarrassment.

"And that I did so because you told me to. Before you came I had already begun to see that it would be impossible to remain with her—for the reasons you gave me; but I wouldn't admit it—I wouldn't let you see that I understood what you meant."

"Ah, I might have trusted you to find your own way out—don't overwhelm me with the sense of my officiousness!"

His light tone, in which, had her nerves been steadier, she would have recognized the mere effort to bridge over an awkward moment, jarred on her passionate desire to be understood. In her strange state of extra-lucidity, which gave her the sense of being already at the heart of the situation, it seemed incredible that any one should think it necessary to linger in the conventional outskirts of word-play and evasion.

"It was not that—I was not ungrateful," she insisted. But the power of expression failed her suddenly; she felt a tremor in her throat, and two tears gathered and fell slowly from her eyes.

Selden moved forward and took her hand. "You are very tired. Why won't you sit down and let me make you comfortable?"

He drew her to the armchair near the fire, and placed a cushion behind her shoulders.

"And now you must let me make you some tea: you know I always have that amount of hospitality at my command."

She shook her head, and two more tears ran over. But she did not weep easily, and the long habit of self-control reasserted itself, though she was still too tremulous to speak.

"You know I can coax the water to boil in five minutes," Selden continued, speaking as though she were a troubled child.

His words recalled the vision of that other afternoon when they had sat together over his tea-table and talked jestingly of her future. There were moments when that day seemed more remote than any other event in her life; and yet she could always relive it in its minutest detail.

She made a gesture of refusal. "No: I drink too much tea. I would rather sit quiet—I must go in a moment," she added confusedly.

Selden continued to stand near her, leaning against the mantelpiece. The tinge of constraint was beginning to be more distinctly perceptible under the friendly ease of his manner. Her self-absorption had not allowed her to perceive it at first; but now that her consciousness was once more putting forth its eager feelers, she saw that her presence was becoming an embarrassment to him. Such a situation can be saved only by an immediate outrush of feeling; and on Selden's side the determining impulse was still lacking.

The discovery did not disturb Lily as it might once have done. She had passed beyond the phase of well-bred reciprocity, in which every demonstration must be scrupulously proportioned to the emotion it elicits, and generosity of feeling is the only ostentation condemned. But the sense of loneliness returned with redoubled force as she saw herself forever shut out from Selden's inmost self. She had come to him with no definite purpose; the mere longing to see him had directed her; but the secret hope she had carried with her suddenly revealed itself in its death-pang.

"I must go," she repeated, making a motion to rise from her chair. "But I may not see you again for a long time, and I wanted to tell you that I have never forgotten the things you said to me at Bellomont, and that sometimes—sometimes when I seemed farthest from remembering them—they have helped me, and kept me from mistakes; kept me from really becoming what many people have thought me."

Strive as she would to put some order in her thoughts, the words would not come more clearly; yet she felt that she could not leave him without trying to make him understand that she had saved herself whole from the seeming ruin of her life.

A change had come over Selden's face as she spoke. Its guarded look had yielded to an expression still untinged by personal emotion, but full of a gentle understanding.

"I am glad to have you tell me that; but nothing I have said has really made the difference. The difference is in yourself—it will always be there. And since it *is* there, it can't really matter to you what people think: you are so sure that your friends will always understand you."

"Ah, don't say that—don't say that what you have told me has made no difference. It seems to shut me out—to leave me all alone with the other people." She had risen and stood before him, once more completely mastered by the inner urgency of the moment. The consciousness of his half-divined reluctance had vanished. Whether he wished it or not, he must see her wholly for once before they parted.

Her voice had gathered strength, and she looked him gravely in the eyes as she continued. "Once—twice—you gave me the chance to escape from my life, and I refused it: refused it because I was a coward. Afterward I saw my mistake—I saw I could never be happy with what had contented me before. But it was too late: you had judged me—I understood. It was too late for happiness—but not too late to be helped by the thought of what I had missed. That is all I have lived on—don't take it from me now! Even in my worst moments it has been like a little light in the darkness. Some women are strong enough to be good by themselves, but I needed the help of your belief in me. Perhaps I might have resisted a great temptation, but the little ones would have pulled me down. And then I remembered—I remembered your saying that such a life could never satisfy me; and I was ashamed to admit to myself that it could. That is what you did for me—that is what I wanted to thank you for. I wanted to tell you that I have always remembered; and that I have tried—tried hard . . ."

She broke off suddenly. Her tears had risen again, and in drawing out her handkerchief her fingers touched the packet in the folds of her dress. A wave of color suffused her, and the words died on her lips. Then she lifted her eyes to his and went on in an altered voice.

"I have tried hard—but life is difficult, and I am a very useless person. I can hardly be said to have an independent existence. I was just a screw or a cog in the great machine I called life, and when I dropped out of it I found I was of no use anywhere else. What can one do when one finds that one only fits into one hole? One must get back to it or be thrown out into the rubbish heap—and you don't know what it's like in the rubbish heap!"

Her lips wavered into a smile—she had been distracted by the whimsical remembrance of the confidences she had made to him, two years earlier, in that very room. Then she had been planning to marry Percy Gryce—what was it she was planning now?

The blood had risen strongly under Selden's dark skin, but his emotion showed itself only in an added seriousness of manner.

"You have something to tell me—do you mean to marry?" he said abruptly.

Lily's eyes did not falter, but a look of wonder, of puzzled self-interrogation, formed itself slowly in their depths. In the light of his question, she had paused to ask herself if her decision had really been taken when she entered the room.

"You always told me I should have to come to it sooner or later!" she said with a faint smile.

"And you have come to it now?"

"I shall have to come to it—presently. But there is something else I must come to first." She paused again, trying to transmit to her voice the steadiness of her recovered smile. "There is some one I must say goodbye to. Oh, not *you*—we are sure to see each other again—but the Lily Bart you knew. I have kept her with me all this time, but now we are going to part, and I have brought her back to you—I am going to leave her here. When I go out presently she will not go with me. I shall like to think that she has stayed with you—and she'll be no trouble, she'll take up no room."

She went toward him, and put out her hand, still smiling. "Will you let her stay with you?" she asked.

He caught her hand, and she felt in his the vibration of feeling that had not yet risen to his lips. "Lily—can't I help you?" he exclaimed.

She looked at him gently. "Do you remember what you said to me once? That you could help me only by loving me? Well—you did love me for a moment; and it helped me. It has always helped me. But the moment is gone—it was I who let it go. And one must go on living. Goodbye."

She laid her other hand on his, and they looked at each other with a kind of solemnity, as though they stood in the presence of death. Something in truth lay dead between them—the love she had killed in him and could no longer call to life. But something lived between them also, and leaped up in her like an imperishable flame: it was the love his love had kindled, the passion of her soul for his.

In its light everything else dwindled and fell away from her. She understood now that she could not go forth and leave her old self with him: that self must indeed live on in his presence, but it must still continue to be hers.

Selden had retained her hand, and continued to scrutinize her with a strange sense of foreboding. The external aspect of the situation had vanished for him as completely as for her: he felt it only as one of those rare moments which lift the veil from their faces as they pass.

"Lily," he said in a low voice, "you mustn't speak in this way. I can't let you go without knowing what you mean to do. Things may change—but they don't pass. You can never go out of my life."

She met his eyes with an illumined look. "No," she said. "I see that now. Let us always be friends. Then I shall feel safe, whatever happens."

"Whatever happens? What do you mean? What is going to happen?"

She turned away quietly and walked toward the hearth.

"Nothing at present—except that I am very cold, and that before I go you must make up the fire for me."

She knelt on the hearthrug, stretching her hands to the embers. Puzzled by the sudden change in her tone, he mechanically gathered a handful of wood from the basket and tossed it on the fire. As he did so, he noticed how thin her hands looked against the rising light of the flames. He saw too, under the loose lines of her dress, how the curves of her figure had shrunk to angularity; he remembered long afterward how the red play of the flame sharpened the depression of her nostrils, and intensified the blackness of the shadows which struck up from her cheekbones to her eyes. She knelt there for a few moments in silence; a silence which he dared not break. When she rose he fancied that he saw her draw something from her dress and drop it into the fire; but he hardly noticed the gesture at the time. His faculties seemed tranced, and he was still groping for the word to break the spell.

She went up to him and laid her hands on his shoulders. "Goodbye," she said, and as he bent over her she touched his forehead with her lips.

XIII

THE street-lamps were lit, but the rain had ceased, and there was a momentary revival of light in the upper sky.

Lily walked on unconscious of her surroundings. She was still treading the buoyant ether which emanates from the high moments of life. But gradually it shrank away from her and she felt the dull pavement beneath her feet. The sense of weariness returned with accumulated force, and for a moment she felt that she could walk no farther. She had reached the corner of Forty-first Street and Fifth Avenue, and she remembered that in Bryant Park there were seats where she might rest.

That melancholy pleasure-ground was almost deserted when she entered it, and she sank down on an empty bench in the glare of an electric street-lamp. The warmth of the fire had passed out of her veins, and she told herself that she must not sit long in the penetrating dampness which struck up from the wet asphalt. But her will-power seemed to have spent itself in a last great effort, and she was lost in the blank reaction which follows on all unwonted expenditure of energy. And besides, what was there to go home to? Nothing but the silence of her cheerless room—that silence of the night which may be more racking to tired nerves than the most discordant noises: that, and the bottle of chloral by her bed. The thought of the chloral was the only spot of light in the dark prospect: she could feel its lulling influence stealing over her already. But she was troubled by the thought that it was losing its power—she dared not go back to it too soon. Of late the sleep it had brought her had been more broken and less profound; there had been nights when she was perpetually floating up through it to consciousness. What if the effect of the drug should gradually fail, as all narcotics were said to fail? She remembered the chemist's warning against increasing the dose; and she had heard before of the capricious and incalculable action of the drug. Her dread of returning to a sleepless night was so great that she lingered on, hoping that excessive weariness would reinforce the waning power of the chloral.

Night had now closed in, and the roar of traffic in Forty-second Street was dying out. As complete darkness fell on the square the lingering occupants of the benches rose and dispersed; but now and then a stray figure, hurrying homeward, struck across the path where Lily sat, looming black for a moment in the white circle of electric light. One or two of these passers-by slackened their pace to glance curiously at her lonely figure; but she was hardly conscious of their scrutiny.

Suddenly, however, she became aware that one of the passing shadows remained stationary between her line of vision and the gleaming asphalt; and raising her eyes she saw a young woman bending over her.

"Excuse me—are you sick?—Why, it's Miss Bart!" a half-familiar voice exclaimed.

Lily looked up. The speaker was a poorly-dressed young woman with a bundle under her arm. Her face had the air of unwholesome refinement which ill-health and overwork may produce, but its common prettiness was redeemed by the strong and generous curve of the lips.

"You don't remember me," she continued, brightening with the pleasure of recognition, "but I'd know you anywhere, I've thought of you such a lot. I guess my folks all know your name by heart. I was one of the girls at Miss Farish's club—you helped me to go to the country that time I had lung-trouble. My name's Nettie Struther. It was Nettie Crane then—but I daresay you don't remember that either."

Yes: Lily was beginning to remember. The episode of Nettie Crane's timely rescue from disease had been one of the most satisfying incidents of her connection with Gerty's charitable work. She had furnished the girl with the means to go to a sanatorium in the mountains: it struck her now with a peculiar irony that the money she had used had been Gus Trenor's.

She tried to reply, to assure the speaker that she had not forgotten; but her voice failed in the effort, and she felt herself sinking under a great wave of physical weakness. Nettie Struther, with a startled exclamation, sat down and slipped a shabbily-clad arm behind her back.

"Why, Miss Bart, you *are* sick. Just lean on me a little till you feel better."

A faint glow of returning strength seemed to pass into Lily from the pressure of the supporting arm.

"I'm only tired—it is nothing," she found voice to say in a moment; and then, as she met the timid appeal of her companion's eyes, she added involuntarily: "I have been unhappy—in great trouble."

"*You* in trouble? I've always thought of you as being so high up, where everything was just grand. Sometimes, when I felt real mean, and got to wondering why things were so queerly fixed in the world, I used to remember that *you* were having a lovely time, anyhow, and that seemed to show there was a kind of justice somewhere. But you mustn't sit here too long—it's fearfully damp. Don't you feel strong enough to walk on a little ways now?" she broke off.

"Yes—yes; I must go home," Lily murmured, rising.

Her eyes rested wonderingly on the thin shabby figure at her side. She had known Nettie Crane as one of the discouraged victims of over-work and anaemic parentage: one of the superfluous fragments of life destined to be swept prematurely into that social refuse-heap of which Lily had so lately expressed her dread. But Nettie Struther's frail envelope was now alive with hope and energy: whatever fate the future reserved for her, she would not be cast into the refuse-heap without a struggle.

"I am very glad to have seen you," Lily continued, summoning a smile to her unsteady lips. "It will be my turn to think of you as happy—and the world will seem a less unjust place to me too."

"Oh, but I can't leave you like this—you're not fit to go home alone. And I can't go with you either!" Nettie Struther wailed with a start of recollection. "You see, it's my husband's night-shift—he's a motor-man—and the friend I leave the baby with has to step upstairs to get *her* husband's supper at seven. I didn't tell you I had a baby, did I? She'll be four months old day after tomorrow, and to look at her you wouldn't think I'd ever had a sick day. I'd give anything to show you the baby, Miss Bart, and we live right down the street here—it's only three blocks off." She lifted her eyes tentatively to Lily's face, and then added with a burst of courage: "Why won't you get right into the cars and come home with me while I get baby's supper? It's real warm in our kitchen, and you can rest there, and I'll take *you* home as soon as ever she drops off to sleep."

It *was* warm in the kitchen, which, when Nettie Struther's match had made a flame leap from the gas-jet above the table, revealed itself to Lily as extraordinarily small and almost miraculously clean. A fire shone through the polished flanks of the iron stove, and near it stood a crib in which a baby was sitting upright, with incipient anxiety struggling for expression on a countenance still placid with sleep.

Having passionately celebrated her reunion with her offspring, and excused herself in cryptic language for the lateness of her return, Nettie restored the baby to the crib and shyly invited Miss Bart to the rocking-chair near the stove.

"We've got a parlor too," she explained with pardonable pride; "but I guess it's warmer in here, and I don't want to leave you alone while I'm getting baby's supper."

On receiving Lily's assurance that she much preferred the friendly proximity of the kitchen fire, Mrs. Struther proceeded to prepare a bottle of infantile food, which she tenderly applied to the baby's impatient lips; and while the ensuing degustation went on, she seated herself with a beaming countenance beside her visitor.

"You're sure you won't let me warm up a drop of coffee for you, Miss Bart? There's some of baby's fresh milk left over—well, maybe you'd rather just sit quiet and rest a little while. It's too lovely having you here. I've thought of it so often that I can't believe it's really come true. I've said to George again and again: 'I just wish Miss Bart could see me *now*—' and I used to watch for your name in the papers, and we'd talk over what you were doing, and read the descriptions of the dresses you wore. I haven't seen your name for a long time, though, and I began to be afraid you were sick, and it worried me so that George said I'd get sick myself, fretting about it." Her lips broke into a reminiscent smile. "Well, I can't afford to be sick again, that's a fact: the last spell nearly finished me. When you sent me off that time I never thought I'd come back alive, and I didn't much care if I did. You see I didn't know about George and the baby then."

She paused to readjust the bottle to the child's bubbling mouth.

"You precious—don't you be in too much of a hurry! Was it mad with mommer for getting its supper so late? Marry Anto'nette—that's what we call her: after the French queen in that play at the Garden—I told George the actress reminded me of you, and that made me fancy the name . . . I never thought I'd get married, you know, and I'd never have had the heart to go on working just for myself."

She broke off again, and meeting the encouragement in Lily's eyes, went on, with a flush rising under her anaemic skin: "You see I wasn't only just *sick* that time you sent me off—I was dreadfully unhappy too. I'd known a gentleman where I was employed—I don't know as you remember I did typewriting in a big importing firm—and—well—I thought we were to be married: he'd gone steady with me six months and given me his mother's wedding ring. But I presume he was too stylish for me—he traveled for the firm, and had seen a great deal of society. Work girls aren't looked after the way you are, and they don't always know how to look after themselves. I didn't . . . and it pretty near killed me when he went away and left off writing . . . It was then I came down sick—I thought it was the end of everything. I guess it would have been if you hadn't sent me off. But when I found I was getting well I began to take heart in spite of myself. And then, when I got back home, George came round and asked me to marry him. At first I thought I couldn't, because we'd been brought up together, and I knew he knew about me. But after a while I began to see that made it easier. I never could have told another man, and I'd never have married without telling; but if George cared for me enough to have me as I was, I didn't see why I shouldn't begin over again—and I did."

The strength of the victory shone forth from her as she lifted her irradiated face from the child on her knees.

"But, mercy, I didn't mean to go on like this about myself, with you sitting there looking so fagged out. Only it's so lovely having you here, and letting you see just how you've helped me." The baby had sunk back blissfully replete, and Mrs. Struther softly rose to lay the bottle aside. Then she paused before Miss Bart.

"I only wish I could help *you*—but I suppose there's nothing on earth I could do," she murmured wistfully.

Lily, instead of answering, rose with a smile and held out her arms; and the mother, understanding the gesture, laid her child in them.

The baby, feeling herself detached from her habitual anchorage, made an instinctive motion of resistance; but the soothing influences of digestion prevailed, and Lily felt the soft weight sink trustfully against her breast. The child's confidence in its safety thrilled her with a sense of warmth and returning life, and she bent over, wondering at the rosy blur of the little face, the empty clearness of the eyes, the vague tendrilly motions of the folding and unfolding fingers. At first the burden in her arms seemed as light as a pink cloud or a heap of down, but as she continued to hold it the weight increased, sinking deeper, and penetrating her with a strange sense of weakness, as though the child entered into her and became a part of herself.

She looked up, and saw Nettie's eyes resting on her with tenderness and exultation.

"Wouldn't it be too lovely for anything if she could grow up to be just like you? Of course I know she never *could*—but mothers are always dreaming the craziest things for their children."

Lily clasped the child close for a moment and laid her back in her mother's arms.

"Oh, she must not do that—I should be afraid to come and see her too often!" she said with a smile; and then, resisting Mrs. Struther's anxious offer of companionship, and reiterating the promise that of course she would come back soon, and make George's acquaintance, and see the baby in her bath, she passed out of the kitchen and went alone down the tenement stairs.

As she reached the street she realized that she felt stronger and happier: the little episode had done her good. It was the first time she had ever come across the results of her spasmodic benevolence, and the surprised sense of human fellowship took the mortal chill from her heart.

It was not till she entered her own door that she felt the reaction of a deeper loneliness. It was long after seven o'clock, and the light and odors proceeding from the basement made it manifest that the boarding-house dinner had begun. She hastened up to her room, lit the gas, and began to dress. She did not mean to pamper herself any longer, to go without food because her surroundings made it unpalatable. Since it was her fate to live in a boarding-house, she must learn to fall in with the conditions of the life. Nevertheless she was glad that, when she descended to the heat and glare of the dining-room, the repast was nearly over.

In her own room again, she was seized with a sudden fever of activity. For weeks past she had been too listless and indifferent to set her possessions in order, but now she began to examine systematically the contents of her drawers and cupboard. She had a few handsome dresses left—survivals of her last phase of splendor, on the Sabrina and in London—but when she had been obliged to part with her maid she had given the woman a generous share of her cast-off apparel. The remaining dresses, though they had lost their freshness, still kept the long unerring lines, the sweep and amplitude of the great artist's stroke, and as she spread them out on the bed the scenes in which they had been worn rose vividly before her. An association lurked in every fold: each fall of lace and gleam of embroidery was like a letter in the record of her past. She was startled to find how the atmosphere of her old life enveloped her. But, after all, it was the life she had been made for: every dawning tendency in her had been carefully directed toward it, all her interests and activities had been taught to center around it. She was like some rare flower grown for exhibition, a flower from which every bud had been nipped except the crowning blossom of her beauty.

Last of all, she drew forth from the bottom of her trunk a heap of white drapery which fell shapelessly across her arm. It was the Reynolds dress she had worn in the Bry *tableaux*. It had been impossible for her to give it away, but she had never seen it since that night, and the long flexible folds, as she shook them out, gave forth an odor of violets which came to her like a breath from the flower-edged fountain where she had stood with Lawrence Selden and disowned her fate. She put back the dresses one by one, laying away with each some gleam of light, some note of laughter, some stray waft from the rosy shores of pleasure. She was still in a state of highly-wrought impressionability, and every hint of the past sent a lingering tremor along her nerves.

She had just closed her trunk on the white folds of the Reynolds dress when she heard a tap at her door, and the red fist of the Irish maid-servant thrust in a belated letter. Carrying it to the light, Lily read with surprise the address stamped on the upper corner of the envelope. It was a business communication from the office of her aunt's executors, and she wondered what unexpected development had caused them to break silence before the appointed time.

She opened the envelope and a check fluttered to the floor. As she stooped to pick it up the blood rushed to her face. The check represented the full amount of Mrs. Peniston's legacy, and the letter accompanying it explained that the executors, having adjusted the business of the estate with less delay than they had expected, had decided to anticipate the date fixed for the payment of the bequests.

Lily sat down beside the desk at the foot of her bed, and spreading out the check, read over and over the *ten thousand dollars* written across it in a steely business hand. Ten months earlier the amount it stood for had represented the depths of penury; but her standard of values had changed in the interval, and now visions of wealth lurked in every flourish of the pen. As she continued to gaze at it, she felt the glitter of the visions mounting to her brain, and after a while she lifted the lid of the desk and slipped the magic formula out of sight. It was easier to think without those five figures dancing before her eyes; and she had a great deal of thinking to do before she slept.

She opened her check-book, and plunged into such anxious calculations as had prolonged her vigil at Bellomont on the night when she had decided to marry Percy Gryce. Poverty simplifies book-keeping, and her financial situation was easier to ascertain than it had been then; but she had not yet learned the control of money, and during her transient phase of luxury at the Emporium she had slipped back into habits of extravagance which still impaired her slender balance. A careful examination of her check-book, and of the unpaid bills in her desk, showed that, when the latter had been settled, she would have barely enough to live on for the next three or four months; and even after that, if she were to continue her present way of living, without earning any additional money, all incidental expenses must be reduced to the vanishing point. She hid her eyes with a shudder, beholding herself at the entrance of that ever-narrowing perspective down which she had seen Miss Silverton's dowdy figure take its despondent way.

It was no longer, however, from the vision of material poverty that she turned with the greatest shrinking. She had a sense of deeper impoverishment—of an inner destitution compared to which outward conditions dwindled into insignificance. It was indeed miserable to be poor—to look forward to a shabby, anxious middle-age, leading by dreary degrees of economy and self-denial to gradual absorption in the dingy communal existence of the boarding-house. But there was something more miserable still—it was the clutch of solitude at her heart, the sense of being swept like a stray uprooted growth down the heedless current of the years. That was the feeling which possessed her now—the feeling of being something rootless and ephemeral, mere spin-drift of the whirling surface of existence, without anything to which the poor little tentacles of self could cling before the awful flood submerged them. And as she looked back she saw that there had never been a time when she had had any real relation to life. Her parents too had been rootless, blown hither and thither on every wind of fashion, without any personal existence to shelter them from its shifting gusts. She herself had grown up without any one spot of earth being dearer to her than another: there was no center of early pieties, of grave endearing traditions, to which her heart could revert and from which it could draw strength for itself and tenderness for others. In whatever form a slowly-accumulated past lives in the blood—whether in the concrete image of the old house stored with visual memories, or in the conception of the house not built with hands, but made up of inherited passions and loyalties—it has the same power of broadening and deepening the individual existence, of attaching it by mysterious links of kinship to all the mighty sum of human striving.

Such a vision of the solidarity of life had never before come to Lily. She had had a premonition of it in the blind motions of her mating-instinct; but they had been checked by the disintegrating influences of the life about her. All the men and women she knew were like atoms whirling away from each other in some wild centrifugal dance: her first glimpse of the continuity of life had come to her that evening in Nettie Struther's kitchen.

The poor little working-girl who had found strength to gather up the fragments of her life, and build herself a shelter with them, seemed to Lily to have reached the central truth of existence. It was a meager enough life, on the grim edge of poverty, with scant margin for possibilities of sickness or mischance, but it had the frail audacious permanence of a bird's nest built on the edge of a cliff—a mere wisp of leaves and straw, yet so put together that the lives entrusted to it may hang safely over the abyss.

Yes—but it had taken two to build the nest; the man's faith as well as the woman's courage. Lily remembered Nettie's words: *I knew he knew about me*. Her husband's faith in her had made her renewal possible—it is so easy for a woman to become what the man she loves believes her to be! Well—Selden had twice been ready to stake his faith on Lily Bart; but the third trial had been too severe for his endurance. The very quality of his love had made it the more impossible to recall to life. If it had been a simple instinct of the blood, the power of her beauty might have revived it. But the fact that it struck deeper, that it was inextricably wound up with inherited habits of thought and feeling, made it as impossible to restore to growth as a deep-rooted plant torn from its bed. Selden had given her of his best; but he was as incapable as herself of an uncritical return to former states of feeling.

There remained to her, as she had told him, the uplifting memory of his faith in her; but she had not reached the age when a woman can live on her memories. As she held Nettie Struther's child in her arms the frozen currents of youth had loosed themselves and run warm in her veins: the old life-hunger possessed her, and all her being clamored for its share of personal happiness. Yes—it was happiness she still wanted, and the glimpse she had caught of it made everything else of no account. One by one she had detached herself from the baser possibilities, and she saw that nothing now remained to her but the emptiness of renunciation.

It was growing late, and an immense weariness once more possessed her. It was not the stealing sense of sleep, but a vivid wakeful fatigue, a wan lucidity of mind against which all the possibilities of the future were shadowed forth gigantically. She was appalled by the intense clearness of the vision; she seemed to have broken through the merciful veil which intervenes between intention and action, and to see exactly what she would do in all the long days to come. There was the check in her desk, for instance—she meant to use it in paying her debt to Trenor; but she foresaw that when the morning came she would put off doing so, would slip into gradual tolerance of the debt. The thought terrified her—she dreaded to fall from the height of her last moment with Lawrence Selden. But how could she trust herself to keep her footing? She knew the strength of the opposing impulses—she could feel the countless hands of habit dragging her back into some fresh compromise with fate. She felt an intense longing to prolong, to perpetuate, the momentary exaltation of her spirit. If only life could end now—end on this tragic yet sweet vision of lost possibilities, which gave her a sense of kinship with all the loving and foregoing in the world!

She reached out suddenly and, drawing the check from her writing-desk, enclosed it in an envelope which she addressed to her bank. She then wrote out a check for Trenor, and placing it, without an accompanying word, in an envelope inscribed with his name, laid the two letters side by side on her desk. After that she continued to sit at the table, sorting her papers and writing, till the intense silence of the house reminded her of the lateness of the hour. In the street the noise of wheels had ceased, and the rumble of the "elevated" came only at long intervals through the deep unnatural hush. In the mysterious nocturnal separation from all outward signs of life, she felt herself more strangely confronted with her fate. The sensation made her brain reel, and she tried to shut out consciousness by pressing her hands against her eyes. But the terrible silence and emptiness seemed to symbolize her future—she felt as though the house, the street, the world were all empty, and she alone left sentient in a lifeless universe.

But this was the verge of delirium . . . she had never hung so near the dizzy brink of the unreal. Sleep was what she wanted—she remembered that she had not closed her eyes for two nights. The little bottle was at her bedside, waiting to lay its spell upon her. She rose and undressed hastily, hungering now for the touch of her pillow. She felt so profoundly tired that she thought she must fall asleep at once; but as soon as she had lain down every nerve started once more into separate wakefulness. It was as though a great blaze of electric light had been turned on in her head, and her poor little anguished self shrank and cowered in it, without knowing where to take refuge.

She had not imagined that such a multiplication of wakefulness was possible: her whole past was reenacting itself at a hundred different points of consciousness. Where was the drug that could still this legion of insurgent nerves? The sense of exhaustion would have been sweet compared to this shrill beat of activities; but weariness had dropped from her as though some cruel stimulant had been forced into her veins.

She could bear it—yes, she could bear it; but what strength would be left her the next day? Perspective had disappeared—the next day pressed close upon her, and on its heels came the days that were to follow—they swarmed about her like a shrieking mob. She must shut them out for a few hours; she must take a brief bath of oblivion. She put out her hand, and measured the soothing drops into a glass; but as she did so, she knew they would be powerless against the supernatural lucidity of her brain. She had long since raised the dose to its highest limit, but tonight she felt she must increase it. She knew she took a slight risk in doing so—she remembered the

But this was the verge of delirium. . . .

chemist's warning. If sleep came at all, it might be a sleep without waking. But after all that was but one chance in a hundred: the action of the drug was incalculable, and the addition of a few drops to the regular dose would probably do no more than procure for her the rest she so desperately needed. . . .

She did not, in truth, consider the question very closely—the physical craving for sleep was her only sustained sensation. Her mind shrank from the glare of thought as instinctively as eyes contract in a blaze of light—darkness, darkness was what she must have at any cost. She raised herself in bed and swallowed the contents of the glass; then she blew out her candle and lay down.

She lay very still, waiting with a sensuous pleasure for the first effects of the soporific. She knew in advance what form they would take—the gradual cessation of the inner throb, the soft approach of passiveness, as though an invisible hand made magic passes over her in the darkness. The very slowness and hesitancy of the effect increased its fascination: it was delicious to lean over and look down into the dim abysses of unconsciousness. Tonight the drug seemed to work more slowly than usual: each passionate pulse had to be stilled in turn, and it was long before she felt them dropping into abeyance, like sentinels falling asleep at their posts. But gradually the sense of complete subjugation came over her, and she wondered languidly what had made her feel so uneasy and excited. She saw now that there was nothing to be excited about—she had returned to her normal view of life. Tomorrow would not be so difficult after all: she felt sure that she would have the strength to meet it. She did not quite remember what it was that she had been afraid to meet, but the uncertainty no longer troubled her. She had been unhappy, and now she was happy—she had felt herself alone, and now the sense of loneliness had vanished.

She stirred once, and turned on her side, and as she did so, she suddenly understood why she did not feel herself alone. It was odd—but Nettie Struther's child was lying on her arm: she felt the pressure of its little head against her shoulder. She did not know how it had come there, but she felt no great surprise at the fact, only a gentle penetrating thrill of warmth and pleasure. She settled herself into an easier position, hollowing her arm to pillow the round downy head, and holding her breath lest a sound should disturb the sleeping child.

As she lay there she said to herself that there was something she must tell Selden, some word she had found that should make life clear between them. She tried to repeat the word, which lingered vague and luminous on the far edge of thought—she was afraid of not remembering it when she woke; and if she could only remember it and say it to him, she felt that everything would be well.

Slowly the thought of the word faded, and sleep began to enfold her. She struggled faintly against it, feeling that she ought to keep awake on account of the baby; but even this feeling was gradually lost in an indistinct sense of drowsy peace, through which, of a sudden, a dark flash of loneliness and terror tore its way.

She started up again, cold and trembling with the shock: for a moment she seemed to have lost her hold of the child. But no—she was mistaken—the tender pressure of its body was still close to hers: the recovered warmth flowed through her once more, she yielded to it, sank into it, and slept.

XIV

THE next morning rose mild and bright, with a promise of summer in the air. The sunlight slanted joyously down Lily's street, mellowed the blistered house-front, gilded the paintless railings of the door-step, and struck prismatic glories from the panes of her darkened window.

When such a day coincides with the inner mood there is intoxication in its breath; and Selden, hastening along the street through the squalor of its morning confidences, felt himself thrilling with a youthful sense of adventure. He had cut loose from the familiar shores of habit, and launched himself on uncharted seas of emotion; all the old tests and measures were left behind, and his course was to be shaped by new stars.

That course, for the moment, led merely to Miss Bart's boarding-house; but its shabby door-step had suddenly become the threshold of the untried. As he approached he looked up at the triple row of windows, wondering boyishly which one of them was hers. It was nine o'clock, and the house, being tenanted by workers, already showed an awakened front to the street. He remembered afterward having noticed that only one blind was down. He noticed too that there was a pot of pansies on one of the window sills, and at once concluded that the window must be hers: it was inevitable that he should connect her with the one touch of beauty in the dingy scene.

Nine o'clock was an early hour for a visit, but Selden had passed beyond all such conventional observances. He only knew that he must see Lily Bart at once—he had found the word he meant to say to her, and it could not wait another moment to be said. It was strange that it had not come to his lips sooner—that he had let her pass from him the evening before without being able to speak it. But what did that matter, now that a new day had come? It was not a word for twilight, but for the morning.

Selden ran eagerly up the steps and pulled the bell; and even in his state of self-absorption it came as a sharp surprise to him that the door should open so promptly. It was still more of a surprise to see, as he entered, that it had been opened by Gerty Farish—and that behind her, in an agitated blur, several other figures ominously loomed.

"Lawrence!" Gerty cried in a strange voice, "how could you get here so quickly?"—and the trembling hand she laid on him seemed instantly to close about his heart.

He noticed the other faces, vague with fear and conjecture—he saw the landlady's imposing bulk sway professionally toward him; but he shrank back, putting up his hand, while his eyes mechanically mounted the steep black walnut stairs, up which he was immediately aware that his cousin was about to lead him.

A voice in the background said that the doctor might be back at any minute—and that nothing, upstairs, was to be disturbed. Some one else exclaimed: "It was the greatest mercy——" then Selden felt that Gerty had taken him gently by the hand, and that they were to be suffered to go up alone.

In silence they mounted the three flights, and walked along the passage to a closed door. Gerty opened the door, and Selden went in after her. Though the blind was down, the irresistible sunlight poured a tempered golden flood into the room, and in its light Selden saw a narrow bed along the wall, and on the bed, with motionless hands and calm unrecognizing face, the semblance of Lily Bart.

That it was her real self, every pulse in him ardently denied. Her real self had lain warm on his heart but a few hours earlier—what had he to do with this estranged and tranquil face which, for the first time, neither paled nor brightened at his coming?

Gerty, strangely tranquil too, with the conscious self-control of one who has ministered to much pain, stood by the bed, speaking gently, as if transmitting a final message.

"The doctor found a bottle of chloral—she had been sleeping badly for a long time, and she must have taken an over-dose by mistake. . . . There is no doubt of that—no doubt—there will be no question—he has been very kind. I told him that you and I would like to be left alone with her—to go over her things before any one else comes. I know it is what she would have wished."

Selden was hardly conscious of what she said. He stood looking down on the sleeping face which seemed to lie like a delicate impalpable mask over the living lineaments he had known. He felt that the real Lily was still there, close to him, yet invisible and inaccessible; and the tenuity of the barrier between them mocked him with a sense of helplessness. There had never been more than a little impalpable barrier between them—and yet he had suffered it to keep them apart! And now, though it seemed slighter and frailer than ever, it had suddenly hardened to adamant, and he might beat his life out against it in vain.

He had dropped on his knees beside the bed, but a touch from Gerty aroused him. He stood up, and as their eyes met he was struck by the extraordinary light in his cousin's face.

"You understand what the doctor has gone for? He has promised that there shall be no trouble—but of course the formalities must be gone through. And I asked him to give us time to look through her things first——"

He nodded, and she glanced about the small bare room. "It won't take long," she concluded.

"No—it won't take long," he agreed.

She held his hand in hers a moment longer, and then, with a last look at the bed, moved silently toward the door. On the threshold she paused to add: "You will find me downstairs if you want me."

Selden roused himself to detain her. "But why are you going? She would have wished——"

Gerty shook her head with a smile. "No: this is what she would have wished——" and as she spoke a light broke through Selden's stony misery, and he saw deep into the hidden things of love.

The door closed on Gerty, and he stood alone with the motionless sleeper on the bed. His impulse was to return to her side, to fall on his knees, and rest his throbbing head against the peaceful cheek on the pillow. They had never been at peace together, they two; and now he felt himself drawn downward into the strange mysterious depths of her tranquillity.

But he remembered Gerty's warning words—he knew that, though time had ceased in this room, its feet were hastening relentlessly toward the door. Gerty had given him this supreme half-hour, and he must use it as she willed.

He turned and looked about him, sternly compelling himself to regain his consciousness of outward things. There was very little furniture in the room. The shabby chest of drawers was spread with a lace cover, and set out with a few gold-topped boxes and bottles, a rose-colored pin-cushion, a glass tray strewn with tortoise-shell hair-pins—he shrank from the poignant intimacy of these trifles, and from the blank surface of the toilet-mirror above them.

These were the only traces of luxury, of that clinging to the minute observance of personal seemliness, which showed what her other renunciations must have cost. There was no other token of her personality about the room, unless it showed itself in the scrupulous neatness of the scant articles of furniture: a washing-stand, two chairs, a small writing-desk, and the little table near the bed. On this table stood the empty bottle and glass, and from these also he averted his eyes.

The desk was closed, but on its slanting lid lay two letters which he took up. One bore the address of a bank, and as it was stamped and sealed, Selden, after a moment's hesitation, laid it aside. On the other letter he read Gus Trenor's name; and the flap of the envelope was still ungummed.

Temptation leapt on him like the stab of a knife. He staggered under it, steadying himself against the desk. Why had she been writing to Trenor—writing, presumably, just after their parting of the previous evening? The thought unhallowed the memory of that last hour, made a mock of the word he had come to speak, and defiled even the reconciling silence upon which it fell. He felt himself flung back on all the ugly uncertainties from which he thought he had cast loose forever. After all, what did he know of her life? Only as much as she had chosen to show him, and measured by the world's estimate, how little that was! By what right—the letter in his hand seemed to ask—by what right was it he who now passed into her confidence through the gate which death had left unbarred? His heart cried out that it was by right of their last hour together, the hour when she herself had placed the key in his hand. Yes—but what if the letter to Trenor had been written afterward?

He put it from him with sudden loathing, and setting his lips, addressed himself resolutely to what remained of his task. After all, that task would be easier to perform, now that his personal stake in it was annulled.

He raised the lid of the desk, and saw within it a check-book and a few packets of bills and letters, arranged with the orderly precision which characterized all her personal habits. He looked through the letters first, because it was the most difficult part of the work. They proved to be few and unimportant, but among them he found, with a strange commotion of the heart, the note he had written her the day after the Brys' entertainment.

"When may I come to you?"—his words overwhelmed him with a realization of the cowardice which had driven him from her at the very moment of attainment. Yes—he had always feared his fate, and he was too honest to disown his cowardice now; for had not all his old doubts started to life again at the mere sight of Trenor's name?

He laid the note in his card-case, folding it away carefully, as something made precious by the fact that she had held it so; then, growing once more aware of the lapse of time, he continued his examination of the papers.

To his surprise, he found that all the bills were receipted; there was not an unpaid account among them. He opened the check-book, and saw that, the very night before, a check of ten thousand dollars from Mrs. Peniston's executors had been entered in it. The legacy, then, had been paid sooner than Gerty had led him to expect. But, turning another page or two, he discovered with astonishment that, in spite of this recent accession of funds, the balance had already declined to a few dollars. A rapid glance at the stubs of the last checks, all of which bore the date of the previous day, showed that between four or five hundred dollars of the legacy had been spent in the settlement of bills, while the remaining thousands were comprehended in one check, made out, at the same time, to Charles Augustus Trenor.

Selden laid the book aside, and sank into the chair beside the desk. He leaned his elbows on it, and hid his face in his hands. The bitter waters of life surged high about him, their sterile taste was on his lips. Did the check to Trenor explain the mystery or deepen it? At first his mind refused to act—he felt only the taint of such a transaction between a man like Trenor and a girl like Lily Bart. Then, gradually, his troubled vision cleared, old hints and rumors came back to him, and out of the very insinuations he had feared to probe, he constructed an explanation of the mystery. It was true, then, that she had taken money from Trenor; but true also, as the contents of the little desk declared, that the obligation had been intolerable to her, and that at the first opportunity she had freed herself from it, though the act left her face to face with bare unmitigated poverty.

That was all he knew—all he could hope to unravel of the story. The mute lips on the pillow refused him more than this—unless indeed they had told him the rest in the kiss they had left upon his forehead. Yes, he could now read into that farewell all that his heart craved to find there; he could even draw from it courage not to accuse himself for having failed to reach the height of his opportunity.

He saw that all the conditions of life had conspired to keep them apart; since his very detachment from the external influences which swayed her had increased his spiritual fastidiousness, and made it more difficult for him to live and love uncritically. But at least he *had* loved her—had been willing to stake his future on his faith in her—and if the moment had been fated to pass from them before they could seize it, he saw now that, for both, it had been saved whole out of the ruin of their lives.

It was this moment of love, this fleeting victory over themselves, which had kept them from atrophy and extinction; which, in her, had reached out to him in every struggle against the influence of her surroundings, and in him, had kept alive the faith that now drew him penitent and reconciled to her side.

He knelt by the bed and bent over her, draining their last moment to its lees; and in the silence there passed between them the word which made all clear.

Tales of Men and Ghosts

The Bolted Door

I

HUBERT GRANICE, pacing the length of his pleasant lamp-lit library, paused to compare his watch with the clock on the chimney-piece.

Three minutes to eight.

In exactly three minutes Mr. Peter Ascham, of the eminent legal firm of Ascham and Pettilow, would have his punctual hand on the door-bell of the flat.

It was a comfort to reflect that Ascham was so punctual—the suspense was beginning to make his host nervous. And the sound of the door-bell would be the beginning of the end—after that there'd be no going back, by God—no going back!

Granice resumed his pacing. Each time he reached the end of the room opposite the door he caught his reflection in the Florentine mirror above the fine old *crédence* he had picked up at Dijon—saw himself spare, quick-moving, carefully brushed and dressed, but furrowed, gray about the temples, with a stoop which he corrected by a spasmodic straightening of the shoulders whenever a glass confronted him: a tired middle-aged man, baffled, beaten, worn out.

As he summed himself up thus for the third or fourth time the door opened and he turned with a thrill of relief to greet his guest. But it was only the man-servant who entered, advancing silently over the mossy surface of the old Turkey rug.

"Mr. Ascham telephones, sir, to say he's unexpectedly detained and can't be here till eight-thirty."

Granice made a curt gesture of annoyance. It was becoming harder and harder for him to control these reflexes. He turned on his heel, tossing to the servant over his shoulder: "Very good. Put off dinner."

Down his spine he felt the man's injured stare. Mr. Granice had always been so mild-spoken to his people—no doubt the odd change in his manner had already been noticed and discussed below stairs. And very likely they suspected the cause. He stood drumming on the writing-table till he heard the servant go out; then he threw himself into a chair, propping his elbows on the table and resting his chin on his locked hands.

Another half hour alone with it!

He wondered irritably what could have detained his guest. Some professional matter, no doubt—the punctilious lawyer would have allowed nothing less to interfere with a dinner engagement, more especially since Granice, in his note, had said: "I shall want a little business chat afterward."

But what professional matter could have come up at that unprofessional hour? Perhaps some other soul in misery had called on the lawyer; and, after all, Granice's note had given no hint of his own need! No doubt Ascham thought he merely wanted to make another change in his will. Since he had come into his little property, ten years earlier, Granice had been perpetually tinkering with his will.

Suddenly another thought pulled him up, sending a flush to his temples. He remembered a word he had tossed to the lawyer some six weeks earlier, at the Century Club. "Yes—my play's as good as taken. I shall be calling on you soon to go over the contract. Those theatrical chaps are so slippery—I won't trust anybody but you to tie the knot for me!" That, of course, was what Ascham would think he was wanted for. Granice, at the idea, broke into an audible laugh—a queer stage-laugh, like the cackle of a baffled villain in a melodrama. The absurdity, the unnaturalness of the sound abashed him, and he compressed his lips angrily. Would he take to soliloquy next?

He lowered his arms and pulled open the upper drawer of the writing-table. In the right-hand corner lay a manuscript, bound in paper folders, and tied with a string beneath which a letter had been slipped. Next to the manuscript was a revolver. Granice stared a moment at these oddly associated objects; then he took the letter from under the string and slowly began to open it. He had known he should do so from the moment his hand touched the drawer. Whenever his eye fell on that letter some relentless force compelled him to reread it.

It was dated about four weeks back, under the letterhead of "The Diversity Theatre."

> "MY DEAR MR. GRANICE:
>
> "I have given the matter my best consideration for the last month, and it's no use—the play won't do. I have talked it over with Miss Melrose—and you know there isn't a gamer artist on our stage—and I regret to tell you she feels just as I do about it. It isn't the poetry that scares her—or me either. We both want to do all we can to help along the poetic drama—we believe the public's ready for it, and we're willing to take a big financial risk in order to be the first to give them what they want. *But we don't believe they could be made to want this*. The fact is, there isn't enough drama in your play to the allowance of poetry—the thing drags all through. You've got a big idea, but it's not out of swaddling clothes.
>
> "If this was your first play I'd say: *Try again*. But it has been just the same with all the others you've shown me. And you remember the result of 'The Lee Shore,' where you carried all the expenses of production yourself, and we couldn't fill the theater for a week. Yet 'The Lee Shore' was a modern problem play—much easier to swing than blank verse. It isn't as if you hadn't tried all kinds——"

Granice folded the letter and put it carefully back into the envelope. Why on earth was he rereading it, when he knew every phrase in it by heart, when for a month past he had seen it, night after night, stand out in letters of flame against the darkness of his sleepless lids?

"It has been just the same with all the others you've shown me."

That was the way they dismissed ten years of passionate unremitting work!

"You remember the result of 'The Lee Shore.'"

Good God—as if he were likely to forget it! He relived it all now in a drowning flash: the persistent rejection of the play, his resolve to put it on at his own cost, to spend ten thousand dollars of his inheritance on testing his chance of success—the fever of preparation, the dry-mouthed agony of the "first night," the flat fall, the stupid press, his secret rush to Europe to escape the condolence of his friends!

"It isn't as if you hadn't tried all kinds."

No—he had tried all kinds: comedy, tragedy, prose and verse, the light curtain-raiser, the short sharp drama, the bourgeois-realistic and the lyrical-romantic—finally deciding that he would no longer "prostitute his talent" to win popularity, but would impose on the public his own theory of art in the form of five acts of blank verse. Yes, he had offered them everything— and always with the same result.

Ten years of it—ten years of dogged work and unrelieved failure. The ten years from forty to fifty—the best ten years of his life! And if one counted the years before, the years of dreams, assimilation, preparation—then call it half a man's lifetime: half a man's lifetime thrown away!

And what was he to do with the remaining half? Well, he had settled that, thank God! He turned and glanced anxiously at the clock. Ten minutes past eight—only ten minutes had been consumed in that stormy rush through his past! And he must wait another twenty minutes for Ascham. It was one of the worst symptoms of his case that, in proportion as he had grown to shrink from human company, he dreaded more and more to be alone . . . But why the devil was he waiting for Ascham? Why didn't he cut the knot himself? Since he was so unutterably sick of the whole business, why did he have to call in an outsider to rid him of this nightmare of living?

He opened the drawer again and laid his hand on the revolver. It was a slim ivory toy—just the instrument for a tired sufferer to give himself a "hypodermic" with. Granice raised it in one hand, while with the other he felt under the thin hair at the back of his head, between the ear and the nape. He knew just where to place the muzzle: he had once got a surgeon to show him. And as he found the spot, and lifted the revolver to it, the inevitable phenomenon occurred. The hand that held the weapon began to shake, the tremor passed into his arm, his heart gave a leap which sent up a wave of deadly nausea to his throat, he smelt the powder, he sickened at the crash of the bullet through his skull, and a sweat broke out over his forehead and ran down his quivering face . . .

He laid away the revolver and, pulling out his handkerchief, passed it tremulously over his brow and temples. It was of no use—he knew he could never do it in that way. His attempts at self-destruction were as futile as his snatches at fame! He couldn't make himself a real life, and he couldn't get rid of the life he had. And that was why he had sent for Ascham to help him . . . .

The lawyer, over the cheese and Burgundy, began to excuse himself for his delay.

"I didn't like to say anything while your man was about; but the fact is, I was sent for on a rather unusual matter——"

"Oh, it's all right," said Granice cheerfully. He was beginning to feel the reaction that food and company always produced in him. It was not any recovered pleasure in life that he felt, but only a deeper withdrawal into himself. It was easier to go on automatically with the social gestures than to uncover to any human eye the abyss within him.

"My dear fellow, it's sacrilege to keep a dinner waiting—especially the production of an artist like yours." Mr. Ascham sipped his Burgundy luxuriously. "But the fact is, Mrs. Ashgrove sent for me."

Granice raised his head with a movement of surprise. For a moment he was shaken out of his self-absorption.

"Mrs. Ashgrove?"

Ascham smiled. "I thought you'd be interested; I know your passion for *causes célèbres*. And this promises to be one. Of course it's out of our line entirely—we never touch criminal cases. But she wanted to consult me as a friend. Ashgrove was a distant connection of my wife's. And, by Jove, it is a queer case!" The servant reentered, and Ascham snapped his lips shut.

Would the gentlemen have their coffee in the dining room?

"No—serve it in the library," said Granice, rising. He led the way back to the curtained confidential room. He was really curious to hear what Ascham had to tell him.

While the coffee and cigars were being served he fidgeted about, glancing at his letters—the usual meaningless notes and bills—and picking up the evening paper. As he unfolded it a headline caught his eye.

"ROSE MELROSE WANTS TO PLAY POETRY.
"THINKS SHE HAS FOUND HER POET."

He read on with a thumping heart—found the name of a young author he had barely heard of, saw the title of a play, a "poetic drama," dance before his eyes, and dropped the paper, sick, disgusted. It was true, then—she *was* "game"—it was not the manner but the matter she mistrusted!

Granice turned to the servant, who seemed to be purposely lingering. "I shan't need you this evening, Flint. I'll lock up myself."

He fancied that the man's acquiescence implied surprise. What was going on, Flint seemed to wonder, that Mr. Granice should want him out of the way? Probably he would find a pretext for coming back to see. Granice suddenly felt himself enveloped in a network of espionage.

As the door closed he threw himself into an armchair and leaned forward to take a light from Ascham's cigar.

"Tell me about Mrs. Ashgrove," he said, seeming to himself to speak stiffly, as if his lips were cracked.

"Mrs. Ashgrove? Well, there's not much to *tell.*"

"And you couldn't if there were?" Granice smiled.

"Probably not. As a matter of fact, she wanted my advice about her choice of counsel. There was nothing especially confidential in our talk."

"And what's your impression, now you've seen her?"

"My impression is, very distinctly, *that nothing will ever be known.*"

"Ah——?" Granice murmured, puffing at his cigar.

"I'm more and more convinced that whoever poisoned Ashgrove knew his business, and will consequently never be found out. That's a capital cigar you've given me."

"You like it? I get them over from Cuba." Granice examined his own reflectively. "Then you believe in the theory that the clever criminals never *are* caught?"

"Of course I do. Look about you—look back for the last dozen years—none of the big murder problems are ever solved." The lawyer ruminated behind his blue cloud. "Why, take the instance in your own family: I'd forgotten I had an illustration at hand! Take old Joseph Lenman's murder—do you suppose that will ever be explained?"

As the words dropped from Ascham's lips his host looked about the library, and every object in it stared back at him with a stale unescapable familiarity. How sick he was of looking at that room! It was as dull as the face of a wife one has tired of. He cleared his throat slowly; then he turned his head to the lawyer and said: "I could explain the Lenman murder myself."

Ascham's eye kindled: he shared Granice's interest in criminal cases.

"By Jove! You've had a theory all this time? It's odd you never mentioned it. Go ahead and tell me. There are certain features in the Lenman case not unlike this Ashgrove affair, and your idea may be a help."

Granice paused and his eye reverted instinctively to the table drawer in which the revolver and the manuscript lay side by side. What if he were to try another appeal to Rose Melrose? Then he looked at the notes and bills on the table, and the horror of taking up again the lifeless routine of life—of performing the same automatic gestures another day—dispelled his fleeting impulse.

"It's not an idea. I *know* who murdered Joseph Lenman."

Ascham settled himself comfortably in his chair, prepared for enjoyment.

"You *know?* Well, who did?" he laughed.

"I did," said Granice, rising to his feet.

He stood before Ascham, and the lawyer lay back, staring up at him. Then he broke into another laugh.

"Why, this is glorious! You murdered him, did you? To inherit his money, I suppose? Better and better! Go on, my boy! Unbosom yourself! Tell me all about it! Confession is good for the soul."

Granice waited till the lawyer had shaken the last peal of laughter from his throat; then he repeated doggedly: "I murdered him."

The two men looked at each other for a long moment, and this time Ascham did not laugh.

"Granice!"

"I murdered him—to get his money, as you say."

There was another pause, and Granice, with a vague sense of amusement, saw his guest's look gradually change from pleasantry to apprehension.

"What's the joke, my dear fellow? I fail to see."

"It's not a joke. It's the truth. I murdered him." He had spoken painfully at first, as if there were a knot in his throat; but each time he repeated the words he found they were easier to say.

Ascham laid down his cigar. "What's the matter? Aren't you well? What on earth are you driving at?"

"I'm perfectly well. But I murdered my cousin, Joseph Lenman, and I want it known that I murdered him."

"You want it known?"

"Yes. That's why I sent for you. I'm sick of living, and when I try to kill myself I funk it." He spoke quite naturally now, as if the knot in his throat had been untied.

"Good Lord—good Lord," the lawyer gasped.

"But I suppose," Granice continued, "there's no doubt this would be murder in the first degree? I'm sure of the chair if I own up?"

Ascham drew a long breath; then he said slowly: "Sit down, Granice. Let's talk."

II

GRANICE told his story simply, connectedly.

He began by a quick survey of his early years—the years of drudgery and privation. His father, a charming man who could never say "no," had so signally failed to say it on certain essential occasions that when he died he left an illegitimate family and a mortgaged estate. His lawful kin found themselves hanging over a gulf of debt, and young Granice, to support his mother and sister, had to leave Harvard and bury himself at eighteen in a broker's office. He loathed his work, and he was always poor, always worried and often ill. A few years later his mother died, but his sister, a helpless creature, remained on his hands. His own health gave out, and he had to go away for six months, and work harder than ever when he came back. He had no knack for business, no head for figures, no dimmest insight into the mysteries of commerce. He wanted to travel and write—those were his inmost longings. And as the years dragged on, and he neared middle-age without making any more money, or acquiring any firmer health, a sick despair possessed him. He tried writing, but he always came home from the office so tired that his brain could not work. For half the year he did not reach his dim uptown flat till after dark, and could only "brush up" for dinner, and afterward lie on the lounge with his pipe, while his sister droned through the evening paper. Sometimes he spent an evening at the theater; or he dined out, or, more rarely, strayed off with an acquaintance or two in quest of what is known as "pleasure." And in summer, when he and Kate went to the sea-side for a month, he dozed through the days in utter weariness. Once he fell in love with a charming girl—but what had he to offer her, in God's name? She seemed to like him, and in common decency he had to drop out of the running. Apparently no one replaced him, for she never married, but grew stoutish, grayish, philanthropic—yet how sweet she had been when he first kissed her! One more wasted life, he reflected . . .

But the stage had always been his master-passion. He would have sold his soul for the time and freedom to write plays! It was *in him*—he could not remember when it had not been his deepest-seated instinct. As the years passed it became a morbid, a relentless obsession—yet with every year the material conditions were more and more against it. He felt himself growing middle-aged, and he watched the reflection of the process in his sister's wasted face. At eighteen she had been pretty, and as full of enthusiasm as he. Now she was sour, trivial, insignificant—she had missed her chance of life. And she had no resources, poor creature, was fashioned simply for the primitive functions she had been denied the chance to fulfill! It exasperated him to think of it—and to reflect that even now a little travel, a little health, a little money, might transform her, make her young and desirable . . . The chief fruit of his experience was that there is no such fixed state as age or youth—there is only health as against sickness, wealth as against poverty; and age or youth as the outcome of the lot one draws.

At this point in his narrative Granice stood up, and went to lean against the mantel-piece, looking down at Ascham, who had not moved from his seat, or changed his attitude of spellbound attention.

"Then came the summer when we went to Wrenfield to be near old Lenman—my mother's cousin, as you know. Some of the family always mounted guard over him—generally a niece or so. But that year they were all scattered, and one of the nieces offered to lend us her cottage if we'd relieve her of duty for two months. It was a nuisance for me, of course, for Wrenfield is two hours from town; but my mother, who was a slave to family observances, had always been good to the old man, so it was natural that we should be called on—and there was the saving of rent and the good air for Kate. So we went.

"You never knew Joseph Lenman? Well, picture to yourself an

amoeba, or some primitive organism of that sort, under a Titan's microscope. He was large, undifferentiated, inert—since I could remember him he had done nothing but take his temperature and read the *Churchman*. Oh, and cultivate melons—that was his hobby. Not vulgar out-of-door melons—his were grown under glass. He had acres of it at Wrenfield—his big kitchen-garden was surrounded by blinking battalions of greenhouses. And in nearly all of them melons were grown: early melons and late, French, English, domestic—dwarf melons and monsters: every shape, color and variety. They were petted and nursed like children—a staff of trained attendants waited on them. I'm not sure they didn't have a doctor to take their temperature; at any rate the place was full of thermometers. And they didn't sprawl on the ground like ordinary melons; they were trained against the glass like nectarines, and each melon hung in a net which sustained its weight and left it free on all sides to the sun and air . . .

"It used to strike me sometimes that old Lenman was just like one of his own melons—the pale-fleshed English kind. His life, apathetic and motionless, hung in a net of gold, in an equable warm ventilated atmosphere, high above earthly worries. The cardinal rule of his existence was not to let himself be 'worried'. . . I remember his advising me to try it myself, one day when I spoke to him about Kate's bad health and her need of a change. 'I always make it a rule not to let myself worry,' he said complacently. 'It's the worst thing for the liver—and you look to me as if you had a liver. Take my advice and be cheerful. You'll make yourself happier and others too.' And all he had to do was to write a check, and send the poor girl off for a holiday!

"The hardest part of it was that the money half-belonged to us already. The old skin-flint only had it for life, in trust for us and the others. But his life was a good deal sounder than mine or Kate's—and one could picture him taking extra care of it for the joke of keeping us waiting. I always felt that the sight of our hungry eyes was a tonic to him.

"Well, I tried to see if I couldn't reach him through his vanity. I flattered him, feigned a passionate interest in his melons. And he was taken in, and used to discourse on them by the hour. On fine days he was driven to the greenhouses in his pony-chair, and waddled through them, prodding and leering at the fruit, like a fat Turk in his seraglio. When he bragged to me of the expense of growing them I was reminded of a hideous old Lothario bragging of what his pleasures cost. And the resemblance was completed by the fact that he couldn't eat as much as a mouthful of his melons—had lived for years on buttermilk and toast. 'But, after all, it's my only hobby—why shouldn't I indulge it?' he said sentimentally. As if I'd ever been able to indulge any of mine! On the keep of those melons Kate and I could have lived like gods . . .

"One day toward the end of the summer, when Kate was too unwell to drag herself up to the big house, she asked me to go and spend the afternoon with cousin Joseph. It was a lovely soft September afternoon—a day to lie under a Roman stone-pine, with one's eyes on the sky, and let the cosmic harmonies rush through one. Perhaps the vision was suggested by the fact that, as I entered cousin Joseph's hideous black walnut library, I passed one of the under-gardeners, a handsome Italian, who dashed out in such a hurry that he nearly knocked me down. I remember thinking it queer that the fellow, whom I had often seen about the melon-houses, did not bow to me or even seem to see me.

"Cousin Joseph sat in his usual seat, behind the darkened windows, his fat hands folded on his protuberant waistcoat, the last number of the *Churchman* at his elbow, and near it, on a huge dish, a melon—the fattest melon I'd ever seen. As I looked at it I pictured the ecstasy of contemplation from which I must have roused him, and congratulated myself on finding him in such a mood, since I had made up my mind to ask him a favor. Then I noticed that his face, instead of looking as calm as an egg-shell, was distorted and whimpering—and without stopping to greet me he pointed passionately to the melon.

"'Look at it, look at it—did you ever see such a beauty? Such firmness—roundness—such delicious smoothness to the touch?' It was as if he had said 'she' instead of 'it,' and when he put out his senile hand and touched the melon I positively had to look the other way.

"Then he told me what had happened. The Italian under-gardener, who had been specially recommended for the melon-houses—though it was against my cousin's principles to employ a Papist—had been assigned to the care of the monster: for it had revealed itself, early in its existence, as destined to become a monster, to surpass its plumpest pulpiest sisters, carry off prizes at agricultural shows, and be photographed and celebrated in every gardening paper in the land. The Italian had done well—seemed to have a sense of responsibility. And that very morning he had been ordered to pick the melon, which was to be shown next day at the county fair, and to bring it in for Mr. Lenman to gaze on its blonde virginity. But in picking it, what had the damned scoundrelly Jesuit done but drop it—drop it crash on the spout of a watering-pot, so that it received a deep gash in its firm pale rotundity, and was henceforth but a bruised, ruined, fallen melon?

"The old man's rage was fearful in its impotence—he shook, spluttered and strangled with it. He had just had the Italian up and had sacked him on the spot, without wages or character—had threatened to have him arrested if he was ever caught prowling about Wrenfield. 'By God, and I'll do it—I'll write to Washington—I'll have the pauper scoundrel deported! I'll show him what money can do!' As likely as not there was some murderous Blackhand business under it—it would be found that the fellow was a member of a 'gang.' Those Italians would murder you for a quarter. He meant to have the police look into it . . . And then he grew frightened at his own excitement. 'But I must calm myself,' he said. He took his temperature, rang for his drops, and turned to the *Churchman*. He had been reading an article on Nestorianism when the melon was brought in. He asked me to go on with it, and I read to him for an hour, in the dim close room, with a fat fly buzzing stealthily about the fallen melon.

"All the while one phrase of the old man's buzzed in my brain like the fly about the melon. *'I'll show him what money can do!'* Good heaven! If *I* could but show the old man! If I could make him see his power of giving happiness as a new outlet for his monstrous egotism! I tried to tell him something about my situation and Kate's—spoke of my ill-health, my unsuccessful drudgery, my longing to write, to make myself a name—I stammered out an entreaty for a loan. 'I can guarantee to repay you, sir—I've a half-written play as security . . .'

"I shall never forget his glassy stare. His face had grown as smooth as an egg-shell again—his eyes peered over his fat cheeks like sentinels over a slippery rampart.

"'A half-written play—a play of *yours* as security?' He looked at me almost fearfully, as if detecting the first symptoms of insanity.

'Do you understand anything of business?' he inquired. I laughed and answered: 'No, not much.'

"He leaned back with closed lids. 'All this excitement has been too much for me,' he said. 'If you'll excuse me, I'll prepare for my nap.' And I stumbled out of the room, blindly, like the Italian."

Granice moved away from the mantel-piece, and walked across to the tray set out with decanters and soda-water. He poured himself a tall glass of soda-water, emptied it, and glanced at Ascham's dead cigar.

"Better light another," he suggested.

The lawyer shook his head, and Granice went on with his tale. He told of his mounting obsession—how the murderous impulse had waked in him on the instant of his cousin's refusal, and he had muttered to himself: "By God, if you won't, I'll make you." He spoke more tranquilly as the narrative proceeded, as though his rage had died down once the resolve to act on it was taken. He applied his whole mind to the question of how the old man was to be "disposed of." Suddenly he remembered the outcry: "Those Italians would murder you for a quarter!" But no definite project presented itself: he simply waited for an inspiration.

Granice and his sister moved to town a day or two afterward. But the cousins, who had returned, kept them informed of the old man's condition. One day, about three weeks later, Granice, on getting home, found Kate excited over a report from Wrenfield. The Italian had been there again—had somehow slipped into the house, made his way up to the library, and "used threatening language." The house-keeper found cousin Joseph gasping, the whites of his eyes showing "something awful." The doctor was sent for, and the attack warded off; and the police had ordered the Italian from the neighborhood.

But cousin Joseph, thereafter, languished, had "nerves," and lost his taste for toast and buttermilk. The doctor called in a colleague, and the consultation amused and excited the old man—he became once more an important figure. The medical men reassured the family—too completely!—and to the patient they recommended a more varied diet: advised him to take whatever "tempted him." And so one day, tremulously, prayerfully, he decided on a tiny bit of melon. It was brought up with ceremony, and consumed in the presence of the house-keeper and a hovering cousin; and twenty minutes later he was dead . . .

"But you remember the circumstances," Granice went on; "how suspicion turned at once on the Italian? In spite of the hint the police had given him he had been seen hanging about the house since 'the scene.' It was said that he had tender relations with the kitchen-maid, and the rest seemed easy to explain. But when they looked round to ask him for the explanation he was gone—gone clean out of sight. He had been 'warned' to leave Wrenfield, and he had taken the warning so to heart that no one ever laid eyes on him again."

Granice paused. He had dropped into a chair opposite the lawyer's, and he sat for a moment, his head thrown back, looking about the familiar room. Everything in it had grown grimacing and alien, and each strange insistent object seemed craning forward from its place to hear him.

"It was I who put the stuff in the melon," he said. "And I don't want you to think I'm sorry for it. This isn't 'remorse,' understand. I'm glad the old skin-flint is dead—I'm glad the others have their money. But mine's no use to me any more. My sister married miserably, and died. And I've never had what I wanted."

Ascham continued to stare; then he said: "What on earth was your object, then?"

"Why, to *get* what I wanted—what I fancied was in reach! I wanted change, rest, *life*, for both of us—wanted, above all, for myself, the chance to write! I traveled, got back my health, and came home to tie myself up to my work. And I've slaved at it steadily for ten years without reward—without the most distant hope of success! Nobody will look at my stuff. And now I'm fifty, and I'm beaten, and I know it." His chin dropped forward on his breast. "I want to chuck the whole business," he ended.

III

IT was after midnight when Ascham left.

His hand on Granice's shoulder, as he turned to go—"District Attorney be hanged; see a doctor, see a doctor!" he had cried; and so, with an exaggerated laugh, had pulled on his coat and departed.

Granice turned back into the library. It had never occurred to him that Ascham would not believe his story. For three hours he had explained, elucidated, patiently and painfully gone over every detail—but without once breaking down the iron incredulity of the lawyer's eye.

At first Ascham had feigned to be convinced—but that, as Granice now perceived, was simply to get him to expose himself, to entrap him into contradictions. And when the attempt failed, when Granice triumphantly met and refuted each disconcerting question, the lawyer dropped the mask, and broke out with a good-humored laugh: "By Jove, Granice you'll write a successful play yet. The way you've worked this all out is a marvel."

Granice swung about furiously—that last sneer about the play inflamed him. Was all the world in a conspiracy to deride his failure?

"I did it, I did it," he muttered, his rage spending itself against the impenetrable surface of the other's mockery; and Ascham answered with a quieting smile: "Ever read any of those books on hallucinations? I've got a fairly good medico-legal library. I could send you one or two if you like . . ."

Left alone, Granice cowered down in the chair before his writing-table. He understood that Ascham thought him off his head.

"Good God—what if they all think me crazy?"

The horror of it broke out over him in a cold sweat—he sat there and shook, his eyes hidden in his hands. But gradually, as he began to rehearse his story for the thousandth time, he saw again how incontrovertible it was, and felt sure that any criminal lawyer would believe him.

"That's the trouble—Ascham's not a criminal lawyer. And then he's a friend. What a fool I was to talk to a friend! Even if he did believe me, he'd never let me see it—his instinct would be to cover the whole thing up . . . But in that case—if he *did* believe me—he might think it a kindness to get me shut up in an asylum . . ." Granice began to tremble again. "Good heaven! If he should bring in an expert—one of those damned alienists! Ascham and Pettilow can do anything—their word always goes. If Ascham drops a hint that I'd better be shut up, I'll be in a strait-jacket by tomorrow! And he'd do it from the kindest motives—be quite right to do it if he thinks I'm a murderer!"

The vision froze him to his chair. He pressed his fists to his bursting temples and tried to think. For the first time he hoped that Ascham had not believed his story.

"But he did—he did! I can see it now—I noticed what a queer eye he cocked at me. Good God, what shall I do—what shall I do?"

He started up and looked at the clock. Half-past one. What if Ascham should think the case urgent, rout out an alienist, and come back with him? Granice jumped to his feet, and his gesture brushed the morning paper from the table. As he stooped to pick it up the movement started a new train of association.

He sat down again, and reached for the telephone book in the rack by his chair.

"Give me three-o-ten . . . yes."

The new idea in his mind had revived his energy. He would act—act at once. It was only by thus planning ahead, committing himself to some unavoidable line of conduct, that he could pull himself through the meaningless days. Each time he reached a fresh decision it was like coming out of a foggy weltering sea into a calm harbor with lights. One of the queerest phases of his long agony was the relief produced by these momentary lulls.

"That the office of the *Investigator?* Yes? Give me Mr. Denver, please . . . Hallo, Denver . . . Yes, Hubert Granice . . . Just caught you? Going straight home? Can I come and see you . . . yes, now . . . have a talk? It's rather urgent . . . yes, might give you some first-rate 'copy'. . . All right!" He hung up the receiver with a laugh. It had been a happy thought to call up the editor of the *Investigator*—Robert Denver was the very man he needed . . .

Granice put out the lights in the library—it was odd how the automatic gestures persisted!—went into the hall, put on his hat and overcoat, and let himself out of the flat. In the hall, a sleepy elevator boy blinked at him and then dropped his head on his arms. Granice passed out into the street. At the corner of Fifth Avenue he hailed a cab, and called out an uptown address. The long thoroughfare stretched before him, dim and deserted, like an ancient avenue of tombs. But from Denver's house a friendly beam fell on the pavement; and as Granice sprang from his cab the editor's electric turned the corner.

The two men grasped hands, and Denver, feeling for his latch-key, ushered Granice into the hall.

"Disturb me? Not a bit. You might have, at ten tomorrow morning . . . but this is my liveliest hour . . . you know my habits of old."

Granice had known Robert Denver for fifteen years—watched his rise through all the stages of journalism to the Olympian pinnacle of the *Investigator*'s editorial office. In the thick-set man with grizzling hair there were few traces left of the hungry-eyed young reporter who, on his way home in the small hours, used to "bob in" on Granice, while the latter sat grinding at his plays. Denver had to pass Granice's flat on the way to his own, and it became a habit, if he saw a light in the window, and Granice's shadow against the blind, to go in, smoke a pipe, and discuss the universe.

"Well—this is like old times—a good old habit reversed." The editor smote his visitor genially on the shoulder. "Reminds me of the nights when I used to rout you out . . . How's the play, by the way? There *is* a play, I suppose? It's as safe to ask you that as to say to some men: 'How's the baby?'"

Denver laughed good-naturedly, and Granice thought how thick and heavy he had grown. It was evident, even to Granice's tortured nerves, that the words had not been uttered in malice—and the fact gave him a new measure of his insignificance. Denver did not even know that he had been a failure! The fact hurt more than Ascham's irony.

"Come in—come in." The editor led the way into a small cheerful room, where there were cigars and decanters. He pushed an arm-chair toward his visitor, and dropped into another with a comfortable groan.

"Now, then—help yourself. And let's hear all about it."

He beamed at Granice over his pipe-bowl, and the latter, lighting his cigar, said to himself: "Success makes men comfortable, but it makes them stupid."

Then he turned, and began: "Denver, I want to tell you——"

The clock ticked rhythmically on the mantel-piece.

The room was gradually filled with drifting blue layers of smoke, and through them the editor's face came and went like the moon through a moving sky. Once the hour struck—then the rhythmical ticking began again. The atmosphere grew denser and heavier, and beads of perspiration began to roll from Granice's forehead.

"Do you mind if I open the window?"

"No. It *is* stuffy in here. Wait—I'll do it myself." Denver pushed down the upper sash, and returned to his chair. "Well—go on," he said, filling another pipe. His composure exasperated Granice.

"There's no use in my going on if you don't believe me."

The editor remained unmoved. "Who says I don't believe you? And how can I tell till you've finished?"

Granice went on, ashamed of his outburst. "It was simple enough, as you'll see. From the day the old man said to me 'Those Italians would murder you for a quarter' I dropped everything and just worked at my scheme. It struck me at once that I must find a way of getting to Wrenfield and back in a night—and that led to the idea of a motor. A motor—that never occurred to you? You wonder where I got the money, I suppose. Well, I had a thousand or so put by, and I nosed around till I found what I wanted—a second-hand racer. I knew how to drive a car, and I tried the thing and found it was all right. Times were bad, and I bought it for my price, and stored it away. Where? Why, in one of those no-questions-asked garages where they keep motors that are not for family use. I had a lively cousin who had put me up to that dodge, and I looked about till I found a queer hole where they took in my car like a baby in a foundling asylum . . . Then I practiced running to Wrenfield and back in a night. I knew the way pretty well, for I'd done it often with the same lively cousin—and in the small hours, too. The distance is over ninety miles, and on the third trial I did it under two hours. But my arms were so lame that I could hardly get dressed the next morning.

"Well, then came the report about the Italian's threats, and I saw I must act . . . I meant to break into the old man's room, shoot him, and get away again. It was a big risk, but I thought I could manage it. Then we heard that he was ill—that there'd been a consultation. Perhaps the fates were going to do it for me! Good Lord, if that could only be!"

Granice stopped and wiped his forehead: the open window did not seem to have cooled the room.

"Then came word that he was better; and the day after, when I came up from my office, I found Kate laughing over the news that he was to try a bit of melon. The house-keeper had just telephoned her—all Wrenfield was in a flutter. The doctor himself had picked out the melon, one of the little French ones that are hardly bigger than a large tomato—and the patient was to eat it at his breakfast the next morning.

"In a flash I saw my chance. It was a bare chance, no more. But I knew the ways of the house—I was sure the melon would be brought in over night and put in the pantry ice-box. If there were only one melon in the ice-box I could be fairly sure it was the one I wanted. Melons didn't lie around loose in that house—every one was known, numbered, catalogued. The old man was beset by the dread that the servants would eat them, and he took all sorts of mean precautions to prevent it. Yes, I felt pretty sure of my melon . . . and poisoning was much safer than shooting. It would have been the devil and all to get into his bedroom without his rousing the house; but I ought to be able to break into the pantry without much trouble.

"It was a cloudy night, too—everything served me. I dined quietly, and sat down at my desk. Kate had one of her usual headaches, and went to bed early. As soon as she was gone I slipped out. I had got together a sort of disguise—red beard and queer-looking ulster. I shoved them into a bag, and went round to the garage. There was no one there but a half-drunken machinist whom I'd never seen before. That served me, too. They were always changing machinists, and this new fellow didn't even bother to ask if the car belonged to me. It was a very easy-going place . . .

"Well, I jumped in, ran up Broadway, and let the car go as soon as I was out of Harlem. Dark as it was, I could trust myself to strike a sharp pace. In the shadow of a wood I stopped a second and got into the beard and ulster. Then away again—it was just eleven-thirty when I got to Wrenfield.

"I left the car in a lane behind the Lenman place, and slipped through the kitchen-garden. The melon-houses winked at me through the dark—I remember thinking that they knew what I wanted to know . . . By the stable a dog came out growling—but he nosed me out, jumped on me, and went back . . . The house was as dark as the grave. I knew everybody went to bed by ten. But there might be a prowling servant—the kitchen-maid might have come down to let in her Italian. I had to risk that, of course. I crept around by the back door and hid in the shrubbery. Then I listened. It was all as silent as death. I crossed over to the house, pried open the pantry window, and climbed in. I had a little electric lamp in my pocket, and shielding it with my cap I groped my way to the ice-box, opened it—and there was the little French melon . . . only one.

"I stopped to listen—I was quite cool. Then I pulled out my bottle of stuff and my syringe, and gave each section of the melon a hypodermic. It was all done inside of three minutes—at ten minutes to twelve I was back in the car. I got out of the lane as quietly as I could, struck a back road, and let the car out as soon as I was beyond the last houses. I only stopped once on the way in, to drop the beard and ulster into a pond. I had a big stone ready to weight them with and they went down plump, like a dead body—and at two I was back at my desk."

Granice stopped speaking and looked across the smoke-fumes at his listener; but Denver's face remained inscrutable.

At length he said: "Why did you want to tell me this?"

The question startled Granice. He was about to explain, as he had explained to Ascham; but suddenly it occurred to him that if his motive had not seemed convincing to the lawyer it would carry much less weight with Denver. Both were successful men, and success does not understand the subtle agony of failure. Granice cast about for another reason.

"Why, I—the thing haunts me . . . remorse, I suppose you'd call it . . ."

Denver struck the ashes from his empty pipe.

"Remorse? Bosh!" he said energetically.

Granice's heart sank. "You don't believe in—*remorse?*"

"Not an atom: in the man of action. The mere fact of your talking of remorse proves to me that you're not the man to have planned and put through such a job."

Granice groaned. "Well—I lied to you about remorse. I've never felt any."

Denver's lips tightened sceptically about his freshly-filled pipe. "What *was* your motive, then? You must have had one."

"I'll tell you—" And Granice began once more to rehearse the story of his failure, of his loathing for life. "Don't say you don't believe me this time . . . that this isn't a real reason!" he stammered out as he ended.

Denver meditated. "No, I won't say that. I've seen too many queer things. There's always a reason for wanting to get out of life—the wonder is that we find so many for staying in!"

Granice's heart grew light. "Then you *do* believe me?"

"Believe that you're sick of the job? Yes. And that you haven't the nerve to pull the trigger? Oh, yes—that's easy enough, too. But all that doesn't make you a murderer—though I don't say it proves you could never have been one."

"I *have* been one, Denver—I swear to you."

"Perhaps." Again the journalist mused. "Just tell me one or two things."

"Oh, go ahead. You won't stump me!" Granice heard himself say with a laugh.

"Well—how did you make all those trial trips without exciting your sister's curiosity? I knew your night habits pretty well at that time, remember. You were seldom out late. Didn't the change in your ways surprise her?"

"No; because she was away at the time. She went to pay several visits in the country after we came back from Wrenfield, and had only been in town a night or two before—before I did the job."

"And that night she went to bed with a headache?"

"Yes—blinding. She didn't know anything when she had that kind. And her room was at the back of the flat."

There was another pause in Denver's interrogatory.

"And when you got back—she didn't hear you? You got in without her knowing it?"

"Yes. I went straight to my work—took it up at the word where I'd left off—*why, Denver, don't you remember?*" Granice passionately interjected.

"Remember——?"

"Yes; how you found me—when you looked in that morning,

between two and three . . . your usual hour . . ?"

"Yes," the editor nodded.

Granice gave a short laugh. "In my old coat—with my pipe: looked as if I'd been working all night, didn't I? Well, I hadn't been in my chair ten minutes!"

Denver uncrossed his legs and then crossed them again. "I didn't know whether *you* remembered that."

"What?"

"My coming in that particular night—or morning."

Granice swung round in his chair. "Why, man alive! That's why I'm here now. Because it was you who spoke for me at the inquest, when they looked round to see what all the old man's heirs had been doing that night—you who testified to having dropped in and found me at my desk as usual . . . I thought *that* would appeal to your journalistic sense if nothing else would!"

Denver smiled. "Oh, my journalistic sense is still susceptible enough—and the idea's picturesque, I grant you: asking the man who proved your alibi to establish your guilt."

"That's it—that's it!" Granice's laugh had a ring of triumph.

"Well, but how about the other chap's testimony—I mean that young doctor: what was his name? Ned Ranney. Don't you remember my testifying that I'd met him at the elevated station, and told him I was on my way to smoke a pipe with you, and his saying: 'All right; you'll find him in. I passed the house two hours ago, and saw his shadow against the blind, as usual.' And the lady with the toothache in the flat across the way: she corroborated his statement, you remember."

"Yes; I remember."

"Well, then?"

"Simple enough. Before starting I rigged up a kind of mannikin with old coats and a cushion—something to cast a shadow on the blind. All you fellows were used to seeing my shadow there in the small hours—I counted on that, and knew you'd take any vague outline as mine."

"Simple enough, as you say. But the woman with the toothache saw the shadow move—you remember she said she saw you sink forward, as if you'd fallen asleep."

"Yes; and she was right. It *did* move. I suppose some extraheavy dray must have jolted by the flimsy building—at any rate, something gave my mannikin a jar, and when I came back he had sunk forward, half over the table."

There was a long silence between the two men. Granice, with a throbbing heart, watched Denver refill his pipe. The editor, at any rate, did not sneer and flout him. After all, journalism gave a deeper insight than the law into the fantastic possibilities of life, prepared one better to allow for the incalculableness of human impulses.

"Well?" Granice faltered out.

Denver stood up with a shrug. "Look here, man—what's wrong with you? Make a clean breast of it! Nerves gone to smash? I'd like to take you to see a chap I know—an ex-prize-fighter—who's a wonder at pulling fellows in your state out of their hole——"

"Oh, oh—" Granice broke in. He stood up also, and the two men eyed each other. "You don't believe me, then?"

"This yarn—how can I? There wasn't a flaw in your alibi."

"But haven't I filled it full of them now?"

Denver shook his head. "I might think so if I hadn't happened to know that you *wanted* to. There's the hitch, don't you see?"

Granice groaned. "No, I didn't. You mean my wanting to be found guilty——?"

"Of course! If somebody else had accused you, the story might have been worth looking into. As it is, a child could have invented it. It doesn't do much credit to your ingenuity."

Granice turned sullenly toward the door. What was the use of arguing? But on the threshold a sudden impulse drew him back. "Look here, Denver—I daresay you're right. But will you do just one thing to prove it? Put my statement in the *Investigator,* just as I've made it. Ridicule it as much as you like. Only give the other fellows a chance at it—men who don't know anything about me. Set them talking and looking about. I don't care a damn whether *you* believe me—what I want is to convince the Grand Jury! I oughtn't to have come to a man who knows me—your cursed incredulity is infectious. I don't put my case well, because I know in advance it's discredited, and I almost end by not believing it myself. That's why I can't convince *you*. It's a vicious circle." He laid a hand on Denver's arm. "Send a stenographer, and put my statement in the paper."

But Denver did not warm to the idea. "My dear fellow, you seem to forget that all the evidence was pretty thoroughly sifted at the time, every possible clue followed up. The public would have been ready enough then to believe that you murdered old Lenman—you or anybody else. All they wanted was a murderer—the most improbable would have served. But your alibi was too confoundedly complete. And nothing you've told me has shaken it." Denver laid his cool hand over the other's burning fingers. "Look here, old fellow, go home and work up a better case—then come in and submit it to the *Investigator.*"

IV

THE perspiration was rolling off Granice's forehead. Every few minutes he had to draw out his handkerchief and wipe the moisture from his face.

For an hour and a half he had been talking steadily, putting his case to the District Attorney. Luckily he had a speaking acquaintance with Allonby, and had obtained, without much difficulty, a private audience on the very day after his talk with Robert Denver. In the interval between he had hurried home, got out of his evening clothes, and gone forth again at once into the dreary dawn. His fear of Ascham and the alienist made it impossible for him to remain in his rooms. And it seemed to him that the only way of averting that hideous peril was to establish, in some sane impartial mind, the proof of his guilt. Even if he had not been so incurably sick of life, the electric chair seemed now the only alternative to the strait-jacket.

As he paused to wipe his forehead he saw the District Attorney glance at his watch. The gesture was significant, and Granice lifted an appealing hand. "I don't expect you to believe me now—but can't you put me under arrest, and have the thing looked into?"

Allonby smiled faintly under his heavy grayish moustache. He had a ruddy face, full and jovial, in which his keen professional eyes seemed to keep watch over impulses not strictly professional.

"Well, I don't know that we need lock you up just yet. But of course I'm bound to look into your statement——"

Granice rose with an exquisite sense of relief. Surely Allonby

"Can't you put me under arrest, and have the thing looked into?"

wouldn't have said that if he hadn't believed him!

"That's all right. Then I needn't detain you. I can be found at any time at my apartment." He gave the address.

The District Attorney smiled again, more openly. "What do you say to leaving it for an hour or two this evening? I'm giving a little supper at Rector's—quiet little affair: just Miss Melrose—I think you know her—and a friend or two; and if you'll join us . . ."

Granice stumbled out of the office without knowing what reply he had made.

He waited for four days—four days of concentrated horror. During the first twenty-four hours the fear of Ascham's alienist dogged him; and as that subsided, it was replaced by the growing conviction that his avowal had made no impression on the District Attorney. Evidently, if he had been going to look into the case, Allonby would have been heard from before now . . . And that mocking invitation to supper showed clearly enough how little the story had impressed him!

Granice was overcome by the futility of any farther attempt to inculpate himself. He was chained to life—a "prisoner of consciousness." Where was it he had read the phrase? Well, he was learning what it meant. In the long night-hours, when his brain seemed ablaze, he was visited by a sense of his fixed identity, of his irreducible, inexpugnable *selfness,* keener, more insidious, more unescapable, than any sensation he had ever known. He had not guessed that the mind was capable of such intricacies of self-realization, of penetrating so deep into its own dark windings. Often he woke from his brief snatches of sleep with the feeling that something material was clinging to him, was on his hands and face, and in his throat—and as his brain cleared he understood that it was the sense of his own personality that stuck to him like some thick viscous substance.

Then, in the first morning hours, he would rise and look out of his window at the awakening activities of the street—at the street-cleaners, the ash-cart drivers, and the other dingy workers flitting by through the sallow winter light. Oh, to be one of them—any of them—to take his chance in any of their skins! They were the toilers—the men whose lot was pitied—the victims wept over and ranted about by altruists and economists; and how thankfully he would have taken up the load of any one of them, if only he might have shaken off his own! But, no—the iron circle of consciousness held them too: each one was handcuffed to his own detested ego. Why wish to be any one man rather than another? The only absolute good was not to be . . . And Flint, coming in to draw his bath, would ask if he preferred his eggs scrambled or poached that morning?

On the fifth day he wrote a long letter to Allonby; and for the succeeding two days he had the occupation of waiting for an answer. He hardly stirred from his rooms in his fear of missing the letter by a moment; but would the District Attorney write, or send a representative: a policeman, a "secret agent," or some other mysterious emissary of the law?

On the third morning Flint, stepping softly—as if, confound it! his master were ill—entered the library where Granice sat behind an unread newspaper, and proffered a card on a tray.

Granice read the name—J. B. Hewson—and underneath, in pencil, "From the District Attorney's office." He started up with a thumping heart, and signed an assent to the servant.

Mr. Hewson was a sallow nondescript man of about fifty—the kind of man of whom one is sure to see a specimen in any crowd. "Just the type of the successful detective," Granice reflected as he shook hands with his visitor.

It was in that character that Mr. Hewson briefly introduced himself. He had been sent by the District Attorney to have "a quiet talk" with Mr. Granice—to ask him to repeat the statement he had made about the Lenman murder.

His manner was so quiet, so reasonable and receptive, that Granice's self-confidence returned. Here was a sensible man—a man who knew his business—it would be easy enough to make him see through that ridiculous alibi! Granice offered Mr. Hewson a cigar, and lighting one himself—to prove his coolness—began again to tell his story.

He was conscious, as he proceeded, of telling it better than ever before. Practice helped, no doubt; and his listener's detached, impartial attitude helped still more. He could see that Hewson, at least, had not decided in advance to disbelieve him, and the sense of being trusted made him more lucid and more consecutive. Yes, this time his words would certainly convince . . .

V

DESPAIRINGLY, Granice gazed up and down the street. Beside him stood a young man with bright prominent eyes, a smooth but not too smoothly-shaven face, and an Irish smile. The young man's nimble glance followed Granice's.

"Sure of the number, are you?" he asked briskly.

"Oh, yes—it was 104."

"Well, then, the new building has swallowed it up—that's certain."

He tilted his head back and surveyed the half-finished front of a brick and limestone flat-house that reared its flimsy elegance above the adjacent row of tottering tenements and stables.

"Dead sure?" he repeated.

"Yes," said Granice, discouraged. "And even if I hadn't been, I know the garage was just opposite Leffler's over there." He pointed across the street to a tumble-down building with a blotched sign on which the words "Livery and Boarding" were still faintly discernible.

The young man glanced at the stable. "Well, that's something—may get a clue there. Leffler's—same name there, anyhow. You remember that name?"

"Yes—distinctly."

Granice had felt a return of confidence since he had enlisted the interest of the *Explorer*'s "smartest" reporter. If there were moments when he hardly believed his own story, there were others when it seemed impossible that every one should not believe it; and young Peter McCarren, peering, listening, questioning, jotting down notes, inspired him with new hope. McCarren had fastened on the case at once, "like a leech," as he phrased it—jumped at it, thrilled to it, and settled down to "draw the last drop of fact from it, and not let go till he had." No one else had treated Granice in that way—even Allonby's detective had not taken a single note. And though a week had elapsed since the visit of that authorized official, nothing had been heard from the District Attorney's office: Allonby had apparently dropped the matter again. But McCarren wasn't going to drop it—not he! He hung on Granice's footsteps. They had spent the greater part of the previous day together, and now they were off again, running down fresh clues.

But at Leffler's they got none, after all. Leffler's was no longer a stable. It was condemned to demolition, and in the respite between sentence and execution it had become a vague place of storage, a hospital for broken-down carriages and carts, presided over by a blear-eyed old woman who knew nothing of Flood's garage across the way—did not even remember what had stood there before the new flat-house began to rise.

"Well—we may run Leffler down somewhere; I've seen harder jobs done," said McCarren, cheerfully noting down the name.

As they walked back toward Sixth Avenue he added, in a less sanguine tone: "I'd undertake now to put the thing through if you could only put me on the track of that cyanide."

Granice's heart sank. Yes—there was the weak spot; he had felt it from the first! But he still hoped to convince McCarren that his case was strong enough without it; and he urged the reporter to come back to his rooms and sum up the facts with him again.

"Sorry, Mr. Granice, but I'm due at the office now. Besides, it'd be no use till I get some fresh stuff to work on. Suppose I call you up tomorrow or next day?"

He plunged into a trolley and left Granice gazing desolately after him.

Two days later he reappeared at the apartment, a shade less jaunty in demeanor.

"Well, Mr. Granice, the stars in their courses are against you, as the bard says. Can't get a trace of Flood, or of Leffler either. And you say you bought the motor through Flood, and sold it through him, too?"

"Yes," said Granice wearily.

"Who bought it, do you know?"

Granice wrinkled his brows. "Why, Flood—yes, Flood himself. I sold it back to him three months later."

"Flood? The devil! And I've ransacked the town for Flood. That kind of business disappears as if the earth had swallowed it."

Granice, discouraged, kept silence.

"That brings us back to the poison," McCarren continued, his notebook out. "Just go over that again, will you?"

And Granice went over it again. It had all been so simple at the time—and he had been so clever in covering up his traces! As soon as he decided on poison he looked about for an acquaintance who manufactured chemicals; and there was Jim Dawes, a Harvard classmate, in the dyeing business—just the man. But at the last moment it occurred to him that suspicion might turn toward so obvious an opportunity, and he decided on a more tortuous course. Another friend, Carrick Venn, a student of medicine whose own ill-health had kept him from the practice of his profession, amused his leisure with experiments in physics, for the execution of which he had set up a simple laboratory. Granice had the habit of dropping in to smoke a cigar with him on Sunday afternoons, and the friends generally sat in Venn's workshop, at the back of the old family house in Stuyvesant Square. Off this workshop was the cupboard of supplies, with its row of deadly bottles. Carrick Venn was an original, a man of restless curious tastes, and his place, on a Sunday, was often full of visitors: a cheerful crowd of journalists, scribblers, painters, experimenters in divers forms of expression. Coming and going among so many, it was easy enough to pass unperceived; and one afternoon Granice, arriving before Venn had returned home, found himself alone in the workshop, and quickly slipping into the cupboard, transferred the drug to his pocket.

But that had happened ten years ago; and Venn, poor fellow, was long since dead of his dragging ailment. His old father was dead, too, the house in Stuyvesant Square had been turned into a boarding-house, and the shifting life of New York had passed its sponge over every trace of their history. Even the optimistic McCarren seemed to acknowledge the hopelessness of seeking for proof in that direction.

"And there's the third door slammed in our faces." He shut his notebook, and throwing back his head, rested his bright inquisitive eyes on Granice's anxious face.

"Look here, Mr. Granice—you see the weak spot, don't you?"

The other made a despairing motion. "I see so many!"

"Yes: but the one that weakens all the others. Why the deuce do you want this thing known? Why do you want to put your head into the noose?"

Granice looked at him hopelessly, trying to take the measure of his quick light irreverent mind. No one so full of a cheerful animal life would believe in the craving for death as a sufficient motive; and Granice racked his brain for one more convincing. But suddenly he saw the reporter's face soften, and melt to an artless sentimentalism.

"Mr. Granice—has the memory of this thing always haunted you?"

Granice stared a moment, and then leapt at the opening. "That's it—the memory of it . . . always . . ."

McCarren nodded vehemently. "Dogged your steps, eh? Wouldn't let you sleep? The time came when you *had* to make a clean breast of it?"

"I had to. Can't you understand?"

The reporter struck his fist on the table. "God, sir! I don't suppose there's a human being with a drop of warm blood in him that can't picture the deadly horrors of remorse——"

The Celtic imagination was aflame, and Granice mutely thanked him for the word. What neither Ascham nor Denver would accept as a conceivable motive the Irish reporter seized on as the most adequate; and, as he said, once one could find a convincing motive, the difficulties of the case became so many incentives to effort.

"Remorse—*remorse,*" he repeated, rolling the word under his tongue with an accent that was a clue to the psychology of the popular drama; and Granice, perversely, said to himself: "If I could only have struck that note I should have been running in six theaters at once."

He saw that from that moment McCarren's professional zeal would be fanned by emotional curiosity; and he profited by the fact to propose that they should dine together, and go on afterward to some music-hall or theater. It was becoming necessary to Granice to feel himself an object of preoccupation, to find himself in another mind. He took a kind of gray penumbral pleasure in riveting McCarren's attention on his case, and to feign the grimaces of moral anguish became an engrossing game. He had not entered a theater for months; but he sat out the meaningless performance, sustained by the sense of the reporter's observation.

Between the acts McCarren amused him with anecdotes about the audience: he knew every one by sight, and could lift the curtain from each physiognomy. Granice listened indulgently. He had lost all interest in his kind, but he knew that he was himself the real center of McCarren's attention, and that every word the latter spoke had an indirect bearing on his own problem.

"See that fellow over there—the little dried-up man in the third row, pulling his moustache? *His* memoirs would be worth publishing," McCarren said suddenly in the last *entr'acte*.

Granice, following his glance, recognized the detective from Allonby's office. For a moment he had the thrilling sense that he was being shadowed.

"Caesar, if *he* could talk——!" McCarren continued. "Know who he is, of course? Dr. John B. Stell, the biggest alienist in the country——"

Granice, with a start, bent again between the heads in front of him. "*That* man—the fourth from the aisle? You're mistaken. That's not Dr. Stell."

McCarren laughed. "Well, guess I've been in court often enough to know Stell when I see him. He testifies in nearly all the big cases where they plead insanity."

A shiver ran down Granice's spine, but he repeated obstinately: "That's not Dr. Stell."

"Not Stell? Why, man, I *know* him. Look—here he comes. If it isn't Stell, he won't speak to me."

The little dried-up man was moving slowly up the aisle. As he neared McCarren he made a gesture of recognition.

"How'do, Doctor Stell? Pretty slim show, ain't it?" the reporter cheerfully flung out at him. And Mr. J. B. Hewson, with a nod of assent, passed on.

Granice sat benumbed. He knew that he had not been mistaken—the man who had just passed was the same man whom Allonby had sent to see him: a physician disguised as a detective. Allonby, then, had thought him insane, like the others—had regarded his confession as the maundering of a maniac. The discovery froze Granice with horror—he saw the madhouse gaping for him.

"Isn't there a man a good deal like him—a detective named J. B. Hewson?"

But he knew in advance what McCarren's answer would be. "Hewson? J. B. Hewson? Never heard of him. But that was J. B. Stell fast enough—I guess he can be trusted to know himself, and you saw he answered to his name."

VI

SOME days passed before Granice could obtain a word with the District Attorney: he began to think that Allonby avoided him.

But when they were face to face Allonby's jovial countenance showed no sign of embarrassment. He waved his visitor to a chair, and leaned across his desk with the encouraging smile of a consulting physician.

Granice broke out at once: "That detective you sent me the other day——"

Allonby raised a deprecating hand.

"——I know: it was Stell the alienist. Why did you do that, Allonby?"

The other's face did not lose its composure. "Because I looked up your story first—and there's nothing in it."

"Nothing in it?" Granice furiously interposed.

"Absolutely nothing. If there is, why the deuce don't you bring me proofs? I know you've been talking to Peter Ascham, and to Denver, and to that little ferret McCarren of the *Explorer*. Have any of them been able to make out a case for you? No. Well, what am I to do?"

Granice's lips began to tremble. "Why did you play me that trick?"

"About Stell? I had to, my dear fellow: it's part of my business. Stell *is* a detective, if you come to that—every doctor is."

The trembling of Granice's lips increased, communicating itself in a long quiver to his facial muscles. He forced a laugh through his dry throat. "Well—and what did he detect?"

"In you? Oh, he thinks it's overwork—overwork and too much smoking. If you look in on him some day at his office he'll show you the record of hundreds of cases like yours, and tell you what treatment he recommends. It's one of the commonest forms of hallucination. Have a cigar, all the same."

"But, Allonby, I killed that man!"

The District Attorney's large hand, outstretched on his desk, had an almost imperceptible gesture, and a moment later, as if in answer to the call of an electric bell, a clerk looked in from the outer office.

"Sorry, my dear fellow—lot of people waiting. Drop in on Stell some morning," Allonby said, shaking hands.

McCarren had to own himself beaten: there was absolutely no flaw in the alibi. And since his duty to his journal obviously forbade his wasting time on insoluble mysteries, he ceased to frequent Granice, who dropped back into a deeper isolation. For a day or two after his visit to Allonby he continued to live in dread of Dr. Stell. Why might not Allonby have deceived him as to the alienist's diagnosis? What if he were really being shadowed, not by a police agent but by a mad-doctor? To have the truth out, he determined to call on Dr. Stell.

The physician received him kindly, and reverted without embarrassment to their previous meeting. "We have to do that occasionally, Mr. Granice; it's one of our methods. And you had given Allonby a fright."

Granice was silent. He would have liked to reaffirm his guilt, to produce the fresh arguments which had occurred to him since his last talk with the physician; but he feared his eagerness might be taken for a symptom of derangement, and he affected to smile away Dr. Stell's allusion.

"You think, then, it's a case of brain-fag—nothing more?"

"Nothing more. I should advise you to knock off tobacco. You smoke a good deal, don't you?"

He developed his treatment, recommending massage, gymnastics, travel, or any form of diversion that did not—that in short——

Granice interrupted him impatiently. "Oh, I loathe all that—and I'm sick of travelling."

"H'm. Then some larger interest—politics, reform, philanthropy? Something to take you out of yourself."

"Yes. I understand," said Granice wearily.

"Above all, don't lose heart. I see hundreds of cases like yours," the doctor added cheerfully from the threshold.

On the doorstep Granice stood still and laughed. Hundreds of cases like his—the case of a man who had committed a murder, who confessed his guilt, and whom no one would believe! Why, there had never been a case like it in the world. What a good figure Stell would have made in a play: the great alienist who couldn't read a man's mind any better than that!

Granice saw huge comic opportunities in the type.

But as he walked away, his fears dispelled, the sense of listlessness returned on him. For the first time since his avowal to Peter Ascham he found himself without an occupation, and understood that he had been carried through the past weeks only by the necessity of constant action. Now his life had once more become a stagnant backwater, and as he stood on the street corner watching the tides of traffic sweep by, he asked himself despairingly how much longer he could endure to float about in the sluggish circle of his consciousness.

The thought of self-destruction came back to him; but again his flesh recoiled. He yearned for death from other hands, but he could never take it from his own. And, aside from his insuperable physical fear, another motive restrained him. He was possessed by the dogged desire to establish the truth of his story. He refused to be swept aside as an irresponsible dreamer—even if he had to kill himself in the end, he would not do so before proving to society that he had deserved death from it.

He began to write long letters to the papers; but after the first had been published and commented on, public curiosity was quelled by a brief statement from the District Attorney's office, and the rest of his communications remained unprinted. Ascham came to see him, and begged him to travel. Robert Denver dropped in, and tried to joke him out of his delusion; till Granice, mistrustful of their motives, began to dread the reappearance of Dr. Stell, and set a guard on his lips. But the words he kept back engendered others and still others in his brain. His inner self became a humming factory of arguments, and he spent long hours reciting and writing down elaborate statements, which he constantly retouched and developed. Then his activity began to languish under the lack of an audience, the sense of being buried beneath deepening drifts of indifference. In a passion of resentment he swore that he would prove himself a murderer, even if he had to commit another crime to do it; and for a night or two the thought flamed red on his sleeplessness. But daylight dispelled it. The determining impulse was lacking and he hated too promiscuously to choose his victim . . . So he was thrown back on the struggle to impose the truth of his story. As fast as one channel closed on him he tried to pierce another through the sliding sands of incredulity. But every issue seemed blocked, and the whole human race leagued together to cheat one man of the right to die.

Thus viewed, the situation became so monstrous that he lost his last shred of self-restraint in contemplating it. What if he were really the victim of some mocking experiment, the center of a ring of holiday-makers jeering at a poor creature in its blind dashes against the solid walls of consciousness? But, no—men were not so uniformly cruel: there were flaws in the close surface of their indifference, cracks of weakness and pity here and there . . .

Granice began to think that his mistake lay in having appealed to persons more or less familiar with his past, and to whom the visible conformities of his life seemed a complete disproof of its one fierce secret deviation. The general tendency was to take for the whole of life the slit seen between the blinders of habit: and in his walk down that narrow vista Granice cut a correct enough figure. To a vision free to follow his whole orbit his story would be more intelligible: it would be easier to convince a chance idler in the street than the trained intelligence hampered by a sense of his antecedents. This idea shot up in him with the tropic luxuriance of each new seed of thought, and he began to walk the streets, and to frequent out-of-the-way chop-houses and bars in his search for the impartial stranger to whom he should disclose himself.

At first every face looked encouragement; but at the crucial moment he always held back. So much was at stake, and it was so essential that his first choice should be decisive. He dreaded stupidity, timidity, intolerance. The imaginative eye, the furrowed brow, were what he sought. He must reveal himself only to a heart versed in the tortuous motions of the human will; and he began to hate the dull benevolence of the average face. Once or twice, obscurely, allusively, he made a beginning—once sitting down by a man in a basement chop-house, another day approaching a lounger on an east-side wharf. But in both cases the premonition of failure checked him on the brink of avowal. His dread of being taken for a man in the clutch of a fixed idea gave him an abnormal keenness in reading the expression of his listeners, and he had provided himself in advance with a series of verbal alternatives, trap-doors of evasion from the first dart of ridicule or suspicion.

He passed the greater part of the day in the streets, coming home at irregular hours, dreading the silence and orderliness of his apartment, and the mute scrutiny of Flint. His real life was spent in a world so remote from this familiar setting that he sometimes had the sense of a living metempsychosis, a furtive passage from one identity to another—yet the other as unescapably himself!

One humiliation he was spared: the desire to live never revived in him. Not for a moment was he tempted to a shabby pact with existing conditions. He wanted to die, wanted it with the fixed unwavering desire which alone attains its end. And still the end eluded him! It would not always, of course—he had full faith in the dark star of his destiny. And he could prove it best by repeating his story, persistently and indefatigably, pouring it into indifferent ears, hammering it into dull brains, till at last it kindled a spark, and some one of the careless millions paused, listened, believed . . .

It was a mild March day, and he had been loitering on the west-side docks, looking at faces. He was becoming an expert in physiognomies: his eagerness no longer made rash darts and awkward recoils. He knew now the face he needed, as clearly as if it had come to him in a vision; and not till he found it would he speak. As he walked eastward through the shabby streets he had a premonition that he should find it that morning. Perhaps it was the promise of spring in the air—certainly he felt calmer than for days . . .

He turned into Washington Square, struck across it obliquely, and walked up University Place. Its heterogeneous passers always attracted him—they were less hurried than in Broadway, less enclosed and classified than in Fifth Avenue. He walked slowly, watching for his face.

At Union Square he had a relapse into discouragement, like a votary who has watched too long for a sign from the altar. Perhaps, after all, he should never find his face . . . The air was languid, and he felt tired. He walked between the bald grass-lots and the twisted trees, making for a seat. Presently he passed a bench on which a girl sat alone, and something as definite as the twitch of a cord caused him to stop before her. He had never dreamed of telling his story to a girl, had hardly looked at the women's faces as they passed. His case was man's work: how could a woman help him? But this girl's face was extraordinary—quiet and wide as an evening sky. It suggested a hundred images of space, distance, mystery, like ships he had seen, as a boy, berthed by a familiar wharf, but with the breath of far seas and strange harbors in their shrouds . . . Certainly this girl would understand. He went up to her, lifting his hat, observing the forms—wishing her to see at once that he was "a gentleman."

"I am a stranger to you," he began, sitting down beside her, "but your face is so extremely intelligent that I feel . . . I feel it is the face I've waited for . . . looked for everywhere; and I want to tell you——"

The girl's eyes widened: she rose to her feet. She was escaping him!

In his dismay he ran a few steps after her, and caught her by the arm.

"Here—wait—listen! Oh, don't scream, you fool!" he shouted out.

He felt a hand on his own arm; turned and confronted a policeman. Instantly he understood that he was being arrested, and something hard within him was loosened and ran to tears.

"Ah, you know—you *know* I'm guilty?"

He was conscious that a crowd was forming, and that the girl had disappeared. But what did he care about the girl? It was the policeman who had understood him. He turned and followed, the crowd at his heels . . .

VII

IN the charming place in which he found himself there were so many sympathetic faces that he felt more than ever convinced of the certainty of making himself heard.

It was a bad blow, at first, to find that he had not been arrested for murder; but Ascham, who had come at once, convinced him that he needed rest, and the time to "review" his statements; it appeared that reiteration had made them a little confused and contradictory. To this end he had readily acquiesced in his removal to a large quiet establishment, with an open space and trees about it, where he had found a number of intelligent companions, some, like himself, engaged in preparing or reviewing statements of their cases,

He understood that he was being arrested; he was conscious that a crowd was forming.

and others ready to lend an attentive ear to his own recital.

For a time he was content to let himself go on the current of this new existence; but although his auditors gave him for the most part an encouraging attention, which, in some, went the length of really brilliant and helpful suggestion, he gradually felt a recurrence of his doubts. Either his hearers were not sincere, or else they had less power to help him than they boasted. His endless conferences resulted in nothing, and the long rest produced an increased mental lucidity which made inaction more and more unbearable. At length he discovered that on certain days visitors from the outer world were admitted to his retreat; and he wrote out long and logically constructed relations of his crime, and furtively slipped them into the hands of these messengers of hope.

This gave him a fresh lease of patience, and he now lived only to watch for the visitors' days, and scan the faces that swept by him like stars seen and lost in the rifts of a hurrying sky.

Mostly, these faces were strange and less intelligent than those of his companions. But they represented his last means of access to the world, a kind of subterranean channel on which he could set his "statements" afloat, like paper boats which a mysterious current might sweep out into the open seas of life.

One day, however, his attention was arrested by a familiar contour, a pair of bright prominent eyes, and a chin insufficiently shaved. He sprang up and stood in the path of Peter McCarren.

The journalist looked at him doubtfully, then held out his hand with a startled "*Why——?*"

"You didn't know me? I'm so changed?" Granice faltered, feeling the rebound of the other's wonder.

"Why, no; but you're looking quieter—smoothed out," McCarren smiled.

"Yes: that's what I'm here for—to rest. And I've taken the opportunity to write out a clearer statement——"

Granice's hand shook so that he could hardly draw the paper from his pocket. As he did so he noticed that the reporter was accompanied by a tall man with compassionate eyes. It came to Granice in a wild thrill of conviction that this was the face he had waited for . . .

"Perhaps your friend—he *is* your friend?—would glance over it—or I could put the case in a few words if you have time?" Granice's voice shook like his hand. If this chance escaped him he felt that his last hope was gone. McCarren and the stranger looked at each other, and the reporter glanced at his watch.

"I'm sorry we can't stay and talk it over now, Mr. Granice; but my friend has an engagement, and we're rather pressed——"

Granice continued to proffer the paper. "I'm sorry—I think I could have explained. But you'll take this, at any rate?"

The stranger looked at him gently. "Certainly—I'll take it." He had his hand out. "Good-bye."

"Good-bye," Granice echoed.

He stood watching the two men move away from him through the long hall; and as he watched them a tear ran down his face. But as soon as they were out of sight he turned and walked toward his room, beginning to hope again, already planning a new statement . . .

Outside the building the two men stood still, and the journalist's companion looked up curiously at the long rows of barred windows.

"So that was Granice?"

"Yes—that was Granice, poor devil," said McCarren.

"Strange case! I suppose there's never been one just like it? He's still absolutely convinced that he committed that murder?"

"Absolutely. Yes."

The stranger reflected. "And there was no conceivable ground for the idea? No one could make out how it started? A quiet conventional sort of fellow like that—where do you suppose he got such a delusion? Did you ever get the least clue to it?"

McCarren stood still, his hands in his pockets, his head cocked up in contemplation of the windows. Then he turned his bright hard gaze on his companion.

"That was the queer part of it. I've never spoken of it—but I *did* get a clue."

"By Jove! That's interesting. What was it?"

McCarren formed his red lips into a whistle. "Why—that it wasn't a delusion."

He produced his effect—the other turned a startled glance on him.

"He murdered the man all right. I tumbled on the truth by the merest accident, when I'd pretty nearly chucked the whole job."

"He murdered him—murdered his cousin?"

"Sure as you live. Only don't split on me. It's about the queerest business I ever ran into . . . *Do about it?* Why, what was I to do? I couldn't hang the poor devil, could I? Lord, but I was glad when they collared him, and had him stowed away safe in there!"

The tall man listened with a grave face, grasping Granice's statement in his hand.

"Here—take this; it makes me sick," he said abruptly, thrusting the paper at the reporter; and the two men turned and walked in silence to the gates.

His Father's Son

I

AFTER his wife's death Mason Grew took the momentous step of selling out his business and moving from Wingfield, Connecticut, to Brooklyn.

For years he had secretly nursed the hope of such a change, but had never dared to suggest it to Mrs. Grew, a woman of immutable habits. Mr. Grew himself was attached to Wingfield, where he had grown up, prospered, and become what the local press described as "prominent." He was attached to his brick house with sandstone trimmings and a cast-iron area-railing neatly sanded to match; to the similar row of houses across the street, with "trolley" wires forming a kind of aerial pathway between, and to the vista closed by the sandstone steeple of the church which he and his wife had always attended, and where their only child had been baptized.

It was hard to snap all these threads of association, yet still harder, now that he was alone, to live so far from his boy. Ronald Grew was practicing law in New York, and there was no more chance of his returning to live at Wingfield than of a river's flowing inland from the sea. Therefore to be near him his father must move; and it was characteristic of Mr. Grew, and of the situation generally, that the translation, when it took place, was to Brooklyn, and not to New York.

"Why you bury yourself in that hole I can't think," had been Ronald's comment; and Mr. Grew simply replied that rents were lower in Brooklyn, and that he had heard of a house there that would suit him. In reality he had said to himself—being the only recipient of his own confidences—that if he went to New York he might be on the boy's mind; whereas, if he lived in Brooklyn, Ronald would always have a good excuse for not popping over to see him every other day. The sociological isolation of Brooklyn, combined with its geographical nearness, presented in fact the precise conditions that Mr. Grew sought. He wanted to be near enough to New York to go there often, to feel under his feet the same pavement that Ronald trod, to sit now and then in the same theaters, and find on his breakfast-table the journals which, with increasing frequency, inserted Ronald's name in the sacred bounds of the society column. It had always been a trial to Mr. Grew to have to wait twenty-four hours to read that "among those present was Mr. Ronald Grew." Now he had it with his coffee, and left it on the breakfast-table to the perusal of a "hired girl" cosmopolitan enough to do it justice. In such ways Brooklyn attested the advantages of its nearness to New York, while remaining, as regards Ronald's duty to his father, as remote and inaccessible as Wingfield.

It was not that Ronald shirked his filial obligations, but rather because of his heavy sense of them, that Mr. Grew so persistently sought to minimize and lighten them. It was he who insisted, to Ronald, on the immense difficulty of getting from New York to Brooklyn.

"Any way you look at it, it makes a big hole in the day; and there's not much use in the ragged rim left. You say you're dining out next Sunday? Then I forbid you to come over here to lunch. Do you understand me, sir? You disobey at the risk of your father's malediction! Where did you say you were dining? With the Waltham Bankshires again? Why, that's the second time in three weeks, ain't it? Big blow-out, I suppose? Gold plate and orchids—opera singers in afterward? Well, you'd be in a nice box if there was a fog on the river, and you got hung up half-way over. That'd be a handsome return for the attention Mrs. Bankshire has shown you—singling out a whipper-snapper like you twice in three weeks! (What's the daughter's name—Daisy?) No, *sir*—don't you come fooling round here next Sunday, or I'll set the dogs on you. And you wouldn't find me in anyhow, come to think of it. I'm lunching out myself, as it happens—yes, sir, *lunching out*. Is there anything especially comic in my lunching out? I don't often do it, you say? Well, that's no reason why I never should. Who with? Why, with—with old Dr. Bleaker: Dr. Eliphalet Bleaker. No, you wouldn't know about him—he's only an old friend of your mother's and mine."

Gradually Ronald's insistence became less difficult to overcome. With his customary sweetness and tact (as Mr. Grew put it) he began to "take the hint," to give in to "the old gentleman's" growing desire for solitude.

"I'm set in my ways, Ronny, that's about the size of it; I like to go tick-ticking along like a clock. I always did. And when you come bouncing in I never feel sure there's enough for dinner—or that I haven't sent Maria out for the evening. And I don't want the neighbors to see me opening my own door to my son. That's the kind of cringing snob I am. Don't give me away, will you? I want 'em to think I keep four or five powdered flunkeys in the hall day and night—same as the lobby of one of those Fifth Avenue hotels. And if you pop over when you're not expected, how am I going to keep up the bluff?"

Ronald yielded after the proper amount of resistance—his intuitive sense, in every social transaction, of the proper amount of force to be expended, was one of the qualities his father most admired in him. Mr. Grew's perceptions in this line were probably more acute than his son suspected. The souls of short thick-set men, with chubby features, mutton-chop whiskers, and pale eyes peering between folds of fat like almond kernels in half-split shells—souls thus encased do not reveal themselves to the casual scrutiny as delicate emotional instruments. But in spite of the disguise in which he walked Mr. Grew vibrated exquisitely in response to every imaginative appeal; and his son Ronald was always stimulating and feeding his imagination.

Ronald in fact constituted Mr. Grew's one escape from the element of mediocrity which had always hemmed him in. To a man so enamored of beauty, and so little qualified to add to its sum total, it was a wonderful privilege to have bestowed on the world such a being. Ronald's resemblance to Mr. Grew's early conception of what he himself would have liked to look might have put new life into the discredited theory of prenatal influences. At any rate, if the young man owed his beauty, his distinction and his winning manner to the dreams of one of his parents, it was certainly to those of Mr. Grew, who, while outwardly devoting his life to the manufacture and dissemination of Grew's Secure Suspender Buckle, moved in an enchanted inward world peopled with all the figures of romance. In this company Mr. Grew cut as brilliant a figure as any of its noble phantoms; and to see his vision of himself projected on the outer world in the shape of a brilliant popular conquering son, seemed, in retrospect, to give to it a belated reality. There were even moments when, forgetting his face, Mr. Grew said to himself that if he'd had "half a chance" he might have done as well as Ronald; but this only fortified his resolve that Ronald should do infinitely better.

Ronald's ability to do well almost equalled his gift of looking well. Mr. Grew constantly affirmed to himself that the boy was "not a genius"; but, barring this slight deficiency, he had almost every gift that a parent could wish. Even at Harvard he had managed to be several desirable things at once—writing poetry in the college magazine, playing delightfully "by ear," acquitting himself creditably of his studies, and yet holding his own in the sporting set that formed, as it were, the gateway of the temple of Society. Mr. Grew's idealism did not preclude the frank desire that his son should pass through that gateway; but the wish was not prompted by material considerations. It was Mr. Grew's notion that, in the rough and hurrying current of a new civilization, the little pools of leisure and enjoyment must nurture delicate growths, material graces as well as moral refinements, likely to be uprooted and swept away by the rush of the main torrent. He based his theory on the fact that he had liked the few "society" people he had met—had found their manners simpler, their voices more agreeable, their views more consonant with his own, than those of the leading citizens of Wingfield. But then he had met very few.

Ronald's sympathies needed no urging in the same direction. He took naturally, dauntlessly, to all the high and exceptional things about which his father's imagination had so long ineffectually hovered—from the start he *was* what Mr. Grew had dreamed of being. And so precise, so detailed, was Mr. Grew's vision of his own imaginary career, that as Ronald grew up, and began to travel in a widening orbit, his father had an almost uncanny sense of the extent to which that career was enacting itself before him. At Harvard, Ronald had done exactly what the hypothetical Mason Grew would have done, had not his actual self, at the same age, been working his way up in old Slagden's button factory—the institution which was later to acquire fame, and even notoriety, as the birthplace of Grew's Secure Suspender Buckle. Afterward, at a period when the actual Grew had passed from the factory to the bookkeeper's desk, his invisible double had been reading law at Columbia—precisely again what Ronald did! But it was when the young man left the paths laid out for him by the parental hand, and cast himself boldly on the world, that his adventures began to bear the most astonishing resemblance to those of the unrealized Mason Grew. It was in New York that the scene of this hypothetical being's first exploits had always been laid; and it was in New York that Ronald was to achieve his first triumph. There was nothing small or timid about Mr. Grew's imagination; it had never stopped at anything between Wingfield and the metropolis. And the real Ronald had the same cosmic vision as his parent. He brushed aside with a contemptuous laugh his mother's entreaty that he should stay at Wingfield and continue the dynasty of the Grew Suspender Buckle. Mr. Grew knew that in reality Ronald winced at the Buckle, loathed it, blushed for his connection with it. Yet it was the Buckle that had seen him through Groton, Harvard and the Law School, and had permitted him to enter the office of a distinguished corporation lawyer, instead of being enslaved to some sordid business with quick returns. The Buckle had been Ronald's fairy godmother—yet his father did not blame him for abhorring and disowning it. Mr. Grew himself often bitterly regretted having attached his own name to the instrument of his material success, though, at the time, his doing so had been the natural expression of his romanticism. When he invented the Buckle, and took out his patent, he and his wife both felt that to bestow their name on it was like naming a battleship or a peak of the Andes.

Mrs. Grew had never learned to know better; but Mr. Grew had discovered his error before Ronald was out of school. He read it first in a black eye of his boy's. Ronald's symmetry had been marred by the insolent fist of a fourth former whom he had chastised for alluding to his father as "Old Buckles"; and when Mr. Grew heard the epithet he understood in a flash that the Buckle was a thing to blush for. It was too late then to dissociate his name from it, or to efface from the hoardings of the entire continent the picture of two gentlemen, one contorting himself in the abject effort to repair a broken brace, while the careless ease of the other's attitude proclaimed his trust in the Secure Suspender Buckle. These records were indelible, but Ronald could at least be spared all direct connection with them; and that day Mr. Grew decided that the boy should not return to Wingfield.

"You'll see," he had said to Mrs. Grew, "he'll take right hold in

New York. Ronald's got my knack for taking hold," he added, throwing out his chest.

"But the way you took hold was in business," objected Mrs. Grew, who was large and literal.

Mr. Grew's chest collapsed, and he became suddenly conscious of his comic face in its rim of sandy whisker. "That's not the only way," he said, with a touch of wistfulness which escaped his wife's analysis.

"Well, of course you could have written beautifully," she rejoined with admiring eyes.

"*Written?* Me!" Mr. Grew became sardonic.

"Why, those letters—weren't *they* beautiful, I'd like to know?"

The couple exchanged a glance, innocently allusive and amused on the wife's part, and charged with a sudden tragic significance on the husband's.

"Well, I've got to be going along to the office now," he merely said, dragging himself out of his chair.

This had happened while Ronald was still at school; and now Mrs. Grew slept in the Wingfield cemetery, under a life-size theological virtue of her own choosing, and Mr. Grew's prognostications as to Ronald's ability to "take right hold" in New York were being more and more brilliantly fulfilled.

II

RONALD obeyed his father's injunction not to come to luncheon on the day of the Bankshires' dinner; but in the middle of the following week Mr. Grew was surprised by a telegram from his son.

"Want to see you important matter. Expect me tomorrow afternoon."

Mr. Grew received the telegram after breakfast. To peruse it he had lifted his eye from a paragraph of the morning paper describing a fancy-dress dinner which the Hamilton Gliddens' had given the night before for the house-warming of their new Fifth Avenue palace.

"Among the couples who afterward danced in the Poets' Quadrille were Miss Daisy Bankshire, looking more than usually lovely as Laura, and Mr. Ronald Grew as the young Petrarch."

Petrarch and Laura! Well—if *anything* meant anything, Mr. Grew supposed he knew what that meant. For weeks past he had noticed how constantly the names of the young people were coupled in the society notes he so insatiably devoured. Even the soulless reporter was getting into the habit of uniting them in his lists. And this Laura and Petrarch business was almost an announcement . . .

Mr. Grew dropped the telegram, wiped his eyeglasses, and reread the paragraph. "Miss Daisy Bankshire . . . more than usually lovely . . ." Yes; she *was* lovely. He had often seen her photograph in the papers—seen her represented in every attitude of the mundane game: fondling her prize bulldog, taking a fence on her thoroughbred, dancing a *gavotte,* all patches and plumes, or fingering a guitar, all tulle and lilies; and once he had caught a glimpse of her at the theater. Hearing that Ronald was going to a fashionable first-night with the Bankshires, Mr. Grew had for once overcome his repugnance to following his son's movements, and had secured for himself, under the shadow of the balcony, a stall whence he could observe the Bankshire box without fear of detection. Ronald had never known of his father's presence; and for three blessed hours Mr. Grew had watched his boy's handsome dark head bent above the fair hair and averted shoulder that were all he could catch of Miss Bankshire's beauties.

He recalled the vision now; and with it came, as usual, its ghostly double: the vision of his young self bending above such a shoulder and such shining hair. Needless to say that the real Mason Grew had never found himself in so enviable a situation. The late Mrs. Grew had no more resembled Miss Daisy Bankshire than he had looked like the happy victorious Ronald. And the mystery was that from their dull faces, their dull endearments, the miracle of Ronald should have sprung. It was almost—fantastically—as if the boy had been a changeling, child of a Latmian night, whom the divine companion of Mr. Grew's early reveries had secretly laid in the cradle of the Wingfield bedroom while Mr. and Mrs. Grew slept the sleep of conjugal indifference.

The young Mason Grew had not at first accepted this astral episode as the complete cancelling of his claims on romance. He too had grasped at the high-hung glory; and, with his tendency to reach too far when he reached at all, had singled out the prettiest girl in Wingfield. When he recalled his stammered confession of love his face still tingled under her cool bright stare. His audacity had struck her dumb; and when she recovered her voice it was to fling a taunt at him.

"Don't be too discouraged, you know—have you ever thought of trying Addie Wicks?"

All Wingfield would have understood the gibe: Addie Wicks was the dullest girl in town. And a year later he had married Addie Wicks . . .

He looked up from the perusal of Ronald's telegram with this memory in his mind. Now at last his dream was coming true! His boy would taste of the joys that had mocked his thwarted youth and his dull middle-age. And it was fitting that they should be realized in Ronald's destiny. Ronald was made to take happiness boldly by the hand and lead it home like a bride. He had the carriage, the confidence, the high faith in his fortune, that compel the willful stars. And, thanks to the Buckle, he would also have the background of material elegance that became his conquering person. Since Mr. Grew had retired from business his investments had prospered, and he had been saving up his income for just such a purpose. His own wants were few: he had brought the Wingfield furniture to Brooklyn, and his sitting-room was a replica of that in which the long years of his married life had been spent. Even the florid carpet on which Ronald's first footsteps had been taken was carefully matched when it became too threadbare. And on the marble center-table, with its beaded cover and bunch of dyed pampas grass, lay the illustrated Longfellow and the copy of Ingersoll's lectures which represented literature to Mr. Grew when he had led home his bride. In the light of Ronald's romance, Mr. Grew found himself reliving, with mingled pain and tenderness, all the poor prosaic incidents of his own personal history. Curiously enough, with this new splendor on them they began to emit a faint ray of their own. His wife's armchair, in its usual place by the fire, recalled her placid unperceiving presence, seated opposite to him during the long drowsy years; and he felt her kindness, her equanimity, where formerly he had only ached at her obtuseness.

And from the chair he glanced up at the discolored photograph on the wall above, with a withered laurel wreath suspended on a corner of the frame. The photograph represented a young man with a poetic necktie and untrammelled hair, leaning against a Gothic chair-back, a roll of music in his hand; and beneath was scrawled a bar of Chopin, with the words: *"Adieu, Adèle."*

The portrait was that of the great pianist, Fortuné Dolbrowski; and its presence on the wall of Mr. Grew's sitting-room commemorated the only exquisite hour of his life save that of Ronald's birth. It was some time before the latter event, a few months only after Mr. Grew's marriage, that he had taken his wife to New York to hear the great Dolbrowski. Their evening had been magically beautiful, and even Addie, roused from her usual inexpressiveness, had waked into a momentary semblance of life. "I never—I never——" she gasped out when they had regained their hotel bedroom, and sat staring back entranced at the evening's vision. Her large face was pink and tremulous, and she sat with her hands on her knees, forgetting to roll up her bonnet strings and prepare her curl-papers.

"I'd like to *write* him just how I felt—I wisht I knew how!" she burst out in a final effervescence of emotion.

Her husband lifted his head and looked at her.

"Would you? I feel that way too," he said with a sheepish laugh. And they continued to stare at each other through a transfiguring mist of sound.

The scene rose before Mr. Grew as he gazed up at the pianist's photograph. "Well, I owe her that anyhow—poor Addie!" he said, with a smile at the inconsequences of fate. With Ronald's telegram in his hand he was in a mood to count his mercies.

III

"A clear twenty-five thousand a year: that's what you can tell 'em with my compliments," said Mr. Grew, glancing complacently across the center-table at his boy.

It struck him that Ronald's gift for looking his part in life had never so completely expressed itself. Other young men, at such a moment, would have been red, damp, tight about the collar; but Ronald's cheek was a shade paler, and the contrast made his dark eyes more expressive.

"A clear twenty-five thousand; yes, sir—that's what I always meant you to have."

Mr. Grew leaned carelessly back, his hands thrust in his pockets, as though to divert attention from the agitation of his features. He had often pictured himself rolling out that phrase to Ronald, and now that it was on his lips he could not control their tremor.

Ronald listened in silence, lifting a hand to his slight moustache, as though he, too, wished to hide some involuntary betrayal of emotion. At first Mr. Grew took his silence for an expression of gratified surprise; but as it prolonged itself it became less easy to interpret.

"I—see here, my boy; did you expect more? Isn't it enough?" Mr. Grew cleared his throat. "Do *they* expect more?" he asked nervously. He was hardly able to face the pain of inflicting a disappointment on Ronald at the very moment when he had counted on putting the final touch to his bliss.

Ronald moved uneasily in his chair and his eyes wandered upward to the laurel-wreathed photograph of the pianist.

"*Is* it the money, Ronald? Speak out, my boy. We'll see, we'll look round—I'll manage somehow."

"No, no," the young man interrupted, abruptly raising his hand as though to check his father.

Mr. Grew recovered his cheerfulness. "Well, what's the trouble then, if *she's* willing?"

Ronald shifted his position again and finally rose from his seat and wandered across the room.

"Father," he said, coming back, "there's something I've got to tell you. I can't take your money."

Mr. Grew sat speechless a moment, staring blankly at his son; then he emitted a laugh. "My money? What are you talking about? What's this about my money? Why, it ain't *mine,* Ronny; it's all yours—every cent of it!"

The young man met his tender look with a gesture of tragic refusal.

"No, no, it's not mine—not even in the sense you mean. Not in any sense. Can't you understand my feeling so?"

"Feeling so? I don't know how you're feeling. I don't know what you're talking about. Are you too proud to touch any money you haven't earned? Is that what you're trying to tell me?"

"No. It's not that. You must know——"

Mr. Grew flushed to the rim of his bristling whiskers. "Know? Know *what?* Can't you speak out?"

Ronald hesitated, and the two faced each other for a long strained moment, during which Mr. Grew's congested countenance grew gradually pale again.

"What's the meaning of this? Is it because you've done something . . . something you're ashamed of . . . ashamed to tell me?" he gasped; and walking around the table he laid his hand gently on his son's shoulder. "There's nothing you can't tell me, my boy."

"It's not that. Why do you make it so hard for me?" Ronald broke out with passion. "You must have known this was sure to happen sooner or later."

"Happen? What was sure to hap——?" Mr. Grew's question wavered on his lip and passed into a tremulous laugh. "Is it something *I've* done that you don't approve of? Is it—is it *the Buckle* you're ashamed of, Ronald Grew?"

Ronald laughed too, impatiently. "The Buckle? No, I'm not ashamed of the Buckle; not any more than you are," he returned with a flush. "But I'm ashamed of all I owe to it—all I owe to you—when—when——" He broke off and took a few distracted steps across the room. "You might make this easier for me," he protested, turning back to his father.

"Make what easier? I know less and less what you're driving at," Mr. Grew groaned.

Ronald's walk had once more brought him beneath the photograph on the wall. He lifted his head for a moment and looked at it; then he looked again at Mr. Grew.

"Do you suppose I haven't always known?"

"Known——?"

"Even before you gave me those letters at the time of my mother's death—even before that, I suspected. I don't know how it began . . . perhaps from little things you let drop . . . you and she . . . and resemblances that I couldn't help seeing . . . in myself . . . How on earth could you suppose I *shouldn't guess?* I always thought you gave me the letters as a way of telling me——"

Mr. Grew rose slowly from his chair. "The letters? Do you mean Dolbrowski's letters?"

Ronald nodded with white lips. "You must remember giving them to me the day after the funeral."

Mr. Grew nodded back. "Of course. I wanted you to have everything your mother valued."

"Well—how could I help knowing after that?"

"Knowing *what?"* Mr. Grew stood staring helplessly at his son. Suddenly his look caught at a clue that seemed to confront it with a deeper difficulty.

"You thought—you thought those letters . . . Dolbrowski's letters . . . you thought they meant . . ."

"Oh, it wasn't only the letters. There were so many other signs. My love of music—my—all my feelings about life . . . and art . . . And when you gave me the letters I thought you must mean me to know."

Mr. Grew had grown quiet. His lips were firm, and his small eyes looked out steadily from their creased lids.

"To know that you were Fortuné Dolbrowski's son?"

Ronald made a mute sign of assent.

"I see. And what did you intend to do?"

"I meant to wait till I could earn my living, and then repay you . . . as far as I can ever repay you . . . for what you'd spent on me . . . But now that there's a chance of my marrying . . . and that your generosity overwhelms me . . . I'm obliged to speak."

"I see," said Mr. Grew again. He let himself down into his chair, looking steadily and not unkindly at the young man. "Sit down too, Ronald. Let's talk."

Ronald made a protesting movement. "Is anything to be gained by it? You can't change me—change what I feel. The reading of those letters transformed my whole life—I was a boy till then: they made a man of me. From that moment I understood myself." He paused, and then looked up at Mr. Grew's face. "Don't imagine that I don't appreciate your kindness—your extraordinary generosity. But I can't go through life in disguise. And I want you to know that I have not won Daisy under false pretenses——"

Mr. Grew started up with the first expletive Ronald had ever heard on his lips.

"You damned young fool, you, you haven't *told* her——?"

Ronald raised his head with pride. "Oh, you don't know her, sir! She thinks no worse of me for knowing my secret. She is above and beyond all such conventional prejudices. She's *proud* of my parentage—" he straightened his slim young shoulders—"as I'm proud of it . . . yes, sir, proud of it . . ."

Mr. Grew sank back into his seat with a dry laugh. "Well, you ought to be. You come of good stock. And you're your father's son, every inch of you!" He laughed again, as though the humor of the situation grew on him with its closer contemplation.

"Yes, I've always felt that," Ronald murmured, gravely.

"Your father's son, and no mistake." Mr. Grew leaned forward. "You're the son of as big a fool as yourself. And here he sits, Ronald Grew!"

The young man's color deepened to crimson; but his reply was checked by Mr. Grew's decisive gesture. "Here he sits, with all your young nonsense still alive in him. Don't you begin to see the likeness? If you don't I'll tell you the story of those letters."

Ronald stared. "What do you mean? Don't they tell their own story?"

"I supposed they did when I gave them to you; but you've given it a twist that needs straightening out." Mr. Grew squared his elbows on the table, and looked at the young man across the gift-books and dyed pampas grass. "I wrote all the letters that Dolbrowski answered."

Ronald gave back his look in frowning perplexity. "*You wrote* them? I don't understand. His letters are all addressed to my mother."

"Yes. And he thought he was corresponding with her."

"But my mother—what did she think?"

Mr. Grew hesitated, puckering his thick lids. "Well, I guess she kinder thought it was a joke. Your mother didn't think about things much."

Ronald continued to bend a puzzled frown on the question. "I don't understand," he reiterated.

Mr. Grew cleared his throat with a nervous laugh. "Well, I don't know as you ever will—*quite*. But this is the way it came about. I had a toughish time of it when I was young. Oh, I don't mean so much the fight I had to put up to make my way—there was always plenty of fight in me. But inside of myself it was kinder lonesome. And the outside didn't attract callers." He laughed again, with an apologetic gesture toward his broad blinking face. "When I went round with the other young fellows I was always the forlorn hope—the one that had to eat the drumsticks and dance with the left-overs. As sure as there was a blighter at a picnic I had to swing her, and feed her, and drive her home. And all the time I was mad after all the things you've got—poetry and music and all the joy-forever business. So there were the pair of us—my face and my imagination—chained together, and fighting, and hating each other like poison.

"Then your mother came along and took pity on me. It sets up a gawky fellow to find a girl who ain't ashamed to be seen walking with him Sundays. And I was grateful to your mother, and we got along first-rate. Only I couldn't say things to her—and she couldn't answer. Well—one day, a few months after we were married, Dolbrowski came to New York, and the whole place went wild about him. I'd never heard any good music, but I'd always had an inkling of what it must be like, though I couldn't tell you to this day how I knew. Well, your mother read about him in the papers too, and she thought it'd be the swagger thing to go to New York and hear him play—so we went . . . I'll never forget that evening. Your mother wasn't easily stirred up—she never seemed to need to let off steam. But that night she seemed to understand the way I felt. And when we got back to the hotel she said to me: 'I'd like to tell him how I feel. I'd like to sit right down and write to him.'

"'Would you?' I said. 'So would I.'

"There was paper and pens there before us, and I pulled a sheet toward me, and began to write. 'Is this what you'd like to say to him?' I asked her when the letter was done. And she got pink and said: 'I don't understand it, but it's lovely.' And she copied it out and signed her name to it, and sent it."

Mr. Grew paused, and Ronald sat silent, with lowered eyes.

"That's how it began; and that's where I thought it would end. But it didn't, because Dolbrowski answered. His first letter was dated January 10, 1872. I guess you'll find I'm correct. Well, I went back to hear him again, and I wrote him after the performance, and he answered again. And after that we kept it up for six months. Your mother always copied the letters and signed them. She seemed to think it was a kinder joke, and she was proud of his answering my letters. But she never went back to New York to hear him, though I saved up enough to give her the treat again. She was too lazy, and she let me go without her. I heard him three times in New York; and in the spring he came to Wingfield and played once at the Academy. Your mother was sick and couldn't go; so I went alone. After the performance I meant to get one of the directors to take me in to see him; but when the time came, I just went back home and wrote to him instead. And the month after, before he went back to Europe, he sent your mother a last little note, and that picture hanging up there . . ."

Mr. Grew paused again, and both men lifted their eyes to the photograph.

"Is that all?" Ronald slowly asked.

"That's all—every bit of it," said Mr. Grew.

"And my mother—my mother never even spoke to Dolbrowski?"

"Never. She never even saw him but that once in New York at his concert."

The blood crept again to Ronald's face. "Are you sure of that, sir?" he asked in a trembling voice.

"Sure as I am that I'm sitting here. Why, she was too lazy to look at his letters after the first novelty wore off. She copied the answers just to humor me—but she always said she couldn't understand what we wrote."

"But how could you go on with such a correspondence? It's incredible!"

Mr. Grew looked at his son thoughtfully. "I suppose it is, to you. You've only had to put out your hand and get the things I was starving for—music, and good talk, and ideas. Those letters gave me all that. You've read them, and you know that Dolbrowski was not only a great musician but a great man. There was nothing beautiful he didn't see, nothing fine he didn't feel. For six months I breathed his air, and I've lived on it ever since. Do you begin to understand a little now?"

"Yes—a little. But why write in my mother's name? Why make it appear like a sentimental correspondence?"

Mr. Grew reddened to his bald temples. "Why, I tell you it began that way, as a kinder joke. And when I saw that the first letter pleased and interested him, I was afraid to tell him—I *couldn't* tell him. Do you suppose he'd gone on writing if he'd ever seen me, Ronny?"

Ronald suddenly looked at him with new eyes. "But he must have thought your letters very beautiful—to go on as he did," he broke out.

"Well—I did my best," said Mr. Grew modestly.

Ronald pursued his idea. "Where *are* all your letters, I wonder? Weren't they returned to you at his death?"

Mr. Grew laughed. "Lord, no. I guess he had trunks and trunks full of better ones. I guess Queens and Empresses wrote to him."

"I should have liked to see your letters," the young man insisted.

"Well, they weren't bad," said Mr. Grew drily. "But I'll tell you one thing, Ronny," he added. Ronald raised his head with a quick glance, and Mr. Grew continued: "I'll tell you where the best of those letters is—it's in *you*. If it hadn't been for that one look at life I couldn't have made you what you are. Oh, I know you've done a good deal of your own making—but I've been there behind you all the time. And you'll never know the work I've spared you and the time I've saved you. Fortuné Dolbrowski helped me do that. I never saw things in little again after I'd looked at 'em with him. And I tried to give you the big view from the start . . . So that's what became of my letters."

Mr. Grew paused, and for a long time Ronald sat motionless, his elbows on the table, his face dropped on his hands.

Suddenly Mr. Grew's touch fell on his shoulder.

"Look at here, Ronald Grew—do you want me to tell you how you're feeling at this minute? Just a mite let down, after all, at the idea that you ain't the romantic figure you'd got to think yourself . . . Well, that's natural enough, too; but I'll tell you what it proves. It proves you're my son right enough, if any more proof was needed. For it's just the kind of fool nonsense I used to feel at your age—and if there's anybody here to laugh at it's myself, and not you. And you can laugh at me just as much as you like . . ."

The Daunt Diana

I

"WHAT'S become of the Daunt Diana? You mean to say you never heard the sequel?"

Ringham Finney threw himself back into his chair with the smile of the collector who has a good thing to show. He knew he had a good listener, at any rate. I don't think much of Ringham's snuff-boxes, but his anecdotes are usually worthwhile. He's a psychologist astray among *bibelots,* and the best bits he brings back from his raids on Christie's and the Hôtel Drouot are the fragments of human nature he picks up on those historic battlefields. If his *flair* in enamel had been half as good we should have heard of the Finney collection by this time.

He really has—queer fatuous investigator!—an unusually sensitive touch for the human texture, and the specimens he gathers into his museum of memories have almost always some mark of the rare and chosen. I felt, therefore, that I was really to be congratulated on the fact that I didn't know what had become of the Daunt Diana, and on having before me a long evening in which to learn. I had just led my friend back, after an excellent dinner at Foyot's, to the shabby pleasant sitting-room of my *Rive Gauche* hotel; and I knew that, once I had settled him in a good armchair, and put a box of cigars at his elbow, I could trust him not to budge till I had the story.

II

YOU remember old Neave, of course? Little Humphrey Neave, I mean. We used to see him pottering about Rome years ago. He lived in two rooms over a wine shop, on polenta and lentils, and prowled among the refuse of the Ripetta whenever he had a few coppers to spend. But you've been out of the collector's world for so long that you may not know what happened to him afterward . . .

He was always a queer chap, Neave; years older than you and me, of course—and even when I first knew him, in my raw Roman days, he produced on me an unusual impression of age and experience. I don't think I've ever known anyone who was at once so intelligent and so simple. It's the precise combination that results in romance; and poor little Neave was romantic.

He told me once how he'd come to Rome. He was *originaire* of Mystic, Connecticut—and he wanted to get as far away from it as possible. Rome seemed as far as anything on the same planet could be; and after he'd worried his way through Harvard—with shifts and shavings that you and I can't imagine—he contrived to be sent to Switzerland as tutor to a chap who'd failed in his examinations. With only the Alps between, he wasn't likely to turn back; and he got another fellow to take his pupil home, and struck out on foot for the seven hills.

I'm telling you these early details merely to give you a notion of the man. There was a cool persistency and a head-long courage in his dash for Rome that one wouldn't have guessed in the pottering chap we used to know. Once on the spot, he got more tutoring, managed to make himself a name for coaxing balky youths to take their fences, and was finally able to take up the more congenial task of expounding "the antiquities" to cultured travellers. I call it more congenial—but how it must have seared his soul! Fancy unveiling the sacred scars of Time to ladies who murmur: "Was this *actually* the spot—?" while they absently feel for their hat-pins! He used to say that nothing kept him at it but the exquisite thought of accumulating the lire for his collection. For the Neave collection, my dear fellow, began early, began almost with his Roman life, began in a series of little nameless odds and ends, broken trinkets, torn embroideries, the amputated extremities of maimed marbles: things that even the rag-picker had pitched away when he sifted his haul. But they weren't nameless or meaningless to Neave; his strength lay in his instinct for identifying, putting together, seeing significant relations. He was a regular Cuvier of bric-a-brac. And during those early years, when he had time to brood over trifles and note imperceptible differences, he gradually sharpened his instinct, and made it into the delicate and redoubtable instrument it is. Before he had a thousand francs' worth of *anticaglie* to his name he began to be known as an expert, and the big dealers were glad to consult him. But we're getting no nearer the Daunt Diana . . .

Well, some fifteen years ago, in London, I ran across Neave at Christie's. He was the same little man we'd known, effaced, bleached, indistinct, like a poor "impression"—as unnoticeable as one of his own early finds, yet, like them, with a *quality,* if one had an eye for it. He told me he still lived in Rome, and had contrived, by persistent self-denial, to get a few bits together—"piecemeal, little by little, with fasting and prayer; and I mean the fasting literally!" he said.

He had run over to London for his annual "look-round"—I fancy one or another of the big collectors usually paid his journey—and when we met he was on his way to see the Daunt collection. You know old Daunt was a surly brute, and the things weren't easily seen; but he had heard Neave was in London, and had sent—yes, actually sent!—for him to come and give his opinion on a few bits, including the Diana. The little man bore himself discreetly, but you can imagine how proud he was! In his exultation he asked me to come with him—"Oh, I've the *grandes et petites entrées,* my dear fellow: I've made my conditions—" and so it happened that I saw the first meeting between Humphrey Neave and his fate.

For that collection was his fate: or, one may say, it was embodied in the Diana who was queen and goddess of the realm. Yes—I shall always be glad I was with Neave when he had his first look at the Diana. I see him now, blinking at her through his white lashes, and stroking his wisp of a moustache to hide a twitch of the muscles.

It was all very quiet, but it was the *coup de foudre*. I could see that by the way his hands worked when he turned away and began to examine the other things. You remember Neave's hands—thin and dry, with long inquisitive fingers thrown out like antennae? Whatever they hold—bronze or lace, enamel or glass—they seem to acquire the very texture of the thing, and to draw out of it, by every fingertip, the essence it has secreted. Well, that day, as he moved about among Daunt's treasures, the Diana followed him everywhere. He didn't look back at her—he gave himself to the business he was there for—but whatever he touched, he felt her. And on the threshold he turned and gave her his first free look—the kind of look that says: "*You're mine.*"

It amused me at the time—the idea of little Neave making eyes at any of Daunt's belongings. He might as well have coquetted with the Kohinoor. And the same idea seemed to strike him; for as we turned away from the big house in Belgravia he glanced up at it and said, with a bitterness I'd never heard in him: "Good Lord! To think of that lumpy fool having those things to handle! Did you notice his stupid stumps of fingers? I suppose he blunted them gouging nuggets out of gold fields. And in exchange for the nuggets he gets all that in a year—only has to hold out his callous palm to have that ripe sphere of beauty drop into it! That's my idea of heaven—to have a great collection drop into one's hand, as success, or love, or any of the big shining things, suddenly drop on some men. And I've had to worry along for nearly fifty years, saving and paring, and haggling and managing, to get here a bit and there a bit—and not one perfection in the lot! It's enough to poison a man's life."

The outbreak was so unlike Neave that I remember every word of it: remember, too, saying in answer: "But, look here, Neave, you wouldn't take Daunt's hands for yours, I imagine?"

He stared a moment and smiled. "Have all that, and grope my way through it like a blind cave fish? What a question! But the sense that it's always the blind fish that live in that kind of aquarium is what makes anarchists, sir!" He looked back from the corner of the square, where we had paused while he delivered himself of this remarkable metaphor. "God, I'd like to throw a bomb at that place, and be in at the looting!"

And with that, on the way home, he unpacked his grievance—

"I shall always be glad I was with Neave when he had his first look at the Diana."

pulled the bandage off the wound, and showed me the ugly mark it made on his little white soul.

It wasn't the struggling, screwing, stinting, self-denying that galled him—it was the smallness of the result. It was, in short, the old tragedy of the discrepancy between a man's wants and his power to gratify them. Neave's taste was too fine for his means—was like some strange, delicate, capricious animal, that he cherished and pampered and couldn't satisfy.

"Don't you know those little glittering lizards that die if they're not fed on some rare tropical fly? Well, my taste's like that, with one important difference—if it doesn't get its fly, it simply turns and feeds on *me*. Oh, it doesn't die, my taste—worse luck! It gets larger and stronger and more fastidious, and takes a bigger bite of me—that's all."

That was all. Year by year, day by day, he had made himself into this delicate register of perceptions and sensations—as far above the ordinary human faculty of appreciation as some scientific registering instrument is beyond the rough human senses—only to find that the beauty which alone could satisfy him was unattainable, that he was never to know the last deep identification which only possession can give. He had trained himself, in short, to feel, in the rare great thing—such an utterance of beauty as the Daunt Diana, say—a hundred elements of perfection, a hundred *reasons why,* imperceptible, inexplicable even, to the average "artistic" sense; he had reached this point by a long process of discrimination and rejection, the renewed great refusals of the intelligence which perpetually asks more, which will make no pact with its self of yesterday, and is never to be beguiled from its purpose by the wiles of the next-best-thing. Oh, it's a poignant case, but not a common one; for the next-best-thing usually wins . . .

You see, the worst of Neave's state was the fact of his not being a mere collector, even the collector raised to his highest pitch. The whole thing was blent in him with poetry—his imagination had romanticized the acquisitive instinct, as the religious feeling of the Middle Ages turned passion into love. And yet his could never be the abstract enjoyment of the philosopher who says: "This or that object is really mine because I'm capable of appreciating it." Neave *wanted* what he appreciated—wanted it with his touch and his sight as well as with his brain.

It was hardly a year afterward that, coming back from a long tour in India, I picked up a London paper and read the amazing headline: "Mr. Humphrey Neave buys the Daunt collection . . . " I rubbed my eyes and read again. Yes, it could only be our old friend Humphrey. "An American living in Rome . . . one of our most discerning collectors"; there was no mistaking the description. I bolted out to see the first dealer I could find, and there I had the incredible details. Neave had come into a fortune—two or three million dollars, amassed by an uncle who had a corset-factory, and who had attained wealth as the creator of the Mystic Super-straight. (Corset-factory sounds odd, by the way, doesn't it? One had fancied that the corset was a personal, a highly specialized garment, more or less shaped on the form it was to modify; but, after all, the Tanagras were all made from two or three molds—and so, I suppose, are the ladies who wear the Mystic Super-straight.)

The uncle had a son, and Neave had never dreamed of seeing a penny of the money; but the son died suddenly, and the father followed, leaving a codicil that gave everything to our friend. Humphrey had to go out to "realize" on the corset-factory; and his description of *that . . . !* Well, he came back with his money in his pocket, and the day he landed old Daunt went to smash. It all fitted in like a puzzle. I believe Neave drove straight from Euston to Daunt House: at any rate, within two months the collection was his, and at a price that made the trade sit up. Trust old Daunt for that!

I was in Rome the following spring, and you'd better believe I looked him up. A big porter glared at me from the door of the Palazzo Neave: I had almost to produce my passport to get in. But that wasn't Neave's fault—the poor fellow was so beset by people clamoring to see his collection that he had to barricade himself, literally. When I had mounted the state *Scalone,* and come on him, at the end of half a dozen echoing saloons, in the farthest, smallest *réduit* of the suite, I received the same welcome that he used to give us in his den over the wine shop.

"Well—so you've got her?" I said. For I'd caught sight of the Diana in passing against the bluish blur of an old *verdure*— just the background for her hovering loveliness. Only I rather wondered why she wasn't in the room where he sat.

He smiled. "Yes, I've got her," he returned, more calmly than I had expected.

"And all the rest of the loot?"

"Yes. I had to buy the lump."

"Had to? But you wanted to, didn't you? You used to say it was your idea of heaven—to stretch out your hand and have a great ripe sphere of beauty drop into it. I'm quoting your own words, by the way."

Neave blinked and stroked his seedy moustache. "Oh, yes. I remember the phrase. It's true—it is the last luxury." He paused, as if seeking a pretext for his lack of warmth. "The thing that bothered me was having to move. I couldn't cram all the stuff into my old quarters."

"Well, I should say not! This is rather a better setting."

He got up. "Come and take a look round. I want to show you two or three things—new attributions I've made. I'm doing the catalogue over."

The interest of showing me the things seemed to dispel the vague apathy I had felt in him. He grew keen again in detailing his redistribution of values, and above all in convicting old Daunt and his advisers of their repeated aberrations of judgment. "The miracle is that he should have got such things, knowing as little as he did what he was getting. And the egregious asses who bought for him were no better, were worse in fact, since they had all sorts of humbugging wrong reasons for admiring what old Daunt simply coveted because it belonged to some other rich man."

Never had Neave had so wondrous a field for the exercise of his perfected faculty; and I saw then how in the real, the great collector's appreciations the keenest scientific perception is suffused with imaginative sensibility, and how it is to the latter undefinable quality that in the last resort he trusts himself.

Nevertheless, I still felt the shadow of that hovering apathy, and he knew I felt it, and was always breaking off to give me reasons for it. For one thing, he wasn't used to his new quarters—hated their bigness and formality; then the requests to show his things drove him mad. "The women—oh, the women!" he wailed, and interrupted himself to describe a heavy-footed German princess who had marched past his treasures as if she were reviewing a cavalry regiment, applying an unmodulated *Mugneeficent* to everything from

the engraved gems to the Hercules torso.

"Not that she was half as bad as the other kind," he added, as if with a last effort at optimism. "The kind who discriminate and say: 'I'm not sure if it's Botticelli or Cellini I mean, but *one of that school,* at any rate.' And the worst of all are the ones who know—up to a certain point: have the schools, and the dates and the jargon pat, and yet wouldn't recognize a Phidias if it stood where they hadn't expected it."

He had all my sympathy, poor Neave; yet these were trials inseparable from the collector's lot, and not always without their secret compensations. Certainly they did not wholly explain my friend's state of mind; and for a moment I wondered if it were due to some strange disillusionment as to the quality of his treasures. But no! the Daunt collection was almost above criticism; and as we passed from one object to another I saw there was no mistaking the genuineness of Neave's pride in his possessions. The ripe sphere of beauty was his, and he had found no flaw in it as yet . . .

A year later came the amazing announcement that the Daunt collection was for sale. At first we all supposed it was a case of weeding out (though how old Daunt would have raged at the thought of anybody's weeding *his* collection!) But no—the catalogue corrected that idea. Every stick and stone was to go under the hammer. The news ran like wildfire from Rome to Berlin, from Paris to London and New York. Was Neave ruined, then? Wrong again—the dealers nosed that out in no time. He was simply selling because he chose to sell; and in due time the things came up at Christie's.

But you may be sure the trade had found an answer to the riddle; and the answer was that, on close inspection, Neave had found the things less good than he had supposed. It was a preposterous answer—but then there was no other. Neave, by this time, was pretty generally acknowledged to have the sharpest *flair* of any collector in Europe, and if he didn't choose to keep the Daunt collection it could be only because he had reason to think he could do better.

In a flash this report had gone the rounds, and the buyers were on their guard. I had run over to London to see the thing through, and it was the queerest sale I ever was at. Some of the things held their own, but a lot—and a few of the best among them—went for half their value. You see, they'd been locked up in old Daunt's house for nearly twenty years, and hardly shown to any one, so that the whole younger generation of dealers and collectors knew of them only by hearsay. Then you know the effect of suggestion in such cases. The undefinable sense we were speaking of is a ticklish instrument, easily thrown out of gear by a sudden fall of temperature; and the sharpest experts grow shy and self-distrustful when the cold current of depreciation touches them. The sale was a slaughter—and when I saw the Daunt Diana fall at the wink of a little third-rate *brocanteur* from Vienna I turned sick at the folly of my kind.

For my part, I had never believed that Neave had sold the collection because he'd "found it out"; and within a year my incredulity was justified. As soon as the things were put in circulation they were known for the marvels that they are. There was hardly a poor bit in the lot; and my wonder grew at Neave's madness. All over Europe, dealers began to fight for the spoils; and all kinds of stuff were palmed off on the unsuspecting as fragments of the Daunt collection!

Meantime, what was Neave doing? For a long time I didn't hear, and chance kept me from returning to Rome. But one day, in Paris, I ran across a dealer who had captured for a song one of the best Florentine bronzes in the Daunt collection—a marvellous *plaquette* of Donatello's. I asked him what had become of it, and he said with a grin: "I sold it the other day," naming a price that staggered me.

"Ye gods! Who paid you that for it?"

His grin broadened, and he answered: "Neave."

"*Neave?* Humphrey Neave?"

"Didn't you know he was buying back his things?"

"Nonsense!"

"He is though. Not in his own name—but he's doing it."

And he *was,* do you know—and at prices that would have made a sane man shudder! A few weeks later I ran across his tracks in London, where he was trying to get hold of a Penicaud enamel—another of his scattered treasures. Then I hunted him down at his hotel, and had it out with him.

"Look here, Neave, what are you up to?"

He wouldn't tell me at first: stared and laughed and denied. But I took him off to dine, and after dinner, while we smoked, I happened to mention casually that I had a pull over the man who had the Penicaud—and at that he broke down and confessed.

"Yes, I'm buying them back, Finney—it's true." He laughed nervously, twitching his moustache. And then he let me have the story.

"You know how I'd hungered and thirsted for the *real thing*—you quoted my own phrase to me once, about the 'ripe sphere of beauty.' So when I got my money, and Daunt lost his, almost at the same moment, I saw the hand of Providence in it. I knew that, even if I'd been younger, and had had more time, I could never hope, nowadays, to form such a collection as *that*. There was the ripe sphere, within reach; and I took it. But when I got it, and began to live with it, I found out my mistake. The transaction was a *mariage de convenance*—there'd been no wooing, no winning. Each of my little old bits—the rubbish I chucked out to make room for Daunt's glories—had its own personal history, the drama of my relation to it, of the discovery, the struggle, the capture, the first divine moment of possession. There was a romantic secret between us. And then I had absorbed its beauties one by one, they had become a part of my imagination, they held me by a hundred threads of far-reaching association. And suddenly I had expected to create this kind of personal tie between myself and a roomful of new cold alien presences—things staring at me vacantly from the depths of unknown pasts! Can you fancy a more preposterous hope? Why, my other things, my own things had wooed me as passionately as I wooed them: there was a certain little Italian bronze, a little Venus, who had drawn me, drawn me, drawn me, imploring me to rescue her from her unspeakable surroundings in a vulgar bric-a-brac shop at Biarritz, where she shrank out of sight among sham Sèvres and Dutch silver, as one has seen certain women—rare, shy, exquisite—made almost invisible by the vulgar splendors surrounding them. Well! that little Venus, who was just a specious seventeenth century attempt at an 'antique,' but who had penetrated me with her leading grace, touched me by the easily guessed story of her obscure anonymous origin, was more to me imaginatively—yes! more—than the cold bought beauty of the Daunt Diana . . ."

"The Daunt Diana!" I broke in. "Hold up, Neave—*the Daunt Diana?*"

He smiled contemptuously. "A professional beauty, my dear fellow—expected every head to be turned when she came into a room."

"Oh, Neave," I groaned.

"Yes, I know. You're thinking of what we felt that day we first saw her in London. Many a poor devil has sold his soul as the result of such a first sight! Well, I sold her instead. Do you want the truth about her? *Elle était bête à pleurer.*"

He laughed, and turned away with a shrug of disenchantment.

"And so you're impenitent?" I insisted. "And yet you're buying some of the things back?"

Neave laughed again, ironically. "I knew you'd find me out and call me to account. Well, yes: I'm buying back." He stood before me, half sheepish, half defiant. "I'm buying back because there's nothing else as good in the market. And because I've a queer feeling that, this time, they'll be *mine*. But I'm ruining myself at the game!" he confessed.

It was true: Neave was ruining himself. And he's gone on ruining himself ever since, till now the job's pretty nearly done. Bit by bit, year by year, he has gathered in his scattered treasures, at higher prices than the dealers ever dreamed of getting for them. There are fabulous details in the story of his quest. Now and then I ran across him, and was able to help him recover a fragment; and it was touching to see his delight in the moment of reunion. Finally, about two years ago, we met in Paris, and he told me he had got back all the important pieces except the Diana.

"The Diana? But you told me you didn't care for her."

"Didn't care?" He leaned across the restaurant table that divided us. "Well, no, in a sense I didn't. I wanted her to want me, you see; and she didn't then! Whereas now she's crying to me to come to her. You know where she is?" he broke off.

Yes, I knew: in the center of Mrs. Willy P. Goldmark's yellow-and-gold drawing-room, under a thousand-candle-power chandelier, with reflectors aimed at her from every point of the compass. I had seen her, wincing and shivering there in her outraged nudity, at one of the Goldmark "crushes."

"But you can't get her, Neave," I objected.

"No, I can't get her," he said.

Well, last month I was in Rome, for the first time in six or seven years, and of course I looked about for Neave. The Palazzo Neave was let to some rich Russians, and the new porter didn't know where the proprietor lived. But I got on his trail easily enough, and it led me to a strange old place in the Trastevere, a crevassed black palace turned tenement house, and fluttering with pauper linen. I found Neave under the leads, in two or three cold rooms that smelt of the *cuisine* of all his neighbors: a poor shrunken figure, smaller and shabbier than ever, yet more alive than when we had made the tour of his collection in the Palazzo Neave.

The collection was around him again, not displayed in tall cabinets and on marble tables, but huddled on shelves, perched on chairs, crammed in corners, putting the gleam of bronze, the lustre of marble, the opalescence of old glass, into all the angles of his dim rooms. There they were, the presences that had stared at him down the vistas of Daunt House, and shone in cold transplanted beauty under his own cornices: there they were, gathered about him in humble promiscuity, like superb wild creatures tamed to become the familiars of some harmless wizard.

As we went from bit to bit, as he lifted one piece after another, and held it to the light, I saw in his hands the same tremor that I had noticed when he first handled the same objects at Daunt House. All his life was in his fingertips, and it seemed to communicate life to the things he touched. But you'll think me infected by his mysticism if I tell you they gained new beauty while he held them . . .

We went the rounds slowly and reverently; and then, when I supposed our inspection was over, and was turning to take my leave, he opened a door I had not noticed, and showed me into a room beyond. It was a mere monastic cell, scarcely large enough for his narrow bed and the chest which probably held his few clothes; but there, in a niche, at the foot of the bed—there stood the Daunt Diana.

I gasped at the sight and turned to him; and he looked back at me without speaking.

"In the name of magic, Neave, how did you do it?"

He smiled as if from the depths of some secret rapture. "Call it magic, if you like; but I ruined myself doing it," he said.

I stared at him in silence, breathless with the madness of it; and suddenly, red to the ears, he flung out his confession. "I lied to you that day in London—the day I said I didn't care for her. I always cared—always worshipped—always wanted her. But she wasn't mine then, and I knew it, and she knew it . . . and now at last we understand each other." He looked at me shyly, and then glanced about the bare room. "The setting isn't worthy of her, I know; she was meant for glories I can't give her; but beautiful things, my dear Finney, like beautiful spirits, live in houses not made with hands . . ."

His face shone with an extraordinary kind of light as he spoke; and I saw he'd got hold of the secret we're all after. No, the setting isn't worthy of her, if you like. The rooms are as shabby and mean as those we used to see him in years ago over the wine shop. I'm not sure they're not shabbier and meaner. But she rules there at last, she shines and hovers there above him, and there at night, I doubt not, comes down from her cloud to give him the Latmian kiss . . .

The Debt

I

YOU remember—it's not so long ago—the talk there was about Dredge's "Arrival of the Fittest"? The talk has subsided, but the book of course remains: stands up, in fact, as the tallest thing of its kind since—well, I'd almost said since "The Origin of Species."

I'm not wrong, at any rate, in calling it the most important contribution yet made to the development of the Darwinian theory, or rather to the solution of the awkward problem about which that theory has had to make such a circuit. Dredge's hypothesis will be contested, may one day be disproved; but at least it has swept out of the way all previous conjectures, including of course Lanfear's great attempt; and for our generation of scientific investigators it will serve as the first safe bridge across a murderous black whirlpool.

It's all very interesting—there are few things more stirring to the imagination than that projection of the new hypothesis, light as a cobweb and strong as steel, across the intellectual abyss; but, for an idle observer of human motives, the other, the personal, side of Dredge's case is even more interesting and arresting.

Personal side? You didn't know there was one? Pictured him simply as a thinking machine, a highly specialized instrument of precision, the result of a long series of "adaptations," as his own jargon would put it? Well, I don't wonder—if you've met him. He does give the impression of being something out of his own laboratory: a delicate instrument that reveals wonders to the initiated, but is useless in an ordinary hand.

In his youth it was just the other way. I knew him twenty years ago, as an awkward lad whom young Archie Lanfear had picked up at college, and brought home for a visit. I happened to be staying at the Lanfears' when the boys arrived, and I shall never forget Dredge's first appearance on the scene. You know the Lanfears always lived very simply. That summer they had gone to Buzzard's Bay, in order that Professor Lanfear should be near the Biological Station at Wood's Holl, and they were picnicking in a kind of sketchy bungalow without any attempt at luxury. But Galen Dredge couldn't have been more awe-struck if he'd been suddenly plunged into a Fifth Avenue ballroom. He nearly knocked his head against the low doorway, and in dodging this peril trod heavily on Mabel Lanfear's foot, and became hopelessly entangled in her mother's draperies—though how he managed it I never knew, for Mrs. Lanfear's dowdy muslins ran to no excess of train.

When the Professor himself came in it was ten times worse, and I saw then that Dredge's emotion was a tribute to the great man's presence. That made the boy interesting, and I began to watch. Archie, always enthusiastic but vague, had said: "Oh, he's a tremendous chap—you'll see—" but I hadn't expected to see quite so early. Lanfear's vision, of course, was sharper than mine; and the next morning he had carried Dredge off to the Biological Station. That was the way it began.

Dredge is the son of a Baptist minister. He comes from East Lethe, New York State, and was working his way through college—waiting at White Mountain hotels in summer—when Archie Lanfear ran across him. There were eight children in the family, and the mother was an invalid. Dredge never had a penny from his father after he was fourteen; but his mother wanted him to be a scholar, and "kept at him," as he put it, in the hope of his going back to "teach school" at East Lethe. He developed slowly, as the scientific mind generally does, and was still adrift about himself and his tendencies when Archie took him down to Buzzard's Bay. But he had read Lanfear's "Utility and Variation," and had always been a patient and curious observer of nature. And his first meeting with Lanfear explained him to himself. It didn't, however, enable him to explain himself to others, and for a long time he remained, to all but Lanfear, an object of incredulity and conjecture.

"*Why* my husband wants him about—" poor Mrs. Lanfear, the kindest of women, privately lamented to her friends; for Dredge, at that time—they kept him all summer at the bungalow— had one of the most encumbering personalities you can imagine. He was as inexpressive as he is today, and yet oddly obtrusive: one of those uncomfortable presences whose silence is an interruption.

The poor Lanfears almost died of him that summer, and the pity of it was that he never suspected it, but continued to lavish on them a floundering devotion as inconvenient as the endearments of a dripping dog. He was full of all sorts of raw enthusiasms, which he forced on any one who would listen when his first shyness had worn off. You can't see him spouting sentimental poetry, can you? Yet I've known him to petrify a whole group of Mrs. Lanfear's callers by suddenly discharging on them, in the strident drawl of his state, "Barbara Frietchie" or "The Queen of the May." His taste in literature was uniformly bad, but very definite, and far more dogmatic than his views on biological questions. In his scientific judgments he showed, even then, a temperance remarkable in one so young; but in literature he was a furious propagandist, aggressive, disputatious, and extremely sensitive to adverse opinion.

Lanfear, of course, had been struck from the first by his gift of observation, and by the fact that his eagerness to learn was offset by his reluctance to conclude. I remember Lanfear's telling me that he had never known a lad of Dredge's age who gave such promise of uniting an aptitude for general ideas with the plodding patience of the observer. Of course when Lanfear talked like that of a young biologist his fate was sealed. There could be no question of Dredge's going back to "teach school" at East Lethe. He must take a course in biology at Columbia, spend his vacations at the Wood's Holl laboratory, and then, if possible, go to Germany for a year or two.

All this meant his virtual adoption by the Lanfears. Most of Lanfear's fortune went in helping young students to a start, and he devoted a liberal subsidy to Dredge.

"Dredge will be my biggest dividend—you'll see!" he used to say, in the chrysalis days when poor Galen was known to the world of science only as a slouching presence in Mrs. Lanfear's drawing-room. And Dredge, it must be said, took his obligations simply, with the dignity, and quiet consciousness of his own worth, which in such cases saves the beneficiary from abjectness. He seemed to trust himself as fully as Lanfear trusted him.

The comic part of it was that his only idea of making what is known as "a return" was to devote himself to the Professor's family.

When I hear pretty women lamenting that they can't coax Professor Dredge out of his laboratory I remember Mabel Lanfear's cry to me: "If Galen would only keep away!" When Mabel fell on the ice and broke her leg, Galen walked seven miles in a blizzard to get a surgeon; but if he did her this service one day in the year, he bored her by being in the way for the other three hundred and sixty-four. One would have imagined at that time that he thought his perpetual presence the greatest gift he could bestow; for, except on the occasion of his fetching the surgeon, I don't remember his taking any other way of expressing his gratitude.

In love with Mabel? Not a bit! But the queer thing was that he *did* have a passion in those days—a blind hopeless passion for Mrs. Lanfear! Yes: I know what I'm saying. I mean Mrs. Lanfear, the Professor's wife, poor Mrs. Lanfear, with her tight hair and her loose shape, her blameless brow and earnest eye-glasses, and her perpetual air of mild misapprehension. I can see Dredge cowering, long and many-jointed, in a small drawing-room chair, one square-toed shoe coiled round an exposed ankle, his knees clasped in a knot of knuckles, and his spectacles perpetually seeking Mrs. Lanfear's eye-glasses. I never knew if the poor lady was aware of the sentiment she inspired, but her children observed it, and it provoked them to irreverent mirth. Galen was the predestined butt of Mabel and Archie; and secure in their mother's obtuseness, and in her worshipper's timidity, they allowed themselves a latitude of banter that sometimes made their audience shiver. Dredge meanwhile was going on obstinately with his work. Now and then he had fits of idleness, when he lapsed into a state of sulky inertia from which even Lanfear's remonstrances could not rouse him. Once, just before an examination, he suddenly went off to the Maine woods for two weeks, came back, and failed to pass. I don't know if his benefactor ever lost hope; but at times his confidence must have been sorely strained. The queer part of it was that when Dredge emerged from these eclipses he seemed keener and more active than ever. His slowly growing intelligence probably needed its periodical pauses of assimilation; and Lanfear was wonderfully patient.

At last Dredge finished his course and went to Germany; and when he came back he was a new man—was, in fact, the Dredge we all know. He seemed to have shed his encumbering personality, and have come to life as a disembodied intelligence. His fidelity to

His spectacles perpetually sought Mrs. Lanfear's eye-glasses.

the Lanfears was unchanged; but he showed it negatively, by his discretions and abstentions. I have an idea that Mabel was less disposed to laugh at him, might even have been induced to softer sentiments; but I doubt if Dredge even noticed the change. As for his ex-goddess, he seemed to regard her as a motherly household divinity, the guardian genius of the darning needle; but on Professor Lanfear he looked with a deepening reverence. If the rest of the family had diminished in his eyes, its head had grown even greater.

II

FROM that day Dredge's progress continued steadily. If not always perceptible to the untrained eye, in Lanfear's sight it never flagged, and the great man began to associate Dredge with his work, and to lean on him more and more. Lanfear's health was already failing, and in my confidential talks with him I saw how he counted on Dredge to continue and develop his teachings. If he did not describe the young man as his predestined Huxley, it was because any such comparison between himself and his great predecessors would have been distasteful to him; but he evidently felt that it would be Dredge's part to reveal him to posterity. And the young man seemed at that time to take the same view. When he was not busy about Lanfear's work he was recording their conversations with the diligence of a biographer and the accuracy of a naturalist. Any attempt to question Lanfear's theories or to minimize his achievement, roused in his disciple the only flashes of wrath I have ever seen a scientific discussion provoke in him. In defending his master he became almost as intemperate as in the early period of his literary passions.

Such filial devotion must have been all the more precious to Lanfear because, about that time, it became evident that Archie would never carry on his father's work. He had begun brilliantly, you may remember, by a little paper on *Limulus Polyphemus* that attracted a good deal of notice when it appeared; but gradually his zoological ardor yielded to a passion for the violin, which was followed by a plunge into physics. At present, after a side-glance at the drama, I understand he's devoting what is left of his father's money to archaeological explorations in Asia Minor.

"Archie's got a delightful little mind," Lanfear used to say to me, rather wistfully, "but it's just a highly polished surface held up to the show as it passes. Dredge's mind takes in only a bit at a time, but the bit stays, and other bits are joined to it, in a hard mosaic of fact, of which imagination weaves the pattern. I saw just how it would be years ago, where my boy used to take my meaning in a flash, and answer me with clever objections, while Galen disappeared into one of his fathomless silences, and then came to the surface like a dripping retriever, a long way beyond Archie's objections, and with an answer to them in his mouth."

It was about this time that the crowning satisfaction of Lanfear's career came to him: I mean, of course, John Weyman's gift to Columbia of the Lanfear Laboratory, and the founding, in connection with it, of a chair of Experimental Evolution. Weyman had always taken an interest in Lanfear's work, but no one had supposed that his interest would express itself so magnificently. The honor came to Lanfear at a time when he was fighting an accumulation of troubles: failing health, the money difficulties resulting from his irrepressible generosity, his disappointment about Archie's career, and perhaps also the persistent attacks of the new school of German zoologists.

"If I hadn't Galen I should feel the game was up," he said to me once, in a fit of half-real, half-mocking despondency. "But he'll do what I haven't time to do myself, and what my boy can't do for me."

That meant that he would answer the critics, and triumphantly reaffirm Lanfear's theory, which had been rudely shaken, but not dislodged.

"A scientific hypothesis lasts till there's something else to put in its place. People who want to get across a river will use the old bridge till the new one's built. And I don't see any one who's particularly anxious, in this case, to take a contract for the new one," Lanfear ended; and I remember answering with a laugh: "Not while Horatius Dredge holds the other."

It was generally known that Lanfear had not long to live, and the Laboratory was hardly opened before the question of his successor in the chair of Experimental Evolution began to be a matter of public discussion. It was conceded that whoever followed him ought to be a man of achieved reputation, some one carrying, as the French say, a considerable "baggage." At the same time, even Lanfear's critics felt that he should be succeeded by a man who held his views and would continue his teaching. This was not in itself a difficulty, for German criticism had so far been mainly negative, and there were plenty of good men who, while they questioned the permanent validity of Lanfear's conclusions, were yet ready to accept them for their provisional usefulness. And then there was the added inducement of the Laboratory! The Columbia Professor of Experimental Evolution has at his disposal the most complete instrument of biological research that modern ingenuity has yet produced; and it's not only in theology or politics *que Paris vaut bien une messe!* There was no trouble about finding a candidate; but the whole thing turned on Lanfear's decision, since it was tacitly understood that, by Weyman's wish, he was to select his successor. And what a cry there was when he selected Galen Dredge!

Not in the scientific world, though. The specialists were beginning to know about Dredge. His remarkable paper on Sexual Dimorphism had been translated into several languages, and a furious polemic had broken out over it. When a young fellow can get the big men fighting over him his future is pretty well assured. But Dredge was only thirty-four, and some people seemed to feel that there was a kind of deflected nepotism in Lanfear's choice.

"If he could choose Dredge he might as well have chosen his own son," I've heard it said; and the irony was that Archie—will you believe it?—actually thought so himself! But Lanfear had Weyman behind him, and when the end came the Faculty at once appointed Galen Dredge to the chair of Experimental Evolution.

For the first two years things went quietly, along accustomed lines. Dredge simply continued the course which Lanfear's death had interrupted. He lectured well even then, with a persuasive simplicity surprising in the inarticulate creature one knew him for. But haven't you noticed that certain personalities reveal themselves only in the more impersonal relations of life? It's as if they woke only to collective contacts, and the single consciousness were an unmeaning fragment to them.

If there was anything to criticize in that first part of the course, it was the avoidance of general ideas, of those brilliant rockets of conjecture that Lanfear's students were used to seeing him fling across the darkness. I remember once saying this to Archie, who, having forgotten his absurd disappointment, had returned to his old allegiance to Dredge.

"Oh, that's Galen all over. He doesn't want to jump into the ring till he has a big swishing knock-down argument in his fist. He'll wait twenty years if he has to. That's his strength: he's never afraid to wait."

I thought this shrewd of Archie, as well as generous; and I saw the wisdom of Dredge's course. As Lanfear himself had said, his theory was safe enough till somebody found a more attractive one; and before that day Dredge would probably have accumulated sufficient proof to crystallize the fluid hypothesis.

III

THE third winter I was off collecting in Central America, and didn't get back till Dredge's course had been going for a couple of months. The very day I turned up in town Archie Lanfear descended on me with a summons from his mother. I was wanted at once at a family council.

I found the Lanfear ladies in a state of explosive distress, which Archie's own indignation hardly made more intelligible. But gradually I put together their fragmentary charges, and learned that Dredge's lectures were turning into an organized assault on his master's doctrine.

"It amounts to just this," Archie said, controlling his women with the masterful gesture of the weak man. "Galen has simply turned round and betrayed my father."

"Just for a handful of silver he left us," Mabel sobbed in parenthesis, while Mrs. Lanfear tearfully cited Hamlet.

Archie silenced them again. "The ugly part of it is that he must have had this up his sleeve for years. He must have known when he was asked to succeed my father what use he meant to make of his opportunity. What he's doing isn't the result of a hasty conclusion: it means years of work and preparation."

Archie broke off to explain himself. He had returned from Europe the week before, and had learned on arriving that Dredge's lectures were stirring the world of science as nothing had stirred it since Lanfear's "Utility and Variation." And the incredible affront was that they owed their success to the fact of being an attempted refutation of Lanfear's great work.

I own that I was staggered: the case looked ugly, as Archie said. And there was a veil of reticence, of secrecy, about Dredge, that always kept his conduct in a half-light of uncertainty. Of some men one would have said off-hand: "It's impossible!" But one couldn't affirm it of him.

Archie hadn't seen him as yet; and Mrs. Lanfear had sent for me because she wished me to be present at the interview between the two men. The Lanfear ladies had a touching belief in Archie's violence: they thought him as terrible as a natural force. My own idea was that if there were any broken bones they wouldn't be Dredge's; but I was too curious as to the outcome not to be glad to offer my services as moderator.

First, however, I wanted to hear one of the lectures; and I went the next afternoon. The hall was jammed, and I saw, as soon as Dredge appeared, what increased security and ease the sympathy of his audience had given him. He had been clear the year before, now he was also eloquent. The lecture was a remarkable effort: you'll find the gist of it in Chapter VII of "The Arrival of the Fittest." Archie sat at my side in a white rage; he was too intelligent not to measure the extent of the disaster. And I was almost as indignant as he when we went to see Dredge the next day.

I saw at a glance that the latter suspected nothing; and it was characteristic of him that he began by questioning me about my finds, and only afterward turned to reproach Archie for having been back a week without letting him know.

"You know I'm up to my neck in this job. Why in the world didn't you hunt me up before this?"

The question was exasperating, and I could understand Archie's stammer of wrath.

"Hunt you up? Hunt you up? What the deuce are you made of,

to ask me such a question instead of wondering why I'm here now?"

Dredge bent his slow calm scrutiny on his friend's agitated face; then he turned to me.

"What's the matter?" he said simply.

"The matter?" shrieked Archie, his fist hovering excitedly above the desk by which he stood; but Dredge, with unwonted quickness, caught the fist as it descended.

"Careful—I've got a *Kallima* in that jar there." He pushed a chair forward, and added quietly: "Sit down."

Archie, ignoring the gesture, towered pale and avenging in his place; and Dredge, after a moment, took the chair himself.

"The matter?" Archie reiterated. "Are you so lost to all sense of decency and honor that you can put that question in good faith? Don't you really know what's the matter?"

Dredge smiled slowly. "There are so few things one really *knows.*"

"Oh, damn your scientific hair-splitting! Don't you know you're insulting my father's memory?"

Dredge thoughtfully turned his spectacles from one of us to the other.

"Oh, that's it, is it? Then you'd better sit down. If you don't see at once it'll take some time to make you."

Archie burst into an ironic laugh.

"I rather think it will!" he retorted.

"Sit down, Archie," I said, setting the example; and he obeyed, with a gesture that made his consent a protest.

Dredge seemed to notice nothing beyond the fact that his visitors were seated. He reached for his pipe, and filled it with the care which the habit of delicate manipulations gave to all the motions of his long knotty hands.

"It's about the lectures?" he said.

Archie's answer was a deep scornful breath.

"You've only been back a week, so you've only heard one, I suppose?"

"It was not necessary to hear even that one. You must know the talk they're making. If notoriety is what you're after—"

"Well, I'm not sorry to make a noise," said Dredge, putting a match to his pipe.

Archie bounded in his chair. "There's no easier way of doing it than to attack a man who can't answer you!"

Dredge raised a sobering hand. "Hold on. Perhaps you and I don't mean the same thing. Tell me first what's in your mind."

The question steadied Archie, who turned on Dredge a countenance really eloquent with filial indignation.

"It's an odd question for you to ask; it makes me wonder what's in *yours*. Not much thought of my father, at any rate, or you couldn't stand in his place and use the chance he's given you to push yourself at his expense."

Dredge received this in silence, puffing slowly at his pipe.

"Is that the way it strikes you?" he asked at length.

"God! It's the way it would strike most men."

He turned to me. "You too?"

"I can see how Archie feels," I said.

"That I am attacking his father's memory to glorify myself?"

"Well, not precisely: I think what he really feels is that, if your convictions didn't permit you to continue his father's teaching, you might perhaps have done better to sever your connection with the Lanfear lectureship."

"Then you and he regard the Lanfear lectureship as having been founded to perpetuate a dogma, not to try and get at the truth?"

"Certainly not," Archie broke in. "But there's a question of taste, of delicacy, involved in the case that can't be decided on abstract principles. We know as well as you that my father meant the laboratory and the lectureship to serve the ends of science, at whatever cost to his own special convictions; what we feel—and you don't seem to—is that you're the last man to put them to that particular use; and I don't want to remind you why."

A slight redness rose through Dredge's sallow skin. "You needn't," he said. "It's because he pulled me out of my hole, woke me up, made me, shoved me off from the shore. Because he saved me ten or twenty years of muddled effort, and put me where I am at an age when my best working years are still ahead of me. Every one knows that's what your father did for me, but I'm the only person who knows the time and trouble it took."

It was well said, and I glanced quickly at Archie, who was never closed to generous emotions.

"Well, then——?" he said, flushing also.

"Well, then," Dredge continued, his voice deepening and losing its nasal edge, "I had to pay him back, didn't I?"

The sudden drop flung Archie back on his prepared attitude of irony. "It would be the natural inference—with most men."

"Just so. And I'm not so very different. I knew your father wanted a successor—some one who'd try and tie up the loose ends. And I took the lectureship with that object."

"And you're using it to tear the whole fabric to pieces!"

Dredge paused to relight his pipe. "Looks that way," he conceded, "This year anyhow."

"This year——?" Archie echoed.

"Yes. When I took up the job I saw it just as your father left it. Or rather, I didn't see any other way of going on with it. The change came gradually, as I worked."

"Gradually? So that you had time to look round you, to know where you were, to see that you were fatally committed to undoing the work he had done?"

"Oh, yes—I had time," Dredge conceded.

"And yet you kept the chair and went on with the course?"

Dredge refilled his pipe, and then turned in his seat so that he looked squarely at Archie.

"What would your father have done in my place?" he asked.

"In your place——?"

"Yes: supposing he'd found out the things I've found out in the last year or two. You'll see what they are, and how much they count, if you'll run over the report of the lectures. If your father'd been alive he might have come across the same facts just as easily."

There was a silence which Archie at last broke by saying: "But he didn't, and you did. There's the difference."

"The difference? What difference? Would your father have suppressed the facts if he'd found them? It's *you* who insult his memory by implying it! And if I'd brought them to him, would he have used his hold over me to get me to suppress them?"

"Certainly not. But can't you see it's his death that makes the difference? He's not here to defend his case."

Dredge laughed, but not unkindly. "My dear Archie, your father wasn't one of the kind who bother to defend their case. Men like him are the masters, not the servants, of their theories. They respect an idea only as long as it's of use to them; when its usefulness ends they chuck it out. And that's what your father would have done."

Archie reddened. "Don't you assume a good deal in taking it for granted that he would have had to do so in this particular case?"

Dredge reflected. "Yes: I was going too far. Each of us can only answer for himself. But to my mind your father's theory is refuted."

"And you don't hesitate to be the man to do it?"

"Should I have been of any use if I had? And did your father ever ask anything of me but to be of as much use as I could?"

It was Archie's turn to reflect. "No. That was what he always wanted, of course."

"That's the way I've always felt. The first day he took me away from East Lethe I knew the debt I was piling up against him, and I never had any doubt as to how I'd pay it, or how he'd want it paid. He didn't pick me out and train me for any object but to carry on the light. Do you suppose he'd have wanted me to snuff it out because it happened to light up a fact *he* didn't fancy? I'm using *his* oil to feed my torch with: yes, but it isn't really his torch or mine, or his oil or mine: they belong to each of us till we drop and hand them on."

Archie turned a sobered glance on him. "I see your point. But if the job had to be done I don't see that you need have done it from his chair."

"There's where we differ. If I did it at all I had to do it in the best way, and with all the authority his backing gave me. If I owe your father anything, I owe him that. It would have made him sick to see the job badly done. And don't you see that the way to honor him, and show what he's done for science, was to spare no advantage in my attack on him—that I'm proving the strength of his position by the desperateness of my assault?" Dredge paused and squared his lounging shoulders. "After all," he added, "he's not down yet, and if I leave him standing I guess it'll be some time before anybody else cares to tackle him."

There was a silence between the two men; then Dredge continued in a lighter tone: "There's one thing, though, that we're both in danger of forgetting: and that is how little, in the long run, it all counts either way." He smiled a little at Archie's indignant gesture. "The most we can any of us do—even by such a magnificent effort as your father's—is to turn the great marching army a hair's breadth nearer what seems to us the right direction; if one of us drops out, here and there, the loss of headway's hardly perceptible. And that's what I'm coming to now."

He rose from his seat, and walked across to the hearth; then, cautiously resting his shoulder-blades against the mantel-shelf jammed with miscellaneous specimens, he bent his musing spectacles on Archie.

"Your father would have understood why I've done what I'm doing; but that's no reason why the rest of you should. And I rather think it's the rest of you who've suffered most from me. He always knew what I was *there for,* and that must have been some comfort even when I was most in the way; but I was just an ordinary nuisance to you and your mother and Mabel. You were all too kind to let me see it at the time, but I've seen it since, and it makes me feel that, after all, the settling of this matter lies with you. If it hurts you to have me go on with my examination of your father's theory, I'm ready to drop the lectures tomorrow, and trust to the Lanfear Laboratory to breed up a young chap who'll knock us both out in time. You've only got to say the word."

There was a pause while Dredge turned and laid his extinguished pipe carefully between a jar of embryo sea-urchins and a colony of regenerating planarians.

Then Archie rose and held out his hand.

"No" he said simply; "go on."

Full Circle

I

GEOFFREY BETTON woke rather late—so late that the winter sunlight sliding across his bedroom carpet struck his eyes as he turned on the pillow.

Strett, the valet, had been in, drawn the bath in the adjoining dressing-room, placed the crystal and silver cigarette-box at his side, put a match to the fire, and thrown open the windows to the bright morning air. It brought in, on the glitter of sun, all the crisp morning noises—those piercing notes of the American thoroughfare that seem to take a sharper vibration from the clearness of the medium through which they pass.

Betton raised himself languidly. That was the voice of Fifth Avenue below his windows. He remembered that, when he moved into his rooms eighteen months before, the sound had been like music to him: the complex orchestration to which the tune of his new life was set. Now it filled him with disgust and weariness, since it had become the symbol of the hurry and noise of that new life. He had been far less hurried in the old days when he had to be up at seven, and down at the office sharp at nine. Now that he got up when he chose, and his life had no fixed framework of duties, the hours hunted him like a pack of blood-hounds.

He dropped back on his pillow with a groan. Yes—not a year ago there had been a positively sensuous joy in getting out of bed, feeling under his bare feet the softness of the warm red carpet, and entering the shining sanctuary where his great porcelain bath proffered its renovating flood. But then a year ago he could still call up the horror of the communal plunge at his earlier lodgings: the listening for other bathers, the dodging of shrouded ladies in "crimping"-pins, the cold wait on the landing, the descent into a blotchy tin bath, and the effort to identify one's soap and nailbrush among the promiscuous implements of ablution. That memory had faded now, and Betton saw only the dark hours to which his tiled temple of refreshment formed a kind of glittering antechamber. For after his bath came his breakfast, and on the breakfast tray his letters. His letters!

He remembered—and *that* memory had not faded!—the thrill with which, in the early days of his celebrity, he had opened the first missive in a strange feminine hand: the letter beginning: "I wonder if you'll mind an unknown reader's telling you all that your book has been to her?"

Mind? Ye gods, he minded now! For more than a year after the publication of "Diadems and Faggots" the letters, the inane indiscriminate letters of commendation, of criticism, of interrogation, had poured in on him by every post. Hundreds of unknown readers had told him with unsparing detail all that his book had been to them. And the wonder of it was, when all was said and done, that it had really been so little—that when their thick broth of praise was strained through the author's searching vanity there remained to him so small a sediment of definite specific understanding! No—it was always the same thing, over and over and over again—the same vague gush of adjectives, the same incorrigible tendency to estimate his effort according to each writer's personal preferences, instead of regarding it as a work of art, a thing to be measured by fixed standards!

He smiled to think how little, at first, he had felt the vanity of it all. He had found a savor even in the grosser evidences of popularity: the advertisements of his book, the daily shower of "clippings," the sense that, when he entered a restaurant or a theater, people nudged each other and said "That's Betton." Yes, the publicity had been sweet to him—at first. He had been touched by the sympathy of his fellow-men: had thought indulgently of the world, as a better place than the failures and the dyspeptics would acknowledge. And then his success began to submerge him: he gasped under the thickening shower of letters. His admirers were really unappeasable. And they wanted him to do such ridiculous things—to give lectures, to head movements, to be tendered receptions, to speak at banquets, to address mothers, to plead for orphans, to go up in balloons, to lead the struggle for sterilized milk. They wanted his photograph for literary supplements, his autograph for charity bazaars, his name on committees, literary, educational, and social; above all, they wanted his opinion on everything: on Christianity, Buddhism, tight lacing, the drug habit, democratic government, female suffrage and love. Perhaps the chief benefit of this demand was his incidentally learning from it how few opinions he really had: the only one that remained with him was a rooted horror of all forms of correspondence. He had been unspeakably thankful when the letters began to fall off.

"Diadems and Faggots" was now two years old, and the moment was at hand when its author might have counted on regaining the blessed shelter of oblivion—if only he had not written another book! For it was the worst part of his plight that the result of his first folly had goaded him to the perpetration of the next—that one of the incentives (hideous thought!) to his new work had been the desire to extend and perpetuate his popularity. And this very week the book was to come out, and the letters, the cursed letters, would begin again!

Wistfully, almost plaintively, he looked at the breakfast-tray with which Strett presently appeared. It bore only two notes and the morning journals, but he knew that within the week it would groan under its epistolary burden. The very newspapers flung the fact at him as he opened them.

READY ON MONDAY.
GEOFFREY BETTON'S NEW NOVEL
ABUNDANCE.
BY THE AUTHOR OF "DIADEMS AND FAGGOTS."
FIRST EDITION OF ONE HUNDRED AND FIFTY THOUSAND
ALREADY SOLD OUT.
ORDER NOW.

A hundred and fifty thousand volumes! And an average of three readers to each! Half a million of people would be reading him within a week, and every one of them would write to him, and their friends and relations would write too. He laid down the paper with a shudder.

The two notes looked harmless enough, and the caligraphy of one was vaguely familiar. He opened the envelope and looked at the signature: *Duncan Vyse*. He had not seen the name in years—what on earth could Duncan Vyse have to say? He ran over the page and dropped it with a wondering exclamation, which the watchful Strett, re-entering, met by a tentative "Yes, sir?"

"Nothing. Yes—that is—" Betton picked up the note. "There's a gentleman, a Mr. Vyse, coming at ten."

Strett glanced at the clock. "Yes, sir. You'll remember that ten was the hour you appointed for the secretaries to call, sir."

Betton nodded. "I'll see Mr. Vyse first. My clothes, please."

As he got into them, in the state of nervous hurry that had become almost chronic with him, he continued to think about Duncan Vyse. They had seen a great deal of each other for the few years after both had left Harvard: the hard happy years when Betton had been grinding at his business and Vyse—poor devil!—trying to write. The novelist recalled his friend's attempts with a smile; then the memory of one small volume came back to him. It was a novel: "The Lifted Lamp." There was stuff in that, certainly. He remembered Vyse's tossing it down on his table with a gesture of despair when it came back from the last publisher. Betton, taking it up indifferently, had sat riveted till daylight. When he ended, the impression was so strong that he said to himself: "I'll tell Apthorn about it—I'll go and see him tomorrow." His own secret literary yearnings increased his desire to champion Vyse, to see him triumph over the dullness and timidity of the publishers. Apthorn was the youngest of the guild, still capable of opinions and the courage of them, a personal friend of Betton's, and, as it happened, the man afterward to become known as the privileged publisher of "Diadems and Faggots." Unluckily the next day something unexpected turned up, and Betton forgot about Vyse and his manuscript. He continued to forget for a month, and then came a note from Vyse, who was ill, and wrote to ask what his friend had done. Betton did not like to say "I've done nothing," so he left the note unanswered, and vowed again: "I'll see Apthorn."

The following day he was called to the West on business, and was away a month. When he came back, there was a third note from Vyse, who was still ill, and desperately hard up. "I'll take anything for the book, if they'll advance me two hundred dollars." Betton, full of compunction, would gladly have advanced the sum himself; but he was hard up too, and could only swear inwardly: "I'll write to Apthorn." Then he glanced again at the manuscript, and reflected:

"No—there are things in it that need explaining. I'd better see him."

Once he went so far as to telephone Apthorn, but the publisher was out. Then he finally and completely forgot.

One Sunday he went out of town, and on his return, rummaging among the papers on his desk, he missed "The Lifted Lamp," which had been gathering dust there for half a year. What the deuce could have become of it? Betton spent a feverish hour in vainly increasing the disorder of his documents, and then bethought himself of calling the maid-servant, who first indignantly denied having touched anything ("I can see that's true from the dust," Betton scathingly remarked), and then mentioned with hauteur that a young lady had called in his absence and asked to be allowed to get a book.

"A lady? Did you let her come up?"

"She said somebody'd sent her."

Vyse, of course—Vyse had sent her for his manuscript! He was always mixed up with some woman, and it was just like him to send the girl of the moment to Betton's lodgings, with instructions to force the door in his absence. Vyse had never been remarkable for delicacy. Betton, furious, glanced over his table to see if any of his own effects were missing—one couldn't tell, with the company Vyse kept!—and then dismissed the matter from his mind, with a vague sense of magnanimity in doing so. He felt himself exonerated by Vyse's conduct.

The sense of magnanimity was still uppermost when the valet opened the door to announce "Mr. Vyse," and Betton, a moment later, crossed the threshold of his pleasant library.

His first thought was that the man facing him from the hearth-rug was the very Duncan Vyse of old: small, starved, bleached-looking, with the same sidelong movements, the same air of anemic truculence. Only he had grown shabbier, and bald.

Betton held out a hospitable hand.

"This is a good surprise! Glad you looked me up, my dear fellow."

Vyse's palm was damp and bony: he had always had a disagreeable hand.

"You got my note? You know what I've come for?"

"About the secretaryship? (Sit down.) Is that really serious?"

Betton lowered himself luxuriously into one of his vast Maple arm-chairs. He had grown stouter in the last year, and the cushion behind him fitted comfortably into the crease of his nape. As he leaned back he caught sight of his image in the mirror between the windows, and reflected uneasily that Vyse would not find *him* unchanged.

"Serious?" Vyse rejoined. "Why not? Aren't *you?"*

"Oh, perfectly." Betton laughed apologetically. "Only—well, the fact is, you may not understand what rubbish a secretary of mine would have to deal with. In advertising for one I never imagined—I didn't aspire to any one above the ordinary hack."

"I'm the ordinary hack," said Vyse drily.

Betton's affable gesture protested. "My dear fellow——. You see it's not business—what I'm in now," he continued with a laugh.

Vyse's thin lips seemed to form a noiseless "*Isn't* it?" which they instantly transposed into the audible reply: "I judged from your advertisement that you want some one to relieve you in your literary work. Dictation, short-hand—that kind of thing?"

"Well, no: not that either. I type my own things. What I'm looking for is somebody who won't be above tackling my correspondence."

Vyse looked slightly surprised. "I should be glad of the job," he then said.

Betton began to feel a vague embarrassment. He had supposed that such a proposal would be instantly rejected. "It would be only for an hour or two a day—if you're doing any writing of your own?" he threw out interrogatively.

"No. I've given all that up. I'm in an office now—business. But it doesn't take all my time, or pay enough to keep me alive."

"In that case, my dear fellow—if you could come every morning; but it's mostly awful bosh, you know," Betton again broke off, with growing awkwardness.

Vyse glanced at him humorously. "What you want me to write?"

"Well, that depends——" Betton sketched the obligatory smile. "But I was thinking of the letters you'll have to answer. Letters about my books, you know—I've another one appearing next week. And I want to be beforehand now—dam the flood before it swamps me. Have you any idea of the deluge of stuff that people write to a successful novelist?"

As Betton spoke, he saw a tinge of red on Vyse's thin cheek, and his own reflected it in a richer glow of shame.

"'I mean—I mean——" he stammered helplessly.

"No, I haven't," said Vyse; "but it will be awfully jolly finding out."

There was a pause, groping and desperate on Betton's part, sardonically calm on his visitor's.

"You—you've given up writing altogether?" Betton continued.

"Yes; we've changed places, as it were." Vyse paused. "But about these letters—you dictate the answers?"

"Lord, no! That's the reason why I said I wanted somebody—er—well used to writing. I don't want to have anything to do with them—not a thing! You'll have to answer them as if they were written to *you*——"

Betton pulled himself up again, and rising in confusion jerked open one of the drawers of his writing-table.

"Here—this kind of rubbish," he said, tossing a packet of letters onto Vyse's knee.

"Oh—you keep them, do you?" said Vyse simply.

"I—well—some of them; a few of the funniest only."

Vyse slipped off the band and began to open the letters. While he was glancing over them Betton again caught his own reflection in the glass, and asked himself what impression he had made on his visitor. It occurred to him for the first time that his high-colored well-fed person presented the image of commercial rather than of intellectual achievement. He did not look like his own idea of the author of "Diadems and Faggots"—and he wondered why.

Vyse laid the letters aside. "I think I can do it—if you'll give me a notion of the tone I'm to take."

"The tone?"

"Yes—that is, if you expect me to sign your name."

"Oh, of course you're to sign for me. As for the tone, say just what you'd—well, say all you can without encouraging them to answer."

Vyse rose from his seat. "I could submit a few specimens," he suggested.

"Oh, as to that—you always wrote better than I do," said Betton handsomely.

"I've never had this kind of thing to write. When do you wish me to begin?" Vyse inquired, ignoring the tribute.

"The book's out on Monday. The deluge will probably begin about three days after. Will you turn up on Thursday at this hour?" Betton held his hand out with real heartiness. "It was great luck for me, your striking that advertisement. Don't be too harsh with my correspondents—I owe them something for having brought us together."

"I'm the ordinary hack," said Vyse drily.

II

THE deluge began punctually on the Thursday, and Vyse, arriving as punctually, had an impressive pile of letters to attack. Betton, on his way to the Park for a ride, came into the library, smoking the cigarette of indolence, to look over his secretary's shoulder.

"How many of 'em? Twenty? Good Lord! It's going to be worse than 'Diadems.' I've just had my first quiet breakfast in two years—time to read the papers and loaf. How I used to dread the sight of my letter-box! Now I shan't know that I have one."

He leaned over Vyse's chair, and the secretary handed him a letter.

"Here's rather an exceptional one—lady, evidently. I thought you might want to answer it yourself——"

"Exceptional?" Betton ran over the mauve pages and tossed them down. "Why, my dear man, I get hundreds like that. You'll have to be pretty short with her, or she'll send her photograph."

He clapped Vyse on the shoulder and turned away, humming a tune. "Stay to luncheon," he called back gaily from the threshold.

After luncheon Vyse insisted on showing a few of his answers to the first batch of letters. "If I've struck the note I won't bother you again," he urged; and Betton groaningly consented.

"My dear fellow, they're beautiful—too beautiful. I'll be let in for a correspondence with every one of these people."

Vyse, in reply, mused for a while above a blank sheet. "All right—how's this?" he said, after another interval of rapid writing.

Betton glanced over the page. "By George—by George! Won't she *see* it?" he exulted, between fear and rapture.

"It's wonderful how little people see," said Vyse reassuringly.

The letters continued to pour in for several weeks after the appearance of "Abundance." For five or six blissful days Betton did not even have his mail brought to him, trusting to Vyse to single out his personal correspondence, and to deal with the rest of the letters

according to their agreement. During those days he luxuriated in a sense of wild and lawless freedom; then gradually, he began to feel the need of fresh restraints to break, and learned that the zest of liberty lies in the escape from specific obligations. At first he was conscious only of a vague hunger but in time the craving resolved itself into a shame-faced desire to see his letters.

"After all, I hated them only because I had to answer them"; and he told Vyse carelessly that he wished all his letters submitted to him before the secretary answered them.

The first morning he pushed aside those beginning: "I have just laid down 'Abundance' after a third reading," or: "Every day for the last month I have been telephoning my bookseller to know when your novel would be out." But little by little the freshness of his interest revived, and even this stereotyped homage began to arrest his eye. At last a day came when he read all the letters, from the first word to the last, as he had done when "Diadems and Faggots" appeared. It was really a pleasure to read them, now that he was relieved of the burden of replying: his new relation to his correspondents had the glow of a love-affair unchilled by the contingency of marriage.

One day it struck him that the letters were coming in more slowly and in smaller numbers. Certainly there had been more of a rush when "Diadems and Faggots" came out. Betton began to wonder if Vyse were exercising an unauthorized discrimination, and keeping back the communications he deemed least important. This conjecture carried the novelist straight to his library, where he found Vyse bending over the writing-table with his usual inscrutable pale smile. But once there, Betton hardly knew how to frame his question, and blundered into an inquiry for a missing invitation.

"There's a note—a personal note—I ought to have had this morning. Sure you haven't kept it back by mistake among the others?"

Vyse laid down his pen. "The others? But I never keep back any."

Betton had foreseen the answer. "Not even the worst twaddle about my book?" he suggested lightly, pushing the papers about.

"Nothing. I understood you wanted to go over them all first."

"Well, perhaps it's safer," Betton conceded, as if the idea were new to him. With an embarrassed hand he continued to turn over the letters at Vyse's elbow.

"Those are yesterday's," said the secretary; "here are today's," he added, pointing to a meager trio.

"H'm—only these?" Betton took them and looked them over lingeringly. "I don't see what the deuce that chap means about the first part of 'Abundance' 'certainly justifying the title'—do you?"

Vyse was silent, and the novelist continued irritably: "Damned cheek, his writing, if he doesn't like the book. Who cares what he thinks about it, anyhow?"

And his morning ride was embittered by the discovery that it was unexpectedly disagreeable to have Vyse read any letters which did not express unqualified praise of his books. He began to fancy that there was a latent rancor, a kind of baffled sneer, under Vyse's manner; and he decided to return to the practice of having his mail brought straight to his room. In that way he could edit the letters before his secretary saw them.

Vyse made no comment on the change, and Betton was reduced to wondering whether his imperturbable composure were the mask of complete indifference or of a watchful jealousy. The latter view being more agreeable to his employer's self-esteem, the next step was to conclude that Vyse had not forgotten the episode of "The Lifted Lamp," and would naturally take a vindictive joy in any unfavorable judgments passed on his rival's work. This did not simplify the situation, for there was no denying that unfavorable criticisms preponderated in Betton's correspondence. "Abundance" was neither meeting with the unrestricted welcome of "Diadems and Faggots," nor enjoying the alternative of an animated controversy: it was simply found dull, and readers said so in language not too tactfully tempered by comparisons with its predecessor. To withhold unfavorable comments from Vyse was, therefore, to make it appear that correspondence about the book had died out; and its author, mindful of his unguarded predictions, found this even more embarrassing. The simplest solution would be to get rid of Vyse; and to this end Betton began to address his energies.

One evening, finding himself unexpectedly disengaged, he asked Vyse to dine; it had occurred to him that, in the course of an after-dinner chat, he might hint his feeling that the work he had offered his friend was unworthy so accomplished a hand.

Vyse surprised him by a momentary hesitation. "I may not have time to dress."

Betton brushed the objection aside. "What's the odds? We'll dine here—and as late as you like."

Vyse thanked him, and appeared, punctually at eight, in all the shabbiness of his daily wear. He looked paler and more shyly truculent than usual, and Betton, from the height of his florid stature, said to himself, with the sudden professional instinct for "type": "He might be an agent of something—a chap who carries deadly secrets."

Vyse, it was to appear, did carry a deadly secret; but one less perilous to society than to himself. He was simply poor—unpardonably, irremediably poor. Everything failed him, had always failed him: whatever he put his hand to went to bits.

This was the confession that, reluctantly, yet with a kind of white-lipped bravado, he flung at Betton in answer to the latter's tentative suggestion that, really, the letter-answering job wasn't worth bothering him with—a thing that any type-writer could do.

"If you mean that you're paying me more than it's worth, I'll take less," Vyse rushed out after a pause.

"Oh, my dear fellow——" Betton protested, flushing.

"What *do* you mean, then? Don't I answer the letters as you want them answered?"

Betton anxiously stroked his silken ankle. "You do it beautifully, too beautifully. I mean what I say: the work's not worthy of you. I'm ashamed to ask you——"

"Oh, hang shame," Vyse interrupted. "Do you know why I said I shouldn't have time to dress tonight? Because I haven't any evening clothes. As a matter of fact, I haven't much but the clothes I stand in. One thing after another's gone against me; all the infernal ingenuities of chance. It's been a slow Chinese torture, the kind where they keep you alive to have more fun killing you." He straightened himself with a sudden blush. "Oh, I'm all right now—getting on capitally. But I'm still walking rather a narrow plank; and if I do your work well enough—if I take your idea——"

Betton stared into the fire without answering. He knew next to nothing of Vyse's history, of the mischance or mismanagement that had brought him, with his brains and his training, to so unlikely a pass. But a pang of compunction shot through him as he remembered the manuscript of "The Lifted Lamp" gathering dust on his table for half a year.

"Not that it would have made any earthly difference—since he's evidently never been able to get the thing published." But this reflection did not wholly console Betton, and he found it impossible, at the moment, to tell Vyse that his services were not needed.

III

DURING the ensuing weeks the letters grew fewer and fewer, and Betton foresaw the approach of the fatal day when his secretary, in common decency, would have to say: "I can't draw my pay for doing nothing."

What a triumph for Vyse!

The thought was intolerable, and Betton cursed his weakness in not having dismissed the fellow before such a possibility arose.

"If I tell him I've no use for him now, he'll see straight through it, of course;—and then, hang it, he looks so poor!"

This consideration came after the other, but Betton, in rearranging them, put it first, because he thought it looked better there, and also because he immediately perceived its value in justifying a plan of action that was beginning to take shape in his mind.

"Poor devil, I'm damned if I don't do it for him!" said Betton, sitting down at his desk.

Three or four days later he sent word to Vyse that he didn't care to go over the letters any longer, and that they would once more be carried directly to the library.

The next time he lounged in, on his way to his morning ride, he found his secretary's pen in active motion.

"A lot today," Vyse told him cheerfully.

His tone irritated Betton: it had the inane optimism of the physician reassuring a discouraged patient.

"Oh, Lord—I thought it was almost over," groaned the novelist.

"No: they've just got their second wind. Here's one from a Chicago publisher—never heard the name—offering you thirty per cent. on your next novel, with an advance royalty of twenty thousand. And here's a chap who wants to syndicate it for a bunch of Sunday papers: big offer, too. That's from Ann Arbor. And this—oh, *this* one's funny!"

He held up a small scented sheet to Betton, who made no movement to receive it.

"Funny? Why's it funny?" he growled.

"Well, it's from a girl—a lady—and she thinks she's the only person who understands 'Abundance'—has the clue to it. Says she's never seen a book so misrepresented by the critics——"

"Ha, ha! That *is* good!" Betton agreed with too loud a laugh.

"This one's from a lady, too—married woman. Says she's misunderstood, and would like to correspond."

"Oh, Lord," said Betton.—"What are you looking at?" he added sharply, as Vyse continued to bend his blinking gaze on the letters.

"I was only thinking I'd never seen such short letters from women. Neither one fills the first page."

"Well, what of that?" queried Betton.

Vyse reflected. "I'd like to meet a woman like that," he said wearily; and Betton laughed again.

The letters continued to pour in, and there could be no farther question of dispensing with Vyse's services. But one morning, about three weeks later, the latter asked for a word with his employer, and Betton, on entering the library, found his secretary with half a dozen documents spread out before him.

"What's up?" queried Betton, with a touch of impatience.

Vyse was attentively scanning the outspread letters.

"I don't know: can't make out." His voice had a faint note of embarrassment. "Do you remember a note signed *Hester Macklin* that came three or four weeks ago? Married—misunderstood—Western army post—wanted to correspond?"

Betton seemed to grope among his memories; then he assented vaguely.

"A short note," Vyse went on: "the whole story in half a page. The shortness struck me so much—and the directness—that I wrote her: wrote in my own name, I mean."

"In your own name?" Betton stood amazed; then he broke into a groan.

"Good Lord, Vyse—you're incorrigible!"

The secretary pulled his thin moustache with a nervous laugh. "If you mean I'm an ass, you're right. Look here." He held out an envelope stamped with the words: "Dead Letter Office." "My effusion has come back to me marked 'unknown.' There's no such person at the address she gave you."

Betton seemed for an instant to share his secretary's embarrassment; then he burst into an uproarious laugh.

"Hoax, was it? That's rough on you, old fellow!"

Vyse shrugged his shoulders. "Yes; but the interesting question is—why on earth didn't *your* answer come back, too?"

"My answer?"

"The official one—the one I wrote in your name. If she's unknown, what's become of *that?*"

Betton's eyes were wrinkled by amusement. "Perhaps she hadn't disappeared then."

Vyse disregarded the conjecture. "Look here—I believe all these letters are a hoax," he broke out.

Betton stared at him with a face that turned slowly red and angry. "What are you talking about? All what letters?"

"These I've got spread out here: I've been comparing them. And I believe they're all written by one man."

Betton's redness turned to a purple that made his ruddy moustache seem pale. "What the devil are you driving at?" he asked.

"Well, just look at it," Vyse persisted, still bent above the letters. "I've been studying them carefully—those that have come within the last two or three weeks—and there's a queer likeness in the writing of some of them. The *g*'s are all like cork-screws. And the same phrases keep recurring—the Ann Arbor news-agent uses the same expressions as the President of the Girl's College at Euphorbia, Maine."

Betton laughed. "Aren't the critics always groaning over the shrinkage of the national vocabulary? Of course we all use the same expressions."

"Yes," said Vyse obstinately. "But how about using the same *g*'s?"

Betton laughed again, but Vyse continued without heeding him: "Look here, Betton—could Strett have written them?"

"Strett?" Betton roared. *"Strett?"* He threw himself into his armchair to shake out his mirth at greater ease.

"I'll tell you why. Strett always posts all my answers. He comes in for them every day before I leave. He posted the letter to the misunderstood party—the letter from *you* that the Dead Letter Office didn't return. I posted my own letter to her; and that came back."

A measurable silence followed the emission of this ingenious conjecture; then Betton observed with gentle irony: "Extremely neat. And of course it's no business of yours to supply any valid motive for this remarkable attention on my valet's part."

Vyse cast on him a slanting glance.

"If you've found that human conduct's generally based on valid motives——!"

"Well, outside of mad-houses it's supposed to be not quite incalculable."

Vyse had an odd smile under his thin moustache. "Every house is a mad-house at some time or another."

Betton rose with a careless shake of the shoulders. "This one will be if I talk to you much longer," he said, moving away with a laugh.

IV

BETTON did not for a moment believe that Vyse suspected the valet of having written the letters.

"Why the devil don't he say out what he thinks? He was always a tortuous chap," he grumbled inwardly.

The sense of being held under the lens of Vyse's mute scrutiny became more and more exasperating. Betton, by this time, had squared his shoulders to the fact that "Abundance" was a failure with the public: a confessed and glaring failure. The press told him so openly, and his friends emphasized the fact by their circumlocutions and evasions. Betton minded it a good deal more than he had expected, but not nearly as much as he minded Vyse's knowing it. That remained the central twinge in his diffused discomfort. And the problem of getting rid of his secretary once more engaged him.

He had set aside all sentimental pretexts for retaining Vyse; but a practical argument replaced them. "If I ship him now he'll think it's because I'm ashamed to have him see that I'm not getting any more letters."

For the letters had ceased again, almost abruptly, since Vyse had hazarded the conjecture that they were the product of Strett's devoted pen. Betton had reverted only once to the subject—to ask ironically, a day or two later, "Is Strett writing to me as much as ever?"—and, on Vyse's replying with a neutral head-shake, had added, laughing: "If you suspect *him* you'll be thinking next that I write the letters myself!"

"There are very few today," said Vyse, with an irritating evasiveness; and Betton rejoined squarely: "Oh, they'll stop soon. The book's a failure."

A few mornings later he felt a rush of shame at his own tergiversations, and stalked into the library with Vyse's sentence on his tongue.

Vyse was sitting at the table making pencil-sketches of a girl's profile. Apparently there was nothing else for him to do.

"Is that your idea of Hester Macklin?" asked Betton jovially, leaning over him.

Vyse started back with one of his anemic blushes. "I was hoping you'd be in. I wanted to speak to you. There've been no letters the last day or two," he explained.

Betton drew a quick breath of relief. The man had some sense of decency, then! He meant to dismiss himself.

"I told you so, my dear fellow; the book's a flat failure," he said, almost gaily.

Vyse made a deprecating gesture. "I don't know that I should regard the absence of letters as the final test. But I wanted to ask you if there isn't something else I can do on the days when there's no writing." He turned his glance toward the book-lined walls.

"Don't you want your library catalogued?" he asked insidiously.

"Had it done last year, thanks." Betton glanced away from Vyse's face. It was piteous how he needed the job!

"I see . . . Of course this is just a temporary lull in the letters. They'll begin again—as they did before. The people who read carefully read slowly—you haven't heard yet what *they* think."

Betton felt a rush of puerile joy at the suggestion. Actually, he hadn't thought of that!

"There was a big second crop after 'Diadems and Faggots,'" he mused aloud.

"Of course. Wait and see," said Vyse confidently.

The letters in fact began again—more gradually and in smaller numbers. But their quality was different, as Vyse had predicted. And in two cases Betton's correspondents, not content to compress into one rapid communication the thoughts inspired by his work, developed their views in a succession of really remarkable letters. One of the writers was a professor in a Western college; the other was a girl in Florida. In their language, their point of view, their reasons for appreciating "Abundance," they differed almost diametrically; but this only made the unanimity of their approval the more striking. The rush of correspondence evoked by Betton's earlier novel had produced nothing so personal, so exceptional as these communications. He had gulped the praise of "Diadems and Faggots" as undiscriminatingly as it was offered; now he knew for the first time the subtler pleasures of the palate. He tried to feign indifference, even to himself; and to Vyse he made no sign. But gradually he felt a desire to know what his secretary thought of the letters, and, above all, what he was saying in reply to them. And he resented acutely the possibility of Vyse's starting one of his clandestine correspondences with the girl in Florida. Vyse's notorious lack of delicacy had never been more vividly present to Betton's imagination; and he made up his mind to answer the letters himself.

He would keep Vyse on, of course: there were other communications that the secretary could attend to. And, if necessary, Betton would invent an occupation: he cursed his stupidity in having betrayed the fact that his books were already catalogued.

Vyse showed no surprise when Betton announced his intention of dealing personally with the two correspondents who showed so flattering a reluctance to take their leave. But Betton immediately read a criticism in his lack of comment, and put forth, on a note of challenge: "After all, one must be decent."

Vyse looked at him with an evanescent smile. "You'll have to explain that you didn't write the first answers." Betton halted. "Well—I—I more or less dictated them, didn't I?"

"Oh, virtually, they're yours, of course."

"You think I can put it that way?"

"Why not?" The secretary absently drew an arabesque on the blotting-pad. "Of course they'll keep it up longer if you write yourself," he suggested.

Betton blushed, but faced the issue. "Hang it all, I shan't be sorry. They interest me. They're remarkable letters." And Vyse, without observation, returned to his writings.

The spring, that year, was delicious to Betton. His college professor continued to address him tersely but cogently at fixed intervals, and twice a week eight serried pages came from Florida. There were other letters, too; he had the solace of feeling that at last "Abundance" was making its way, was reaching the people who, as Vyse said, read slowly because they read intelligently. But welcome as were all these proofs of his restored authority they were but the background of his happiness. His life revolved for the moment about the personality of his two chief correspondents. The professor's letters satisfied his craving for intellectual recognition, and the satisfaction he felt in them proved how completely he had lost faith in himself. He blushed to think that his opinion of his work had been swayed by the shallow judgments of a public whose taste he despised. Was it possible that he had allowed himself to think less well of "Abundance" because it was not to the taste of the average novel-reader? Such false humility was less excusable than the crudest appetite for praise: it was ridiculous to try to do conscientious work if one's self-esteem were at the mercy of popular judgments. All this the professor's letters delicately and indirectly conveyed to Betton, with the result that the author of "Abundance" began to recognize in it the ripest flower of his genius.

But if the professor understood his book, the girl from Florida understood *him;* and Betton was fully alive to the superior qualities of discernment which this implied. For his lovely correspondent his novel was but the starting point, the pretext of her discourse: he himself was her real object, and he had the delicious sense, as their exchange of thoughts proceeded, that she was interested in "Abundance" because of its author, rather than in the author because of his book. Of course she laid stress on the fact that his ideas were the object of her contemplation; but Betton's agreeable person had permitted him some insight into the incorrigible subjectiveness of female judgments, and he was pleasantly aware, from the lady's tone, that she guessed him to be neither old nor ridiculous. And suddenly he wrote to ask if he might see her . . .

The answer was long in coming. Betton fidgeted at the delay, watched, wondered, fumed; then he received the one word "Impossible."

He wrote back more urgently, and awaited the reply with increasing eagerness. A certain shyness had kept him from once more modifying the instructions regarding his mail, and Strett still carried the letters directly to Vyse. The hour when he knew they were passing under the latter's eyes was now becoming intolerable to Betton, and it was a relief when the secretary, suddenly advised of his father's illness, asked permission to absent himself for a fortnight.

Vyse departed just after Betton had despatched to Florida his second missive of entreaty, and for ten days he tasted the joy of a first perusal of his letters. The answer from Florida was not among them; but Betton said to himself "She's thinking it over," and delay, in that light, seemed favorable. So charming, in fact, was this phase of sentimental suspense that he felt a start of resentment when a telegram apprised him one morning that Vyse would return to his post that day.

Betton had slept later than usual, and, springing out of bed with the telegram in his hand, he learned from the clock that his secretary was due in half an hour. He reflected that the morning's mail must long since be in; and, too impatient to wait for its appearance with his breakfast-tray, he threw on a dressing-gown and went to the library. There lay the letters, half a dozen of them: but his eyes flew to one envelope, and as he tore it open a warm wave rocked his heart.

The letter was dated a few days after its writer must have received his own: it had all the qualities of grace and insight to which his unknown friend had accustomed him, but it contained no allusion, however indirect, to the special purport of his appeal. Even a vanity less ingenious than Betton's might have read in the lady's silence one of the most familiar motions of consent; but the smile provoked by this inference faded as he turned to his other letters. For the upper-most bore the superscription "Dead Letter Office," and the document that fell from it was his own last letter from Florida.

Betton studied the ironic "Unknown " for an appreciable space of time; then he broke into a laugh. He had suddenly recalled Vyse's similar experience with "Hester Macklin," and the light he was able to throw on that episode was searching enough to penetrate all the dark corners of his own adventure. He felt a rush of heat to the ears; catching sight of himself in the glass, he saw a ridiculous congested countenance, and dropped into a chair to hide it between his fists. He was roused by the opening of the door, and Vyse appeared.

"Oh, I beg pardon—you're ill?" said the secretary.

Betton's only answer was an inarticulate murmur of derision; then he pushed forward the letter with the imprint of the Dead Letter Office.

"Look at that," he jeered.

Vyse peered at the envelope, and turned it over slowly in his hands. Betton's eyes, fixed on him, saw his face decompose like a substance touched by some powerful acid. He clung to the envelope as if to gain time.

"It's from the young lady you've been writing to at Swazee Springs?" he asked at length.

"It's from the young lady I've been writing to at Swazee Springs."

"Well—I suppose she's gone away," continued Vyse, rebuilding his countenance rapidly.

"Yes; and in a community numbering perhaps a hundred and fifty souls, including the dogs and chickens, the local post-office is so ignorant of her movements that my letter has to be sent to the Dead Letter Office."

Vyse meditated on this; then he laughed in turn.

"After all, the same thing happened to me—with 'Hester Macklin,' I mean," he suggested sheepishly.

"Just so," said Betton, bringing down his clenched fist on the table. *"Just so,"* he repeated, in italics.

He caught his secretary's glance, and held it with his own for a moment. Then he dropped it as, in pity, one releases something seared and squirming.

"The very day my letter was returned from Swazee Springs she wrote me this from there," he said, holding up the last Florida missive.

"Ha! That's funny," said Vyse, with a damp forehead.

"Yes, it's funny," said Betton. He leaned back, his hands in his pockets, staring up at the ceiling, and noticing a crack in the cornice. Vyse, at the corner of the writing-table, waited.

"Shall I get to work?" he began, after a silence measurable by minutes. Betton's gaze descended from the cornice.

"I've got your seat, haven't I?" he said politely, rising and moving away from the table.

Vyse, with a quick gleam of relief, slipped into the vacant chair, and began to stir about among the papers.

"How's your father?" Betton asked from the hearth.

"Oh, better—better, thank you. He'll pull out of it."

"But you had a sharp scare for a day or two?"

"Yes—it was touch and go when I got there."

Another pause, while Vyse began to classify the letters.

"And I suppose," Betton continued in a steady tone, "your anxiety made you forget your usual precautions—whatever they were—about this Florida correspondence, and before you'd had time to prevent it the Swazee post-office blundered?"

Vyse lifted his head with a quick movement. "What do you mean?" he asked, pushing back his chair.

"I mean that you saw I couldn't live without flattery, and that you've been ladling it out to me to earn your keep."

Vyse sat motionless and shrunken, digging the blotting-pad with his pen. "What on earth are you driving at?" he repeated.

"Though why the deuce," Betton continued in the same steady tone, "you should need to do this kind of work when you've got such faculties at your service—those letters were wonderful, my dear fellow! Why in the world don't you write novels, instead of writing to other people about them?"

Vyse straightened himself with an effort. "What are you talking about, Betton? Why the devil do you think I wrote those letters?"

Betton held back his answer with a brooding face. "Because I wrote 'Hester Macklin's'—to myself!"

Vyse sat stock-still, without the least outcry of wonder. "Well—?" he finally said, in a low tone.

"And because you found me out (you see, you can't even feign surprise!)—because you saw through it at a glance, knew at once that the letters were faked. And when you'd foolishly put me on my guard by pointing out to me that they were a clumsy forgery, and had then suddenly guessed that I was the forger, you drew the natural inference that I had to have popular aproval, or at least had to make you think I had it. You saw that, to me, the worst thing about the failure of the book was having you know it was a failure. And so you applied your superior—your immeasurably superior—abilities to carrying on the humbug, and deceiving me as I'd tried to deceive you. And you did it so successfully that I don't see why the devil you haven't made your fortune writing novels!"

Vyse remained silent, his head slightly bent under the mounting tide of Betton's denunciation.

"The way you differentiated your people—characterized them—avoided my stupid mistake of making the women's letters too short and too logical, of letting my different correspondents use the same expressions: the amount of ingenuity and art you wasted on it! I swear, Vyse, I'm sorry that damned post-office went back on you," Betton went on, piling up the waves of his irony.

But at this height they suddenly paused, drew back on themselves, and began to recede before the sight of Vyse's misery. Something warm and emotional in Betton's nature—a lurking kindliness, perhaps, for any one who tried to soothe and smooth his writhing ego—softened his eye as it rested on the figure of his secretary.

"Look here, Vyse—I'm not sorry—not altogether sorry this has happened!" He moved across the room, and laid his hand on Vyse's drooping shoulder. "In a queer illogical way it evens up things, as it were. I did you a shabby turn once, years ago—oh, out of sheer carelessness, of course—about that novel of yours I promised to give to Apthorn. If I *had* given it, it might not have made any difference—I'm not sure it wasn't too good for success—but anyhow, I dare say you thought my personal influence might have helped you, might at least have got you a quicker hearing. Perhaps you thought it was because the thing *was* so good that I kept it back, that I felt some nasty jealousy of your superiority. I swear to you it wasn't that—I clean forgot it. And one day when I came home it was gone: you'd sent and taken it away. And I've always thought since that you might have owed me a grudge—and not unjustly; so this . . . this business of the letters . . . the sympathy you've shown . . . for I suppose it *is* sympathy . . . ?"

Vyse startled and checked him by a queer crackling laugh.

"It's *not* sympathy?" broke in Betton, the moisture drying out of his voice. He withdrew his hand from Vyse's shoulder. "What is it, then? The joy of uncovering my nakedness? An eye for an eye? Is it *that?*"

Vyse rose from his seat, and with a mechanical gesture swept into a heap all the letters he had sorted.

"I'm stone broke, and wanted to keep my job—that's what it is," he said wearily . . .

The Legend

I

ARTHUR BERNALD could never afterward recall just when the first conjecture flashed on him: oddly enough, there was no record of it in the agitated jottings of his diary. But, as it seemed to him in retrospect, he had always felt that the queer man at the Wades' must be John Pellerin, if only for the negative reason that he couldn't imaginably be any one else. It was impossible, in the confused pattern of the century's intellectual life, to fit the stranger in anywhere, save in the big gap which, some five and twenty years earlier, had been left by Pellerin's disappearance; and conversely, such a man as the Wades' visitor couldn't have lived for sixty years without filling, somewhere in space, a nearly equivalent void.

At all events, it was certainly not to Doctor Wade or to his mother that Bernald owed the hint: the good unconscious Wades, one of whose chief charms in the young man's eyes was that they remained so robustly untainted by Pellerinism, in spite of the fact that Doctor Wade's younger brother, Howland, was among its most impudently flourishing high-priests.

The incident had begun by Bernald's running across Doctor Robert Wade one hot summer night at the University Club, and by Wade's saying, in the tone of unprofessional laxity which the shadowy stillness of the place invited: "I got hold of a queer fish at St. Martin's the other day—case of heat-prostration picked up in Central Park. When we'd patched him up I found he had nowhere to go, and not a dollar in his pocket, and I sent him down to our place at Portchester to rebuild."

The opening roused his hearer's attention. Bob Wade had an instinctive sense of values that Bernald had learned to trust.

"What sort of chap? Young or old?"

"Oh, every age—full of years, and yet with a lot left. He called himself sixty on the books."

"Sixty's a good age for some kinds of living. And age is purely subjective. How has he used his sixty years?"

"Well—part of them in educating himself, apparently. He's a scholar—humanities, languages, and so forth."

"Oh—decayed gentleman," Bernald murmured, disappointed.

"Decayed? Not much!" cried the doctor with his accustomed literalness. "I only mentioned that side of Winterman—his name's Winterman—because it was the side my mother noticed first. I suppose women generally do. But it's only a part—a small part. The man's the big thing."

"Really big?"

"Well—there again . . . When I took him down to the country, looking rather like a tramp from a 'Shelter,' with an untrimmed beard, and a suit of reach-me-downs he'd slept round the Park in for a week, I felt sure my mother'd carry the silver up to her room, and send for the gardener's dog to sleep in the hall. But she didn't."

"I see. 'Women and children love him.' Oh, Wade!" Bernald groaned.

"Not a bit of it! You're out again. We don't love him, either of us. But we *feel* him—the air's charged with him. You'll see."

And Bernald agreed that he *would* see, the following Sunday. Wade's inarticulate attempts to characterize the stranger had struck his friend. The human revelation had for Bernald a poignant and ever-renewed interest, which his trade, as the dramatic critic of a daily paper, had hitherto failed to diminish. And he knew that Bob Wade, simple and undefiled by literature—Bernald's specific affliction—had a free and personal way of judging men, and the diviner's knack of reaching their hidden springs. During the days that followed, the young doctor gave Bernald further details about John Winterman: details not of fact—for in that respect the stranger's reticence was baffling—but of impression. It appeared that Winterman, while lying insensible in the Park, had been robbed of the few dollars he possessed; and on leaving the hospital, still weak and half-blind, he had quite simply and unprotestingly accepted the Wades' offer to give him shelter till such time as he should be strong enough to work.

"But what's his work?" Bernald interjected. "Hasn't he at least told you that?"

"Well, writing. Some kind of writing." Doctor Bob always became vague when he approached the confines of literature. "He means to take it up again as soon as his eyes get right."

Bernald groaned again. 'Oh, Lord—that finishes him; and *me!* He's looking for a publisher, of course—he wants a 'favorable notice.' I won't come!"

"He hasn't written a line for twenty years."

"A line of *what?* What kind of literature can one keep corked up for twenty years?"

Wade surprised him. "The real kind, I should say. But I don't know Winterman's line," the doctor added. "He speaks of the things he used to write merely as 'stuff that wouldn't sell.' He has a wonderfully confidential way of *not* telling one things. But he says he'll have to do something for his living as soon as his eyes are patched up, and that writing is the only trade he knows. The queer thing is that he seems pretty sure of selling *now.* He even talked of buying the bungalow of us, with an acre or two about it."

"The bungalow? What's that?"

"The studio down by the shore that we built for Howland when he thought he meant to paint." (Howland Wade, as Bernald knew, had experienced various "calls.") "Since he's taken to writing nobody's been near the place. I offered it to Winterman, and he camps there—cooks his meals, does his own housekeeping, and never comes up to the house except in the evenings, when he joins us on the verandah, in the dark, and smokes while my mother knits."

"A discreet visitor, eh?"

"More than he need be. My mother actually wanted him to stay on in the house—in her pink chintz room. Think of it! But he says houses smother him. I take it he's lived for years in the open."

"In the open where?"

"I can't make out, except that it was somewhere in the East. 'East of everything—beyond the day-spring. In places not on the map.' That's the way he put it; and when I said: 'You've been an explorer, then?' he smiled in his beard, and answered: 'Yes; that's it—an explorer.' Yet he doesn't strike me as a man of action: hasn't the hands or the eyes."

"What sort of hands and eyes has he?"

Wade reflected. His range of observation was not large, but within its limits it was exact and could give an account of itself.

"He's worked a lot with his hands, but that's not what they were made for. I should say they were extraordinarily delicate conductors of sensation. And his eye—his eye too. He hasn't used it to dominate people: he didn't care to. He simply looks through 'em all like windows. Makes me feel like the fellows who think they're made of glass. The mitigating circumstance is that he seems to see such a glorious landscape through me." Wade grinned at the thought of serving such a purpose.

"I see. I'll come on Sunday and be looked through!" Bernald cried.

II

BERNALD came on two successive Sundays; and the second time he lingered till the Tuesday.

"Here he comes!" Wade had said, the first evening, as the two young men, with Wade's mother, sat on the verandah, with the Virginian creeper drawing, between the arches, its black arabesques against a moon-lined sky.

Bernald heard a step on the gravel, and saw the red flit of a cigar through the shrubs. Then a loosely-moving figure obscured the patch of sky between the creepers, and the spark became the center of a dim bearded face, in which Bernald, through the darkness, discerned only a broad white gleam of forehead.

It was the young man's subsequent impression that Winterman had not spoken much that first evening; at any rate, Bernald himself remembered chiefly what the Wades had said. And this was the more curious because he had come for the purpose of studying their visitor, and because there was nothing to distract his attention in Wade's slow phrases or his mother's artless comments. He reflected afterward that there must have been a mysteriously fertilizing quality in the stranger's silence: it had brooded over their talk like a rain-cloud over a dry country.

"*And his eye—his eye, too. He hasn't used it to dominate people. He simply looks through 'em all like windows.*"

Mrs. Wade, apparently fearing that her son might have given Bernald an exaggerated notion of their visitor's importance, had hastened to qualify it before the latter appeared.

"He's not what you or Howland would call intellectual—" (Bernald winced at the coupling of the names)—"not in the least *literary;* though he told Bob he used to write. I don't think, though, it could have been what Howland would call writing." Mrs. Wade always named her younger son with a reverential drop of the voice. She viewed literature much as she did Providence, as an inscrutable mystery; and she spoke of Howland as a dedicated being, set apart to perform secret rites within the veil of the sanctuary.

"I shouldn't say he had a quick mind," she continued, reverting to Winterman. "Sometimes he hardly seems to follow what we're saying. But he's got such sound ideas—when he does speak he's never silly. And clever people sometimes *are,* don't you think so?" Bernald sighed an unqualified assent. "And he's so capable. The other day something went wrong with the kitchen range, just as I was expecting some friends of Bob's for dinner; and do you know, when Mr. Winterman heard we were in trouble, he came and took a look, and knew at once what to do? I told him it was a dreadful pity he wasn't married!"

Close on midnight, when the session on the verandah ended, and the two young men were strolling down to the bungalow at Winterman's side, Bernald's mind reverted to the image of the fertilizing cloud. There was something brooding, pregnant, in the silent presence beside him: he had, in place of any circumscribing personal impression, a large hovering sense of manifold latent meanings. And he felt a thrill of relief when, half-way down the lawn, Doctor Bob was checked by a voice that called him back to the telephone.

"Now I'll be with him alone!" thought Bernald, with a throb like a lover's.

Under the low rafters of the bungalow Winterman had to grope for the lamp on his desk, and as its light struck up into his face Bernald's sense of the rareness of the opportunity increased. He couldn't have said why, for the face, with its bossed forehead, its shabby greyish beard and blunt Socratic nose, made no direct appeal to the eye. It seemed rather like a stage on which remarkable things might be enacted, like some shaggy moorland landscape dependent for form and expression on the clouds rolling over it, and the bursts of light between; and one of these flashed out in the smile with which Winterman, as if in answer to his companion's thought, said simply, as he turned to fill his pipe: "Now we'll talk."

So he'd known all along that they hadn't yet—and had guessed that, with Bernald, one might!

The young man's sudden glow of pleasure left him for a moment unable to meet the challenge; and in that moment he felt the sweep of something winged and summoning. His spirit rose to it with a rush, but just as he felt himself poised between the ascending pinions, the door opened and Bob Wade reappeared.

"Too bad! I'm so sorry! It was from Howland, to say he can't come tomorrow after all." The doctor panted out his news with honest grief.

"I tried my best to pull it off for you, Winterman; and my brother *wants* to come—he's keen to talk to you and see what he can do. But you see he's so tremendously in demand. He'll try for another Sunday later on."

Winterman gave an untroubled nod. "Oh, he'll find me here. I shall work my time out slowly." He waved his hand toward the scattered sheets on the kitchen table which formed his desk.

"Not slowly enough to suit us," Wade answered hospitably. "Only, if Howland could have come he might have given you a tip or two—put you on the right track—shown you how to get in touch with the public."

Winterman, his hands in his pockets, lounged against the bare pine walls, twisting his pipe under his beard. "Does your brother enjoy the privilege of that contact?" he questioned gravely.

Wade stared a little. "Oh, of course Howland's not what you'd call a *popular* writer; he despises that kind of thing. But whatever he says goes with—well, with the chaps who count; and every one tells me he's written *the* book on Pellerin. You must read it when you get back your eyes." He paused, as if to let the name sink in, but Winterman drew at his pipe with a blank face. "You must have heard of Pellerin, I suppose?" the doctor continued. "I've never read a word of him myself: he's too big a proposition for *me*. But one can't escape the talk about him. I have him crammed down my throat even in hospital. The internes read him at the clinics. He tumbles out of the nurses' pockets. The patients keep him under their pillows.

Oh, with most of them, of course, it's just a craze, like the last new game or puzzle: they don't understand him in the least. Howland says that even now, twenty-five years after his death, and with his books in everybody's hands, there are not twenty people who really understand Pellerin; and Howland ought to know, if anybody does. He's—what's their great word?—*interpreted* him. You must get Howland to put you through a course of Pellerin."

And as the young men, having taken leave of Winterman, retraced their way across the lawn, Wade continued to develop the theme of his brother's accomplishments.

"I wish I *could* get Howland to take an interest in Winterman: this is the third Sunday he's chucked us. Of course he does get bored with people consulting him about their writings—but I believe if he could only talk to Winterman he'd see something in him, as we do. And it would be such a god-send to the poor devil to have some one to advise him about his work. I'm going to make a desperate effort to get Howland here next Sunday."

It was then that Bernald vowed to himself that he would return the next Sunday at all costs. He hardly knew whether he was prompted by the impulse to shield Winterman from Howland Wade's ineptitude, or by the desire to see the latter abandon himself to the full shamelessness of its display; but of one fact he was assured—and that was of the existence in Winterman of some quality which would provoke Howland to the amplest exercise of his fatuity. "How he'll draw him—how he'll draw him!" Bernald chuckled, with a security the more unaccountable that his one glimpse of Winterman had shown the latter only as a passive subject for observation; and he felt himself avenged in advance for the injury of Howland Wade's existence.

III

THAT this hope was to be frustrated Bernald learned from Howland Wade's own lips, the day before the two young men were to have met at Portchester.

"I can't really, my dear fellow," the Interpreter lisped, passing a polished hand over the faded smoothness of his face. "Oh, an authentic engagement, I assure you: otherwise, to oblige old Bob I'd submit cheerfully to looking over his foundling's literature. But I'm pledged this week to the Pellerin Society of Kenosha: I had a hand in founding it, and for two years now they've been patiently waiting for a word from me—the *Fiat Lux,* so to speak. You see it's a ministry, Bernald—I assure you, I look upon my calling quite religiously."

As Bernald listened, his disappointment gradually changed to relief. Howland, on trial, always turned out to be too insufferable, and the pleasure of watching his antics was invariably lost in the impulse to put a sanguinary end to them.

"If he'd only kept his beastly pink hands off Pellerin," Bernald sighed, thinking for the hundredth time of the thick manuscript condemned to perpetual incarceration in his own desk by the publication of Howland's "definitive" work on the great man. One couldn't, *after* Howland Wade, expose one's self to the derision of writing about Pellerin: the eagerness with which Wade's book had been devoured proved, not that the public had enough appetite for another, but simply that, for a stomach so undiscriminating, anything better than Wade had given it would be too good. And Bernald, in the confidence that his own work was open to this objection, had stoically locked it up. Yet if he had resigned himself to the fact that Wade's book existed, and was already passing into the immortality of perpetual republication, he could not, after repeated trials, adjust himself to the author's talk about Pellerin. When Wade wrote of the great dead he was egregious, but in conversation he was familiar and fond. It might have been supposed that one of the beauties of Pellerin's hidden life and mysterious taking off would have been to guard him from the fingering of anecdote; but biographers like Howland Wade are born to rise above such obstacles. He might be vague or inaccurate in dealing with the few recorded events of his subject's life; but when he left fact for conjecture no one had a firmer footing. Whole chapters in his volume were constructed in the conditional mood and made up of hypothetical detail; and in talk, by the very law of the process, hypothesis became affirmation, and he was ready to tell you confidentially the exact circumstances of Pellerin's death, and of the "distressing incident" leading up to it. Bernald himself not only questioned the form under which this incident was shaping itself before posterity, but the very fact of its occurrence: he had never been able to discover any break in the dense cloud enveloping Pellerin's end. He had gone away—that was all that any of them knew: he who had so little, at any time, been with them or of them; and his going had so slightly stirred the public consciousness that the news of his death, laconically imparted from afar, had dropped unheeded into the universal scrap-basket, to be long afterward fished out, with all its details missing, when some enquiring spirit first became aware, by chance encounter with a volume in a London book-stall, not only that such a man as John Pellerin had died, but that he had ever lived, or written.

It need hardly be noted that Howland Wade had not been the pioneer in question: his had been the safer part of swelling the chorus when it rose, and gradually drowning the other voices by his own. He had pitched his note so screamingly, and held it so long, that he was now the accepted authority on Pellerin, not only in the land which had given birth to his genius but in the Europe which had first acclaimed it; and it was the central point of pain in Bernald's sense of the situation that a man who had so yearned for silence should have his grave piped over by such a voice as Wade's.

Bernald's talk with the Interpreter had revived this ache to the momentary exclusion of other sensations; and he was still sore with it when, the next afternoon, he arrived at Portchester for his second Sunday with the Wades.

At the station he had the surprise of seeing Winterman's face on the platform, and of hearing from him that Doctor Bob had been called away to assist at an operation in a distant town.

"Mrs. Wade wanted to put you off, but I believe the message came too late; so she sent me down to break the news to you," said Winterman, holding out his hand.

Perhaps because they were the first conventional words that Bernald had heard him speak, the young man was struck by the quality his intonation gave them.

"She wanted to send a carriage," Winterman added, "but I told her we'd walk back through the woods." He looked at Bernald with a kindliness that flushed the young man with pleasure.

"Are you strong enough? It's not too far?"

"Oh, no. I'm pulling myself together. Getting back to work is the slowest part of the business: not on account of my eyes—I can use them now, though not for reading; but some of the links between things are missing. It's a kind of broken spectrum . . . here, that boy will look after your bag."

The walk through the woods remained in Bernald's memory as an enchanted hour. He used the word literally, as descriptive of the way in which Winterman's contact changed the face of things, or perhaps restored them to their deeper meanings. And the scene they traversed—one of those little untended woods that still, in America, fringe the tawdry skirts of civilization—acquired, as a background to Winterman, the hush of a spot aware of transcendent visitings. Did he talk, or did he make Bernald talk? The young man never knew. He recalled only a sense of lightness and liberation, as if the hard walls of individuality had melted, and he were merged in the poet's deeper interfusion, yet without losing the least sharp edge of self. This general impression resolved itself afterward into the sense of Winterman's wide elemental range. His thought encircled things like the horizon at sea. He didn't, as it happened, touch on lofty themes—Bernald was gleefully aware that, to Howland Wade, their talk would hardly have been Talk at all—but Winterman's mind, applied to lowly topics, was like a lens that brought out microscopic delicacies and differences.

The lack of Sunday trains kept Doctor Bob for two days on the scene of his surgical duties, and during those two days Bernald seized every moment of communion with his friend's guest. Winterman, as Wade had said, was reticent concerning his personal affairs, or rather concerning the practical and material questions to which the term is generally applied. But it was evident that, in Winterman's case, the usual classification must be reversed, and that the discussion of ideas carried one much farther into his intimacy than familiarity with the incidents of his life.

"That's exactly what Howland Wade and his tribe have never understood about Pellerin: that it's much less important to know how, or even why, he disapp——"

Bernald pulled himself up with a jerk, and turned to look full at his companion. It was late on the Monday evening, and the two men, after an hour's chat on the verandah to the tune of Mrs. Wade's knitting-needles, had bidden their hostess good-night and strolled back to the bungalow together.

"Come and have a pipe before you turn in," Winterman had said; and they had sat on together till midnight, with the door of the bungalow open on the heaving moonlit bay, and summer insects bumping against the chimney of the lamp. Winterman had just bent down to refill his pipe from the jar on the table, and Bernald, jerking about to catch him in the circle of lamplight, sat speechless, staring at a fact that seemed suddenly to have substituted itself for Winterman's face, or rather to have taken on its features.

"No, they never saw that Pellerin's ideas *were* Pellerin . . ." He continued to stare at Winterman. "Just as this man's ideas are—why, *are* Pellerin!"

The thought uttered itself in a kind of inner shout, and Bernald started upright with the violent impact of his conclusion. Again and again in the last forty-eight hours he had exclaimed to himself: "This is as good as Pellerin." Why hadn't he said till now: "This *is* Pellerin"? . . . Surprising as the answer was, he had no choice but to take it. He hadn't said so simply because Winterman was *better than Pellerin*—that there was so much more of him, so to speak. Yes; but—it came to Bernald in a flash—wouldn't there by this time have been any amount more of Pellerin? . . . The young man felt actually dizzy with the thought. That was it—there was the solution of the problem! This man was Pellerin, and more than Pellerin! It was so fantastic and yet so unanswerable that he burst into a sudden laugh.

Winterman, at the same moment, brought his palm down with a crash on the pile of manuscript covering the desk.

"What's the matter?" Bernald cried.

"My match wasn't out. In another minute the destruction of the library of Alexandria would have been a trifle compared to what you'd have seen." Winterman, with his large deep laugh, shook out the smoldering sheets. "And I should have been a pensioner on Doctor Bob the Lord knows how much longer!"

Bernald looked at him intently. "You've really got going again? The thing's actually getting into shape?"

"This particular thing *is* in shape. I drove at it hard all last week, thinking our friend's brother would be down on Sunday, and might look it over."

Bernald had to repress the tendency to another wild laugh.

"Howland—you meant to show *Howland* what you've done?"

Winterman, looming against the moonlight, slowly turned a dusky shaggy head toward him.

"Isn't it a good thing to do?"

Bernald wavered, torn between loyalty to his friends and the grotesqueness of answering in the affirmative. After all, it was none of his business to furnish Winterman with an estimate of Howland Wade.

"Well, you see, you've never told me what your line *is,*" he answered, temporizing.

"No, because nobody's ever told *me*. It's exactly what I want to find out," said the other genially.

"And you expect Wade——?"

"Why, I gathered from our good Doctor that it's his trade. Doesn't he explain—interpret?"

"In his own domain—which is Pellerinism."

Winterman gazed out musingly upon the moon-touched dusk of waters. "And what *is* Pellerinism?" he asked.

Bernald sprang to his feet with a cry. "Ah, I don't know—but you're Pellerin!"

They stood for a minute facing each other, among the uncertain swaying shadows of the room, with the sea breathing through it as something immense and inarticulate breathed through young Bernald's thoughts; then Winterman threw up his arms with a humorous gesture.

"Don't shoot!" he said.

IV

DAWN found them there, and the sun laid its beams on the rough floor of the bungalow, before either of the men was conscious of the passage of time. Bernald, vaguely trying to define his own state in retrospect, could only phrase it: "I floated . . . floated . . ."

The gist of fact at the core of the extraordinary experience was simply that John Pellerin, twenty-five years earlier, had voluntarily disappeared, causing the rumor of his death to be reported to an inattentive world; and that now he had come back to see what that world had made of him.

"You'll hardly believe it of me; I hardly believe it of myself; but I went away in a rage of disappointment, of wounded pride—no, vanity! I don't know which cut deepest—the sneers or the silence—but between them, there wasn't an inch of me that wasn't raw. I had just the one thing in me: the message, the cry, the revelation. But nobody saw and nobody listened. Nobody wanted what I had to give. I was like a poor devil of a tramp looking for shelter on a bitter night, in a town with every door bolted and all the windows dark. And suddenly I felt that the easiest thing would be to lie down and go to sleep in the snow. Perhaps I'd a vague notion that if they found me there at daylight, frozen stiff, the pathetic spectacle might produce a reaction, a feeling of remorse . . . So I took care to be found! Well, a good many thousand people die every day on the face of the globe; and I soon discovered that I was simply one of the thousands; and when I made that discovery I really died—and stayed dead a year or two . . . When I came to life again I was off on the under side of the world, in regions unaware of what we know as 'the public.' Have you any notion how it shifts the point of view to wake under new constellations? I advise any who's been in love with a woman under Cassiopeia to go and think about her under the Southern Cross . . . It's the only way to tell the pivotal truths from the others . . . I didn't believe in my theory any less—there was my triumph and my vindication! It held out, resisted, measured itself with the stars. But I didn't care a snap of my finger whether anybody else believed in it, or even knew it had been formulated. It escaped out of my books—my poor still-born books—like Psyche from the chrysalis, and soared away into the blue, and lived there. I knew then how it frees an idea to be ignored; how apprehension circumscribes and deforms it . . . Once I'd learned that, it was easy enough to turn to and shift for myself. I was sure now that my idea would live: the good ones are self-supporting. And meanwhile *I* had to learn to be so; and I tried my hand at a number of things . . . adventurous, menial, commercial . . . It's not a bad thing for a man to have to live his life—and we nearly all manage to dodge it. Our first round with the Sphinx may strike something out of us—a book or a picture or a symphony; and we're amazed at our feat, and go on letting that first work breed others, as some animal forms reproduce each other without renewed fertilization. So there we are, committed to our first guess at the riddle; and our works look as like as successive impressions of the same plate, each with the lines a little fainter; whereas they ought to be—if we touch earth between times—as different from each other as those other creatures—jelly-fish, aren't they, of a kind? —where successive generations produce new forms, and it takes a zoologist to see the hidden likeness . . .

"Well, I proved my first guess, off there in the wilds, and it lived, and grew, and took care of itself. And I said, 'Some day it will make itself heard; but by that time my atoms will have waltzed into a new pattern.' Then, in Cashmere one day, I met a fellow in a caravan, with a dog-eared book in his pocket. He said he never stirred without it—wanted to know where I'd been, never to have heard of it. It was *my guess*—in its twentieth edition! . . . The globe spun round at that, and all of a sudden I was under the old stars. That's the way it happens when the ballast of vanity shifts! I'd lived a third of a life out there, unconscious of human opinion—because I supposed it was unconscious of *me*. But now—now! Oh, it was different. I wanted to know what they said . . . Not exactly that, either: I wanted to know *what I'd made them say.* There's a difference . . . And here I am," said John Pellerin, with a pull at his pipe.

So much Bernald retained of his companion's actual narrative; the rest was swept away under the tide of wonder that rose and submerged him as Pellerin—at some indefinitely later stage of their talk—picked up his manuscript and began to read. Bernald sat opposite, his elbows propped on the table, his eyes fixed on the swaying waters outside, from which the moon gradually faded, leaving them to make a denser blackness in the night. As Pellerin read, this density of blackness—which never for a moment seemed inert or unalive—was attenuated by imperceptible degrees, till a greyish pallor replaced it; then the pallor breathed and brightened, and suddenly dawn was on the sea.

Something of the same nature went on in the young man's mind while he watched and listened. He was conscious of a gradually withdrawing light, of an interval of obscurity full of the stir of invisible forces, and then of the victorious flush of day. And as the light rose, he saw how far he had traveled and what wonders the night had prepared. Pellerin had been right in saying that his first idea had survived, had borne the test of time; but he had given his hearer no hint of the extent to which it had been enlarged and modified, of the fresh implications it now unfolded. In a brief flash of retrospection Bernald saw the earlier books dwindle and fall into their place as mere precursors of this fuller revelation; then, with a leap of rage, he pictured Howland Wade's pink hands on the new treasure, and his prophetic feet upon the lecture platform.

V

"IT won't do—oh, he let him down as gently as possible; but it appears it simply won't do."

Doctor Bob imparted the ineluctable fact to Bernald while the two men, accidentally meeting at their club a few nights later, sat together over the dinner they had immediately agreed to share.

Bernald had left Portchester the morning after his strange discovery, and he and Bob Wade had not seen each other since. And now Bernald, moved by an irresistible instinct of postponement, had waited for his companion to bring up Winterman's name, and had even executed several conversational diversions in the hope of delaying its mention. For how could one talk of Winterman with the thought of Pellerin swelling one's breast?

"Yes; the very day Howland got back from Kenosha I brought the manuscript to town, and got him to read it. And yesterday evening I nailed him, and dragged an answer out of him."

"Then Howland hasn't seen Winterman yet?"

"No. He said: 'Before you let him loose on me I'll go over the stuff, and see if it's at all worthwhile.'"

Bernald drew a freer breath. "And he found it wasn't?"

"Between ourselves, he found it was of no account at all. Queer, isn't it, when the *man* . . . but of course literature's another proposition. Howland says it's one of the cases where an idea might seem original and striking if one didn't happen to be able to trace its descent. And this is straight out of bosh—by Pellerin . . . Yes: Pellerin. It seems that everything in the article that isn't pure nonsense is just Pellerinism. Howland thinks Winterman must have been tremendously struck by Pellerin's writings, and have lived too much out of the world to know that they've become the textbooks of modern thought. Otherwise, of course, he'd have taken more trouble to disguise his plagiarisms."

"I see," Bernald mused. "Yet you say there *is* an original element?"

"Yes; but unluckily it's no good."

"It's not—conceivably—in any sense a development of Pellerin's idea: a logical step farther?"

"*Logical?* Howland says it's twaddle at white heat."

Bernald sat silent, divided between the satisfaction of seeing the Interpreter rush upon his fate, and the despair of knowing that the state of mind he represented was indestructible. Then both emotions were swept away on a wave of pure joy, as he reflected that now, at last, Howland Wade had given him back John Pellerin.

The possession was one he did not mean to part with lightly; and the dread of its being torn from him constrained him to extraordinary precautions.

"You've told Winterman, I suppose? How did he take it?"

"Why, unexpectedly, as he does most things. You can never tell which way he'll jump. I thought he'd take a high tone, or else laugh it off; but he did neither. He seemed awfully cast down. I wished myself well out of the job when I saw how cut up he was."

Bernald thrilled at the words. Pellerin had shared his own pang, then—the "old woe of the world" at the perpetuity of human dullness!

"But what did he say to the charge of plagiarism—if you made it?"

"Oh, I told him straight out what Howland said. I thought it fairer. And his answer to that was the rummest part of all."

"What was it?" Bernald questioned, with a tremor.

"He said: 'That's queer, for I've never read Pellerin.'"

Bernald drew a deep breath. "Well—and I suppose you believed him?"

"I believed him, because I know him. But the public won't—the critics won't. And if the plagiarism is a pure coincidence it's just as bad for him as if it were a straight steal—isn't it?"

Bernald sighed his acquiescence.

"It bothers me awfully," Wade continued, knitting his kindly brows, "because I could see what a blow it was to him. He's got to earn his living, and I don't suppose he knows how to do anything but write. At his age it's hard to start fresh. I put that to Howland—asked him if there wasn't a chance he might do better if he only had a little encouragement. I can't help feeling he's got the essential thing in him. But of course I'm no judge when it comes to books. And Howland says it would be cruel to give him any hope." Wade paused, turned his wineglass about under a meditative stare, and then leaned across the table toward Bernald. "Look here—do you know what I've proposed to Winterman? That he should come to town with me tomorrow and go in the evening to hear Howland lecture to the Uplift Club. They're to meet at Mrs. Beecher Bain's, and Howland is to repeat the lecture that he gave the other day before the Pellerin Society at Kenosha. It will give Winterman a chance to get some notion of what Pellerin *was:* he'll get it much straighter from Howland than if he tried to plough through Pellerin's books. And then afterward—as if accidentally—I thought I might bring him and Howland together. If Howland could only see him and hear him talk, there's no knowing what might come of it. He couldn't help feeling the man's force, as we do; and he might give him a pointer—tell him what line to take. Anyhow, it would please Winterman, and take the edge off his disappointment. I saw that as soon as I proposed it."

"Some one who's never heard of Pellerin?"

Mrs. Beecher Bain, large, smiling, diffuse, reached out through the incoming throng on her threshold to detain Bernald with the question as he was about to move past her in the wake of his companion.

"Oh, keep straight on, Mr. Winterman!" she interrupted herself to call after the latter. "Into the back drawing-room, please! And remember, you're to sit next to me—in the corner on the left, close under the platform."

She renewed her interrogative clutch on Bernald's sleeve. "Most curious! Doctor Wade has been telling me all about your friend—how remarkable you all think him. And it's actually true that he's never heard of Pellerin? Of course as soon as Doctor Wade told me *that,* I said 'Bring him!' It will be so extraordinarily interesting to watch the first impression.—Yes, do follow him, dear Mr. Bernald, and be sure that you and he secure the seats next to me. Of course Alice Fosdick insists on being with us. She was wild with excitement when I told her she was to meet some one who'd never heard of Pellerin!"

On the indulgent lips of Mrs. Beecher Bain conjecture speedily passed into affirmation; and as Bernald's companion, broad and shaggy in his visible new evening clothes, moved down the length of the crowded rooms, he was already, to the ladies drawing aside their skirts to let him pass, the interesting Huron of the fable.

How far he was aware of the character ascribed to him it was impossible for Bernald to discover. He was as unconscious as a tree or a cloud, and his observer had never known any one so alive to human contacts and yet so secure from them. But the scene was playing such a lively tune on Bernald's own sensibilities that for the moment he could not adjust himself to the probable effect it produced on his companion. The young man, of late, had made but rare appearances in the group of which Mrs. Beecher Bain was one of the most indefatigable hostesses, and the Uplift Club the chief medium of expression. To a critic, obliged by his trade to cultivate convictions, it was the essence of luxury to leave them at home in his hours of ease; and Bernald gave his preference to circles in which less finality of judgment prevailed, and it was consequently less embarrassing to be caught without an opinion.

But in his fresher days he had known the spell of the Uplift Club and the thrill of moving among the Emancipated; and he felt an odd sense of rejuvenation as he looked at the rows of faces packed about the embowered platform from which Howland Wade was presently to hand down the eternal verities. Many of these countenances belonged to the old days, when the gospel of Pellerin was unknown, and had required considerable intellectual courage to avow one's acceptance of the very doctrines he had since demolished. The latter moral revolution seemed to have been accepted as submissively as a change in hair-dressing; and it even struck Bernald that, in the case of many of the assembled ladies, their convictions were rather newer than their clothes.

One of the most interesting examples of this readiness of adaptation was actually, in the person of Miss Alice Fosdick, brushing his elbow with exotic amulets, and enveloping him in Arabian odors, as she leaned forward to murmur her sympathetic sense of the situation. Miss Fosdick, who was one of the most advanced exponents of Pellerinism, had large eyes and a plaintive mouth, and Bernald had always fancied that she might have been pretty if she had not been perpetually explaining things.

"Yes, I know—Isabella Bain told me all about him. (He can't hear us, can he?) And I wonder if you realize how remarkably interesting it is that we should have such an opportunity *now*—I mean the opportunity to see the impression of Pellerinism on a perfectly fresh mind. (You must introduce him as soon as the lecture's over.) I explained that to Isabella as soon as she showed me Doctor Wade's note. Of course you see why, don't you?" Bernald made a faint motion of acquiescence, which she instantly swept aside. "At least I think I can *make you see why.* (If you're sure he can't hear?) Why, it's just this—Pellerinism is in danger of becoming a truism. Oh, it's an awful thing to say! But then I'm not afraid of saying awful things! I rather believe it's my mission. What I mean is, that we're getting into the way of taking Pellerin for granted—as we do the air we breathe. We don't sufficiently lead our *conscious life* in him—we're gradually letting him become subliminal." She swayed closer to the young man, and he saw that she was making a graceful attempt to throw her explanatory net over his companion, who, evading Mrs. Bain's hospitable signal, had cautiously wedged himself into a seat between Bernald and the wall.

"*Did* you hear what I was saying, Mr. Winterman? (Yes, I know who you are, of course!) Oh, well, I don't really mind if you did.

I was talking about you—about you and Pellerin. I was explaining to Mr. Bernald that what we need at this very minute is a Pellerin revival; and we need some one like you—to whom his message comes as a wonderful new interpretation of life—to lead the revival, and rouse us out of our apathy . . .

"You see," she went on winningly, "it's not only the big public that needs it (of course *their* Pellerin isn't ours!) It's we, his disciples, his interpreters, we who discovered him and gave him to the world—we, the Chosen People, the Custodians of the Sacred Books, as Howland Wade calls us—it's *we* who are in perpetual danger of sinking back into the old stagnant ideals, and practicing the Seven Deadly Virtues; it's *we* who need to count our mercies, and realize anew what he's done for us, and what we ought to do for him! And it's for that reason that I urged Mr. Wade to speak here, in the very inner sanctuary of Pellerinism, exactly as he would speak to the uninitiated—to repeat, simply, his Kenosha lecture, 'What Pellerinism Means'; and we ought all, I think, to listen to him with the hearts of little children—just as you will, Mr. Winterman—as if he were telling us new things, and we——"

"Alice, *dear*——" Mrs. Bain murmured with a warning gesture; and Howland Wade, emerging between the palms, took the center of the platform.

A pang of commiseration shot through Bernald as he saw him there, so innocent and so exposed. His plump pulpy body, which made his evening dress fall into intimate and wrapper-like folds, was like a wide surface spread to the shafts of irony; and the ripples of his voice seemed to enlarge the vulnerable area as he leaned forward, poised on confidential fingertips, to say persuasively: "Let me try to tell you what Pellerinism means."

Bernald moved restlessly in his seat. He had the sense of being a party to something not wholly honorable. He ought not to have come; he ought not to have let his companion come. Yet how could he have done otherwise? John Pellerin's secret was his own. As long as he chose to remain John Winterman it was no one's business to gainsay him; and Bernald's scruples were really justifiable only in respect of his own presence on the scene. But even in this respect he ceased to feel them as soon as Howland Wade began to speak.

VI

IT had been arranged that Pellerin, after the meeting of the Uplift Club, should join Bernald at his rooms and spend the night there, instead of returning to Portchester. The plan had been eagerly elaborated by the young man, but he had been unprepared for the alacrity with which his wonderful friend accepted it. He was beginning to see that it was a part of Pellerin's wonderfulness to fall in, quite simply and naturally, with any arrangements made for his convenience, or tending to promote the convenience of others. Bernald perceived that his docility in such matters was proportioned to the force of resistance which, for nearly half a lifetime, had kept him, with his back to the wall, fighting alone against the powers of darkness. In such a scale of values how little the small daily alternatives must weigh!

At the close of Howland Wade's discourse, Bernald, charged with his prodigious secret, had felt the need to escape for an instant from the liberated rush of talk. The interest of watching Pellerin was so perilously great that the watcher felt it might, at any moment, betray him. He lingered in the drawing-room long enough to see his friend enclosed in a mounting tide, above which Mrs. Beecher Bain and Miss Fosdick actively waved their conversational tridents; then he took refuge, at the back of the house, in a small dim library where, in his younger days, he had discussed personal immortality and the problem of consciousness with beautiful girls whose names he could not remember.

In this retreat he surprised Mr. Beecher Bain, a quiet man with a mild brow, who was smoking a surreptitious cigar over the last number of the *Strand*. Mr. Bain, at Bernald's approach, dissembled the *Strand* under a copy of the *Hibbert Journal,* but tendered his cigar-case with the remark that stocks were heavy again; and Bernald blissfully abandoned himself to this unexpected contact with reality.

On his return to the drawing-rooms he found that the tide had set toward the supper-table, and when it finally carried him thither it was to land him in the welcoming arms of Bob Wade.

"Hullo, old man! Where have you been all this time?—Winterman? Oh, *he's* talking to Howland: yes, I managed it finally. I believe Mrs. Bain has steered them into the library, so that they shan't be disturbed. I gave her an idea of the situation, and she was awfully kind. We'd better leave them alone, don't you think? I'm trying to get a croquette for Miss Fosdick."

Bernald's secret leapt in his bosom, and he devoted himself to the task of distributing sandwiches and champagne while his pulses danced to the tune of the cosmic laughter. The vision of Pellerin and his Interpreter, face to face at last, had a Titanic grandeur that dwarfed all other comedy. "And I shall hear of it presently; in an hour or two he'll be telling me about it. And that hour will be all mine—mine and his!" The dizziness of the thought made it difficult for Bernald to preserve the balance of the supper-plates he was distributing. Life had for him at that moment the completeness which seems to defy disintegration.

The throng in the dining-room was thickening, and Bernald's efforts as purveyor were interrupted by frequent appeals, from ladies who had reached repleteness, that he should sit down and tell them all about his interesting friend. Winterman's fame, trumpeted abroad by Miss Fosdick, had reached the four corners of the Uplift Club, and Bernald found himself fabricating *de toutes pièces* a Winterman legend which should in some degree respond to the Club's demand for the human document. When at length he had acquitted himself of this obligation, and was free to work his way back through the lessening groups into the drawing-room, he was at last rewarded by a glimpse of his friend, who, still densely encompassed, towered in the center of the room in all his sovereign ugliness.

Their eyes met across the crowd; but Bernald gathered only perplexity from the encounter. What were Pellerin's eyes saying to him? What orders, what confidences, what indefinable apprehension did their long look impart? The young man was still trying to decipher their message when he felt a tap on the arm, and turned to meet the rueful gaze of Bob Wade, whose meaning lay clearly enough on the surface of his good blue stare.

"Well, it won't work—it won't work," the doctor groaned.

"What won't?"

"I mean with Howland. Winterman won't. Howland doesn't take to him. Says he's crude—frightfully crude. And you know Howland hates crudeness."

"Oh, I know," Bernald exulted. It was the word he had waited for—he saw it now! Once more he was lost in wonder at Howland's miraculous faculty for always, as the naturalists said, being true to type.

"So I'm afraid it's all up with his chance of writing. At least *I* can do no more," said Wade, discouraged.

Bernald pressed him for further details. "Does Winterman seem to mind much? Did you hear his version?"

"His version?"

"I mean what he said to Howland."

"Why, no. What the deuce was there for him to say?"

"What indeed? I think I'll take him home," said Bernald gaily.

He turned away to join the circle from which, a few minutes before, Pellerin's eyes had vainly and enigmatically signalled to him; but the circle had dispersed, and Pellerin himself was not in sight.

Bernald, looking about him, saw that during his brief aside with Wade the party had passed into the final phase of dissolution. People still delayed, in diminishing groups, but the current had set toward the doors, and every moment or two it bore away a few more lingerers. Bernald, from his post, commanded the clearing perspective of the two drawing-rooms, and a rapid survey of their length sufficed to assure him that Pellerin was not in either. Taking leave of Wade, the young man made his way back to the drawing-room, where only a few hardened feasters remained, and then passed on to the library which had been the scene of the late momentous colloquy. But the library too was empty, and drifting back to the inner drawing-room Bernald found Mrs. Beecher Bain domestically putting out the candles on the mantel-piece.

"Dear Mr. Bernald! Do sit down and have a little chat. What a wonderful privilege it has been! I don't know when I've had such an intense impression."

She made way for him, in a corner of the sofa to which she had sunk; and he echoed her vaguely: "You *were* impressed, then?"

"I can't express to you how it affected me! As Alice said, it was a resurrection—it was as if John Pellerin were actually here in the room with us!"

Bernald turned on her with a half-audible gasp. "You felt that, dear Mrs. Bain?"

"We all felt it—every one of us! I don't wonder the Greeks—it *was* the Greeks?—regarded eloquence as a supernatural power. As Alice says, when one looked at Howland Wade one understood what they meant by the Afflatus."

Bernald rose and held out his hand. "Oh, I see—it was Howland who made you feel as if Pellerin were in the room? And he made Miss Fosdick feel so too?"

"Why, of course. But why are you rushing off?"

"Because I must hunt up my friend, who's not used to such late hours."

"Your friend?" Mrs. Bain had to collect her thoughts. "Oh, Mr. Winterman, you mean? But he's gone already."

"Gone?" Bernald exclaimed, with an odd twinge of foreboding. Remembering Pellerin's signal across the crowd, he reproached himself for not having answered it more promptly. There had been a summons in the look—and it was certainly strange that his friend should have left the house without him.

"Are you quite sure?" he asked, with a startled glance at the clock.

"Oh, perfectly. He went half an hour ago. But you needn't hurry away on his account, for Alice Fosdick carried him off with her. I saw them leave together."

"Carried him off? She took him home with her, you mean?"

"Yes. You know what strange hours she keeps. She told me she was going to give him a Welsh rabbit, and explain Pellerinism to him."

"Oh, if she's going to explain——" Bernald murmured. But his amazement at the news struggled with a confused impatience to reach his rooms in time to be there for his friend's arrival. There could be no stranger spectacle beneath the stars than that of John Pellerin carried off by Miss Fosdick, and listening, in the small hours, to her elucidation of his doctrines; but Bernald knew enough of his sex to be aware that such an experiment may appear less humorous to its subject than to the detached observer. Even the Uplift Club and its connotations might benefit by the attraction of the unknown; and it was conceivable that to a traveller from Mesopotamia Miss Fosdick might present elements of interest which she had lost for the frequenters of Fifth Avenue. There was, at any rate, no denying that the affair had become unexpectedly complex, and that its farther development promised to be rich in comedy.

In the contemplation of these possibilities Bernald sat over his fire, listening for Pellerin's ring. He had arranged his modest quarters with the reverent care of a celebrant awaiting the descent of his deity. He guessed Pellerin to be careless of visual detail, but sensitive to the happy blending of sensuous impressions: to the spell of lamplight on books, and of a deep chair placed where one could watch the fire. The chair was there, and Bernald, facing it across the hearth, already saw it filled by Pellerin's lounging figure. The autumn dawn came late, and even now they had before them the promise of some untroubled hours. Bernald, sitting there alone in the warm stillness of his room, and in the profounder hush of his expectancy, was conscious of gathering up all his sensibilities and perceptions into one exquisitely-adjusted instrument of notation. Until now he had tasted Pellerin's society only in unpremeditated snatches and had always left him with a sense, on his own part, of waste and shortcoming. Now, in the lull of this dedicated hour, he felt that he should miss nothing, and forget nothing, of the initiation that awaited him. And catching sight of Pellerin's pipe, he rose and laid it carefully on a table by the arm-chair . . .

"No. I've never had any news of him," Bernald heard himself repeating. He spoke in a low tone, and with the automatic utterance that alone made it possible to say the words.

They were addressed to Miss Fosdick, into whose neighborhood chance had thrown him at a dinner, a year or so later than their encounter at the Uplift Club. Hitherto he had successfully, and intentionally, avoided Miss Fosdick, not from any animosity toward that unconscious instrument of fate, but from an intense reluctance to pronounce the words which he knew he should have to speak if they met.

Now, as it turned out, his chief surprise was that she should wait so long to make him speak them. All through the dinner she had swept him along on a rapid current of talk which showed no tendency to linger or turn back upon the past. At first he ascribed her reserve to a sense of delicacy with which he reproached himself for not having credited her; then he saw that she had been carried so far beyond the point at which they had last faced each other, that she was finally borne back to it only by the merest hazard of associated ideas. For it appeared that the very next evening, at Mrs. Beecher Bain's, a Hindu Mahatma was to lecture to the Uplift Club on the Limits of the Subliminal; and it was owing to no less a person than Howland Wade that this exceptional privilege had been obtained.

"Of course Howland's known all over the world as the interpreter of Pellerinism, and the Aga Gautch, who had absolutely declined to speak anywhere in public, wrote to Isabella that he could not refuse anything that Mr. Wade asked. Did you know that Howland's lecture, 'What Pellerinism Means,' has been translated into twenty-two languages, and gone into a fifth edition in Icelandic? Why, that reminds me," Miss Fosdick broke off—"I've never heard what became of your queer friend—what was his name?—whom you and Bob Wade accused me of spiriting away the night that Howland gave that very lecture at Hatty Bain's. And I've never seen *you* since you rushed into the house the next morning and dragged me out of bed to know what I'd done with him!"

With a sharp effort Bernald gathered himself together to have it out. "Well, what *did* you do with him?" he retorted.

She laughed her appreciation of his humor. "Just what I told you, of course. I said good-bye to him on Isabella's door-step."

Bernald looked at her. "It's really true, then, that he didn't go home with you?"

She bantered back: "Have you suspected me, all this time, of hiding his remains in the cellar?" And with a droop of her fine lids she added: "I wish he *had* come home with me, for he was rather interesting, and there were things about Pellerinism that I think I could have explained to him."

Bernald helped himself to a nectarine, and Miss Fosdick continued on a note of amused curiosity: "So you've really never had any news of him since that night?"

"No—I've never had any news of him."

"Not the least little message?"

"Not the least little message."

"Or a rumor or report of any kind?"

"Or a rumor or report of any kind."

Miss Fosdick's interest seemed to be revived by the undeniable strangeness of the case. "It's rather creepy, isn't it? What *could* have happened? You don't suppose he could have been waylaid and murdered?" she asked with brightening eyes.

Bernald shook his head serenely. "No. I'm sure he's safe—quite safe."

"But if you're sure, you must know something."

"No. I know nothing," he repeated.

She scanned him incredulously. "But what's your theory—for you must have a theory? What in the world can have become of him?"

Bernald returned her look and hesitated. "Do you happen to remember the last thing he said to you—the very last, on the doorstep, when he left you?"

"The last thing?" She poised her fork above the peach on her plate. "I don't think he said anything. Oh, yes—when I reminded him that he'd solemnly promised to come back with me and have a little talk he said he couldn't because he was going home."

"Well, then, I suppose," said Bernald, "he went home."

She glanced at him as if suspecting a trap. "Dear me, how flat! I always inclined to a mysterious murder. But of course you know more of him than you say."

She began to cut her peach, but paused above a lifted bit to ask, with a renewal of animation in her expressive eyes: "By the way, had you heard that Howland Wade has been gradually getting farther and farther away from Pellerinism? It seems he's begun to feel that there's a Positivist element in it which is narrowing to any one who has gone at all deeply into the Wisdom of the East. He was intensely interesting about it the other day, and of course I *do* see what he feels . . . Oh, it's too long to tell you now; but if you could manage to come in to tea some afternoon soon—any day but Wednesday—I should so like to explain—"

The Eyes

I

WE had been put in the mood for ghosts, that evening, after an excellent dinner at our old friend Culwin's, by a tale of Fred Murchard's—the narrative of a strange personal visitation.

Seen through the haze of our cigars, and by the drowsy gleam of a coal fire, Culwin's library, with its oak walls and dark old bindings, made a good setting for such evocations; and ghostly experiences at first hand being, after Murchard's opening, the only kind acceptable to us, we proceeded to take stock of our group and tax each member for a contribution. There were eight of us, and seven contrived, in a manner more or less adequate, to fulfill the condition imposed. It surprised us all to find that we could muster such a show of supernatural impressions, for none of us, excepting Murchard himself and young Phil Frenham—whose story was the slightest of the lot—had the habit of sending our souls into the invisible. So that, on the whole, we had every reason to be proud of our seven "exhibits," and none of us would have dreamed of expecting an eighth from our host.

Our old friend, Mr. Andrew Culwin, who had sat back in his arm-chair, listening and blinking through the smoke circles with the cheerful tolerance of a wise old idol, was not the kind of man likely to be favored with such contacts, though he had imagination enough to enjoy, without envying, the superior privileges of his guests. By age and by education he belonged to the stout Positivist tradition, and his habit of thought had been formed in the days of the epic struggle between physics and metaphysics. But he had been, then and always, essentially a spectator, a humorous detached observer of the immense muddled variety show of life, slipping out of his seat now and then for a brief dip into the convivialities at the back of the house, but never, as far as one knew, showing the least desire to jump on the stage and do a "turn."

Among his contemporaries there lingered a vague tradition of his having, at a remote period, and in a romantic clime, been wounded in a duel; but this legend no more tallied with what we younger men knew of his character than my mother's assertion that he had once been "a charming little man with nice eyes" corresponded to any possible reconstitution of his physiognomy.

"He never can have looked like anything but a bundle of sticks," Murchard had once said of him. "Or a phosphorescent log, rather," someone else amended; and we recognized the happiness of this description of his small squat trunk, with the red blink of the eyes in a face like mottled bark. He had always been possessed of a leisure which he had nursed and protected, instead of squandering it in vain activities. His carefully guarded hours had been devoted to the cultivation of a fine intelligence and a few judiciously chosen habits; and none of the disturbances common to human experience seemed to have crossed his sky. Nevertheless, his dispassionate survey of the universe had not raised his opinion of that costly experiment, and his study of the human race seemed to have resulted in the conclusion that all men were superfluous, and women necessary only because some one had to do the cooking. On the importance of this point his convictions were absolute, and gastronomy was the only science which he revered as a dogma. It must be owned that his little dinners were a strong argument in favor of this view, besides being a reason—though not the main one—for the fidelity of his friends.

Mentally he exercised a hospitality less seductive but no less stimulating. His mind was like a forum, or some open meeting-place for the exchange of ideas: somewhat cold and draughty, but light, spacious and orderly—a kind of academic grove from which all the leaves have fallen. In this privileged area a dozen of us were wont to stretch our muscles and expand our lungs; and, as if to prolong as much as possible the tradition of what we felt to be a vanishing institution, one or two neophytes were now and then added to our band.

Young Phil Frenham was the last, and the most interesting, of these recruits, and a good example of Murchard's somewhat morbid assertion that our old friend "liked 'em juicy." It was indeed a fact that Culwin, for all his dryness, specially tasted the lyric qualities in youth. As he was far too good an Epicurean to nip the flowers of soul which he gathered for his garden, his friendship was not a disintegrating influence: on the contrary, it forced the young idea to robuster bloom. And in Phil Frenham he had a good subject for experimentation. The boy was really intelligent, and the soundness of his nature was like the pure paste under a fine glaze. Culwin had fished him out of a fog of family dullness, and pulled him up to a peak in Darien; and the adventure hadn't hurt him a bit. Indeed the skill with which Culwin had contrived to stimulate his curiosities without robbing them of their bloom of awe seemed to me a sufficient answer to Murchard's ogreish metaphor. There was nothing hectic in Frenham's efflorescence, and his old friend had not laid even a finger-tip on the sacred stupidities. One wanted no better proof of that than the fact that Frenham still reverenced them in Culwin.

"There's a side of him you fellows don't see. *I* believe that story about the duel!" he declared; and it was of the very essence of this belief that it should impel him—just as our little party was dispersing—to turn back to our host with the joking demand: "And now you've got to tell us about *your* ghost!"

The outer door had closed on Murchard and the others; only Frenham and I remained; and the devoted servant who presided over Culwin's destinies, having brought a fresh supply of soda-water, had been laconically ordered to bed.

Culwin's sociability was a night-blooming flower, and we knew that he expected the nucleus of his group to tighten around him after midnight. But Frenham's appeal seemed to disconcert him comically, and he rose from the chair in which he had just reseated himself after his farewells in the hall.

"*My* ghost? Do you suppose I'm fool enough to go to the expense of keeping one of my own, when there are so many charming ones in my friends' closets?—Take another cigar," he said, revolving toward me with a laugh.

Frenham laughed too, pulling up his slender height before the chimney-piece as he turned to face his short bristling friend.

"Oh," he said, "you'd never be content to share if you met one you really liked."

Culwin had dropped back into his arm-chair, his shock head

embedded in the hollow of worn leather, his little eyes glimmering over a fresh cigar.

"Liked—*liked?* Good Lord!" he growled.

"Ah, you *have,* then!" Frenham pounced on him in the same instant, with a side-glance of victory at me; but Culwin cowered gnomelike among his cushions, dissembling himself in a protective cloud of smoke.

"What's the use of denying it? You've seen everything, so of course you've seen a ghost!" his young friend persisted, talking intrepidly into the cloud. "Or, if you haven't seen one, it's only because you've seen two!"

The form of the challenge seemed to strike our host. He shot his head out of the mist with a queer tortoise-like motion he sometimes had, and blinked approvingly at Frenham.

"That's it," he flung at us on a shrill jerk of laughter; "it's only because I've seen two!"

The words were so unexpected that they dropped down and down into a deep silence, while we continued to stare at each other over Culwin's head, and Culwin stared at his ghosts. At length Frenham, without speaking, threw himself into the chair on the other side of the hearth, and leaned forward with his listening smile . . .

II

"OH, of course they're not show ghosts—a collector wouldn't think anything of them . . . Don't let me raise your hopes . . . their one merit is their numerical strength: the exceptional fact of their being two. But, as against this, I'm bound to admit that at any moment I could probably have exorcised them both by asking my doctor for a prescription, or my oculist for a pair of spectacles. Only, as I never could make up my mind whether to go to the doctor or the oculist—whether I was afflicted by an optical or a digestive delusion—I left them to pursue their interesting double life, though at times they made mine exceedingly uncomfortable . . .

"Yes—uncomfortable; and you know how I hate to be uncomfortable! But it was part of my stupid pride, when the thing began, not to admit that I could be disturbed by the trifling matter of seeing two——

"And then I'd no reason, really, to suppose I was ill. As far as I knew I was simply bored—horribly bored. But it was part of my boredom—I remember—that I was feeling so uncommonly well, and didn't know how on earth to work off my surplus energy. I had come back from a long journey—down in South America and Mexico—and had settled down for the winter near New York, with an old aunt who had known Washington Irving and corresponded with N. P. Willis. She lived, not far from Irvington, in a damp Gothic villa, overhung by Norway spruces, and looking exactly like a memorial emblem done in hair. Her personal appearance was in keeping with this image, and her own hair—of which there was little left—might have been sacrificed to the manufacture of the emblem.

"I had just reached the end of an agitated year, with considerable arrears to make up in money and emotion; and theoretically it seemed as though my aunt's mild hospitality would be as beneficial to my nerves as to my purse. But the deuce of it was that as soon as I felt myself safe and sheltered my energy began to revive; and how was I to work it off inside of a memorial emblem? I had, at that time, the illusion that sustained intellectual effort could engage a man's whole activity; and I decided to write a great book—I forget about what. My aunt, impressed by my plan, gave up to me her Gothic library, filled with classics bound in black cloth and daguerreotypes of faded celebrities; and I sat down at my desk to win myself a place among their number. And to facilitate my task she lent me a cousin to copy my manuscript.

"The cousin was a nice girl, and I had an idea that a nice girl was just what I needed to restore my faith in human nature, and principally in myself. She was neither beautiful nor intelligent—poor Alice Nowell!— but it interested me to see any woman content to be so uninteresting, and I wanted to find out the secret of her content. In doing this I handled it rather rashly, and put it out of joint—oh, just for a moment! There's no fatuity in telling you this, for the poor girl had never seen any one but cousins . . .

"Well, I was sorry for what I'd done, of course, and confoundedly bothered as to how I should put it straight. She was staying in the house, and one evening, after my aunt had gone to bed, she came down to the library to fetch a book she'd mislaid, like any artless heroine on the shelves behind us. She was pink-nosed and flustered, and it suddenly occurred to me that her hair, though it was fairly thick and pretty, would look exactly like my aunt's when she grew older. I was glad I had noticed this, for it made it easier for me to decide to do what was right; and when I had found the book she hadn't lost I told her I was leaving for Europe that week.

"Europe was terribly far off in those days, and Alice knew at once what I meant. She didn't take it in the least as I'd expected—it would have been easier if she had. She held her book very tight, and turned away a moment to wind up the lamp on my desk—it had a ground glass shade with vine leaves, and glass drops around the edge, I remember. Then she came back, held out her hand, and said: 'Good-bye.' And as she said it she looked straight at me and kissed me. I had never felt anything as fresh and shy and brave as her kiss. It was worse than any reproach, and it made me ashamed to deserve a reproach from her. I said to myself: 'I'll marry her, and when my aunt dies she'll leave us this house, and I'll sit here at the desk and go on with my book; and Alice will sit over there with her embroidery and look at me as she's looking now. And life will go on like that for any number of years.' The prospect frightened me a little, but at the time it didn't frighten me as much as doing anything to hurt her; and ten minutes later she had my seal ring on her finger, and my promise that when I went abroad she should go with me.

"You'll wonder why I'm enlarging on this incident. It's because the evening on which it took place was the very evening on which I first saw the queer sight I've spoken of. Being at that time an ardent believer in a necessary sequence between cause and effect I naturally tried to trace some kind of link between what had just happened to me in my aunt's library, and what was to happen a few hours later on the same night; and so the coincidence between the two events always remained in my mind.

"I went up to bed with rather a heavy heart, for I was bowed under the weight of the first good action I had ever consciously committed; and young as I was, I saw the gravity of my situation. Don't imagine from this that I had hitherto been an instrument of destruction. I had been merely a harmless young man, who had followed his bent and declined all collaboration with Providence. Now I had suddenly undertaken to promote the moral order of the world, and I felt a good deal like the trustful spectator who has given his gold watch to the conjurer, and doesn't know in what shape he'll get it back when the trick is over . . . Still, a glow of self-righteousness tempered my fears, and I said to myself as I undressed that when I'd got used to being good it probably wouldn't make me as nervous as it did at the start. And by the time I was in bed, and had blown out my candle, I felt that I really *was* getting used to it, and that, as far as I'd got, it was not unlike sinking down into one of my aunt's very softest wool mattresses.

"I closed my eyes on this image, and when I opened them it must have been a good deal later, for my room had grown cold, and intensely still. I was waked by the queer feeling we all know—the feeling that there was something in the room that hadn't been there when I fell asleep. I sat up and strained my eyes into the darkness. The room was pitch black, and at first I saw nothing; but gradually a vague glimmer at the foot of the bed turned into two eyes staring back at me. I couldn't distinguish the features attached to them, but as I looked the eyes grew more and more distinct; they gave out a light of their own.

"The sensation of being thus gazed at was far from pleasant, and you might suppose that my first impulse would have been to jump out of bed and hurl myself on the invisible figure attached to the eyes. But it wasn't—my impulse was simply to lie still . . . I can't say whether this was due to an immediate sense of the uncanny nature of the apparition—to the certainty that if I did jump out of bed I should hurl myself on nothing—or merely to the benumbing effect of the eyes themselves. They were the very worst eyes I've ever seen: a man's eyes—but what a man! My first thought was that he must be frightfully old. The orbits were sunk, and the thick red-lined lids hung over the eyeballs like blinds of which the cords are broken. One lid drooped a little lower than the other, with the effect of a crooked leer; and between these folds of flesh, with their scant bristle of lashes, the eyes themselves, small glassy disks with an agate-like rim, looked like sea-pebbles in the grip of a starfish.

"But the age of the eyes was not the most unpleasant thing about them. What turned me sick was their expression of vicious security. I don't know how else to describe the fact that they seemed to belong to a man who had done a lot of harm in his life, but had always kept just inside the danger lines. They were not the eyes of a coward, but of some one much too clever to take risks; and my gorge rose at their look of base astuteness. Yet even that wasn't the worst; for as we continued to scan each other I saw in them a tinge of derision, and felt myself to be its object.

"At that I was seized by an impulse of rage that jerked me to my feet and pitched me straight at the unseen figure. But of course there wasn't any figure there, and my fists struck at emptiness. Ashamed and cold, I groped about for a match and lit the candles. The room looked just as usual—as I had known it would; and I crawled back to bed, and blew out the lights.

"As soon as the room was dark again the eyes reappeared; and I now applied myself to explaining them on scientific principles. At first I thought the illusion might have been caused by the glow of the last embers in the chimney; but the fireplace was on the other side of my bed, and so placed that the fire could not be reflected in my toilet glass, which was the only mirror in the room. Then it struck me that I might have been tricked by the reflection of the embers in some polished bit of wood or metal; and though I couldn't discover any object of the sort in my line of vision, I got up again, groped my way to the hearth, and covered what was left of the fire. But as soon as I was back in bed the eyes were back at its foot.

"They were an hallucination, then: that was plain. But the fact that they were not due to any external dupery didn't make them a bit pleasanter. For if they were a projection of my inner consciousness, what the deuce was the matter with that organ? I had gone deeply enough into the mystery of morbid pathological states to picture the conditions under which an exploring mind might lay itself open to such a midnight admonition; but I couldn't fit it to my present case. I had never felt more normal, mentally and physically; and the only unusual fact in my situation—that of having assured the happiness of an amiable girl—did not seem of a kind to summon unclean spirits about my pillow. But there were the eyes still looking at me . . .

"I shut mine, and tried to evoke a vision of Alice Nowell's. They were not remarkable eyes, but they were as wholesome as fresh water, and if she had had more imagination—or longer lashes—their expression might have been interesting. As it was, they did not prove very efficacious, and in a few moments I perceived that they had mysteriously changed into the eyes at the foot of the bed. It exasperated me more to feel these glaring at me through my shut lids than to see them, and I opened my eyes again and looked straight into their hateful stare . . .

"And so it went on all night. I can't tell you what that night was like, nor how long it lasted. Have you ever lain in bed, hopelessly wide awake, and tried to keep your eyes shut, knowing that if you opened 'em you'd see something you dreaded and loathed? It sounds easy, but it's devilish hard. Those eyes hung there and drew me. I had the *vertige de l'abîme,* and their red lids were the edge of my abyss . . . I had known nervous hours before: hours when I'd felt the wind of danger in my neck; but never this kind of strain. It wasn't that the eyes were awful; they hadn't the majesty of the powers of darkness. But they had—how shall I say?—a physical effect that was the equivalent of a bad smell: their look left a smear like a snail's. And I didn't see what business they had with me, anyhow—and I stared and stared, trying to find out . . .

"I don't know what effect they were trying to produce; but the effect they *did* produce was that of making me pack my portmanteau and bolt to town early the next morning. I left a note for my aunt, explaining that I was ill and had gone to see my doctor; and as a matter of fact I did feel uncommonly ill—the night seemed to have pumped all the blood out of me. But when I reached town I didn't go to the doctor's. I went to a friend's rooms, and threw myself on a bed, and slept for ten heavenly hours. When I woke it was the middle of the night, and I turned cold at the thought of what might be waiting for me. I sat up, shaking, and stared into the darkness; but there wasn't a break in its blessed surface, and when I saw that the eyes were not there I dropped back into another long sleep.

"I had left no word for Alice when I fled, because I meant to go back the next morning. But the next morning I was too exhausted to stir. As the day went on the exhaustion increased, instead of wearing off like the fatigue left by an ordinary night of insomnia: the effect of the eyes seemed to be cumulative, and the thought of seeing them again grew intolerable. For two days I fought my dread; and on the third evening I pulled myself together and decided to go back the next morning. I felt a good deal happier as soon as I'd decided, for I knew that my abrupt disappearance, and the strangeness of my not writing, must have been very distressing to poor Alice. I went to bed with an easy mind, and fell asleep at once; but in the middle of the night I woke, and there were the eyes . . .

"Well, I simply couldn't face them; and instead of going back to my aunt's I bundled a few things into a trunk and jumped aboard the first steamer for England. I was so dead tired when I got on board that I crawled straight into my berth, and slept most of the way over; and I can't tell you the bliss it was to wake from those long dreamless stretches and look fearlessly into the dark, *knowing* that I shouldn't see the eyes . . .

"I stayed abroad for a year, and then I stayed for another; and during that time I never had a glimpse of them. That was enough reason for prolonging my stay if I'd been on a desert island. Another was, of course, that I had perfectly come to see, on the voyage over, the complete impossibility of my marrying Alice Nowell. The fact that I had been so slow in making this discovery annoyed me, and made me want to avoid explanations. The bliss of escaping at one stroke from the eyes, and from this other embarrassment, gave my freedom an extraordinary zest; and the longer I savored it the better I liked its taste.

"The eyes had burned such a hole in my consciousness that for a long time I went on puzzling over the nature of the apparition, and wondering if it would ever come back. But as time passed I lost this dread, and retained only the precision of the image. Then that faded in its turn.

"The second year found me settled in Rome, where I was planning, I believe, to write another great book—a definitive work on Etruscan influences in Italian art. At any rate, I'd found some pretext of the kind for taking a sunny apartment in the Piazza di Spagna and dabbling about in the Forum; and there, one morning, a charming youth came to me. As he stood there in the warm light, slender and smooth and hyacinthine, he might have stepped from a ruined altar—one to Antinous, say; but he'd come instead from New York, with a letter (of all people) from Alice Nowell. The letter—the first I'd had from her since our break—was simply a line introducing her young cousin, Gilbert Noyes, and appealing to me to befriend him. It appeared, poor lad, that he 'had talent,' and 'wanted to write'; and, an obdurate family having insisted that his calligraphy should take the form of double entry, Alice had intervened to win him six months' respite, during which he was to travel abroad on a meager pittance, and somehow prove his ability to increase it by his pen. The quaint conditions of the test struck me first: it seemed about as conclusive as a medieval 'ordeal.' Then I was touched by her having sent him to me. I had always wanted to do her some service, to justify myself in my own eyes rather than hers; and here was a beautiful occasion.

"I imagine it's safe to lay down the general principle that predestined geniuses don't, as a rule, appear before one in the spring sunshine of the Forum looking like one of its banished gods. At any rate, poor Noyes wasn't a predestined genius. But he *was* beautiful to see, and charming as a comrade. It was only when he began to talk literature that my heart failed me. I knew all the symptoms so well—the things he had 'in him,' and the things outside him that impinged! There's the real test, after all. It was always—punctually, inevitably, with the inexorableness of a mechanical law—it was *always* the wrong thing that struck him. I grew to find a certain fascination in deciding in advance exactly which wrong thing he'd select; and I acquired an astonishing skill at the game . . .

"The worst of it was that his *bêtise* wasn't of the too obvious sort. Ladies who met him at picnics thought him intellectual; and even at dinners he passed for clever. I, who had him under the microscope, fancied now and then that he might develop some kind of a slim talent, something that he could make 'do' and be happy on; and wasn't that, after all, what I was concerned with? He was so charming—he continued to be so charming—that he called forth all my charity in support of this argument; and for the first few months I really believed there was a chance for him . . .

"Those months were delightful. Noyes was constantly with me, and the more I saw of him the better I liked him. His stupidity was a natural grace—it was as beautiful, really, as his eyelashes. And he was so gay, so affectionate, and so happy with me, that telling him the truth would have been about as pleasant as slitting the throat of some gentle animal. At first I used to wonder what had put into that radiant head the detestable delusion that it held a brain. Then I began to see that it was simply protective mimicry—an instinctive ruse to get away from family life and an office desk. Not that Gilbert didn't—dear lad!—believe in himself. There wasn't a trace of hypocrisy in him. He was sure that his 'call' was irresistible, while to me it was the saving grace of his situation that it *wasn't,* and that a little money, a little leisure, a little pleasure would have turned him into an inoffensive idler. Unluckily, however, there was no hope of money, and with the alternative of the office desk before him he couldn't postpone his attempt at literature. The stuff he turned out was deplorable, and I see now that I knew it from the first. Still, the absurdity of deciding a man's whole future on a first trial seemed to justify me in withholding my verdict, and perhaps even in encouraging him a little, on the ground that the human plant generally needs warmth to flower.

"At any rate, I proceeded on that principle, and carried it to the point of getting his term of probation extended. When I left Rome he went with me, and we idled away a delicious summer between Capri and Venice. I said to myself: 'If he has anything in him, it will come out now,' and it *did.* He was never more enchanting and enchanted. There were moments of our pilgrimage when beauty born of murmuring sound seemed actually to pass into his face—but only to issue forth in a flood of the palest ink . . .

"Well, the time came to turn off the tap; and I knew there was no hand but mine to do it. We were back in Rome, and I had taken him to stay with me, not wanting him to be alone in his *pension* when he had to face the necessity of renouncing his ambition. I hadn't, of course, relied solely on my own judgment in deciding to advise him to drop literature. I had sent his stuff to various people—editors and critics—and they had always sent it back with the same chilling lack of comment. Really there was nothing on earth to say——

"I confess I never felt more shabbily than I did on the day when I decided to have it out with Gilbert. It was well enough to tell myself that it was my duty to knock the poor boy's hopes into splinters—but I'd like to know what act of gratuitous cruelty hasn't been justified on that plea? I've always shrunk from usurping the functions of Providence, and when I have to exercise them I decidedly prefer that it shouldn't be on an errand of destruction. Besides, in the last issue, who was I to decide, even after a year's trial, if poor Gilbert had it in him or not?

"The more I looked at the part I'd resolved to play, the less I liked it; and I liked it still less when Gilbert sat opposite me, with his head thrown back in the lamp-light, just as Phil's is now . . . I'd been going over his last manuscript, and he knew it, and he knew that his future hung on my verdict—we'd tacitly agreed to that. The manuscript lay between us, on my table—a novel, his first novel, if you please!—and he reached over and laid his hand on it, and looked up at me with all his life in the look.

"I stood up and cleared my throat, trying to keep my eyes away from his face and on the manuscript.

"'The fact is, my dear Gilbert,' I began——

"I saw him turn pale, but he was up and facing me in an instant.

"'Oh, look here, don't take on so, my dear fellow! I'm not so awfully cut up as all that!' His hands were on my shoulders, and he was laughing down on me from his full height, with a kind of mortally-stricken gaiety that drove the knife into my side.

"He was too beautifully brave for me to keep up any humbug about my duty. And it came over me suddenly how I should hurt others in hurting him: myself first, since sending him home meant losing him; but more particularly poor Alice Nowell, to whom I had so longed to prove my good faith and my desire to serve her. It really seemed like failing her twice to fail Gilbert——

"But my intuition was like one of those lightning flashes that encircle the whole horizon, and in the same instant I saw what I might be letting myself in for if I didn't tell the truth. I said to myself: 'I shall have him for life'—and I'd never yet seen anyone, man or woman, whom I was quite sure of wanting on those terms. Well, this impulse of egotism decided me. I was ashamed of it, and to get away from it I took a leap that landed me straight in Gilbert's arms.

"'The thing's all right, and you're all wrong!' I shouted up at him; and as he hugged me, and I laughed and shook in his clutch, I had for a minute the sense of self-complacency that is supposed to attend the footsteps of the just. Hang it all, making people happy *has* its charms——

"Gilbert, of course, was for celebrating his emancipation in some spectacular manner; but I sent him away alone to explode his emotions, and went to bed to sleep off mine. As I undressed I began to wonder what their after-taste would be—so many of the finest don't keep! Still, I wasn't sorry, and I meant to empty the bottle, even if it *did* turn a trifle flat.

"After I got into bed I lay for a long time smiling at the memory of his eyes—his blissful eyes . . . Then I fell asleep, and when I woke the room was deathly cold, and I sat up with a jerk—and there were *the other eyes* . . .

"It was three years since I'd seen them, but I'd thought of them so often that I fancied they could never take me unawares again. Now, with their red sneer on me, I knew that I had never really believed they would come back, and that I was as defenseless as ever against them . . . As before, it was the insane irrelevance of their coming that made it so horrible. What the deuce were they after, to leap out at me at such a time? I had lived more or less carelessly in the years since I'd seen them, though my worst indiscretions were not dark enough to invite the searchings of their infernal glare; but at this particular moment I was really in what might have been called a state of grace; and I can't tell you how the fact added to their horror . . .

"But it's not enough to say they were as bad as before: they were worse. Worse by just so much as I'd learned of life in the interval; by all the damnable implications my wider experience read into them. I saw now what I hadn't seen before: that they were eyes which had grown hideous gradually, which had built up their baseness coral-wise, bit by bit, out of a series of small turpitudes slowly accumulated through the industrious years. Yes—it came to me that what made them so bad was that they'd grown bad so slowly . . .

"There they hung in the darkness, their swollen lids dropped across the little watery bulbs rolling loose in the orbits, and the puff of flesh making a muddy shadow underneath—and as their stare moved with my movements, there came over me a sense of their tacit complicity, of a deep hidden understanding between us that was worse than the first shock of their strangeness. Not that I understood them; but that they made it so clear that some day I should . . . Yes, that was the worst part of it, decidedly; and it was the feeling that became stronger each time they came back . . .

"For they got into the damnable habit of coming back. They reminded me of vampires with a taste for young flesh, they seemed so to gloat over the taste of a good conscience. Every night for a month they came to claim their morsel of mine: since I'd made Gilbert happy they simply wouldn't loosen their fangs. The coincidence almost made me hate him, poor lad, fortuitous as I felt it to be. I puzzled over it a good deal, but couldn't find any hint of an

"*When I awoke, the room was deathly cold, and I sat up with a jerk—there were* the other eyes."

explanation except in the chance of his association with Alice Nowell. But then the eyes had let up on me the moment I had abandoned her, so they could hardly be the emissaries of a woman scorned, even if one could have pictured poor Alice charging such spirits to avenge her. That set me thinking, and I began to wonder if they would let up on me if I abandoned Gilbert. The temptation was insidious, and I had to stiffen myself against it; but really, dear boy! he was too charming to be sacrificed to such demons. And so, after all, I never found out what they wanted . . ."

III

THE fire crumbled, sending up a flash which threw into relief the narrator's gnarled face under its grey-black stubble. Pressed into the hollow of the chair-back, it stood out an instant like an intaglio of yellowish red-veined stone, with spots of enamel for the eyes; then the fire sank and it became once more a dim Rembrandtish blur.

Phil Frenham, sitting in a low chair on the opposite side of the hearth, one long arm propped on the table behind him, one hand supporting his thrown-back head, and his eyes fixed on his old friend's face, had not moved since the tale began. He continued to maintain his silent immobility after Culwin had ceased to speak, and it was I who, with a vague sense of disappointment at the sudden drop of the story, finally asked: "But how long did you keep on seeing them?"

Culwin, so sunk into his chair that he seemed like a heap of his own empty clothes, stirred a little, as if in surprise at my question. He appeared to have half-forgotten what he had been telling us.

"How long? Oh, off and on all that winter. It was infernal. I never got used to them. I grew really ill."

Frenham shifted his attitude, and as he did so his elbow struck against a small mirror in a bronze frame standing on the table behind him. He turned and changed its angle slightly; then he resumed his former attitude, his dark head thrown back on his lifted palm, his eyes intent on Culwin's face. Something in his silent gaze embarrassed me, and as if to divert attention from it I pressed on with another question:

"And you never tried sacrificing Noyes?"

"Oh, no. The fact is I didn't have to. He did it for me, poor boy!"

"Did it for you? How do you mean?"

"He wore me out—wore everybody out. He kept on pouring out his lamentable twaddle, and hawking it up and down the place till he became a thing of terror. I tried to wean him from writing—oh, ever so gently, you understand, by throwing him with agreeable people, giving him a chance to make himself felt, to come to a sense of what he *really* had to give. I'd foreseen this solution from the beginning—felt sure that, once the first ardor of authorship was quenched, he'd drop into his place as a charming parasitic thing, the kind of chronic Cherubino for whom, in old societies, there's always a seat at table, and a shelter behind the ladies' skirts. I saw him take his place as 'the poet': the poet who doesn't write. One knows the type in every drawing-room. Living in that way doesn't cost much—I'd worked it all out in my mind, and felt sure that, with a little help, he could manage it for the next few years; and meanwhile he'd be sure to marry. I saw him married to a widow, rather older, with a good cook and a well-run house. And I actually had my eye on the widow . . . Meanwhile I did everything to help the transition—lent him money to ease his conscience, introduced him to pretty women to make him forget his vows. But nothing would do him: he had but one idea in his beautiful obstinate head. He wanted the laurel and not the rose, and he kept on repeating Gautier's axiom, and battering and filing at his limp prose till he'd spread it out over Lord knows how many hundred pages. Now and then he would send a barrelful to a publisher, and of course it would always come back.

"At first it didn't matter—he thought he was 'misunderstood.' He took the attitudes of genius, and whenever an opus came home he wrote another to keep it company. Then he had a reaction of despair, and accused me of deceiving him, and Lord knows what. I got angry at that, and told him it was he who had deceived himself. He'd come to me determined to write, and I'd done my best to help him. That was the extent of my offense, and I'd done it for his cousin's sake, not his.

"That seemed to strike home, and he didn't answer for a minute. Then he said: 'My time's up and my money's up. What do you think I'd better do?'

"'I think you'd better not be an ass,' I said.

"'What do you mean by being an ass?' he asked.

"I took a letter from my desk and held it out to him.

"'I mean refusing this offer of Mrs. Ellinger's: to be her secretary at a salary of five thousand dollars. There may be a lot more in it than that.'

"He flung out his hand with a violence that struck the letter from mine. 'Oh, I know well enough what's in it!' he said, red to the roots of his hair.

"'And what's the answer, if you know?' I asked.

"He made none at the minute, but turned away slowly to the door. There, with his hand on the threshold, he stopped to say, almost under his breath: 'Then you really think my stuff's no good?'

"I was tired and exasperated, and I laughed. I don't defend my laugh—it was in wretched taste. But I must plead in extenuation that the boy was a fool, and that I'd done my best for him—I really had.

"He went out of the room, shutting the door quietly after him. That afternoon I left for Frascati, where I'd promised to spend the Sunday with some friends. I was glad to escape from Gilbert, and by the same token, as I learned that night, I had also escaped from the eyes. I dropped into the same lethargic sleep that had come to me before when I left off seeing them; and when I woke the next morning, in my peaceful room above the ilexes, I felt the utter weariness and deep relief that always followed on that sleep. I put in two blessed nights at Frascati, and when I got back to my rooms in Rome I found that Gilbert had gone . . . Oh, nothing tragic had happened—the episode never rose to *that*. He'd simply packed his manuscripts and left for America—for his family and the Wall Street desk. He left a decent enough note to tell me of his decision, and behaved altogether, in the circumstances, as little like a fool as it is possible for a fool to behave . . ."

IV

CULWIN paused again, and Frenham still sat motionless, the dusky contour of his young head reflected in the mirror at his back.

"And what became of Noyes afterward?" I finally asked, still disquieted by a sense of incompleteness, by the need of some connecting thread between the parallel lines of the tale.

Culwin twitched his shoulders. "Oh, nothing became of him—because he became nothing. There could be no question of 'becoming' about it. He vegetated in an office, I believe, and finally got a clerkship in a consulate, and married drearily in China. I saw him once in Hong Kong, years afterward. He was fat and hadn't shaved. I was told he drank. He didn't recognize me."

"And the eyes?" I asked, after another pause which Frenham's continued silence made oppressive.

Culwin, stroking his chin, blinked at me meditatively through the shadows. "I never saw them after my last talk with Gilbert. Put two and two together if you can. For my part, I haven't found the link."

He rose, his hands in his pockets, and walked stiffly over to the table on which reviving drinks had been set out.

"You must be parched after this dry tale. Here, help yourself, my dear fellow. Here, Phil——" He turned back to the hearth.

Frenham made no response to his host's hospitable summons. He still sat in his low chair without moving, but as Culwin advanced toward him, their eyes met in a long look; after which the young man, turning suddenly, flung his arms across the table behind him, and dropped his face upon them.

Culwin, at the unexpected gesture, stopped short, a flush on his face.

"Phil—what the deuce? Why, have the eyes scared *you?* My dear boy—my dear fellow—I never had such a tribute to my literary ability, never!"

He broke into a chuckle at the thought, and halted on the hearth-rug, his hands still in his pockets, gazing down at the youth's bowed head. Then, as Frenham still made no answer, he moved a step or two nearer.

"Cheer up, my dear Phil! It's years since I've seen them—apparently I've done nothing lately bad enough to call them out of chaos. Unless my present evocation of them has made *you* see them; which would be their worst stroke yet!"

His bantering appeal quivered off into an uneasy laugh, and he moved still nearer, bending over Frenham, and laying his gouty hands on the lad's shoulders.

"Phil, my dear boy, really—what's the matter? Why don't you answer? *Have* you seen the eyes?"

Frenham's face was still hidden, and from where I stood behind Culwin I saw the latter, as if under the rebuff of this unaccountable attitude, draw back slowly from his friend. As he did so, the light of the lamp on the table fell full on his congested face, and I caught its reflection in the mirror behind Frenham's head.

Culwin saw the reflection also. He paused, his face level with the mirror, as if scarcely recognizing the countenance in it as his own. But as he looked his expression gradually changed, and for an appreciable space of time he and the image in the glass confronted each other with a glare of slowly gathering hate. Then Culwin let go on Frenham's shoulders, and drew back a step . . .

Frenham, his face still hidden, did not stir.

The Blond Beast

I

IT had been almost too easy—that was young Millner's first feeling, as he stood again on the Spence doorstep, the great moment of his interview behind him, and Fifth Avenue rolling its grimy Pacolus at his feet.

Halting here in the winter light, with the clang of the vestibule doors in his ears, and his eyes carried down the perspective of the packed interminable thoroughfare, he even dared to remember Rastignac's apostrophe to Paris, and to hazard recklessly under his small fair moustache: "Who knows?"

He, Hugh Millner, at any rate, knew a good deal already: a good deal more than he had imagined it possible to learn in half an hour's talk with a man like Orlando G. Spence; and the loud-rumoring city spread out before him seemed to grin like an accomplice who knew the rest.

A gust of wind, whirling down from the dizzy height of the building on the next corner, drove through his shabby overcoat and compelled him to clutch hurriedly at his hat. It was a bitter January day, a day of fierce light and air, when the sunshine cut like icicles and the wind sucked one into black gulfs at the street corners. But Millner's complacency was like a warm lining to his coat, and having steadied his hat he continued to stand on the Spence threshold, lost in the vision revealed to him from the Pisgah of its marble steps. Yes, it was wonderful what the vision showed him . . . In his absorption he might have frozen fast to the doorstep if the Rhadamanthine portals behind him had not suddenly opened to let out a slim fur-coated figure, the figure, as he perceived, of the youth whom he had caught in the act of withdrawal as he entered Mr. Spence's study, and whom the latter, with a wave of his affable hand, had detained to introduce as "my son Draper."

It was characteristic of the odd friendliness of the whole scene that the great man should have thought it worth while to call back and name his heir to a mere humble applicant like Millner; and that the heir should shed on him, from a pale high-browed face, a smile of such deprecating kindness. It was characteristic, equally, of Millner, that he should at once mark the narrowness of the shoulders sustaining this ingenuous head; a narrowness, as he now observed, imperfectly concealed by the fur collar of young Spence's expensive and badly cut coat. But the face took on, as the youth smiled his pleasure at their second meeting, a look of almost plaintive goodwill: the kind of look that Millner scorned and yet could never quite resist.

"Mr. Millner? Are you—er—waiting?" the lad asked, with an intention of serviceableness that was like a finer echo of his father's cordiality.

"For my motor? No," Millner jested in his frank free voice. "The fact is, I was just standing here lost in the contemplation of my luck"—and as his companion's pale blue eyes seemed to shape a question: "my extraordinary luck," he explained, "in having been engaged as your father's secretary."

"Oh," the other rejoined, with a faint color in his cheek. "I'm so glad," he murmured; "but I was sure—" He stopped, and the two looked kindly at each other.

Millner averted his gaze first, almost fearful of its betraying the added sense of his own strength and dexterity which he drew from the contrast of the other's frailness.

"Sure? How could any one be sure? I don't believe in it yet!" he laughed out in the irony of his triumph.

The boy's words did not sound like a mere civility—Millner felt in them an homage to his power.

"Oh, yes: I was sure," young Draper repeated. "Sure as soon as I saw you, I mean."

Millner tingled again with this tribute to his physical straightness and bloom. Yes, he looked his part, hang it—he looked it!

But his companion still lingered, a shy sociability in his eye.

"If you're walking, then, may I go along a little way?" And he nodded southward down the shabby gaudy avenue.

That, again, was part of the wild comedy of the hour—that Millner should descend the Spence steps at young Spence's side, and stroll down Fifth Avenue with him at the proudest moment of the afternoon; O. G. Spence's secretary walking abroad with O. G. Spence's heir! He had the scientific detachment to pull out his watch and furtively note the hour. Yes—it was exactly forty minutes since he had rung the Spence door-bell and handed his card to a gelid footman, who, openly sceptical of his claim to be received, had left him unceremoniously planted on the cold tessellations of the vestibule.

("Some day," Millner grinned to himself, "I think I'll take that footman as furnace-man—or to do the boots." And he pictured his marble palace rising from the earth to form the mausoleum of a footman's pride.) Only forty minutes ago! And now he had his opportunity fast! And he never meant to let it go! It was incredible, what had happened in the interval. He had gone up the Spence steps an unknown young man, out of a job, and with no substantial hope of getting into one: a needy young man with a mother and two sisters to be helped, and a lengthening figure of debt that stood by his bed through the anxious nights. And he went down the steps with his present assured, and his future lit by the hues of the rainbow above the pot of gold. Certainly a fellow who made his way at that rate had it "in him," and could afford to trust his star. Descending from this joyous flight he stooped his ear to the discourse of young Spence.

"My father'll work you rather hard, you know: but you look as if you wouldn't mind that."

Millner pulled up his inches with the self-consciousness of the man who has none to waste. "Oh, no, I shan't mind that: I don't mind any amount of work if it leads to something."

"Just so," Draper Spence assented eagerly. "That's what I feel. And you'll find that whatever my father undertakes leads to such awfully fine things."

Millner tightened his lips on a grin. He was thinking only of where the work would lead him, not in the least of where it might land the eminent Orlando G. Spence. But he looked at his companion sympathetically.

"You're a philanthropist like your father, I see?"

"Oh, I don't know." They had paused at a crossing, and young Draper, with a dubious air, stood striking his agate-headed stick against the curb-stone. "I believe in a purpose, don't you?" he asked, lifting his blue eyes suddenly to Millner's face.

"A purpose? I should rather say so! I believe in nothing else," cried Millner, feeling as if his were something he could grip in his hand and swing like a club.

Young Spence seemed relieved. "Yes—I tie up to that. There *is* a Purpose. And so, after all, even if I don't agree with my father on minor points . . ." He colored quickly, and looked again at Millner. "I should like to talk to you about this some day."

Millner smothered another smile. "We'll have lots of talks, I hope."

"Oh, if you can spare the time—!" said Draper, almost humbly.

"Why, I shall be there on tap!"

"For father, not me." Draper hesitated, with another self-confessing smile. "Father thinks I talk too much—that I keep going in and out of things. He doesn't believe in analyzing: he thinks it's destructive. But it hasn't destroyed my ideals." He looked wistfully up and down the clanging street. "And that's the main thing, isn't it? I mean, that one should have an Ideal." He turned back almost gaily to Millner. "I suspect you're a revolutionist too!"

"Revolutionist? Rather! I belong to the Red Syndicate and the Black Hand!" Millner joyfully assented.

Young Draper chuckled at the enormity of the joke. "First rate! We'll have incendiary meetings!" He pulled an elaborately armorial watch from under his enfolding furs. "I'm so sorry, but I must say good-bye—this is my street," he explained.

Millner, with a faint twinge of envy, glanced across at the colonnaded marble edifice on the farther corner.

"Going to the club?" he said carelessly.

His companion looked surprised. "Oh, no: I never go *there*. It's too boring." And he jerked out, after one of the pauses in which he seemed rather breathlessly to measure the chances of his listener's indulgence: "I'm just going over to a little Bible Class I have in Tenth Avenue."

Millner, for a moment or two, stood watching the slim figure wind its way through the mass of vehicles to the opposite corner; then he pursued his own course down Fifth Avenue, measuring his steps to the rhythmic refrain: "It's too easy—it's too easy—it's too easy!"

His own destination being the small faded flat off University Place where three tender females awaited the result of his mission, he had time, on the way home, after abandoning himself to a general sense of triumph, to dwell specifically on the various aspects of his achievement. Viewed materially and practically, it was a thing to be proud of; yet it was chiefly on aesthetic grounds—because he had done so exactly what he had set out to do—that he glowed with pride at the afternoon's work. For, after all, any young man with the proper "pull" might have applied to Orlando G. Spence for the post of secretary, and might even have penetrated as far as the great man's study; but that he, Hugh Millner, should not only have forced his way to this fastness, but have established, within a short half hour, his right to remain there permanently: well, this, if it proved anything, proved that the first rule of success was to know how to live up to one's principles.

"One must have a plan—one must have a plan," the young man murmured, looking with pity at the vague faces which the crowd bore past him, and feeling almost impelled to detain them and expound his doctrine. But the planlessness of average human nature was of course the measure of his opportunity; and he smiled to think that every purposeless face he met was a guarantee of his own advancement, a rung in the ladder he meant to climb.

Yes, the whole secret of success was to know what one wanted to do, and not to be afraid to do it. His own history was proving that already. He had not been afraid to give up his small but safe position in a real-estate office for the precarious adventure of a private secretaryship; and his first glimpse of his new employer had convinced him that he had not mistaken his calling. When one has a "way" with one—as, in all modesty, Millner knew he had—not to utilize it is a stupid waste of force. And when he learned that Orlando G. Spence was in search of a private secretary who should be able to give him intelligent assistance in the execution of his philanthropic schemes, the young man felt that his hour had come. It was no part of his plan to associate himself with one of the masters of finance: he had a notion that minnows who go to a whale to learn how to grow bigger are likely to be swallowed in the process. The opportunity of a clever young man with a cool head and no prejudices (this again was drawn from life) lay rather in making himself indispensable to one of the beneficent rich, and in using the timidities and conformities of his patron as the means of his own advancement. Young Millner felt no scruples about formulating these principles to himself. It was not for nothing that, in his college days, he had hunted the hypothetical "moral sense" to its lair, and dragged from their concealment the various self-advancing sentiments dissembled under it. His strength lay in his precocious insight into the springs of action, and in his refusal to classify them according to the accepted moral and social sanctions. He had to the full the courage of his lack of convictions.

To a young man so untrammelled by prejudice it was self-evident that helpless philanthropists like Orlando G. Spence were just as much the natural diet of the strong as the lamb is of the wolf. It was pleasanter to eat than to be eaten, in a world where, as yet, there seemed to be no third alternative; and any scruples one might feel as to the temporary discomfort of one's victim were speedily dispelled by that larger scientific view which took into account the social destructiveness of the benevolent. Millner was persuaded that every individual woe mitigated by the philanthropy of Orlando G. Spence added just so much to the sum-total of human inefficiency, and it was one of his favorite subjects of speculation to picture the innumerable social evils that may follow upon the rescue of one infant from Mount Taygetus.

"We're all born to prey on each other, and pity for suffering is one of the most elementary stages of egotism. Until one has passed beyond, and acquired a taste for the more complex forms of the instinct——"

He stopped suddenly, checked in his advance by a sallow wisp of a dog which had plunged through the press of vehicles to hurl itself between his legs. Millner did not dislike animals, though he preferred that they should be healthy and handsome. The dog under his feet was neither. Its cringing contour showed an injudicious mingling of races, and its meager coat betrayed the deplorable habit of sleeping in coal-holes and subsisting on an innutritious diet. In addition to these disadvantages, its shrinking and inconsequent movements revealed a congenital weakness of character which, even under more favorable conditions, would hardly have qualified it to become a useful member of society; and Millner was not sorry to notice that it moved with a limp of the hind leg that probably doomed it to speedy extinction.

The absurdity of such an animal's attempting to cross Fifth Avenue at the most crowded hour of the afternoon struck him as only less great than the irony of its having been permitted to achieve the feat; and he stood a moment looking at it, and wondering what had moved it to the attempt. It was really a perfect type of the human derelict which Orlando G. Spence and his kind were devoting their millions to perpetuate, and he reflected how much better Nature knew her business in dealing with the superfluous quadruped.

A lady advancing in the opposite direction evidently took a less dispassionate view of the case, for she paused to remark emotionally: "Oh, you poor thing!" while she stooped to caress the object of her sympathy. The dog, with characteristic lack of discrimination, viewed her gesture with suspicion, and met it with a snarl. The lady turned pale and shrank away, a chivalrous male repelled the animal with his umbrella, and two idle boys backed his actions by a vigorous "Hi!" The object of these demonstrations, apparently attributing them not to his own unsocial conduct, but merely to the chronic hostility of the universe, dashed wildly around the corner into a side street, and as it did so Millner noticed that the lame leg left a slight trail of blood. Irresistibly, he turned the corner to see what would happen next. It was clear that the animal itself had no plan; but after several inconsequent and contradictory movements it plunged down an area, where it backed up against the iron gate, forlornly and foolishly at bay.

Millner, still following, looked down at it, and wondered. Then he whistled, just to see if it would come; but this only caused it to start up tremblingly, with desperate turns of the head that measured the chances of escape.

"Oh, hang it, you poor devil, stay there if you like!" the young man murmured, walking away.

A few yards off he looked back, and saw that the dog had made a rush out of the area and was limping down the street. The idle boys were in the offing, and he disliked the thought of leaving them in control of the situation. Softly, with infinite precautions, he began to follow the dog. He did not know why he was doing it, but the impulse was overmastering. For a moment he seemed to be gaining upon his quarry, but with a cunning sense of his approach it suddenly turned and hobbled across the frozen grass-plot adjoining a shuttered house. Against the wall at the back of the plot it cowered down in a dirty snow-drift, as if disheartened by the struggle. Millner stood outside the railings and looked at it. He reflected that under the shelter of the winter dusk it might have the luck to remain there unmolested, and that in the morning it would probably be dead. This was so obviously the best solution that he began to move away again; but as he did so the idle boys confronted him.

"Ketch yer dog for yer, boss?" they grinned.

Millner consigned them to the devil, and stood watching till the first stage of the journey had carried them around the nearest corner; then, after pausing to look once more up and down the empty street, he laid his hand on the railing, and vaulted over it into the grass-plot. As he did so, he reflected that, since pity for suffering was one of the most primitive forms of egotism, he ought to have remembered that it was necessarily one of the most tenacious.

II

"MY chief aim in life?" Orlando G. Spence repeated. He threw himself back in his chair, straightened the tortoise-shell *pince-nez* on his short thick nose, and beamed down the luncheon table at the two young men who shared his repast.

His glance rested on his son Draper, seated opposite him behind a barrier of Georgian silver and orchids; but his words were addressed to his secretary who, stylograph in hand, had turned from the seductions of a mushroom *soufflé* to jot down, for the Sunday *Investigator,* an outline of his employer's views and intentions respecting the newly endowed Orlando G. Spence College for Missionaries. It was Mr. Spence's practice to receive in person the journalists privileged to impart his opinions to the world; but during the last few months—and especially since the vast project of the Missionary College had been in process of development—the pressure of business and beneficence had necessitated Millner's frequent intervention, and compelled the secretary to snatch the sense of his patron's elucubrations between the courses of their rapid meals.

Young Millner had a healthy appetite, and it was not one of his least sacrifices to be so often obliged to curb it in the interest of his advancement; but whenever he waved aside one of the triumphs of Mr. Spence's chef he was conscious of rising a step in his employer's favor. Mr. Spence did not despise the pleasures of the table, though he appeared to regard them as the reward of success rather than as the alleviation of effort; and it increased his sense of his secretary's merit to note how keenly the young man enjoyed the fare which he was so frequently obliged to deny himself. Draper, having subsisted since infancy on a diet of truffles and terrapin, consumed such delicacies with the insensibility of a traveller swallowing a railway sandwich; but Millner never made the mistake of concealing from Mr. Spence his sense of what he was losing when duty constrained him to exchange the fork for the pen.

"My chief aim in life?" Mr. Spence repeated, removing his eye-glass and swinging it thoughtfully on his finger. ("I'm sorry you should miss this *soufflé,* Millner: it's worth while.) Why, I suppose I might say that my chief aim in life is to leave the world better than I found it. Yes: I don't know that I could put it better than that. To leave the world better than I found it. It wouldn't be a bad idea to use that as a headline. *'Wants to leave the world better than he found it.'* It's exactly the point I should like to make in this talk for the *Investigator* about the College."

Mr. Spence paused, and his glance once more reverted to his son, who, having pushed aside his plate, sat watching Millner with a dreamy intensity.

"And it's the point I want to make with you, too, Draper," his father continued, while he turned over with a critical fork the plump and perfectly matched asparagus which a footman was presenting to his notice. "I want to make you feel that nothing else counts in comparison with that—no amount of literary success or intellectual celebrity."

"Oh, I *do* feel that," Draper murmured, with one of his quick blushes, and a glance that wavered between his father and Millner. The secretary kept his eyes on his notes, and young Spence continued, after a pause: "Only the thing is—isn't it?—to try and find out just what *does* make the world better?"

"To *try* to find out?" his father echoed compassionately. "It's not necessary to try very hard. Goodness is what makes the world better."

"Yes, yes, of course," his son interposed; "but the question is, what *is* good——"

Mr. Spence, with a darkening brow, brought his fist down emphatically on the damask. "I'll thank you not to blaspheme, my son!"

Draper's head reared itself a trifle higher on his thin neck. "I was not going to blaspheme; only there may be different ways——"

"There's where you're mistaken, Draper. There's only one way: there's my way," said Mr. Spence in a tone of unshaken conviction.

"I know, father; I see what you mean. But don't you see that even your way wouldn't be the right way for you if you ceased to believe that it was?"

His father looked at him with mingled bewilderment and reprobation. "Do you mean to say that the fact of goodness depends on my conception of it, and not on God Almighty's?"

"I do . . . yes . . . in a certain sense . . ." young Draper falteringly maintained; and Mr. Spence turned with a discouraged gesture toward his secretary.

"I don't understand your scientific jargon, Draper; and I don't want to.—What's the next point, Millner? (No; no *Savarin*. Bring the fruit—and the coffee with it.)"

Millner, keenly aware that an aromatic *Savarin au rhum* was describing an arc behind his head previous to being rushed back to the pantry under young Draper's indifferent eye, stiffened himself against this last assault, and read out firmly: *"What relation do you consider that a man's business conduct should bear to his religious and domestic life?"*

Mr. Spence meditated for a moment. "Why, that's a stupid question. It goes over the same ground as the other one. A man ought to do good with his money—that's all. Go on."

At this point the butler's murmur in his ear caused him to push back his chair, and to arrest Millner's interrogatory by a rapid gesture. "Yes; I'm coming. Hold the wire." Mr. Spence rose and plunged into the adjoining "office," where a telephone and a Remington divided the attention of a young lady in spectacles who was preparing for Zenana work in the East.

As the door closed, the butler, having placed the coffee and liqueurs on the table, withdrew in the wake of his battalion, and the two young men were left alone beneath the Rembrandts and Hobbemas that looked down upon the dining-table.

There was a moment's silence between them; then young Spence, leaning across the table, said in the lowered tone of intimacy: "Why do you suppose he dodged that last question?"

Millner, who had taken an opulent purple fig from the fruit-dish nearest him, paused in surprise in the act of hurrying it to his lips.

"I mean," Draper hastened on, "the question as to the relation between business and private morality. It's such an interesting one, and he's just the person who ought to tackle it."

Millner, despatching the fig, glanced down at his notes. "I don't think your father meant to dodge the question," he returned.

Young Draper continued to look at him.

"You think he imagined that his answer really covers the ground?"

"As much as it needs to be covered."

The son of the house glanced away with a sigh. "You know things about him that I don't," he said wistfully, but without a tinge of resentment.

"Oh, as to that—(may I give myself some coffee?)" Millner, in his walk around the table to fill his cup, paused a moment to lay an affectionate hand on Draper's shoulder. "Perhaps I know him *better,* in a sense: outsiders often get a more accurate focus."

Draper seemed to consider this. "And your idea is that he acts on principles he has never thought of testing or defining?"

Millner looked up quickly, and for an instant their glances crossed. "How do you mean?"

"I mean: that he's an inconscient instrument of goodness, as it were? A—a sort of blindly beneficent force?"

The other smiled. "That's not a bad definition. I know one thing about him, at any rate: he's awfully upset at your having chucked your Bible Class."

A shadow fell on young Spence's candid brow. "I know. But what can I do about it? That's what I was thinking of just now when I tried to show him that goodness, in a certain sense, is purely subjective: that one can't do good against one's principles." Again his glance appealed to Millner. "*You* understand me, don't you?"

Millner stirred his coffee in a silence not unclouded by perplexity. "Theoretically, perhaps. It's a pretty question, certainly. But I also understand your father's feeling that it hasn't much to do with life: especially now that he's got to make a speech in connection with the founding of this Missionary College. He may think that any hint of internecine strife will weaken his prestige. Mightn't you have waited a little longer?"

"How could I, when I might have been expected to take a part in this performance? To talk, and say things I didn't mean? That was exactly what made me decide not to wait."

The door opened and Mr. Spence re-entered the room. As he did so his son rose as if to leave it.

"Where are you off to, Draper?" the banker asked.

"I'm in rather a hurry, sir——"

Mr. Spence looked at his watch. "You can't be in more of a hurry than I am; and I've got seven minutes and a half." He seated himself behind the coffee-tray, lit a cigar, laid his watch on the table, and signed to Draper to resume his place. "No, Millner, don't you go; I want you both." He turned to the secretary. "You know that Draper's given up his Bible Class? I understand it's not from the pressure of engagements"—Mr. Spence's narrow lips took an ironic curve under the straight-clipped stubble of his moustache—"it's on principle, he tells me. He's *principled* against doing good!"

Draper lifted a protesting hand. "It's not exactly that, father——"

"I know: you'll get off some scientific quibble that I don't understand. I've never had time to go in for intellectual hair-splitting. I've found too many people down in the mire who needed a hand to pull them out. A busy man has to take his choice between helping his fellow-men and theorizing about them. I've preferred to help. (You might take that down for the *Investigator,* Millner.) And I thank God I've never stopped to ask what made me want to do good. I've just yielded to the impulse—that's all." Mr. Spence turned back to his son. "Better men than either of us have been satisfied with that creed, my boy."

Draper was silent, and Mr. Spence once more addressed himself to his secretary. "Millner, you're a reader: I've caught you at it. And I know this boy talks to you. What have you got to say? Do you suppose a Bible Class ever *hurt* anybody?"

Millner paused a moment, feeling all through his nervous system the fateful tremor of the balance. "That's what I was just trying to tell him, sir——"

"Ah; you were? That's good. Then I'll only say one thing more. Your doing what you've done at this particular moment hurts me more, Draper, than your teaching the gospel of Jesus could possibly have hurt those young men over in Tenth Avenue." Mr. Spence arose and restored his watch to his pocket. "I shall want you in twenty minutes, Millner."

The door closed on him, and for a while the two young men sat silent behind their cigar fumes. Then Draper Spence broke out, with a catch in his throat: "That's what I can't bear, Millner, what I simply can't *bear:* to hurt him, to hurt his faith in *me!* It's an awful responsibility, isn't it, to tamper with anybody's faith in anything?"

III

THE twenty minutes prolonged themselves to forty, the forty to fifty, and the fifty to an hour; and still Millner waited for Mr. Spence's summons.

During the two years of his secretaryship the young man had learned the significance of such postponements. Mr. Spence's days were organized like a railway time-table, and a delay of an hour implied a casualty as far-reaching as the breaking down of an express. Of the cause of the present derangement Hugh Millner was ignorant; and the experience of the last months allowed him to fluctuate between conflicting conjectures. All were based on the indisputable fact that Mr. Spence was "bothered"—had for some time past been "bothered." And it was one of Millner's discoveries that an extremely parsimonious use of the emotions underlay Mr. Spence's expansive manner and fraternal phraseology, and that he did not throw away his feelings any more than (for all his philanthropy) he threw away his money. If he was bothered, then, it could be only because a careful survey of his situation had forced on him some unpleasant fact with which he was not immediately prepared to deal; and any unpreparedness on Mr. Spence's part was also a significant symptom.

Obviously, Millner's original conception of his employer's character had suffered extensive modification; but no final outline had replaced the first conjectural image. The two years spent in Mr. Spence's service had produced too many contradictory impressions to be fitted into any clear pattern; and the chief lesson Millner had learned from them was that life was less of an exact science, and character a more incalculable element, than he had been taught in the schools. In the light of this revised impression, his own footing seemed less secure than he had imagined, and the rungs of the ladder he was climbing more slippery than they had looked from below. He was not without the reassuring sense of having made himself, in certain small ways, necessary to Mr. Spence; and this conviction was confirmed by Draper's reiterated assurance of his father's appreciation. But Millner had begun to suspect that one might be necessary to Mr. Spence one day, and a superfluity, if not an obstacle, the next; and that it would take superhuman astuteness to foresee how and when the change would occur. Every fluctuation of the great man's mood was therefore anxiously noted by the young meteorologist in his service; and this observer's vigilance was now strained to the utmost by the little cloud, no bigger than a man's hand, adumbrated by the banker's unpunctuality.

When Mr. Spence finally appeared, his aspect did not tend to dissipate the cloud. He wore what Millner had learned to call his "back-door face": a blank barred countenance, in which only an occasional twitch of the lids behind his glasses suggested that some one was on the watch. In this mood Mr. Spence usually seemed unconscious of his secretary's presence, or aware of it only as an arm terminating in a pen. Millner, accustomed on such occasions to exist merely as a function, sat waiting for the click of the spring that should set him in action; but the pressure not being applied, he finally hazarded: "Are we to go on with the *Investigator,* sir?"

Mr. Spence, who had been pacing up and down between the desk and the fireplace, threw himself into his usual seat at Millner's elbow.

"I don't understand this new notion of Draper's," he said abruptly. "Where's he got it from? No one ever learned irreligion in my household."

He turned his eyes on Millner, who had the sense of being scrutinized through a ground-glass window which left him visible while it concealed his observer. The young man let his pen describe two or three vague patterns on the sheet before him.

"Draper has ideas——" he risked at last.

Mr. Spence looked hard at him. "That's all right," he said. "I want my son to have everything. But what's the point of mixing up

When Mr. Spence finally appeared, his aspect did not tend to dissipate the cloud.

ideas and principles? I've seen fellows who did that, and they were generally trying to borrow five dollars to get away from the sheriff. What's all this talk about goodness? Goodness isn't an idea. It's a fact. It's as solid as a business proposition. And it's Draper's duty, as the son of a wealthy man, and the prospective steward of a great fortune, to elevate the standards of other young men—of young men who haven't had his opportunities. The rich ought to preach contentment, and to set the example themselves. We have our cares, but we ought to conceal them. We ought to be cheerful, and accept things as they are—not go about sowing dissent and restlessness. What has Draper got to give these boys in his Bible Class, that's so much better than what he wants to take from them? That's the question I'd like to have answered."

Mr. Spence, carried away by his own eloquence, had removed his *pince-nez* and was twirling it about his extended forefinger with the gesture habitual to him when he spoke in public. After a pause, he went on, with a drop to the level of private intercourse: "I tell you this because I know you have a good deal of influence with Draper. He has a high opinion of your brains. But you're a practical fellow, and you must see what I mean. Try to make Draper see it. Make him understand how it looks to have him drop his Bible Class just at this particular time. It was his own choice to take up religious teaching among young men. He began with our office-boys, and then the work spread and was blessed. I was almost alarmed, at one time, at the way it took hold of him: when the papers began to talk about him as a formative influence I was afraid he'd lose his head and go into the church. Luckily he tried University Settlement first; but just as I thought he was settling down to that, he took to worrying about the Higher Criticism, and saying he couldn't go on teaching fairy-tales as history. I can't see that any good ever came of criticizing what our parents believed, and it's a queer time for Draper to criticize *my* belief just as I'm backing it to the extent of five millions."

Millner remained silent; and, as though his silence were an argument, Mr. Spence continued combatively: "Draper's always talking about some distinction between religion and morality. I don't understand what he means. I got my morals out of the Bible, and I guess there's enough left in it for Draper. If religion won't make a man moral, I don't see why irreligion should. And he talks about using his mind—well, can't he use that in Wall Street? A man can get a good deal farther in life watching the market than picking holes in Genesis; and he can do more good too. There's a time for everything; and Draper seems to me to have mixed up week-days with Sunday."

Mr. Spence replaced his eye-glasses, and stretching his hand to the silver box at his elbow, extracted from it one of the long cigars sheathed in gold-leaf which were reserved for his private consumption. The secretary hastened to tender him a match, and for a moment he puffed in silence. When he spoke again it was in a different note.

"I've got about all the bother I can handle just now, without this nonsense of Draper's. That was one of the Trustees of the College with me. It seems the *Flashlight* has been trying to stir up a fuss——" Mr. Spence paused, and turned his *pince-nez* on his secretary. "You haven't heard from them?" he asked.

"From the *Flashlight?* No." Millner's surprise was genuine.

He detected a gleam of relief behind Mr. Spence's glasses. "It may be just malicious talk. That's the worst of good works; they bring out all the meanness in human nature. And then there are always women mixed up in them, and there never was a woman yet who understood the difference between philanthropy and business." He drew again at his cigar, and then, with an unwonted movement, leaned forward and absently pushed the box toward Millner. "Help yourself," he said.

Millner, as mechanically, took one of the virginally cinctured cigars, and began to undo its wrappings. It was the first time he had ever been privileged to detach that golden girdle, and nothing could have given him a better measure of the importance of the situation, and of the degree to which he was apparently involved in it. "You remember that San Pablo rubber business? That's what they've been raking up," said Mr. Spence.

Millner paused in the act of striking a match. Then, with an appreciable effort of the will, he completed the gesture, applied the flame to his cigar, and took a long inhalation. The cigar was certainly delicious.

Mr. Spence, drawing a little closer, leaned forward and touched him on the arm. The touch caused Millner to turn his head, and for an instant the glance of the two men crossed at short range. Millner was conscious, first, of a nearer view than he had ever had of his employer's face, and of its vaguely suggesting a seamed sandstone head, the kind of thing that lies in a corner in the court of a museum, and in which only the round enamelled eyes have resisted the wear of time. His next feeling was that he had now reached the moment to which the offer of the cigar had been a prelude. He had always known that, sooner or later, such a moment would come; all his life, in a sense, had been a preparation for it. But in entering Mr. Spence's service he had not foreseen that it would present itself in this form. He had seen himself consciously guiding that gentleman up to the moment, rather than being thrust into it by a stronger hand. And his first act of reflection was the resolve that, in the end, his hand should prove the stronger of the two. This was followed, almost immediately, by the idea that to be stronger than Mr. Spence's it would have to be very strong indeed. It was odd that he should feel this, since—as far as verbal communication went—it was Mr. Spence who was asking for his support. In a theoretical statement of the case the banker would have figured as being at Millner's mercy; but one of the queerest things about experience was the way it made light of theory. Millner felt now as though he were being crushed by some inexorable engine of which he had been playing with the lever . . .

He had always been intensely interested in observing his own reactions, and had regarded this faculty of self-detachment as of immense advantage in such a career as he had planned. He felt this still, even in the act of noting his own bewilderment—felt it the more in contrast to the odd unconsciousness of Mr. Spence's attitude, of the incredible candor of his self-abasement and self-abandonment. It was clear that Mr. Spence was not troubled by the repercussion of his actions in the consciousness of others; and this looked like a weakness—unless it were, instead, a great strength . . .

Through the hum of these swarming thoughts Mr. Spence's voice was going on. "That's literally the only rag of proof they've got; and they got it by one of those nasty accidents that nobody can guard against. I don't care how conscientiously a man attends to business, he can't always protect himself against meddlesome people. I don't pretend to know how the letter came into their hands; but they've got it; and they mean to use it—and they mean to say that you wrote it for me, and that you knew what it was about when you wrote it . . . They'll probably be after you tomorrow——"

Mr. Spence, restoring his cigar to his lips, puffed at it slowly. In the pause that followed there was an instant during which the universe seemed to Hugh Millner like a sounding-board bent above his single consciousness. If he spoke, what thunders would be sent back to him from that intently listening vastness?

"You see?" said Mr. Spence.

The universal ear bent closer, as if to catch the least articulation of Millner's narrowed lips; but when he opened them it was merely to reinsert his cigar, and for a short space nothing passed between the two men but a mute exchange of smoke-rings.

"What do you mean to do? There's the point," Mr. Spence at length sent through the rings.

Oh, yes, the point was there, as distinctly before Millner as the tip of his expensive cigar: he had seen it coming quite as soon as Mr. Spence. But the sense of the formidable echo which his least answer would rouse kept him doggedly, and almost helplessly, silent. To let Mr. Spence talk on as long as possible was no doubt the best way of gaining time; but Millner knew that his silence was really due to his dread of the echo. Suddenly, however, in a reaction of impatience at his own indecision, he began to speak.

The sound of his voice cleared his mind and strengthened his resolve. It was odd how the word seemed to shape the act, though one knew how ancillary it really was. As he talked, it was as if the globe had swung around, and he himself were upright on its axis, with Mr. Spence underneath, on his head. Through the ensuing interchange of concise and rapid speech there sounded in Millner's ears the refrain to which he had walked down Fifth Avenue after his first talk with Mr. Spence: "It's too easy—it's too easy—it's too easy." Yes, it was even easier than he had expected. His sensation was that of the skillful carver who feels his blade sink into a tender joint.

As he went on talking, this surprised sense of mastery was like wine in his veins. Mr. Spence was at his mercy, after all—that was what it came to; but this new view of the case did not lessen Millner's sense of Mr. Spence's strength, it merely revealed to him his own superiority. Mr. Spence was even stronger than he had suspected. There could be no better proof of that than his faith in Millner's power to grasp the situation, and his tacit recognition of the young man's right to make the most of it. Millner felt that Mr. Spence would have despised him even more for not using his advantage than for not seeing it; and this homage to his capacity nerved him to greater alertness, and made the concluding moments of their talk as physically exhilarating as some hotly contested game.

When the conclusion was reached, and Millner stood at the goal, the golden trophy in his grasp, his first conscious thought was one of regret that the struggle was over. He would have liked to prolong their talk for the purely aesthetic pleasure of making Mr. Spence lose time, and, better still, of making him forget that he was losing it. The sense of advantage that the situation conferred was so great that when Mr. Spence rose it was as if Millner were dismissing him, and when he reached his hand toward the cigar-box it seemed to be one of Millner's cigars that he was taking.

IV

THERE had been only one condition attached to the transaction: Millner was to speak to Draper about the Bible Class.

The condition was easy to fulfill. Millner was confident of his power to deflect his young friend's purpose; and he knew the opportunity would be given him before the day was over. His professional duties despatched, he had only to go up to his room to wait. Draper nearly always looked in on him for a moment before dinner: it was the hour most propitious to their elliptic interchange of words and silences.

Meanwhile, the waiting was an occupation in itself. Millner looked about his room with new eyes. Since the first thrill of initiation into its complicated comforts—the shower-bath, the telephone, the many-jointed reading-lamp and the vast mirrored presses through which he was always hunting his scant outfit—Millner's room had interested him no more than a railway-carriage in which he might have been travelling. But now it had acquired a sort of historic significance as the witness of the astounding change in his fate. It was Corsica, it was Brienne—it was the kind of spot that posterity might yet mark with a tablet. Then he reflected that he should soon be leaving it, and the lustre of its monumental mahogany was veiled in pathos.

Why indeed should he linger on in bondage? He perceived with a certain surprise that the only thing he should regret would be leaving Draper . . .

It was odd, it was inconsequent, it was almost exasperating, that such a regret should obscure his triumph. Why in the world should he suddenly take to regretting Draper? If there were any logic in human likings, it should be to Mr. Spence that he inclined. Draper, dear lad, had the illusion of an "intellectual sympathy" between them; but that, Millner knew, was an affair of reading and not of character. Draper's temerities would always be of that kind; whereas his own—well, his own, put to the proof, had now definitely classed him with Mr. Spence rather than with Mr. Spence's son. It was a consequence of this new condition—of his having thus distinctly and irrevocably classed himself—that, when Draper at length brought upon the scene his shy shamble and his wistful smile, Millner, for the first time, had to steel himself against them instead of yielding to their charm.

In the new order upon which he had entered, one principle of the old survived: the point of honor between allies. And Millner had promised Mr. Spence to speak to Draper about his Bible Class . . .

Draper, thrown back in his chair, and swinging a loose leg across a meager knee, listened with his habitual gravity. His downcast eyes seemed to pursue the vision which Millner's words evoked; and the words, to their speaker, took on a new sound as that candid consciousness refracted them.

"You know, dear boy, I perfectly see your father's point. It's naturally distressing to him, at this particular time, to have any hint of civil war leak out——"

Draper sat upright, laying his lank legs knee to knee.

"That's it, then? I thought that was it!"

Millner raised a surprised glance. "*What's* it?"

"That it should be at this particular time——"

"Why, naturally, as I say! Just as he's making, as it were, his public profession of faith. You know, to men like your father convictions are irreducible elements—they can't be split up and differently combined. And your exegetical scruples seem to him to strike at the very root of his convictions."

Draper pulled himself to his feet and shuffled across the room. Then he turned about, and stood before his friend.

"Is it that—or is it this?" he said; and with the word he drew a letter from his pocket and proffered it silently to Millner.

The latter, as he unfolded it, was first aware of an intense surprise at the young man's abruptness of tone and gesture. Usually Draper fluttered long about his point before making it; and his sudden movement seemed as mechanical as the impulsion conveyed by some strong spring. The spring, of course, was in the letter; and to it Millner turned his wondering glance, feeling the while that, by some curious cleavage of perception, he was continuing to watch Draper while he read.

"Oh, the beasts!" he cried.

He and Draper were face to face across the sheet which had dropped between them. The youth's features were tightened by a smile that was like the ligature of a wound. He looked white and withered.

"Ah—you knew, then?"

Millner sat still, and after a moment Draper turned from him, walked to the hearth, and leaned against the chimney, propping his chin on his hands. Millner, his head thrown back, stared up at the ceiling, which had suddenly become to him the image of the universal sounding-board hanging over his consciousness.

"You knew, then?" Draper repeated.

Millner remained silent. He had perceived, with the surprise of a mathematician working out a new problem, that the lie which Mr. Spence had just bought of him was exactly the one he could give of his own free will to Mr. Spence's son. This discovery gave the world a strange new topsy-turvyness, and set Millner's theories spinning about his brain like the cabin furniture of a tossing ship.

"You *knew,*" said Draper, in a tone of quiet affirmation.

Millner righted himself, and grasped the arms of his chair as if that too were reeling. "About this blackguardly charge?"

Draper was studying him intently. "What does it matter if it's blackguardly?"

"Matter——?" Millner stammered.

"It's that, of course, in any case. But the point is whether it's true or not." Draper bent down, and picking up the crumpled letter, smoothed it out between his fingers. "The point is, whether my father, when he was publicly denouncing the peonage abuses on the San Pablo plantations over a year ago, had actually sold out his stock, as he announced at the time; or whether, as they say here—how do they put it?—he had simply transferred it to a dummy till the scandal should blow over, and has meanwhile gone on drawing his forty per cent. interest on five thousand shares? There's the point."

Millner had never before heard his young friend put a case with such unadorned precision. His language was like that of Mr. Spence making a statement to a committee meeting; and the resemblance to his father flashed out with ironic incongruity.

"You see why I've brought this letter to you—I couldn't go to *him* with it!" Draper's voice faltered, and the resemblance vanished as suddenly as it had appeared.

"No; you couldn't go to him with it," said Millner, to gain time.

"And since they say here that *you* know: that they've got your letter proving it——" The muscles of Draper's face quivered as if a blinding light had been swept over it. "For God's sake, Millner—it's all right?"

"It's all right," said Millner, rising to his feet.

Draper caught him by the wrist. "You're sure—you're absolutely sure?"

"Sure. They know they've got nothing to go on."

Draper fell back a step and looked almost sternly at his friend. "That's not what I mean. I don't care a straw what they think they've got to go on. I want to know if my father's all right. If he is, they can say what they please."

Millner, again, felt himself under the concentrated scrutiny of the ceiling. "Of course, of course. I understand."

"You understand? Then why don't you answer?"

Millner looked compassionately at the boy's struggling face. Decidedly, the battle was to the strong, and he was not sorry to be on the side of the legions. But Draper's pain was as awkward as a material obstacle, as something that one stumbled over in a race.

"You know what I'm driving at, Millner." Again Mr. Spence's committee-meeting tone sounded oddly through his son's strained voice. "If my father's so awfully upset about my giving up my Bible Class, and letting it be known that I do so on conscientious grounds, is it because he's afraid it may be considered a criticism on something *he* has done which—which won't bear the test of the doctrines he believes in?"

Draper, with the last question, squared himself in front of Millner, as if suspecting that the latter meant to evade it by flight. But Millner had never felt more disposed to stand his ground than at that moment.

"No—by Jove, no! It's not *that.*" His relief almost escaped him in a cry, as he lifted his head to give back Draper's look.

"On your honor?" the other passionately pressed him.

"Oh, on anybody's you like—on *yours!*" Millner could hardly restrain a laugh of relief. It was vertiginous to find himself spared, after all, the need of an altruistic lie: he perceived that they were the kind he least liked.

Draper took a deep breath. "You don't—Millner, a lot depends on this—you don't really think my father has any ulterior motive?"

"I think he has none but his horror of seeing you go straight to perdition!"

They looked at each other again, and Draper's tension was suddenly relieved by a free boyish laugh. "It's his convictions—it's just his funny old convictions?"

"It's that, and nothing else on earth!"

Draper turned back to the arm-chair he had left, and let his narrow figure sink down into it as into a bath. Then he looked over at Millner with a smile. "I can see that I've been worrying him horribly. So he really thinks I'm on the road to perdition? Of course you can fancy what a sick minute I had when I thought it might be this other reason—the damnable insinuation in this letter." Draper crumpled the paper in his hand, and leaned forward to toss it into the coals of the grate. "I ought to have known better, of course. I ought to have remembered that, as you say, my father can't conceive how conduct may be independent of creed. That's where I was stupid—and rather base. But that letter made me dizzy—I couldn't think. Even now I can't very clearly. I'm not sure what *my* convictions require of me: they seem to me so much less to be considered than his! When I've done half the good to people that he has, it will be time enough to begin attacking their beliefs. Meanwhile—meanwhile I can't touch his . . ." Draper leaned forward, stretching his lank arms along his knees. His face was as clear as a spring sky. "I *won't* touch them, Millner—Go and tell him so . . ."

V

IN the study a half hour later Mr. Spence, watch in hand, was doling out his minutes again. The peril conjured, he had recovered his dominion over time. He turned his commanding eye-glasses on Millner.

"It's all settled, then? Tell Draper I'm sorry not to see him again tonight—but I'm to speak at the dinner of the Legal Relief Association, and I'm due there in five minutes. You and he dine alone here, I suppose? Tell him I appreciate what he's done. Some day he'll see that to leave the world better than we find it is the best we can hope to do. (You've finished the notes for the *Investigator?* Be sure you don't forget that phrase.) Well, good evening: that's all, I think."

Smooth and compact in his glossy evening clothes, Mr. Spence advanced toward the study door; but as he reached it, his secretary stood there before him.

"It's not quite all, Mr. Spence."

Mr. Spence turned on him a look in which impatience was faintly tinged with apprehension. "What else is there? It's two and a half minutes to eight."

Millner stood his ground. "It won't take longer than that. I want to tell you that, if you can conveniently replace me, I'd like—there are reasons why I shall have to leave you."

Millner was conscious of reddening as he spoke. His redness deepened under Mr. Spence's dispassionate scrutiny. He saw at once that the banker was not surprised at his announcement.

"Well, I suppose that's natural enough. You'll want to make a start for yourself now. Only, of course, for the sake of appearances——"

"Oh, certainly," Millner hastily agreed.

"Well, then: is that all?" Mr. Spence repeated.

"Nearly." Millner paused, as if in search of an appropriate formula.

But after a moment he gave up the search, and pulled from his pocket an envelope which he held out to his employer. "I merely want to give this back to you."

The hand which Mr. Spence had extended dropped to his side, and his sand-colored face grew chalky.

"Give it back?" His voice was as thick as Millner's. "What's happened? Is the bargain off?"

"Oh, no. I've given you my word."

"Your word?" Mr. Spence lowered at him. "I'd like to know what that's worth!"

Millner continued to hold out the envelope. "You do know, now. It's worth *that*. It's worth my place."

Mr. Spence, standing motionless before him, hesitated for an appreciable space of time. His lips parted once or twice under their square-clipped stubble, and at last emitted: "You'd better say at once how much more you want."

Millner broke into a laugh. "Oh, I've got all I want—all and more!"

"What—from the others? Are you crazy?"

"No, you are," said Millner with a sudden recovery of composure. "But you're safe—you're as safe as you'll ever be. Only I don't care to take this for making you so."

Mr. Spence slowly moistened his lips with his tongue, and removing his *pince-nez,* took a long hard look at Millner.

"I don't understand. What other guaranty have I got?"

"That I mean what I say?" Millner glanced past the banker's figure at his rich densely colored background of Spanish leather and mahogany. He remembered that it was from this very threshold that he had first seen Mr. Spence's son.

"What guaranty? You've got Draper!" he said.

Afterward

I

"OH, there *is* one, of course, but you'll never know it."

The assertion, laughingly flung out six months earlier in a bright June garden, came back to Mary Boyne with a new perception of its significance as she stood, in the December dusk, waiting for the lamps to be brought into the library.

The words had been spoken by their friend Alida Stair, as they sat at tea on her lawn at Pangbourne, in reference to the very house of which the library in question was the central, the pivotal "feature." Mary Boyne and her husband, in quest of a country place in one of the southern or southwestern counties, had, on their arrival in England, carried their problem straight to Alida Stair, who had successfully solved it in her own case; but it was not until they had rejected, almost capriciously, several practical and judicious suggestions that she threw out: "Well, there's Lyng, in Dorsetshire. It belongs to Hugo's cousins, and you can get it for a song."

The reason she gave for its being obtainable on these terms—its remoteness from a station, its lack of electric light, hot-water pipes, and other vulgar necessities—were exactly those pleading in its favor with two romantic Americans perversely in search of the economic drawbacks which were associated, in their tradition, with unusual architectural felicities.

"I should never believe I was living in an old house unless I was thoroughly uncomfortable," Ned Boyne, the more extravagant of the two, had jocosely insisted; "the least hint of 'convenience' would make me think it had been bought out of an exhibition, with the pieces numbered, and set up again." And they had proceeded to enumerate, with humorous precision, their various doubts and demands, refusing to believe that the house their cousin recommended was *really* Tudor till they learned it had no heating system, or that the village church was literally in the grounds till she assured them of the deplorable uncertainty of the water-supply.

"It's too uncomfortable to be true!" Edward Boyne had continued to exult as the avowal of each disadvantage was successively wrung from her; but he had cut short his rhapsody to ask, with a relapse to distrust: "And the ghost? You've been concealing from us the fact that there is no ghost!"

Mary, at the moment, had laughed with him, yet almost with her laugh, being possessed of several sets of independent perceptions, had been struck by a note of flatness in Alida's answering hilarity.

"Oh, Dorsetshire's full of ghosts, you know."

"Yes, yes; but that won't do. I don't want to have to drive ten miles to see somebody else's ghost. I want one of my own on the premises. *Is* there a ghost at Lyng?"

His rejoinder had made Alida laugh again, and it was then that she had flung back tantalizingly: "Oh, there *is* one, of course, but you'll never know it."

"Never know it?" Boyne pulled her up. "But what in the world constitutes a ghost except the fact of its being known for one?"

"I can't say. But that's the story."

"That there's a ghost, but that nobody knows it's a ghost?"

"Well—not till afterward, at any rate."

"Till afterward?"

"Not till long long afterward."

"But if it's once been identified as an unearthly visitant, why hasn't its *signalement* been handed down in the family? How has it managed to preserve its incognito?"

Alida could only shake her head. "Don't ask me. But it has."

"And then suddenly—" Mary spoke up as if from cavernous depths of divination— "suddenly, long afterward, one says to one's self *'That was it?'*"

She was startled at the sepulchral sound with which her question fell on the banter of the other two, and she saw the shadow of the same surprise flit across Alida's pupils. "I suppose so. One just has to wait."

"Oh, hang waiting!" Ned broke in. "Life's too short for a ghost who can only be enjoyed in retrospect. Can't we do better than that, Mary?"

But it turned out that in the event they were not destined to, for within three months of their conversation with Mrs. Stair they were settled at Lyng, and the life they had yearned for, to the point of planning it in advance in all its daily details, had actually begun for them.

It was to sit, in the thick December dusk, by just such a wide-hooded fireplace, under just such black oak rafters, with the sense that beyond the mullioned panes the downs were darkened to a deeper solitude: it was for the ultimate indulgence of such sensations that Mary Boyne, abruptly exiled from New York by her husband's business, had endured for nearly fourteen years the soul-deadening ugliness of a Middle Western town, and that Boyne had ground on doggedly at his engineering till, with a suddenness that still made her blink, the prodigious windfall of the Blue Star Mine had put them at a stroke in possession of life and the leisure to taste it. They had never for a moment meant their new state to be one of idleness; but they meant to give themselves only to harmonious activities. She had her vision of painting and gardening (against a background of grey walls), he dreamed of the production of his long-planned book on the "Economic Basis of Culture"; and with such absorbing work ahead no existence could be too sequestered: they could not get far enough from the world, or plunge deep enough into the past.

Dorsetshire had attracted them from the first by an air of remoteness out of all proportion to its geographical position. But to the Boynes it was one of the ever-recurring wonders of the whole incredibly compressed island—a nest of counties, as they put it—that for the production of its effects so little of a given quality went so far: that so few miles made a distance, and so short a distance a difference.

"It's that," Ned had once enthusiastically explained, "that gives such depth to their effects, such relief to their contrasts. They've been able to lay the butter so thick on every delicious mouthful."

The butter had certainly been laid on thick at Lyng: the old house hidden under a shoulder of the downs had almost all the finer marks of commerce with a protracted past. The mere fact that it was neither large nor exceptional made it, to the Boynes, abound the more completely in its special charm—the charm of having been for centuries a deep dim reservoir of life. The life had probably not been of the most vivid order: for long periods, no doubt, it had fallen as noiselessly into the past as the quiet drizzle of autumn fell, hour after hour, into the fish-pond between the yews; but these back-waters of existence sometimes breed, in their sluggish depths, strange acuities of emotion, and Mary Boyne had felt from the first the mysterious stir of intenser memories.

The feeling had never been stronger than on this particular afternoon when, waiting in the library for the lamps to come, she rose from her seat and stood among the shadows of the hearth. Her husband had gone off, after luncheon, for one of his long tramps on the downs. She had noticed of late that he preferred to go alone; and, in the tried security of their personal relations, had been driven to conclude that his book was bothering him, and that he needed the afternoons to turn over in solitude the problems left from the morning's work. Certainly the book was not going as smoothly as she had thought it would, and there were lines of perplexity between his eyes such as had never been there in his engineering days. He had often, then, looked fagged to the verge of illness, but the native demon of "worry" had never branded his brow. Yet the few pages he had so far read to her—the introduction, and a summary of the opening chapter—showed a firm hold on his subject, and an increasing confidence in his powers.

The fact threw her into deeper perplexity, since, now that he had done with "business" and its disturbing contingencies, the one other possible source of anxiety was eliminated. Unless it were his health, then? But physically he had gained since they had come to Dorsetshire, grown robuster, ruddier and fresher-eyed. It was only within the last week that she had felt in him the undefinable change which made her restless in his absence, and as tongue-tied in his presence as though it were *she* who had a secret to keep from him!

The thought that there *was* a secret somewhere between them struck her with a sudden rap of wonder, and she looked about her down the long room.

"Can it be the house?" she mused.

The room itself might have been full of secrets. They seemed to be piling themselves up, as evening fell, like the layers and layers of velvet shadow dropping from the low ceiling, the rows of books, the smoke-blurred sculpture of the hearth.

Its special charm—the charm of having been for centuries a deep dim reservoir of life.

"Why, of course—the house is haunted!" she reflected.

The ghost—Alida's imperceptible ghost—after figuring largely in the banter of their first month or two at Lyng, had been gradually left aside as too ineffectual for imaginative use. Mary had, indeed, as became the tenant of a haunted house, made the customary inquiries among her rural neighbors, but, beyond a vague "They dü say so, Ma'am," the villagers had nothing to impart. The elusive specter had apparently never had sufficient identity for a legend to crystallize about it, and after a time the Boynes had set the matter down to their profit-and-loss account, agreeing that Lyng was one of the few houses good enough in itself to dispense with supernatural enhancements.

"And I suppose, poor ineffectual demon, that's why it beats its beautiful wings in vain in the void," Mary had laughingly concluded.

"Or, rather," Ned answered in the same strain, "why, amid so much that's ghostly, it can never affirm its separate existence as *the* ghost." And thereupon their invisible housemate had finally dropped out of their references, which were numerous enough to make them soon unaware of the loss.

Now, as she stood on the hearth, the subject of their earlier curiosity revived in her with a new sense of its meaning—a sense gradually acquired through daily contact with the scene of the lurking mystery. It was the house itself, of course, that possessed the ghost-seeing faculty, that communed visually but secretly with its own past; if one could only get into close enough communion with the house, one might surprise its secret, and acquire the ghost-sight on one's own account. Perhaps, in his long hours in this very room, where she never trespassed till the afternoon, her husband *had* acquired it already, and was silently carrying about the weight of whatever it had revealed to him. Mary was too well versed in the code of the spectral world not to know that one could not talk about the ghosts one saw: to do so was almost as great a breach of taste as to name a lady in a club. But this explanation did not really satisfy her. "What, after all, except for the fun of the shudder," she reflected, "would he really care for any of their old ghosts?" And thence she was thrown back once more on the fundamental dilemma: the fact that one's greater or less susceptibility to spectral influences had no particular bearing on the case, since, when one *did* see a ghost at Lyng, one did not know it.

"Not till long afterward," Alida Stair had said. Well, supposing Ned *had* seen one when they first came, and had known only within the last week what had happened to him? More and more under the spell of the hour, she threw back her thoughts to the early days of their tenancy, but at first only to recall a lively confusion of unpacking, settling, arranging of books, and calling to each other from remote corners of the house as, treasure after treasure, it revealed itself to them. It was in this particular connection that she presently recalled a certain soft afternoon of the previous October, when, passing from the first rapturous flurry of exploration to a detailed inspection of the old house, she had pressed (like a novel heroine) a panel that opened on a flight of corkscrew stairs leading to a flat ledge of the roof—the roof which, from below, seemed to slope away on all sides too abruptly for any but practiced feet to scale.

The view from this hidden coign was enchanting, and she had flown down to snatch Ned from his papers and give him the freedom of her discovery. She remembered still how, standing at her side, he had passed his arm about her while their gaze flew to the long tossed horizon-line of the downs, and then dropped contentedly back to trace the arabesque of yew hedges about the fish-pond, and the shadow of the cedar on the lawn.

"And now the other way," he had said, turning her about within his arm; and closely pressed to him, she had absorbed, like some long satisfying draught, the picture of the grey-walled court, the squat lions on the gates, and the lime-avenue reaching up to the highroad under the downs.

It was just then, while they gazed and held each other, that she had felt his arm relax, and heard a sharp "Hullo!" that made her turn to glance at him.

Distinctly, yes, she now recalled that she had seen, as she glanced, a shadow of anxiety, of perplexity, rather, fall across his face; and, following his eyes, had beheld the figure of a man—a man in loose greyish clothes, as it appeared to her—who was sauntering down the lime-avenue to the court with the doubtful gait of a stranger who seeks his way. Her short-sighted eyes had given her but a blurred impression of slightness and greyishness, with something foreign, or at least unlocal, in the cut of the figure or its dress; but her husband had apparently seen more—seen enough to make him push past her with a hasty "Wait!" and dash down the stairs without pausing to give her a hand.

A slight tendency to dizziness obliged her, after a provisional clutch at the chimney against which they had been leaning, to follow him first more cautiously; and when she had reached the landing she paused again, for a less definite reason, leaning over the banister to strain her eyes through the silence of the brown sun-flecked depths. She lingered there till, somewhere in those depths, she heard the closing of a door; then, mechanically impelled, she went down the shallow flights of steps till she reached the lower hall.

The front door stood open on the sunlight of the court, and hall and court were empty. The library door was open, too, and after listening in vain for any sound of voices within, she crossed the threshold, and found her husband alone, vaguely fingering the papers on his desk.

He looked up, as if surprised at her entrance, but the shadow of anxiety had passed from his face, leaving it even, as she fancied, a little brighter and clearer than usual.

"What was it? Who was it?" she asked.

"Who?" he repeated, with the surprise still all on his side.

"The man we saw coming toward the house."

He seemed to reflect. "The man? Why, I thought I saw Peters; I dashed after him to say a word about the stable drains, but he had disappeared before I could get down."

"Disappeared? But he seemed to be walking so slowly when we saw him."

Boyne shrugged his shoulders. "So I thought; but he must have got up steam in the interval. What do you say to our trying a scramble up Meldon Steep before sunset?"

That was all. At the time the occurrence had been less than nothing, had, indeed, been immediately obliterated by the magic of their first vision from Meldon Steep, a height which they had dreamed of climbing ever since they had first seen its bare spine rising above the roof of Lyng. Doubtless it was the mere fact of the other incident's having occurred on the very day of their ascent to Meldon that had kept it stored away in the fold of memory from which it now emerged; for in itself it had no mark of the portentous. At the moment there could have been nothing more natural than that Ned should dash himself from the roof in the pursuit of dilatory tradesmen. It was the period when they were always on the watch for one or the other of the specialists employed about the place; always lying in wait for them, and rushing out at them with questions, reproaches or reminders. And certainly in the distance the grey figure had looked like Peters.

Yet now, as she reviewed the scene, she felt her husband's explanation of it to have been invalidated by the look of anxiety on his face. Why had the familiar appearance of Peters made him anxious? Why, above all, if it was of such prime necessity to confer with him on the subject of the stable drains, had the failure to find him produced such a look of relief? Mary could not say that any one of these questions had occurred to her at the time, yet, from the promptness with which they now marshalled themselves at her summons, she had a sense that they must all along have been there, waiting their hour.

II

WEARY with her thoughts, she moved to the window. The library was now quite dark, and she was surprised to see how much faint light the outer world still held.

As she peered out into it across the court, a figure shaped itself far down the perspective of bare limes: it looked a mere blot of deeper grey in the greyness, and for an instant, as it moved toward her, her heart thumped to the thought "It's the ghost!"

She had time, in that long instant, to feel suddenly that the man of whom, two months earlier, she had had a distant vision from the roof, was now, at his predestined hour, about to reveal himself as *not* having been Peters; and her spirit sank under the impending fear of the disclosure. But almost with the next tick of the clock the figure, gaining substance and character, showed itself even to her weak sight as her husband's; and she turned to meet him, as he entered, with the confession of her folly.

"It's really too absurd," she laughed out, "but I never *can* remember!"

"Remember what?" Boyne questioned as they drew together.

"That when one sees the Lyng ghost one never knows it."

Her hand was on his sleeve, and he kept it there, but with no response in his gesture or in the lines of his preoccupied face.

"Did you think you'd seen it?" he asked, after an appreciable interval.

"Why, I actually took *you* for it, my dear, in my mad determination to spot it!"

"Me—just now?" His arm dropped away, and he turned from her with a faint echo of her laugh. "Really, dearest, you'd better give it up, if that's the best you can do."

"Oh, yes, I give it up. Have *you?*" she asked, turning round on him abruptly.

The parlor-maid had entered with letters and a lamp, and the light struck up into Boyne's face as he bent above the tray she presented.

"Have *you?*" Mary perversely insisted, when the servant had disappeared on her errand of illumination.

"Have I what?" he rejoined absently, the light bringing out the sharp stamp of worry between his brows as he turned over the letters.

"Given up trying to see the ghost." Her heart beat a little at the experiment she was making.

Her husband, laying his letters aside, moved away into the shadow of the hearth.

"I never tried," he said, tearing open the wrapper of a newspaper.

"Well, of course," Mary persisted, "the exasperating thing is that there's no use trying, since one can't be sure till so long afterward."

He was unfolding the paper as if he had hardly heard her; but after a pause, during which the sheets rustled spasmodically between his hands, he looked up to ask, "Have you any idea *how long?*"

Mary had sunk into a low chair beside the fireplace. From her seat she glanced over, startled, at her husband's profile, which was projected against the circle of lamplight.

"No; none. Have *you?*" she retorted, repeating her former phrase with an added stress of intention.

Boyne crumpled the paper into a bunch, and then, inconsequently, turned back with it toward the lamp.

"Lord, no! I only meant," he explained, with a faint tinge of impatience, "is there any legend, any tradition, as to that?"

"Not that I know of," she answered; but the impulse to add "What makes you ask?" was checked by the reappearance of the parlor-maid, with tea and a second lamp.

With the dispersal of shadows, and the repetition of the daily domestic office, Mary Boyne felt herself less oppressed by that sense of something mutely imminent which had darkened her afternoon. For a few moments she gave herself to the details of her task, and when she looked up from it she was struck to the point of bewilderment by the change in her husband's face. He had seated himself near the farther lamp, and was absorbed in the perusal of his letters; but was it something he had found in them, or merely the shifting of her own point of view, that had restored his features to their normal aspect? The longer she looked the more definitely the change affirmed itself. The lines of tension had vanished, and such traces of fatigue as lingered were of the kind easily attributable to steady mental effort. He glanced up, as if drawn by her gaze, and met her eyes with a smile.

"I'm dying for my tea, you know; and here's a letter for you," he said.

She took the letter he held out in exchange for the cup she proffered him, and, returning to her seat, broke the seal with the languid gesture of the reader whose interests are all enclosed in the circle of one cherished presence.

Her next conscious motion was that of starting to her feet, the letter falling to them as she rose, while she held out to her husband a newspaper clipping.

"Ned! What's this? What does it mean?"

He had risen at the same instant, almost as if hearing her cry before she uttered it; and for a perceptible space of time he and she studied each other, like adversaries watching for an advantage, across the space between her chair and his desk.

"What's what? You fairly made me jump!" Boyne said at length, moving toward her with a sudden half-exasperated laugh. The shadow of apprehension was on his face again, not now a look of fixed foreboding, but a shifting vigilance of lips and eyes that gave her the sense of his feeling himself invisibly surrounded.

Her hand shook so that she could hardly give him the clipping.

"This article—from the *Waukesha Sentinel*—that a man named Elwell has brought suit against you—that there was something wrong about the Blue Star Mine. I can't understand more than half."

They continued to face each other as she spoke, and to her astonishment she saw that her words had the almost immediate effect of dissipating the strained watchfulness of his look.

"Oh, *that!*" He glanced down the printed slip, and then folded it with the gesture of one who handles something harmless and familiar. "What's the matter with you this afternoon, Mary? I thought you'd got bad news."

She stood before him with her undefinable terror subsiding slowly under the reassurance of his tone.

"You knew about this, then—it's all right?"

"Certainly I knew about it; and it's all right."

"But what *is* it? I don't understand. What does this man accuse you of?"

"Pretty nearly every crime in the calendar." Boyne had tossed the clipping down, and thrown himself into an arm-chair near the fire. "Do you want to hear the story? It's not particularly interesting—just a squabble over interests in the Blue Star."

"But who is this Elwell? I don't know the name."

"Oh, he's a fellow I put into it—gave him a hand up. I told you all about him at the time."

"I daresay. I must have forgotten." Vainly she strained back among her memories. "But if you helped him, why does he make this return?"

"Probably some shyster lawyer got hold of him and talked him over. It's all rather technical and complicated. I thought that kind of thing bored you."

His wife felt a sting of compunction. Theoretically, she deprecated the American wife's detachment from her husband's professional interests, but in practice she had always found it difficult to fix her attention on Boyne's report of the transactions in which his varied interests involved him. Besides, she had felt during their years of exile, that, in a community where the amenities of living could be obtained only at the cost of efforts as arduous as her husband's professional labors, such brief leisure as he and she could command should be used as an escape from immediate preoccupations, a flight to the life they always dreamed of living. Once or twice, now that this new life had actually drawn its magic circle about them, she had asked herself if she had done right; but hitherto such conjectures had been no more than the retrospective excursions of an active fancy. Now, for the first time, it startled her a little to find how little she knew of the material foundation on which her happiness was built.

She glanced at her husband, and was again reassured by the composure of his face; yet she felt the need of more definite grounds for her reassurance.

"But doesn't this suit worry you? Why have you never spoken to me about it?"

He answered both questions at once. "I didn't speak of it at first because it *did* worry me—annoyed me, rather. But it's all ancient history now. Your correspondent must have got hold of a back number of the *Sentinel.*"

She felt a quick thrill of relief. "You mean it's over? He's lost his case?"

There was a just perceptible delay in Boyne's reply. "The suit's been withdrawn—that's all."

But she persisted, as if to exonerate herself from the inward charge of being too easily put off. "Withdrawn it because he saw he had no chance?"

"Oh, he had no chance," Boyne answered.

She was still struggling with a dimly felt perplexity at the back of her thoughts.

"How long ago was it withdrawn?"

He paused, as if with a slight return of his former uncertainty. "I've just had the news now; but I've been expecting it."

"Just now—in one of your letters?"

"Yes; in one of my letters."

She made no answer, and was aware only, after a short interval of waiting, that he had risen, and, strolling across the room, had placed himself on the sofa at her side. She felt him, as he did so, pass an arm about her, she felt his hand seek hers and clasp it, and turning slowly, drawn by the warmth of his cheek, she met his smiling eyes.

"It's all right—it's all right?" she questioned, through the flood of her dissolving doubts; and "I give you my word it was never righter!" he laughed back at her, holding her close.

III

ONE of the strangest things she was afterward to recall out of all the next day's strangeness was the sudden and complete recovery of her sense of security.

It was in the air when she woke in her low-ceiled, dusky room; it went with her downstairs to the breakfast-table, flashed out at her from the fire, and reduplicated itself from the flanks of the urn and the sturdy flutings of the Georgian teapot. It was as if, in some roundabout way, all her diffused fears of the previous day, with their moment of sharp concentration about the newspaper article—as if this dim questioning of the future, and startled return upon the past, had between them liquidated the arrears of some haunting moral obligation. If she had indeed been careless of her husband's affairs, it was, her new state seemed to prove, because her faith in him instinctively justified such carelessness; and his right to her faith had now affirmed itself in the very face of menace and suspicion. She had never seen him more untroubled, more naturally and unconsciously himself, than after the cross-examination to which she had subjected him: it was almost as if he had been aware of her doubts, and had wanted the air cleared as much as she did.

It was as clear, thank Heaven! as the bright outer light that surprised her almost with a touch of summer when she issued from the house for her daily round of the gardens. She had left Boyne at his desk, indulging herself, as she passed the library door, by a last peep at his quiet face, where he bent, pipe in mouth, above his papers; and now she had her own morning's task to perform. The task involved, on such charmed winter days, almost as much happy loitering about the different quarters of her demesne as if spring were already at work there. There were such endless possibilities still before her, such opportunities to bring out the latent graces of the old place, without a single irreverent touch of alteration, that the winter was all too short to plan what spring and autumn executed. And her recovered sense of safety gave, on this particular morning, a peculiar zest to her progress through the sweet still place. She went first to the kitchen-garden, where the espaliered pear-trees drew complicated patterns on the walls, and pigeons were fluttering and preening about the silvery-slated roof of their cot. There was something wrong about the piping of the hot-house, and she was expecting an authority from Dorchester, who was to drive out between trains and make a diagnosis of the boiler. But when she dipped into the damp heat of the greenhouses, among the spiced scents and waxy pinks and reds of old-fashioned exotics—even the flora of Lyng was in the note!—she learned that the great man had not arrived, and, the day being too rare to waste in an artificial atmosphere, she came out again and paced along the springy turf of the bowling-green to the gardens behind the house. At their farther end rose a grass terrace, looking across the fish-pond and yew hedges to the long house-front with its twisted chimney-stacks and blue roof angles all drenched in the pale gold moisture of the air.

Seen thus, across the level tracery of the gardens, it sent her, from open windows and hospitably smoking chimneys, the look of some warm human presence, of a mind slowly ripened on a sunny wall of experience. She had never before had such a sense of her intimacy with it, such a conviction that its secrets were all beneficent, kept, as they said to children, "for one's good," such a trust in its power to gather up her life and Ned's into the harmonious pattern of the long long story it sat there weaving in the sun.

She heard steps behind her, and turned, expecting to see the gardener accompanied by the engineer from Dorchester. But only one figure was in sight, that of a youngish slightly built man, who, for reasons she could not on the spot have given, did not remotely resemble her notion of an authority on hot-house boilers. The newcomer, on seeing her, lifted his hat, and paused with the air of a gentleman—perhaps a traveller—who wishes to make it known that his intrusion is involuntary. Lyng occasionally attracted the more cultivated traveller, and Mary half-expected to see the stranger dissemble a camera, or justify his presence by producing it. But he made no gesture of any sort, and after a moment she asked, in a tone responding to the courteous hesitation of his attitude: "Is there any one you wish to see?"

"I came to see Mr. Boyne," he answered. His intonation, rather than his accent, was faintly American, and Mary, at the note, looked at him more closely. The brim of his soft felt hat cast a shade on his face, which, thus obscured, wore to her short-sighted gaze a look of seriousness, as of a person arriving "on business," and civilly but firmly aware of his rights.

Past experience had made her equally sensible to such claims; but she was jealous of her husband's morning hours, and doubtful of his having given any one the right to intrude on them.

"Have you an appointment with my husband?" she asked.

The visitor hesitated, as if unprepared for the question.

"I think he expects me," he replied.

It was Mary's turn to hesitate. "You see this is his time for work: he never sees any one in the morning."

He looked at her a moment without answering; then, as if accepting her decision, he began to move away. As he turned, Mary saw him pause and glance up at the peaceful house-front. Something in his air suggested weariness and disappointment, the dejection of the traveller who has come from far off and whose hours are limited by the time-table. It occurred to her that if this were the case her refusal might have made his errand vain, and a sense of compunction caused her to hasten after him.

"May I ask if you have come a long way?"

He gave her the same grave look. "Yes—I have come a long way."

"Then, if you'll go to the house, no doubt my husband will see you now. You'll find him in the library."

She did not know why she had added the last phrase, except from a vague impulse to atone for her previous inhospitality. The visitor seemed about to express his thanks, but her attention was distracted by the approach of the gardener with a companion who bore all the marks of being the expert from Dorchester.

"This way," she said, waving the stranger to the house; and an instant later she had forgotten him in the absorption of her meeting with the boiler-maker. The encounter led to such far-reaching results that the engineer ended by finding it expedient to ignore his train, and Mary was beguiled into spending the remainder of the morning in absorbed confabulation among the flower-pots. When the colloquy ended, she was surprised to find that it was nearly luncheon-time, and she half expected, as she hurried back to the house, to see her husband coming out to meet her. But she found no one in the court but an under-gardener raking the gravel, and the hall, when she entered it, was so silent that she guessed Boyne to be still at work.

Not wishing to disturb him, she turned into the drawing-room, and there, at her writing-table, lost herself in renewed calculations of the outlay to which the morning's conference had pledged her. The fact that she could permit herself such follies had not yet lost its novelty; and somehow, in contrast to the vague fears of the previous days, it now seemed an element of her recovered security, of the sense that, as Ned had said, things in general had never been "righter."

She was still luxuriating in a lavish play of figures when the parlor-maid, from the threshold, roused her with an enquiry as to the expediency of serving luncheon. It was one of their jokes that Trimmle announced luncheon as if she were divulging a state secret, and Mary, intent upon her papers, merely murmured an absent-minded assent.

She felt Trimmle wavering doubtfully on the threshold, as if in rebuke of such unconsidered assent; then her retreating steps sounded down the passage, and Mary, pushing away her papers, crossed the hall and went to the library door. It was still closed, and she wavered in her turn, disliking to disturb her husband, yet anxious that he should not exceed his usual measure of work. As she stood there, balancing her impulses, Trimmle returned with the announcement of luncheon, and Mary, thus impelled, opened the library door.

Boyne was not at his desk, and she peered about her, expecting to discover him before the book-shelves, somewhere down the length of the room; but her call brought no response, and gradually it became clear to her that he was not there.

She turned back to the parlor-maid.

"Mr. Boyne must be upstairs. Please tell him that luncheon is ready."

Trimmle appeared to hesitate between the obvious duty of obedience and an equally obvious conviction of the foolishness of the injunction laid on her. The struggle resulted in her saying: "If you please, Madam, Mr. Boyne's not upstairs."

"Not in his room? Are you sure?"

"I'm sure, Madam."

Mary consulted the clock. "Where is he, then?"

"He's gone out," Trimmle announced, with the superior air of one who has respectfully waited for the question that a well-ordered mind would have put first.

Mary's conjecture had been right, then. Boyne must have gone to the gardens to meet her, and since she had missed him, it was clear that he had taken the shorter way by the south door, instead of going round to the court. She crossed the hall to the French window opening directly on the yew garden, but the parlor-maid, after another moment of inner conflict, decided to bring out: "Please, Madam, Mr. Boyne didn't go that way."

Mary turned back. "Where *did* he go? And when?"

"He went out of the front door, up the drive, Madam." It was a matter of principle with Trimmle never to answer more than one question at a time.

"Up the drive? At this hour?" Mary went to the door herself, and glanced across the court through the tunnel of bare limes. But its perspective was as empty as when she had scanned it on entering.

"Did Mr. Boyne leave no message?"

Trimmle seemed to surrender herself to a last struggle with the forces of chaos.

"No, Madam. He just went out with the gentleman."

"The gentleman? What gentleman?" Mary wheeled about, as if to front this new factor.

"The gentleman who called, Madam," said Trimmle resignedly.

"When did a gentleman call? Do explain yourself, Trimmle!"

Only the fact that Mary was very hungry, and that she wanted to consult her husband about the greenhouses, would have caused her to lay so unusual an injunction on her attendant; and even now she was detached enough to note in Trimmle's eye the dawning defiance of the respectful subordinate who has been pressed too hard.

"I couldn't exactly say the hour, Madam, because I didn't let the gentleman in," she replied, with an air of discreetly ignoring the irregularity of her mistress's course.

"You didn't let him in?"

"No, Madam. When the bell rang I was dressing, and Agnes——"

"Go and ask Agnes, then," said Mary.

Trimmle still wore her look of patient magnanimity. "Agnes would not know, Madam, for she had unfortunately burnt her hand in trimming the wick of the new lamp from town"—Trimmle, as Mary was aware, had always been opposed to the new lamp—"and so Mrs. Dockett sent the kitchen-maid instead."

Mary looked again at the clock. "It's after two! Go and ask the kitchen-maid if Mr. Boyne left any word."

She went into luncheon without waiting, and Trimmle presently brought her there the kitchen-maid's statement that the gentleman had called about eleven o'clock, and that Mr. Boyne had gone out with him without leaving any message. The kitchen-maid did not even know the caller's name, for he had written it on a slip of paper, which he had folded and handed to her, with the injunction to deliver it at once to Mr. Boyne.

Mary finished her luncheon, still wondering, and when it was over, and Trimmle had brought the coffee to the drawing-room, her wonder had deepened to a first faint twinge of disquietude. It was unlike Boyne to absent himself without explanation at so unwonted an hour, and the difficulty of identifying the visitor whose summons he had apparently obeyed made his disappearance the more unaccountable. Mary Boyne's experience as the wife of a busy engineer, subject to sudden calls and compelled to keep irregular hours, had trained her to the philosophic acceptance of surprises, but since Boyne's withdrawal from business he had adopted a Benedictine regularity of life. As if to make up for the dispersed and agitated years, with their "stand-up" lunches, and dinners rattled down to the joltings of the dining-cars, he cultivated the last refinements of punctuality and monotony, discouraging his wife's fancy for the unexpected, and declaring that to a delicate taste there were infinite gradations of pleasure in the recurrences of habit.

Still, since no life can completely defend itself from the unforeseen, it was evident that all Boyne's precautions would sooner or later prove unavailable, and Mary concluded that he had cut short a tiresome visit by walking with his caller to the station, or at least accompanying him for part of the way.

This conclusion relieved her from farther preoccupation, and she went out herself to take up her conference with the gardener. Thence she walked to the village post-office, a mile or so away; and when she turned toward home the early twilight was setting in.

She had taken a foot-path across the downs, and as Boyne, meanwhile, had probably returned from the station by the highroad, there was little likelihood of their meeting. She felt sure, however, of his having reached the house before her; so sure that, when she entered it herself, without even pausing to inquire of Trimmle, she made directly for the library. But the library was still empty, and with an unwonted exactness of visual memory she observed that the papers on her husband's desk lay precisely as they had lain when she had gone in to call him to luncheon.

Then of a sudden she was seized by a vague dread of the unknown. She had closed the door behind her on entering, and as she stood alone in the long silent room, her dread seemed to take shape and sound, to be there breathing and lurking among the shadows. Her short-sighted eyes strained through them, half-discerning an actual presence, something aloof, that watched and knew; and in the recoil from that intangible presence she threw herself on the bell-rope and gave it a sharp pull.

The sharp summons brought Trimmle in precipitately with a lamp, and Mary breathed again at this sobering reappearance of the usual.

"You may bring tea if Mr. Boyne is in," she said, to justify her ring.

"Very well, Madam. But Mr. Boyne is not in," said Trimmle, putting down the lamp.

"Not in? You mean he's come back and gone out again?"

"No, Madam. He's never been back."

The dread stirred again, and Mary knew that now it had her fast.

"Not since he went out with—the gentleman?"

"Not since he went out with the gentleman."

"But who *was* the gentleman?" Mary insisted, with the shrill note of some one trying to be heard through a confusion of noises.

"That I couldn't say, Madam." Trimmle, standing there by the lamp, seemed suddenly to grow less round and rosy, as though eclipsed by the same creeping shade of apprehension.

"But the kitchen-maid knows—wasn't it the kitchen-maid who let him in?"

"She doesn't know either, Madam, for he wrote his name on a folded paper."

Mary, through her agitation, was aware that they were both designating the unknown visitor by a vague pronoun, instead of the conventional formula which, till then, had kept their allusions within the bounds of conformity. And at the same moment her mind caught at the suggestion of the folded paper.

"But he must have a name! Where's the paper?"

She moved to the desk, and began to turn over the documents that littered it. The first that caught her eye was an unfinished letter in her husband's hand, with his pen lying across it, as though dropped there at a sudden summons.

"My dear Parvis"—who was Parvis?—"I have just received your letter announcing Elwell's death, and while I suppose there is now no farther risk of trouble, it might be safer——"

She tossed the sheet aside, and continued her search; but no folded paper was discoverable among the letters and pages of manuscript which had been swept together in a heap, as if by a hurried or a startled gesture.

"But the kitchen-maid *saw* him. Send her here," she commanded, wondering at her dullness in not thinking sooner of so simple a solution.

Trimmle vanished in a flash, as if thankful to be out of the room, and when she reappeared, conducting the agitated underling, Mary had regained her self-possession, and had her questions ready.

The gentleman was a stranger, yes—that she understood. But what had he said? And, above all, what had he looked like? The first question was easily enough answered, for the disconcerting reason that he had said so little—had merely asked for Mr. Boyne, and, scribbling something on a bit of paper, had requested that it should at once be carried in to him.

"Then you don't know what he wrote? You're not sure it *was* his name?"

The kitchen-maid was not sure, but supposed it was, since he had written it in answer to her inquiry as to whom she should announce.

"And when you carried the paper in to Mr. Boyne, what did he say?"

The kitchen-maid did not think that Mr. Boyne had said anything, but she could not be sure, for just as she had handed him the paper and he was opening it, she had become aware that the visitor had followed her into the library, and she had slipped out, leaving the two gentlemen together.

"But then, if you left them in the library, how do you know that they went out of the house?"

This question plunged the witness into a momentary inarticulateness, from which she was rescued by Trimmle, who, by means of ingenious circumlocutions, elicited the statement that before she could cross the hall to the back passage she had heard the two gentlemen behind her, and had seen them go out of the front door together.

"Then, if you saw the strange gentleman twice, you must be able to tell me what he looked like."

But with this final challenge to her powers of expression it became clear that the limit of the kitchen-maid's endurance had been reached. The obligation of going to the front door to "show in" a visitor was in itself so subversive of the fundamental order of things that it had thrown her faculties into hopeless disarray, and she could only stammer out, after various panting efforts: "His hat, mum, was different-like, as you might say——"

"Different? How different?" Mary flashed out, her own mind, in the same instant, leaping back to an image left on it that morning, and then lost under layers of subsequent impressions.

"His hat had a wide brim, you mean? and his face was pale—a youngish face?" Mary pressed her, with a white-lipped intensity of interrogation. But if the kitchen-maid found any adequate answer to this challenge, it was swept away for her listener down the rushing current of her own convictions. The stranger—the stranger in the garden! Why had Mary not thought of him before? She needed no one now to tell her that it was he who had called for her husband and gone away with him. But who was he, and why had Boyne obeyed him?

IV

IT leaped out at her suddenly, like a grin out of the dark, that they had often called England so little—"such a confoundedly hard place to get lost in."

A confoundedly hard place to get lost in! That had been her husband's phrase. And now, with the whole machinery of official investigation sweeping its flashlights from shore to shore, and across the dividing straits; now, with Boyne's name blazing from the walls of every town and village, his portrait (how that wrung her!) hawked up and down the country like the image of a hunted criminal; now the little compact populous island, so policed, surveyed and administered, revealed itself as a Sphinx-like guardian of abysmal mysteries, staring back into his wife's anguished eyes as if with the wicked joy of knowing something they would never know!

In the fortnight since Boyne's disappearance there had been no word of him, no trace of his movements. Even the usual misleading reports that raise expectancy in tortured bosoms had been few and fleeting. No one but the kitchen-maid had seen Boyne leave the house, and no one else had seen "the gentleman" who accompanied him. All enquiries in the neighborhood failed to elicit the memory of a stranger's presence that day in the neighborhood of Lyng. And no one had met Edward Boyne, either alone or in company, in any of the neighboring villages, or on the road across the downs, or at either of the local railway-stations. The sunny English noon had swallowed him as completely as if he had gone out into Cimmerian night.

Mary, while every official means of investigation was working at its highest pressure, had ransacked her husband's papers for any trace of antecedent complications, of entanglements or obligations unknown to her, that might throw a ray into the darkness. But if any such had existed in the background of Boyne's life, they had vanished like the slip of paper on which the visitor had written his name. There remained no possible thread of guidance except—if it were indeed an exception—the letter which Boyne had apparently been in the act of writing when he received his mysterious summons. That letter, read and reread by his wife, and submitted by her to the police, yielded little enough to feed conjecture.

"I have just heard of Elwell's death, and while I suppose there is now no farther risk of trouble, it might be safer——" That was all. The "risk of trouble" was easily explained by the newspaper clipping which had apprised Mary of the suit brought against her husband by one of his associates in the Blue Star enterprise. The only new information conveyed by the letter was the fact of its showing Boyne, when he wrote it, to be still apprehensive of the results of the suit, though he had told his wife that it had been withdrawn, and though the letter itself proved that the plaintiff was dead. It took several days of cabling to fix the identity of the "Parvis" to whom the fragment was addressed, but even after these enquiries had shown him to be a Waukesha lawyer, no new facts concerning the Elwell suit were elicited. He appeared to have had no direct concern in it, but to have been conversant with the facts merely as an acquaintance, and possible intermediary; and he declared himself unable to guess with what object Boyne intended to seek his assistance.

This negative information, sole fruit of the first fortnight's search, was not increased by a jot during the slow weeks that followed. Mary knew that the investigations were still being carried on, but she had a vague sense of their gradually slackening, as the actual march of time seemed to slacken. It was as though the days, flying horror-struck from the shrouded image of the one inscrutable day, gained assurance as the distance lengthened, till at last they fell back into their normal gait. And so with the human imaginations at work on the dark event. No doubt it occupied them still, but week by week and hour by hour it grew less absorbing, took up less space, was slowly but inevitably crowded out of the foreground of consciousness by the new problems perpetually bubbling up from the cloudy caldron of human experience.

Even Mary Boyne's consciousness gradually felt the same lowering of velocity. It still swayed with the incessant oscillations of conjecture; but they were slower, more rhythmical in their beat. There were even moments of weariness when, like the victim of some poison which leaves the brain clear, but holds the body motionless, she saw herself domesticated with the Horror, accepting its perpetual presence as one of the fixed conditions of life.

These moments lengthened into hours and days, till she passed into a phase of stolid acquiescence. She watched the routine of daily life with the incurious eye of a savage on whom the meaningless processes of civilization make but the faintest impression. She had come to regard herself as part of the routine, a spoke of the wheel, revolving with its motion; she felt almost like the furniture of the room in which she sat, an insensate object to be dusted and pushed about with the chairs and tables. And this deepening apathy held her fast at Lyng, in spite of the entreaties of friends and the usual medical recommendation of "change." Her friends supposed that her refusal to move was inspired by the belief that her husband would one day return to the spot from which he had vanished, and a beautiful legend grew up about this imaginary state of waiting.

But in reality she had no such belief: the depths of anguish enclosing her were no longer lighted by flashes of hope. She was sure that Boyne would never come back, that he had gone out of her sight as completely as if Death itself had waited that day on the threshold. She had even renounced, one by one, the various theories as to his disappearance which had been advanced by the press, the police, and her own agonized imagination. In sheer lassitude her mind turned from these alternatives of horror, and sank back into the blank fact that he was gone.

No, she would never know what had become of him—no one would ever know. But the house *knew;* the library in which she spent her long lonely evenings knew. For it was here that the last scene had been enacted, here that the stranger had come, and spoken the word which had caused Boyne to rise and follow him. The floor she trod had felt his tread; the books on the shelves had seen his face; and there were moments when the intense consciousness of the old dusky walls seemed about to break out into some audible revelation of their secret. But the revelation never came, and she knew it would never come. Lyng was not one of the garrulous old houses that betray the secrets entrusted to them. Its very legend proved that it had always been the mute accomplice, the incorruptible custodian, of the mysteries it had surprised. And Mary Boyne, sitting face to face with its silence, felt the futility of seeking to break it by any human means.

V

"I DON'T say it *wasn't* straight, and yet I don't say it *was* straight. It was business."

Mary, at the words, lifted her head with a start, and looked intently at the speaker.

When, half an hour before, a card with "Mr. Parvis" on it had been brought up to her, she had been immediately aware that the name had been a part of her consciousness ever since she had read it at the head of Boyne's unfinished letter. In the library she had found awaiting her a small sallow man with a bald head and gold eye-glasses, and it sent a tremor through her to know that this was the person to whom her husband's last known thought had been directed.

Parvis, civilly, but without vain preamble—in the manner of a man who has his watch in his hand—had set forth the object of his visit. He had "run over" to England on business, and finding himself in the neighborhood of Dorchester, had not wished to leave it without paying his respects to Mrs. Boyne; and without asking her, if the occasion offered, what she meant to do about Bob Elwell's family.

The words touched the spring of some obscure dread in Mary's bosom. Did her visitor, after all, know what Boyne had meant by his unfinished phrase? She asked for an elucidation of his question, and noticed at once that he seemed surprised at her continued ignorance of the subject. Was it possible that she really knew as little as she said?

"I know nothing—you must tell me," she faltered out; and her visitor thereupon proceeded to unfold his story. It threw, even to her confused perceptions, and imperfectly initiated vision, a lurid glare on the whole hazy episode of the Blue Star Mine. Her husband had made his money in that brilliant speculation at the cost of "getting ahead" of some one less alert to seize the chance; and the victim of his ingenuity was young Robert Elwell, who had "put him on" to the Blue Star scheme.

Parvis, at Mary's first cry, had thrown her a sobering glance through his impartial glasses.

"Bob Elwell wasn't smart enough, that's all; if he had been, he might have turned round and served Boyne the same way. It's the kind of thing that happens every day in business. I guess it's what the scientists call the survival of the fittest—see?" said Mr. Parvis, evidently pleased with the aptness of his analogy.

Mary felt a physical shrinking from the next question she tried to frame: it was as though the words on her lips had a taste that nauseated her.

"But then—you accuse my husband of doing something dishonorable?"

Mr. Parvis surveyed the question dispassionately. "Oh, no, I don't. I don't even say it wasn't straight." He glanced up and down the long lines of books, as if one of them might have supplied him with the definition he sought. "I don't say it *wasn't* straight, and yet I don't say it *was* straight. It was business." After all, no definition in his category could be more comprehensive than that.

Mary sat staring at him with a look of terror. He seemed to her like the indifferent emissary of some evil power.

"But Mr. Elwell's lawyers apparently did not take your view, since I suppose the suit was withdrawn by their advice."

"Oh, yes; they knew he hadn't a leg to stand on, technically. It was when they advised him to withdraw the suit that he got desperate. You see, he'd borrowed most of the money he lost in the Blue Star, and he was up a tree. That's why he shot himself when they told him he had no show."

The horror was sweeping over Mary in great deafening waves.

"He shot himself? He killed himself because of *that?"*

"Well, he didn't kill himself, exactly. He dragged on two months before he died." Parvis emitted the statement as unemotionally as a gramophone grinding out its "record."

"You mean that he tried to kill himself, and failed? And tried again?"

"Oh, he didn't have to *try* again," said Parvis grimly.

They sat opposite each other in silence, he swinging his eye-glasses thoughtfully about his finger, she, motionless, her arms stretched along her knees in an attitude of rigid tension.

"But if you knew all this," she began at length, hardly able to force her voice above a whisper, "how is it that when I wrote you at the time of my husband's disappearance you said you didn't understand his letter?"

Parvis received this without perceptible embarrassment: "Why, I didn't understand it—strictly speaking. And it wasn't the time to talk about it, if I had. The Elwell business was settled when the suit was withdrawn. Nothing I could have told you would have helped you to find your husband."

Mary continued to scrutinize him. "Then why are you telling me now?"

Still Parvis did not hesitate. "Well, to begin with, I supposed you knew more than you appear to—I mean about the circumstances of Elwell's death. And then people are talking of it now; the whole matter's been raked up again. And I thought if you didn't know you ought to."

She remained silent, and he continued: "You see, it's only come out lately what a bad state Elwell's affairs were in. His wife's a proud woman, and she fought on as long as she could, going out to work, and taking sewing at home when she got too sick—something with the heart, I believe. But she had his mother to look after, and the children, and she broke down under it, and finally had to ask for help. That called attention to the case, and the papers took it up, and a subscription was started. Everybody out there liked Bob Elwell, and most of the prominent names in the place are down on the list, and people began to wonder why——"

Parvis broke off to fumble in an inner pocket. "Here," he continued, "here's an account of the whole thing from the *Sentinel*—a little sensational, of course. But I guess you'd better look it over."

He held out a newspaper to Mary, who unfolded it slowly, remembering, as she did so, the evening when, in that same room, the perusal of a clipping from the *Sentinel* had first shaken the depths of her security.

As she opened the paper, her eyes, shrinking from the glaring headlines, "Widow of Boyne's Victim Forced to Appeal for Aid," ran down the column of text to two portraits inserted in it. The first was her husband's, taken from a photograph made the year they had come to England. It was the picture of him that she liked best, the one that stood on the writing-table upstairs in her bedroom. As the eyes in the photograph met hers, she felt it would be impossible to read what was said of him, and closed her lids with the sharpness of the pain.

"I thought if you felt disposed to put your name down——" she heard Parvis continue.

She opened her eyes with an effort, and they fell on the other portrait. It was that of a youngish man, slightly built, with features somewhat blurred by the shadow of a projecting hat-brim. Where had she seen that outline before? She stared at it confusedly, her heart hammering in her ears. Then she gave a cry.

"This is the man—the man who came for my husband!"

She heard Parvis start to his feet, and was dimly aware that she had slipped backward into the corner of the sofa, and that he was bending above her in alarm. She straightened herself, and reached out for the paper, which she had dropped.

"It's the man! I should know him anywhere!" she persisted in a voice that sounded to her own ears like a scream.

Parvis's answer seemed to come to her from far off, down endless fog-muffled windings.

"Mrs. Boyne, you're not very well. Shall I call somebody? Shall I get a glass of water?"

"No, no, no!" She threw herself toward him, her hand frantically clutching the newspaper. "I tell you, it's the man! I *know* him! He spoke to me in the garden!"

Parvis took the journal from her, directing his glasses to the portrait. "It can't be, Mrs. Boyne. It's Robert Elwell."

"Robert Elwell?" Her white stare seemed to travel into space. "Then it was Robert Elwell who came for him."

"Came for Boyne? The day he went away from here?" Parvis's voice dropped as hers rose. He bent over, laying a fraternal hand on her, as if to coax her gently back into her seat. "Why, Elwell was dead! Don't you remember?"

Mary sat with her eyes fixed on the picture, unconscious of what he was saying.

"Don't you remember Boyne's unfinished letter to me—the one you found on his desk that day? It was written just after he'd heard of Elwell's death." She noticed an odd shake in Parvis's unemotional voice. "Surely you remember!" he urged her.

Yes, she remembered: that was the profoundest horror of it. Elwell had died the day before her husband's disappearance; and this was Elwell's portrait; and it was the portrait of the man who had spoken to her in the garden. She lifted her head and looked slowly about the library. The library could have borne witness that it was also the portrait of the man who had come in that day to call Boyne from his unfinished letter. Through the misty surgings of her brain she heard the faint boom of half-forgotten words—words spoken by Alida Stair on the lawn at Pangbourne before Boyne and his wife had ever seen the house at Lyng, or had imagined that they might one day live there.

"This was the man who spoke to me," she repeated.

She looked again at Parvis. He was trying to conceal his disturbance under what he probably imagined to be an expression of indulgent commiseration; but the edges of his lips were blue. "He thinks me mad; but I'm not mad," she reflected; and suddenly there flashed upon her a way of justifying her strange affirmation.

She sat quiet, controlling the quiver of her lips, and waiting till she could trust her voice; then she said, looking straight at Parvis: "Will you answer me one question, please? When was it that Robert Elwell tried to kill himself?"

"When—when?" Parvis stammered.

"Yes; the date. Please try to remember."

She saw that he was growing still more afraid of her. "I have a reason," she insisted.

"Yes, yes. Only I can't remember. About two months before, I should say."

"I want the date," she repeated.

Parvis picked up the newspaper. "We might see here," he said, still humoring her. He ran his eyes down the page. "Here it is. Last October—the——"

She caught the words from him. "The 20th, wasn't it?" With a sharp look at her, he verified. "Yes, the 20th. Then you *did* know?"

"I know now." Her gaze continued to travel past him. "Sunday, the 20th—that was the day he came first."

Parvis's voice was almost inaudible. "Came *here* first?"

"Yes."

"You saw him twice, then?"

"Yes, twice." She just breathed it at him. "He came first on the 20th of October. I remember the date because it was the day we went up Meldon Steep for the first time." She felt a faint gasp of inward laughter at the thought that but for that she might have forgotten.

Parvis continued to scrutinize her, as if trying to intercept her gaze.

"We saw him from the roof," she went on. "He came down the lime-avenue toward the house. He was dressed just as he is in that picture. My husband saw him first. He was frightened, and ran down ahead of me; but there was no one there. He had vanished."

"Elwell had vanished?" Parvis faltered.

"Yes." Their two whispers seemed to grope for each other. "I couldn't think what had happened. I see now. He *tried* to come then; but he wasn't dead enough—he couldn't reach us. He had to wait for two months to die; and then he came back again—and Ned went with him."

She nodded at Parvis with the look of triumph of a child who has worked out a difficult puzzle. But suddenly she lifted her hands with a desperate gesture, pressing them to her temples.

"Oh, my God! I sent him to Ned—I told him where to go! I sent him to this room!" she screamed.

She felt the walls of books rush toward her, like inward falling ruins; and she heard Parvis, a long way off, through the ruins, crying to her, and struggling to get at her. But she was numb to his touch, she did not know what he was saying. Through the tumult she heard but one clear note, the voice of Alida Stair, speaking on the lawn at Pangbourne.

"You won't know till afterward," it said. "You won't know till long, long afterward."

The Letters

I

UP the hill from the station at St.-Cloud, Lizzie West climbed in the cold spring sunshine. As she breasted the incline, she noticed the first waves of wistaria over courtyard railings and the high lights of new foliage against the walls of ivy-matted gardens; and she thought again, as she had thought a hundred times before, that she had never seen so beautiful a spring.

She was on her way to the Deerings' house, in a street near the hilltop; and every step was dear and familiar to her. She went there five times a week to teach little Juliet Deering, the daughter of Mr. Vincent Deering, the distinguished American artist. Juliet had been her pupil for two years, and day after day, during this time, Lizzie West had mounted the hill in all weathers; sometimes with her umbrella bent against the rain, sometimes with her frail cotton parasol unfurled beneath a fiery sun, sometimes with the snow soaking through her boots or a bitter wind piercing her thin jacket, sometimes with the dust whirling about her and bleaching the flowers of the poor little hat that had to "carry her through" till next summer.

At first the ascent had seemed tedious enough, as dull as the trudge to her other lessons. Lizzie was not a heaven-sent teacher; she had no born zeal for her calling, and though she dealt kindly and dutifully with her pupils, she did not fly to them on winged feet. But one day something had happened to change the face of life, and since then the climb to the Deering house had seemed like a dream-flight up a heavenly stairway.

Her heart beat faster as she remembered it—no longer in a tumult of fright and self-reproach, but softly, happily, as if brooding over a possession that none could take from her.

It was on a day of the previous October that she had stopped, after Juliet's lesson, to ask if she might speak to Juliet's papa. One had always to apply to Mr. Deering if there was anything to be said about the lessons. Mrs. Deering lay on her lounge upstairs, reading relays of dog-eared novels, the choice of which she left to the cook and the nurse, who were always fetching them for her from the *cabinet de lecture;* and it was understood in the house that she was not to be "bothered" about Juliet. Mr. Deering's interest in his daughter was fitful rather than consecutive; but at least he was approachable, and listened sympathetically, if a little absently, stroking his long fair moustache, while Lizzie stated her difficulty or put in her plea for maps or copy-books.

"Yes, yes—of course—whatever you think right," he would always assent, sometimes drawing a five-franc piece from his pocket, and laying it carelessly on the table, or oftener saying, with his charming smile: "Get what you please, and just put it on your account, you know."

But this time Lizzie had not come to ask for maps or copy-books, or even to hint, in crimson misery—as once, poor soul! she had had to do—that Mr. Deering had overlooked her last little account—had probably not noticed that she had left it, some two months earlier, on a corner of his littered writing-table. That hour had been bad enough, though he had done his best to carry it off gallantly and gaily; but this was infinitely worse. For she had come to complain of her pupil; to say that, much as she loved little Juliet, it was useless, unless Mr. Deering could "do something," to go on with the lessons.

"It wouldn't be honest—I should be robbing you; I'm not sure that I haven't already," she half laughed, through mounting tears, as she put her case. Little Juliet would not work, would not obey. Her poor little drifting existence floated aimlessly between the kitchen and the *lingerie,* and all the groping tendrils of her curiosity were fastened about the life of the backstairs.

It was the same kind of curiosity that Mrs. Deering, overhead in her drug-scented room, lavished on her dog-eared novels and on the "society notes" of the morning paper; but since Juliet's horizon was not yet wide enough to embrace these loftier objects, her interest was centered in the anecdotes that Celeste and Suzanne brought back from the market and the library. That these were not always of an edifying nature the child's artless rattle too often betrayed; but unhappily they occupied her fancy to the complete exclusion of such nourishing items as dates and dynasties, and the sources of the principal European rivers.

At length the crisis became so acute that poor Lizzie felt herself bound to resign her charge or ask Mr. Deering's intervention; and for Juliet's sake she chose the harder alternative. It *was* hard to speak to him not only because one hated to confess one's failure, and hated still more to ascribe it to such vulgar causes, but because one blushed to bring them to the notice of a spirit engaged with higher things. Mr. Deering was very busy at that moment: he had a new picture "on." And Lizzie entered the studio with the flutter of one profanely intruding on some sacred rite; she almost heard the rustle of retreating wings as she approached.

And then—and then—how differently it had all turned out! Perhaps it wouldn't have, if she hadn't been such a goose—she who so seldom cried, so prided herself on a stoic control of her little twittering cageful of "feelings." But if she had cried, it was because he had looked at her so kindly, and because she had nevertheless felt him so pained and shamed by what she said. The pain, of course, lay for both in the implication behind her words—in the one word she left unspoken. If little Juliet was as she was, it was because of the mother upstairs—the mother who had given the child her frivolous impulses, and grudged her the care that might have corrected them. The case so obviously revolved in its own vicious circle that when Mr. Deering had murmured, "Of course if my wife were not an invalid," they both turned with a spring to the flagrant "bad example" of Celeste and Suzanne, fastening on that with a mutual insistence that ended in his crying out: "All the more, then, how can you leave her to them?"

"But if I do her no good?" Lizzie wailed; and it was then that, when he took her hand and assured her gently, "But you do, you do!"—it was then that, in the traditional phrase, she "broke down," and her poor little protest quivered off into tears.

"You do *me* good, at any rate—you make the house seem less like a desert," she heard him say; and the next moment she felt herself drawn to him, and they kissed each other through her weeping.

They kissed each other—there was the new fact. One does not, if one is a poor little teacher living in Mme. Clopin's Pension Suisse at Passy, and if one has pretty brown hair and eyes that reach out trustfully to other eyes—one does not, under these common but defenseless conditions, arrive at the age of twenty-five without being now and then kissed—waylaid once by a noisy student between two doors, surprised once by one's grey-bearded professor as one bent over the "theme" he was correcting—but these episodes, if they tarnish the surface, do not reach the heart: it is not the kiss endured, but the kiss returned, that lives. And Lizzie West's first kiss was for Vincent Deering.

As she drew back from it, something new awoke in her—something deeper than the fright and the shame, and the penitent thought of Mrs. Deering. A sleeping germ of life thrilled and unfolded, and started out to seek the sun.

She might have felt differently, perhaps—the shame and penitence might have prevailed—had she not known him so kind and tender, and guessed him so baffled, poor and disappointed. She knew the failure of his married life, and she divined a corresponding failure in his artistic career. Lizzie, who had made her own faltering snatch at the same laurels, brought her thwarted proficiency to bear on the question of his pictures, which she judged to be remarkable, but suspected of having somehow failed to affirm their merit publicly. She understood that he had tasted an earlier moment of success: a *mention,* a medal, something official and tangible; then the tide of publicity had somehow set the other way, and left him stranded in a noble isolation. It was incredible that anyone so naturally eminent and exceptional should have been subject to the same vulgar necessities that governed her own life, should have known poverty and obscurity and indifference. But she gathered that this had been the case, and felt that it formed the miraculous link between them. For through what medium less revealing than that of shared misfortune would he ever have perceived so inconspicuous an object as herself? And she recalled now how gently his eyes had rested on her from the first—the grey eyes that might have seemed mocking if they had not seemed so gentle.

She remembered how kindly he had met her the first day, when Mrs. Deering's inevitable headache had prevented her receiving the new teacher. Insensibly he had led Lizzie to talk of herself and his questions had at once revealed his interest in the little stranded compatriot doomed to earn a precarious living so far from her native shore. Sweet as the moment of unburdening had been, she wondered afterward what had determined it: how she, so shy and sequestered, had found herself letting slip her whole poverty-stricken story, even to the avowal of the ineffectual "artistic" tendencies that had drawn her to Paris, and had then left her there to the dry task of tuition. She wondered at first, but she understood now; she understood everything after he had kissed her. It was simply because he was as kind as he was great.

She thought of this now as she mounted the hill in the spring sunshine, and she thought of all that had happened since. The intervening months, as she looked back at them, were merged in a vast golden haze, through which here and there rose the outline of a shining island. The haze was the general enveloping sense of his love, and the shining islands were the days they had spent together. They had never kissed again under his own roof. Lizzie's professional honor had a keen edge, but she had been spared the necessity of making him feel it. It was of the essence of her fatality that he always "understood" when his failing to do so might have imperilled his hold on her.

But her Thursdays and Sundays were free, and it soon became a habit to give them to him. She knew, for her peace of mind, only too much about pictures, and galleries and churches had been the one outlet from the greyness of her personal conditions. For poetry, too, and the other imaginative forms of literature, she had always felt more than she had hitherto had occasion to betray; and now all these folded sympathies shot out their tendrils to the light. Mr. Deering knew how to express with unmatched clearness the thoughts that trembled in her mind: to talk with him was to soar up into the azure on the outspread wings of his intelligence, and look down, dizzily yet clearly, on all the wonders and glories of the world. She was a little ashamed, sometimes, to find how few definite impressions she brought back from these flights; but that was doubtless because her heart beat so fast when he was near, and his smile made his words seem like a long quiver of light. Afterward, in quieter hours, fragments of their talk emerged in her memory with wondrous precision, every syllable as minutely chiselled as some of the delicate objects in crystal or ivory that he pointed out in the museums they frequented. It was always a puzzle to Lizzie that some of their hours should be so blurred and others so vivid.

She was reliving all these memories with unusual distinctness, because it was a fortnight since she had seen her friend. Mrs. Deering, some six weeks previously, had gone to visit a relative at St.-Raphaël; and, after she had been a month absent, her husband and the little girl had joined her. Lizzie's adieux to Deering had been made on a rainy afternoon in the damp corridors of the Aquarium at the Trocadéro. She could not receive him at her own *pension*. That a teacher should be visited by the father of a pupil, especially when that father was still, as Madame Clopin said, *si bien,* was against that lady's austere Helvetian code. And from Deering's first tentative hint of another solution Lizzie had recoiled in a wild flurry of all her scruples. He took her "No, no, *no!*" as he took all her twists and turns of conscience, with eyes half-tender and half-mocking, and an instant acquiescence which was the finest homage to the "lady" she felt he divined and honored in her.

So they continued to meet in museums and galleries, or to extend, on fine days, their explorations to the suburbs, where now and then, in the solitude of grove or garden, the kiss renewed itself, fleeting, isolated, or prolonged in a shy pressure of the hand. But on the day of his leave-taking the rain kept them under cover; and as they threaded the subterranean windings of the Aquarium, and Lizzie gazed unseeingly at the grotesque faces glaring at her through walls of glass, she felt like a drowned wretch at the bottom of the sea, with all her sunlit memories rolling over her like the waves of its surface.

"You'll never see him again—never see him again," the waves boomed in her ears through his last words; and when she had said good-bye to him at the corner, and had scrambled, wet and shivering, into the Passy omnibus, its grinding wheels took up the derisive burden—"Never see him, never see him again."

All that was only two weeks ago, and here she was, as happy as a lark, mounting the hill to his door in the fresh spring sunshine! So weak a heart did not deserve such a radiant fate; and Lizzie said to herself that she would never again distrust her star.

II

THE cracked bell tinkled sweetly through her heart as she stood listening for Juliet's feet. Juliet, anticipating the laggard Suzanne, almost always opened the door for her governess, not from any eagerness to hasten the hour of her studies, but from the irrepressible desire to see what was going on in the street. But doubtless on this occasion some unusually absorbing incident had detained the child below-stairs; for Lizzie, after vainly waiting for a step, had to give the bell a second twitch. Even a third produced no response, and Lizzie, full of dawning fears, drew back to look up at the house. She saw that the studio shutters stood wide, and then noticed, without surprise, that Mrs. Deering's were still unopened. No doubt Mrs. Deering was resting after the fatigue of the journey. Instinctively Lizzie's eyes turned again to the studio window; and as she looked, she saw Deering approach it. He caught sight of her, and an instant later was at the door. He looked paler than usual, and she noticed that he wore a black coat.

"I rang and rang—where is Juliet?" she asked.

He looked at her gravely; then, without answering, he led her down the passage to the studio, and closed the door when she had entered.

"My wife is dead—she died suddenly ten days ago. Didn't you see it in the papers?" he said.

Lizzie, with a cry, sank down on the rickety divan propped against the wall. She seldom saw a newspaper, since she could not afford one for her own perusal, and those supplied to the Pension Clopin were usually in the hands of its more privileged lodgers till long after the hour when she set out on her morning round.

"No; I didn't see it," she stammered.

Deering was silent. He stood twisting an unlit cigarette in his hand, and looking down at her with a gaze that was both constrained and hesitating.

She, too, felt the constraint of the situation, the impossibility of finding words which, after what had passed between them, should seem neither false nor heartless; and at last she exclaimed, standing up: "Poor little Juliet! Can't I go to her?"

"Juliet is not here. I left her at St.-Raphaël with the relations with whom my wife was staying."

"Oh," Lizzie murmured, feeling vaguely that this added to the difficulty of the moment. How differently she had pictured their meeting!

"I'm so—so sorry for her!" she faltered.

Deering made no reply, but, turning on his heel, walked the length of the studio and halted before the picture on the easel. It was the landscape he had begun the previous autumn, with the intention of sending it to the Salon that spring. But it was still unfinished—seemed, indeed, hardly more advanced than on the fateful October day when Lizzie, standing before it for the first time, had confessed her inability to deal with Juliet. Perhaps the same thought struck its creator, for he broke into a dry laugh and turned from the easel with a shrug.

Under his protracted silence Lizzie roused herself to the fact that, since her pupil was absent, there was no reason for her remaining any longer; and as Deering approached her she rose and said with an effort: "I'll go, then. You'll send for me when she comes back?"

Deering still hesitated, tormenting the cigarette between his fingers.

"She's not coming back—not at present."

Lizzie heard him with a drop of the heart. Was everything to be changed in their lives? Of course; how could she have dreamed it would be otherwise? She could only stupidly repeat: "Not coming back? Not this spring?"

"Probably not, since our friends are so good as to keep her. The fact is, I've got to go to America. My wife left a little property, a few pennies, that I must go and see to—for the child."

Lizzie stood before him, a cold knife in her breast. "I see—I see," she reiterated, feeling all the while that she strained her eyes into utter blackness.

"It's a nuisance, having to pull up stakes," he went on, with a fretful glance about the studio.

She lifted her eyes to his face. "Shall you be gone long?" she took courage to ask.

"There again—I can't tell. It's all so mixed up." He met her look for an incredibly long strange moment. "I hate to go!" he murmured abruptly.

Lizzie felt a rush of moisture to her lashes, and the familiar wave of weakness at her heart. She raised her hand to her face with an instinctive gesture, and as she did so he held out his arms.

"Come here, Lizzie!" he said.

And she went—went with a sweet wild throb of liberation, with the sense that at last the house was his, that *she* was his, if he wanted her; that never again would that silent presence in the room above constrain and shame her rapture.

He pushed back her veil and covered her face with kisses. "Don't cry, you little goose!" he said.

III

THAT they must see each other before his departure, in some place less exposed than their usual haunts, was as clear to Lizzie as it appeared to be to Deering. His expressing the wish seemed, indeed, the sweetest testimony to the quality of his feeling, since, in the first weeks of the most perfunctory widowerhood, a man of his stamp is presumed to abstain from light adventures. If, then, he wished so much to be quietly and gravely with her, it could be only for reasons she did not call by name, but of which she felt the sacred tremor in her heart; and it would have seemed to her vain and vulgar to put forward, at such a moment, the conventional objections with which such little exposed existences defend the treasure of their freshness.

In such a mood as this one may descend from the Passy omnibus at the corner of the Pont de la Concorde (she had not let him fetch her in a cab) with a sense of dedication almost solemn, and may advance to meet one's fate, in the shape of a gentleman of melancholy elegance, with an auto-taxi at his call, as one has advanced to the altar-steps in some girlish bridal vision.

Even the experienced waiter ushering them into an upper room of the quiet restaurant on the Seine could hardly have supposed their quest for privacy to be based on the familiar motive, so soberly did Deering give his orders, while his companion sat small and grave at his side. She did not, indeed, mean to let her distress obscure their hour together: she was already learning that Deering shrank from sadness. He should see that she had courage and gaiety to face their coming separation, and yet give herself meanwhile to this completer nearness; but she waited, as always, for him to strike the opening note.

Looking back at it later, she wondered at the sweetness of the hour. Her heart was unversed in happiness, but he had found the tone to lull her fears, and make her trust her fate for any golden wonder. Deepest of all, he gave her the sense of something tacit and established between them, as if his tenderness were a habit of the heart hardly needing the support of outward proof.

Such proof as he offered came, therefore, as a kind of crowning luxury, the flowering of a profoundly rooted sentiment; and here again the instinctive reserves and defenses would have seemed to vulgarize what his confidence ennobled. But if all the tender casuistries of her heart were at his service, he took no grave advantage of them. Even when they sat alone after dinner, with the lights of the river trembling through their one low window, and the rumor of Paris enclosing them in a heart of silence, he seemed, as much as herself, under the spell of hallowing influences. She felt it most of all as she yielded to the arm he presently put about her, to the long caress he laid on her lips and eyes: not a word or gesture missed the note of quiet understanding, or cast a doubt, in retrospect, on the pact they sealed with their last look.

That pact, as she reviewed it through a sleepless night, seemed to have consisted mainly, on his part, in pleadings for full and frequent news of her, on hers in the promise that it should be given as often as he wrote to ask it. She did not wish to show too much eagerness, too great a desire to affirm and define her hold on him. Her life had given her a certain acquaintance with the arts of defense: girls in her situation were supposed to know them all, and to use them as occasion called. But Lizzie's very need of them had intensified her disdain. Just because she was so poor, and had always, materially, so to count her change and calculate her margin, she would at least know the joy of emotional prodigality, and give her heart as recklessly as the rich their millions. She was sure now that Deering loved her, and if he had seized the occasion of their farewell to give her some definitely worded sign of his feeling—if, more plainly, he had asked her to marry him—his doing so would have seemed less a proof of his sincerity than of his suspecting in her the need of such a warrant. That he had abstained seemed to show that he trusted her as she trusted him, and that they were one most of all in this complete security of understanding.

She had tried to make him guess all this in the chariness of her promise to write. She would write; of course she would. But he would be busy, preoccupied, on the move: it was for him to let her know when he wished a word, to spare her the embarrassment of ill-timed intrusions.

"Intrusions?" He had smiled the word away. "You can't well intrude, my darling, on a heart where you're already established to the complete exclusion of other lodgers." And then, taking her hands, and looking up from them into her happy dizzy eyes: "You don't know much about being in love, do you, Lizzie?" he laughingly ended.

It seemed easy enough to reject this imputation in a kiss; but she wondered afterward if she had not deserved it. Was she really cold and conventional, and did other women give more richly and recklessly? She found that it was possible to turn about every one of her reserves and delicacies so that they looked like selfish scruples and petty pruderies, and at this game she came in time to exhaust all the resources of casuistry.

Meanwhile the first days after Deering's departure wore a soft refracted light like the radiance lingering after sunset. *He,* at any rate, was taxable with no reserves, no calculations, and his letters of farewell, from train and steamer, filled her with long murmurs and echoes of his presence. How he loved her, how he loved her—and how he knew how to tell her so!

She was not sure of possessing the same gift. Unused to the expression of personal emotion, she wavered between the impulse to pour out all she felt and the fear lest her extravagance should amuse or even bore him. She never lost the sense that what was to her the central crisis of experience must be a mere episode in a life so predestined as his to romantic incidents. All that she felt and said would be subjected to the test of comparison with what others had already given him: from all quarters of the globe she saw passionate missives winging their way toward Deering, for whom her poor little swallow-flight of devotion could certainly not make a summer. But such moments were succeeded by others in which she raised her head and dared affirm her conviction that no woman had ever loved him just as she had, and that none, therefore, had probably found just such things to say to him. And this conviction strengthened the other less solidly based belief that *he* also, for the same reason, had found new accents to express his tenderness, and that the three letters she wore all day in her shabby blouse, and hid all night beneath her pillow, not only surpassed in beauty, but differed in quality from, all he had ever penned for other eyes.

They gave her, at any rate, during the weeks that she wore them on her heart, sensations more complex and delicate than Deering's actual presence had ever produced. To be with him was always like breasting a bright rough sea that blinded while it buoyed her; but his letters formed a still pool of contemplation, above which she could bend, and see the reflection of the sky, and the myriad movements of the life that flitted and gleamed below the surface. The wealth of this hidden life—that was what most surprised her! She had had no inkling of it, but had kept on along the narrow track of habit, like a traveller climbing a road in a fog, and suddenly finding himself on a sunlit crag between leagues of sky and dizzy depths of valley. And the odd thing was that all the people about her—the whole world of the Passy pension—seemed plodding along the same dull path, preoccupied with the pebbles underfoot, and unaware of the glory beyond the fog!

There were hours of exultation, when she longed to cry out to them what one saw from the summit—and hours of abasement, when she asked herself why *her* feet had been guided there, while others, no doubt as worthy, stumbled and blundered in obscurity. She felt, in particular, an urgent pity for the two or three other girls at Mme. Clopin's—girls older, duller, less alive than she, and by that very token more thrown upon her sympathy. Would they ever know? Had they ever known?—those were the questions that haunted her as she crossed her companions on the stairs, faced them at the dinner-table, and listened to their poor pining talk in the dimly-lit slippery-seated *salon*. One of the girls was Swiss, another English;

a third, Andora Macy, was a young lady from the Southern States who was studying French with the ultimate object of imparting it to the inmates of a girls' school at Macon, Georgia.

Andora Macy was pale, faded, immature. She had a drooping accent, and a manner which fluctuated between arch audacity and fits of panicky hauteur. She yearned to be admired, and feared to be insulted; and yet seemed wistfully conscious that she was destined to miss both these extremes of sensation, or to enjoy them only in the experiences of her more privileged friends.

It was perhaps for this reason that she took a tender interest in Lizzie, who had shrunk from her at first, as the depressing image of her own probable future, but to whom she now suddenly became an object of sentimental pity.

IV

MISS MACY'S room was next to Miss West's, and the Southerner's knock often appealed to Lizzie's hospitality when Mme. Clopin's early curfew had driven her boarders from the *salon*. It sounded thus one evening, just as Lizzie, tired from an unusually long day of tuition, was in the act of removing her dress. She was in too indulgent a mood to withhold her "Come in," and as Miss Macy crossed the threshold, Lizzie felt that Vincent Deering's first letter—the letter from the train—had slipped from her bosom to the floor.

Miss Macy, as promptly aware, darted forward to recover it. Lizzie stooped also, instinctively jealous of her touch; but the visitor reached the letter first, and as she seized it, Lizzie knew that she had seen whence it fell, and was weaving round the incident a rapid web of romance.

Lizzie blushed with annoyance. "It's too stupid, having no pockets! If one gets a letter as one is going out in the morning, one has to carry it in one's blouse all day."

Miss Macy looked at her fondly. "It's warm from your heart!"

she breathed, reluctantly yielding up the missive.

Lizzie laughed, for she knew it was the letter that had warmed her heart. Poor Andora Macy! *She* would never know. Her bleak bosom would never take fire from such a contact. Lizzie looked at her with kind eyes, chafing at the injustice of fate.

The next evening, on her return home, she found her friend hovering in the entrance hall.

"I thought you'd like me to put this in your own hand," Andora whispered significantly, pressing a letter upon Lizzie. "I couldn't *bear* to see it lying on the table with the others."

It was Deering's letter from the steamer. Lizzie blushed to the forehead, but without resenting Andora's divination. She could not have breathed a word of her bliss, but she was not sorry to have it guessed, and pity for Andora's destitution yielded to the pleasure of using it as a mirror for her own abundance.

Deering wrote again on reaching New York, a long fond dissatisfied letter, vague in its indication to his own projects, specific in the expression of his love. Lizzie brooded over every syllable till they formed the undercurrent of all her waking thoughts, and murmured through her midnight dreams; but she would have been happier if they had shed some definite light on the future.

That would come, no doubt, when he had had time to look about and get his bearings. She counted the days that must elapse before she received his next letter, and stole down early to peep at the papers, and learn when the next American mail was due. At length the happy date arrived, and she hurried distractedly through the day's work, trying to conceal her impatience by the endearments she bestowed upon her pupils. It was easier, in her present mood, to kiss them than to keep them at their grammars.

That evening, on Mme. Clopin's threshold, her heart beat so wildly that she had to lean a moment against the door-post before entering. But on the hall table, where the letters lay, there was none for her.

She went over them with an impatient hand, her heart dropping down and down, as she had sometimes fallen down an endless stairway in a dream—the very same stairway up which she had seemed to fly when she climbed the long hill to Deering's door. Then it struck her that Andora might have found and secreted her letter, and with a spring she was on the actual stairs, and rattling Miss Macy's door-handle.

"You've a letter for me, haven't you?" she panted.

Miss Macy enclosed her in attenuated arms. "Oh, darling, did you expect another?"

"Do give it to me!" Lizzie pleaded with eager eyes.

"But I haven't any! There hasn't been a sign of a letter for you."

"I know there is. There *must* be," Lizzie cried, stamping her foot.

"But, dearest, I've *watched* for you, and there's been nothing."

Day after day, for the ensuing weeks, the same scene re-enacted itself with endless variations. Lizzie, after the first sharp spasm of disappointment, made no effort to conceal her anxiety from Miss Macy, and the fond Andora was charged to keep a vigilant eye upon the postman's coming, and to spy on the *bonne* for possible negligence or perfidy. But these elaborate precautions remained fruitless, and no letter from Deering came.

During the first fortnight of silence, Lizzie exhausted all the ingenuities of explanation. She marvelled afterward at the reasons she had found for Deering's silence: there were moments when she almost argued herself into thinking it more natural than his continuing to write. There was only one reason which her intelligence rejected; and that was the possibility that he had forgotten her, that the whole episode had faded from his mind like a breath from a mirror. From that she resolutely averted her thoughts, conscious that if she suffered herself to contemplate it, the motive power of life would fail, and she would no longer understand why she rose in the morning and lay down at night.

If she had had leisure to indulge her anguish she might have been unable to keep such speculations at bay. But she had to be up and working: the *blanchisseuse* had to be paid, and Mme. Clopin's weekly bill, and all the little "extras" that even her frugal habits had to reckon with. And in the depths of her thought dwelt the dogging fear of illness and incapacity, goading her to work while she could. She hardly remembered the time when she had been without that fear; it was second nature now, and it kept her on her feet when other incentives might have failed. In the blankness of her misery she felt no dread of death; but the horror of being ill and "dependent" was in her blood.

In the first weeks of silence she wrote again and again to Deering,

Lizzie brooded over every syllable till they formed the undercurrent of all her waking thoughts.

entreating him for a word, for a mere sign of life. From the first she had shrunk from seeming to assert any claim on his future, yet in her bewilderment she now charged herself with having been too possessive, too exacting in her tone. She told herself that his fastidiousness shrank from any but a "light touch," and that hers had not been light enough. She should have kept to the character of the "little friend," the artless consciousness in which tormented genius may find an escape from its complexities; and instead, she had dramatized their relation, exaggerated her own part in it, presumed, forsooth, to share the front of the stage with him, instead of being content to serve as scenery or chorus.

But though, to herself, she admitted, and even insisted on, the episodical nature of the experience, on the fact that for Deering it could be no more than an incident, she was still convinced that his sentiment for her, however fugitive, had been genuine.

His had not been the attitude of the unscrupulous male seeking a vulgar "advantage." For a moment he had really needed her, and if he was silent now, it was perhaps because he feared that she had mistaken the nature of the need, and built vain hopes on its possible duration.

It was of the essence of Lizzie's devotion that it sought, instinctively, the larger freedom of its object; she could not conceive of love under any form of exaction or compulsion. To make this clear to Deering became an overwhelming need, and in a last short letter she explicitly freed him from whatever sentimental obligation its predecessors might have seemed to impose. In this communication she playfully accused herself of having unwittingly sentimentalized their relation, affecting, in self-defense, a retrospective astuteness, a sense of the impermanence of the tenderer sentiments, that almost put Deering in the position of having mistaken coquetry for surrender. And she ended, gracefully, with a plea for the continuance of the friendly regard which she had "always understood" to be the basis of their sympathy. The document, when completed, seemed to her worthy of what she conceived to be Deering's conception of a woman of the world—and she found a spectral satisfaction in the thought of making her final appearance before him in this distinguished character. But she was never destined to learn what effect the appearance produced; for the letter, like those it sought to excuse, remained unanswered.

V

THE fresh spring sunshine which had so often attended Lizzie West on her dusty climb up the hill of St.-Cloud, beamed on her, some two years later in a scene and a situation of altered import.

Its rays, filtered through the horse-chestnuts of the Champs Elysées, shone on the gravelled circle about Laurent's restaurant; and Miss West, seated at a table within that privileged space, presented to the light a hat much better able to sustain its scrutiny than those which had shaded the brow of Juliet Deering's instructress.

Her dress was in keeping with the hat, and both belonged to a situation rife with such possibilities as the act of a leisurely luncheon at Laurent's in the opening week of the Salon. Her companions, of both sexes, confirmed this impression by an appropriateness of attire and an ease of manner implying the largest range of selection between the forms of Parisian idleness; and even Andora Macy, seated opposite, as in the place of co-hostess or companion, reflected, in coy greys and mauves, the festal note of the occasion.

This note reverberated persistently in the ears of a solitary gentleman straining for glimpses of the group from a table wedged in the remotest corner of the garden; but to Miss West herself the occurrence did not rise above the usual. For nearly a year she had been acquiring the habit of such situations, and the act of offering a luncheon at Laurent's to her cousins, the Harvey Mearses of Providence, and their friend Mr. Jackson Benn, produced in her no emotion beyond the languid glow which Mr. Benn's presence was beginning to impart to such scenes.

"It's frightful, the way you've got used to it," Andora Macy had wailed, in the first days of her friend's transfigured fortunes, when Lizzie West had waked one morning to find herself among the heirs of an ancient miserly cousin whose testamentary dispositions had formed, since her earliest childhood, the subject of pleasantry and conjecture in her own improvident family. Old Hezron Mears had never given any sign of life to the luckless Wests; had perhaps hardly been conscious of including them in the carefully drawn will which, following the old American convention, scrupulously divided his millions among his kin. It was by a mere genealogical accident that Lizzie, falling just within the golden circle, found herself possessed of a pittance sufficient to release her from the prospect of a long grey future in Mme. Clopin's *pension*.

The release had seemed wonderful at first; yet she presently found that it had destroyed her former world without giving her a new one. On the ruins of the old *pension* life bloomed the only flower that had ever sweetened her path; and beyond the sense of present ease, and the removal of anxiety for the future, her reconstructed existence blossomed with no compensating joys. She had hoped great things from the opportunity to rest, to travel, to look about her, above all, in various artful feminine ways, to be "nice" to the companions of her less privileged state; but such widenings of scope left her, as it were, but the more conscious of the empty margin of personal life beyond them. It was not till she woke to the leisure of her new days that she had the full sense of what was gone from them.

Their very emptiness made her strain to pack them with transient sensations: she was like the possessor of an unfurnished house, with random furniture and bric-a-brac perpetually pouring in "on approval." It was in this experimental character that Mr. Jackson Benn had fixed her attention, and the languid effort of her imagination to adjust him to her taste was seconded by the fond complicity of Andora, and by the smiling approval of her cousins. Lizzie did not discourage these attempts: she suffered serenely Andora's allusions to Mr. Benn's infatuation, and Mrs. Mears's boasts of his business standing. All the better if they could drape his narrow square-shouldered frame and round unwinking countenance in the trailing mists of sentiment: Lizzie looked and listened, not unhopeful of the miracle.

"I never saw anything like the way these Frenchmen stare! Doesn't it make you nervous, Lizzie?" Mrs. Mears broke out suddenly, ruffling her feather boa about an outraged bosom. Mrs. Mears was still in that stage of development when her country-women taste to the full the peril of being exposed to the gaze of the licentious Gaul.

Lizzie roused herself from the contemplation of Mr. Benn's round baby cheeks and the square blue jaw resting on his perpendicular collar. "Is someone staring at me?" she asked.

"Don't turn round, whatever you do! There—just over there, between the rhododendrons—the tall blond man alone at that table. Really, Harvey, I think you ought to speak to the head waiter, or something; though I suppose in one of these places they'd only laugh at you," Mrs. Mears shudderingly concluded.

Her husband, as if inclining to this probability, continued the undisturbed dissection of his chicken wing, but Mr. Benn, perhaps conscious that his situation demanded a more punctilious attitude, sternly revolved upon the parapet of his high collar in the direction of Mrs. Mears's glance.

"What, that fellow all alone over there? Why, *he's* not French; he's an American," he then proclaimed with a perceptible relaxing of the muscles.

"Oh!" murmured Mrs. Mears, as perceptibly disappointed, and Mr. Benn continued: "He came over on the steamer with me. He's some kind of an artist—a fellow named Deering. He was staring at me, I guess: wondering whether I was going to remember him. Why, how d' 'e do? How are you? Why, yes, of course; with pleasure—my friends, Mrs. Harvey Mears—Mr. Mears; my friends, Miss Macy and Miss West."

"I have the pleasure of knowing Miss West," said Vincent Deering with a smile.

VI

EVEN through his smile Lizzie had seen, in the first moment, how changed he was; and the impression of the change deepened to the point of pain when, a few days later, in reply to his brief note, she granted him a private hour.

That the first sight of his writing—the first answer to her letters—should have come, after three long years, in the shape of this impersonal line, too curt to be called humble, yet revealing a consciousness of the past in the studied avoidance of its language! As she read, her mind flashed back over what she had dreamed his letters would be, over the exquisite answers she had composed above his name. There was nothing exquisite in the lines before her; but dormant nerves began to throb again at the mere touch of the paper he had touched, and she threw the note into the fire before she dared to reply to it.

Now that he was actually before her again, he became, as usual, the one live spot in her consciousness. Once more her tormented self sank back passive and numb, but now with all its power of suffering mysteriously transferred to the presence, so known yet so unknown, at the opposite corner of her hearth. She was still Lizzie West and he was still Vincent Deering; but the Styx rolled between them, and she saw his face through its fog. It was his face, really, rather than his words, that told her, as she furtively studied it, the tale of failure and discouragement which had so blurred its handsome lines. She kept, afterward, no precise memory of the details of his narrative: the pain it evidently cost him to impart it was so much the sharpest fact in her new vision of him. Confusedly, however, she gathered that on reaching America he had found his wife's small property gravely impaired; and that, while lingering on to secure what remained of it, he had contrived to sell a picture or two, and had even known a moment of success, during which he received orders and set up a studio. Then the tide had ebbed, his work had remained on his hands, and a tedious illness, with its miserable sequel of debt, soon wiped out his advantage. There followed a period of eclipse, during which she inferred that he had tried his hand at divers means of livelihood, accepting employment from a fashionable house-decorator, designing wall-papers, illustrating magazine articles, and acting for a time—she dimly understood—as the social tout of a new hotel desirous of advertising its restaurant. These disjointed facts were strung on a slender thread of personal allusions—references to friends who had been kind (jealously, she guessed them to be women), and to enemies who had schemed against him. But, true to his tradition of "correctness," he carefully avoided the mention of names, and left her imagination to grope dimly through a crowded world in which there seemed little room for her small shy presence.

As she listened, her private grievance vanished beneath the sense of his unhappiness. Nothing he had said explained or excused his conduct to her; but he had suffered, he had been lonely, had been humiliated, and she felt, with a fierce maternal rage, that there was no possible justification for any scheme of things in which such facts were possible. She could not have said why: she simply knew that it hurt too much to see him hurt.

Gradually it came to her that her absence of resentment was due to her having so definitely settled her own future. She was glad she had decided—as she now felt she had—to marry Jackson Benn, if only for the sense of detachment it gave her in dealing with Vincent Deering. Her personal safety insured her the requisite impartiality, and justified her in lingering as long as she chose over the last lines of a chapter to which her own act had fixed the close. Any lingering hesitations as to the finality of this decision were dispelled by the need of making it known to Deering, and when her visitor paused in his reminiscences to say, with a sigh, "But many things have happened to you too," the words did not so much evoke the sense of her altered fortunes as the image of the suitor to whom she was about to entrust them.

"Yes, many things; it's three years," she answered.

Deering sat leaning forward, in his sad exiled elegance, his eyes gently bent on hers; and at his side she saw the form of Mr. Jackson Benn, with shoulders preternaturally squared by the cut of his tight black coat, and a tall shiny collar sustaining his baby cheeks and hard blue chin. Then the vision faded as Deering began to speak.

"Three years," he repeated musingly. "I've so often wondered what they'd brought you."

She lifted her head with a blush, and the terrified wish that he should not—at the cost of all his notions of correctness—lapse into the blunder of becoming "personal."

"You've wondered?" she smiled back bravely.

"Do you suppose I haven't?" His look dwelt on her. "Yes, I dare say that *was* what you thought of me."

She had her answer pat—"Why, frankly, you know, I *didn't* think of you at all." But the mounting tide of her memories swept it indignantly away. If it was his correctness to ignore, it could never be hers to disavow!

"*Was* that what you thought of me?" she heard him repeat in a tone of sad insistence; and at that, with a lift of her head, she resolutely answered: "How could I know what to think? I had no word from you."

If she had expected, and perhaps almost hoped, that this answer would create a difficulty for him, the gaze of quiet fortitude with which he met it proved that she had underestimated his resources.

"No, you had no word. I kept my vow," he said.

"Your vow?"

"That you *shouldn't* have a word—not a syllable. Oh, I kept it through everything!"

Lizzie's heart was sounding in her ears the old confused rumor of the sea of life, but through it she desperately tried to distinguish the still small voice of reason.

"What was your vow? Why shouldn't I have had a syllable from you?"

He sat motionless, still holding her with a look so gentle that it almost seemed forgiving.

Then, abruptly, he rose, and crossing the space between them, sat down in a chair at her side. The movement might have implied a forgetfulness of changed conditions, and Lizzie, as if thus viewing it, drew slightly back; but he appeared not to notice her recoil, and his eyes, at last leaving her face, slowly and approvingly made the round of the small bright drawing-room. "This is charming. Yes, things *have* changed for you," he said.

A moment before, she had prayed that he might be spared the error of a vain return upon the past. It was as if all her retrospective tenderness, dreading to see him at such a disadvantage, rose up to protect him from it. But his evasiveness exasperated her, and suddenly she felt the desire to hold him fast, face to face with his own words.

Before she could repeat her question, however, he had met her with another.

"You *did* think of me, then? Why are you afraid to tell me that you did?"

The unexpectedness of the challenge wrung a cry from her. "Didn't my letters tell you so enough?"

"Ah—your letters—" Keeping her gaze on his with unrelenting fixity, she could detect in him no confusion, not the least quiver of a nerve. He only gazed back at her more sadly.

"They went everywhere with me—your letters," he said.

"Yet you never answered them." At last the accusation trembled to her lips.

"Yet I never answered them."

"Did you ever so much as read them, I wonder?"

All the demons of self-torture were up in her now, and she loosed them on him as if to escape from their rage.

Deering hardly seemed to hear her question. He merely shifted his attitude, leaning a little nearer to her, but without attempting, by the least gesture, to remind her of the privileges which such nearness had once implied.

"There were beautiful, wonderful things in them," he said, smiling.

She felt herself stiffen under his smile. "You've waited three years to tell me so!"

He looked at her with grave surprise. "And do you resent my telling you, even now?"

His parries were incredible. They left her with a sense of thrusting at emptiness, and a desperate, almost vindictive desire to drive him against the wall and pin him there.

"No. Only I wonder you should take the trouble to tell me, when at the time——"

And now, with a sudden turn, he gave her the final surprise of meeting her squarely on her own ground.

"When at the time I didn't? But how *could* I—at the time?"

"Why couldn't you? You've not yet told me."

He gave her again his look of disarming patience. "Do I need to? Hasn't my whole wretched story told you?"

"Told me why you never answered my letters?"

"Yes—since I could only answer them in one way: by protesting my love and my longing."

There was a pause, of resigned expectancy on his part, on hers of a wild, confused reconstruction of her shattered past. "You mean, then, that you didn't write because——"

"Because I found, when I reached America, that I was a pauper; that my wife's money was gone, and that what I could earn—I've so little gift that way!—was barely enough to keep Juliet clothed and educated. It was as if an iron door had been locked and barred between us."

Lizzie felt herself driven back, panting, on the last defenses of her incredulity. "You might at least have told me—have explained. Do you think I shouldn't have understood?"

He did not hesitate. "You would have understood. It wasn't that."

"What was it then?" she quavered.

"It's wonderful you shouldn't see! Simply that I couldn't write you *that*. Anything else—not *that!*"

"And so you preferred to let me suffer?"

There was a shade of reproach in his eyes. "I suffered too," he said.

It was his first direct appeal to her compassion, and for a moment it nearly unsettled the delicate poise of her sympathies, and sent them trembling in the direction of scorn and irony. But even as the impulse rose it was stayed by another sensation. Once again, as so often in the past, she became aware of a fact which, in his absence, she always failed to reckon with; the fact of the deep irreducible difference between his image in her mind and his actual self—the mysterious alteration in her judgment produced by the inflections of his voice, the look of his eyes, the whole complex pressure of his personality. She had phrased it once, self-reproachfully, by saying to herself that she "never could remember him—" so completely did the sight of him supersede the counterfeit about which her fancy wove its perpetual wonders. Bright and breathing as that counterfeit was, it became a figment of the mind at the touch of his presence, and on this occasion the immediate result was to cause her to feel his possible unhappiness with an intensity beside which her private injury paled.

"I suffered horribly," he repeated, "and all the more that I couldn't make a sign, couldn't cry out my misery. There was only one escape from it all—to hold my tongue, and pray that you might hate me."

The blood rushed to Lizzie's forehead. "Hate you—you prayed that I might hate you?"

He rose from his seat, and moving closer, lifted her hand in his. "Yes; because your letters showed me that if you didn't, you'd be unhappier still."

Her hand lay motionless, with the warmth of his flowing through it, and her thoughts, too—her poor fluttering stormy thoughts—felt themselves suddenly penetrated by the same soft current of communion.

"And I meant to keep my resolve," he went on, slowly releasing his clasp. "I meant to keep it even after the random stream of things swept me back here, in your way; but when I saw you the other day I felt that what had been possible at a distance was impossible now that we were near each other. How could I see you, and let you hate me?"

He had moved away, but not to resume his seat. He merely paused at a little distance, his hand resting on a chair-back, in the transient attitude that precedes departure.

Lizzie's heart contracted. He was going, then, and this was his farewell. He was going, and she could find no word to detain him but the senseless stammer: "I never hated you."

He considered her with a faint smile. "It's not necessary, at any rate, that you should do so now. Time and circumstances have made me so harmless—that's exactly why I've dared to venture back. And I wanted to tell you how I rejoice in your good fortune. It's the only obstacle between us that I can't bring myself to wish away."

Lizzie sat silent, spell-bound, as she listened, by the sudden evocation of Mr. Jackson Benn. He stood there again, between herself and Deering, perpendicular and reproachful, but less solid and sharply outlined than before, with a look in his small hard eyes that desperately wailed for re-embodiment.

Deering was continuing his farewell speech. "You're rich now—you're free. You will marry." She saw him holding out his hand.

"It's not true that I'm engaged!" she broke out. They were the last words she had meant to utter; they were hardly related to her conscious thoughts; but she felt her whole will gathered up in the irrepressible impulse to repudiate and fling away from her forever the spectral claim of Mr. Jackson Benn.

VII

IT was the firm conviction of Andora Macy that every object in the Vincent Deerings' charming little house at Neuilly had been expressly designed for the Deerings' son to play with.

The house was full of pretty things, some not obviously applicable to the purpose; but Miss Macy's casuistry was equal to the baby's appetite, and the baby's mother was no match for them in the art of defending her possessions. There were moments, in fact, when she almost fell in with Andora's summary division of her works of art into articles safe or unsafe for the baby to lick, or resisted it only to the extent of occasionally substituting some less precious, or less perishable, object for the particular fragility on which her son's desire was fixed. And it was with this intention that, on a certain spring morning—which wore the added luster of being the baby's second birthday—she had murmured, with her mouth in his curls, and one hand holding a bit of Chelsea above his clutch: "Wouldn't he rather have that beautiful shiny thing in Aunt Andora's hand?"

The two friends were together in Lizzie's morning-room—the room she had chosen, on acquiring the house, because, when she sat there, she could hear Deering's step as he paced up and down before his easel in the studio she had built for him. His step had been less regularly audible than she had hoped, for, after three years of wedded bliss, he had somehow failed to settle down to the great work which was to result from that state; but even when she did not hear him she knew that he was there, above her head, stretched out on the old divan from St.-Cloud, and smoking countless cigarettes while he skimmed the morning papers; and the sense of his nearness had not yet lost its first keen edge of wonder.

Lizzie herself, on the day in question, was engaged in a more arduous task than the study of the morning's news. She had never unlearned the habit of orderly activity, and the trait she least understood in her husband's character was his way of letting the loose ends of life hang as they would. She had been disposed to ascribe this to the chronic incoherence of his first ménage; but now she knew that, though he basked under her beneficent rule, he would never feel any impulse to further its work. He liked to see things fall into place about him at a wave of her wand; but his enjoyment of her household magic in no way diminished his smiling irresponsibility, and it was with one of its least amiable consequences that his wife and her friend were now dealing.

Before them stood two travel-worn trunks and a distended portmanteau, which had shed their heterogeneous contents over Lizzie's rosy carpet. They represented the hostages left by her husband on his somewhat precipitate departure from a New York boarding-house, and redeemed by her on her learning, in a curt letter from his landlady, that the latter was not disposed to regard them as an equivalent for the arrears of Deering's board.

Lizzie had not been shocked by the discovery that her husband had left America in debt. She had too sad an acquaintance with the economic strain to see any humiliation in such accidents; but it offended her sense of order that he should not have liquidated his obligation in the three years since their marriage. He took her remonstrance with his usual good humor, and left her to forward the liberating draft, though her delicacy had provided him with a bank-account which assured his personal independence. Lizzie had discharged the duty without repugnance, since she knew that his delegating it to her was the result of his indolence and not of any design on her exchequer. Deering was not dazzled by money; his altered fortunes had tempted him to no excesses: he was simply too lazy to draw the check, as he had been too lazy to remember the debt it cancelled.

"No, dear! No!" Lizzie lifted the Chelsea higher. "Can't you find something for him, Andora, among that rubbish over there? Where's the beaded bag you had in your hand? I don't think it could hurt him to lick that."

Miss Macy, bag in hand, rose from her knees, and stumbled across the room through the frayed garments and old studio properties. Before the group of mother and son she fell into a rapturous attitude.

"Do look at him reach for it, the tyrant! Isn't he just like the young Napoleon?"

Lizzie laughed and swung her son in air. "Dangle it before him, Andora. If you let him have it too quickly, he won't care for it. He's just like any man, I think."

Andora slowly lowered the bag till the heir of the Deerings closed his masterful fist upon it. "There—my Chelsea's safe!" Lizzie smiled, setting her boy on the floor, and watching him stagger away with his booty.

Andora stood beside her, watching too. "Do you know where that bag came from, Lizzie?"

Mrs. Deering, bent above a pile of discollared shirts, shook an inattentive head. "I never saw such wicked washing! There isn't one that's fit to mend. The bag? No; I've not the least idea."

Andora surveyed her incredulously. "Doesn't it make you utterly miserable to think that some woman may have made it for him?"

Lizzie, still bowed in scrutiny above the shirts, broke into a laugh.

"Really, Andora, really! Six, seven, nine; no, there isn't even a dozen. There isn't a whole dozen of *anything*. I don't see how men live alone."

Andora broodingly pursued her theme. "Do you mean to tell me it doesn't make you jealous to handle these things of his that other women may have given him?"

Lizzie shook her head again, and, straightening herself with a smile, tossed a bundle in her friend's direction. "No, I don't feel jealous. Here, count these socks for me, like a darling."

Andora moaned "Don't you feel *anything at all?"* as the socks landed in her hollow bosom; but Lizzie, intent upon her task, tranquilly continued to unfold and sort. She felt a great deal as she did so, but her feelings were too deep and delicate for the simplifying processes of speech. She only knew that each article she drew from the trunks sent through her the long tremor of Deering's touch. It was part of her wonderful new life that everything belonging to him contained an infinitesimal fraction of himself—a fraction becoming visible in the warmth of her love as certain secret elements become visible in rare intensities of temperature. And in the case of the objects before her, poor shabby witnesses of his days of failure, what they gave out acquired a special poignancy from its contrast to his present cherished state. His shirts were all in round dozens now, and washed as carefully as old lace. As for his socks, she knew the pattern of every pair, and would have liked to see the washerwoman who dared to mislay one, or bring it home with the colors "run"! And in these homely tokens of his well-being she saw the symbol of what her tenderness had brought him. He was safe in it, encompassed by it, morally and materially, and she defied the embattled powers of malice to reach him through the armor of her love. Such feelings, however, were not communicable, even had one desired to express them: they were no more to be distinguished from the sense of life itself than bees from the lime-blossoms in which they murmur.

"Oh, do *look* at him, Lizzie! He's found out how to open the bag!"

Lizzie lifted her head to look a moment at her son, throned on a heap of studio rubbish, with Andora before him on adoring knees. She thought vaguely "Poor Andora!" and then resumed the discouraged inspection of a buttonless white waistcoat. The next sound she was conscious of was an excited exclamation from her friend.

"Why, Lizzie, do you know what he used the bag for? To keep your letters in!"

Lizzie looked up more quickly. She was aware that Andora's pronoun had changed its object, and was now applied to Deering. And it struck her as odd, and slightly disagreeable, that a letter of hers should be found among the rubbish abandoned in her husband's New York lodgings.

"How funny! Give it to me, please."

"Give it to Aunt Andora, darling! Here—look inside, and see what else a big, big boy can find there!—Yes, here's another! Why, why——"

Lizzie rose with a shade of impatience and crossed the floor to the romping group beside the other trunk.

"What is it? Give me the letters, please." As she spoke, she suddenly recalled the day when, in Mme. Clopin's *pension,* she had addressed a similar behest to Andora Macy.

Andora lifted to her a look of startled conjecture. "Why, this one's never been opened! Do you suppose that awful woman could have kept it from him?"

Lizzie laughed. Andora's imaginings were really puerile! "What awful woman? His landlady? Don't be such a goose, Andora. How can it have been kept back from him, when we've found it among his things?"

"Yes; but then why was it never opened?"

Andora held out the letter, and Lizzie took it. The writing was hers; the envelope bore the Passy postmark; and it was unopened. She looked at it with a sharp drop of the heart.

"Why, so are the others—all unopened!" Andora threw out on a rising note; but Lizzie, stooping over, checked her.

"Give them to me, please."

"Oh, Lizzie, Lizzie—" Andora, on her knees, held back the packet, her pale face paler with anger and compassion. "Lizzie, they're the letters I used to post for you—the letters he never answered! *Look!*"

"Give them back to me, please." Lizzie possessed herself of the letters.

The two women faced each other, Andora still kneeling, Lizzie motionless before her. The blood had rushed to her face, humming in her ears, and forcing itself into the veins of her temples. Then it ebbed, and she felt cold and weak.

"It must have been some plot—some conspiracy," Andora cried, so fired by the ecstasy of invention that for the moment she seemed lost to all but the aesthetic aspect of the case.

Lizzie averted her eyes with an effort, and they rested on the boy, who sat at her feet placidly sucking the tassels of the bag. His mother stooped and extracted them from his rosy mouth, which a cry of wrath immediately filled. She lifted him in her arms, and for the first time no current of life ran from his body into hers. He felt heavy and clumsy, like some other woman's child; and his screams annoyed her.

"Take him away, please, Andora."

"Oh, Lizzie, Lizzie!" Andora wailed.

Lizzie held out the child, and Andora, struggling to her feet, received him.

"I know just how you feel," she gasped, above the baby's head.

Lizzie, in some dark hollow of herself, heard the faint echo of a laugh. Andora always thought she knew how people felt!

"Tell Marthe to take him with her when she fetches Juliet home from school."

"Yes, yes." Andora gloated on her. "If you'd only give way, my darling!"

The baby, howling, dived over Andora's shoulder for the bag.

"Oh, *take* him!" his mother ordered.

Andora, from the door, cried out: "I'll be back at once. Remember, love, you're not alone!"

But Lizzie insisted, "Go with them—I wish you to go with them," in the tone to which Miss Macy had never learned the answer.

The door closed on her reproachful back, and Lizzie stood alone. She looked about the disordered room, which offered a dreary image of the havoc of her life. An hour or two ago, everything about her had been so exquisitely ordered, without and within: her thoughts and her emotions had all been outspread before her like jewels laid away symmetrically in a collector's cabinet. Now they had been tossed down helter-skelter among the rubbish there on the floor, and had themselves turned to rubbish like the rest. Yes, there lay her life at her feet, among all that tarnished trash.

She picked up her letters, ten in all, and examined the flaps of the envelopes. Not one had been opened—not one. As she looked, every word she had written fluttered to life, and every feeling prompting it sent a tremor through her. With vertiginous speed and microscopic distinctness of vision she was reliving that whole period of her life, stripping bare again the ruin over which the drift of three happy years had fallen.

She laughed at Andora's notion of a conspiracy—of the letters having been "kept back." She required no extraneous aid in deciphering the mystery: her three years' experience of Deering shed on it all the light she needed. And yet a moment before she had believed herself to be perfectly happy! Now it was the worst part of her pain that it did not really surprise her.

She knew so well how it must have happened. The letters had reached him when he was busy, occupied with something else, and had been put aside to be read at some future time—a time which never came. Perhaps on the steamer, even, he had met "some one else"—the "some one" who lurks, veiled and ominous, in the background of every woman's thoughts about her lover. Or perhaps he had been merely forgetful. She knew now that the sensations which he seemed to feel most intensely left no reverberations in his memory—that he did not relive either his pleasures or his pains. She needed no better proof than the lightness of his conduct toward his daughter. He seemed to have taken it for granted that Juliet would remain indefinitely with the friends who had received her after her mother's death, and it was at Lizzie's suggestion that the little girl was brought home and that they had established themselves at Neuilly to be near her school. But Juliet once with them, he became the model of a tender father, and Lizzie wondered that he had not felt the child's absence, since he seemed so affectionately aware of her presence.

Lizzie had noted all this in Juliet's case, but had taken for granted that her own was different; that she formed, for Deering, the exception which every woman secretly supposes herself to form in the experience of the man she loves. She had learned by this time that she could not modify his habits; but she imagined that she had deepened his sensibilities, had furnished him with an "ideal"—angelic function! And she now saw that the fact of her letters—her unanswered letters—having, on his own assurance, "meant so much" to him, had been the basis on which this beautiful fabric was reared.

There they lay now, the letters, precisely as when they had left her hands. He had not had time to read them; and there had been a moment in her past when that discovery would have been to her the sharpest pang imaginable. She had traveled far beyond that point. She could have forgiven him now for having forgotten her; but she could never forgive him for having deceived her.

She sat down, and looked again about the room. Suddenly she heard his step overhead, and her heart contracted. She was afraid that he was coming down to her. She sprang up and bolted the door; then she dropped into the nearest chair, tremulous and exhausted, as if the act had required an immense effort. A moment later she heard him on the stairs, and her tremor broke into a fit of shaking. "I loathe you—I loathe you!" she cried.

She listened apprehensively for his touch on the handle of the door. He would come in, humming a tune, to ask some idle question and lay a caress on her hair. But no, the door was bolted; she was safe. She continued to listen, and the step passed on. He had not been coming to her, then. He must have gone downstairs to fetch something—another newspaper, perhaps. He seemed to read little else, and she sometimes wondered when he had found time to store the material that used to serve for their famous "literary" talks. The wonder shot through her again, barbed with a sneer. At that moment it seemed to her that everything he had ever done and been was a lie.

She heard the house door close, and started up. Was he going out? It was not his habit to leave the house in the morning.

She crossed the room to the window, and saw him walking, with a quick decided step, between the lilacs to the gate. What could have called him forth at that unusual hour? It was odd that he should not have told her. The fact that she thought it odd suddenly showed her how closely their lives were interwoven. She had become a habit to him, and he was fond of his habits. But to her it was as if a stranger had opened the gate and gone out. She wondered what he would feel if he knew that she felt *that*.

"In an hour he will know," she said to herself, with a kind of fierce exultation; and immediately she began to dramatize the scene. As soon as he came in she meant to call him up to her room and hand him the letters without a word. For a moment she gloated on the picture; then her imagination recoiled. She was humiliated by the thought of humiliating him. She wanted to keep his image intact; she would not see him.

He had lied to her about her letters—had lied to her when he found it to his interest to regain her favor. Yes, there was the point to hold fast. He had sought her out when he learned that she was rich. Perhaps he had come back from America on purpose to marry her; no doubt he had come back on purpose. It was incredible that she had not seen this at the time. She turned sick at the thought of her fatuity and of the grossness of his arts. Well, the event proved that they were all he needed . . . But why had he gone out at such an hour? She was irritated to find herself still preoccupied by his comings and goings.

Turning from the window, she sat down again. She wondered what she meant to do next . . . No, she would not show him the letters; she would simply leave them on his table and go away. She would leave the house with her boy and Andora. It was a relief to feel a definite plan forming itself in her mind—something that her uprooted thoughts could fasten on. She would go away, of course; and meanwhile, in order not to see him, she would feign a headache, and remain in her room till after luncheon. Then she and Andora would pack a few things, and fly with the child while he was dawdling about upstairs in the studio. When one's house fell, one fled from the ruins: nothing could be simpler, more inevitable.

Her thoughts were checked by the impossibility of picturing what would happen next. Try as she would, she could not see herself and the child away from Deering. But that, of course, was because of her nervous weakness. She had youth, money, energy: all the trumps were on her side. It was much more difficult to imagine what would become of Deering. He was so dependent on her, and they had been so happy together! It struck her as illogical and even immoral, and yet she knew he had been happy with her. It never happened like that in novels: happiness "built on a lie" always crumbled, burying the presumptuous architect beneath its ruins. According to the laws of fiction, Deering, having deceived her once, would inevitably have gone on deceiving her. Yet she knew he had not gone on deceiving her . . .

She tried again to picture her new life. Her friends, of course, would rally about her. But the prospect left her cold; she did not want them to rally. She wanted only one thing—the life she had been living before she had given her baby the embroidered bag to play with. Oh, why had she given him the bag? She had been so happy, they had all been so happy! Every nerve in her clamored for her lost happiness, angrily, irrationally, as the boy had clamored for his bag! It was horrible to know too much; there was always blood in the foundations. Parents "kept things" from children—protected them from all the dark secrets of pain and evil. And was any life livable unless it were thus protected? Could anyone look in the Medusa's face and live?

But why should she leave the house, since it was hers? Here, with her boy and Andora, she could still make for herself the semblance of a life. It was Deering who would have to go; he would understand that as soon as he saw the letters.

She saw him going—leaving the house as he had left it just now. She saw the gate closing on him for the last time. Now her vision was acute enough: she saw him as distinctly as if he were in the room. Ah, he would not like returning to the old life of privations and expedients! And yet she knew he would not plead with her.

Suddenly a new thought seized her. What if Andora had rushed to him with the tale of the discovery of the letters—with the "Fly, you are discovered!" of romantic fiction? What if he *had* left her for good? It would not be unlike him, after all. For all his sweetness he was always evasive and inscrutable. He might have said to himself that he would forestall her action, and place himself at once on the defensive. It might be that she *had* seen him go out of the gate for the last time.

She looked about the room again, as if the thought had given it a new aspect. Yes, this alone could explain her husband's going out. It was past twelve o'clock, their usual luncheon hour, and he was scrupulously punctual at meals, and gently reproachful if she kept him waiting. Only some unwonted event could have caused him to leave the house at such an hour and with such marks of haste. Well, perhaps it was better that Andora should have spoken. She mistrusted her own courage; she almost hoped the deed had been done for her. Yet her next sensation was one of confused resentment. She said to herself "Why has Andora interfered?" She felt baffled and angry, as though her prey had escaped her. If Deering had been in the house she would have gone to him instantly and overwhelmed him with her scorn. But he had gone out, and she did not know where he had gone, and oddly mingled with her anger against him was the latent instinct of vigilance, the solicitude of the woman accustomed to watch over the man she loves. It would be strange never to feel that solicitude again, never to hear him say, with his hand on her hair: "You foolish child, were you worried? Am I late?"

The sense of his touch was so real that she stiffened herself against it, flinging back her head as if to throw off his hand. The mere thought of his caress was hateful; yet she felt it in all her veins. Yes, she felt it, but with horror and repugnance. It was something she wanted to escape from, and the fact of struggling against it was what made its hold so strong. It was as though her mind were sounding her body to make sure of its allegiance, spying on it for any secret movement of revolt . . .

To escape from the sensation, she rose and went again to the window. No one was in sight. But presently the gate began to swing back, and her heart gave a leap—she knew not whether up or down. A moment later the gate opened to admit a perambulator, propelled by the nurse and flanked by Juliet and Andora. Lizzie's eyes rested on the familiar group as if she had never seen it before, and she stood motionless, instead of flying down to meet the children.

Suddenly there was a step on the stairs, and she heard Andora's knock. She unbolted the door, and was strained to her friend's emaciated bosom.

"My darling!" Miss Macy cried. "'Remember you have your child—and me!"

Lizzie loosened herself. She looked at Andora with a feeling of estrangement which she could not explain.

"Have you spoken to my husband?" she asked, drawing coldly back.

"Spoken to him? No." Andora stared at her, surprised.

"Then you haven't met him since he went out?"

"No, my love. Is he out? I haven't met him."

Lizzie sat down with a confused sense of relief, which welled up to her throat and made speech difficult.

Suddenly light seemed to come to Andora. "I understand, dearest. You don't feel able to see him yourself. You want me to go to him for you." She looked eagerly about her, scenting the battle. "You're right, darling. As soon as he comes in, I'll go to him. The sooner we get it over, the better."

She followed Lizzie, who had turned restlessly back to the window. As they stood there, the gate moved again, and Deering entered.

"There he is now!" Lizzie felt Andora's excited clutch upon her arm. "Where are the letters? I will go down at once. You allow me to speak for you? You trust my woman's heart? Oh, believe me, darling," Miss Macy panted, "I shall know exactly what to say to him!"

"What to say to him?" Lizzie absently repeated.

As her husband advanced up the path she had a sudden vision of their three years together. Those years were her whole life; everything before them had been colorless and unconscious, like the blind life of the plant before it reaches the surface of the soil. The years had not been exactly what she had dreamed; but if they had taken away certain illusions they had left richer realities in their stead. She understood now that she had gradually adjusted herself to the new image of her husband as he was, as he would always be. He was not the hero of her dreams, but he was the man she loved, and who had loved her. For she saw now, in this last wide flash of pity and initiation, that, as a comely marble may be made out of worthless scraps of mortar, glass, and pebbles, so out of mean mixed substances may be fashioned a love that will bear the stress of life.

More urgently, she felt the pressure of Miss Macy's hand.

"I shall hand him the letters without a word. You may rely, love, on my sense of dignity. I know everything you're feeling at this moment!"

Deering had reached the doorstep. Lizzie watched him in silence till he disappeared under the projecting roof of the porch; then she turned and looked almost compassionately at her friend.

"Oh, poor Andora, you don't know anything—you don't know anything at all!" she said.